Digging Out
Up the Sandbox
Long Division
Torch Song
Generation Without Memory
Your Child's Mind
    (*with Dr. Herman Roiphe*)
Lovingkindness
A Season for Healing

ANNE
ROIPHE

SUMMIT BOOKS
New York • London • Toronto • Sydney • Tokyo • Singapore

THE

PURSUIT

OF

HAPPINESS

A NOVEL

SUMMIT BOOKS
Simon & Schuster Building
Rockefeller Center
1230 Avenue of the Americas
New York, New York 10020

SUMMIT BOOKS and colophon are trademarks
of Simon & Schuster Inc.
Designed by Edith Fowler
Manufactured in the United States of America

10 9 8 7 6 5 4 3 2 1

Library of Congress Cataloging in Publication Data

Roiphe, Anne Richardson, date.
  The pursuit of happiness : a novel / Anne Roiphe.
    p. cm.
  I. Title.
PS3568.O53P8 1991
813'.54—dc20   91-6738
ISBN 0-671-66754-8   CIP

FOR MY DAUGHTER KATIE ROIPHE,
my critic of the first resort,
my friend

The Gruenbaum Family

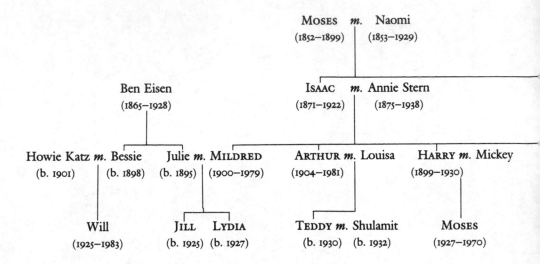

MOSES   *m.*   Naomi
(1852–1899)   (1853–1929)

Ben Eisen   ISAAC   *m.* Annie Stern
(1865–1928)   (1871–1922)   (1875–1938)

Howie Katz *m.* Bessie   Julie *m.* MILDRED   ARTHUR *m.* Louisa   HARRY *m.* Mickey
(b. 1901)   (b. 1898)   (b. 1895) (1900–1979)   (1904–1981)   (1899–1930)

Will   JILL   LYDIA   TEDDY *m.* Shulamit   MOSES
(1925–1983)   (b. 1925) (b. 1927)   (b. 1930) (b. 1932)   (1927–1970)

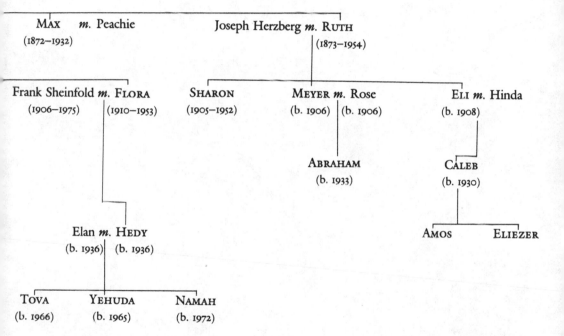

MAX   *m.* Peachie   Joseph Herzberg *m.* RUTH
(1872–1932)   (1873–1954)

Frank Sheinfold *m.* FLORA   SHARON   MEYER *m.* Rose   ELI *m.* Hinda
(1906–1975) (1910–1953)   (1905–1952)   (b. 1906) (b. 1906)   (b. 1908)

                                           ABRAHAM   CALEB
                                           (b. 1933)   (b. 1930)

                Elan *m.* HEDY   AMOS   ELIEZER
                (b. 1936) (b. 1936)

TOVA   YEHUDA   NAMAH
(b. 1966) (b. 1965)   (b. 1972)

In Which the Narrator Introduces the Pursuit

Reader: Over the oceans, up and down the ladders, proud or ashamed, lucky or unlucky, smart or stupid, blundering or swift, giving their hearts away too quickly or not quickly enough, these characters are doing their part to keep the wolf from the door, the earth from returning to water, to keep evolution on an upward swing.

Hedy in the Hadassah Hospital Corridor: Jerusalem, 1990

NO SMOKING, the sign says in Hebrew, in Arabic, and in English. Hedy reads the sign in all its languages and then takes the letters of each word and scrambles them, trying to make other words, designing them on their white background like petals of a flower, like the constellation Orion, like the ring around Neptune, and finally as she closes her eyes the letters fall together in a black mass, a black hole, a density in which there is no room for whirlwinds to speak or bushes to burn. The green doors swing open and a nurse walks past, not looking at her, avoiding Hedy's stare. Inside, behind the green doors, Hedy knows what is happening. The lights above the table are steady. The drip through the tube into Namah's arm is steady. The skull of the child she bore is open. This is more than Hedy wants to see. She walks up and down the corridor. It has been two hours already. The speed of light is 186,000 miles per second. If Namah were a meteor, a fragment of gas and mineral, spinning in the vacancy of starlight, neither up nor down, where would she be? In this time, the time that Hedy has stood in the corridor, refusing the seat her cousin Teddy offered, refusing to look at her husband, who was standing at the door by the large can that was stuffed with green gowns and abandoned sterile paper slippers, Namah, if she were a meteor, would have traveled 1,339,200,000 miles closer or farther from what to where? In two hours Namah could have reached into the orbit of a passing moon or strayed beyond the galaxy. It would depend on where she started.

Hedy, a Twig on the Gruenbaum Family Tree: In Maine, Summer 1942

The child is in her small bed against the wood-paneled wall. The pine boards are not sealed tight enough to prevent the sound of the wind from entering or the cold August air from seeping about the child's head. The child's mother, Flora, sits on her bed in the room next door. She applies paint to her nails, bright red paint, she waves her fingers in the air, drying the polish, listening to the wind, rushing around the corners, slipping over the roof. The branches of the pine trees, their hard cones falling like stones against the window, wipe again and again against the cabin walls. There is too much static on the radio. The announcer's voice fades in and out. The radio, shaped like a small house in the alps, makes gulping explosive noises in an effort to digest and relay its messages. The woman puts on her slippers, pink with feathers on the tips. She wraps herself in a robe. She lights a Camel cigarette and pulls the smoke deep into her lungs. She blows out, little rings, just like the sign above 42nd Street. Maine. Songowood Camp. Adults and children and their nannies spend the summer in the woods. The men come up for a week or two and then take the train back to New York, to businesses and law practices, jobs with agencies named with initials, wartime jobs at desks, buying supplies, manufacturing uniforms, shipping socks and underwear to places in the Pacific, to bases in England and Wales, not heroes exactly, too old to be heroes, men with wives and children, but necessary, some of them freeing up young men, keeping the home fires burning, selling war bonds, making the smokestacks belch and the assembly lines move and Rosy the Riveter rivet. At Camp Songowood they put their feet into sandals and wade into the lake holding their children in their arms. In New York and Washington they wear white shirts and black socks and urge bank accounts to fill and empty like tidal pools at the shore's edge, keeping currency debiting and crediting for those who defend the Stars and Stripes. While their families are away in the woods, the men have dinner at the club, or they do freely things that might in October or May force them to lie.

Camp Songowood, we sing-a-ling-a-ling and ding-a-ling to you. That's the way the children chant at dinner, rattling their knives and forks together as they sing in the long dining room each night. They eat at six o'clock with their nannies. The adults eat later, after a cocktail or two, after a walk by the lake at sunset, after the evening's canasta, mah-jongg, and backgammon games have all been arranged. The nanny lies awake in the dark, listening to the coming storm. She is thinking of Bavaria, of Volkspan, the mountain by her hometown. When the storms came there, her mother, a widow, would cover her face with an apron and pray. Here among the Jews, in Maine, Ursula prayed to the baby Jesus, but she was never sure, among the Jews, whether Jesus remembered her. The storm would pass, other storms had passed, but it was dark in the room, the smallest one in the cabin, the child's bed was wedged next to a bureau, casting a shadow like the head of a wolf whose teeth were bared.

These people had eyes so brown they looked like the plowed earth after the rain. The child had the heavy tartar lids of her father and a dark mole at her temple. It was hard to keep her thick hair brushed. The child cried when the comb pulled through the tangles. Ursula tried to sleep. When the girl woke she would be there.

The child heard the storm first as the wind picked up the shutters and banged them against the shingled walls. She saw the first lightning, a streak, a bolt of yellow force, down from the clouds and on to the ground far on the other side of the lake, and then the deafening howl of the thunder, like the cannon in the war that would not—her mother said it would not—reach her. The child considered. It was only the weather, the clapping together of clouds. The night was dark, the child could see no stars from her window. The child climbed up on her bed and searched the sky for familiar signs, the moon, the tall pine across the path, the neighbor's cabin, painted dark green, like all the other cabins in the camp circle. She could not see anything. It was so dark. She pressed her face to the screen. The wind caught her hair and whipped it across her cheek. Suddenly the whole window was bright with a suspended light, as if a monster had held its breath, poised for a second before opening its jaws. She stood at the window, caught in the light, her pale face stunned, her mind wondering, When the war was over, when the Yanks won, would they still come to Maine for the summers?

The child's mother, Flora, saw the same sheet of lightning. She heard the thunder that followed a few seconds later. It came to her as if the whole earth were opening up, as if the sky had fallen downward and had crashed into her. She felt the sound in her belly, where she had carried one child and lost two others, bloody pools on the bathroom floor. She heard the sound as if the boot of the enemy were above her face. Her father, Isaac Gruenbaum, had told her that a caravan of Gypsies had turned to ash in a thunderstorm outside his town in the old country. She pulled on her cigarette, she turned the dials on her radio. She needed music, the Andrews Sisters, "I'm looking over a four-leaf clover," any-thing, something with a beat that could remind her of bands and silk dresses and waiters serving drinks on silver trays. She poured herself a Scotch and added water from the bathroom tap. The amber liquid slid up the sides of the water glass as she paced back and forth across the knotted pine floor. The goddamn state of Maine was sitting beneath a bolt of lightning, and she was about to be burned. In the city, storms didn't matter, the doorman held an umbrella over your head as you raced toward a taxi, the coats in the coatroom of the Little Club, where she had lunch with her friends would smell moist, wet wool drying in the radiator heat, but a storm would not wake her at night. Here in this cabin, by this lake, didn't water attract lightning? She was tissue and bone, muscle and mucus, exposed to the elements. She watched a moth beat its wings against the screen window; another bolt of lightning and a rip of thunder, the lights in the room flickered and lowered and went out. She was in the dark. The radio was dead. She moved, quickly, a small woman, not yet thirty, with full hips, not quite five feet, a small soft fold of flesh around her waist, a long neck, a sweet roundness to the face. Under the robe, under the powder and the night cream, there was a woman, who had not wanted to spend the night alone, not the night of a storm. She moved through the door and saw the shape of her daughter, lit by a sheet of lightning, standing on her bed looking out the window. She grabbed her from behind.

"Don't stand by an open window, the lightning may get you."

The child turned around to see her mother, lit by the fading flash. The mother's eyes were brown like a pile of fallen leaves, and mascara had smudged at the corners. Her smile despite the waver of the lips was hopeful. The mother pulled her daughter, hands groping in the dark for the bare wood walls, for the bureau, for the doorjamb, back into her own room. Behind her the nanny slept, her hair net tight across her forehead. She placed her daughter in the bed that was shared with her husband when he visited. She climbed in bed with the child and, holding her tightly, said, "Count, count the seconds between the lightning and the thunder, then we will know if the storm is coming closer or going away. When the lightning and the thunder seem to come together, then the storm is over our heads."

The mother and the child watched and counted. The mother trembled in the bed, wrapping her legs, newly waxed, soft and smooth, lightly freckled from the sun, around the child's small frame. She held her daughter in her arms.

"It will go away," said the mother, tugging at the daughter's hair.

"It will go away. It's all right," said the child, "it's only a storm."

When the thunder was directly over head, the mother cried out, "Oh, God!"

The daughter put her thumb in her mouth but said nothing. She thought about burning. Would the lightning strike her head with its sharp point, the way it was drawn in the comics, or would it zigzag to a spot on the floor, perhaps where Ursula was sleeping? Storms, she said to herself, come every summer. The rain is necessary. The clouds are banging together. The earth has no end. It sounds as if the lightning is right here, but the ground is wide. She had been in the big pine woods that surrounded the camp. The lightning is not after me. What is lightning made of? she wondered. What is it good for? she thought. Electricity, she remembered. Lightning was the flashing of electricity, electricity was a friend, it made the icebox cold and the radio hum. Her eyes were blinking too fast. She could feel a small spasm cross her lids. She closed her eyes tightly to stop the twitching. She would not be afraid. Someone must be calm. Someone must think clearly. In her book of nursery rhymes she had seen a child leaning over the top of the crow's nest of a ship, looking out over the sea. Someone must keep watch. She would not cry. Her mother needed her. If the lightning struck and the cabin burst into flames, her mother would need her to lead the way out the door, to hold her hand. Then the count between thunder and lightning grew longer, and the storm was passing on, miles away it rumbled comfortably. The child felt the silk of her mother's nightgown. Later the mother fell asleep, but she was dreaming and her legs and arms flailed in her sleep, and the child was pushed to the edge of the bed, where she hung on as long as she could. Then the daughter pulled the covers up, gently, over her mother's shoulders and tiptoed back, careful in the dark not to knock into the chair or the lamp, into her own bed. There was nothing to be afraid of after all.

The Beginning of the Story: Sulvalki, Poland, 1878

It had begun in the town of Sulvalki, Poland, as Jews were beginning to journey, large numbers of them, driven by the whisperings of their neighbors, carried by the wind of hope. Like flocks of birds that at a certain season feel the warm air under their wings and move on, the Jews were packing.

Reader: Do not assume that all immigrants are the same, that all family stories begin on a boat and end up with a safety-deposit box in Chase Manhattan. Do not assume that this is a tale in which the villains and the heroes are set apart from one another by lines so clear they could be prison bars. Family stories are not morality plays, although they are about morality, how it dips and swings, how it sways and jitterbugs through the generations. We can see that whatever compelled the Gruen-baums from rags to riches and took them on such a rough road leading— well, leading is the point, and that is for the end of the story not the beginning—to their own particular destiny, whatever it was that propelled them along was a cocktail of fate shaken well with their own choices; life on the rocks, it is. Perhaps we are all here only to make good stories, so that one of our own can one day spill the beans, open the closet door, inventing a punch line that replaces random fate with impartial justice. Here at the beginning, Reader, just be patient and don't be too quick with prejudice and assumption. Money is the root of all evil, and it is easier for a camel to pass through the eye of a needle than for a rich man to enter the kingdom of Heaven, as true for a Jew as a Gentile or not true for either, but a homily will not pay the tuition at the best schools, and there is a long way between the flower and the root, and besides, if the streets were not paved with gold, at least they were streets open to anyone fleet of foot, handy with figures, and daring enough to take risks. Also, you had to forget about piety, which after all there was enough of in the old country, and if that was what you wanted, you could have saved yourself a trip. Lucky for the Gruenbaums that they came to America, or else they might have met Ursula's youngest brother, who served in the East and wrote home to his mother complaining about certain unpleasant aspects of his duty that involved the driving of gas vans down forest roads. That is narrative line; one turn places you at risk of a heart attack and another leaves you naked at the bottom of a ditch.

It had begun in the town of Sulvalki, late into the century, its grand stone synagogue, its much grander cathedral, its tiny shuls, its Jewish community ever growing, always pushing at the edges, always wanting something better, the cobblestone streets, the gray ash buildings decorated with stone gargoyles, bunches of stone grapes and wreaths of stone flowers—that was a town to have a beginning or an and in: the Jewish cemetery was crowded but perfectly tended. Some of the dead were buried with small sticks between their fingers so that when the Messiah came it would be easier for them to dig their way through the earth back to Jerusalem. It's not so hard to imagine the Jews of Sulvalki, those waiting in the cemetery, swimming through the geological layers of soil, brushing aside fossils, digging closer and closer to the hot center of the earth and then floating easily upward toward the end of history.

Moses Gruenbaum was a young man who was willing to wait his lifetime through in the back alleys of Sulvalki, on the wooden porch of the house he shared with three other families, with its privy in the back courtyard. He was willing to wait for the wars of Gog of the land of Magog to announce God's presence. He was willing to do his part toward bringing the Messiah by following the laws, by living the life of a pious man, by turning his face and his mind heavenward, by working in his uncle's tailoring shop cutting and snipping and pressing six days a week. However, his wife, Naomi, with their three young children, born one right after another, Isaac, Max, and Ruth, was less content to let theological matters take their inevitable course. She cut out the picture of the

New York harbor from the newspaper, and each night as she served supper she spoke to her children about America.

"In America," she said, "you will not live in the dark streets behind the cathedral, but up front in the sunshine, and you will be able to turn red from the sun just by putting your face to your own window."

Each day Naomi sold buttons and thread and needles from a large basket that sat by her side in the market. She sat on a little stool and called out, in Polish, in Yiddish, "Come get your thread, let nothing go unmended, here is the needle, here is the button, sew, sew for your family, here is your thread." She sang her song, loud and soft, addressed it to one or another passerby; she wasn't above sticking her small foot out into the passageway and tripping a possible customer, and then she would apologize and offer a free needle if the person, picking up their packages, smoothing down their clothing, would consider buying from a poor lady who had children to feed three other needles and a packet of thread, white and orange and black.

The hours were long and the children who waited for her at home, peering down the dark alley for her shape to appear up the hill, amused themselves sometimes by chasing across the street just as a horse would come down the alley pulling a dray with ice or firewood or bricks. The game was to get across the street without being struck by the wheels, whose wide axles made loud creaking, gobbling noises as they rolled over the uneven cobblestones. A game that seems foolish to grown-ups, but one that holds at its heart all the questions of childhood, all the meaning that each small mind was searching for: Will I survive the crush of wheel, can I dare and live, is fate with me or against me? Think of this game as a prayer set in action by the muscles of the foot. It was one of these games that Max didn't win, and his small leg was flattened in an instant. The driver barely paused, he hardly registered the slight swaying of his wheel and the screams that followed. He was thick in his own whiskey and had his own problems anyway.

Moses stood over the bed of his second son and, tears in his eyes, he said to him, "Fool, what kind of game was that, fool?"

The boy was pale as a ghost, and Moses smoothed the bed cover again and again while thinking to himself that he would have to borrow the money for the burial from his uncle. Like a sparrow near to death on the street, its wings stilled, but its eyes still staring as if rescue were still possible, Max looked at his father and instead of seeing his coffin lifted onto the carriage and his mother weeping behind, instead of hearing the words of the kaddish that his brother, Isaac, was already practicing in the kitchen, he said to his father, "Let's go to America."

And his father said, "Like your mother, you fool, I should run with you across the street ahead of the carriage. Leave everything we know for the other side." He stroked his son's hair, and by the time Naomi came home from the market and the doctor came and did what he could, it was clear enough that Max would live, although his condition would never again be perfect.

"What is perfect?" said Naomi. "Compared to living, it is less than nothing." She sang songs of joy while carrying the wood to the stove.

Moses thought that the miracle of Max's life having been saved by a gracious God was a clear sign that the family should stay where they were. Someday perhaps the tailor shop would be his, and each corner of Sulvalki, each alley from which the laundry hung and the smells of cooking came, was an old friend of his, a part of the blood that coursed through his veins. He thought that America was a land for the discontents, the ones whom God had already scratched out of His grand plan. "Who understands God?" he said to Naomi. "Not a simple man like me."

"So let God take care of himself," answered his wife, "and let us get away from the place where the wind comes round the corners and tears the skin off your face, where the peasants have intentions that are not good, and the darkness is a trapdoor through which Jews are always falling."

Moses heard her, but he was not the kind of man to venture out. It was hard for him even to carry the pants to a customer. Before he set out to make his delivery, he would imagine that a peasant who had drunk too much had wandered into the Jewish streets looking for a Jew to knock to the gutter. This had not happened to him personally, but he had seen it happen more than once. He imagined that one of the stone gargoyles that decorated the corners of the cathedral had come loose in the last storm, and that just as he passed it would rock on its stone claws and plummet toward the earth, landing on his head.

But in the shul, where he prayed each morning, he felt that nothing catastrophic could happen to him. His breath came easily. His skin color, always so white, took on almost a pinkish tone. Inside his shul, which was on Egypt Street, he felt safe.

The century was well into its second half, and there were those who said that progress was coming. The breath of wind blowing from the east brought word of new ideas, ideas that might make life good for the Jews. The breath of wind, the winds of change, might . . . who knows what they might?—the Messiah, of course . . . but besides, maybe the neighbors would turn friendly, maybe the Easter tide of bricks and stones would stop, maybe the universities would be open and a Jew could travel like a king. Hope, the umbilical cord of man to his future, ran through the Jewish streets like children on Purim, as if Haman were the last enemy on earth.

Then it happened that a certain Jacob, the son of a rabbi in Brest, who was given to quick swings of temper and injudicious acts with his fists, which was why he was not in Brest, had an argument with a peasant. This Jacob had been sent off to Sulvalki to deal in mirrors, glass, and imitation jewels. On a certain Friday morning he had words in his shop with a man who had thought he could get two mirrors for his new wife for the price of one. The quarrel was nothing unusual in itself. Jacob had yelled and called his customer a pig in the barnyard rolling in his own shit, but the Pole had returned the insult and gone off with his one mirror, and that appeared to be the end of it. But in the evening the Pole was in the tavern and regretted the second mirror he had lost in the morning. Always taking, the Jews, a little here, some there, making a Christian work till the end of his time, always behind, never ahead.

Jewish women and children were in their houses; Shabbat had come, lovely queen, consoler of the poor, bringing the family together by the table laid with white cloth and lit by candle flickering in the window. Moses was in his shul wrapping up his tallis and putting his prayer book away in the velvet case he had been given by his parents on his Bar Mitzvah, when there was a terrible pounding on the door.

"Let us in, you sons of bitches!" screamed the Poles. "You kikes, whose mothers have slept with oxen," they screamed, "open the door!"

The Jews in the shul had narrow chests and pale complexions, they had frail hands that wrote in ledgers. They all had glasses, tied with bits of string around their necks. The young men like Moses had early learned, learned at their mothers' breasts, that words were better than actions, that protection lay in the downward eye and the sloped shoulder. That God had his own plan for the Jews and would protect them or not as He intended. They knew that gangster Jews who swaggered and drank and swore would not have rushed as they did as if one man to the door and pulled the big metal bolt across its barrier. The gangster Jews would not have locked the door and thrown themselves on their knees in prayer. Moses sat on the wooden bench by his desk and put his hands over his ears. He didn't want to hear the banging on the door. Jacob, who would have shouted back at the Poles, Jacob was not in the house of study on a Friday night. He was playing cards with some traveling merchants from Hamburg.

The shul was made of wood, and wood is no barrier to the determined heart. Maybe the scheme began with the Pole whose mirror, wrapped carefully in hay, waited in his cart by the tavern, or maybe the first gesture belonged to the Pole whose wife he had laid on for twenty years and thought a part of himself like his hands and feet, his nose and eyes, had gone to bed with a fever that had arrived on a Friday and left a corpse on a Sunday and although that was three months earlier he still cursed the space in his bed where a woman's buttocks had made a valley in the mattress and he still filled the hours of the night by howling at the moon. Whatever, the men rushed back to the tavern, and grabbing torches lit from the great fireplace that warmed the room, they swung down the street, strong in arm, tall and with strides of men who know that they are outside and someone else is locked in. They took armfuls of hay from a cart as it rolled slowly through the street. While the men inside the shul, hearing little noise, were debating whether or not to open the door and rush for their homes, the fire was lit. The Poles crossed the street to watch the fine dinner they were making of these Sabbath Jews. Slowly the smoke curled under the wooden door. The smoke came from all sides, and the roof too began to smolder as a torch came to rest up near the chimney where in the spring a family of swallows had made their home. The empty nest, with its small twigs, quickly burned, and the planks of the roof caught fire. Another torch lit the pile of wood next to the window, a small window, in which a pane had been broken a while before by a child with a stone and was now covered with black tar paper. The wood-pile stocked high for winter's comfort burned and sent flames up into the night, and the side of the building swelled and little bubbles appeared on the surface of the wood and then burst and began to crackle. Then came the sound of smashing glass, and a torch flew through the small window.

When it was clear to the men inside that the choking in their throats, the smarting in their eyes, was indeed fire, they rushed to the door and pulled back the metal bolt and thrust their bodies against the door. The Poles, who were ready to knock out teeth and break bones, seemed now almost like friends. The enemy was fire and smoke. But when the men leaned on the door it would not fly open as it should. It was wedged in by barrels, barrels of beer taken off the back of a cart that was delivering to the tavern. The Poles had piled the barrels up over the door and were themselves drinking from the open tap of another barrel they had dragged across the street. The Jews on the block had come to their windows to see what was happening. Afraid to leave their homes, they drew their curtains shut and hoped the fire would not spread. They did not know that inside the shul men were hurling themselves at the door, calling out to their God and spitting up, vomit sharing the nasal passages with the smoke and ash that spread quickly through the small room. Moses had thought that God would hold him in His arms to ease his dying. He thought God would rock him as he had cradled his own sons when in the first months their stomachs cramped and their small legs twitched against his chest. Always he had imagined dying as joining his mother and father and the sister who had died in the bed with him when she was three, but now that he was close, now that he could feel his own spittle on his lip, he did not think of his body or his soul or the time when the Messiah would come, things he had much considered before. Now failure flowed through his body. What use was he to his wife and children? What had been the purpose of his twenty-five years of life?

In the back of the shul there was an extension. In it were kept the blankets for the coldest of winter nights, the dust rags used to clean the desks and the buckets that were used to mop the floor. Some of the younger men pushed their way into the small extension, and leaning all together on the inner wall, they smashed their shoulders again and again against the wood. One young man threw a desk at the wall, and the fire, which had started up the back side of the building, had crumbled a supporting beam, and the wall gave way. The men, tumbling one after another, rushed into the little alley behind the building and, climbing over a small fence, made their way out into the Sulvalki night.

Moses felt the cold air and the cooling wind from the northern mountains, and although he could smell the fire on his clothes and although his face was covered with ash and his cheek had been singed by a falling ember as he passed through the opening in the wall, he knew he would live. He could not remember why. It was this question that formed in his chest, first like a sharp pain and then like a stone, a stone worn smooth by the river. He looked up. It was starting to snow. The first snow of the winter, heavy flakes, tentative at first, white paths in the sky lit now by the fire. Snowflakes coming down on the shul and disappearing in the smoke and the heat.

The Jews had come running into the street with buckets of water. The Poles, too, now pulled back the barrels of beer that had blocked the door and, emptying them as fast as possible into the pails, were helping to put out the fire. The police had arrived, and they too were carrying water from wherever they could find it. The fire in the wooden shul could spread, not only to the houses of the Jews, but through the whole town. The street was packed with people, milling about. Quietly, as if noise could attract the evil eye, women searched for their husbands, their sons. The Poles were happy to be putting out the fire. They raised their arms in unison and carried great pails of water. The snow had turned their mood, and now despite a weave to their step they moved close to the fire, daring the flames, the falling boards, to harm them. Gently they pushed the young children back from the rising sparks, and they smiled at the women who stood on the opposite side of the street, snow falling on their shawls. They were eager to save the house next door and the one after that. In the light dusting of snow that soon covered the ground, they moved their big boots back and forth. There is something in a fire that brings people together, and the women of the street brought coffee from their stoves and gave it to the men who were bending and pulling and lifting in the pink-and-orange light of the fire. Jacob and the traveling salesmen had put away their cards and, following the light of the fire had joined in the crowd, passing buckets, calling out to friends and customers. Here were neighbors putting out a fire under the white clouds of snow that kept on falling long after Moses was home and clutching Naomi, telling her over and over that the smell came first and the smoke came second and the door was blocked and the books were burned and the walls came down and that the snow had come, the first snow of winter.

After the fire Jacob sold off his business to his assistant and using the proceeds booked passage on the *Trieste,* third class, so as to arrive in America with expectations. After the fire Moses became very thin, a man whose clothes bagged about his hips and whose work shirt hung across his chest, billowing out with the breeze as if he were a boat about to set sail. After the fire Naomi wept in her bed and Moses tried to comfort her.

"How could you leave the graves of your parents?" he asked.

"Graves," she yelled, sitting up in bed, her tears drying instantly. "Graves are what you think of? Soon enough you will be dead."

"There is no money," said Moses. "I haven't the money for the passage. Money," he said, "money, where will we find the money?" And with that sacred word he tried to touch her full breasts. "At least we have each other," he said.

She allowed him to put his hands on her, but her nipples were flat; they would have fled to the opposite side of her body, hidden behind her spine, if they could.

"I would go," he said, "if we had the money."

"Good," said Naomi, and her body opened to him.

Reader: Before we go on, let us talk about money and Jews. What an old and nasty libel that is, sunk deep into the fabric of medieval life, the Jew as usurer, the Shylock of the marketplace, the pound of flesh taken from a poor angelic spirit, the Jew who provided the grease for the wheeling and the dealing, the fortunes made and lost in trade, in cunning, and the Jew who kept the accounts, who owned no land—he wasn't allowed—who sold and bought from town to town, who put the nails into the limbs that hung from the cross, they said, and have kept saying, while feudal lords counted treasures behind sealed walls, while dukes and counts, plantation owners, tycoons, and moguls slept in beds of goose down and golden thread—the Jews were the ones whose banking habits, so convenient for others, made them ideal runners for the numbers game. Jews and money gave the world a shadow play while the real wheel of fortune spun on and on, a carny hustle that was loaded in the house's favor, the real currency changing hands out of sight of peasant, farmer, workers with collars blue and white and gray. Someone collected gold bowls and jeweled tiaras and prime real estate, and Jews collected pennies and hid them in their stockings so they could pay the ferrymen when they were tossed from land to land. Money may wear a Jewish mask from time to time, but don't be fooled. Real money plays with currencies international, bicoastal, and the sky's the limit. And in this story, which is about money—how could an American story not be about money?—these Jews are little players, set large against the canvas here. Don't forget as they bumble along, looking for royal flushes at the end of rainbows, they are only finger puppets for the real actors, who own steel mills and railroads, chemical companies and airplanes, and live in houses with long driveways lined with great oaks.

Farmers lost their farms in dust and mortgages. Slaves were shackled in the dark belly of sailing ships. Tithes were paid, and women dug for potatoes in the worn dirt. We had poorhouses and debtors prisons, Tiny Tims without milk or apples, and not because anyone wished it, not because everyone was unkind, but because money has its own logic, claims its own victims. Money has a part in my story, been a character, so to speak, with enormous influence, appeal, effect. When I begin at the beginning I think of money, money earned by the sweat of the brow and money longed for, money wasted, money saved, and always money reproducing itself in the ways that money can, parthenogenesis, mitosis benign and malignant. The Jew and the Christian, the black and the white, the Asian and the Indian, we struggle to eat, to shelter, to enjoy. We stumble against each other and think we have found the enemy. The enemy eludes us. Ah, where? who?

My characters have spirits that would soar to the heavens, but they live in the world of exchange and commodity. They need money to nourish their souls. Don't we all?

Naomi stopped selling buttons in the market. She got a job in the House of the Elderly, where the sick and the lame and the abandoned

were kept alive by charity of the rich. She was strong and could carry the
laundry up the four flights of stairs. She was not afraid of stained bed
sheets and babbling men and women. Her salary was small, but one day,
in the distant future, she would feel the spray of the ocean on her arm.

Naomi was on the night shift when Leah appeared. Her neighbor
had carried her up the front steps in his arms, tenderly, as if she were his
own mother, small and withered in his arms. He handed her over to
Naomi and quickly left, slamming the door behind him. "What else could
I do?" he asked.

"You did the right thing," said Naomi.

Leah could no longer get about her house without crawling on the
floor. Her mind was wandering. The smell from her house disturbed the
neighbors. Her son had left for Warsaw many years before.

Naomi carried the old lady to a bed in the room with several other
women, who were now asleep. "Don't be afraid," said Naomi to Leah,
stroking her hair and patting her hand. "We will take good care of you
here. This is a charitable place. You will be fed and cared for better than
in your own home."

"No, no," said Leah, "I want my bed, my own bed, please," she
begged. "Return me, return me."

"I can't," said Naomi, who began undressing her charge, to replace
her worn nightgown with one of the clean white ones worn by all the
inmates of the house.

Leah scratched at Naomi's face and flailed her arms and would not
stop moving like a wild animal caught in a trap. Naomi was tired, and
she knew that this show of spirit was pointless. The old lady would have
to wear the white nightgown, and soon enough she would get used to
it. The noise woke the others, who trembled and called for Naomi to
help them to the bathroom, to get them a drink, to have pity on an old
woman, to let them sleep, to open the window and let in a breeze, to
allow them to die in peace without the yelling of strangers, to bring them
their babies, to let their lovers in the door. A mixture of wish and need
filled the room with noise.

"See what you have done!" Naomi pushed Leah down on the cot.

The pain began in Leah's head, and her hand flew to her scalp as if
she could contain the pain in her palm. It spread down her neck and arm
and grasped at her throat so that she could not scream, although she
tried. The pain rose in her chest and seemed strong enough to split the
bone between her two wilted breasts, spread across her back and under
her ribs as if it were looking for a way to break out, to escape the bond
of her body. Then she closed her eyes. She had time to wonder if this

was death. Would her son remember to say kaddish for her? Did he still know how?

It was death and it came in less than thirty seconds. Naomi shook Leah, trying to get her to open her eyes. The others who recognized the silence of a soul rising, turned reasonable, some returning to sleep, dreams being preferable to the stiffening body on the nearby bed.

"Sweetie, good night," one called to another.

"God keep you till morning," they said.

There was a sour, indecent smell to Leah. Naomi pulled the nightgown down. It would be better, more orderly, if the doctor came and the body were wearing the white gown of the house; and there in the dark she felt the necklace. It was a locket on a long chain. In an instant Naomi had taken it and put it in her own pocket. It would do the old lady no good. Whatever it was worth—a piece of costume glass, a memento of a lost love, a container for a lock of her child's hair—whatever it signified to its owner, it signified no longer, and Naomi had meant Leah well, to clean her, to change her, to get her to sleep in the white nightgown of the house. An orphan who has been raised by the town does not inherit from a parent, and harvesting a little locket, which was not really hers, but then belonged to no one since its owner was cold as stone, was permissible. Perhaps this locket that had fallen into her pocket was God's way of acknowledging that he cared about her, too.

At home at the kitchen table, a small kitchen in which the bathtub sat filled often with the wash that she was always too tired to finish, she took the locket out of her pocket and showed it to Moses, who was about to leave for his cubicle on Carol Street in which he sat sewing and steaming from dawn till dusk. Naomi pulled the locket from her apron pocket.

"Where did you get that?" said Moses.

"From Leah, the baker's widow, whose son is away in Warsaw. She wanted me to have it because I reminded her of the daughter she did not have."

"Open it," said Isaac, who had just come into the room. He was only seven, but his eyes told him that the locket was not a trinket for a child. In the early light of the morning, the gray light of the dawn that found its way to their small window, Isaac saw gold. Naomi used a fingernail but could not pry open the locket, whose oval sides seemed shut. "Never mind," she said.

"Open it," said Isaac. He took it from his mother and with his small teeth bit at the edge until suddenly in his mouth the spring clicked and the locket opened. Isaac took it down from his mouth and held it in the palm of his hand. There was a faded curl of hair, a child's wisp, but that wasn't all. In the locket, cupped in it as if they had been cradled there from the beginning of time, as if the locket were an oyster of extraordinary power, lay three small diamonds.

"We are going," said Naomi as soon as she saw them in her hand. "We are going to America."

The jeweler Chaim bought two of the diamonds from her and the locket as well. With the funds she booked passage. "Naomi," said Moses, "are you sure we shouldn't contact Leah's son? Perhaps these are really his. We should ask the rabbi."

Naomi put her hands over her ears and kicked at the floor. "Mine," she said. "Why do you want to take from me the only present I have ever received?" Moses, ashamed, looked away.

Reader: It may appear in the story thus far that God intended the good fortune of Naomi. It may be that Naomi's lack of moral scruple when it came to an old lady's inheritance was the original sin that shaped the destiny of this family. Or the beginning of this story may contain God's plan to save the Gruenbaums from the gas chambers. Maybe these are stories in which we can find the hand of God turning the pages. But some might say that, despite certain promises exchanged at Sinai, the Gruenbaums were sinking like falling stars across the sky. Nothing magic intervened to protect them, and what happy endings they found they paid for in hard currency. Some would see this story as a record of people whose collective destiny may yet prove dazzling, but whose individual lives lead to nothing more redemptive than the next generation and the one that follows. Banal, yes—ah, the banality of goodness—but how much courage and resistance, how much imagination and determination, how much sorrow and wonder, salts the path and how brave our characters who, unrecognized by the multitudes, unsung in history books, are, like us, people who have the nerve to survive while the Messiah considers and the seasons turn.

Reader: Is it possible that Jacob was wrestling with the angel on a social ladder? That would explain how the ladder stood up even though it was leaning against nothing.

Hedy in Maine: Summer 1942

The child was left with the nanny when her mother went back to the city. With only a few weeks left in August, Flora had to go to a funeral. Flora had kissed her child good-bye and waved to her from the backseat of the Buick that was taking her to the train in Portland. But the child knew, as children know, that her mother dressed in her traveling suit, wobbling in her Cuban heels, had felt as if a door were opening. The child held her mother's hand all the way to the main lodge, smelling the perfume, the lipstick that reminded the child of peppermint candy. The child knew that the lakes of Maine, the tall pines, the ashtray she had made for her mother in day camp in the crafts shop, none of these things would bring her mother back. Her mother had watched as the kitchen boys put her suitcases in the car. She had smoked her last Camel in the wilderness and turned her face homeward. Vacations breed false expectations.

The child, whose name was Hedy, after the movie star Hedy Lamarr, spent the remaining weeks of the summer, a summer in which she grew an inch and gained two pounds and learned how to do the crawl and won the prize in team spirit and sportsmanship—only six years old she knew that you shouldn't cheer for yourself (such things come with being born in America)—imagining her mother, back in New York, sitting by her dressing table, applying dark lines to the eyes, doing crossword puzzles, lying back on her pillows talking on the telephone, having breakfast on a tray that would come in with the maid, a tray with a flower on it, and a china cup with a soft-boiled egg and with muffins and marmalade. Hedy would sit in the bathtub in the small cabin while Ursula scrubbed at her dirty knees, thinking about the tray and the newspaper at the end of her mother's bed and the lace on her nightgown and the way her mother kissed her on the nose, leaving lipstick marks behind, and the way her mother would blow smoke rings for her, one after another. Some days her mother phoned and some days she did not. Hedy always told her mother how fine everything was, what a good day she had. She tried to keep her mother on the line as long as possible, but the connection was bad and their conversations were always cut short. After she talked to her mother, Hedy would go out to play with Michael and maybe his friend Henry. In the fading light among the grasshoppers and fireflies they played a game about Japanese kamikaze pilots and flaming dragons disguised as pine cones that appeared from behind the trunks of trees and hid under fallen leaves. At the end of the game the dragons were boiled in pots and the Japs had worms stuck down their throats, and a particularly wicked Japanese general was always given an enema of castor oil. While they were playing Hedy felt like a dragon herself, breathing fire, flashing prickly scales, leaping rocks, flying to the tops of trees. What was to stop her from eating the whole world for breakfast and drinking the ocean for lunch? But afterward, in her bed, an ache came in Hedy's stomach, not a hunger, not a hunger at all, more of a deadness, a numbness, that was spreading through her limbs, up her body, into her head.

Sometimes she hardly felt she was real at all, and only the hardest work of her own imagination kept her from disappearing entirely.

Late in August, just before Hedy and Ursula boarded the train back to New York, all the children were taken on a nighttime hayride to a great meadow. As the stars glittered across the sky they lay on wool blankets and sang songs and watched the fire that had been built in the middle of their circle.

"Camp Songowood," they sang, "we'll always ding-a-ling to you." And then at the far end of the field great green lights began shooting up to the top of the universe, wide silver lights, and then pink ones shaped like arrows rose after them. The northern half of the sky was blinking and shaking with color. It was the lights off the ice, the Northern Lights of late summer in Maine. Hedy was frightened at first. She was quiet sitting on her blanket and wondering about bombs in Europe and where her mother was at the moment. And then as it went on and the sky seemed to rise and fall with light and Hedy could see the Venus star above her head and the familiar Big Dipper on her right, she lay back, feeling the scratchy wool of her blanket against her cheek. Was Mary the Mother of God watching her, as Ursula said? She reached her hand out for a blade of grass and felt an insect crawl over her thumb. With her other hand she crushed the bug and wiped the black stain against her shirt. Then she buried her face in her lap so no one would see her smile.

Hedy in the Hadassah Hospital: Jerusalem, 1990

Hedy leaned against the wall. She tore the paper napkin that came with her coffee into shreds and let the pieces slip from her hands onto the floor. She felt numb, as if someone had injected a jungle poison into her veins. She rocked gently back on her heels, a gesture of prayer without content. It was hot. She felt flushed, and sweat appeared on her upper lip and dripped down the back of her neck. She thought of Namah, whose face had been scorched at the beach the summer before and whose hands had clenched into fists when her mother, gently, with the tips of her fingers, rubbed cream across the blistered cheeks. The sweetness of Namah's face bent forward, explaining the height of the waves, the friends talking, the beach towel that had slipped, the ice-cream wagon up on the boardwalk, the sweetness of Namah's face, made Hedy tired, suddenly needing sleep.

Inside the operating room, the neurosurgeon was singing, a song from his childhood, something about a bird who tried to wash the moon-light out of his eyes, a song he had learned from his grandmother, who had learned it in the Jewish quarter of Morocco when she was a girl. His patient was young, which was in her favor. Her pulse was strong and her pale skin freckled and smooth. Was she still a virgin? He hoped not, just in case. He worked slowly. Time was not so much the enemy as fatigue and carelessness. His residents, his nurses, handed him what he wanted, followed his instructions, moved the light closer as he wished, and one of them, the one from Arad, she hummed the chorus of his song along with him.

Hedy on Park Avenue: Fall 1942

In the basement of the apartment house on Park Avenue there is a maze of halls all painted dark green, all cement. The halls lead to storage areas where in great cages, cages large enough for lions or bears, lie, gathering dust, hosting spiderwebs, carton boxes and suitcases, old bikes, abandoned dollhouses, tennis rackets with missing strings, mattresses, sofas and lamps, things that have gone out of style, things inherited from parents who had houses in Deal, New Jersey, or Belle Harbor, Queens. Only one bare bulb lights each of these halls, and only the superintendent with his large ring of keys can open the doors. Hedy walks along the hall, rattling the cages with her shoes, staring into the dark rooms, looking for something, something revealing, something exciting, something dead. She walks past the sled room where her sled sits, waiting for winter. Her name is on it. Ursula will take her to the park when the snow comes, although she won't let her go down the large hill with the path between the rocks and trees. The air is musty, chill, and steamy, damp with a smell of mildew and ammonia. Hedy is waiting for the school holiday to be over. She walks in the basement when Ursula thinks she is in her room playing with her dolls. Hedy never plays with dolls. Hedy turns the corner and sees the laundry room. There is Willow, who comes on Thursdays to do the laundry. Willow is a Negro; her brown skin is now glistening with sweat, and she is talking with the other Negro laundresses in the basement. Hedy sits down on a canvas chair, right near Willow. The women, who are bending over a long row of enamel basins, stop talking. Hedy waits for them to start again. Willow turns to her.

"Go upstairs," she says.

"I'll be quiet," Hedy says.

It takes a few minutes, but the women decide to forget about Hedy. They talk.

"Whatcha gonna do with him?"

"Put him out, let him go."

"Who needs that one?"

"She needs him."

Hedy is bored. She asks Willow if she can help put the wet clothes on the rack to dry.

"Girl, get outta here," says Willow. "What you gonna do, be a laundress?" And she laughs.

The other laundresses in their print dresses, some like Willow with flowered scarves wrapped around their heads, their arms full of wet clothes, laugh. Hedy is certain she must be sick. Shame can churn the insides of a child long before it has a shape that can be named.

Hedy takes the elevator, the front elevator. John, the day man, is in full uniform. His buttons shine gold, and his black shoes have been polished to a shine. "Let me drive the elevator," says Hedy. "Just this once."

"Ah, now, miss," says John, "you wouldn't be wanting me to lose me job, would you?" Hedy kicks the dark brown wood paneled elevator wall. "Be a good girl," says John.

Mary opens the door. Her uniform is black with a starched white apron. Mary says not a word to Hedy, as if a ghost had rung the bell and entered the apartment. Mary, whose mother had fourteen children, some of whom Mary herself tended as they died of pneumonia, measles, and diarrhea, has no soft spot for children. While Christ may have suffered them, she herself had enough to do just taking care of herself. Her tiny room in the back of the apartment, next to the cook's behind the kitchen, has its own small bath. This is a good job despite the German governess who has airs and wants her breakfast served off the silver trays, despite the cook who screams in her sleep and wakes Mary night after night.

Hedy goes to the door outside her mother's room. She lies down on the soft carpet and looks under the crack. She can see the peach ruffle of the bedspread. She can see that the curtains are still pulled. Her mother is still asleep. Hedy leans against the door. She knows she is not allowed to wake her mother. In the dark hallway, she curls up. Bears hibernate all winter, they sleep and need no food. Hedy waits for the door to open, for Mary to arrive with her mother's breakfast tray.

Reader: I hear you scoff. Poor little rich girl. I should have had it so good, with maids and cooks and nannies. I hear you. What's this child moping about—let her get a toy or a book or count the pennies in her piggy bank. The rich have no right to lie on the floor and stare at the ceiling as if they were stuck down a well waiting for rescue. So many children, Willow's children, for example, don't have stuffed bears sitting on their bureaus, listen for the steps of mothers or fathers out working long hours trying to pay off the landlord, the doctor, save enough for a winter coat to keep off the cold winds. So why should anyone think about Hedy, who has a gold charm bracelet with a miniature piano with real ivory keys? Forget it. Believe me, Reader, I understand. It's not easy to feel sympathy for Hedy and Flora. We admire the rich even as we despise them for looking better than we do, for not worrying about the things that keep us up at night, the mortgage, the tuition bills, the new tires for the car. Of course we know the rich have their moments of collapse. The youngest and simplest among us know that money doesn't make you happy, but what pleasure stabs the heart as we hear it again and again. So, Reader, enjoy Hedy's drift through her home, feel superior to Flora, who has no idea that her daughter waits outside her door. But remember that a child who presses her face to the carpet hoping to see a glimpse of her mother's ankle under the sheets is a witness to the awakening from the American dream.

The Huddled Masses Afloat: 1880

In the cabin that they shared with six other people on the lowest deck where the portholes looked out only on black waves, the sound of the engines whining and belching, bucking and churning, went on night and day, as relentlessly as Jewish history itself.

As the sun rose over the stern of the ship, Moses made his way toward the third deck where steerage passengers were allowed to take the air, crowded into a small space, with no chairs or blankets, no stewards offering coffee. In the first moments of morning the deck was still quiet. Here and there other men like Moses were taking out their velvet prayer cases and shaking out their taleysim and wrapping them around their shoulders, as if several black birds with white wings had settled on the lurching deck.

"God," said Moses, doubling over with nausea, "I am sick. Your ocean is too large. I am"—and he raised his thin arms in their shirtsleeves up to the warming sky—"I am only Moses, the tailor from Sulvalki." He looked down to see his daughter wrapped in her mother's shawl, leaning against his legs, her arms raised in imitation of his.

"Papa," she said, "look at the sun. It is coming straight to me."

And so it was, a red line on the water bending and dipping from the horizon's edge right to a place in front of them.

"See," said Ruth, "if I move, it follows me." And she ran a few feet away and looked out over the sea. "The sun is making a path to me," she said.

Moses put his hand on the face of the child. What a good soft thing was the skin of a child.

Let Them Eat Cake—Max Gruenbaum on the Boat: 1880

Max looked over the crowded deck and saw his brother sitting beside a woman who was studying English from a grammar book. Boring, thought Max, boring, the whole ocean that rocked and rocked. He swung on a chain that held a lifeboat to the side. An old man with a beard and blanket he carried everywhere with him gave him a kick.

"Don't fool, boychik," he said, not so kindly.

Max moved away and to the head of the stairs, the stairs that went up where he was not allowed to go. The boat swayed. The mist came off the ocean and made it hard to see. The boy was still small, small enough to think that the boat was forever and land the best memory he had. His socks, the ones he'd worn for weeks, were slipping down his ankles. His muffler was stained with the morning's porridge. He began to climb, pulling his weak leg up after the good one. It was good to climb alone into a place where you didn't know what was at the top, where you were forbidden to go. Max was old enough to know that the things that were not allowed were not boring. Up he went; through the bars of the staircase he could see the ocean still moving, going nowhere, nothing changed. He reached the landing. He saw another staircase. Why not. He climbed up the first step, and now he was on his way, maybe to the place where the captain steered the boat. He reached the next landing and saw a lady in fur-lined boots and silver laces sitting on a long chair. She caught his eye.

"Boy," she said, "you don't belong here."

Max moved out of her sight, ran down the side of the ship, and peered in the portholes. He saw a man shaving at a sink, not like down below where the men crowded together, but this man had a bowl all to himself. Max ran his hand over the window to clear the glass. Had he seen clearly? He heard footsteps. He crouched low and crawled along. He saw an open passageway. He was in a kitchen—a grand kitchen where the knives were shining, and bowls of fruit sat on a table, and the pots and pans were bubbling and boiling with the smell of meats and vegetables. He moved along the wall till he saw a table on which a tray of pastries sat: lemon and strawberry, cream and cherry, chocolate icing and buttery cake. He drew in his breath. He jumped for the table and began eating his way across the tray. It was a big tray. He stuffed pastries in his mouth as fast as he could, one after the other, cream oozing out over his small lips. He wanted to take some downstairs, some for later, maybe one for his mother and his sister, but how could cakes survive the journey down the stairs? Better to eat them now. The kitchen was filled with waiters and cooks and dishwashers who hadn't noticed the child. One did.

"Hey boy!" they yelled. "Catch him!" they called.

Max dragged his leg, and it was hard for him to run fast, but he was small and dashed under chairs and hid behind pipes and pressed himself flat and crawled under a net. He ran back and forth among the legs of the first-class passengers, who yelled and tried to hold on to his sleeve. His muffler fell off. He didn't stop to pick it up. Down the stairs he went, falling the last half landing.

"What happened to you, Max?" said his mother, wiping the blood from his bruised leg.

"Nothing," said Max.

Greenhorns, Black Hats, in the Red, White, and Blue: 1880 and On

They found a place to live, and the landlord found Moses a job in a shop that needed men who could work the sewing machine. Naomi he had found a job for, too, in a loft where one hundred women were plucking the feathers of chickens killed according to the kosher rules. Isaac was to stay home and watch over Max and Ruth. It was just as it had been in Sulvalki, only the neighbors lived in one's bedroom and the fire escapes lent a view of the street, and the privy was down three flights of stairs and in a small courtyard that was always damp from pipes that leaked and rain that collected in holes. The sound of coughing was everywhere, and there were feces of horses and humans in the puddles in the streets.

Think how they slept together in one room with the single man, the boarder from the Ukraine, whose aunt was a friend of the landlord, who knew that the new family could use help with the rent. Think of the sounds in the night, not just from their own bedroom, but in the apartment across the way and the one upstairs and the one across the alley whose window looked into theirs. On hot nights the children could watch the adults who chased each other over the bed, calling names that they seemed not to mean because later they would fall into bed together and turn down the lamp and the moaning and groaning and humping and slapping and creaking and banging would begin. Think what Freud would have had to say when passions were part of the darkness that covered the children who were sleeping—or were they? Of course in the morning they could hear their father, his tallis over his shoulders, standing at the window, praising God for the hounds of the forest and the glories of the day; they could hear his voice raised in Hebrew toward the sliver of sky that stood above their building, his voice carrying the words, rocking them back and forth, dipping them into his sadness and releasing them with his hope out the window into the air that so often hung heavy and brown over the street. They could hear other men, too, the one on the floor above them and the one below, not exactly at the same moment, but sometime between dawn and leaving for work, before the line at the privy grew long, the sound of the men with their prayers, linking their fathers to their fathers and backward to the temple before it was burning and the walls were breached by the foxes. The prayers would take away the sound of the night and its animal grunting and its animal breathing— or did it?

Moses found a shul. He found there other men like himself who were surprised in a new land, their minds still working by the clocks of other centuries, still waiting for Messiahs who were intending to lead them east to Jerusalem, not west to California. Naomi found friends among the chicken pluckers, women who spoke English or pieces of it, at least, and she came home with words, new words that she taught to the family. She came home with her fingers raw and her eyesight bleary, but she knew this was the beginning, just the beginning, not the end of the story at all. She was not yet twenty-seven; some of the women in the House for the Elderly were almost a century old. If sometimes at night her body was aching and her courage failed, she felt her small diamond and smiled to herself. She had been favored once and would be favored again. She would find a way.

In Sulvalki Isaac had gone to the cheder. In the winter the air in the small school was heavy with smoke from the wood stove, and in the summer the heat made his eyes close. Only Moses, who could keep any dream going for a millennium, believed that his son Isaac was going to be a scholar, a rabbi. Isaac could see plainly enough that first came food and shelter, then came a piece of cloth for the table, a piece for the body, a hat to cover the head, and that out in the world of men things were being exchanged that made a difference, unlike the words of the rabbi in the cheder that felt to him like so many stones tied to his body, slowing him down when the race had started and he was already late.

In America Moses sent his son Max to the cheder. After three days Max ran away and refused to return. When Moses heard that Max had left the cheder he raised his hand to his son's face. He did not release it. Instead he sat on his chair and stared out the window at the brick wall next door. His eyes were closed. He looked thinner than usual. A muscle on his eye twitched. Max said, "I won't go back. I don't ever want to go back." Max ran down the stairs and was out in the street before anyone could stop him.

"So he'll be an American, an Indian savage," said Naomi, shrugging it off.

But Moses sat still in his chair, and when Isaac heard the milk cart early in the morning, Moses was still sitting, his clothes on, his hands over his ears as if to block out the sounds of the new day. Max did not come back that night. He was gone all day Wednesday, too. Naomi knocked on the doors of all the neighbors.

"It's your fault!" she screamed at Moses. "You shouldn't have sent him to the cheder. We are in America now. You've killed him!" she screamed at Moses, who took his lunch pail and went off to work, his eyes red from lack of sleep.

Thursday night Max came back, and Naomi scolded him, pinched his arm, and yelled at his absence, but not a word was said about returning to the cheder. Moses sighed. America was no place to bring up rabbis.

As Isaac was bringing the coal up the stairs for the stove that sat in the kitchen, he thought that if he were to lean against God, he would fall down, if he were to place himself in God's hands, he would be crushed as those hands folded together. He could not trouble himself about the destiny of the Jews, the fate of the people; he had enough to do without the chanting of old men ringing in his ears. These thoughts he kept to himself.

Ruth went to the settlement house, where she took free piano lessons once a week. Max was out in the streets with a gang of boys who filched apples from the carts, cigarettes from the corner kiosk, and who wandered as far uptown as the Italian streets, where they sometimes returned with bloody noses, bruises on their arms. Max followed the group of boys, always a little behind because of his limp. Once they entered Spring Street where the Italians lived, and Max picked up an empty bottle of seltzer that was rattling against the curb and threw it at a group of Italian boys standing outside a candy store. Within minutes the names were flying, and Max was called a little kike and told to get back in his zoo with the other kikes. The other boys moved forward to meet the Italians, who were boys like themselves not so long in America, not so big yet, but big enough. Only this being an Italian street, there were more of them than of Jews, and fists flew about, and Max sat on the curb, watching.

The Italians made the Jews run. They were outnumbered, they were not yet the fighters of their imaginations. But as the group headed for the corner, the Italians in pursuit, a Jew named Moshe tripped on his own shoelace and fell to the ground. Within a few seconds he was surrounded. His friends had disappeared around the corner. Only Max, who was sitting on the gutter edge, hiding behind an ice cart, was still there. The biggest Italian leaned over Moshe and, pressing his thumb into his eye and his other hand on his throat, pushed down. Moshe screamed, the scream of the cornered, the scream of the wounded, the scream of the victim who knows his mother cannot save him. In a moment, as Max peered between the legs of the others, there was blood all over the fallen Jew's face, and his eye, with the sound of a flopping fish, had popped from his head and lay on the street by his thrashing head.

"God, Holy Jesus," shouted the Italians, and they too ran off in the other direction. "Kikes," they yelled as they ran. "Christ killers," one called, and the others laughed, or perhaps it wasn't laughter so much as the gurgle of excitement, the nausea at the sight of blood and a rising fear: what if the Irish got them one night in the wrong street, outnumbered?

Max had stayed home several days after that incident. He claimed he was sick to his stomach, but Isaac, who heard things that Naomi and Moses did not, knew that Max had thrown a bottle of seltzer and that he had started it all.

"You're too small for fighting," said Isaac. "It wasn't your fault, you didn't hurt anyone."

But Max was not sure if God were watching or not, if God understood that if one leg were not as long as the other, you could not be a fighter, if David had conquered Goliath, should he not have rushed into the street and knocked the Italian from behind and kicked the greasy wop in the groin? He should have. Max stayed home because he was ashamed. But shame, like sorrow, wears thin, and Max returned to the streets. Moshe, known all over the neighborhood thereafter as Moshe the Blind, had been taken to the hospital by the owner of the ice cart, whose sister had married a Jew and who couldn't bear the sound of the boy crying out for his mother in the half darkness that would be his portion ever after.

As the weather got colder, Max spent more time playing cards in the back of the candy store with his pals. He learned, allowing an extra second for his bad leg, allowing a moment to roll on the ground, to jump on the trolley at 3rd Street and jump off before the conductor could catch hold of his jacket. He learned to speak English faster than his brother, who had found a job with a towel and sheet peddler on Orchard Street making package after package in the back of the stall where the light rarely came and he could only hear the echoes of the customers' voices.

Isaac brought home every penny he earned and watched as his mother figured the accounts. He watched as she saved—"in case we should need," she would say.

When Moses came home, up the stairs, he put his head on the table and slept. One night he woke as the stars were high in the sky, where of course he could not see them, and he woke his wife, who was spread out across the bed, her bosoms heaving and the hair she wore in the old country under a scarf, now loose on the pillow, and he said to her, "Naomi, my love, you have the diamond, let's return to Sulvalki. I want to go back."

Naomi's hand went to her waist, where the diamond was protected in its familiar place. "You go back," she said, "but without me and the children. We are Americans now. Go back," she said, "I don't care." She shouted her words, her voice cracking, so high was her pitch, so hard was her larynx working, and the boarder who was asleep on his cot and dreaming of his wife who would come to him soon, woke and yelled out for quiet.

"A man has to earn in the day," he said, and the children woke and huddled together, Ruth with her hand on Isaac's arm. They listened in the dark to their mother, who repeated over and over as if she wanted her words to go up to heavens, to be recorded there in the Book of Judgment.

"Go already," she said. "What use are you to me here, a mouth to feed?" That wasn't true, she needed his paycheck. Isaac felt his mouth dry and his fingers cold.

"All right," said Moses, "be quiet, my love, we'll stay."

And that's how it was for a while for the Gruenbaums in America. A Promised Land that needed some tilling before it would yield up its promise, a Promised Land that had already been claimed by someone else before you had arrived, a Promised Land that was a gift that you had to earn, a promise with clauses and subclauses and fine print that turned out to be consequences, payments due. Nothing new about that.

Christmas on Park Avenue: 1943

It was the week before Christmas. Ursula was supposed to take Hedy downtown to see Santa Claus, to see the windows in the stores where elves and toy reindeer spun on circular platforms while snowflakes fell on dolls and stuffed animals all preparing for Christmas morning and dancing at parties or riding in toy trains or waving from the windows of toy carriages. But Ursula had caught Hedy's cold, so that they could not go, not today, not tomorrow, maybe never.

Hedy went to sleep thinking of Christmas, of the baby Jesus born in the manger: of Santa Claus, who came down the chimney and brought presents to good boys and girls. Of course Hedy didn't believe that part. This year was to be their first Christmas. Ursula was going to buy a tree, and her mother had brought presents. Hedy and Ursula would have Christmas in their room because Jews were not supposed to have Christmas at all, but Hedy's mother had always wanted a tree, Hedy had heard her tell Ursula that. Ursula was to go to midnight mass and then have the morning off after the celebration with Hedy. This year they would have Christmas like everybody else. Hedy had read " 'Twas the Night Before Christmas," and she could recite it by heart, the eight tiny reindeer, the finger by the side of the nose, and the dreams of sugar plums that danced in the head.

When she woke in the morning, there on her dresser table a Christmas scene awaited her. Cotton batting had covered the table, small mirrors were made into ice ponds, and little figures, a man in a top hat, a woman with a blue dress, were skating, little houses with chimneys, with Christmas wreaths on their small doors, dotted the hills that had been sloped up and down over the dresser top. A small policeman stood by a train, and in the center of the snow stood a white church, its doors open. Inside, when Hedy picked it up, one could see the tiny people in their pews, the stained-glass window behind the preacher. In the top of the steeple a real little bell rang when the church was tipped from side to side. Silver sparkling flecks were embedded in the cotton as if the light of the sun had caught the snow in its first fall. Hedy saw a bunch of carolers, who were holding open a miniature song book, and their mouths were open as they serenaded the people inside one of the houses. There was a small bakery with rolls in the window, and a horse with a sled pulled a group of children behind the church. There was a manger with the three kings and the three wise men kneeling in the cotton snow, and nestled in the hay was a tiny basket in which the baby Jesus rested, a doll wrapped in cloth, the size of a fingernail.

Hedy stood in front of her dresser, amazed. Ursula had made this for her. She had kept it a secret. Hedy considered the baby. She picked him up carefully and unwound the cloth that wrapped him. A tiny doll rested in the palm of her hand. She bent down and kissed it. What do you do with babies? she wondered. You bathe them, she thought. She went into the bathroom and turned on the water. She put her hand under the faucet, holding the doll between her fingers. The force of the water washed the tiny doll out of her hand. In a split second the baby Jesus went down the open drain. Hedy stared at the empty sink. The baby Jesus was gone. She went back to her dresser. There the scene was just as she had left it. The skaters on the mirror, the miniature houses covered with snow, the tiny manger, only now there was no baby Jesus in the hay.

Ursula came into the room. She had expected the child to be happy. Hedy was quiet and could not lift up her eyes. She did not say, "Thank you." Her hands were held together as if they might fly off if she let them free. Ursula looked at the scene on the dresser. "Where is the baby Jesus?" she asked. Hedy said nothing.

Ursula walked out of the room. She slammed the bathroom door. The sound was loud, and it took Hedy by the throat. There was a terrible silence in her room, an emptiness, as if the furniture and clothes, her dolls and her stuffed animals, had all been scooped away and there was nothing except bare walls to look at and no one would come to bring her breakfast.

Several hours later Ursula returned. Her lips were thin and white. Her face was ashen. Her eyes behind her thick glasses had turned gray like stone. Ursula picked up all the little houses, the mirror, and the figures and put them in a paper bag. She swept up the cotton batting, and the hills of snow disappeared; she took away the train and the carolers and the church and the small green trees, even the one with the star on the top. Ursula slammed the door again. She had planned the surprise for so long, she had bought the little figures out of her own money. She had expected the child to shout with excitement, she had expected that she would put her arms around her and that the Christmas spirit would have entered the house of these Jews. Ursula thought of her home; her village looked like the scene she had made, almost. There would be smells of cookies, and her uncles would be preparing the goose. Ursula in a foreign land was saving money each week, but she was living with the enemy and that was clear enough. Ursula was loyal to the brook that had run down to the river through her mother's field, and she was loyal to her priest, who had once called her Ursula, a little bird of spring, because she sang as she waited for him to walk with her to her aunt's house. Ursula had received mail up until a few years ago, and now the mail had stopped. Each of the war years she did as she had the previous fifteen— she sent presents to her mother through the International Red Cross and mailed them in September. But she had not heard from her family. Perhaps the Americans had killed them all. Ursula thought of her farm with weeds growing in the corn and string bean patch, she thought of her mother lying dead across the kitchen table with blood at the throat. She had always said, It didn't matter what nationality you were, if you were a good person, that's what counted; but sometimes it did matter which side of the border you slept on. Sometimes Ursula thought she should have gone home when the streets of Yorkville filled with young Germans raising their fists and the Bund passed out literature on the corner of 86th Street and Third Avenue; she had promised the young man who had invited her to a meeting that she would come, but then she hadn't. Now Ursula packed away the entire miniature village except for the small church with a tiny bell that actually rang, which she put in her own bureau drawer, the one Hedy was forbidden ever to open.

Reader: I remind you that Sigmund Freud's family celebrated only two holidays: Christmas and Easter. He believed in the ability of man to invent God, and he accepted the civilizing values of festivals and customs. He profoundly and truthfully with all of his being believed in the power of reason and science, but we have no holidays celebrating those, so he adopted the common Christian pageants, out of convenience, out of conformity, out of a desire—admit it, dear Freud—to be an esteemed member of Viennese society, or to pretend that he was.

So the Gruenbaums, buying a Christmas wreath, wrapping presents in red and green and hiding them in the top shelf of closets, they who did not believe in the value of reason and science, how much more likely it was that they would turn to their neighbors and, being modern, imitate the followers of Paul the Apostle. Each generation was entitled to its own decisions, the one didn't follow the other like sheep, at least not in America, at least not in the twentieth century, when science was promising to cure everything and the sky was not the limit anymore. I remind you that our current passion for ethnic multiplicity—Pakistani mittens and Indian food and Mexican piñatas at children's birthday parties, Thai bells on teenagers and high-fashion models in the turbans of the Persian bazaar, models in fact with black skin and Watusi ancestors, menorahs in Central Park—this is all new, this brotherhood of custom, this united nations of style. Back in the forties, when the Christmas tree came into the Gruenbaum house, first in Hedy's room and eventually into the living room, where it stood in front of the Chinese screen the decorator had purchased at a bargain, the tree lights flashing on the turquoise walls that were painted with gold trim, there was only one America visible and indivisible to all, and it celebrated Christmas. Also: Hedy was sorry, truly sorry, that the baby Jesus had fallen down the drain.

Adversity: 1882

In the third August, while over the sidewalks and in the gutters the crumpled wrappers of pickles, ices, and knishes bloomed and the fire escapes were crowded with children who lay on quilts sleeping under the slits of sky that appeared between the buildings, the sighs of those who dreamed of golems, ships that tossed in storms and darkness that never receded, rose through the smells of beer, ammonia, cabbage, and human sweat, barrels of human sweat, into the city night, Ruth turned over on the mattress she shared with Isaac and Max, a mattress they had pulled to the edge of the window but could not fit out onto the fire escape, and scratched her leg. Isaac woke and put out his hand to soothe his sister. Her arm was burning hot. Of course she was hot, he thought, the bricks of the building were practically embers and the air was steam, swallowing, breathing, everyone walked with a weight in his lungs, ash and steam. But Ruth's skin was searing. Her hair was wet. Isaac whispered to Ruth, "What is it?"

"I think," she said, "I'm sick." And so she was.

Isaac pulled a towel down from a hook on the wall and went down to the sink. He washed his sister's face and hands. The moon was full. A stream of moonlight fell down over the fire escape and over the children at the window. Isaac saw his sister's face, and he closed his eyes and turned his head toward the wall. There were blisters on her cheeks, only three now, but more would come. Pox was a word that was whispered in every house; in every shop someone had heard of a case, and the month of August had multiplied the whispering. Isaac held his sister's hand. He should pray. His father when he awoke would pray. Isaac wanted to pray, but all the words that came to mind were curses, and those he kept to himself as he wiped his sister's lips with the towel. The moon slipped down behind the buildings on Avenue B, and the sky lightened with the approach of dawn, and Ruth closed her eyes and the fever carried her into sleep or a thing like sleep that is not so much rest as pause, while more blisters formed under her armpits and in the creases behind the backs of her knees.

Isaac let his parents sleep. The doctor could not be called until morning, and in the quiet of the hour he could look at Ruth and imagine that the blisters were fading, that it was some other rash, some other illness. If the Angel of Death had appeared on the fire escape, there where his mother had draped her cleaning rags, he would tear its heart out of its chest before he would let it near his sister. It was a fight he would lose, and he saw himself crushed on the small balcony, his face, too, covered with blisters. He clenched his teeth so he would not cry and waited for the sound of the milk cart as it clattered down the street and his mother, still thinking that today would be the same as yesterday, rose from her bed and headed out the door down the stairs to the privy in the courtyard.

When in the first light of morning Naomi saw her daughter, she screamed. Max heard the sound and pulled himself close to the wall and closed his eyes tightly. Moses sat on the edge of his bed and his hands shook as he lay the straps of the tefillin over his forearm.

"Get the doctor," Naomi shouted at her husband. "Forget about praying today."

Moses shook his head. She pushed him. Moses continued as if he had not been touched. Naomi pinched his neck. He brushed her hand away as if an insect had settled there. Isaac ran to get the doctor. Ruth's breathing was raspy. Her face was white, and her eyes were hardly open.

Max dressed and went into the street. He said not a word to anyone. All through the day when he thought no one was looking he put a hand to his forehead. He was hot, but no hotter, no stickier, than the others. He felt across his neck, no blisters. He limped, his back was crooked, what more could God want from him? Max was ten. He had seen enough to know that more was surely possible, that one pain did not guarantee exemption from another. He went to the tobacco shop, where the widow Schultz asked him to carry a sandwich and a bottle of whiskey up to the fourth floor. There a man opened the door, and Max saw the whore, Goodie, with her ass in the air and stockings on the floor. The man shut the door before Max could see all he wanted. The widow gave him a cigarette. In the alley, under the line of laundry that mercifully dripped down, Max smoked and, holding the cigarette between his lips, used his hands to quickly examine his private parts—no blisters. He returned in the evening, hungry for his supper. He jumped up the stairs two at a time, favoring his good leg, extending his arms as if they were wings to keep balance. Then he thought of Ruth and a wave of regret washed over him. Why her? Why not somebody else, someone who had never given him an extra bite of her food, who had never played cards with him, watched his tricks and laughed? And then as he propelled himself up the stairs, a second wave rolled over. It was not him, not him, he was fine. He couldn't help it, a shout of joy came from his throat, a shout so loud that Mrs. Moscowitz opened her door and glared at him.

The doctor, already sweating from the heat of the new day, needed only a second. He attached his white mask to his face, and with heavy gloves he turned his young patient over on her back and pulled up her gown. Two more pox were forming at the base of the child's spine. He took refuge in arithmetic; the eighth case he had seen this week, the one-hundredth case in a four-block area. It had started with four in the Italian block over by the river. Now it was moving, jumping buildings, skipping parks, doubling in strength each day, sixteen, thirty-two, forty-eight. If he were mayor, he would announce an epidemic. He would evacuate the area. Send all the families to the country. What does a doctor think when he sees a little girl, no more than eight years old, with those blisters on her face? She would have been pretty, he thought. She would have had children, and there are enough children here already. He stopped thinking about her at all. He didn't ask her name or offer her a sweet from his bag. He told Naomi about cleaning the floors with lye. He told her to scrub her utensils with water she had boiled on the stove. He told her to burn the child's clothing, burn it all. He told Moses that the quarantine wagon would come and take his daughter to the Hospital for Infectious Diseases. He forbade the family to visit. They allow no visitors there, he said, visitors return sick and the numbers are burdensome enough.

Moses leaned over his daughter. He saw the blisters on her cheeks. "I will go to the hospital with her," he said. "God will protect me."

"Just the way God protected your daughter?" said the doctor, who was impatient with the candles lit by the pictures of Mary a few streets over and impatient with the Jews, who persisted in thinking they would receive special treatment.

Moses remembered the burning shul and was silent. Your family needs you here, said the doctor. To Naomi, he said, "Take care of your other children. If they show signs, call me immediately."

"Will Jews be the nurses in the hospital?" asked Moses as the doctor was closing the door.

"Of course," said the doctor, who knew that the Hospital for Infectious Diseases was staffed by the Carmelite nuns of Brooklyn, a group whose numbers were decreasing and whose surviving members bore signs of the pox on their bodies. "Of course, it is a Jewish hospital," said the doctor, almost running down the stairs.

But Isaac, who had not missed a day of work since the time several years before when he had offered his services to the linen man on Orchard Street, had waited for the doctor at the front door. He grabbed the doctor by the arm. "My sister will be afraid," he said. "I know my sister, she will be afraid if she is sent alone. She's only a child."

The doctor peeled Isaac's hand off his arm and then in one quick motion felt the boy's glands on either side of his neck. "Stay here and help your mother," he said. "No reason for her to lose two children."

Within an hour the cart with its red cross painted on its side, its wooden stretchers banging with each lurch of the horse, came down the street, stopping in front of the Gruenbaum building. Two men, one wearing a white mask, the other his face covered with the red pits that marked those who survived the disease, his ears bent forward as if they had been incorrectly anchored to his head, climbed down, tied the horse to a lamppost, and pushed their way past the peering neighbors into the building. Isaac patted the horse on the nose. He moved casually, as if he had no purpose other than boyish curiosity, to the back of the cart, its wheels that had rattled over the cobblestones, had stilled the Jewish voice, bringing each nerve to attention.

While the driver and his pockmarked assistant bounced the wooden stretcher on which Ruth had been strapped into the back of the cart, Isaac lay flat against the floor, an old wool blanket pulled up over his head. As soon as the cart began to move he pulled the blanket down and leaned forward to his sister, who was staring at the shaking sky, her eyes glazed and without focus.

"Water," she said to Isaac when she saw him. She put out her hand and held his sleeve. "Water," she said again. But Isaac had no water.

The horse stopped and was tied up again. The men came and pulled another stretcher from the stack. "Go," said Ruth. "Go now, please go." But Isaac knew she did not mean it. It was said the same way she told him that her eyes were fine and it was all right that she was working late helping her mother, who had taken a second job, sewing beads onto velvet patches that would be turned into pocketbooks for fancy ladies.

The men came back to the wagon. Isaac again hid under the wool blanket, breathing quietly as the heat of the day put its hand around his throat. A young man was lifted into the cart. He screamed out, "No, No, don't take me! I'm not sick. I'll get better. I don't have it. I don't!"

The driver and his assistant paid no attention to the thrashing and the noise. "Ave Maria," said the man, and began to mumble a prayer. It could not be, then, as his father's friend Shmuel had said, that the pox was a punishment for the Jews because they had abandoned their fathers' ways and knelt before the golden calf in this desert that was America.

"Nonsense," his mother had said. "You think God has nothing better to do than see if the Jews are eating right?" She had laughed. His father had looked down at the ground. He had not contradicted his wife; that he never did in front of the children.

"Water," said the young man as soon as he saw Isaac curled in his corner of the wagon. But Isaac had none.

They came to a pier. The horse was tied to a pillar. Isaac heard the men climb down from their bench. They would chase him away. They would carry his sister off, and he would never find her again. Ruth stared at him. Her face swollen now, and blisters appeared above her lip. Isaac thought about hiding under the blanket and then slipping away after the men had carried out the stretchers. He thought about walking back to Mott Street. It would be a long walk. It might take a day or two, but he would find his way. He would go home to his mother and father and tell them that he had gone with Ruth to the hospital. He could go back to folding his linens and calling to the customers and opening and closing the little shop. He could listen to his father spilling the tap water over his hands, saying to his wife, as he had every morning of the summer, softly so she wouldn't think he was rude, "So this is your America, so hot a man's liver melts and his beard crawls under his chin." He could watch Max and his friends round the corner and smash into the grocer's apple cart sending red and green apples rolling across the street. If he kept his eye on Max, he would see his brother picking up apples and stuffing them in his shirt and hopping off after his friends down the alley. Isaac wanted to go home, but his sister was staring at him. If it were his body lying there and Ruth beside him, he would never let her go—his sister, who knew what he thought even if he did not speak, who had placed her hand in his and never questioned his strength, who believed everything he told her even when he himself was uncertain.

The wagon side dropped down. A sudden shaft of sunlight brought with it a solid wall of heat. Isaac gasped as he saw the men reach for his sister's stretcher and pull it forward. Ruth put out her arms toward him, and he found his body moving forward with her, and then he made his decision—or his decision was made for him. He pulled Ruth off her wooden shaft, out from under the strap that had been loosely placed over her small hips, and held her in his arms. Her hot body rested against his, making his shirt wet. Her head was buried in his chest when the men jumped into the wagon to see why the stretcher had emerged without the child they had placed on it.

"You can't take her without me," shouted Isaac. He was only twelve years old, and his voice chose that moment to emerge from his throat like a string on a violin that strains and snaps.

"One girl child with the pox, that's what we picked up," said the driver.

"I'm staying with her," repeated Isaac, and this time the squeak was louder. "She's my sister," he added, "my sister."

The assistant scrambled across the wagon floor and grabbed Isaac's arm. "You got some nerve, kid," he said. "I could smash your brains out right here."

Isaac kicked, he struck out with his free hand. He bared his teeth and, snarling, tried to bite the arm that was squeezing his chest, forcing his backbone into a wooden rail.

"A Jew kid," said the driver, spitting on the cobblestones. "Probably has the pox same as his sister. Let him go with her, one less Jew kid hanging around." The assistant opened his fingers, and Isaac felt his arm throbbing.

Isaac rode the ferry to the small island in the middle of the East River. The shores of Manhattan stretched out before him, and Isaac remembered the ship that had brought them there. Then he had been eager to land; now he wished to stay at sea forever. Isaac standing at the rail could see the farms and the cows grazing in Harlem. He leaned against the side of the boat and felt the breeze blow over the water. He watched the white foam churning in the propellor's blades.

The ferry docked. The assistant tied the rope to the iron standard on the pier. Boards were missing from the dock, and the men jumped about, testing the firmness of the wood before resting their weight. As the boat bobbed at the dock, Isaac leaned over the side and filled his hands with water. He spilled drops over his sister's face. He wet her hands with his wet hands. The men picked up the other stretcher, whose occupant was now in a deep sleep. The assistant pushed the boat hard with his legs, and when Isaac stood up to jump to the pier, the distance seemed long; the entire length of the rope was several times his height. "Can't swim?" called the assistant. "You're dying anyhow, so you might as well drown," he shouted at Isaac.

On the shore Ruth picked up her head and looked for her brother. Isaac leapt as far as he could, but it was not far enough. He fell in the water, which tasted dank and bitter in his mouth. He flailed with his hands and kicked with his feet. He did not know how to swim, and he gulped water into his mouth. The dock was only a few feet away. He felt his feet in his shoes go down toward the bottom, and suddenly they were resting on mud. It was shallow. He walked to the dock and pulled himself up, scratching his hands on some splinters of broken wood. The men laughed. "I'm here," he said to Ruth. "Don't worry, I'm here."

Two nuns pulled back the steel door at the hospital's entrance. They were not surprised to see the man on the stretcher. They were not surprised to see the little girl, shivering from her fever, curled up with her arms wrapped around her knees. But the boy, the apparently healthy boy whose clothes were soaking wet, whose shoes were filled with mud, who insisted on staying beside his sister, this they had not seen before.

The hospital itself was an old fort. The original walls had been built by the Dutch against the intentions of the British. It was a logical place to quarantine the dangerously ill. The rectangular openings in the wall were converted to narrow windows that brought shafts of light down the stone corridors. The rotting floors were replaced with the latest in brick and stone. Wide, deep closets were built to store the blankets and the sheets and the trays and the china and the pitchers that were necessary for the care of the thirsty and the feverish. The city had rebuilt the fortress this time to keep disease out of the streets, to make a house of the dying so the living could be safe. There across the water it was hoped the dread disease could only run in circles. Clothing of the dead was burned in a giant furnace in the basement. The dead were shrouded and buried one on top of another, quickly, at the edge of the island, and their families told they could never visit the graves upon penalty of joining the dead themselves. The nuns from the parish in Brooklyn that had lost so many of its novitiates to an outbreak of pox had proved able caretakers, conductors of the passage between the breathing and the nonbreathing. Everyone, regardless of religion, was given the last rites. Those of the dying who were aware of what was happening usually didn't mind. Who knew for sure what was coming next? When Isaac, however, saw the nuns in their habits, the white hoods, the long black robes, the crosses rising and falling with the heaving motion of the breasts, he lost his courage. He was only twelve years old, and tears came to his eyes.

Ruth was placed in a bed on a ward with thirty other cots. They were all filled with children, all without their mothers and fathers, some already orphaned by the disease, some whose parents lay on other wards, some whose mothers had abandoned them on the streets when they had seen the first red blisters on their skin, some whose mothers were now begging God, "Spare him and I'll never have sex again, spare him and I'll give away my engagement ring, spare her and I'll never ask anything else of You for the rest of my life," bargains, deals, negotiations, all one-sided.

Ruth's bed was by a window, a small opening in the brick that was now covered with glass. Isaac, if he stood on the balls of his feet and pulled himself up with his hands, could just see the water that swirled around the island, changing colors with the time of day and the clouds that came and went. Sometimes he saw a ship, a ferry carrying the stricken to the island, or a tugboat pushing a barge loaded with coal, or a cargo ship testing its seaworthiness on a sail around Manhattan.

The nuns tried to send him home. But each time one approached him he would throw himself on his sister's bed and hang on to the sides with all his strength. He would close his eyes and wait for the sound of the nun's boots going away from the bed. The nuns brought him a blanket to sleep on, and they brought bread and milk and an apple on a tray and left it at the side of the bed. One fat nun with hair on her chin kept trying to touch his forehead, to see if he were sick.

"Are you hot, boy?" she would say. He would keep his eyes closed and toss his head so her hand could not rest on him. "Not yet, I think," she would say. "Mary, Mother of God, protect you," she would mumble, and move on.

No scratching of blisters; it will make it worse, said the nuns to Ruth. When they saw that Ruth's blisters had broken and the child could not keep her fingers from rubbing and pulling at the sores, they tied her hands with straps to the sides of the cot. Isaac wanted to take the straps off his sister's arms, but the nuns had told him that she would make herself worse if she pulled at her skin. "Maybe she will live," one had said. "We don't want more holes than is necessary." So Isaac had stood there while his sister pulled at her arms in the straps and waved her fingers trying to reach her skin. Most of the other children in the ward were also strapped down. Some of them cried and some of them were silent. When Isaac passed the beds of the silent ones, he was most afraid.

It was the boredom that was the hardest part of all. Ruth could not talk to him. He told her what was happening. He described to her the ward and the other children and the section at the far end with cribs and babies who cried and cried and then were silent until the nuns came and carried them away and new babies were placed in the cribs. He told her about the ships that he could see from the window, and he exaggerated their grandeur, the size of the sails, the wooden hulls, the colors of the flags they flew. But the hours dragged on and on. The mornings turned into afternoons, and the light in the ward grew dimmer and dimmer and the nuns moved back and forth like trains on a track, and he began to predict their coming and to know their walks. He amused himself by jumping along the corridor, by counting everything in sight, the numbers of legs on the cots, the numbers of tables at the end of the corridor, the numbers of bricks in the wall, the numbers of candles in their holders. The numbers of blisters on the bodies of the children on either side of Ruth. For her part Ruth dozed or moaned or lay still as if she had no thoughts, as if she had no mind. This scared Isaac the most, and when she did this he would promise her things: when she got well he would take her uptown to see where the rich people lived. This was a thing he had not yet dared himself but intended one day to do. He would make money and buy her a ring with a diamond in it just like the one their mother kept in a pouch at her waist. He would buy her a house with a piano when he was grown up. He would talk and talk till at last she would look at him and focus her eyes and smile, not a big smile, not a recognizable smile, but a thing with the mouth that was meant to reassure him, I'm still here. And it did. Time blurred and the days began to seem like years and a little like it was on the ship crossing the Atlantic. It seemed not to matter how long it had been or how much longer it would be, it just went on and on as if he had no past, no place outside the hospital, and no future to go to, as if the entire world were in this place and nothing would ever change. He felt as if his legs were losing their strength, as if he couldn't remember his mother or his father, not without a great effort. It was as if the boat that had brought them across had lost its motor midway and was tossing about on the waters, day and night, night and day, what difference did it make?

Sister Abigail looked at him carefully each time she passed, and finally on the third day, when she had brought him a portion of cereal and a piece of bread, he dared to look at her. Her face was smooth, the part that he could see of it. Her blue eyes seemed clear, as if whatever she wanted, she had. She asked him if his mother wasn't missing him and if it wouldn't be better to go home and let her take care of Ruth. She would do it very well, she promised him. Ruth had gotten sicker in the days since their arrival at the hospital. She had blisters all over her body now, and her face was a mass of pus. Her arms and legs shook, and sometimes she seemed to be freezing and Isaac had given her his blanket, and at other times she begged him to take all the covers off. She slept and woke and called for water, and Isaac held her hand and brought her water from the pitcher at the end of the ward, and sometimes he stopped and gave other children water.

The little boy in the bed next to Ruth screamed in a language Isaac did not know. Isaac tried to speak to him, but the child either did not hear or did not understand. Isaac tried Yiddish, and the child still ignored him. He tried Polish, and the child did not respond. In the middle of the night there was a hurrying of nuns down the corridor, and when Isaac picked up his head from the blanket on the floor beside his sister's bed where he was sleeping, he saw the sheets pulled back and the boy lying naked on the cot, and his eyes were open but his body was still. The nuns folded his arms, and with a candle in their hands, a candle that cast shadows across the walls, they were singing in a whispering kind of way. Isaac understood that the boy whose name he had never learned was dead.

His sister had eaten only a spoonful or two of porridge in three days.

Her ribs were showing through her skin. Once a day Sister Abigail had come to change Ruth's gown, and Isaac had helped her because Ruth could not sit up herself, could not pull her own arms through the rough cotton shirt. Isaac had seen his sister's ribs, and he had asked Sister Abigail, following her down the corridor, "Will Ruth die?"

Sister Abigail had said to him, "If Christ takes such an innocent child, she will live forever in the Heavenly Kingdom, and one day, when it is the right time, you will be there with her for all eternity."

Isaac had not wanted to offend Sister Abigail and so he had not told her of his conviction, the one he had formed while sitting on the fire escape and watching the roaches pull at a piece of bread he had left in the cracks, that the flicker of life that was in him would be extinguished one day, once and for all, because God must consider him a roach, a crawling moving thing, an eating eliminating thing, one that could be crushed and forgotten.

In the night Isaac had trouble sleeping because the noises on the ward continued, the crying of children, the walking up and down of nuns, and the scraping of the legs of cots against the floor and the banging of the tin cups used to carry the water back and forth. During the day when the dim light entered the ward through the high thin openings that served as windows, turning the air gray and landing in patches on the stone floor, Isaac often fell asleep on his blanket spread out beside his sister's bed. The sleep came from exhaustion and from boredom, the sense of not belonging, of drifting between, that is spawned by long journeys and long illnesses. But Isaac, though he grew thinner and paler from his incarceration, did not get sick, although he sat on the edge of his sister's bed, though he breathed the heavy air of the ward in which the heat and the disease mingled, brewed, floated.

Sister Abigail asked Isaac to help her remove the sheets from a bed on which a child had died, to ready it for the next child. At first Isaac moved his limbs slowly, stiffly, not like a boy at all; but after a while, when the requests were repeated, Isaac came back to himself and furled the sheet out into the air with a snap and carried the old sheets off to the laundry room, where the nuns placed them in great vats of water and stirred them with huge ladles. He always ran up and down the stone stairs so as to get back to Ruth as soon as possible. If she did not see him, because he was away from her bed, she closed her eyes and sank further into her sunken, pus-filled face. Once Isaac came to her bed and for a moment didn't recognize her; it wasn't only the strange shape of her face and the limpness of her arms, but her very body looked unfamiliar, as if she were another girl, any girl; and this frightened him. It was hours before Sister Abigail could coax him back into his role as her valued assistant, her extra pair of hands.

Isaac had disappeared. Moses and Naomi knew, knew without evidence, knew even before one of the neighbors reported seeing him hovering at the side of the quarantine wagon, that he had gone with Ruth. He had done what they had wished to do. They knew too that not only had one child been taken to the hospital, the hospital in the middle of the river from which few returned, but that their son, their oldest son, the one on whom they could depend, the one for whom the world of America was being endured, the one whose English was better than theirs, far better, was in the hospital, his young face covered like his sister's with pox, tossing on a cot, uncomforted by mother or father.

No word came from the hospital. Naomi went to the doctor's office. She waited three hours and gave up a day's work to speak to the doctor. He had not received information on Ruth; they would send him a certificate when she died, but no such certificate had appeared. The mails were slow, next week might bring it. No word on her son. The doctor was furious. "You let him go with her?" These people, these people he was giving his life to help, were ignorant, careless of life, and their children ran wild, did what they wanted, caused trouble everywhere, had no respect for their parents, for doctors or teachers; little better than savages, they ran in the streets. The doctor promised Naomi that he would send his assistant to her house to bring word of her children as soon as it came to him.

For Naomi the days passed in a stupor, unable to mourn the not yet dead, to tear her clothing and let the tears flow, to rage at the betrayal of her plans, the indifference of a God she had never trusted, to blame herself for taking the diamonds that had been Leah's, for violating the body of the dead, for bringing punishment on herself, for coming to America, for wanting when she should have bowed her head and accepted, for taking Moses away from his tailor shop, which his feet could find in his sleep, for wanting whatever it was she had wanted that ended in the death of her son and the death of her daughter. Since she couldn't mourn because she had not yet heard of their death, she could only imagine her children, lying on cots, untended, calling for her, alone, feeling alone as if she had left them in the forest by the town. Naomi lay in bed at night, not sleeping—the heat, of course, but not just the heat, the burning of a grief that could not yet become a grief kept her eyes open. The evil eye has fallen on the family, she would sigh, the evil eye has brought Lilith into our house, and she has stolen our children. Strange about Naomi, whose prayers were limited, her belief in Lilith, the demon wife of Adam, had survived her more skeptical musings.

Moses, too, lay awake, pulled as far away from his wife as the small bed would allow. He kept his hands folded across his chest, finger locked into finger as if to prevent them from striking out, striking out at who or at what? Moses felt only a churning and a nausea in his stomach, a tightness in his chest that made breathing difficult. If this was the beginning of the pox, so be it, he thought. He had no desire to wake in the morning and look at the mattress still pulled by the fire escape and see there only one child instead of three. His daughter, his beautiful daughter, whose face when she slept had made him think of an angel, was now away from him, and that left a space, a hollow space inside, one that he knew would never be filled.

The fear in the house might have brought Naomi and Moses closer together; after all, the thing that was hovering over them both, the absence of the children, caused them both to feel as if they were lost, themselves abandoned in the dark of the forest. But instead Moses said to Naomi in a quiet voice, "America. You were the one who said it was good here. Our children will be corpses. Isn't that fine, this thing that you wanted?"

He turned his face to the wall, and she looked at him with her new American eyes and saw that he was small, and his hands that she had once thought were strong and steady were filled with veins and brown spots and his beard was thin like the hair on top of his head, gone like a meadow prepared for sowing. This, I am going to spend the rest of my life with, she thought. Better I should have the pox.

He sat alone at the table they used for all purposes and put his head in his hands. This woman, he said, is my wife, and I owe her my desire and my tenderness. But the words did not alter the hardness he felt when he looked at her square back moving about, carrying things here and there, telling everything in the room just what it should be and where it should go. He tried: "We could go home, take the diamond and go home to Sulvalki," he said. But Naomi said nothing. She had nothing to say. He understood her silence to mean "Never" when actually it only meant "Don't speak when I can't hear."

Reader: Do you believe that God has sent his scourge down on the Jews of the Lower East Side for straying from the ways of their fathers? Probably not. Do you believe that God has marked out the house of the Gruenbaums for the pox, to test them, to experiment with their morality, their loyalty, the way He once toyed with Job? Probably not. Do you believe that God has forgotten the Gruenbaums and the pox is as eager to succeed in evolutionary terms as anything else that feeds, reproduces, dies on the globe? Probably. Do you believe in the evil eye, in Lilith and her demons wreaking havoc on the human body and soul? You don't? Have you a better explanation?

Sometime into the second week when Isaac was following Sister Abigail to the storage room in which the large pails used for human waste were kept, she turned around and looked at him.

"Boy, you're getting too thin. You need some food. I'm taking you in the kitchen for a real meal, a meal for a healthy child." He went with her down some back stairs and through a basement passage into the kitchen, where the blocks of ice that had been brought over by boat in the morning had melted across the floor, forcing them to walk through sheets of water to reach the other side of the room.

"Here is where we eat," said Sister Abigail, and sat Isaac down at the foot of a long wooden table. She opened a cupboard door and found for him a pear, a round and perfect pear, a slice of heavy bread, and a piece of orange cheese.

"Eat," she said to him, but he sat, unable to move his hands. Hunger had left him.

"Are you hot?" she said to him, and for the tenth time that morning felt his forehead. "You are not sick," she said. "Eat."

Isaac wanted to do what she asked. He had grown used to her strange habit. He had accustomed himself even to the cross that hung around her neck, even to the crosses that hung on either end of all the wards with the figure of Jesus pinned, arms and legs, splash of blood down the rib cage, painted eyes that followed him as he walked up and down. He had learned the individual faces of the nuns, he could tell who was walking through the ward at night just by listening to their footsteps and the weight they placed on the floor and the speed with which they traveled. He had learned to look right into Sister Abigail's eyes, where there was an absence of the thing that made his mother's face change from moment to moment, lines appear and disappear, lips puff and flatten, as if the seasons were changing all the time. In Sister Abigail's face the color stayed the same, the distance between the features stayed the same, as if a storm had passed and the sea was now calm and still. Isaac stared and stared at Sister Abigail as if her face, the steady paleness of her eyes, could release him and his sister from this place and return them safely home.

"Eat," said Sister Abigail.

"I can't," said the boy.

Suddenly there were tears in Sister Abigail's eyes. Just two, they dropped slowly down her cheeks. She sat there quietly, her hands folded in her lap. "Home," she said, "where I grew up, there was never enough food, not enough for the baby to eat, not enough for my brothers, and so one had legs that were bent and crooked and one had the mind of simpleton, and we had to watch him always that he would not fall into the creek or walk into the road and get lost or put his hand in the fire. All across the place that was my home there was hunger. Every year my da planted potatoes, but then the rains did not come and whatever we grew we had to give to others, the tax collector, the manor house, the doctor. And we sat around the table at night and there was warmth because we had a fire, but there was no food, no cereal for the baby, who screamed. Across the whole village there were children in every house who went to bed at night with their stomachs curled up in knots. In every house the parents stirred the water to make a soup with roots and grass and whatever else fell from the trees at the edge of the woods, and the soup left the children with blotches on their skin, and every day the church bells rang and another small coffin was taken out to the fields— my sister Elizabeth, my sister Mavis—there was plenty of space for the dead because nothing was growing. They sent me away to the nuns in America when I was eight so that I could eat, so that they could eat my portion at home. I do not like to see a child who does not eat when there is food. It is like slapping God in the face. It is like returning the gift of life, and those who want it cannot take it and so it is wasted, spilt. Do you understand me, child?" Sister Abigail leaned across to Isaac. "I am talking to you," she said. "You eat."

Isaac took a bite of the pear, he took a bite of the bread. In moments he discovered he was indeed hungry, and he ate everything she had set before him, and she brought him a glass of milk and another piece of cheese. Then she smiled at him.

"The pox will not take you because you are too stuffed."

One night as Isaac was tossing on his blanket, as Ruth, who seemed a little better, slept, as the cries in the ward rose and fell, Sister Abigail came to Isaac and said to him, "As long as you're awake, as long as this is my night to sit up on the ward, I will teach you about Christ the Lord."

"Jews," said Isaac, and by "Jews" he meant his father, whose image came to him, his beard and his payess, his black hat and his black coat. "Jews," said Isaac, "do not believe in Jesus. We think there is only one God, and his name is Adonai."

"Well," Sister Abigail said, "that is a matter of opinion, and you could always change yours. Let me read you a story."

And so in a corner at the far end of the ward where the nuns kept a chair and a table, Sister Abigail read aloud, Matthew, Mark, Luke, and John. By the time she was finished—they were interrupted many times, screaming children whose nightmares were coming true, children in need of water, of the tin pot that Sister Abigail would not let Isaac touch for fear of infection—the first light of day was turning the river a sweet pink.

"What do you think?" she said to Isaac.

"It's a sad story," said Isaac.

"Yes," said Sister Abigail, "it is that, but the ending," she said, "it ends with salvation for everyone."

"I know sad stories, too," said Isaac, "but stories do not change anything."

"Oh, they do," said Sister Abigail, "they change everything."

Isaac looked at the nun, and there was no doubt that he felt love, that this was his first love. Nevertheless, despite the stirring of his heart, the desire to please the object of his affections, despite the color of her eyes, which seemed to him unlike any he had ever seen before, his convictions were his convictions. "Stories," he said, "do not help a person make money, and money," he said, "would have brought food to your house and saved your sisters Elizabeth and Mavis and all the others."

Sister Abigail was not offended. "I'll read it to you again," she said, "when next it is my turn to stay the night."

Isaac rather hoped she wouldn't because in truth the words, or perhaps it was her voice, the way it rose and fell in strange patterns, made him struggle against sleep, made him rub his eyes to pay attention, made his mind wander to the linen cart and the customers and the street that was his home.

In the third week Ruth sat up in bed and her fever dropped. Sister Abigail was pleased. Isaac had hardly hoped for this; so many had been carried away, delivered to the cart that took them to the back of the island where the great pits were, where the fires burned their clothing, that he could hardly believe that Ruth, his sister, had managed to be one of those who would cross the river again, whose arms stopped trembling, whose thin bodies began to rest on their beds as if gathering strength instead of preparing for the separation of the spirit from the flesh. Ruth began to speak.

"How long have we been here? Can we go home? Today? Tomorrow? I am fine," she said, though her legs were too weak to stand on.

There was something else, something that frightened Isaac so much that he couldn't bear to think about it. The pox: the pox had not reached into her lungs and prevented them from pumping, it had not circled her heart and squeezed it into silence, it had not curled her liver or punctured her brain, but it had dug deep into her flesh. And her face, the face that had once promised a woman, a mother, now was full of holes and red and scarred, and the pus still oozed from some of the blisters, and the others between the eyes, over the lips, on the bridge of the nose, gave Ruth—Ruth, who had played with her friend Reba on the balcony and planned to name her children Deborah, Jeremiah, and Aaron—the face of a girl no man would touch and a girl who would stand in the shadows and hide herself for the rest of her life. Isaac had not realized how much he had loved his sister's face, like his, but not quite, a mouth that tilted up, a long nose, but one that fit in her oval face, and eyes that were soft brown, that grew darker with sorrow and lighter with joy. He looked at his sister in the bed at the quarantine hospital, and he knew he would never see her again as she had been. If he did not know her, if she were not still small, he might even be frightened of her, a monster look, a thing that grew in dank cellars, that was what she looked like. Was surviving the fever such a good thing? Sister Abigail said yes, but Isaac did not believe everything Sister Abigail said.

Sister Abigail stood at the end of Ruth's bed. "Ruth," she said, "do you know what the soul is? Jews believe in the soul, don't they?"

"The spark of life, that's what you mean," said Ruth, whose father had told her this.

"And God, God gave you this soul to take good care of, did he not?" Ruth nodded. "Your soul is beautiful," said Sister Abigail. "It is beautiful because you are a good girl."

Isaac kicked the end of the cot with his shoe. This was the moment he had been dreading. This was the part where Sister Abigail would begin to lie. "You have lived through a sickness that has taken many other children. You are a very lucky girl." Isaac knew that Jews had many ways of saying things so that the edges would be covered. Now he knew that was true of nuns, too. "But" said Abigail, "the beauty of the body, the beauty that is only given to people for a short while, only a thing of the surface, a thing that distracts from the truth, that you do not have anymore."

Ruth had known; she had known but had not wanted to know. She had seen the others on the cots with the pus and red marks. "No," said Ruth, "I am a pretty girl." She looked at Isaac. "Tell her I'm pretty," she said.

Isaac stood up and glared at Sister Abigail. "She's pretty," he said. "She was sick, but now she's well, and we're going home."

"No," said Sister Abigail, "she cannot live with a lie; others will tell her soon enough." Isaac felt a throbbing in his ears, and his legs felt weak. "Tell her, Isaac," said Sister Abigail. "You brought her here, you will have to take her the rest of the journey."

Ruth looked at him. His face was pale. "I can't," he said. But Ruth knew anyway. She knew by herself. She put her hands over her face and felt the ridges. She could not imagine it all—the other children turning away, the end of the games in the schoolyard . . . the end of the promise of pleasure, of a young man bringing flowers, of walks with a hand around her shoulder, years of tending the children of others, of being without a home of her own. She only knew that everything had changed, everything that could have been was now denied, and she was more frightened of tomorrow than she had been of dying, and what had she done, what was the cause, why? These thoughts were not so clear as the tears that flowed from her eyes would indicate.

"Don't cry," said Isaac, "please."

"Jesus Christ will take you if you wish," said Sister Abigail. "You can come to the Convent of the Carmelites any time now or when you are older, and I will make sure that you become one of us. Jesus cares only about your soul and not about your face."

Isaac heard the kindness in the words, but certain other things he also knew. He said, "I will take care of Ruth. She is my sister."

And so they rode the ferry in the other direction, and Isaac said good-bye to Sister Abigail and promised never to forget her, and she told him he was a fine boy, even though he was Jewish, and he looked in her eyes and knew that she found him worthy. He would never tell his father about his friendship with Sister Abigail.

Naomi and Moses had not been told of the survival of their children, the one with the illness and the one who went with her. No notification of any sort had arrived at the doctor's office. Moses was at work, Naomi was at work, the children let themselves in the apartment and sat at the table and waited.

When Naomi saw her daughter she screamed. Her relief was mixed with regret. A daughter who looked like Ruth would be a burden forever, would be alone forever, and when she thought of her child and the aloneness that waited for her, she thought about going back to Sulvalki. What difference did it make where they were buried?

"Your God," she whispered to Moses when they were in bed, "I wish I could rip His eyes out."

Moses said nothing, but silently he begged the Almighty to forgive his wife, to protect his daughter, to let him die before he saw her a grown woman without a marriage. When Moses saw his daughter, he wrapped her in his arms and said, "The face is the least important part of a person." But there were tears in his eyes, and his daughter saw them because they did not stop for days and days.

As for Isaac, Naomi and Moses were relieved that he had survived, but they couldn't help complain about the way he had left, without a word, without a good-bye, possibly forever. Was this what family meant, just till you choose, just till something else comes along? They understood, of course, but for Naomi there remained a question about her oldest son. Who was he, anyway? Would he always be there when she needed him? He was a boy. It would have been better if his face were raw while Ruth's stayed smooth. Unreasonable as it was, Naomi loved her son less for his clear skin.

As for Max, he looked at his sister and thought she was ugly, uglier even than he with his leg and the curve of his back. The thought was pleasing and unpleasing at the same time.

As for Ruth, she stopped going to school because the children ran from her. Her friend Reba, who had played with her on the fire escape, never again knocked on the door.

Isaac had dreams about Sister Abigail in which she removed the habit that framed her face and her hair, which he imagined was blond, fell down on her shoulders and he touched it with his fingers.

Temptations Not Resisted, or the Evil Inclination Has Its Way: 1882–1885

When Ruth came home from the hospital, the summer was still boiling in the streets, but something had changed in the house. There was an additional silence from the room her parents shared. Max had been in a fight and his eye was black, and he said over and over, "I'll give you one in the mouth, you son of a bitch," to no one in particular. Naomi woke each morning and lay still in her bed extra moments, keeping her eyes shut as if to push the day away. Her black hair was no longer so carefully combed. When she came up the stairs in the evening, her body felt heavy as lead and she used her arms on the banister to pull her weight up floor to floor. Moses came home for a quick supper at the table and then sometimes without saying a word to anyone would disappear down the stairs again. He went to the shul on Avenue C, where the tailor who worked at the bench next to his had introduced him to a new group that studied two by two by the candlelight in the basement room that had been given them by Devorah, the landlady, whose husband had died falling off the roof he had tried to repair himself, leaving her with property

and possibilities. She had a father whom she brought from the old country, who moaned and whined about under her feet until she established
a study group for him, a place where he could pretend he had not crossed
the ocean at his daughter's bidding.

Devorah was still young. Her breasts were full and high. Her voice
was soft as a young child's, and in the evening when the men were talking
she would bring tea downstairs for each. She would grasp the spoon with
her small, pudgy hands and stir the sugar in the glass, and she would
look at each man as she offered the refreshment as if he and he alone held
the secret to her happiness. She had a smell, of flour and pastry and jam.
The sweetness was not Moses's imagination. She worked during the day
in a bakery, and the white flakes of flour stuck to the strands of her hair,
and there was the aroma in her dress and her apron of things in the oven
melting and oozing together. She had wide hips that swung from side
to side as she walked, and there was a fold of flesh above her waist that
seemed like an extra pillow stuffed under her dress. Her eyes were pale,
gray as the sea that Moses had prayed beside as the sun came up over
the horizon's edge and the boat moved across the Atlantic.

One day as the men were discussing the concept of the stealing of
the mind, the thing that made a cheat as evil as a murderer, the landlady
called down the cellar stairs, "Someone come help me. I have cut my
finger."

All the men jumped to their feet. Her father, first of all, but he was
older and his legs moved slowly. Moses was sitting nearest the stairs, and
he bolted up them as if he had been called by an angel to receive his
reward. The other men sat back down and resumed their discussion.
Moses came into the kitchen and saw Devorah holding her finger over a
bowl while blood was pouring out. He grabbed a cloth from the table
and held her finger tightly. She was pale with fright. The knife had fallen
to the floor.

"Silly me, silly me, how stupid I am," she said over and over.

But holding her finger in his hand, close as he was to her, Moses
felt a great stirring in his loins, a great forbidden, sinful stirring that
moved up his body, into his mouth, and made even his nose tingle and
his ears shine. He looked away from her. He would not smile at her when
she said, "Thank you for helping me, you are such a kind gentleman.
Does your wife appreciate how good you are?"

When the bleeding appeared to stop, and she sat down at the table
holding the napkin herself around her wound, Moses backed away, prepared to go downstairs. "What a fine shape of a man you are," she said
to him, and looked down at her feet, little plump feet whose calves he

could see beneath her skirt, puffed out over the tops of her boots. "Come sit with me awhile," she said, and Moses did, though he knew he shouldn't.

"Do you like me?" she asked him, and he nodded, even though he knew he shouldn't. His head was spinning. He felt dizzy with guilt. "Would you like a roll?" she said to him. "This is baked fresh this morning, and I take home the ones we do not sell. It is soft inside and crusty outside, just the way a roll should be."

Moses accepted the roll, even though he knew it was wrong. He bit into the top and crumbs fell into his beard, and Devorah put out her hand, the one that had not been cut, and brushed them away. Moses felt that he understood nothing, that he knew nothing of good and bad and the world that he lived in, that he was a child with everything ahead of him.

"You like the roll?" said Devorah. "You could have another."

This was the kind of thing that happened to other men, the kind of thing he had heard about in his shop, as the fellows boasted of going home from the dances with a lady who took them behind the stairs or into the park and left them thirsty but full. He had when hearing those stories always thanked God for his Naomi, small and hard, whose body was his when he needed. But lately it had not been so easy to do what he should. His body had been in bed beside Naomi and had not obeyed his own command. The ruined face of the child intruded between them. Naomi was always there if he needed, but need was not the same as this thing that was moving, crawling between him and Devorah. It could not have the name of love, and Moses did not have any other name for it. Because it had no word, it grew in him and dominated his thoughts.

Isaac had been the assistant to the linen man for three years. He knew where to take his cart, he knew what to say to the women who rushed past him, not yet knowing that they needed a new cloth for their table, not yet understanding how good a bargain they would get if they would just pause for a moment and let him explain the value of the embroidery, the numbers of stitches in each small flower, and the extra napkins that he would throw in, free, if they just asked.

Isaac had grown from a boy to the beginnings of manhood. His voice cracked now as he called out to passersby, and sometimes he would lose his voice altogether, but this made the ladies smile; they would pinch his cheek, they would look at his sturdy body and say, "I have a daughter for you, when you're ready." "I have a sister you can meet in a few years." Sometimes they gave him a prune or a raisin.

The cart owner, who housed his wares in the back of his shop on

Orchard Street, was grateful for his young assistant, and although he kept him counting inventory well into the early darkness when the men who worked in other shops were already home for dinner, and although he paid him only the wages of a child, he knew he was getting a man's worth from the boy. Things went well. He decided to expand. "That's what it is all about," he explained to Isaac, who listened carefully. "Expand. If you sell more than you have before your profit is higher and if you risk a little to expand even more, then you will gain even more in profit because small in America is bad, can be outsold by a bigger cart, by a bigger store who can sell cheaper because he sells more. So I will get bigger, and that is why we have come to America, because in America there is no end to how big my store can become."

Isaac listened. The linen man rented the cubicle next to the one he already held. Before Yom Kippur he rented the next cubicle, too, and he bought linens to fill all the space he now possessed, enough linens to drown an entire block in cloth, and he had Isaac staying late into the night, when others were already asleep, folding and folding and counting and marking tags on the merchandise.

"Bigger," said the linen man, "is better." And Isaac, in a kind of fever and fascination, folded and folded. Bigger, he said to himself, bigger is better, but who will buy all this? He worried for his boss. Is he right? Isaac entered his sales into the account book, and he saw that money was owed. "Money owed was a hand on the throat," his father had always said. "Money owed is a way to the grave," his father had said when his mother had pressed him to borrow and start his own tailor shop. "Money owed is the way a man becomes a slave to another," he had said, and Isaac's mother had shrugged. "You could sell the diamond," Moses had said to his wife, and Isaac had heard his mother's reply, like a blast of cold wind when you open the door in February:

"Not yet, not now. The diamond is not to be sold. Borrow," said his mother.

"Maybe," said his father, and so things stayed as they were.

"So," said Moses to Naomi one morning as they were standing by the stove, drinking the hot coffee Naomi had just made, "my study group starts early, I won't be home for dinner."

"Should I give you an extra piece of bread in your lunch box?" asked Naomi.

"No," said Moses, "I have enough as it is."

"All right," said Naomi with a shrug. She looked at him in the morning light, still a young man whose shoulders stooped and whose eyes behind his glasses blinked with the nervousness of the man who watches his stitches go up and down the cloth; yet there remained in the set of his chin, in the slope of his nose, the groom she had taken so many years ago, the man whose bed she had shared for all her adult life. The hair on the front of his head had fallen on his shoulders, fallen in the tub, fallen on the sheets, and above his forehead a shiny white patch was extending back over his ears. The bare skin, covered to the world by a hat, made his face paler. She could see the veins in his skull where the blood pulsed round his body. It frightened her, how thin the wall between outside and inside was, how fragile his head, how open to the sky he was. She reached her hand out to him. "Remember to smile today," she said. So many days the man went without a smile, as if there were nothing but tragedy on this earth.

Her touch, gentle as it was, made him feel sour. He pulled back his hand. She was a good woman who would never understand the filling of his chest when Devorah came toward him. She would not know why he was tempted, and God, his God, was permitting this temptation, this evil thought that would not go out of his head, not when he lay next to his own wife and tried to dissolve the image of the other's body and not when he was working and tried to think of nothing but the shape of the cloth and the motion of the machine, not when he was studying the word of the teachers who had gone before: now the images of Devorah bending down to pick up a napkin from the floor or reaching up to open a window or leaning forward over her tray with the glasses of tea would intrude on his thoughts, and he would stumble over the Hebrew words and miss the vowels and with heavy tongue stand the discussion on its head. Was the pox that had taken the face of his child, was that pox not enough punishment for him?

Naomi went to the loft that morning with a shadow at her back, something she had left undone, something that was unclean in her house, something with her children that was not as it should be. Although she did not know what was in Moses's head, she knew that the ground was not as steady as before.

Moses looked over his shoulder as he walked to work as if he expected Naomi to follow him down the street. He feared that the orphan he had taken for his bride knew that the graves of her parents, those two crooked stones that were tended by the gardener who weeded and pressed the earth, were soon to be violated by her husband.

In the house on Avenue C where Devorah and her pious father lived, the widow waited eagerly for her visitor. She had come home early from work and had placed a strawberry bun in the oven. Its fruity smell rose through the house and just as she had planned reached its fullness and ripeness, so that one could almost taste it as one breathed, when Moses rang the bell. She had slipped him a note the week before, placing it discreetly in his pocket. In the privy in the yard at the back of the house, he had taken the note from his pocket, and standing there above the opening, he felt faint, as if he could drop into the hole and, with all the other decaying matter, with the flies that circled round and round, lie in the moist earth and rot. He had torn the note up after reading it and sent the pieces down after his stream of urine, into the darkness where they belonged. He had blushed as he walked home, so much so that one of his study companions asked him if he were feeling quite well.

"My heart," he had said. "My heart is not as steady as it should be." And the other had nodded: Whose heart was as steady as it should be, and what man could walk the streets without fear that he might drop to the ground, the beating thing in the chest stilled at any moment? It was the way of the body since the exile from Paradise. Any man who thought he was an exception, that his lungs would go on pumping forever, such a man missed the pleasure. The pleasure was in surviving another day, or so Moses's companion explained as they walked in the early evening heat around the lampposts that had been lit just moments before, around the prostitutes who gathered on B and 3rd, calling out to men, good men with beards and hats and lunch boxes in their hands, "Hey, good-looking, look over here, like what you see?"

The note had requested this meeting, this hour earlier than the study group. The old man was in his room on the fourth floor, taking a nap after his dinner. Devorah asked Moses if he would like to see her bedroom. Yes, he nodded, although he knew he should say no. He followed her up the stairs, watching the motion of her legs, the lift of her rear as it raised itself to greet each new step.

"I am married," he said as they crossed the threshold.

"I know," said Devorah. "I don't want to marry you. A husband is a nuisance, needs to be fed and cleaned and clothed and fetched for and worried over if his nose turns red with cold or his chest fills with phlegm. I've had a husband. Your wife can have you. I just want an hour here or there, that seems reasonable, yes?"

Devorah opened the bodice of her dress and revealed two huge breasts, larger than any Moses ever dreamed of, and he had dreamed of breasts bending over him, calling to him with their nipples straight and dark, but never like this, real breasts waiting for his touch, his mouth to move forward.

"This is not right," said Moses, clutching his lunch box as if it were the Torah, but his Torah was downstairs in a box waiting for the others to arrive.

"All right," said Devorah, "then go home to your family, I'll find someone else to play with me." And she opened her mouth and smiled, and she was missing two teeth in the back, but the moist red tongue flickered against her palate and her smile was so easy, so unlike any smile that Moses could return, that he moved all at once toward her, his arms flapping, his shirt coming out of his pants. Tears in his eyes, for reasons he could not explain, ran down his cheeks, and his glasses fell off onto the wooden floor, and when he bent to pick them up he saw all her legs right up to the top. He fell on the bed in a near swoon, and she undressed him carefully, respectfully, slowly, as one would a corpse.

The fading sun came through the window, now a slash of rose and silver fell across his head, and his bald pate looked like a strawberry itself resting on the widow's pillow. She leaned over him, lying there stunned, his arms stretched out over the edges of the bed, and she put her face over his and began to lick the bald white spot on his head. As she moved from one end to the other, her tongue left behind a trail of moisture. His wide chest with its white skin lay across the bed like a stone, like a stone that knew its place.

With effort, with the feeling of a man rising from the grave, with the smell of buns and flour on his chest and a thankfulness for creation that he had never had so genuinely before, Moses dressed and went downstairs and was at his place at the table of study when the old man wearing a thin shirt with an open neck to catch what breeze was possible came into the room and opened his own book, saying the prayers that precede the act of learning. The Hebrew words floated up over the wooden beams and the kerosene lamp flickered, and Moses felt his guilt grow like the lumps that appear in old women's stomachs and swell to a resting place above their ribs and finally carry them off to death, misshapen mockeries of their girlhood. At the same time another feeling flowed in his fingers as they traced the words on the page; it was a feeling that had to be named, because as a descendant of Adam, Moses was in the habit of naming things. He called this feeling, which came unbidden into this place of study, joy, and he smiled, he smiled as he had never smiled before. Thou shalt not commit adultery, he thought to himself, but in every circumstance, even when it does no harm? How can a man obey his God if God sends down the pox onto the face of little children? And then Moses added, because he had been thinking this a long time, And if God allows the burning of the shul, what harm can a small, only once, never again, twenty minutes, of man and woman be? Forgiveness must be possible; on Yom Kippur I will repent, and with that thought, Moses smiled again.

• • •

Naomi said to herself that when the redness of the scars faded, Ruth's face would look better, almost normal, perhaps. In her dreams she saw her daughter as she was before the illness, white and smooth, soft brown eyes and long lashees and white hands that reached up for her mother, white shoulders in the bath with clear water running over them. Naomi looked in the window of the store downstairs and saw her own face with its dark circles under the eyes and the strands of hair that flew out from under her comb.

"Go downstairs and play with the other children," she said to Ruth, who shook her head and sat by the fire escape sewing, sewing beads on fabric. "You'll ruin your eyes, you'll go blind, too," said Naomi, but Ruth didn't move. "Go to the settlement house and play the piano," said Naomi. "The piano doesn't care about the pox."

But Ruth didn't want to play the piano anymore. There were marks on the back of her hands and her fingers felt stiff, and she had no need of music, none at all. The child slept some of each day on the mattress, almost as if she were still sick. At night she was awake, and, more comfortable in the darkness, she walked about the apartment, played an imaginary game with the spoons, who all became members of a family, a family that was always in peril of fire, drowning, being murdered by Cossacks who came with their boots and broke all the dishes . . . but at the last minute, in the early hours of the morning, something, some invisible force, guided by Ruth's hand, saved the spoon family for another night of calamity.

Isaac noticed that the linen man was getting so thin that his trousers hung wide around his waist and his chest had sunk beneath his shirt and the suspenders seem to dangle down. The linen man had developed a cough. His checks were red, and now he often had to sit down while he gave Isaac instructions. He allowed Isaac to do all the heavy work, all the lifting and packing and unpacking. The double store, the double cart, the expansion that had been such a good idea, wearied him now. His wife came to the store and brought him soup for lunch, and he would pretend to drink it in front of her; but as soon as she left he spilled it out, vegetables and broth, out onto the street.

One day the linen man was standing on a ladder in the store putting away the curtains that Isaac had not been able to sell that morning. There were many of them. The women had to buy food first and then clothes for their young and then for themselves, enough for the cold weather, and last, last on the budget, was the tablecloth for the Sabbath meal, for

Passover, to impress the relatives. Very few who walked the streets had the pennies for the tablecloths and the towels and the lace that Isaac was now selling. They stopped by his cart, they offered him an apple. They looked at each cloth as he unfolded it for them, but then they would tell him, I'll buy it next week, after Purim, before Pesach, in time for Rosh Hashonah, and they did not buy. Bring the prices down, said Isaac, but still they did not buy. They had bought before when the store was small, but then the goods were not so fine and did not cost so much. The boxes the linen man had ordered for his expansion kept coming, and each week they had to find a new place to keep the goods that were not selling. The linen man coughed and coughed and the red spots on his checks grew darker and sometimes Isaac could see that his legs trembled.

"I'm fine," he said, "this is a temporary thing. Business will get better." To Isaac he said, "Young man, you will be my first assistant when we open another store farther uptown, maybe as good as Fourteenth Street."

Isaac could hardly move around the store, the pile of curtains in red, blue, and yellow that had arrived the week before still lay in their boxes, and he had not been able to sell one pair from his cart.

"Here," said the linen man, "take one home to your mother," and that week he did not pay Isaac at all.

Naomi was happy with the pink curtains that hung from her window. "See," she said to Moses, "America is already bringing us good." The curtains quickly were stained with the ash of the city, with the floating dust that turned the air gray. Naomi stayed up later than ever and washed her curtains and ironed their pleats. "See," she said to Moses, "in America the curtains are not just straight down." She told Mrs. Moscowitz, whom she invited in, that the curtains were a gift from her son, who was doing well in the linen shop.

But a few weeks later the linen man did not appear at the store, and Isaac opened up without him. He did not come in the afternoon or the next day, and then his wife came and said he was in bed and could not come to the store. She asked Isaac what she could do to help him in the store. Isaac did not know what to say. If he took the cart out on the street, he sold nothing. If he stayed in the store, he sold only a few items, a face cloth, napkins for a wedding present, an occasional curtain to someone from another neighborhood looking for a bargain.

The linen man's wife had the children to look after. She had a sick husband in bed. She did not stay long. The next day the woman did not come, and the day after she did not come. At the end of the week just before Shabbos when the storekeepers were bringing down their shutters and the last of the carts were pulled into the alleys and the street was quieting down for the evening, she appeared.

"He is gone," she said.

The widow closed the store forever. She had Isaac pack everything up, and she had him put all the packages on the carts and pull them to the post office and send everything back that was not stained or soiled by the air or the dust. She sat in the back room and read the account book, and she told Isaac that he should pull the shutters down even though it was only noon and that she was going home to her mother in Vilna, she was taking the children and leaving as soon as possible.

"America is a wild place," she said, "for pigs and Indians. Jews will be eaten here, like cows grazing, they will guzzle up the Jews. I am going home to my mother," she said.

"What about my pay?" said Isaac.

"There is nothing," said the widow, and although Isaac knew there was something, he also knew that widows had needs.

"Give me one of the carts," said Isaac. "Let me have a cart for my pay, no one will buy it from you." That was not quite true, but the widow, who had never asked her husband if the carts could be sold if he died, gave the cart to Isaac instead of pay.

"You were good to my husband," she said, and kissed him on the cheek. She was a young widow, and something moved in Isaac's groin, a filling and a rising that startled him. Something about the young widow reminded him of Sister Abigail. So startled was he that he turned his face away from his benefactress, but not before she caught the blush that rose from his cheeks and spread across his high forehead. Seeing the young boy, his arms hanging stiffly at his side, gave her the first occasion since her husband's death to feel a momentary lightness in her mind, a possibility of a future.

So it was that three years after his arrival in America Isaac Gruenbaum was the owner of a cart—an empty cart, as his mother pointed out, and no one to pay him at the end of each week. But Isaac was sure he understood it all, things you need, things you must have, things at a price you can pay, and the profit, the profit would not go to the linen man— expand, but not too fast, only if you're healthy and have time; grow, but don't stretch. Everything over the cost of the goods would be his, and with that thought Isaac's heart leaped and pounded and skipped beats. His eyes shone and he held his sister's hands in his and promised again, A piano, Ruth, a piano for you. You have my word.

Reader: You think that Isaac should have turned his attention to education, to things of the spirit, to art, perhaps, to collecting canvases of the sort that today you can find in stores on the same Avenues A and B where Isaac had pulled his linen cart. Perhaps you agree with Moses that the boy should have been Bar Mitzvahed. He should have stayed in cheder and at least learned his portion of the haftorah and stood before a congregation and become a Jewish man who would bind the words of the Lord on his forehead and his forearm each day. But, Reader, you forget that economics precedes religion; worship grew out of eating, not the other way around. The luxuries of space and form and philosophy, beauty and charity, that another generation would enjoy were not considerations for the boy from Sulvalki. That boy did not even have the right pictures in his head to dream of tennis courts and racquetball, croquet and badminton. The boy woke each morning to the sound of the milk cart on the cobblestones below, heard the barrels of merchandise crossing and banging over the streets, saw that his mother's diamond was like his father's tallis, only it had more power, more potential power, to protect them all.

Isaac asked his father if he could go with him to work one day.

"What do you want with me?" said his father.

"Just to come to the loft, see where you work. Maybe I too will learn to be a tailor."

Moses hesitated. His son was now almost as tall as he was. A grown boy should not go with his father to his place of work. It was not done. None of the other men arrived with their children.

Isaac looked at his father. "Papa," he said, "Why not?"

And Moses could not think of a reason, and he had certain other things on his mind that made him want to please his wife, his children, in any way he could. So Isaac went with Moses up the five flights of stairs, through the metal door, and onto the long narrow floor where fifty men were sitting at machines. Soon the buzzing sound of the needle moving back and forth made it hard to hear the words of the man at the table next to you, and the boss didn't like talking on his time, and the men got up and went to the bathroom up on the roof as often as they thought they could, and on the stairs they waved their fingers, squeezed their hands, and tried to press the cramps away from the backs of their necks, from the middle of their spines, from the center of their chests.

Isaac went to find the boss. "How about," he said to him, "how about I take some of your pants and jackets and sell them from my cart."

"One cart," said the boss. "It's not worth my time to give them to you. I sell to the stores, I sell to Mendelssohn, who has three carts already. I have an order for New Jersey. I don't need to give to you."

But Isaac stood there. "Give me seventy-five suits, and if I don't sell them all in a week, I will work for you for free for a month." The man laughed, a deal that could not be missed, it was win or win, and he gave Isaac his hand.

Moses was relieved when Isaac left the loft. He didn't want the boy to spend the entire day there, watching him cut and stitch. He didn't want Isaac to see him, there in his seat, fifth from the window, harnessed like an animal to a plow, moving his feet up and down on the pedals as the light outside grew and faded and the steel pipe in front of him grew dark and cast its shadow across his face. Also, he didn't want the boy to go with him after work when he hurried to his house of study, where he would arrive an hour early and the widow would be waiting for him and would pull him upstairs to the now familiar room and he would undress as fast as possible and then lie on the quilt as she would pour a little hot tea into his mouth and begin to tug at the hairs he had growing in private places. He discovered that if he touched her on the top of her mound, she would moan, and the moan would fly in his ears like a call to action, like an angel's summons, and his body would rise and fill and astound him with its possibilities.

Naomi asked him where he ate, so many dinners had he missed. I am not in need of dinner, he said. Naomi worried that his appetite was gone. She felt his forehead in bed. She looked at him carefully for signs of wasting, lumps that should not be there, a catch in the breathing, the cough that wasted the linen man and others she knew. She looked under his arms into the pits and around the groin for rashes. But he seemed all right. He slept calmly, the sleep of a good child. Moses continued to lose hair, and the space above his forehead increased and became shiny and clear. Sometimes when he slept beside Naomi and she looked at his head on the pillow as the early morning white came across the fire escape onto the bed, she would put her fingers gently on his skull; so close to his brains were her hands, she felt she could pierce the cover in a moment and expose his mind, all bloody and curled to the day. The thought was a frightening one, and after its appearance Naomi would pinch herself for thinking strange things and scold herself for wasting time when she should be moving her arms and legs in a purposeful direction. Moses was not ill, she concluded; at least he was not yet ill.

Isaac sold the seventy-five pairs of pants. He sold them by working from early in the morning till late at night. He sold them by placing his cart in the best spots. He had a fight with an old man who sold pots and pans from a place up by the candy store at the corner that he believed was his, and on the morning when he arrived and found Isaac there, his pants piled high on his cart, he screamed at him and he cursed him and he brought down the evil eye on the boy and he demanded the name of his parents and he attempted to push him out of the way. He pulled his own cart into the middle of the street, and then, pushing it as fast as he could, he rammed into the side of Isaac's cart. A crowd watched.

Isaac took care to keep his body out of the way of the man and his cart, but he did not answer him. He just went on scanning the crowd for customers. "Beautiful pants," he said, almost crooning, "just right for the mister who needs a new pair. Why should he be shabby in this America, where every man can hold up his head as high as another? Here is a blue pair to match someone's blue eyes, is that not so? And here is a jacket that a Mr. Rockefeller might envy." As he talked on, the old man approached him from behind and threw his arm around his neck. He was not a strong man or a big man, but he was an exceedingly angry man, and Isaac felt the air disappear from his lungs and he turned red in the face and he began to kick with his feet. He fell backward and the man fell under him and released his arm for a second, and Isaac jumped up and, yelling for all he was worth, said, "My spot, now it's my spot! Old man, find another." He picked up the dung that was in the gutter still warm from the horse that had passed only moments before and he flung it in the face of the man on the ground. The crowd roared in appreciation. What next? They waited for the old man to get to his feet and return the favor, but the man had had enough.

"Cossack!" he screamed as he wiped his face with his sleeve. "Goy!" he shrieked as he moved his cart off to another block.

A man patted Isaac on the shoulder. "So you are a merchant," said the man, who sold hats, "like me."

The older fellows said, "Watch out for that one, he probably picks pockets."

But Isaac just smiled at everyone. He had his own cart, he had the best spot on the most important street, and the women who picked up his suits and inspected them carefully in the sunlight and ran their fingers over the weave of the fabric, they smiled at him. The gold they had expected to find on the streets of the Lower East Side was only, they now understood, the reflection of sun on the droppings of horses as they lumbered by—and the young man, at least, he knew what to do with it. So the women smiled at him. How much better to throw it than to catch it, said one while purchasing a fine suit of the best wool.

Moses's eyes had always been watery from the long hours over the machine. They were rimmed in red, and sometimes he had infections that brought a crust and caused them to stay closed in the morning when he woke. Now something new happened to Moses's eyes. They seemed to blink constantly; a small swift contraction began at the upper lid and swiftly gathered across the top of the eye. If you looked right in his face, it appeared as if a small ripple had crossed his lids, and then it would happen again and again as if a hint of a storm were stirring up the waters of a lake. The blinking made it hard for Moses to work. It would take him longer to fit the sleeve into the jacket vest and to follow the lines of chalk on the buttonholes. He occasionally made mistakes. Stop that blinking, said his boss, and so alarmed was Moses at the thought of losing his job that he managed not to blink when the boss was looking. He found a way when he was working to bend his head, practically placing his nose above the needle shaft so that even the man at the nearest table could not see if he was blinking or not. He was blinking because he could not stop it.

"What is it?" said Naomi. "Do your eyes hurt? You are getting sick from skipping so many meals, you must eat dinner, you are getting sick!" she screamed.

"No," said Moses, who never raised his voice to his wife, "I'm fine. I've never felt better."

And that was true, too. Naomi noticed that between blinks his pale eyes were calm and even had a shine, a light she had not seen in all their years together.

Ruth sat in her father's lap at night and she said to him, "Papa, I think you are happy tonight, your eyes are soft when you look at me."

"I am happy," said Moses, "when you are with me."

And that too was true. She would always carry the scars from the pox and her face would never hold a man and she would never know what he knew with Devorah, but perhaps she would stay with him and nurse him in his old age. God, perhaps, had a plan when he gave the illness to Ruth, perhaps inside the punishment lay the reward? After the exile would come the return—was that not so? The thought that Ruth would be his forever increased the light in his eyes, the light that others could only see between the blinking that went on and on; even in his sleep now, the contractions followed one after another across his closed eyelids.

Isaac sold more than seventy-five suits in a week. He pulled the heavy cart through the streets, catching the last shopper, the last man walking home from work, the ones who had stopped for a glass of tea, the ones who were dragging their feet because something in the rooms that waited for them, could bear waiting.

"I know suits," he said to his customers, "and these suits are the best."

"How could you know suits?" said a lady wrapped in shawls against the cold. "You should be home with your mama." She pushed him in the shoulder but bought a suit anyway.

Max found trouble, or trouble found Max, depending on your view of history. He had been playing cards in the back of the cigar store, which also sold milk and the *Forward,* with his friends, Abe and Solly. A girl, maybe fifteen years old, came running into the alley and knocked over the crate on which they had their cards. Max had a good hand, and he was furious and began yelling at the girl. She was sobbing and choking, and when she saw that the alley was a dead end, she sank to the ground and whimpered into the dirt. There she put her face on the cigarette butts, the spilled beer, and the other oozing things that lay on the ground. The boys saw that she had ripped her dress, ripped it so bad that her undergarments showed, and they were all see-through anyway. So Abe and Solly were picking up cards and swearing at the girl, and Max bent down to her.

"Watch where you're running, you clumsy ox," he said to her in English and then in Yiddish just to be sure she understood.

Something in his tone restored the girl, and she picked up her head and said to him, "Here, hold this. Keep it for me. I'll come back and get it tomorrow." She pressed a wallet into his hand.

Max took it, quickly slipped it into his pocket. He patted the girl on the shoulder and was just thinking about moving his hand down her chest, so his friends would envy him later, when a man came out the back door, grabbed the girl by the throat, and shoved her against the wall. Solly and Abe bolted. Max stood there.

"Stop that, mister," Max said. "That's a girl." The man was shaking her and hitting her head against the wall. The girl was screaming for her mother. Max kicked the man in the back of his legs. "Don't hit girls," Max said.

"Go away, go," the girl said to him.

The man didn't turn around, but his jacket flapped up and Max saw that he had a gun tucked under his belt. Max ran. Once he was home, sitting on his fire escape, he opened the wallet. It belonged to one Jacob Brest and it contained twenty dollars. A fortune. But not his—the girl's, and maybe not the girl's.

The next afternoon he was in the alley waiting for the girl to return. He thought he might ask for a reward. He imagined she would give him something, something good for holding the wallet for her. He had seen her garters pressing against her thighs, and he thought that perhaps he would see more in the future.

The back door to the cigar store opened and the man, Jacob Brest, appeared. He picked up Max by the arms and demanded his wallet. "She gave it to you. She told me so. The whore, the stinking whore. She works for me and she tried to rob me. You try to rob me and you'll end up with her wrapped in a blanket, dumped in the river. You hear me, kid?"

The man put Max down on the ground, and Max reached into his pocket and pulled out the wallet and returned it with a flourish. "I was hoping you'd come," he said. "I didn't know where to find you. But if this is yours, perhaps you would give me a small reward for taking such good care of it?"

"Where you from, kid?" the man asked. Max said Sulvalki. "Oh, yeah," said the man, "I spent some time in that town."

Which was how Max got to be the one to bring messages from Jacob to the girls who lived in the house on Barlow Street, to run errands for them, bringing them beer and tea and cigarettes. The girls would give him a tip when he came, and sometimes they let him have a feel of some hip or some nipple that was poking out here and there. Which is how it happened that one night when Naomi thought that Max was asleep on the mattress with Isaac and Ruth, he was found by the police, who had been bought off by Jacob, but not enough or not recently or someone in the precinct was putting on pressure for a show, and the wagons came and they took all the occupants, including some kid who kept saying he was innocent and had been lost and had just knocked on the door but was found in one of the back rooms drinking beer with a young lady who was only wearing a necklace of seashells and a green girdle with red feathers glued on. Moses wept and Naomi slapped Max in the face, right in front of everyone at the station house when they came for him in the morning. The police had threatened to send him away forever, and Max had been so scared that he even prayed to God to save him, although he knew he was not in such good standing with God.

Naomi read the *Forward,* and she saw the fashions that were advertised there. She worked with the other women who had all arrived from the same part of the world and shared the same tongue, but they still spoke English to one another, each picking up mistakes from the other. Naomi stopped covering her hair in public after six months. It is not American to do that, she told Moses, who shrugged. In fact, he liked it better, to see his wife's black hair piled on her head and reflecting the light of the sun or the shimmer of the kerosene lamps that hung at each corner and were lit in the evening by the lamplighter, who walked through the streets with his long pole and his pail and who sometimes sang the aria from *Rigoletto* if the night were especially balmy.

Naomi had stopped going to the mikvah after a year. "It isn't nec- essary," she said. "I'm clean enough without a prayer."

Moses was not happy about it. "These are our laws, our ways," he said.

She tugged at his nose and rubbed her hands in his hair, wiping off the strands that remained on her palm. "I promise you," she said, "God does not care. I am a good woman, and that's enough." In fact, Naomi stopped going to the mikvah because she was worried about her diamond. In the bath she was forced to hide her pouch in the apron of her dress, and she was afraid, afraid all the time, that someone would steal it, someone would know, would shake out her pockets and find her treasure. She could not enjoy the warm water or the soaping under the breasts or the woman who handed her a towel. Comfort only came when she re- turned to her cubicle and found her dress and felt in the pocket for her diamond and it was there, her link to the future, her hope for her children, her superiority over others who did not know what she held, small and glowing in her hand, in the privacy of night, when Moses was sleeping, when the children were sleeping, and when only her conscience cried aloud in the darkness . . . and a conscience one could sing to sleep with lullabies and other excuses.

Now, after Ruth had returned from the hospital and Moses began to blink in his own incessant way, Naomi, on her way home, walked from the loft to the Italian street where the butchers had red blood flowing into the sidewalks and the pastry stores had little cakes with red cherries on the top and at Christmastime the windows were filled with evergreen and figures of Jesus in his cradle and glowing candles. She went to the butcher and bought one pound of bacon. The boss had expanded the pocketbook loft and had added a floor and hired some Italians, and Naomi had met one of them as the women waited in line for the privy. The Italian girl had spoken that morning of her mother making bacon and the smell coming through the whole house and chasing away the Devil, who hated bacon because it brought so much happiness. Naomi knew that bacon was pork, was the forbidden food, but she did not know if it was wide or narrow, yellow or brown, or what you did to make it cook.

"How," she asked her co-worker, "did your mother make the bacon?" And she was told.

That afternoon Naomi, in a stranger's territory, aware that the people on the street were looking at her, Jew woman, went into the butcher's and ordered a pound of bacon. When Moses came home he could smell the strange odor as soon as he opened the downstairs door.

Mrs. Moscowitz opened her door and, peering at Moses through a sliver, shouted at him, "You'd better do something with your wife before God strikes this whole building down."

Isaac was still out with his cart of jackets and pants. Ruth was sitting on the chair in the kitchen playing with her spoons, talking to them. "Children, dear," she was saying, "let me clean your faces." Max was hanging out the fire escape throwing something against the window across the way.

Moses said to his wife, "What is it? What are you doing?"

"Don't you know bacon when you smell it?" she said. "I am frying it for our dinner."

"Pork?" said Moses, and sank down on the bed. "You have made pork in this house, in our pan?"

"Yes," said Naomi, "American bacon. It tastes good, even," she said.

"But it is forbidden," said Moses. "The dishes will be mixed, will be impure." Moses looked at his wife, there were tears in his eyes. His blink was flickering like a dying flame. "What will the rabbi say, what would my uncle say? Everything in this house will be impure."

"So," said Naomi, "who is pure?"

What she knew, what she didn't, Moses couldn't tell. Naomi turned the bacon over in the pan. Moses blinked and blinked. He wished he could go to Devorah's. There it was still glatt kosher, and a man of God could put the food in his mouth without risking his eternal soul. It was the demon in Naomi, he thought; it was the tragedy of her daughter, he thought. It was his fault, he knew.

That was the end of the keeping of the kosher kitchen. The plates for the meat and the dairy were put away together, and Max laughed at the turn of his father's lips when he put his spoon to his mouth.

Moses prayed to his God. Early, earlier than usual, Moses rose from the bed he shared with his wife and went to the roof of the building. There he looked down on the tangle of fire escapes, the swing of the laundry from ropes, the cans in the alley, and the papers that blew against the dark brick walls as if clinging for their lives, an instant's reprieve before being sent on their way. The air was cold and he had not brought his jacket with him. He felt the wind cutting across his shoulder blades and icing his thighs and freezing his groin. There was the problem. There was the impurity. He took out his tallis from its velvet case and swung it over his shoulders, in a gesture repeated so frequently that it had acquired a grace, a speed, an aspect of dance, as if the arc of his arm and the arc of the tallis, with its fringe and its blue strips at the base, together formed a prayer, a gesture to God of the flight of man's imagination. The wind blew off his hat and he had to tuck it under his arm. He stood there on the roof like a bird, a bald-headed man in his shirtsleeves, on a January day staring up at the first light of day, coming white and icy off the East River, shining on the metal funnels, reflecting in the smoke that began to rise from the chimneys as coal blistered and burned in stoves. Ahead of him lay a forest of chimneys, red brick, black with soot, crumbling with time, some leaning, some already falling, and the black of the roof peeling and chipping. If he looked down, down to the space between his building and the next, he saw how far he could fall, how easy it would be to just edge his foot over the rim. He stepped backward, and standing in the middle of the roof, looking to the morning moon, which hung like an unburied body, drained of its soul in the west, a cloud of a moon with a swollen shape that was neither round nor crescent but a thing in between, he prayed to God. First the prayers he must say, and then he spoke to his God.

"Forgive Naomi," he begged. "She has been orphaned and her daughter was ill with the pox and she thought she had lost her son and the other one with the gangsters. She works hard in the loft and she doesn't mean the disrespect that comes from her mouth. The matter of pork and the dishes confused does not tell you about her innocence. She is innocent," he said to his God, knowing that she was guilty at least of bringing the bacon into the house. "I am the one who is guilty," he said, "and I will change. I will never go to Devorah's bed again. I will find a new place of study. I will change, you will see. Forgive this family, O God, whose mercy is unending as the horizon, who created all things, forgive the weak creature of your making and let us start again, even though it is not yet the days of awe, I am returning to you."

The cold air blew. The tallis fringes flapped in the wind. Moses blinked his eyes and the tears that formed were from the cold as much as from the heart. He folded up his tallis and his tefillin and he stood a moment on the roof looking at the metallic globe of sun that now appeared low on the left. It appeared to be dead. The rays returned into itself. It floated in the sky like a memory of a sun, like a prayer from the mouth of man in whose kitchen the smell of bacon lingered.

He had indeed decided not to go to his house of study anymore, not to see Devorah bending over the desks with the tray of tea, not to watch her legs rising up the stairs, never again to break the commandment; but by the end of the day when the work was winding down and the dark blue jacket he had been making lacked only the last buttonholes, it seemed to him that it would not be so bad to go once more and to tell Devorah that he could no longer come. It was better than letting her wait for him at the window and feel the sharp cut of disappointment.

When he thought of her disappointment, his own rose in his throat, and he decided to go as usual. Once she let him in the door and led him upstairs, she quickly slipped his suspenders off his shoulders and pressed her palms against the center of his wide chest. In moments they were undressed, the two of them, goose bumps on their flesh from the cold air, and he did not have time to talk the matter over with her before she had blown in his ear and he had touched, just gently with his thumb and forefinger, her right nipple, which then followed his hand and went wherever he wanted. She lay down on the bed with her face in the pillow and invited him to rub her large white buttocks. He leaned over her and with his tongue went into forbidden places, something she had taught him, something she had learned from her late husband, and something he found so evil that it made his stomach turn and his flesh fill with joy as never before. Everything in Devorah's bedroom was wrong, and everything was good. Oh, God, he thought as he sank into the occasion, this morning I said no, but this evening my strength is gone. He came from behind her and found her opening. This, he understood, must be why the first temple fell and the second temple fell and the Jews are still wandering in exile. But at that moment the exile felt more like a homecoming, a fact that caused Moses to utter such a harsh sound from his throat that Devorah did not know if he was calling out in pleasure or in pain.

Hedy in the Corridor of the Hadassah Hospital: Jerusalem, 1990

Her husband's white shirt was open at the collar, and his neck and the top of his chest showed patches of red. Sweat dripped from his forehead. He held his glasses in his hand and swung them up and down like a pendulum. He had come from the education council, where he was sitting on a committee. She had told the secretary that it was an emergency. "He must be here," she had shouted into the telephone. When he came, Hedy was not glad to see him. What use was he, after all? She was wearing an old cotton dress, the one she wore to work at her desk at home. She had on sandals that were scuffed with use. Should she have changed? Was there an outfit that would influence the events in the operating room? Her mother had believed in lucky dresses. If she wore a particular dress and had a bad time or lost money at cards, she would never wear that dress again. Hedy remembered the closet with lucky shoes and lucky hats, which sometimes changed their status and became unlucky shoes and unlucky hats. Hedy, who believed in reason, owned no lucky clothes. She carried her blue pocketbook, now hanging from the orange plastic chair she could have been sitting on if she weren't too restless to sit, if she didn't prefer standing so that she could keep her back to her husband and her son, Yehuda, who had been called out in the middle of a chemistry exam. He stood at his father's side, his hands curled into fists stuck into his pockets, with formulas leaking through his mind. Hedy turned her back on her older daughter, Tova, the medical student whose wedding they had just celebrated in May. Hedy looked at the clock in the corridor.

"You didn't have to come," said Hedy.

"Of course I had to come," said Tova. "She's my sister."

In Which a Further Journey Is Taken: 1886

Moses was only a tailor, one of fifty in the shop, and Isaac was only the owner of a single cart, and Naomi worked in the pocketbook loft, and Ruth strung beads sitting by the fire escape, disappearing into the back room if anyone came to the apartment door. The family income was steady, adequate for food and shelter, without the luxury of a warm coat or gloves or more than a chicken for every third Shabbos. Naomi wanted more.

"Isaac," she said, "could you have two carts and get Max to pull one?"

Isaac sighed. Max would never stay by his cart. On the few occasions when he had asked him to help, Max had grown bored and jumped up and down and bothered the customers as they went through the piles on the cart. And then he disappeared, just for a moment, he said, but he had come back hours later. He left apple cores in the back of the cart, where they rotted and caused the jackets to smell like last night's garbage. "Maybe a store," said Isaac. "Maybe I can rent a store and sell from there, and that would be a way."

He went to his supplier, who was Moses's boss, and he said to him, "I want a store. I want to do better, I can sell more of your jackets if you give me the money for the first two months' rent on a store."

The boss looked at Isaac. He saw a boy, a boy with a serious face, with wide lips that curved downward, with legs and arms that did not yet know how to move together. The boss laughed. "No," he said, "not yet."

Isaac came back the following week and said to him again, "I want to rent a store."

But the boss said, "No. No, no," when Isaac appeared at the doorway of his office at one end of the large loft. "I am not throwing my money out," he yelled. "I am not lending it. What do you think I am, a bank?"

Isaac went to the bank that had just opened. The banker, Ben Eisen, was an immigrant who until recently had been working in the cigar factory. The bank was running on nerve. Its capital was small. It took Isaac three hours of sitting before the banker in the office with the green-shaded lamp would see him.

The banker, who was very young himself, only a few years older than Isaac, looked at the boy. "Have you been to school?" he said.

"No," said Isaac.

"No," said the banker, who also had not been to school. "You're too young. The possibility of loss is too high."

Isaac said to his mother, "I cannot get the money to rent the store. Sell the diamond for me."

Naomi reached her hand down to her waist. Through the folds of her dress she felt the small stone. "No," she said, "this is for us when we really need it."

The boss was tired of Isaac appearing at his office with his request unchanged. The next time Isaac came he said, "I have a cousin who has gone to a town in Pennsylvania, and he sells household goods to the miners in the town and he is making a good living. He is saving money. Maybe you should go to Pennsylvania and sell to the miners, pants, suits for church. Miners need pants, and I will make them special for you to sell, and you can sell them from door to door, from your cart, and when you have saved enough, then you can come back to New York and rent your store, maybe on Fifth Avenue, who knows."

The boss opened his desk drawer and took out a map of America, and for the first time Isaac saw the whole expanse, the Mississippi River, the mountain ranges of Colorado, the mitten that was Wisconsin, the Great Lakes that dipped up and down, the finger that was Florida, and the states in the middle with names that Isaac was not sure how to pronounce. "A great country of which New York is just a small part and the Lower East Side an even smaller place. Opportunity lies there," said the boss, waving his hand across the map. Isaac saw the reds and blues and oranges of the colors of each state unfold.

"Your father will never agree," said Naomi.

Ruth brought her brother a glass of tea. "If you think we should go, I will talk to Papa," she said.

Moses came home late. He sat down at the table and listened to his son: "We will go and I will sell to the miners and you can help me, you can make things for me to sell. This is our chance. Our first big chance." Moses looked at his un–Bar Mitzvahed son, his face unsmiling as always. Isaac searched his father's face. Moses put his head in his hands and tried to steady his blinking eyes; the contractions came one after another. It was God's answer to his prayer. They would move away from Devorah, from the shul, from the pork. His son, his Isaac, was leading him toward God.

So they all went to Pansville. They traveled by train. Max rode on the steps between the cars. He ran up and down the aisles. He dragged his bad leg behind him, and he screamed every time he saw a cow or a horse in the distance. "America!" he shouted. "There, out there!" The conductor boxed him on the ears, but that didn't stop Max from standing up on the seats and calling out to the other passengers, in his accent that still hummed of Yiddish, had a few Italian words in it, and came through the nose, translated, strangled, but English nevertheless, "We are going to Pansville, Pennsylvania, and I am going to have a horse of my own." The other passengers, some of them turned their faces away, and some of them grimaced; the invasion of the Jews was heading west and some of them didn't like it and some were indifferent, and Isaac thought to himself that they all would buy from him, every last passenger on the train, if the price were right.

It turned out to be true that in Pansville the boss's cousin was doing fairly well. He had a store, right on Main Street, that sold knives and forks, bowls and pots, and he was glad, this Abraham Vishniac, to have another Jewish family in town. He helped them take their bags to the apartment he had found for them, right by the railroad tracks in a house that rocked on its foundation each time the trains went by, that had a well in the back and the water for the bath had to be heated on the stove and the man who owned the house was a drunkard whose binges always ended in a flinging of things about the kitchen. His wife had died and his children had left home and the upstairs apartment was small but good enough.

"We are beginning, Mama," said Isaac.

"But in a place with only one other Jewish family," said Naomi, who missed the talk in the shop, who missed the sound of the street and was afraid of the man downstairs.

"These are not Poles," said Isaac, "these are Americans like you and me. They are poor people, too, who work for a living, and they will appreciate that I bring them honest goods."

Moses sat in his new apartment, stunned by the change in his life, by the unknown he was about to face. If they starved, if Isaac sold nothing, if he could find no work, what then? He wanted only to go back to Sulvalki and his uncle's tailor shop with its green curtains that separated him from the customers and its familiar smell of sausage and beer that floated in the doorway from the tavern across the street. He also wanted to go back to Devorah. He dreamed of a large roll being removed from the oven on a shovel and puffed and powdered, with the smell of fresh bread. It was in the shape of Devorah, her breasts each with a cherry embedded in the nipple, waiting for him. He woke crying. Did David dream of Bathsheba as a roll? What terrible punishments had David endured?

As the train had sped away from New York City, away from the scenes of his recent pleasure, his ache had increased, but his blinking had slowed. The contractions were less frequent. He was able for the first time in months to see clearly, and that brought him some comfort.

"It's the country air, it is better for the eyes," said Naomi. And it was.

Hedy Waits for Her Father to Take Her to the Park: 1942

Hedy was sitting in the hall on the red velvet Louis Quatorze chair. Above her head the sconces with crystal beads and gold loops hung, and all around her the red-and-white silk wallpaper marched in thick stripes. If she closed her eyes tightly and then tilted her head, she could make the bands appear to lean and tip. It was Saturday afternoon and her mother was playing cards and Ursula was visiting Shinki, Ursula's friend from the park, who came from a village outside of Hamburg; when the two women were together the sound of German flowed like a gentle river above the children's heads, the sounds of cows in the barns and snow melting on the hills and edelweiss pushing up the dark soil and gray leather pants and sweaters with tassels and the banging of dishes in wooden tubs and the ringing of the church bell, the sound of German Hedy heard as a lullaby.

Today the cook was in the kitchen but had already told Hedy she couldn't sit there all afternoon. Hedy was waiting for her father to come home. He was supposed to be there at four o'clock. He was going to take her to the park and go climbing on the rocks with her. Hedy went into her room and looked at the clock. It was already quarter to five. It was too late to go to out. It would get dark soon. She could already see the sky above Park Avenue bleaching out its colors, sending shadows like plumes of smoke across the streets, where the doormen leaned against the silver poles that supported the awnings.

Hedy returned to her chair and waited. Any minute she would hear the key in the lock. He would walk to the closet, hang up his coat, and turn to her. He would say, "I'm sorry, but the game at the club went on longer than I thought it would." Or he would say, "I'm sorry, I had to make a phone call." He made many phone calls, his head tucked down and away from her and his hand over his mouth. When they went walking together, he would stop at pay phones and say, "Just a moment," and he would put in his nickel and turn his back to her. She would wait. His back was strong. He was tall and his suede gloves were soft and she kept up with him, stretching her legs, leaping and sometimes running so he would not have to slow down, so he would make the light at the corner, so that he could keep going just as if she weren't there at his side. When they went to the park he would lead her up to the lake where there was a castle surrounded by piles of rocks and dirt and a steep path that wound up the face of the castle and ended at the turret. It was a weather station, no longer in use. Now that there was a war on and people had lost their romantic affection for things of the Continent, the Parks Department had allowed the stones of the castle to crumble and weeds to grow between the cracks. Hedy and her father would climb to the top. Higher, he would say. You can make that leap, he would call if she hesitated. Up there on the rocks, as he stood above her, offering a hand for a difficult jump at the top, she felt as if she could do anything he asked. She was as strong as he was, as brave as he was, or she would be one day. His black hair lay flat and slicked down on his head, and he held his fedora in his hand and gestured out to the people who now looked small walking around the base of the lake. He said, "Look at them walking around in a circle while we were climbing up."

Once, he had picked up a stone and held it in his hand. He lifted his arm, ready to throw. "I could hit that baby carriage," he said. Hedy saw the sunlight on her father's camel-hair coat and she saw the dark glint in his eye. She leaned her head against him. She wanted him to pick her up, to wrap his coat around her to keep off the wind that blew around them, making it hard for her to stand up straight. But he wasn't that kind of father. He moved to another rock, away from her, one she could not reach without going way down a rickety path and then returning up a steep slope. She was cold but didn't want to say so. She thought about trying to reach the rock her father was on, but her leather leggings with all their straps and clips made it hard for her to bend her knees. The wind turned her nose red and her eyes began to water. Her checkered hat had ear flaps that she had loosened so that she could hear her father's instructions as they climbed. Now she tried to fasten the velvet ribbon under her chin, but her fingers in the thick gloves were too clumsy, so the cold blew into her ears, shutting out all other sounds. Her father stood on his rock like a Norse god from her book, as if he could have a thunderbolt in his hand, as if he could make the skies rip open and the rains come rushing down.

"Look," she shouted to him, "I found a round pebble, it's perfectly round like the sun." She held out the pebble to him, an offering, a bid. He stared at the pebble in her hand and then came to her ledge. He took the pebble and put it in his pocket.

"You're my kind of girl," he said. He started down the rocks, and sliding on her leggings, feeling the bunched-up places where her skirt had been tucked in, she followed as fast as she could.

Today, Hedy listened for the door to open, she willed the door to open, she concentrated only on the sound of the key and the lock and the door moving forward toward her. She pushed all other thoughts aside and thought only of the door and its opening, and she believed that if she concentrated enough, she could bring her father home.

The door opened. Her mother entered. "You're still waiting." she said. "He promised me he would come back and get you this afternoon." Hedy's mother took off her fox fur, the head with the little paws and the beady eyes that Hedy petted and fondled and held close to her heart as if her own heartbeat could restore the heat to the beast, release it for its run in the darkest foliage of the farthest forest. Hedy's mother took off her hat with the veil and said to her daughter, "Let me get a drink and then I'll tell you how I won forty dollars this afternoon."

Hedy followed her mother to the den, although she kept listening for the door, for the footsteps, for the sound of his voice in the hall. His hands were large. His legs were long. He was the prince of her darkness, the lord of her awakening, the duke of her manor, and the jailer of her prison as well as the knight of her escape, and she wished for him, a sword of rubies and diamonds: a kingdom equal to his stride.

Success in Pansville: 1886

The railroad that connected Pansville with the West also ran east, back to New York. Four times a day the trains, throwing black smoke into the air, grinding metal wheels on tracks, passed by the small house the Gruenbaums lived in. When the whistle blew and the train approached the red-brick station, everything in the house shook. The chairs rocked and the dishes bounced in the cupboard and the legs of the beds squealed as they scraped against the floor. The windows shook in their frames, and for a few seconds the floor seemed about to buckle. The Gruenbaums learned how to steady themselves, to rock on their heels and float with the motion and then to resume when the train had passed and the sound of clacking and banging and shaking had faded, to pick up their conversation, to continue to serve dinner, to bathe in the tub in the kitchen, to button clothes, to iron clothes, to wash clothes, clothes that were always gray. Black ash would fall through the open window and cover the sheets and the chairs and the sills. Naomi washed and mopped and brushed it away and still more would come, and her dreams, dreams that had before been full of oranges and pinks and yellows, were now only gray, gray flowers, gray rivers, gray skies.

On Main Street was the Congregational church, the post office, the general grocery, and the hardware store owned by Abraham Vishniac. There was the school with its three rooms and its yard with old boxes rotting from the rain and logs for the children to climb over and a swing, a swing with its broken seat that banged against the wooden pole in the wind. There was a blacksmith and a doctor's ofice and a vet's office and a big white building that housed the offices of the mine and backed right up on the railroad where the coal was loaded onto freight cars and hitched to the trains that carried it away. The minister's house had a cupola and a parapet. Up on the hill, overlooking a stream that ran blue in summer and white in winter, sat the house of the owner of the mill. He and his family were often away, traveling. It was said that they had an apartment in Paris. Near the big house were other white houses, freshly painted, with shutters of black and green. These belonged to the accountant, the vice president of the mine, and the unmarried daughter of the engineer who had discovered the riches inside the mountain some eighty years before. On the other side of the valley, up from the railroad tracks, were streets lined with small houses. Some of them had leaning walls. None of them had indoor plumbing. The white clapboard was chipped and splintered, and the windows were often covered with tar paper. It was here that the miners lived with their wives and their children. It was through these streets that Isaac and his father traveled every day, pulling their cart with them loaded with pants for the miners, pants for the boys, and pants for the old men whose faces were lined from years in the pits and black dirt, coal dust crusted in the crevices under the eyes, above the lips, and beside the nose. Business was good. Business was very good, and Isaac sold as many pants each week as he could carry through the streets. The profit margin was high.

At Christmastime, when the music from the church floated down the square, and the carolers gathered by the mine ofices and the store offered candy canes and dolls and toy trains for the children and evergreen was hung on the lampposts, Naomi remembered Sulvalki and the Jewish streets, where the smells were one's own and there was safety in numbers. Had she been right after all: was America a place for Jews? In the general store Isaac found a Christmas card; it pictured a Madonna holding a baby who was wrapped in a gold cloth. He looked at it a long time. He offered to go into the woods and gather firewood for the owner of the store. He went at night, when the family was at supper. For a week he gathered wood. In return he was given the card. He wrote in it, "Merry Christmas, to my friend." He bought a stamp at the post office, and the postmaster, a man with a crossed eye and a hand that shook, read the address on the envelope: Sister Abigail, Hospital for Infectious Diseases, New York City.

"You got a sister in New York?" he asked.

"Yes," said Isaac.

Ruth hardly ever left the apartment. Isaac told her stories in the evening. He told her about the baby who had only one arm, whose mother let him into the kitchen although she was only wearing a slip and her stockings. He told Ruth about the widow who had bought a pair of pants from Isaac even though her husband was dead and her sons had moved away. She hung the pants up in the closet, "in case. One never knows," she said. "A man can make a sudden appearance; it could be." Isaac told Ruth how the woman's lips had trembled and how many teeth she was missing.

Moses, whose eyes had completely recovered, walked about like a man without a purpose, a man who had forgotten what he was doing here and who had made no plans for tomorrow.

"What is the matter with you?" said Naomi. "You sit in the chair like a sick person. We are making money. We are doing well. What is the matter with you?"

Moses just nodded his head. "It's all right, Naomi," he said. "It's all right."

He did his duty by her. A man, it says in the Talmud, must do for his wife, but as his body rose and fell on hers and the covers were pulled to keep the warmth in, he realized that even in exile one could be exiled. Little diasporas existed inside of bigger ones; such was the inventiveness of the Lord.

Max limped out into the streets and looked for a fellow to share a beer with, but the town boys did not like his accent, did not like the slope of his chin and the shuffle of his gait. They knew a Jew when they saw one, and a Jew was a thing that came from the other side and whose irregular habits did not belong in a place where the mines tunneled ever deeper into the mountains, and the miners' sons knew where they would go, what they would do, when their time came. The mine whistle blew in the morning and in the evening, and the whole town flowed together, toward the mine, away from the mine; but the small Jew boy watched by the schoolyard as the others tossed a ball in the air, and they laughed at him, the way he talked, the way he walked. Once they found him smoking behind the general store. They kicked him and rubbed his face in the dirt, and he got a cut on his chin that his mother bathed in water and alcohol later that night.

"Bastards," said Max.

"What language," said his mother.

"Better to go back to New York," said Max.

"Better to go back to New York," said Moses.

"No," said Isaac. "We are doing well here."

"No," said Naomi, "Isaac says we are doing well. You think," she said to Max, "you couldn't get a cut on your chin in New York?"

There wasn't enough money for a horse. Max knew he would not have a horse, not now. He thought about horses, though, he visited them at the blacksmith's shop. He smelled their skin, he smelled their droppings. He dreamed about horses galloping through the hills, riderless horses, who followed their whim while the wind lifted up their manes and flowed through their wide nostrils.

Hedy Learns to Throw a Baseball: 1944

It was September and the Dodgers were in a bad spot, the bad spot that had been going on for weeks. Their hitters were sleepy. Their outfield dropped balls. The Duke bumbled and sprained his ankle. The sportscasters had colds. Jerry the doorman was in a state of gloom. Hedy made a promise to God. She would never ask for a favor again if only her team broke the spell. The next day it happened, two in the bleachers, an incredible catch off the wall, and a win that made the blood rush to the face. Jerry the doorman taught Hedy how to throw overarm, like a boy. He pulled her arm back in the socket, and she did it. However it was in Mudville, there was joy on Park Avenue.

Opportunity Knocks Hard: 1890

In the first spring of their stay in Pansville, Moses discovered while waiting for Isaac one day a patch of purple flowers and he saw an extraordinary butterfly with velvet wings of brazen colors.

"Thank you, God," said Moses, "for the creatures of the world you have brought before me."

When Isaac came out of the house he found Moses on his knees in the wet grass. There were tears running down his cheeks. "Look," said Moses, "at the flowers."

"Get off the wet grass. Your trousers will be stained. You'll be ill," said Isaac, who wanted to visit each house on four more streets that afternoon.

As time passed Moses discovered the clouds took on different shapes over the low mountains that fringed the town. He could tell rain clouds and storm clouds, and in the winter he knew when snow was coming. He knew the names of the trees. That is to say, he had noticed the different leaves, the different blossoms on each, and had given them pet names, names from Sulvalki, the name of his mother and her sister and the name of the street on which he was born.

Moses never took off his black coat and he never went out in public without his hat on his head because even in Pansville God was watching over everything, although he didn't forget the fire in the shul in Sulvalki.

At four o'clock one winter afternoon the sirens from the mines blew and blew, calling for help. There had been an accident. Not a small one as before, but a major cave-in, and the women rushed from their houses and stood outside the mines wrapped in their shawls with their small children, white-faced, clinging to their skirts. The doctor came and stood helplessly on a scaffold above the mine entrance and waited. Men and boys, even Moses and Isaac, were digging down through the side of the mountain to reach the spot where the walls of coal had collapsed and the smell of gas had filled the tunnels and the men whose heavy shoes bore them down toward the center of the earth breathed or had stopped breathing, now part of the mountain they had invaded. Three days passed and no one in the town bought anything. Everyone went to the mouth of the mine and waited. Max and Isaac and Moses were there when the first bodies were carried out and the women held each other's hands and the children cried. There was talk of unsafe conditions and neglect, and the men who stood about on the hills now wearing their Sunday clothes out of respect for the dead and the dying grumbled, and there was talk of striking the mine and there was talk of the owners closing the mine because of the expense involved in reopening and there was talk of un- employment, and the bells of the church rang with each body discovered and at night the town was so quiet that when a woman cried out, her neighbors heard her and opened their doors and rushed from house to house, and small children wandered in front doors and asked for food and were fed.

Max went to the mouth of the mine the night before they declared the rescue effort over, and the men stood around watching the ground as if it might open and belch out their friends, their fathers and brothers who lay entombed miles below. Max sat on a rock away from the other boys, some of whom were wearing black ribbons on their jackets. One was holdng his sister's arm, trying to stop her from digging in the dirt with her fingernails. So the God of the goy is like our God, he thought. No God, he thought. No God at all, and that made him kick at the rock. Bastard, he said to the sky.

That night by the fires that kept watch, Max found a girl. A local girl named Beatrice who was slow of wit and easy with her favors. Her father and two brothers were down in the mine, and she had come to stand vigil. Her hair hung in wisps over her face. Her eyes were soft blue in the flickering light. There were stars in the sky. She smelled of powder and peppermint. She put her hand on his arm, and he shivered. She smiled, one tooth was missing.

"They are digging," said Max. "They will get them before dawn."

"I don't think so," she said. "It's farther down than you think. I've been there. Once one of my brothers took me down. I was dressed as a boy."

Max thought of her standing naked in her house putting on trousers. His blood raced to his organ. He would take of her. She didn't need her father or her brothers. She wandered down a gully and Max wandered after her, and he touched her hips as he eased himself into the dirt. He was hard as the rocks under his back. He felt tall, tall as the pine behind them that shook in the wind.

The morning came and the mine whistles didn't blow and the crews of men stood around, dark lines of exhaustion in their faces. They brought the last few men, coughing and knees buckled and gray as death. They brought up a body; someone's heart had stopped in the darkness. Beatrice's father was there, trying to smile into the sun. Later they sent down dynamite and exploded the rocks, closing off the area where the men they hadn't reached had breathed their last. Now the mine was a tomb as well as a mine. Moses stood on the rocks at the mouth of the mine where the men had returned to work, disappearing in lines into the cave, and said the kaddish. He added, "May ye be comforted among all the mourners of Zion and Jerusalem." What could it hurt?

Beatrice and Max met by the swings in the schoolyard. Beatrice was in trouble. Max sighed. Her father was angry and wanted to kill Max. "I'll marry you," said Max, who dreamed about her every night and didn't care what anyone thought.

Moses banged his head against the wall. Naomi screamed, "You can't marry a girl like that, not one of us."

Beatrice's father was at the door in the evening with some of his friends. He wanted to take Max into the woods and give him what he deserved. "Jews," the men yelled, "get outta here!" Someone else would marry Beatrice. "Go," said Beatrice's father, smashing his hand against Moses's chest. Moses struggled to his feet. Isaac raised his fists up. A train went by. Everything clattered. The train wheels turned.

"Go back where you came from," said the men who stood behind Beatrice's father.

Naomi picked up a dish and was ready to throw it. Moses was shaking. Max said, "I want to marry her." Naomi threw her dish at Max.

In Which a Friendly Banker Makes All the Difference: 1890

On the way back to New York Moses shivered when he thought of Orchard Street where a certain woman might still be, handing the men of the study group hot tea and brushing curls of hair off her wide damp forehead.

Ruth didn't mind their sudden departure. She hardly ever left the apartment. If her mother made her go to the store or walk to the corner, she kept her head down and her arms up over her face, and if young people came by, she turned around and fled for her home. "Papa," said Ruth on the train going east, "we will be together wherever we are."

"In New York," said Isaac, "I will get you a piano."

Max kept on dreaming of Beatrice long after their return. She was a girl whose skinny legs made him tremble, whose baby he had fathered but not fathered. Moses said to him, "You have a child." Naomi said to him, "You're not married, so you have no child." Isaac said, "We have savings."

When the family returned to the Lower East Side after their stay in Pansville, Isaac was a young man with a deep voice and wide shoulders, and while his broad forehead and his wide lips were like his father's, his eyes had a light in them closer to his mother's, and he walked down Hester Street heading toward Essex with a stride that meant work lay ahead, work lay behind, and his moment had come. He went to Ben Eisen the banker for the second time in his life. Now Ben Eisen welcomed him into his office, listened to the young man, and nodded his head. He had already granted hundreds of these loans, and he rarely made a mistake.

The village in which Ben Eisen had lived with his parents in the Ukraine had unfortunately been right on the road to the Black Sea, and a band of Cossacks off to join forces with their commander wandered through in the early morning, pulling men at prayer out into the street and beating them till they fell in the gutter and didn't move, shooting horses tied up in barns, spilling books out of the shul, smashing the window of the Belzer rebbe. Ten of them grabbed the rebbe's young wife and carried her off to the marketplace. There on the butcher's counter, where the day before the women of the town had purchased their chickens, they tore off her dress, held her down, and, turning her over forward and backward, entered her again and again. Her screams were heard in the cellars where the Jews were hiding, pressed up against the darkened walls, bolts and chains drawn. Men with payess wet with sweat prayed and rolled their hands into fists and swung them in the air, as if they could, as if they knew how to, protect the women and the children who listened to the rebbe's wife as she called for mercy to the unmerciful who sucked at her breasts and pulled at her hair in their excitement, who bit her shoulders and smashed themselves against her buttocks as if she were withholding a kernel of pleasure, keeping it for herself deep within. When they were done—and it took a long time—they saw the woman, dirtied, bloodied, legs stained with fluids and eyes wild and lips bruised and swollen, and they despised the portrait of themselves that lay thrashing, weeping, before them; and despising the sight, one pulled a gun and shot the woman in the head and another shot her in the stomach and one urinated on the doorpost of the butcher's shop, and then they tucked in their blouses and smoothed down their hair and put on their jackets. The Jews in their houses heard the shots and the other shots that rang as the Cossacks mounted their horses and left the town, and it was then that Ben Eisen's father decided to send his son, three years before his Bar Mitzvah, to his cousin in New York. What could be saved, should be saved.

This was the story that Ben Eisen told to his cousin in New York when he arrived shortly after New Year's in 1880. His cousin looked at the ten-year-old boy who would need to be fed and whose arms were not strong and whose eyes squinted in the daylight of his new American home, and he said, "Go to work or else you will starve." And so Ben Eisen went to work with his cousin in the cigar factory. He rose early in the morning and came back late at night, his fingers stained with tobacco, tobacco that he had been rolling and twisting and placing in its cover, stuffing as if it were a sausage, all day long. Ben Eisen was not yet twelve when he figured that if he saved his money and gave only what was required to his cousin for room and board, he would one day be a rich man. He ran favors for the older men in the factory. He would bring them water from the barrel at the head of the stairs and he would share his cheese that he had wrapped in newspaper for his lunch with anyone who asked. He looked people directly in the eye and he was respectful to them all, and the men, who themselves had been boys, often alone in the world, would pat him on the shoulder, would greet him with a wave when they passed on the street, would reward him with a cube of sugar or a sip of tea. Up and down the aisles of the factory he was known as a good boy, a boy you could trust, a boy who learned English fast, who learned anything you taught him and never forgot. He could write letters, and sometimes he would write to the old country for the men, a letter to a wife, a letter to a mother, a letter that said, I am well, and I wait for you, and did not say that the hours were long and days felt empty and the distance made the purpose of the journey fade. He wrote letters too that broke off marriage proposals, that brought unfortunate news of deaths both real and pretend, that bragged of wealth that had not been accumulated and some that had. He wrote the letters for free, but he gathered goodwill, and goodwill is capital. It is a treasure that doubles its worth in half the time of other assets. Goodwill can be hoarded indefinitely. If he missed his mother and his sisters, if he felt his father had been wrong to send him off, loading him and a sack of clothing onto a cart headed for Bremen with the money for a ticket in his pocket and an address printed on the back of a family photograph taken before his birth, he never said so to another living soul. His childhood had ended, as if he were a bird and shoved off the branch into flight, and his letters home were reassuring and money became the subject of his visions, and his savings that grew each week, this was his comfort and his rock.

When Ben Eisen was sixteen years old and had been working in the cigar factory for over seven years, he sat on his bed in his cousin's apartment. His cousin now had a wife and a new baby, and they wanted his bed. They said it was time for him to go out on his own, and it was. He was a short boy with a barrel of a chest like his father. He had his mother's clear eyes that looked right through you, expecting the best. He wasted no time wishing he had something he didn't. He believed that wishes were wasteful. Waste was a sin. He believed that honesty would win him friends, and friends were the key to survival. He could hardly remember his mother's face. Perhaps because his parents were gone, he was freer than most men to think well of himself. He never considered whether others would approve of him. He supplied his own approval. He had no parents to drink up his love, to make him wary of strangers, to consume his obligations, to make him wonder if he was worthy. He had instant responses. His guard was not up. He had a deep laugh that came easy. His handshake was warm and offered to everyone. He looked people in the eye and expected they would like him. He liked them, anyone who touched his arm, who told him a story, who gave him a glass of tea. He felt close, very close, to anyone who pulled up a chair, who walked a block with him. That was his gift, and he made the most of it. He knew what it was like to live on a wage. He could cry at a sad story. He understood that peril was everywhere, and his smile flashed into dark corners like a charm against the evil eye. He understood about the evil eye, that's why he was trusted. When it was time to atone he tried but could think of nothing he had done wrong.

He counted the money he had saved, and it was enough. He went to the building at the corner and he talked the landlord into renting him the ground floor, and there he hung out a sign. New World Bank, it said in bold letters. Underneath it repeated the name in Yiddish and so the sign was understood. Landsman, it said, here your money will be safe. And safety had become an important matter. Thieves. Yes, Jewish thieves were running up the fire escapes and opening the windows and searching among the socks and grabbing a pendant here, a week's wages there, a pinky ring from a grandmother, a memento of a mother's dress with faded yellow ribbons on a piece of lace. Thieves were selling things in the markets out in Brooklyn, off the carts on Orchard Street, things that belonged to others. In America there was money to be made and there were others willing to take it away. People were worried and changed their hiding places to a new one each day. When they came home at night, the first thing they did was look for the change they had placed in the sugar bowl, in the shaving kit, in the extra pair of shoes that they hid under the bed. So when Ben Eisen hung up his sign and it was known that he had a safe, a big iron safe with a padlock with a combination, his fellow workers at the cigar factory, who had shared his lunch, told him jokes, and watched him grow from a skinny boy to a young man who called you by name, asked after your children, who knew about the value of money and how many hours it took to get the pile high enough to spill between the thumb and forefinger into the palm of the hand, even though he was young they brought him their savings to keep. He had a packet for each with the name of the depositor written on it. He had a good word for everyone who stopped in his store and talked with him at his desk. He charged just a few pennies for his reassurance that all was well with the savings, but the pennies mounted. In the evening he would sit on his bed at the back of the store and count again and again, the things in the safe, the things that the safe could hold. He slept near the safe and woke with a start if a cat cried in the street or he heard footsteps outside his window. He slept with an ax by his side, never doubting that if trouble came, he could protect his own. Security was important for a new bank. In the early evening he would stretch his body and swing his ax above his head. He would stand out on the steps and swing his ax around and around. Everyone in the neighborhood knew that Ben Eisen had an ax and kept it by his bed and the bed was placed near the safe.

Hyman Resnik from Pinsk was the first to ask for a loan. He wanted to open a restaurant. He had sold knishes from a cart, but now he was too old for the handles. His shoulders ached and his legs had begun to shake. He had a son who could help him wait tables and a wife who would cook in the kitchen. Ben Eisen did the accounting. He knew what the interest need be and he made his loan and he collected each week. Soon there were others wanting a loan, and then he had to hire an assistant, and the New World Bank moved to offices on Canal Street and Ben Eisen's bed moved with it, and everyone in the neighborhood brought their money to the bank because in the front at a very big desk, with a chair that swiveled around so he could watch his employees and wave to his customers out the window, Ben Eisen sat and his face, which spoke of home, wherever home might truly be, his face was there and made his guarantee unnecessary.

Moses had asked Naomi if she should not put her diamond in the bank of the boy Ben Eisen, but she had clasped her waist and screamed at him. "Never," she said, "will this leave my side." So Moses put in the bank only his savings and that of his son, Isaac. Before Ben Eisen was twenty years old he had become a banker, with a teller's cage and a guard whom he paid to spend nights by the deposit boxes.

He agreed to lend Isaac the money to buy out the business where Moses had first worked, where Isaac had come some years before begging for a chance to take a few pairs of pants out on his cart. Isaac had hired some women to begin to sew. His mother had wanted to work in the shop, but he had told her no, she was the mother of the owner and it would not be right to have her on the floor. He wanted her home, leaning out the window, preparing food, keeping Ruth company—Ruth, whose days were so solitary that sometimes the thought of them made his neck bend as if a hand were pressing down on the top of his head.

He walked through the streets of the Lower East Side, changed only by the different names of the merchants; the new arrivals were still coming, children with circles of alarm around their dark, astonished eyes. His English was accented, but there was nothing he needed to say that he couldn't. He knew cloth, as only a man who had spent his childhood lifting linens, carrying pants, folding pants, putting pants in rows, selecting pants, talking about pants, for summer, for winter, for dress, for work, could know. He knew prices. He knew how they went up and down and how important it was to keep rent low and expenses minimal and how it mattered who you knew, who would help you, who was your friend and who was your enemy, and who to count on and who to avoid, and how to move ahead when an opening appeared and how to retreat when inner sirens warned. He knew how to look a customer in the eye and tell him the truth. Without that pair of pants, good fortune will avoid you. He had his own way of saying that, but it succeeded again and again. He knew how to talk to the women who worked for him. Not like slaves, not like women dispensable, interchangeable, but women with names like his mother, Naomi, like his sister, Ruth, women who had children at home, as he was once a child at home. He paid them no more than the going wage, he provided no extra time for drawing a deep breath of cool air on the roof. He allowed no extra pay without extra hours. He fired anyone who was sick more than a few days, and he fired anyone who made mistakes, even those he had called sweetheart only the week before. He knew how to keep the floor humming and the pants and the jackets mounting up on the tables in the back and to move them quickly out to the stores. He knew all this because he had been watching, he had been planning all the time in Pansville, making, he had decided, the pants and the jackets himself; that's where the profit lay.

Moses Loses His Virtue a Second Time: 1891

In the loft there was nothing for Moses to do. Isaac wouldn't let him sew with the other men, although he knew how and was perfectly able, even though his blink had returned. "It will save a wage," said Moses.

"Nonsense," said Isaac, who understood about authority and order and bosses. "I am the boss and you are my father."

So Moses drifted out of the loft and spent his days drinking tea at a cafe on the corner. He missed the mountains of Pansville, more than he missed the forest around Sulvalki where he had gone on picnics as a child with his mother and father. Then he had not noticed how the ferns grew close to the dark earth and the mushrooms, brown-edged, pleated underneath, snapped beneath his step. He missed the crocuses that the miners' wives planted in their window boxes. He missed the red-and-blue birds, particularly the blue one with the white tail and the terrible croak in his voice that reminded Moses that true prophets are hard to recognize. He had known that it would not be a good thing to come back to New York.

He found the house that belonged to Devorah, and he sat on the stoop across the street, just another man in a black hat and coat sitting in the sunshine on a spring day. He stretched out his toes and let his legs hang limp in their sockets. He prayed to God to send him on his way. But his way seemed to be unclear, and the hours went by and as the sky over the Hudson turned pink, and the smell of cabbage, fish, and urine filled the air, Moses found himself on Devorah's step.

"You," she said, and pulled him in through the door. "You left, just like that, without a word." She did not seem pleased to see him. She hated him for his desertion. Just as well, he thought. Better, he thought, and with a hollow feeling in his chest turned to go. "So where are you going now, you fart-ass?" she said to him, holding tight to his arm. She wants me to stay, he thought. "So speak," she said. "Why are you back on my doorstep? I saw you, out the window, sitting there. He's coming, I said, but you didn't. All day you looked up at my window. So what is it you want now?" she asked.

Moses heard a softening in her voice; she released her fingers a little, realizing that he wasn't fleeing out the door.

"So," he said, "you missed me?"

He wasn't as welcome as before. Now there was someone else, the owner of the kosher bakery on Mott Street, who seemed to have rights over his, and really, how could he complain? For over four years he had disappeared, not a note, not a postcard, not a word sent with a traveling salesman. Devorah had not wanted to spend her best years mourning yet another man. "What is a man, anyway," she said to Moses, "but a thing between legs and an ass that gives heat in the winter?"

Moses was shocked by her words. His Naomi would never say anything personal like that at all. But the shock was not unpleasant, not so unpleasant at all, and Moses didn't complain when she shooed him away from her door or asked him to wait on the stoop across the street even if it were raining or the wind was blowing so hard it seemed as if God were about to speak, some rebuke to Moses, some request, perhaps. The baker came early in the morning, after his loaves were taken out of the ovens. He came on holidays and sometimes in the afternoon. Moses was fit in between. Devorah's father had died in the meanwhile.

"The funeral," she said, "was beautiful. All the men who had studied the Talmud with him, they came and carried the coffin into the streets and put him on the cart that went out to the cemetery in Queens." Thank God her father had thought to take a plot with the other Lvovniks who had arrived on the Lower East Side. "Only a few pennies a year," she said, "and he saved me such an expense."

Moses realized he had no plot, and he would place the burden on Naomi. For a moment he worried. But then he remembered that Isaac had a loft and was talking about taking over another floor of their building. He was wearing suits these days, good suits. He would be able to bury his father.

"You young turd," Devorah had said. "Stop planning your death. It will come soon enough." And she pulled back her comforter and knocked him down—yes, knocked him down as if he were a recalcitrant child. How he loved it, sitting on top of her, watching her breasts flop to the sides and then heave up toward him. It was wicked, it was terrible, it was forbidden, the most forbidden, it made him feel like he was indeed made in God's image.

Moses rejoined the study group that had moved from the basement into the parlor and had taken on an additional man to fill the place he had so abruptly vacated, and they pulled up another chair and continued. They were making their way through Kings for the tenth time.

Then Devorah found out that Isaac was doing well: more than well, in fact. "Your wife," said Devorah, "she has a silk dress, I suppose?"

It was true. Isaac had bought his mother one. It rustled, it swept against the floor. It had pleats in the front and panels embroidered with roses in the back. Naomi caressed it again and again, and Moses, who watched her silently, wished he had brought her the box, that his son, his son who could do everything, had not done this.

"So I should have a dress of silk, too," said Devorah, and Moses saw the justice in her demand. He asked Isaac for the money, promising to return it soon, and Isaac gave the money to his father so that Devorah could have a silk dress, although he thought it was so that his father's study group could have a Torah of their own and a new mishnah because the old book had become worn with the turning of the pages and the grease of the fingertips.

What Some People Might Call a Miracle: 1895

Isaac had bought a piano for Ruth. It had come one day and the men had brought it up by attaching pulleys and ropes and lifting it up to their floor. It was a miracle, the piano, both having it and the way it came in the apartment, like manna from heaven. Isaac had known that Ruth could not wait much longer and so against his habit of frugality, against his habit of caution, he had risked the expense. And so far, so he consoled himself, he met all the payments and even one extra, one ahead. In his black book, which he notched and he nibbled with his pen, he marked off the months till the piano was hers alone.

Ruth began once again to take piano lessons from a teacher at the settlement house. She went through the streets by herself, with her head bent down and her face covered by a thick veil. She had grown into a tall young woman, whose body was neglected by its owner. She never looked in the mirror or let her hands slide over the rising curves or along her legs. Her mother sewed her dresses, and she put on anything she was given. She still spoke in a small child's voice and her smile, while generous, wide, and promising, was seen only by her brothers, her parents, and now her piano teacher. Her head was bent, away from everyone else. In the evenings when Max would leave the apartment, clean-shaven, bare-headed, an animal smell coming from the pits of his arms and a light in his eye, Ruth would sit down on the shining stool and practice her finger exercises on the piano. Mozart and Chopin, the simplified version, the sonatas of Liszt, these she was learning.

Isaac too was going out in the evenings. He came home earlier than Max, who sometimes never came home at all. Isaac would often walk up the stairs and open the apartment door and see his sister, still in her clothes, asleep in a chair, the sheets of music in her lap. It had been a daring thing to buy the piano, to make the payments that were due each week. He had told Ruth that it was not absolutely hers till he had paid for it all. But to see Ruth's hands on the keyboard, to hear the notes, even the stumbling, the repetitions, brought him peace. Everything was possible. He wrote down the amounts he owed each week, the payment to the landlord for the apartment, for the loft, to the eighteen women who now worked for him, sewing pants on machines he was also paying for, and the salaries of the salesmen, one of whom was Max, who never sold as much as the other salesmen, but was after all his brother, and the lights and the key to the bathroom that the landlord made him pay extra for, and the boxes in which to pack the pants and the balls of string, which also cost per box, and the three boys who packed in the back of the loft. When he added up his costs he was frightened, but never for more than a moment. If you looked down, you could fall. His loft was known for good work, and his pants, and his jackets with the name *Gruenbaum* sewn into the back of each, were making a name for themselves not just in the stores along Orchard Street, where shirts and pants, dresses and sweaters, of all sizes hung from poles out over the rising dirt of the gutters, but in real stores on 14th Street and even in a fancy men's shop on 24th Street that had taken its first order.

Moses would listen in the evening to his daughter as the sounds of the piano, the simple sounds of the first-level student, floated above the kitchen table, and he would smile at Naomi. "It is good, isn't it, that she plays."

Naomi shrugged her shoulders. It was better than her sitting and staring at the wall, better than her lying for hours on her bed, the way she had ever since Isaac had told her to stop sewing for the pocketbook factory. It was still not what a mother wants, what a mother who has raised a daughter expects, no admirers, no chance to tell stories about boys, to teach her daughter the things she knew. "Your God," said Naomi to Moses, "has His favorites."

Moses understood and would put his hand on his wife's shoulder and sigh. What could a man do to alter whom God favored and whom he despised?

Downstairs across the courtyard, a young man, new to America, was listening to Ruth play the piano. He was the assistant to the rabbi, and he slept on a cot in a small room in the back of the ground-floor apartment. Joseph Herzberg was training to be the eighth rabbi in his family. The first had been a follower of the Baal Shem Tov, the first Hasidic rabbi, who believed that all Jews could speak directly to God, and a disciple in his court. The Herzbergs had not been the most famous of the followers, the most honored, or the most talked about, but they had been there, generation after generation. In Vilna they had been attacked by the Mitnaggedim, the rabbinic authorities opposed to the mystic Baal Shem, and forced to leave. In Grodno they had found a home, and the first son, or sometimes the second, had followed in his father's steps and studied at the court of the most learned and the most pious of the neighboring Hasidim. It was known about the Herzbergs that while none of them had brilliance, none had memories that stunned the community as did others, they had voices that carried the message of the people right to the Throne itself, voices so strange and sad, so ripe and soft, so firm and full, that angels themselves stopped their song to listen when a Herzberg threw back his head and, pulling air into the deepest recess of his lungs, began the prayer melody, the *niggun*. The Herzberg rabbis, all the generations of them, were not often courted for their fine opinions on disputes of property, of law, of ritual endeavor. They were often ignored when the other rabbis took up the threads of an ethical tangle, but when word came from the outside that the crops had failed and the peasants were angry or the court of the czar had decreed new hardships or the yellow fever had appeared again or the money to support the orphanage had been stolen or the bodies of Jewish boys had been found mutilated on the road, then the rabbinical court arrived at the home of the Herzberg rabbi and together they prayed, and the sound of the Herzberg rabbi, calling to his God, breaking through the layers of human corruption, out into the upper levels of cloud and star and moon, and beyond to the site of Paradise, where man could not go without madness or death, that voice was said to bring each Jewish soul into the other, so that there were no longer multiple Jews, quarreling, self-interested, needy, and frightened on earth, but just Jew, a singular essence, a thing alive in its parts but together in one soul, a Jew that was all Jews who called to his God for mercy and redemption.

In the town of Grodno where the Herzbergs were living, Joseph's father was the rabbi of the shul on Catherine Street and his mother was a pious woman, who knew the answers to the questions that were sometimes brought to her husband; sometimes he would leave his study and go to the kitchen and find his wife, herself the daughter of the distinguished rabbi from Bratslov, a descendant of the famous Rabbi Nachman, and she would prompt him, tell him the source, remind him of something he had forgotten. One day a Jew, a peddler who came from far away, came to their house and told the rabbi that he had been robbed, robbed of all his goods in the forest outside of town, where he had pulled up his horse for a rest.

"I know the robbers," said the peddler, "I know their names because they called to each other while they tied me up, they laughed at me for not carrying a gun or a knife, and they took my shoes and cut my feet."

"How terrible," said the rabbi.

"God forgive them," said his wife.

"And they were Jews," said the peddler.

"No," said the rabbi.

"Not Jews," said his wife.

"Yes," said the peddler, "and they live here in this town. They boasted that they were not afraid, no one dared turn them in to the authorities. They had brothers, so many brothers that whoever reported them would be killed, and the authorities, they don't care what Jews do to Jews." And the peddler, whose feet were bandaged and who slid about the room on his knees, called out to Rabbi Benjamin Herzberg to bring justice down on the heads of those who had robbed him.

Although he had said, "No, no, not Jews," to the peddler, the rabbi was not surprised, his *no* was rhetorical, categorical, loyal, not meant as a reflection of reality, because he knew about the Babel brothers, who lived in the town, doing just as they pleased, knocking the heads of old men together, taking from carts, pulling purses away from women in the market, and sometimes surprising a merchant with jewels or furs on his way to or from the town. These Jews were bandits. That night he sat at the dinner table and looked at his children, the oldest of whom, his only son, Joseph, had a voice that was unmistakable. Rabbi Benjamin Herzberg took it into his head that he would save the Jews of Grodno from the fallen Jews who preyed on them. His wife thought that this was not wise, that trouble, more trouble, would come, but a man, a rabbi whose voice was the Herzberg voice, did not always listen to his wife but obeyed the stirring of his soul.

The next day, hat in hand, his shoulders bowed, his step soft, he entered the government office of the czar's representative, who had a secretary and a golden seal emblazoned above his door. "What do you want, Jew?" asked the secretary.

"Can't you take care of them without bothering us?" said the czar's representative.

"Filthy Jew," said the czar's secretary. "Your own people are beasts, not fit, not fit at all."

"But," said Rabbi Herzberg, his voice never rising above a whisper, "if they take everything from us, then what will they do? They will take from you, and in fact, I have heard that it is they, the Babel brothers, who have made off with the pouch carrying the tax rubles to Moscow that was sent only a week ago." This Rabbi Herzberg had not heard, though it was possible, very possible, and as he said it he became convinced that he was telling the truth.

"Ah . . ." The head of the czar's representatives wheeled around. "I should have known it was the Jews. I declare a tax to replace the lost money, on every Jewish head in Grodno."

Rabbi Herzberg trembled; what had he done to his people? But after a moment's thought the czar's representative said, "We will get them, all of them."

That night a troop of soldiers appeared at the house of the brothers Babel, and before the sky began to lighten they knocked in the door and pulled them from their beds. They tried to fight off the invaders, so it was said, but they were in their nightclothes and their swords were hung up by the kitchen stove and they had drunk too much the night before; although they punched and kicked and howled, most of them were caught. The youngest brother was shot and the fifth brother ran off into the forest and perhaps the sixth also escaped. The czar's soldiers smashed everything in the house and ripped the mezuzah from the doorpost and stuck it in the mouth of the dead brother, or so it was said.

"It was Rabbi Herzberg who told us your pockets were bulging with rubles and rubies," said the czar's sergeant at arms to the surviving brothers as they stood tied up and shivering in the cold light of the dawn.

And the Babel brothers were put in chains and sent far away, and the Jewish community of Grodno willingly paid the taxes that had been missing, and the rich Jews paid for the poor Jews, and the tax was considered by all as well worth the cost; the bandits, the criminals, the Jews without Jewish souls, were gone. But they were not quite gone. The one in the forest and a cousin from Pinsk and the one who broke away from his jailers and leapt from the train that was carrying him east out of sight of civilized peoples, into the snows of punishment, they met in the forest and vowed vengeance on Rabbi Herzberg. They were Jews and they knew about the Herzberg voice, so they sent a note with a small boy, who appeared at the kitchen door one spring afternoon. The note said that they were coming, coming soon in the night, and they would take Joseph Herzberg and cut his larynx so that never again would the Herzberg voice be heard; they would cut up his cords and mince them into a thousand pieces and spread them from Moscow to Vilna so that even when the Messiah came they could not be found, and it would be the end of the Herzberg family, the end forever.

The family sat in the rabbi's study. Joseph, who was only seventeen, put his face in his older sister's lap as his father wept, and his mother, whose eyes were dry, said over and over, "It was not our business to tell on those thieves. Why couldn't you just sing your songs and let others go tattle on their fellow Jews?"

The next week Joseph, who had planned to marry the daughter of a rabbi who had been selected for him years before, who had intended to continue his studies at his new father-in-law's yeshiva, found himself, for the sake of his voice, for the sake of the larynx that made his family famous, with a ticket, steerage class, to America. America, the land of the godless, the land where heathen ways ruled, a land where no one would appreciate the history of his family or the importance of his vocal cords and he would be alone ever after.

His father had embraced him and given him his grandfather's tallis that had remained wrapped in velvet in the closet all these years. His mother had clung to him, begging her husband to change his mind and take them all to America, which he would not do because the Jews of Grodno needed him. Joseph's mother wanted to go on her knees to the authorities, begging them to chase away the criminals who waited in the woods to cut her son's throat. His mother could not part with him and she could not let him stay, and she spent the last three days of his life in Russia throwing up in the outhouse, retching her guts into the hole in the ground and cursing God for giving her son the Herzberg voice, which was a present that he couldn't return.

Joseph Herzberg, small for his age, thin, with wisps of a beard that barely covered his chin, that floated above his lip like the down on a newly hatched chicken, with knees that bent in toward each other, with pale eyes that had never before seen beyond the edges of Grodno where the dirt road led over a hill and disappeared, arrived in America. He found a job in a cheder in the basement of the synagogue on Eldridge Street. He slept in the room behind the coal bin and washed in the rabbi's kitchen in the house next door, and it was here, two years after his arrival, after taking his weekly bath in the tin tub that was brought for him by the rabbi's wife, lying down on his cot, that he heard Ruth practicing the piano.

Joseph Herzberg sang out the small barred window above the back room where he slept. He sang all the melodies he had learned from his father, the evening prayers, the blessings for bread and wine and newborn sons and mezuzahs as they were placed over the doorposts. He sang the prayers for the holidays, the prayers that welcomed Shabbos, and the prayers that begged for mercy on Yom Kippur and the ones that made promises to God and the ones that entreated God to remember the virtue of the supplicant, to remember the covenant and the special relationship of pleader to Creator that had existed since the days of yore. Joseph Herzberg sang to remember his father and his mother and his sisters, from whom no word had come in many months. He ate his food at the table with the rabbi. The rebbetzin worried over his thinness and gave him an extra blanket in the winter, but he missed his mother's hands, his sisters' voices, the home as a place where he would not be overlooked.

One night he heard the tinkle of the piano keys from the building next door. The sound came from the fourth floor, not experienced, not flowing, only one hand was moving, but pure, a melodic line, each note distinct, a Mozart sonata. He had never heard it before. He had never heard Mozart or Beethoven or Bach before. The press of the chords as Ruth tentatively added the left hand came down over his head, and feelings rose in his body that he could not name but were surely less of God and more of man than he had ever known before.

If he had seen her first, seen her before he heard her, would everything have been different? The matter is decided by the quirks of individual taste, by the fact that he was nearsighted, and much of the world, even with the glasses he had worn back in Grodno, was often blurred and leaning. Add to that the loneliness of the young man, and the fact that he had been taught all his life that beauty was a thing to be found in the spirit of God, the queen that had separated from her king and remained on this earth only as a reflection. Perhaps if he had passed Ruth coming out of her building on her way to a piano lesson, or seen her walking in the dusk as she sometimes was convinced to do with Isaac on her arm, he might have been overcome by the bend in her shoulders, by the way her hands were clasped at her waist, or by the way the dress that Naomi had made for her clung demurely to her breasts, which, all unaware of themselves, promised sweet things to a young man who had yet to make friends in his new country, a place he still thought of as his land of exile, a private diaspora arranged just for him.

Night after night, morning after morning, between his teaching small boys the letters of the Hebrew alphabet, how to read when the vowels were not printed on the page, he would run to his window, hoping she was at the piano. The rebbetzin told him about the girl on the fourth floor whose face had been marked by the pox and whose brother was in the suit business, doing well, they said. "Not such a religious family," said the rebbetzin. "Not for you," she said. "They walk around with bare heads, they eat whatever they please, they have forgotten." And the rebbetzin held her hand to her heart. "What you must never forget, for your father's sake, for your mother's sake."

Joseph Herzberg might have been content to let the years go by as he listened to the piano above him, but a letter arrived from the surviving Herzberg sister, who was visiting cousins in Vilna on the night that the Cossacks came to her town, set fire to the beard of Benjamin Herzberg, and carried off his wife into the forest, where her body was never found. The three remaining sisters were used by the entire barracks, and they drowned themselves in the morning in the river. When Joseph read the letter, he wept and he tore his lapels and the rabbi prayed with him and the rebbetzin's eyes were red as she patted him on the head over and over. Joseph Herzberg was an orphan, and there would be no more Herzbergs, after seven generations of steadfastness, if he did not stir himself and become the man that his father expected.

So it was that the rebbetzin appeared at the door of the Gruenbaum family and invited them all to tea. Ruth made an excuse, she never went out, she explained, turning her head away.

"Nonsense," said the rebbetzin. "You are coming to tea. There is a young man who has listened to your piano playing and he wants to meet you."

"No," said Ruth, although she had heard him singing, night after night, after she was through with her practicing; she had heard him, and his voice had brought her to the window with a pillow for her head, so that she could hear better. The Hebrew words she did not understand, but the meaning was clear, the notes, unlike the notes of her piano, were like the sound of her father's breath. She knew about Joseph, although she had dared only to wish that he continue to live in the little room in the back of the rabbi's office so that she could go on listening to him sing for the rest of her life.

"Then you must invite us to tea," said the rebbetzin, looking at Naomi, who grasped at the straw that was being offered, who flung herself about the room like a woman visited by an angel. Yes, she would arrange a tea, a tea with cakes, she promised, although she was calculating the expense of the baking even as she was closing the door.

When the rabbi and his wife and his young assistant appeared at the apartment for tea and her mother opened the door, Ruth walked right into the center of the room. She held her head up straight, and she did not wear the veil she had always worn in public. Her hair was pulled back off over her ears, showing the red lumps that sprawled across her forehead. She stared at Joseph as he looked at her. She stood by the window with the full sunlight falling across her features. She kept her lips tightly closed and her eyes focused on a distant point above the doorpost.

Joseph went to her side. "What is it," he said, "the things that you play on the piano? We did not have them at home." His English was flavored with a heavy accent. He switched to Yiddish and said, "I sing, I am the eighth member of my family to sing. We are disciples—direct, that is—of the Baal Shem."

"Oh," said Ruth, who did not know who the Baal Shem was. "Did he teach you to sing?" Joseph explained about the Baal Shem. "In America, we have not known him," said Ruth.

"I will teach you," he said, "if you will play the piano for me."

Ruth looked in his face. Was he pitying her? She backed away. She would have run out the door, but Joseph blocked her way.

"You are not pretty," he said. "I am more afraid of your face than I thought I would be, but I have heard the music in your hands and I know you, and I will prove to you that I am worthy of the sounds that you make."

"I am ugly," said Ruth.

"Yes," said Joseph, "that's true."

And he sat down and she sat down by his side, and it was settled between them shortly afterward. The neighbors talked not so kindly about the match, but Moses hugged himself again and again. Who would have thought? Who could have hoped? "Papa," said Ruth, "he sings better than you do."

Moses put his arm around his child, and tears were in his eyes. "I thought you would take care of me in my old age," he muttered in her ear, "but this, this is better."

It was strange for Ruth, all the rules of the religion that Joseph thought so important. But she followed his instructions, although her mother made faces and her brother Max laughed at her when she covered her arms in the summer as her husband wished. Joseph Herzberg was not happy with his wife's family, but he loved his wife, and each morning when he wrapped the tefillin round his arm, he thanked God again for bringing him such happiness. Each night when he put on his cotton pajamas and climbed into bed, he reached for the place in the bed where his wife was curled and he put his arms around her and ran his fingers over her face. "Come to me, little one," he would say. "You are beautiful beyond my dreams, and I want to touch you so that I know you are real and will stay with me." This speech he made again and again, in a thousand different ways; sometimes he said it in English, sometimes he said it in Yiddish, and sometimes he sang to her the whole of the Song of Songs in Hebrew, and he said that she was like the people of Israel, marked by suffering, but with a soul as fine as the finest silk. He would move her legs apart and enter her, mounting on her body and singing all the while and touching everything, everywhere. Ruth loved Joseph, and her body would open for him, night after night, except when she was bleeding and it was forbidden, and on those nights he talked to her instead and told her stories of his childhood and they spoke of their children and they talked about money and how to save more.

Hedy Sleeps Alone: 1943

The pediatrician was concerned because he had no name for Hedy's rash. It wouldn't go away. It couldn't be identified. The child was always scratching, and there were open sores on her arms and legs and splotches of red across her cheeks. Hedy wanted a dog. She wanted a cat. She wanted something soft to take into bed, something that needed her. Flora was afraid of dogs, even small dogs. Ursula thought all animals belonged in the barn. Ursula liked goats, but you couldn't have a goat on Park Avenue. Flora said that cats suffocated people as they slept or slashed at your legs with their claws. Flora said that dogs got rabid and foamed at the mouth. Flora bought Hedy a china dog that sat on her bureau. It was a black Scottie, like Fala, the president's dog. It had a pink china tongue. Hedy scratched.

Max Makes A Fateful Choice: 1897

He was short. He had a limp. He had a smile that cracked open his round face and made others check their wallets, put their hands in their pocket to secure their watches. His eyes shone with excitement. Nothing was boring. Nothing was finished or over. He might yet get a horse. He had a lock of black hair that fell across his forehead, and he plastered it down in the evening with water. He put his head out the window and watched the girls go by. He studied their fannies as they wiggled past. He watched in the loft as their breasts hung over the sewing tables, and he ran his tongue across his lips. Each one was delicious. Each curve, each fold, each soft upper arm as it reached for a bolt of fabric or stretched up or down. He was an admirer of the scent of women, especially when they perspired in the summer, showing wet circles under their arms. He liked their hair piled up on the head. He liked it when wisps came down over ears or followed the bend of the neck. He liked it when hair hung loose and blew in the wind, and he liked it wet after the bath, sticking to the back of bare shoulders.

This last he saw in the house where the whores lived. Jacob Brest ran several pleasure palaces, one only a block away from the Gruenbaum loft. His son Ira was now in the business with him. Ira had slapped Max on the back when he saw him again.

"So," he said, "come play cards with the boys." And Max did. He won enough to buy Ruth a wedding present, silver candlesticks that made everyone gasp, made Isaac question him carefully about where and how much and warn him against taking off the books. The card game was in the back room. The whores floated through the main drawing room in their slips and bare feet in the morning. In the evening they wore black lace stockings, pink girdles, and feather boas that shed on all the furniture.

A new girl from Lodz, who wasn't more than sixteen—Peachie, Jacob had called her when he introduced her to the others—took Max's fancy. Peachie had light red hair and green eyes, and she held her arms across her chest as if to hide what had grown very large and seemed to tilt her young form forward, throwing her off balance. Max took her into her cubicle and wiped the tears that flowed from her eyes because this was not what she expected of America, but a person had to eat and she had no one, no one except Ira, Jacob's son, to take care of her. Max put his head into her lap and touched her so gently that she cried some more. He paid for the hour and then a second, and then he declared to Peachie that he was in love, and she smiled at him. There was a red blotch on her chin.

"I'm hungry," she said. "I'm always hungry, but I'm not supposed to eat until later."

"I'll feed you," said Max. "I'll feed you for the rest of your life."

"You've paid," she said. "You can say anything you want."

"Say it," he said to her, "say you love me. You must love me." She was willing. If she wasn't a willing girl, she wouldn't have ended up in Jacob's house in the first place.

Max showed up at the house at lunchtime. He was there at closing time. He had circles under his eyes and he fell asleep at work, only to wake and go back to the house. Peachie worked. He couldn't afford her day and night.

Jacob laughed at him. "Try another one," he said. "Each one has charm. I'm old enough to be your father, I'm telling you, don't get stuck on one. They're whores, not women."

Max would have lunged for Jacob despite his small size, except that these remarks were made just as he was holding a full house and the pot was high. So he kept his face clear of expression, but under the table his short leg bounced up and down in a nervous tremor.

Ira Brest said, "You can have her any time you want, house price."

Isaac was furious. "You cannot marry a whore," he said. "They have diseases. It will break Papa's heart. You cannot think of marrying a whore."

Max laughed at his brother. "Smile," he said to him, "you are going to get a sister-in-law with the most beautiful breasts in America."

Naomi forbade it. Moses looked at his son in horror. "She did it for money, what she did, it's a sin before God. She's not a virgin," he added. But for reasons of his own he didn't say anything else.

Isaac said, "She just wants your part of the business. She knows the business is good."

"She thinks I'm a gambler," said Max. "She doesn't know about the pants." Which wasn't quite true, because even whores have access to information and even whores want to better themselves. Peachie, who was thin as a needle except for her breasts, had never been to school, worked in her widowed mother's fruit stall in Lodz until her mother married again and her aunt had given her money to go to America, still had enough brains to see that opportunity was knocking.

Naomi cried at the wedding. Moses gave the bride away, and Isaac stood at his brother's side. Peachie was wearing a white dress and had violet flowers in her veil. Her wide green eyes stared without flinching at the others in the family. Tough if they didn't like her. Tough if it made Jacob mad to have her leave so suddenly. Tough if her regular customers would have to switch to someone else. Who cared if Max were shorter than she by many inches? Who cared if he limped? They were going to live happily ever after.

Hedy in the Corridor of the Hadassah Hospital: Jerusalem, 1990

Hedy's husband brings her a cup of coffee. He put milk in it and plenty of sugar. She holds it in her hands but does not drink. Her thick hair is now gray and held in place with a flowered scarf. Once her hair flew wild about her head and her bangs grew long over her eyes.

It is still daylight outside, but in the hospital corridor the electric light hangs from its fixture and glows clear and white. There are no windows in this area outside the operating room. There are chairs for family, and a silver ashtray stands on a long stem. There is a photograph of the Dead Sea and bathers dunking their arms in the sharp, sulfurous waters in the year 1927. The bathing suits hang down to the knees, and the clouds over Jordan are dark as if the day were about to turn. On the left side of the photograph a cabana stands with its striped panels blowing in the air. Hedy looks at the picture but doesn't see it. If Namah survives, but survives as a vegetable, helpless, without the question in her eyes, without the arms that moved up and down to make a point, without memory or with too much memory, what then?

Hedy remembers that when she was a child she had gone to the elevator one morning and, standing in the hall, had suddenly shivered and known that this was the day she would get polio. When she woke the next morning and was fine, she repeated the thought in front of the elevator door, in case her anticipation had protected her the day before. Gradually she added a list of other illnesses, arthritis, pneumonia, bone cancer, a heart attack, and each day as she survived more and more disasters listed quickly as the elevator rose up to her floor, she grew more secure that her magic would protect her. If she imagined a calamity and truly feared it, she would be spared. Now she is a scientist, a professor, a woman who understands deductive and inductive reasoning, who believes in rational causes and logical sequences; still her mind races on, calling up pictures of her child strapped to a bed, breathing through a tube, being fed by a nurse, babbling in baby talk, her brain no more functional than that of a lizard sunning itself on rock. If she anticipates the worst, perhaps it won't happen.

Hedy's husband stands near her. He touches her shoulder. She startles. She stares at him. She does not want him to touch her or to speak.

Isaac Nearly Misses the Boat: 1897

A thousand small decisions, and the payroll was expanded. Isaac now rented two stories in a small building on Essex Street. He was careful.

He remembered the linen man. He mixed caution with courage and never looked back. If he made a mistake, he corrected it quickly. His eyes flashed out over his workers, checking every detail, watching thread, counting the bolts of fabric as they were stacked against the wall. He was twenty-five years old, and his mother still fixed him lunch to carry to work.

Max said to Isaac, "I'll introduce you to a doll."

"Never mind," said Isaac.

Then into his office on the second-floor loft came Annie Stern. She had brown curly hair and a small cleft in her chin, and she smiled at him shyly. When he interviewed her she touched her heart with her two fingers as she promised to be prompt and swore not to take any scraps from the floor. The gesture touched him. At night he recalled it again and again. Her figure was full, and her bottom eased over the edge of the chair she was sitting on, and when Isaac saw her he gasped with longing. She bent her head over the machine, and he watched as the light from the window threw a rectangular glow across her lap. The rays of the sun slipping down between the buildings had no other purpose than to touch the curve of her cheek, to glide over her forearm and fall still across her round breasts. She stuck the end of her pink tongue between her lips as she threaded her machine. Sometimes she rubbed her eyes with the palms of her hands. Isaac believed that the aching he felt in his groin was the start of an illness whose name he did not know.

She had lunch with the other girls on the roof, and he could hear the clatter of their feet on the stairs. He could hear the laughter that rose up and down, floated in and out, excluding him, the boss, from their jokes. He waited at the base of the stairs. He called her into his office. She sat on the chair. Had she done something wrong? She was pale with shame. No, nothing was wrong, he explained. She could go. He wanted to say something more, but he didn't.

A week or so later it was raining as he was leaving the shop, and he saw Annie with a young man who held an umbrella over her head. They were talking together, and the man had his arm on hers, steadying her as they crossed the puddles. Isaac walked in the streets, miles and miles, through his neighborhood and others, all the way uptown to Fifth Avenue, soaked by the rain. He moved on and on. He was not used to the heat that now surged through his mind. He was new to the feeling of regret that washed over him. He had no words to soothe himself and no language to understand. He raged against the girl who had caused his knees to buckle and tears to come to his eyes.

He looked in the mirror and saw himself for the first time. Was he acceptable? He tried to judge himself through her eyes. He didn't know that his smile was gentle. He didn't know that he had strong arms and his gaze was direct. He didn't know that the girls burst into giggles and blushes as soon as his back was turned. Of course he was the boss, and many women were willing to treat him well.

In the following weeks Annie tilted her head and looked at him carefully as he walked between the machines. He caught her eye. He blushed. He waited for her at lunchtime. He pulled her away from the others. It cost him to ask her out to dinner. It cost him to tell her that he needed her, not for once, but forever. It was hard on him to have to explain that he had never before, but that he wanted, that he hadn't thought of himself as requiring, but he did. It cost him to scale the walls of his privacy and let a stranger see his need. He risked ridicule. He risked her turning her head away. She didn't.

Her parents, behind in the old country, had known she deserved the best; that was why she laughed with such ease, a laugh that Isaac found amazing, unlike the more cautious sound that rose from his own throat.

Naomi was not pleased. "She likes fine things. She'll take from you," she said.

"It's time I was married," Isaac said. "It will be good for the business, you'll see."

Isaac sent a note to Sister Abigail of the Carmelite nuns in Brooklyn, announcing his marriage. There was no answer. The other girls on the machines looked sullen. Why had he picked Annie, the one with the mole on the side of her face? Nothing special about her, they said. But Isaac was happy in the prize that he had won by scaling the walls of himself.

The Firstborn Son: Spring 1899

First there was a miscarriage. Annie had lain in bed for days afterward, staring at the ceiling. Isaac had sat by her side. He could have lost her, he knew. This made him shy.

"It doesn't matter," he said.

This was a mistake. Annie's eyes flashed. "Who are you?" she said. "How dare you come in here?"

Isaac considered. He tried again. "You're fine. You'll be back to yourself in a day or two."

"I'm not fine," she said. She stared at him.

He thought of the child they had lost, not a child yet, exactly, but there was blood and flesh. He felt bile in the back of this throat. "I don't want to think about it," he said.

She looked at him sitting on the chair, his head down and his hands clenched together. It was too hard for him, she understood. "Don't think about it," she said. "Tell me what happened today. Did any new orders come in?"

"Yes," he said, and smiled with relief. His love for her rose to his lips but didn't cross them.

After that the family moved to an apartment building in the Bronx on the Grand Concourse. Naomi and Moses had their own apartment downstairs, and Annie and Isaac had a front view of the trees and the boulevard. The halls were painted yellow, and sparrows and pigeons sat on the fire escape outside their window. Naomi sighed with pleasure each time she approached her doorway. Annie invited her old friends to see her new apartment. She served tea. Her joy in the cups and the saucers, in the napkins that were linen, in the new couch that was covered in satin stripes, was so strong that it might have lifted her right up to the moon that she saw from her bed slipping across the Bronx night after night.

Reader: Respect Annie's joy in the solidness of her possessions. Don't look down on her for not letting anyone sit on the couch in case they might wear out the weave. It's all very well for other generations who have studied Beowulf and organic chemistry in the best schools of the land to wear torn jeans, sleep on futons they throw on the floor, but to Annie the couch and the lamp, the lace doily on the table, were all signs of safety, a nod of God's head in her direction, as certain as if He had spoken himself, a whirlwind on her mahogany dining table. To Annie, who had lived four girls in a room the size of the closet in her new apartment, the linen, the silver sugar bowl, the cup and the saucer, were like the fruits of the harvest, a protection against the return of winter with its long nights and empty cupboards.

Then they had a son. When Harry was born, Isaac had taken the infant in his arms and felt himself opened as never before, as if his new factory burned to the ground in the middle of the night, taking with it all the bolts for the fall jackets, as if his cutters had cut the cloth into useless pieces that didn't match. He had broken out into a sweat, and the midwife took the baby from him, thinking he was ill. Standing at the window of the bedroom he shared with his wife, he trembled as if he were still on the deck of the ship that had brought them over, and the spray of the water had turned icy in the December air; he trembled and had no words for the shaking of his hands. Was it joy he was feeling?

What was in the room with them, now that the child was crying, a soft whimper, a gasp of discontent, a frail red hand closed into a tight fist? Whatever was in the room had no name, it had no shape, but it was the thing that was attached to his child, like the umbilical cord that had been cut but still clung in its shrunken remains to the child's navel. The baby was named Chaim after his wife's dead father, and in English he was named Harry, and Naomi called him Chaimele in Yiddish.

Isaac held his son in his arms at his bris as the mohel lifted his swift hand and Ruth's husband, Joseph, rocked back and forth on his feet and hunched his shoulders over the baby as he said the prayers. Joseph sounded like a man who knew that God had recalled the angels with the flaming swords and unsealed the gates of Eden or would shortly.

As the mohel lifted his knife, Naomi, in the kitchen, realized the ceremony had already begun without her and rushed to put down the china bowl filled with potato salad that she held to her breast. In her haste she missed the countertop and the bowl fell crashing to the floor, and potatoes in their oily dressing slid across the floor. The mohel moved his hand toward the foreskin, but his concentration was shattered both by the sound of the splitting china and the woman's sharp cry, and he took with his small special knife, not just the covering, but a piece, a slice, a scoop of the baby's penis. Blood, red blood, spurted straight up to the sky, falling back on the blue blanket that was under the infant and falling against Isaac, whose white shirt was suddenly stained as a woman's napkin. The child screamed and Isaac turned pale and, holding the baby in his arms, was afraid he would collapse and further hurt the child. So he stood there rigid, pleading, as if things done could be undone, over and over, "Only the foreskin, that's all that was asked, only the foreskin." But it was too late. The baby Chaim would have a penis that slanted, that looked like a potato half sliced for the salad, for the rest of his life.

The doctor came. Isaac kept his hands over his eyes till the doctor declared that nothing crucial had been taken.

"Maybe" said Max, who was thinking to himself that perhaps after all it was better to have daughters than sons, "God wants the whole penis, and that's why the Jews have been punished all these years. God wants more than he gets, and if we gave it to him, maybe he would let up on us." Max grinned at his brother, who was not ready for a theological joke. "Perhaps some idiot at Sinai heard 'foreskin' when the Lord said 'all the skin,' " Max went on. "Perhaps if you offered up the baby's entire penis, God would forgive us. How about it, Isaac? You could be more famous than Abraham."

Isaac looked at his brother without opening his eyes. "Go home, Max," he said. "The party is over."

Max in Debt: 1899

Max took Peachie to the theater, and he kissed her neck and he begged her not to go to St. Louis. "I can give you everything," he said. "Just stay here."

Max was jealous. He was surprised at himself. He hadn't known he would be the type to follow his wife down the street, hiding behind lampposts when she went to the butcher to buy a chicken. He thought he wasn't that kind of man, but he was.

Peachie had a beaded pocketbook, and she swung it at Max. Its silver clip caught him on the end of his nose, and he began to bleed. Peachie took out a handkerchief and patted him there. "Don't be silly," she said. "It's just for a few months."

Peachie was going to visit an aunt who had turned up in America and wanted to see her only niece. Max played cards while she was gone, and he lost a lot. Isaac covered his debt. Max said, "Is it my fault I love her?"

Peachie came back from St. Louis with a black eye, three months pregnant. "Sorry, Max," she said.

Max might have overlooked it. Max might have pretended. But Peachie said the guy was tall and looked like Ira Brest, and she was a sucker for guys who look like that, and Max got mad and took a bite out of her shoulder, which was the first thing he thought to do. He apologized, but Peachie packed up. Some things were too much for a woman who knew how to make her own living. Max wanted to take care of her even after she left, but Peachie didn't want it that way.

"I'm my own woman," she explained, "always have been."

Max rented an apartment for her in Brighton Beach. He sent her money each week, and after she had a baby girl, he tried to get her back to his bed. "The baby needs a name," he said, but Peachie had a new friend who was paying the rent, and she sent Max back his checks. She said she was doing fine.

Max seemed to shrink in size after that. Isaac and Annie invited him to dinner at least twice a week, but he hardly ate a thing. He brought little Harry presents and for the new daughter, Mildred, he brought a silk nightgown.

"It's for a grown woman," said Annie. "The baby can't use it."

"Save it for her," said Max, "she's going to be gorgeous."

"What did you love about Peachie?" asked Isaac.

Max bit his lip and said nothing. What could he say, after all? He brought Arthur, who was born the following year, a pack of cards, trick cards with four aces.

"What a gift for a baby," said Annie, who wasn't really annoyed. What else could she expect from Max?

Max called on Peachie and gave her a rope of pearls. She went back to live with him for a few months with her little girl but then ran off again with a salesman who had a suitcase full of hose. It seemed as if Peachie had no faithful bones. Even money couldn't tie her down. Her attention flagged; one cross word and off she went again and again.

By the time Flora, the last of Isaac and Annie's children, was born, the one who was not so much an afterthought as a surprise, Max had accepted his fate, or so it seemed. He told Annie, "I'm better at cards than at love."

Isaac, however, knew that he wasn't so good at cards. Often Isaac had to bail him out. He wrote out checks for large amounts of money to one Ira Brest, who seemed to be lending as well as winning. "Don't play," begged Isaac.

"I won't," said Max. "I swear to you on our mother's honor, I won't."

Annie laughed. "He will," she said.

The Wages of Sin: 1899

Moses Gruenbaum spent his evenings with the study group. He spent his afternoons with Devorah when she would have him. Increasingly she brushed him aside with one excuse or another: the baker had taken an unexpected holiday. She had to clean the house or she had to go shopping. He was afraid to accompany her. What if a neighbor saw him? What if his sons saw him? What if he was standing by her when Naomi came by? He would wait for Devorah in the street, leaning on the stoops, pretending to be smoking a cigar, stamping his feet against the cold. He would go to a nearby restaurant where he could have a cup of tea and a knish, and he would nurse his tea through the long afternoon. He should not have gone to Pansville, he had lost his place. At home in the night he would sit on the edge of his bed before putting on his nightclothes, and lying next to Naomi, his head would be filled with images of Devorah, spreading, heaving, laughing, her wide arms raised and her hips pushing toward him. What kind of animal am I? he would moan.

"So what's wrong?" asked Naomi, who asked this question of him a thousand times.

"Nothing," he would say. "Nothing's wrong. Must a man always have a smile on his lips like some kind of idiot?" Home for Moses was still Sulvalki.

Naomi tried to be kind. "It's all right," she said to him. "Everything is fine, Isaac says the business goes good and will go better. He's a good son, like his papa, a good man."

This made Moses bite his lip and pound his hands on the bed. "Good, who knows what good is, in this heathen country, in this pack of idol worshipers, who knows good? Not you," said Moses, and jumped into bed with his back to his wife.

She put out a hand for his shaking shoulder. "What's the matter?" she said.

"Nothing is the matter," he said. His eye blink did not get worse, but he developed a cough.

"Stop coughing," said Naomi, "it scares me. Do you have a fever?"

But he said he had none. He was hot and he was cold, but this came from thinking too much about things he should not, about forbidden matters. God punishes me, he thought, with this cough.

Moses took to watching Devorah's house, and he soon found out it wasn't just the baker who had precedence over him, but some others, too, one young boy still in knickers, all of them bareheaded, godless men who took the stairs two at a time and called out to the widow, "Hey, Devorah, open up."

It made Moses angry, this sharing he was forced to do. It's not right, he said to himself. It's not right for a woman to act like an animal in the barn. She should be choosy. A widow all right, need not be alone, but so much together, it's not right. And he told her so, but she sniffed at him, "So who ran off to Pansville, so who has a wife of his own, who this very moment is waiting for you? So who cares what you think? Get out and don't come back." And she threw her jar with all her pins in it, the ones she used to pile her hair up on her head, and the pins spilled all over and she blamed him for making a mess. And so it was between Moses and Devorah.

The others in the study group noticed the cough.

"Go to the doctor," said Shmuel.

"Do us a favor and cough somewhere else," said Edelman.

"So you don't want me," said Moses, and stood up.

"Sit down," said Shmuel, "just go to the doctor."

But Moses didn't want to spend the money. Early one morning Isaac found Moses shivering by the window, even though the day was beginning hot and the breeze was so warm that Isaac had begun to sweat with only the effort of shaving. "Go to the doctor," said Isaac.

"You," said Moses, "think everything can be fixed, will go on always getting better and better, that's what you think with your ignorant American head, that's what you think."

One day he was going to see Devorah. He had prepared for the moment by putting on a clean shirt and a new tie, one that Naomi had bought for him from a cart and said he looked like a real American in, especially he would look like an American if he would take off his hat, but he wouldn't. But he was soaped and scrubbed and ready for Devorah. His clothes hung on his body because lately he had lost so much weight. It didn't matter how much Naomi made him eat. It didn't matter that Devorah pinched his middle and said she missed what used to be there. Sometimes he caught sight of his shadow and saw how it dwindled, and he gasped. If I could stop seeing Devorah, I could gain back the weight, he thought. This is God's punishment. This time he was in her bed when the baker came up the stairs. He had just arrived. The baker came unannounced. His disappointment when he heard the heavy steps of the baker on the stairs was so sharp that it seemed to tear something in his lungs, and he began to cough. The baker was standing over him, trying to pull him to his feet and push him out the door, Devorah was screaming at him to get going, and the coughing wouldn't stop, and this time he felt his mouth fill with warm fluid and he opened his mouth and his blood, blood that belonged in the veins, came out over his beard, red clots, blue-black clots. The baker backed off and turned paler than the dough he had pounded that morning, and Devorah sat down on a chair and put her hands over her face. I deserve it, thought Moses, who collapsed on her bed.

The doctor shook his head. Naomi wept and her eyes were red for days as she tiptoed around him. He seemed to get a little better in the late summer and went for walks along the street with his daughter on his arm, but she was busy hiding her head and hurrying him along, and he could only walk slowly. His legs had lost their strength. The doctor said he should go to the country, and Isaac was trying to figure out how to send him there. He could afford it now. Isaac went over the books carefully. In the Catskills there were places for the sick, and his mother could go, too, and perhaps they would enjoy it. He could certainly afford to send his parents to the country.

In the mountains, where the air was cold and clear, Moses seemed to recover. He gained a few pounds. He went for short walks in the woods and admired each wildflower, each leaf that fell on his head. He watched the sun go down while rocking on the porch with the other guests, and he boasted of his children.

"My daughter, she plays the piano, she's married to a rabbi, despite everything, who would have thought, she's married," he said, "and my son, he has a business. He paid for everything here. And my other son, Max, he has a wife, too." He didn't say everything there was to be said about that wife, but then who impresses new acquaintances with the whole truth? Who needs to give people something to whisper about? "What a wife," said Moses to the others, who shook their heads admiringly. Everyone has secrets, large and small.

When it rained he stayed in the main lodge and listened to the sound on the roof and the window panes. He breathed deeply, and it seemed to him that his lungs were repairing themselves, just because when he prayed each morning he didn't feel the angel's hissing, God's female spirit, the shekinah, shrinking away from him, the fragment of the world that held the spark of his soul breaking into still smaller pieces. He still had dreams about Devorah. He still had hopes that he would return to her bed. He tried to ignore them. He tried to repudiate them. This year, he thought, when he went to shul on Yom Kippur, he would promise, he would mean it, he would do it. This year he would repent in truth. He would mean it as never before, it would save his life. He sat with Naomi by the creek that ran down the back of the hotel's property. "See, Naomi, how the water changes colors because of the rocks underneath, each one different."

"Yes," said Naomi, whose interest in stones was limited, but who was happy to see her husband smile and smile at her. Sometimes, she remembered how he had looked under the *chuppa,* how frightened she had been that he would not like her, that it would be bad between them. And he had tried to be a good husband. It wasn't his fault that here in America he was not so useful, a kind of baggage that she had brought with her, old and worn, reminding of things one didn't necessarily wish to be reminded of. It made her sad how hard he had tried. Naomi sat, her dress folded carefully beneath her, on one of the chairs the hotel provided, and she knitted, a shawl for Ruth, who was moving to Baltimore, where her husband was going to be an assistant rabbi in a little shul. Naomi sighed.

"If I've said or done anything that offended or harmed you," said Moses to Naomi, "please forgive me."

"So what is this?" said Naomi. "Only on Yom Kippur do you say that, and for me you don't need to say it."

"Say it," said Moses, "say you forgive me. All debts are settled between us." So Naomi said it, not once, but over and over, each time he asked.

Moses began to cough again and his cheeks were red and the redness was not from the sun. He was put to bed, and the hotel owner was very disturbed. Perhaps he is too sick to be on vacation, perhaps he should be sent to a hospital. Contagion is not good for business. Tuberculosis is a forbidden word. Moses didn't want to leave the hotel. He looked out the window of his small room on the fourth floor at the maple tree that hugged the side of the huge house, and he watched the sun pass through the leaves. In America, he thought to himself, the sun is brighter than in Poland. In America the leaves are bigger on the trees. Can that be, he wondered, or is my mind going? He could still say all the words of the morning and evening prayers, and while none of the other vacationers were willing to come to his room to join with him, he said them anyway. He could not entreat God for mercy too often.

Naomi said that the Hebrew prayers were soothing to her and that she wished he would tell her the meaning of the words so she could join with him. Moses knew she did not mean that. She meant she was afraid of losing him, a presence she had assumed would be with her forever, like the diamond she still wore at her waist. In the long hours by his bedside while he was waiting for the angel of death, she prayed for his release back into life. He taught her the morning prayer and she repeated the Hebrew sounds after him, stroking his shoulder all the time. She should have been kinder, gentler, given him more respect. She did not beg God to forgive her, that wasn't her habit. She dug her fingernails into her palms and promised that if he recovered, she would fulfill his every wish even before he had wished it. She washed him with a cloth when his fever was high. She knew every corner of his body, the way the flesh under his arms had grown soft and the hair on the groin went in different directions. She touched his body carefully with her fingers and she stroked his chest with the palm of her hand. She remembered him standing over Max's bed when his leg had been crushed by the wagon and she remembered him coming up the stairs with his lunch pail banging against the narrow walls and how in Pansville he brought her a red leaf that had fallen from a tree and told her to save it. She had thrown it out. What could you do with a leaf? She should have kept it. "If I have said or done anything to harm you," she whispered to him, "forgive me."

One night in the middle of the night he called to Naomi, but his voice was faint and she didn't hear him. He choked and leaned forward and tried to get air into his lungs, and he apologized to God for wanting

Devorah at that moment, and he died. His eyes thrust back in his head and his mouth twisted in an effort to get air down the blocked passages in his throat.

Naomi told Isaac and Max and Ruth that his last words had been to praise his children and to wish them prosperity and joy. "He died with a smile on his lips, thinking of you all and the love you had given him in this life," said Naomi. This was not true, but after a few days Naomi believed it to be true. Who after all has the stomach to tell children the truth?

The funeral was small. Isaac didn't want the workers at the loft to leave their machines. He didn't want the cutters to stop cutting, and he didn't want to spend a week in mourning. He covered the mirror over his parents' dresser with cloth and went back to work. The body was buried in a city of tombstones out in Queens. As they walked through the rows and rows of stones, Ruth cried out, "Which one, which line, where is ours, where is he going?" And nobody answered because they weren't quite sure. They had a map marked with numbers, and like sojourners in a forest, they moved cautiously ahead until, looking over her shoulder, Ruth saw a continent of the dead and felt she could not leave her father there, so forgotten among the forgotten. But after all, how could he be buried except as he had lived, one among many, distinguishing marks, none? Ruth wept. Max was silent and still. Naomi was dry-eyed and glared at the men of the study group who came to mourn. She would not accept their kind words. She turned her face away from them as if it were their fault that her husband, in his forty-seventh year, had died, leaving her to spend the rest of her life in a cold and empty bed. Would he have lived to be an old man if they had stayed in Sulvalki as he wanted? Was he vulnerable to disease in America? Nonsense, she thought. It was good she had insisted they come. He liked it in America, more than he let on, she told herself. He had a good life, she told herself.

The men of the study group served as pallbearers, and they lifted the coffin and placed it in the ground. Naomi hated them all because they were living and because they were bringing her comfort among all the mourners of Zion and Jerusalem, and she wanted no part of that comfort. Some people like to mourn alone, so their faces can sag as they wish, so their eyes can go blank when they want, so that they can avoid whatever it is they wish to avoid for however long they like. Naomi had no intention of leaning on shoulders or fainting delicately into open arms. She clenched her teeth and, in the privacy of her bedroom, fondled her diamond and counted her blessings.

Flora Tells Hedy a Story: 1944

Hedy sat on the edge of Flora's bed. It was Saturday. Hedy's father, Frank, had gotten up early and gone to play tennis. He had taken his shower, dressed in his white shirt and pants, and pulled a sweater with purple and blue stripes around the V over his head. Hedy sat soberly on the pink quilt and looked at her mother's hand. One of the long red nails had chipped, two of the others needed polish. The manicurist did not understand what Flora did to ruin her nails each week, but Hedy knew. While Flora talked she nibbled at her fingertips, she pulled at the polish and peeled it off, absentmindedly, unintentionally. The Camel cigarette was lit and rested in the china ashtray by the side of the bed. "Hedy, dear, give me a puff of cigarette now, that's a girl." Ursula was in the other room writing letters to Germany, and Hedy would have all morning alone with her mother, before the guests came to play cards in the afternoon.

Flora told Hedy a story about when she was a little girl and was invited to a party.

The Story: 1915

The Gruenbaum family was living in a big house on Riverside Drive. It had a staircase at the entrance and a maid whose only job was to polish the banister and make it shine. Flora was the youngest of all the children, an afterthought, a reminder that sex has consequences. Flora was plump and small for her age, and whatever she said to her older brothers and sister, they said, "Later," "Not now," or, "Be quiet, we're talking," or, "Who let you in here?" Each night at the dinner table, the maid helped Flora's mother, Annie, serve the meal of choice to each of the brothers and to her husband. Three separate dinners were always cooked so that each of the males could have his choice. The girls, Mildred and Flora, ate whatever was left after the boys had been served. Sometimes Flora was fed in the kitchen. There she was given last night's meal, scraps warmed in pots. Often during the day she would arrive in the kitchen and someone always gave her food, a glass of milk, a little cake, even though she was so round that her brother Arthur called her "pudding" and her brother Harry called her "matzo ball." She ate and she ate, who knew why.

One day an invitation came in the mail from Selma Abromovitz, the daughter of one of the biggest stores in Manhattan. This store had four floors and departments that sold linens and jewelry and toys and clothes for men and women and an escalator and windows that showed glamorous mannequins dressed in fur coats and beaded dresses waving to one another. The store also carried the Gruenbaum suits. Selma Abromovitz was going to celebrate her fifth birthday with a costume party at the store, and Flora, the daughter of the Gruenbaums, was invited.

At last Flora was the center of the conversation. What should she wear to the party? "A fairy costume?"

"A clown's costume," suggested Arthur.

"A frog," suggested Harry.

"A queen," said Flora, "I want to be a queen." "But there will be lots of queens," said Flora's mother, Annie. "I want you to stand out. There's going to be a prize. If you are going to win the prize, you have to have an original costume."

And the debate went round the table. Mildred, who was ten years older than Flora and was already thinking about marriage, suggested a bride's costume. "She has lovely eyes," she said about her sister, "and we could get a dress that would hang so she won't look so fat."

"A pregnant bride is what we'll have," said Arthur, whose mother gave him a look, a look that said that his behavior was despicable, his reference to the unspeakable in front of the child was disgusting, and he was the cleverest, most adorable of men who could never do anything but please.

Mildred said it was hopeless, nothing would do on a child like Flora. Flora didn't mind being teased. The invitation was for her. Selma was having a birthday, and Flora was going to the party.

Otto Fernwald, the head designer of the Gruenbaum Company, the one who had made Gruenbaum Suits practically a household name, was called in. He arrived at the house after dinner one evening with a sketch pad. He only spoke Yiddish and made Mildred giggle when he would roll his eyes to tell her how beautiful she looked in an outfit he had made for her. Flora was delighted when Arthur lifted her up and placed her on the dining table and Otto measured her, height, shoulder to knee, waist to ankle, wrist to collarbone. Annie said to her daughter, No more cake till the party, at the party you can eat cake.

The day before the big event, the first Sunday after Passover, Otto arrived with the costume. Flora was to be dressed as a doll, but not just a doll, a doll in a box, and that was the remarkable original thing about the costume. An hour before the party she was given a special bath by the upstairs maid. Mildred came into the bathroom and told Flora how lucky she was, how everyone was going to be at the Abromovitz store for Selma's party, and how fine her costume was, it would surely win the prize. Flora had always loved Mildred, Mildred best of all, because sometimes Mildred would pick her up and kiss the back of her neck or her nose. "Funny Flora," she would say. Sometimes Mildred would come into Flora's room late at night and wake her up. "Yoo hoo," she would say. "Would you like to stroke my back?" And Flora would roll her pudgy hands down her sister's spine and over her thin hips, and sometimes they both fell asleep in Mildred's bed and when they woke Flora would have one of her hands around Mildred's back and the other in her mouth, sucking her thumb.

The doll's costume was made of pink silk, and it had a lace collar and a bonnet to match. Flora slipped it over her head and looked at herself in the mirror. She was pink all over, pink gloves, and little buttons that were made of mother-of-pearl ran down her sloping chest. The upstairs maid brought her a pair of white stockings. They had tight elastic at the top and bit into her round calves. She tried to roll them down, but the maid forbade her to touch them. "Such beautiful stockings," said the maid.

It was beautiful. It was the best doll's dress she had ever seen. They made her stand still, nothing should be wrinkled, nothing should be spotted. She was given a new pair of shoes, white high shoes with laces up the front. She had socks with a tassel at the top. She is a perfect doll, said her mother, who looked with pride at her daughter. Annie was going, too, and the mothers were going to have tea and cakes on the ground floor while the children played games on the second.

Just before the carriage came to take them to the party, Otto Fernwald himself entered the room carrying the box, the important part of the costume. A box with a cellophane front, with a bottom that had holes in it so that Flora's legs could rest on the floor, was placed over her head. Inside the box Flora looked like a perfect present. The heavy cardboard that had been used to make the sides of the box had been covered in a silk fabric from one of the Gruenbaum trouser linings. It was a paisley pink fabric that matched the dress on the doll inside. Flora began to be alarmed when she realized that she couldn't sit down in the box. She couldn't reach her hands out.

"How will I eat my cake?" she asked her mother. Her voice was muffled by the cellophane.

"Don't worry," said her mother, "you wait till the costume judging is over and then you can take off the box and have a big piece of cake." Flora was already hungry, even though she had just had lunch.

She had to stand in the carriage and was lifted out by the driver. She made an entrance into the store with her mother right behind her.

Immediately she was jostled by little boys with swords at their sides, helmets on their heads, who were screaming and running and chasing one another in circles. Someone picked her up and carried her up the staircase because she could hardly move her feet forward in the box. Each step was tiny, and the box waved from side to side as she took it. Upstairs through her cellophane she could see other little girls, in gowns, in makeup, in hats like her older sister wore, dressed as Mother Goose or puppy dogs or cats. The little girls were playing "ring a round a rosy," and the nursemaids were singing and clapping. Flora wanted to join, but she couldn't move fast enough. She couldn't put out a hand to take another child's. The little girls saw that she was in a box, behind a veil of cellophane. They ignored her. Flora stood at the side of the room, behind the counters that had been pushed aside for the party. Butlers came by with cookies on silver platters. One stopped in front of Flora and she saw the tray and the chocolate cookies, but she couldn't reach out her hands, so the butler passed her by. At a great high table at one end of the room there were glasses with drinks; strawberry and vanilla sodas were waiting with candy-striped straws in them. Children ran up to the table and took them. Flora stood there watching. She looked for her mother, but her mother was downstairs. All around her were strangers, and they were all eating or running or speaking to one another. She stood still. Gradually, slowly, she made her way back toward the stairs.

"Help me," she said to the man at the head who was dressed as a clown. His face frightened her when he bent his head down to have a look. He lifted her to the bottom of the stairs. On the ground floor the ladies were milling about. Flora could only see straight ahead as the sides of the box cut off her vision. She searched for her mother, moving carefully, through the crowd, an inch at a time. A man dressed as a guard at Buckingham Palace bent down to her.

"Little girl, you belong upstairs," he said, and without asking he pushed her back toward the staircase and she was carried back to the second floor, where the games had grown wilder and the boys were chasing the girls and throwing things about the store and the nursemaids were screaming at them. Some children were playing "pin the tail on the donkey," and big stuffed animals, lions and tigers, were being given out for prizes. Flora watched the game. She waited for the judging of the costumes: after that she would be able to eat.

How long was it, really? How much time had passed since Mrs. Annie Gruenbaum and her daughter Flora had arrived at Selma Abromovitz's birthday party? It seemed to Flora as if time had stopped and each second took a year and she was missing her entire life, waiting for the judging of the costumes and the bringing out of the birthday cake. What a cake it would be, she thought. The five candles blazing and roses everywhere and white icing a mile high. Then she began to feel a pressure, a terrible pressure, at the bottom of her belly. A familiar urge came on her, and she didn't know what to do. Wait, she told herself, soon the judging will come and Mother will find me and she will take off the box and I will be all right. But time passed and the other children were flushed from excitement, their hair was damp and their costumes were coming apart in the running about.

A group of little girls, one of whom Flora knew, sat on the floor playing with a jigsaw puzzle. Flora walked over, but she could not sit down. They paid no attention to her. The pressure grew greater and made a small pain at the place where you are not allowed to touch, a little burning pain that said, Pay attention to me. Flora was a big girl, a few months older than Selma Abromovitz. She was no baby, and she would not give in to the need, not at all. She could not, inside the box, put her thumb in her mouth, as much as she longed for its familiar soft bend resting behind her front teeth. She bit her lip. She pressed her thighs close together and for a few moments the pressure disappeared. Then it came back again stronger than ever.

At last the grown-ups came up the staircase, silk dresses, blue and gold, beaded handbags swinging at their sides, hair in buns, pinned with mother-of-pearl combs, sweeping rustling skirts and ruffles, pleats, hours of seamstress work, stitch after stitch embroidering flowers and leaves on bodices that now rose and fell with the excitement of a crowd, of an event, of being there and being seen and seeing.

Flora saw her mother at the top of the stairs. She wanted to run to her, but she could not, so she stood still waiting for her mother to see her, which was not so difficult since she was the only child dressed as a doll in a box.

The music was playing. There were live musicians up on an impro-vised stage calling everyone to attention with cymbals. A clown was juggling balls while a man in black tie and tails announced the judging of the costumes and asked the children to march in a parade in a circle around the floor. They were led by a tiny cart pulled by a shaggy dog in which sat Selma Abromovitz dressed as Betsy Ross with an American flag draped over her lap. The circle was large. The parade went twice around the floor. The judges were all adults who sat in benches up on the stage. Flora walked her slow shuffle step, and other children passed her by. The music played. Balloons floated to the ceiling. Flora looked for her mother among the other mothers, but she could no longer find her. The music played faster, the children marched on. Flora felt the pressure return. If only she could find her mother, she could tell her and they might find a bathroom. Somewhere in the Abromovitz store there must be a bathroom.

The music stopped. The cymbals clanged. Three large clowns went through the crowd of children, tapping many on the shoulder. If you were tapped, you were supposed to sit down. One little boy dressed as Pinocchio, whose long nose had fallen off and dangled round his neck, burst into tears as the clown approached him and he was swept off into his mother's arms.

The music started again. Now the parade was shorter and there fewer children following the cart. Flora felt the pressure so badly, tears came to her eyes and spilled out over her face. Behind the cellophane the judges could not see the tears. They looked like spots of light on the child's face. Confetti was thrown in the air.

The music stopped again and the clowns came out and tapped more children on the shoulders, and a girl dressed as a shepherdess collapsed on the floor and refused to leave. She was carried off kicking. The remaining children began once again to march around. Now there were only a few, and Flora saw her mother, with shining eyes in the first row, encouraging her on with a fluttering of her hands. Flora tried to break out of the small circle and reach her mother, but the clowns who were walking with the children pushed her back in line. Walk they said, straight ahead, walk faster, they said. But Flora could only shuffle along, and so she was the last in the line.

The music stopped. The cymbals sounded. The clowns came out. Flora could see her mother twisting her handkerchief in her hand and the clown passed her by and tapped the child in front of her and the one behind. Now there were only three children left in the middle of a large circle. The judges sat on the stage and stared at the children. The clowns marched around them. Flora could not bear it any longer. She would come apart inside. Everyone was looking at her, so she could not, must not, but she did. What else could she do? The liquid trickled down her legs onto the tops of her white stockings and onto her shoes. It streamed down her legs and made a miniature lake on the floor. She was standing there, as the judges watched her, a yellow stain on her white stockings, a small mishap but a recognizable one, and the other children began to whisper. Suddenly the clown came out and picked her up and carried her out of the center of the circle. Behind where she had been standing a shining wet spot remained, reminding everyone in the room, adult and child, that behind the masks of civilization, biology still ruled. Flora was taken home immediately, before the cake was served.

• • •

When Flora told Hedy this story, she was warning her of dangers that waited ahead, but of course Flora didn't know that, not exactly. She was just talking the way mothers will, not realizing that each word is a rock that daughters carry around ever after, a rock to build a fortress, a rock to throw at someone else, a rock to stand on while crossing rivers. At night when Hedy was going to sleep, she would see in that space between sleep and imagination where dreams began to bud, the box abandoned in her mother's room, a wet spot at the bottom where the cardboard now sagged.

The Fortunes of the Herzberg Family in Baltimore: 1905–1910

When Joseph Herzberg first became the rabbi and the hazan because they needed one for the price of two, of the Beale Street Synagogue in Baltimore, he was still very young and not trained quite the way rabbis had been trained at home. But the older men in the congregation had heard of his family, the famous voice that had once accompanied the Baal Shem as he said his morning prayers. It was true, they whispered to themselves, the Baal Shem's voice, his own voice, with the sweetness of heaven, returned each generation in a Herzberg body. How lucky they were, this poor congregation of immigrants from Lvov and Vitebsk, from Kovno and Grodno, here in Baltimore, in a street of leaning green-and-pink houses, whose front porches sagged and whose windows sat uneasily in their peeling frames, to have secured for themselves a man with such a voice, such a connection, such a miracle in his family.

When Joseph opened the Torah and took up the silver pointer that had been left to him by the original rabbi, who had gone back to Kovno to die where he was born, the congregation would sit up and their eyes would open and their bodies would begin to rock gently back and forth on their heels. In the balcony where the women sat, the talking would die down, not disappear, but diminish. Here in the place where Indians, covered in feathers and rabbit skins, once dug for clams and launched their canoes, the synagogue would tremble with the sound of the winds in the desert at the base of Mt. Sinai and the cymbals and drums of the old temple as the dancers marched in the great hall and the prophets wailed in the marketplaces. And mingled with these ancient resonances came the sound of mourning, constant mourning for the gates of the Garden of Eden, closed till the end of time and the temples sacked and the women sold into slavery. In his voice Joseph, like his father and his father's father, caught the tremor of fear that is constant after the first drawn breath as well as the wisp of wild joy, the joy of an idiot child who doesn't know the afternoon sun will set. All this was Joseph's voice. His wife, Ruth, sat in the balcony, behind the curtain, every Friday service, every Saturday morning, and she quickly became known as a woman who would come to the sick and tend to the elderly and always bake an extra loaf of challah for the hungry. She also gave piano lessons to the children of the neighborhood. Soon the congregation forgot how shocked they were when they first saw that their new rabbi had chosen for a wife a woman with a face so mangled that she wore a thick veil in daylight. Ruth gave funds to the orphans' home, to the unemployed, to the Hospital for Chronic Illnesses, for a kosher kitchen that was run by volunteers from the community. She gave money to the burial society so that the dead could have shrouds of fine linen. She gave anonymously. Isaac thought that the large checks he sent each month allowed his sister luxuries that her husband couldn't provide, but she spent none of the money on herself. What did she need, after all, more than she and Joseph had? That was true until their daughter was six years old.

Ruth played on the piano all during the months of her pregnancy. She was getting better and better, and now she could play Strauss and Debussy and both hands and the pedals worked together to fill the room with what she really meant, meant all the time but could only say with her hands on the piano keys.

The child was named Sharon, and her birth seemed to complete or confirm the miracle of her mother's life. The baby girl's skin was pale and perfect. Ruth ran her fingers over the smooth cheeks over and over. The baby had her mother's soft brown eyes and black hair and when, at a few weeks of age, she smiled, Joseph wept and told his wife that the baby looked like his own mother, his mother who disappeared like a leaf whipped off a tree by a summer storm.

Naomi took the train from New York, a long trip for a woman alone to visit her daughter and her granddaughter, and she looked at the baby and said without surprise, "The baby has Moses's forehead. She has the thick eyelids of a Gruenbaum." It was as if Moses were calling out from beyond the grave, Don't forget me, don't forget me. The baby's face had a wise look, as if she knew more than she possibly could, just lying there in the crib.

Isaac had sent his niece a satin dress and a mother-of-pearl hairbrush. He wrote to his sister: "I haven't words for what is in my heart." Isaac wanted to have the words. If he could have, he would have told her how he wished she lived near him. How he thought of her in the nights when he opened his door, how he thought of her when he had decisions to make, how the touch of her arm on his shoulder came to him sometimes in his sleep. All he said was, "I am glad that all our children are American citizens."

To Joseph, his child was not so much an American citizen as an Israelite born in exile, waiting for the Messiah so that all could return to Paradise.

Was Joseph disappointed that his first child was a girl? Only a little. He explained to Ruth that he must have a son. How else could the voice, the voice that had sung with the Baal Shem, continue into the next generation? His little girl was a joy. His sons would be necessities.

In three years Ruth bore him two sons, named Meyer and Eli, and with the birth of the last she grew ill and the time for recovery was long and the doctor in the hospital in Baltimore where she had been carried sick with fever on the fifth day after the delivery said, No more, and so the Herzberg family was complete.

On her fourth birthday Sharon, who already had been taught how to change the diapers of her brothers, who could help her mother prepare a meal, who had learned the words to the prayer for the Sabbath candles, and who sat often in the synagogue on her papa's lap and listened to him *daven,* opened her mouth and sang the melody she had heard in synagogue that day. Her mother, who was grinding the babies' food in a bowl, stood frozen. Her father heard the sound and looked in horror at his child.

It was pure, it was perfect. Not a note was wrong, and more than that, the edge was there, the weight of time, the worry that would never go away as well as the narrow window opened, always opened, to impossible happiness, it was all there in the notes. The Baal Shem's disciple, within the walls of a four-year-old's larynx, was heard in the small house in Baltimore.

Joseph put his head in his hands. "It can't be," he said. "She's a girl. The voice will not be in a girl."

"Of course not," said Ruth reassuringly. "Don't worry. One of the boys will have it."

The babies gurgled and laughed and tumbled with one another on the floor. The older pushed the younger too hard, and there were tears and a cry that sounded harsh, not like music at all. All night Joseph stayed by the window with his tallis on his shoulders, and he prayed, "Don't let this be, God, don't let me have escaped death in the Ukraine only to have the sound of the Baal Shem's disciple disappear forever in Baltimore."

Sharon found her mother's piano. Her small pudgy fingers picked out notes and she played whole songs. When her father was not home and the boys were sick or tired or restless, she would sing to them and they would quiet down, letting her brush their hair with her pearl-handled brush. If she sang to them, they would close their eyes and fall asleep in their beds.

The boys, Meyer and Eli, learned to read. They learned to read before Sharon, and they taught her the letters and the sounds. "See, they are smart," said Ruth to her husband.

But he was not comforted. Neither boy showed any signs of having a voice. The older emitted only a flat constant nasal sound when he tried, and the younger, who at least heard the notes correctly, could only reproduce them automatically, as if the heart had been removed, as if the shape were there but the sound were dead. Joseph loved his sons just as dearly as if they had been born like he was, a descendant of a long line that went back to the table of the Baal Shem, had taken walks with the Baal Shem in the fields. He loved his daughter Sharon, whose dark hair and pale skin showed him what his wife would have looked like had she not been afflicted. But he did not like to hear his daughter sing. It was as if she were taunting him, as if she were promising him something she could not deliver. It was not fair, he knew it was not fair, it was not her fault, but he did not want her to sing.

Ruth loved her daughter's voice, and when she was six years old she decided for the first time to use her brother's check to fulfill her own desire. She arranged for Sharon to have music lessons, piano and voice, twice a week, three dollars each time, with a Miss Marion Feldman, who was not a member of the synagogue and lived in another part of town altogether and whose name Ruth had cut from the paper where she had advertised herself as a teacher of music for young ladies of talent. Surely Ruth thought her Sharon was one of those. Joseph had said, "No, what does she need it for? You play well enough, you teach other children, teach her."

Ruth said, "I am only an amateur. She needs a real teacher."

"For what?" said Joseph. "What are you doing to her?"

But in the end, this, their first terrible quarrel, ended with Ruth taking Sharon by trolley and by bus and bringing her to Miss Marion Feldman on Tuesday and Thursday afternoon, lessons paid for by Isaac Gruenbaum of New York City.

Joseph never asked how the lessons were going. He never appeared at the recitals Miss Feldman held twice a year. He would no longer let his daughter sit downstairs with him, and she joined the other girls and women in the balcony. She would lean over the edge, her mother holding on to her skirt, peeking up the curtains that hung over the balcony to prevent the men and women from seeing each other. After a while she sat down and paid no attention to the murmurings from downstairs. She would play games with her fingers and sing to herself, and finally her mother would send her outside to wait. Soon she stopped coming at all except on the important holidays.

Bad times came to Joseph and Ruth, and there were whole months when Joseph didn't smile or ask his sons to name the prophets or remember to bless his daughter on the Sabbath. In Baltimore they lived in a Jewish quarter where all their neighbors were Jews from the small shtetls, and while some were kosher and the men wore yarmulkes and hurried to prayers in the evening and others were bareheaded and sat on the stoops in the long hot dusk talking about revolutions and Palestine and the overthrowing of czars and kings, they all spoke Yiddish and they all knew one another as family of sorts, responsible in a way for each other. Especially beloved among them were the learned ones, the rabbis and the scholars, the ones who bridged the abyss between the daily life and the Sabbath queen, who made the covenant come alive for all on the holidays and who reminded each Jew that there still was a purpose, a destiny of unknown grandeur, hiding in Elijah's cloak, in the promises that had been exchanged. So Joseph was not only admired in his shul, but was known in the neighborhood as a pious one, even a holy one, a descendant of those who had sat with the Baal Shem and a man whose voice was proof that some of the zaddiks—the wise men—had made their way into the dazzling light of Paradise and were not blinded or driven mad: but love of a community for its rabbi is never unconditional.

Joseph had been alone in the small shul one Friday afternoon before the evening prayers when into the back wandered a big and dirty Negro with overalls torn at the knee and a haunted look in his eye. Joseph was afraid the man had come to rob the shul of its treasure, the silver Torah plate and the silver cones that were placed gently on the Torah handles when the book was returned to its ark. He was afraid the man was after the candlesticks that stood on either side of the *bimah* or the gold threads that ran through the curtain on the ark.

It was dusty in the shul and the pews, which would be polished for the holidays, were now faded and worn in spots. The one window that looked out into a back alley had just been replaced by blue stained glass with the name of the donating family written in large black letters across the top. Joseph, who was a small man, whose shoulders were narrow and whose arms were like twigs waiting for the wind and rain to bend them toward the earth, was frightened. Not so much for himself—he forgot himself in his urgency to protect the holy objects—but for the disaster he saw coming: torn curtains, defamed Torah, stolen silver, enemies of the Jews trampling them into the dust. Pogrom, pogrom, he wanted to scream in hopes that the janitor who worked only once in a while, and who swept the place out twice a week, might miraculously be within hearing and call for help. Or one of the few men who would appear for the evening prayers might come if he cried out. Instead, he said calmly to the intruder, "What do you want in this house of worship?"

The man, whose heavy frame supported little flesh, and whose eyes were wild with a kind of demon, the demon of drink or fear or madness, Joseph couldn't tell which, sat down on a bench and put his large head in his hands and said to Joseph, "Help me, I'm hungry."

And Joseph heard him and came hurrying toward him. The man sat still and, looking up, opened his palms to the roof, and Joseph saw the pale skin of his palm and the deep crevices lined with dirt and the calluses on the fingers and the dark skin of his body, glistening with sweat. He asked the Negro to come back with him to the room behind the sanctuary, where the wine and crackers were kept for the celebrations that were sometimes held in the basement area after the services for those who could stay the additional moments. Joseph fed the man and gave him wine from a bottle. The wine was a sweet wine, and the man drank it down in a gulp and bent his head and thanked Joseph.

"How did you come to a Jewish place? Why not a church?" said Joseph.

"The churches here don't let Negroes in. Not in the front and not in the back," said the man.

"Why didn't you go to a Negro church in the south side?"

"No," said the man. "Someone says I killed a man, but I didn't, and if I go to the home place, the police, they going to get me."

"Oh," said Joseph.

"I didn't hurt no one," said the man, and Joseph believed him. "Where can I go?" said the man.

"I don't know," said Joseph.

"If they catch me, I be going to the chain gang," said the Negro.

Joseph had heard of prison, of course, and the cold exile of Siberia and the dark dungeons of the czar, and he knew that this America had its bars and its cells, but he had not heard of chain gangs. When the Negro told him, ankles and hands, linked man to man, breaking rock on the road, like beasts that never rest, Joseph said, "No, not in America."

The Negro shook his head. "Shut your eyes, you don't get no flies," he said.

This is how it happened that the shul on M Street had a Negro man living in the basement. A Negro in the basement was why Ruth prepared one extra meal each evening and something for Joseph's lunch and for the stranger whose name was Matthew and who promised Joseph each day that he had done nothing, nothing at all.

The trouble began when the president of the shul showed up one morning to talk to Joseph about some money matters and found a strange black man sleeping in one of the pews, his long legs stretched out and his hands behind his head, just as if he were in a public park or home in his own bed.

"Who is that?" said the president when Joseph appeared. Joseph explained, and the president shook his head. "Get him out of here."

Joseph said, "I don't think I can do that."

The president left and came back with some of the other men in the community, the ones who were just a little better off than the others, whose businesses were flourishing. They told Joseph, Get the nigger out. Joseph said, "Let him be the Shabbos goy. He will clean for us, protect the place, watch over it when I am at home."

"Not a nigra," said the men, "not in Baltimore, we don't do that here."

"In America," said one in a thick Yiddish accent, "we don't mix with the nigras."

"But," said Joseph, "he needs our help. He's innocent and in trouble, just like the Jews driven from their homes.

"But," the others said, "he is dirty and a darky, and we don't want him here."

Joseph did not understand "darky." "He is a Christian, true, but what is wrong with his being dark?" said Joseph. "Abraham's son was dark, the son of Hagar was dark-skinned. The color of your skin says nothing of your holiness before God."

The others looked at him and shook their heads. In Baltimore, they explained, the color of your skin was everything. Savages and slaves, that's what their color told you.

"Slaves," said Joseph. "But we were slaves, too, in Egypt."

The men who were talking to Joseph grew exasperated. "Either he goes or you go," said one who was somewhat tone deaf and didn't appreciate that Joseph had a voice that came from his great-great-grandfather listening to the Baal Shem.

The Negro woke up and ambled down the center aisle toward the men, who were talking about him. They scattered in fear. "Don't worry," said the man, "I don't hurt no one. I never done."

"Get out of here!" screamed the president of the shul, and the man looked at his friend Joseph, who said, "If you chase him away, I will go, too."

The men looked at their feet, and Joseph took out the keys from his coat pocket and he walked out the door, and the Negro followed him to his small house on L Street and slept in the room with his young sons for a month, till he decided to go up north. He said good-bye to the family and hugged Sharon and bounced the boys in the air and said, "Thank you, ma'am," to Ruth and gave Joseph a hug, a hug in which Joseph disappeared, so small was he compared with his guest. Matthew said to Joseph, "You're a true Christian man," and Joseph said, "I'm grateful for your compliment." Ruth smiled at him and told him to come by next time he was in Baltimore. They gave him fifteen dollars that they had hidden in their shoebox for his fare, and Ruth thought to tell him that if he went to New York, maybe her brother would have a job for him, Gruenbaum Suits.

Sharon cried when he left because he had taught her a song that went with hand clapping and feet stamping, and she loved the song, which had to do with chariots and clouds and sounded like her papa but wasn't in Hebrew. He taught her another song about planting things in the ground, and she loved that song, too. She hadn't known before about the growing of things, that somebody put their shoulder on a wheel and pulled the plow. She cried when he left and was only comforted when Ruth took her into bed with her and braided her hair and fed her bread with jam on it. Joseph had no shul and he had no job and he stayed home all day staring sadly out the window, and the house was quiet, even the children were quiet, because they understood that their father was sad.

"Maybe," said Ruth one night at dinner, "you should have told Matthew to go, you lost so much for him."

Joseph, who had not said a word for two days, put down his fork and his knife and said to his wife, "I will tell you a story my father told me, he heard it from the Dubner *maggid*: In Aram, where Sarah and Abraham and their flock and their servants were wandering, pitching their tents here and there, following the rising waters of the occasional river, pulling back against a mountainside to protect against the wind and the darkness, there came to Abraham's tent an angel, but the angel had no wings and had no flaming sword and his hair was not in ringlets but hung limp under his shawl and he limped because he said a beast, a beast in the desert, perhaps a wild boar, had gored his leg and his sore was full of insects that crawled in his skin. He called out to Abraham for water and Sarah came out of her tent and saw the angel who did not look like an angel, and she said to Abraham, He is too dirty, he has a sore that is open. Let the servants take him in their tent, let him wander on in the night, I do not want such a creature in my tent, near my bed, near our sheets and our clothes. On that night Sarah was twenty-five years old, and her eyes flashed and her hair was braided in a thick braid, and Abraham saw the light of the first star as it touched her forehead. The Lord heard Sarah and He wept because this was the angel that had come to tell Sarah that she would be pregnant and give birth to a son. Abraham told his wife that she was wrong to turn the stranger away. She must be hospitable, human to human, in the night when the wind of the desert blew cold and the sands shifted and the stars spun, and Sarah bowed her head, but she complained to her servant, and she turned away from Abraham on their rugs and she set her lips tightly and did not speak, and the angel spent the night in the tent and he was nursed by Sarah's hand as she cleaned his wound and bound it in bandages made from her own linen as her husband bade her do. She did the right thing, but her heart was against it. In the morning the angel left the tent and did not return for sixty years, his message delivered so late because of Sarah's hardness of heart, only a temporary matter, a moment of neglect.

"Who knows," said Joseph to his wife, "who is an angel of the Lord and what his message may be."

"What message is the angel bringing you?" said Ruth. "Did you marry me because you thought I might be an angel under the scars?" Ruth teased her husband, but though her mouth smiled, her eyes were like pillars of salt.

"No," said Joseph, "I did not think you were an angel. I thought you were a shadow of an angel. When Matthew came I did not think the Lord had a message for me, I thought, If I do not take care of the stranger at my gate, then who am I and what is the purpose?"

Ruth was silent. The money was not the real problem. She could write to Isaac and he would send more. Joseph did not like to take from his brother-in-law, but he would not let his children starve.

Joseph found a place some miles away where he could teach Hebrew to little boys. He prepared boys for their Bar Mitzvahs. He missed raising his voice before the congregation. At night in bed, he could no longer touch his wife, and her body seemed to him a reproach, a thing he should want but could no longer. His sadness filled the house like the dampness from the sea, and soon everyone longed for the weather to change.

"Go find another congregation," said Ruth. "Isaac would do something, he wouldn't just wait for fate to come to him."

"I am not your brother," said Joseph, and thought for a moment that he might hate his wife.

Joseph waited. He was shy, and the thought of approaching the well-dressed men of the boards of the synagogues that were multiplying in Baltimore appalled him. Then Ruth began to hear from neighbors and friends that the replacement rabbi had the voice of a toad calling out to its mate in a swamp by the highway. He was demanding a higher salary and wouldn't do weddings or funerals unless he was paid first, and his wife shut the door in the face of Rachel, the old woman who came to beg clothes for her grandchildren and who everyone knew was harmless, though her eyes roamed about in her head and she said strange things about the end of the world. Joseph and Ruth always gave her soup and clothes and invited her stay for the evening.

Eventually the men of the congregation came to Joseph and asked him to return, and he said yes and did not ask for a raise or for a vacation. He said he wanted to hire a Negro, and they agreed. It had all been an unfortunate mistake. Ruth played Chopin on the piano and Sharon sang songs, Matthew's songs, in the yard, and the boys yelled and screamed and punched each other again, and in the nighttime Joseph found his hands on his wife's breasts and he said to her, "Maybe you're an angel after all."

Harry Gives Flora a Sailboat: 1916

Flora's oldest brother, Harry, had a room in the front of the house, and out his window in the wintertime when the trees were bare he could see the river with its barges floating up and down, pushed by tugboats with steam coming from their stacks. He was a heavy boy with a slow walk and a careful, cautious way of standing back and letting others talk. He covered his wandering eye with one hand. If he didn't, he often had double vision. He wanted to be a sailor. He wanted to sail to China and spend long months on the ocean watching the waves change color with the shift in the earth's orbit and the shape of the moon. He wanted to throw a harpoon in the water and haul back a whale, slippery and wild-eyed, gasping as water rushed through its mouth. He was a daydreamer, a boy who wrote lists of things to take on long journeys in the flyleaf of his algebra book. He took walks alone and recited the stories of Kipling to himself. He thought about sailing to India. He thought about the Amazon River, how dark and terrible its crocodile depths and how strange must be the people who fished its muddy bottoms. He was going to be the president of the Gruenbaum Suit Company, and he knew that for a fact. Isaac would put his hand on his son's shoulder and say, Our business is doing well this season, or Our factory in Fall River lost money last month. His mother would say, He's got plans, that one, big plans. His grandmother would pinch his ear and say, One day a lot of people will be working for you. For his tenth birthday he had been given a model sailboat with canvas sails and ropes that went up and down on miniature pulleys. Once Arthur touched the boat's hull and Harry for the first and last time in his life lunged for his brother, kicking him, biting his forearm with his teeth, and screaming as if he himself had been thrown into the sea by the turning of the miniature mast.

When Harry was seventeen, his father took him to work. He was given an office of his own overlooking Seventh Avenue with a window, which if he opened it wide and leaned to the left he could see, between buildings, off in the distance, a ribbon of river, pressing against the cliffs of New Jersey, as it turned from dark blue to pale gray under the passing clouds.

After a week in the office, a week of wearing his new suit and copying the figures his father gave him in a brown leather ledger, he walked into Flora's room around midnight. He woke her up.

"What's the matter?" she said.

"I can't sleep," he said.

"Shall I sing to you?" asked Flora.

"No," said Harry, "please don't."

"Would you like me to read you a story?"

"No," said Harry.

"Would you like me to go downstairs and fix you a sandwich?" Harry nodded.

Flora brought him a big chicken sandwich and sat next to him on the floor while he ate it. Flora touched his cheek where the fine hair of his new beard was just beginning to gather. She leaned on his back and put her head on his shoulder. "Are you sleepy now?" she asked.

He sighed. He left the room and came back holding his sailboat. "I want you to have it," he said. Flora took it in her arms and placed it carefully on her windowsill. She began to shiver. "Why are you trembling like that?" Harry asked.

"No one," said Flora, "will ever again give me such an important present."

"Did anyone?" asked Hedy when she was told this story while she and her mother were waiting for the Fifth Avenue bus to take them downtown where they were meeting Mildred at the Plaza for tea.

"Not yet," said Flora.

Reader: America was built by dreamers, true enough, but dreamers like Isaac, who spent most of their time awake, saved carefully and sprang into action when the time was ripe. America was not built by daydreamers like his son Harry, who had so much to live up to and no mountains of his own to scale, mountains that would strengthen the muscles and hone the nerve. Men like Isaac often have sons like Harry, who give away the ships that would have taken them to darkest Africa, where they might have collected butterflies or gathered shells on a tropical beach. Oedipus killed his father, Chronus ate his sons, but that was myth. In real life the sons of fathers who built up their own small empires just shuffle on, doing what is expected of them, leaving heroics to the past or the distant future.

Meyer Herzberg Shows Signs of Promise: 1915

Ruth and Joseph's eldest son, Meyer, began to read shortly after his second birthday. He had dark curls and black eyes and a wide mouth that puckered and puffed with his every grief, flattened with his pleasures, and split open with a laugh that frightened his father, so open and free was the sound, so unlike the laugh of a child who lived under the law of God. Meyer ran his fingers over his mother's face as if his tiny hands could smooth away her angry skin. He raced ahead of the others in school, but he asked questions, and whatever the answer it was followed by a new question; nothing satisfied him completely.

Ruth was amazed by her first son. She wrote to her brother Isaac in New York. "He asks how the oven works. He looks inside to see if I am telling the truth. He asks about the gas and what is in it. He fills jars with worms and butterflies to see what happens to them when they die."

"Papa," he asked when he was five, "you believe that the bones of the dead will rise when the Messiah comes?"

Joseph looked at his son with a cold dread. What kind of question was that? "Yes," he said, "I believe in what was given to us at Sinai."

"I don't think," said Meyer, "that the soul of the living could still be in the bones of the dead, so long in the dirt; the soul would not last."

Joseph said to his son, "Don't think, just believe. God brings you a whirlwind and you must accept it, the way it is, the way it says."

Meyer pulled at his earlocks. "I don't think so, Papa."

Joseph hugged his son. He gave him a piece of bread with honey. "Darling," he said, "don't worry about it. Promise me you won't worry about it." Meyer promised, but he broke his promise.

When Meyer was nine his father told him that holiness was obeying the law. "For our people," said Joseph, "holy is the man who does as he should, who obeys as he should."

"Holy," said Meyer "is in the mind, is the mind thinking."

"Thinking?" said Joseph. "What do you mean?"

"I don't know yet," said Meyer.

Joseph complained to his wife. "He is without melody, without music. He sings like the pulley over the well in the backyard of my father's house."

"He is a good boy," said Ruth.

"I know," said Joseph, "but in America maybe that is not enough."

Ruth laughed at her husband as he paced back and forth, rattling his tea cup, knocking into the table so the fringed lamp swayed on its base. Ruth sat down at the piano and played Vivaldi for him. She did not get every note right, but the Vivaldi was there, the chords, the rise and fall of the notes, the spaces between as if God were holding his breath.

The Vivaldi made Joseph weak in the knees, and his hands stretched out for Ruth's back and he touched the back of her neck, and his love hit him in the groin, desire and pride, joy and tenderness. Meyer, he decided, would be all right.

Flora Has a Cold and Gives It to Her Brother Arthur: 1916

The house on Riverside Drive was silent. It was Thursday afternoon and the cook was out, and the maid, who had newly arrived from the county of Cork, was in her room praying to the small picture of Jesus she had pinned above her bed. Flora was home in bed with a fever, and her mother had gone out to visit the daughters of Jacob in the old age home as she did every Thursday afternoon, bringing cookies and fruits in baskets and speaking in the Yiddish of her own childhood.

Flora tossed on her sheets. She was hot and her legs ached beneath the creases of her plump knees. Her eyes smarted and she had finished the book that her mother had left by her bedside, a Hardy Boys adventure story that had belonged to Harry, been read by Arthur, spurned by Mildred, and devoured by Flora, who longed to solve a mystery, to bring a killer to justice, to find an embezzler in the office, to make everyone proud of her, to notice her.

The downstairs door slammed shut, and in its slamming there was a fury. The sound carried up the stairs, and Flora thought of kidnappers who would come and wrap her in blankets and carry her off to New Jersey and demand a ransom from her father, who would go white with fear for her life and sell everything he had to bring her back safely. Flora heard the steps on the stair, heavy and slow, rising determinedly. Should she scream, should she hide, should she take her lamp and be prepared to hit the intruder on his head? Would she be violated? Violation, Mildred said, was the worst thing that could happen to a girl. Violation, Flora thought, and certain shivers in certain forbidden places slid unwanted into her mind and she began to cry. Not loud, she was not a foolish girl, just soft tears that came trickling out of her eyes, that made her nose red and damp and caused the thumping in her head to increase.

The steps came nearer up the first landing and onto the second flight, and Flora thought of running to the window and calling for help. What would the Hardy boys have done? What would the Hardy boys do if someone wanted to violate them? Flora wanted a cookie. Her fever was making her sweat and the sweat mingled with her tears, and while ordinarily in most people this condition does not signal hunger, Flora thought of cookies. But food was downstairs in the kitchen, and the intruder was on the stairs.

Flora tried to hide under the bed, but she was too round to fit and her stomach, even when she lay flat on her back and held herself in, stuck on the bottom of the bed. She was too smart to hide in the closet, that's the first place that any kidnapper would think to look for her. She decided on running, running right for the front door, in her nightgown stained from the rice pudding she'd had for lunch, stained from certain sneezes she hadn't managed to catch in the handkerchief her mother had provided. She opened the door of her bedroom, and lowering her head so as not to see what would be too terrifying to see, she charged for the stairs.

There at the top was Arthur, home early from school, home because his Latin teacher had an emergency appointment with his dentist and had dismissed the class before it had begun. Arthur had a dark scowl on his face because the Latin homework had doubled and the afternoon, which could have been filled with such fine things as smoking a cigarette up on Broadway with a friend and looking at girls who pretended to ignore him, was going to be wasted conjugating verbs in a dead language of dead people whose day was over, who in their glory had routed the Jews from their home and whose descendants had tortured the Jews and burned them in fires. What did he want with Latin?

He saw his sister running toward him, and he grabbed her by the shoulders. She screamed, "Please, God, help me!"

Arthur lifted her up in his arms. "What is it? What's wrong?" he said.

She saw it was Arthur. She stopped writhing. She started to cry, and he sat down, there at the top of the stairs, and he held her in his arms and rocked her back and forth. Thank God, none of the guys could see him. He patted her on the back. "It's all right, Flora, it's all right."

She put her wet face against his neck and smelled his boy smell, and she put her hand up to his cheek where he had shaved four days ago and would need to shave again in another week.

"I'll show you a magic trick," he said.

The two of them went into Arthur's room, a place forbidden to Flora. He let her pick a card and put it back in the pack. "Five of hearts," he said, and it was.

"Show me," she begged, "how you did that."

He did. He taught her how to play poker. He taught her how to not to let her eyes tell him the secret of her cards. He didn't get angry when she beat him.

A few days later he came down with her cold. Flora brought him chocolates. She brought him a thick slice of cake that had been her own portion at dinner. After that, late at night, when everyone else was sleeping, Arthur took to waking Flora and playing a few hands of draw or stud with her. She would sit up in bed, rub her eyes, blink from the light, and play however long he liked. He taught her how to shuffle the cards so that they flew in the air. Her pudgy fingers practiced under her school desk, even without the cards, the flipping of the thumbs, the arc of the rising and falling cards. Arthur only regretted that he couldn't send her up against his friends. She would cream them, he thought, she really would. Sometimes a sister and brother find in each other's company a completeness that deserves its own special name.

Meyer Herzberg Becomes a Man and Makes His Own Choices: 1919

Meyer was splendid at his Bar Mitzvah. He did his part perfectly. When Joseph wrapped his son in his own tallis, the one that his father had given him when he fled his home so many years before, that he had worn all these years, and the boy and his father stood together before the open ark, no one in the congregation breathed, as if the tenderness of the moment, the invisible chain holding the past to the future, might overcome them, might cause inexplicable, even terrible, tears to pour.

His mother, who had listened in the front row of the balcony behind the green curtain that had hung there for so many years that it had rust stains from the time the roof leaked and rips in places where the material had aged beyond repair, had bit her lip, heard the pounding in her heart the whole time Meyer was reading his portion, shaking hands with the men of the congregation, sitting and standing and rocking back on his still uncallused heels. To be so proud, to be so happy, to be so rich in the accomplishment of a child, it made her shiver. Would something terrible happen now? Would Lilith, Adam's spurned first wife, come in the night and exact revenge for her pride? She didn't believe in Lilith. But she had heard enough to consider always, if Lilith did fly through the night, how she could protect her children. Ruth thought of her spoon family. No one in her spoon family had ever had a Bar Mitzvah, more's the pity for them, she thought. She wore a kerchief on her head and kept her face down as the men came over to her later and complimented her on her son's existence, his Hebrew, his excellent memory. She thought to thank God that an ugly woman could give birth to a fine son. In the basement of the synagogue they drank wine with the congregation, and there was some bread on a china plate passed out to all.

"That's it," said Meyer to his father. "I have to go to school. I want to study in an American school."

Joseph sat on the chair he had pulled up to the kitchen table and held his hand over his stomach where cramps were beginning. "What can you learn in an American school? What will they teach you that matters?" said Joseph, but he knew that it was over. He could not order this son of his, who was almost his size—his feet were larger, in fact, his arms lifted and fell already like a man's—to go to the yeshiva. If the boy did not want to study the Hebrew text, he could not force his mind where it would not go. Freedom, thought Joseph, this land of freedom is about the freedom to lose everything. "I will lose you," said Joseph.

"No, Papa," said Meyer. "I will always be a good Jew, a Jew of the law, like you."

"Promise?" said Joesph.

"I promise," said Meyer. But he couldn't keep his promise.

The Bank, The Banker, The Banker's Son and Daughter: 1895–1920

Ben Eisen moved the bank, moved it in one bold step, in one week of wagons piled with desks and lamps, with Ben Eisen sitting on top of a dozen safes, his ax in hand, as the horse pulled his weight along Fifth Avenue, past the library and the great stores on Ladies' Mile, and on into the new frontier, the Bronx, the same Grand Concourse that the Jews of the neighborhood were migrating toward, one by one, as they got enough money, as their small businesses flourished, as they learned that the Lower East Side was only a port of entry, not a country unto itself, as their English improved and their desire to be American increased and the streets of New York beckoned, they moved farther from the ocean, from the ships that had brought them, from the mouth of the country, into the Bronx, where there were trees and bigger apartments and an immigrant could hardly believe his good fortune at the running water, the sunlight on the river, the parks that were filled with boys who still called out the rules of the game in Yiddish, but whose birth certificates were made out in English and stored at Chambers Street, arranged alphabetically along with the Rockefellers and the Morgans who went to the opera every week in horse-drawn carriages and summered in Oyster Bay.

Ben Eisen's New World Bank began to take the deposits of the Italians on Hoyt Street and beyond. The Irish, who sent their kids to the Holy Name School on the other side of the park, were still glad to put their money in their own accounts there and to come and talk with Ben Eisen, who always had an encouraging word for a man who wanted to strike out on his own, or wanted a loan for a wedding party, or had a family to bring from the old country. Ben Eisen had become a good judge, something in the face, something in the way a man held his hat in his hands when he talked to him, of who would be able to make the payments and who might not. He gave everyone the benefit of the doubt. He saw good where others might have wondered. He was right most of the time. He hired assistants, and the assistants had assistants, but Ben Eisen himself passed all the applicants, and his mistakes were few. The business was for his son. The bank, the bank with its fortune in its belly, was for his American son and his American daughter.

The family now lived in a large house with servants in the Bronx. His children had not been exiled from the family hearth as he had. They had been given the best parts of the chicken, the finest pieces of the lamb. His son had been given violin lessons and a Bar Mitzvah, an American Bar Mitzvah. His children wore the softest linens and slept on featherbeds in rooms of their own. Through his children, Ben Eisen reclaimed his own childhood. It may be that the parent gives life to the child, but the child can give the parent a second life, another chance at having what was missed. In this way children become parents to their parents and parents become the children of their children. Each chocolate delicacy that Julie put on his plate, or Bessie spooned into her mouth, settled in Ben Eisen's stomach, lending it a fullness it could never have on its own. Ben Eisen had often enough in his early years in America walked past such confections in the windows of cafes and known that they were not for him.

His wife, Elyssa Blau, the daughter of a zipper manufacturer, was a beautiful young woman with a wry smile and a quick way with words. She was fond of puns, in Yiddish and English, and read novels. When they were first seeing each other, Ben Eisen would take her to the theater on Second Avenue. Often he fell asleep in the second act. Sweetly she told him the plot and acted out the parts. He loved to watch her pronounce the words and gesture like an actress. He was proud of his wife, who knew more about some things than he did.

She was not the mother he had expected her to be. She had little patience with children and preferred to shut herself up in her room and read stories. Ben Eisen was sad about that, but he couldn't complain, she did what he asked in most respects. She was a gracious hostess and a sweet companion on his walks. She read the newspapers and knew what was happening. She helped him form opinions that he repeated at work. As the years went by her wit grew drier and her tongue was sharpened sometimes at the expense of Ben Eisen, who shrugged and smiled nervously. Papa, cried Julie when he woke in the night with a fever. Papa, cried Bessie, who was given to unexpected nosebleeds.

Reader: Think how it was to be poor one day and rich the next. Are you the same person? The world doesn't think so. Now the doorman tips his hat to you, now the cabbie asks you where you want to go, now the waiter serves you, and through the glass you see others outside, cold or hungry, without the money to join you at your table. You have different clothes, warm and well cut, and your closet is so full that you make selections based on color, texture, whim. Are you the same person you had been, or have you metamorphosed, caterpillar to butterfly, roe to salmon, seed to corn, dead to alive, or vice versa? Who knows your real place? Who knows who you are? You don't. You can't. The dream of getting rich by hard work and bold guess includes the waking moments when one doesn't know, is it a dream? Am I guilty of sin? Am I the recipient of blind luck, or has the hand of God elected me for future tragedy? What shifted once can shift twice. What was my lot can become my lot again. How hard it is to enjoy with serenity the rapid change of status. Most men and women become dizzy as they too rapidly climb the ladder of success. It is far better to be newly rich than newly poor, but that doesn't mean that those who suddenly find change jangling in their pockets do not have reasons for nervousness, for nightmares of missing trains and falling down holes. No matter how often they pinch themselves they may never wake into reality: which reality, after all? Have pity, Reader, on the newly rich, the suddenly altered, the winners who know they are not worthy and the winners who are confused and the winners who forget themselves in the heady thrill of victory.

The Courtship: 1919

It pleased Ben Eisen when Julie announced that he was going to ask Mildred Gruenbaum to marry him. The matter had not been arranged as it might have been in the old country. Nevertheless, the parents had talked. They had met at tea at the Eisen household one

Sunday. All the parents had made clear what a fine marriage this would be, necessarily bringing together the capital of the Gruenbaum suits and the New World Bank, and the union was approved of by all. Two families prominent in the community—the Gruenbaums already had donated the funds for the hospital foundation on 17th Street, and the Eisens were known by everyone as people of substance, a family of good name.

Isaac watched his daughter Mildred as she moved, all blue silk and fast talking, always smiling, about the room, and he sighed with gratitude. The balance sheets would be good and the future protected, and whatever it was that brought a man and a woman together, the backgrounds were right, the families were good for each other and the grandchildren would have twice as much, be twice as far removed from the back alley of Sulvalki, would be ready to go further into America, higher up its ladders, who knew how far or what was at the top?

Mildred was a tall girl with a long neck and a fine nose with perhaps a small extra bump along the bridge that had come from her mother's side of the family. She had huge blue eyes and dark lashes that rose and fell like the curtains at the opera, lush and promising. She was tall, and her arms were in constant motion, showing off her bracelets, letting her rings catch in the light, pushing her shoulders back and letting her breasts ride high and forward under the lace of her blouse, under the pearl buttons that had been made in Switzerland. She wore oils and perfumes at the back of her earlobes, which were a bit too large and tended to sway with her neck as it moved from side to side. Her hair was a dusty blond that she wore piled up on her head, sometimes with a braid, sometimes in buns that hung above her ears, with strands that would float across her forehead and down the nape of her neck. Her smile was her crucial asset. Her smile was broad and including, and while her teeth were slightly too large and perhaps a little forward in the jaw, when she tilted her head to one side and pulled back her lips, exposing perhaps just a bit too much pink gum, the look of it was sweet, sweet with wicked mixed in. When she smiled and nodded toward someone, that person felt as if a door had opened, a promise had been made, an unexpected bit of money had been found at one's feet. Isaac and his wife, Annie, admired their oldest daughter and understood that she would marry well. As if they had planted a seed in the ground and watched its thin branches bud and green leaves spread and the trunk grow thicker till the tree bore golden pears that one could take to the market and reap a reward.

Isaac drew his daughter aside one morning. It was hard for him to say it, but he tried. "You remind me," he said, "of my sister, Ruth." Mildred hugged her father, but absently; her mind was elsewhere. "I want to say . . . " said Issac, but he paused too long. Mildred was gone.

Mildred's wedding dress was made by a seamstress from Zurich, where her mother had gone by ship the summer before and brought back, in steamer trunks, silks and cottons, lace rippling with white flowers and leaves, bunches of grapes, winding vines, the result of needles and fingers working hour after hour in huts with mud on the floors and cow dung in the yard. Wedding sheets had been ordered from Mordecai the linen man, who arrived with a suitcase of his samples and bowed to the ladies and gave them each a sample handkerchief with a swan embroidered on it, with a small knot for an eye. He even gave Flora a handkerchief, Flora, who was still so young she used it to blow her nose in and it was snatched away from her by the upstairs maid and never returned.

Mildred bobbed her hair. She wasn't one of the first. But she wasn't the last, either, and Julie laughed when he saw her. It promised adventure, this new look of his wife-to-be. He bought her a Packard that came with a chauffeur because Mildred did not know how to drive. She also did not know how to cook or clean, but Julie was not expecting a woman who would put her head over a pot or ruin her hands with lye while scrubbing the floor. He wanted to escort Mildred to events, like the Federation Young People's Dance, like the harvest ball at the country club. He wanted a woman who knew what colors flattered her complexion and which did not, and Mildred was just what he wanted. When she would climb into the backseat of her car, she would pull up her skirt and let him see her stockings and her firm thighs that she squeezed together and opened just a bit. She whispered in his ear. Julie was short and somewhat round and his lips were full as if he had been pouting. He had a dimple in the center of his chin and the beginnings of a second chin that rested against a slightly protruding Adam's apple. His eyes were trusting. Whatever unexpected could happen to such a fine fellow as himself born to the banking family of Eisen? He loved his violin and he would bring it on Thursday nights when he visited his fiancée. He did not have great patience with practicing. He had stubby fingers that got in his way, but still he made music, a little Haydn, a version of Mozart there, and sometimes, knowing that Mildred was not up on such matters, he played them together as one piece. She smiled at him, bent earnestly over his violin, the fine wood, burnished and glowing in the lamplight, his chins tucked firmly down.

After the music he would bring her a glass of wine and kiss her gently on the lips. He kept his hands to himself, although they longed to climb in and out of the folds of her dress. She didn't allow that. He would do whatever she asked because he was the sort who wanted to do what a woman asked, who was grateful that she had chosen him out of the pack of courtiers who had bowed and scraped at her knees. It was a sign, he believed, a sign of his good fortune that he had captured Mildred Gruenbaum, whose smile still made other men pale. It was his hand she was holding when they went out to parties. It was his hand that helped her into the car for the ride home, and it was his hands that would one day roam across the long neck and down below the pearls and into the sweaty places that he was perfectly capable of imagining, although he had admitted that imagination was not his strong suit.

Mildred's mornings were occupied waiting for the postman and then opening the packages, gifts from buyers and salesmen, from button manufacturers to thread manufacturers and their cousins and their aunts, and gifts from businessmen who were old customers of the bank and gifts from businessmen who hoped to be customers of the bank and a box of fruit forks from the staff at the bank and a glass with a picture of William Penn from the foreman of the suit factory in Pansville and a ceramic soap dish from the manager in Fall River and a silver cup from the tailors at the factory in Lower Manhattan, where Mildred had once gone with her father and all the men had said how pretty she was and her father had held her by the shoulder and introduced her to everyone there. How simple it was to have a good time, thought Mildred, stacking the crystal candy dishes up on the dining table next to the silver candlesticks and the soup tureens and the Spode plates and the silver knives and forks with the willow tree pattern.

"See," said Mildred, picking up her little sister and holding her in her arms, "this is what you get for marrying. It's all mine for getting married."

Reader: Think of it. A rubbish room, a junk wagon full of the possessions you once thought valuable and then abandoned . . . the first bicycle, scraped and bent, small and thick, once a parachute to global travel, once a miracle, now a heap of metal, wire rims askew, rubber tires punctured. Ash to ash, dust to dust, molecule to molecule, equally true of the teddy bear that bore your first vomit and the pearls you wore to your sixteenth birthday party and the tennis racket that brought you the junior championship and the wedding presents from a wedding so long ago you can't remember the guests and have now changed partners, moved to a new city, broken those vows and others. We leave behind us a trail of objects, bracelets and kites, bits of Monopoly sets, stereo speakers and sleds, ski boots and ashtrays, as we embrace each new day we leave rotting in closets, in abandoned yards, in trunks, and in pits dug deep in the ground, the stuff of memory, the decaying bits of our snuffed intensities, things that betray our presence on this earth, like the trail of an earthworm through the daffodil bed. If each abandoned thing was tied to the next and the entire string wound around our necks, we would sink into the ground, gone forever, buried by our own possession. The positive effect, the social purpose of our need to have things that we cherish only for the moment and forget in time, is gross national product, inflation, deficit, interest rates, the entire caboodle, which Ben Eisen mastered as his bank added a branch in uptown Manhattan and another in the Flatbush section of Brooklyn, and which all was clear to him without attending business school or even high school. It was clear to him because the motions of money followed the lines of lust and greed logically, followed the path of the earthworm through the garden. What was of value to Stone Age man? His mate, his children? Most likely not. His treasures were pebbles and clubs and skins of the kill, and he probably counted up his goods and kept them safe from intruders and considered himself better than others because of his pile of rocks or his possession of a sharp tusk, one that he abandoned in a rubble of twigs after his next kill. Even Sister Abigail valued her rosary, her prayer book, her flower pot, her corner of the table, the napkin that was hers. Think of man without possessions and you have man without memory, you have no man at all. The Gruenbaum suit business grew and grew because men needed more than one, new ones to match the changing fashions, to meet the changing seasons, because Isaac Gruenbaum knew when to expand and how to make costs and profits line up obediently, because out there in the land of America there was a great desire for new suits even before the old ones were worn out. Things, we are not supposed to care about, objects of desire are not as valuable as matters of spirit, we are told. But no one pays attention. Monks and hermits when they are near their end dream of possessing God or holiness or mercy; even when the object of desire is intangible, possession is the goal. Things are the way we mark our graves while we are still living. Things are the bread crumbs we drop through the forest so that we will be able to find our way back. Possession is the container of our spirit, so much the worse for us.

Flora dreamed of weddings, played weddings with her dolls, but had trouble finding anyone to listen to her as everyone in the household was occupied with Mildred, whose star was shining in the family firmament, dimming the other satellites, the other moons, the other contenders for the sky. Flora had new glasses that slipped down her nose. Her brothers knocked the palms of their hands against her head and scolded her when the glasses dropped to the floor or to her lap on which her stomach sat, full with cookies stolen and otherwise.

Mildred took her best friends to the Plaza, and there they had tea and cakes. Mildred described the salt and pepper shakers she had received from Uncle Max, in the shape of golden lions and their little tails pulled out to make spoons. There were emeralds in the lions' eyes. Mildred smiled and smiled and waved her hand in the air, showing her diamond ring, set in gold with a ruby rim. A pianist at one end of the room, under the fronds of the huge palms, played, and the girls tapped their feet and sipped their tea.

The drawback—there was a drawback, Mildred admitted it, leaning her head forward and whispering to her friends—the drawback was that Julie Eisen had a younger sister who everyone knew was unmarriageable, who would undoubtedly come to dinner at their house night after night, a sour spirit with a grim little toad's face, almost dwarfed; she had a hunch in her shoulders and warts on her chin and hairs growing from brown moles on either side of her nose. An unfortunate girl with a stoop and a glint in her eye that said Don't pity me or I'll spit on you, my saliva right in your mouth. She had small yellow teeth that were bent one over the other and tiny hands that reminded everyone of claws.

"What a sister-in-law!" the girls shrieked with laughter.

"Don't worry," said Mildred, "I'll make her my friend, you'll see. She must have some quality that no one has yet found. I'll find it. We'll be friends, you'll see."

"Poor thing, poor Bessie"—they put their heads together—"a toad," they said, "a real toad for a sister-in-law."

The Banker Plays Matchmaker: 1919

Ben Eisen must be pardoned for loving his daughter. He must be pardoned for what he did for her because what father would not have done the same if he were in the position to do so? When the child was born, he had leaned over the midwife and seen her face all tucked up into itself and her frail form writhing in the midwife's arms and he had known that she needed him, would need him always, and that joy, a share in common good fortune, might escape her forever.

"Babies change," said the midwife.

"She is crumpled from the passage," said his wife.

They named her Bessie. Ben Eisen bought the finest sheets for her bed, the best carved toys for the crib, the thickest carpet for her floor, but he could not change her destiny. It galled him as nothing else in his life ever had. He loved her as he loved no other member of his family, precisely because he was disappointed in her.

After I die, he said to himself, who will smile at the girl, who will bring her presents for her birthday, who will ask her opinion on matters of business, who will hug her in the morning and think of her during the day? The thought of the loneliness of his daughter, the barrenness of her womb, the stretching of her days, without purpose or order, filled him with grief. He could not change that look of desperation in his child's eye, that pull of her mouth that expected so little. The piercing sound of her voice as she commanded the servants and whined at her mother saddened him more. The other girls in her class at the private school made excuses and wouldn't come to the house even when promised visits to the ballet, the opera, the theater, or rides on ponies, because her disposition turned out to be difficult and she made no effort to win friends with her charm. She felt entitled to attention, and when it didn't come she squinted her eyes and turned her head away. She had contempt for those who did not admire her. She would not be a pleader, or a follower, or a handmaiden to some more favored girl. She chose to move through her days alone, alone except for her father, who treated her like a queen, and her brother, who followed his father's lead and behaved toward his sister with respect, if not excessive affection.

Ben Eisen prayed to God. This was not a thing he did often. He went to services with his wife on the High Holidays. He wore a hat in public places because she wished him to. He led the seder at their table each year, although his Hebrew was uncertain and sometimes he bluffed. He worked on the Sabbath. He didn't eat kosher. That was all superstition, baggage from the old country. But still there was something, a God that a Jew had in his heart, one that he spoke to, whom he owed certain things, who would not capriciously harm him, not destroy him as if he were an insect crawling on the plate. So Ben Eisen prayed to his God to help his daughter, to soften her expression, to bring a light into her eyes and perhaps another inch or so on her height. He prayed to his God not to let the child live without knowing the pleasures of being a woman, of holding a baby and resting in the arms of a man. As he explained to God while walking to his office one morning, the riches of the bank and the deposits, which were now in the multimillions and the profits were more than he cared to say, the wealth he had accumulated, which showed itself in the fur on the lapels of his coat, on the gold knocker at the doorpost of his house, meant nothing to him, was a mockery of his hard work, if his child was to be excluded from the people, not a part of the line that began in Sinai and would end when the Messiah came. Did Ben Eisen believe in the coming of the Messiah? He considered it a possibility, and he pleaded with God to bring a miracle to his daughter. If Bessie were to get married, it would take a miracle. Ben Eisen knew that. He was a devoted father, but not a blind one.

When Howard Katz walked into the New World Bank to ask for a loan, he was directed to the president's office. Ben Eisen, rising from his chair, knew that God had not forsaken him.

Howard Katz was a young lawyer, had completed his apprenticeship in a law firm, after graduating from City College. His family lived in Brooklyn. His father delivered milk in a truck, and the entire family had arrived in America from Bialystok only ten years ago, so the fact that Howard Katz had mastered the language, mastered the law, demonstrated his gifts, and these gifts were what Howard Katz was putting up as collateral for a loan.

He needed to open an office, he needed to pay for a desk and a lamp and the first three month's rent. He wanted to open his own office because he had dreams, big dreams, he explained to Ben Eisen. He didn't just want to be an ordinary lawyer, working alongside the businessmen of the community, writing their contracts, holding their hands; he wanted to be a judge. A judge is a pillar of the Constitution, a force for democracy, a partner in the American enterprise of freedom and justice for all. Howard Katz was a dreamer, and he believed in the American experiment. He believed in the law, it was here to protect every citizen, to give truth and decency and dignity to our society. His heroes were Ben Franklin, Abraham Lincoln, and Thomas Jefferson, and he quoted the Bill of Rights to the president of the bank.

"Is there anything more worthwhile in the entire world?" the young man asked. "I intend to devote my life to the defense and the upkeep of those rights." The Constitution, he explained to Ben Eisen, who found the conversation heady, made it possible for Jews to live and prosper and restrained men from the hatred in their hearts. In the history of mankind, there had never been a more remarkable thing than this American experiment, this country whose promise of equality and the pursuit of happiness made Howard Katz shine with the same kind of light that had been in his grandfather's eyes at the court of the Hasidic rebbe in Gratz. The light in both cases was about the ideal, the spirit of human venture, the possibility of perfection, the ideals of justice and godliness, of elevation of human life and elevation of the soul. These visions were both about the repair of the broken world, and Howard Katz and his grandfather alike, although their vocabulary would have differed, both believed that the shards could be pasted together, and the vision of better times made their heads spin.

Ben Eisen looked at the young man and saw him, wrapped in the American flag, rising, rising the way the Jews were rising, climbing purple mountains' majesty. It made his hands tremble with excitement, that dream of America that Howard Katz gave to Ben Eisen, who had been experiencing it all along without knowing it.

Howard Katz wanted to be a judge one day, but Ben Eisen knew and even Howard Katz knew that judges were not selected from the array of candidates because of their love of the Constitution or the Bill of Rights, but because money had been paid to the local clubhouse, the Democratic clubhouse, which made its recommendations, put people on the ballot who could afford it, and made promotions according to contributions of the sort that would certainly exclude a young lawyer, the only son of a father who delivered milk to grocery stores in the Sheepshead Bay section of Brooklyn. Ben Eisen seized his miracle.

"Young man," he said, "I think we can arrange your loan. In time we may even be able to help you find your judgeship." In his head he calculated the going rate for a judgeship was around $35,000, and he might be able to get it for less, considering certain contributions he had already made to the Democratic party's Bronx headquarters, contributions he had made as a sensible businessman who might need consideration in unforeseen circumstances, who certainly needed the goodwill of his neighbors and elected officials.

"It would be an act of loyalty to this wonderful country of ours to find the right spot for you on the bench," he said to Howard Katz, "and you must come home to dinner, to my house for dinner tonight. I have a son around your age and a daughter. I think you will particularly like my daughter. She's a woman of good character." Ben Eisen got up and put his arm around the shoulders of the young man, who was not quite clear on what had been proposed but nevertheless felt a lump in his throat, and he fought back the tears of gratitude that came to his eye. Was he now to have everything he wanted? Was it more than a dream, was it a fact that a Jew in America could become a judge and sit on a high podium beneath the America flag?

"It's a great country," said Ben Eisen to his wife when he came home that night and announced that a guest was invited for dinner, "a country in which everyone has the freedom to get married."

"Yes," said his wife, who was grateful for her husband's elevated mood but was somewhat unclear as to what had caused it.

Howard Katz arrived at the Ben Eisen home in his best suit, although it was ragged at the cuffs and had been patched several times by his mother. He wore a flower in his lapel, and although his black shoes were scuffed and his shirt frayed at the collar, his face was shining with expectations. His opportunity had arrived.

What did he think when he first saw Bessie? Did he understand the proposition that had been offered to him? Bessie sat at the table on the right of her father with her head tucked over her chest like a small crow on a telephone wire, wary of the things above and below, and her eyes inspected the visitor without any particular interest. So many of her brother's friends had come to dinner and then never reappeared. They were polite enough but had made it clear that they were committed, about to go off on a trip; one had claimed medical troubles that would keep him in bed for a year, and another had asked her out to his country club for the July Fourth dance but then had broken his leg while playing baseball with some fraternity brothers and had never called again.

Bessie complained about the roast beef, and the maid had to take her plate out to the kitchen and bring her back a piece of chicken. Bessie said that the chauffeur was drinking and she wanted her father to fire him immediately. Ben Eisen agreed immediately. Julie discussed golf with Howard, who had not had the opportunity to learn the game but was polite and asked the right kinds of questions and admired Julie's handicap after it was explained to him. Howard welcomed the woman's right to vote and asked Bessie if she were pleased. Bessie said it wouldn't change anything and didn't look up from her plate.

Howard had never before been served his meal by anyone other than his mother, and he was afraid that he would do something wrong, use the wrong fork, knock over his glass of water. The napkin in his lap was made of a silk so soft that he wanted to put it to his face and hold it against his cheek. He didn't. He watched Julie and did everything Julie did, including taking two helpings of potatoes and waving away the broccoli. Howard had trouble speaking. He felt as he had the year before, when, determined to become a real New Yorker, he had wandered into St. Patrick's Cathedral on Fifth Avenue. He had become dizzy with the conviction that a giant hand was going to come out of the air and pick him up under his arms and throw him out, intruder in the glories of others. But Ben Eisen gently asked the visitor about his law studies, about his desire to be a judge, and Howard, feeling the older man's interest, his kindness, told him about Oliver Wendell Holmes and the role of the Supreme Court in preserving the checks and balances between the parts of the government. Ben Eisen looked into the young man's earnest eyes and prayed for success. Howard caught Ben Eisen's look and knew it for approval.

After dinner the young people went into the library and played a record that Julie had brought home. Julie held his sister by the waist and pulled her over the Oriental rug. Howard confessed he did not know how to dance at all. He asked Bessie to teach him, but she, who had been instructed by a private tutor, thought he was mocking her and sulked on a chair by the window.

Never mind, thought Howard Katz, who had understood it all. The moment he saw Bessie, he realized that his judgeship was not without a string, that he had not been asked to dinner because he had looked hungry. But then what in this world ever came free, what was without an obstacle to be overcome, and what was ever accomplished without hard work and sacrifice? Never mind, thought Howard Katz, looking at Bessie, who was complaining to her brother that the room was too hot. I'll find a way to your heart, and as for my heart, it belongs to my country and I will always serve it well.

There was a moment in the library when he saw Bessie by the lamp-light, and her complexion seemed to turn chartreuse and he saw how her shoulders bent toward each other in an effort to hide her unpromising chest, that he thought to himself that he ought to be careful, to take his time, to be sure. The sacrifice he would make might be more than he could survive, a man who had liked girls with long legs and had watched, across the fire escape, a woman wash herself, pouring water over her white breasts that hung like two huge moons over a tub in her kitchen. What he had felt then he might never feel again, and that made him sad, even he—the optimist, the believer in progress and the course of human events that had made it possible to overthrow tyranny and forget for all time the inalienable truths—even he could see that sacrifice was not an empty word but promised deprivations and other scaldings. Well, what of it? he thought. I am not the first man to sacrifice for my country.

Julie said, "What about those White Sox?"

Howard said, "I don't believe it, do you?" Julie shook his head.

Reader: Consider Bessie Eisen, not fair of face, not graceful in body or in manner. If she had been a male child, it would have mattered little. She could have been the vice president of the New World Bank and she could have become a champion golfer or the best chess player in the Bronx. She might have mastered billiards and poker and commanded secretaries and assistants and had a wife to rub her back when it was tired and children to command and a place on the board of the country club in Scarsdale and a place on the board of governors of the hospital and the home for the aged and the Federation of Jewish Philanthropies would one day have a dinner in her honor and while the mirror would never have been kind, the scope of her life would have been unlimited. A man without grace is not handicapped, whereas a woman is stripped of her capital, robbed of her opportunity, and worst of all, cannot find it in her heart to forgive herself, to admire herself, when no one else will. Ben Eisen thought he could purchase a husband and in so doing bring peace to his daughter, but how could she not have understood the unspoken bargain that had been sealed that first dinner, sealed before the custard with raspberry sauce arrived at the table? That bargain could bring her respectability, an appearance of normalcy, but it could not give her what every human being considers an inalienable right, the knowledge that one is wanted, desired, needed, by another. Without this, matters remain unsettled, and a lifetime stretches before, without expectations, without variety.

Ben Eisen was not able to save his daughter, but more credit to him that he tried. Reader, I know you are wondering why Bessie didn't take up community work, become an angel of mercy in the hospitals, the settlement houses, or take to the streets for Prohibition, the League of Nations, or homes for unwed mothers. Dear Reader, all of those refuges, places where self-respect can be redeemed and earn interest, were beyond the borders of Bessie's imagination. She had one place and one option and one career, could dream no dream but the one she was given, and the result was as much the fault of those who kept sending for dressmakers who would tuck and nip in the silk as it was the fault of Bessie, who had not learned how to love herself.

Mildred's Wedding: 1920

Mildred was married in the fall of 1920 at the Sherry Netherland Hotel. The guest list included the chairman of the board of Beth Israel Hospital, where her father, Isaac, had just years before taken a shovel and broken the ground. The Jewish press had covered the event, and there was a picture of him on the front page of the *Forward*. His hat covers his bald head, his shoulders are broad, and he wears a coat with a fur collar and has leather gloves on his hands. He does not smile for the camera. His eyes have dark circles under them in the photograph, and his mouth is tight. Something in the way he puts his foot on the shovel, leans his shoulder down, something in the black-and-whiteness of the photograph makes him look like a well-dressed gravedigger instead of a prominent member of the community whose generosity has made it possible for the Jews from the Eastern countries to have a hospital of their own, a place where their own young doctors, despised by the German Jewish establishment at Mt. Sinai Hospital uptown and rejected, of course, by the Gentile hospitals, can find appointments, a place where the kitchen will be kosher for those who need it, a hospital where the nursing staff will speak Yiddish and the poor Jews of the Lower East Side will be greeted at the emergency door with only the ordinary contempt for the ill.

In the photograph Naomi Gruenbaum, a widow, a woman whose hair has turned white, stands draped in a fur coat, with an ermine muff in which her hands are hidden. She seems small—tiny, even—in the background. If you look closely, perhaps with a magnifying glass, you can see that her eyes are wet. Is it just the reflection of light, or has the ceremony, the rabbi who has said the prayers stands with his tallis over his shoulders to the left, reminded her of something? In the gray light of the photograph, the workmen's tools laid on one side, the crowd of dignitaries pushed together on the right, one with a cane, one with a white scarf wrapped around his neck, the conscientious viewer can almost see the bodies, limbs and ears, organs and blood, that will soon tumble through the narrow halls, calling out to their Creator, "Is it for this that I was made in Your image?"

There were glove, shirt, and tie manufacturers at the wedding as well as two button companies represented. One by a teenage stepdaughter of a salesman, who lived in Brighton Beach, Arthur's date for the occasion, a tall, buxom girl named Mickey, a nickname she had given herself from the more proper Miriam, who kept pulling at her dress so that more and more of her chest was exposed. She had huge eyes that struggled to stay open under the weight of makeup she had plastered on her lids. She giggled and she wiggled and she shook the bracelets on her arms, and Arthur thought she was swell. In the coatroom he pressed her into the racks of hanging furs and smeared her lipstick, and made her nipples, which of course he couldn't see, stand up, lean forward, and rub against his starched white shirt.

At the wedding Flora, who was only ten years old, danced with her father. There is a photograph of that. Flora wore a pink dress that came down to her ankles, and she had a corsage of roses in her hair. Her glasses were tied by a velvet ribbon to the back of her head. Her arms were pudgy and the folds around her stomach showed through the shiny satin of her dress. Her father bends his knees and holds her as if she were a young lady. Behind the dancing couple one can see the band on a podium, saxes and trombones, drums and violins. Isaac bends over his youngest child. It is clear from his expression that here is a man dancing with someone he cherishes. Flora is wearing a pearl bracelet that catches the light and sends a white line across the photograph, cutting through her father's bald head and blurring the flowers on the table behind them.

Mildred at her wedding laughed and laughed and kissed all her former boyfriends and danced with everyone and made sure that all her girlfriends sat next to the man of their choice, and she took time to talk to all the bankers, accountants, investment specialists, the Bronx assistant district attorney, the first Jewish DA in America, the dress manufacturers and the shoe manufacturers and all the fabric suppliers and all the store owners, and head buyers, and all the hat manufacturers and the shippers, who sipped champagne and ate from gold-leafed plates heaped with cold salmon and cucumbers. Mildred wore a choker of rubies around her neck, and everyone said her wedding gown was the best of the season. Under the *chuppa* she stood next to Julie without a tremble, without a second thought. The rabbi said the words, Julie stepped on the glass hidden in the napkin, Mildred smiled and smiled and kissed her husband directly, splash in the center of his mouth. A twelve-piece orchestra played "Yes, We Have No Bananas."

"God, what a blessed world this is," Mildred said to her father when she passed him on the dance floor.

Isaac was tired. It seemed to him that he had lived forever, although he was still a young man, only forty-nine, sturdy and seasoned. "What a blessed world," he repeated to himself, but he could not manage the conviction that bounded, like a racehorse four lengths ahead, through his daughter's words.

At Mildred's wedding her aunt Ruth was wearing a blue silk gown with yellow tassels at the hem. She wore a blue hat on her head and a veil, the veil she always wore to prevent the world from seeing what in fact they saw all too clearly, her skin red and raw. Her eyes were dark tonight, and one could see if you looked carefully that once they were beautiful, they had long lashes and a clear gaze, but her left eye had been pulled down as tissue healed and now seemed too close to her nose. Her black hair was piled in a bun at the back. She wore a ruby necklace that was a gift from her brother Isaac, a wedding present to her the day she had married. She had not worn it since. Her husband would not come to the wedding, and she had not pressed him. Her brother Isaac was always kind to him, but there was distance between them. They breathed a different way, one from the other. Her sons, Meyer and Eli, and her daughter, Sharon, had not come with her. Her husband would not allow it. He would not approve of the blue silk dress that his wife wore, the one her sister-in-law had sent her and begged her to wear to the wedding.

Howard Katz had been invited, and he danced with Bessie and sat next to her at the head table with the bride and groom. He put his arm around Bessie's waist. Julie had paid for his dancing lessons as a gift, a gift to a friend, he had said, not a future brother-in-law, but Howard knew why the lessons were paid for and he accepted them. He moved his body self-consciously across the floor. He still counted in his head as he made his steps—one two, one two three.

"So," said Mildred's mother, Annie, to one of her friends, "even Bessie has a partner tonight. For every pot there's a cover." And her friend agreed.

Mildred went out of her way to be nice to Howard Katz, giving him her most dazzling smile. "Join us this summer at Atlantic Beach." she said. "You could take a house and come down on weekends."

Howard did not look at the other girls at the party. He kept his eyes on Bessie, who ordered him to get her a different flavor ice cream, who hardly talked to him, as if he were a nobody, a servant of the family. He pulled his gilt-framed chair closer to her and reached for her hand. She let him take it. What else could she do? What else should he have done?

Harry had no date for his sister's wedding. He was shy. He was round and had thighs far too heavy for a man not yet twenty-two. He wore glasses that pinched on his nose, and one of his eyes was off center, giving him the look of a man who wasn't concentrating, who saw things in the sky, who might in fact be a little unbalanced. His mouth was softly shaped, and he had the thick high forehead of his grandfather and the black eyes of his grandmother. He watched others carefully, wanting to join them, wanting to be a part, but not knowing just how. He envied Arthur, his younger brother, for his easy conversation with old ladies, men, and young girls. He especially envied Arthur his date, Mickey, who bounced up and down the aisles between the tables, seeming never to be able to sit still, whose wide lips were moist with fruit punch, helped by the contents of the silver flask that Arthur kept in his hip pocket. Mickey cooed and bubbled and stuck out her ankles that showed beneath her dress and smiled at Harry as if he were as handsome as his brother, as if he weren't someone most people tended to ignore. Harry's eyes followed Mickey all across the dance floor. He wanted to ask her to dance with him, but he didn't dare. She wouldn't, he just knew she wouldn't.

Arthur told Mickey, "My brother is a great guy, he's going to be president of the company one day, and I'll be the vice president."

Mickey thought everything about the wedding was great, fancy, just the cat's meow, as far away as she could get from Brighton Beach, where her mother took in gentlemen on rainy afternoons and her stepfather sometimes tried to put his hands where he shouldn't and there was only one bathroom and the paint was peeling and her mother shouted at her to pipe down when Mickey jumped out of bed in the morning and yelled, just yelled because it felt good, everything in her felt good, except living in Brighton Beach. Harry brought a large piece of cake to the table. Flora had already finished hers. She stared at her brother's. Harry cut his cake in half and pushed the larger piece onto Flora's plate.

In the ladies' room Mickey said to Flora, "Hey, little girl, tell your brother Harry I think he's swell." Flora told him.

With that Harry found the courage to ask Mickey to dance. Arthur was talking to someone else. He turned around and saw that his brother was smiling into the face of his date. She was touching his cheek just the way moments before her hands had been on his own face, giving him goose bumps all over. Harry was older, but Arthur was the one everyone liked. Arthur was easy with a smile and a kiss. Arthur remembered people's names and what they liked to talk about. Arthur was one of the guys whose golf game was good, who did tricks with his cards. Arthur could be counted on if a fellow was in trouble. Arthur had friends calling him, inviting him out for a game or a party all the time, while Harry was always bumbling about, not sure of just what it was he should say. Girls paid no attention to Harry, who kept his head tilted away from them so they wouldn't notice his wandering eye. Arthur was fond of his brother. Arthur thought he needed protecting, even though Arthur was the younger and Harry the older. He brought Harry along to his parties and told Harry some jokes to tell the guys, but they never came out right. Now Arthur couldn't believe what he saw on the dance floor: the girl he had brought was just snuggling there next to Harry's chest, as if she belonged there. Arthur cut in.

"My date," he said.

Harry looked at him and mumbled, "Sorry." He blushed but didn't move away. "I didn't mean," he said to Arthur, and his face was all covered with pain and confusion.

"You think being older gives you a right?" said Arthur, whose blue eyes were focused very clearly, despite the drink.

Harry shook his head but didn't take his hand off Mickey's arm. She kept on leaning against him just as if Arthur were not there. It took Arthur a moment to sort it all out. He considered punching his brother in his mouth, knocking his glasses to the floor. But he couldn't, not at his sister's wedding. The girl wasn't worth it. He was just fooling around. Who needed her? Not him; he had many, while poor Harry had none.

"I'm going to sit with Flora," he said to Harry. "Go on dancing."

Harry smiled, a trembling smile, and he hugged his brother to his wide chest. "I'll never forget this," he said, "never."

He better not, thought Arthur as he walked to the bar. But he felt good, good enough to ask Flora to dance and to kiss the top of her head when he dipped down.

Max came to Mildred's wedding, and perhaps he shouldn't have. He arrived just in time for the ceremony. He was dressed in spats and a tux, and he carried a white cane with a pearl top. He had a gray high hat and he tossed it up in the air and caught it again when the rabbi began to speak. He brought with him a skinny young woman in a low-cut gown who was obviously not a friend of the family, perhaps a cook or a maid from Ireland or from Scotland. She had tiny ankles and she wore many petticoats that flashed bright colors as she twirled around on the dance floor. She was much younger than Max, younger even than Mildred.

"That's disgusting," said Mildred's mother, Annie, to her best friend. "He's always embarrassing us."

But that wasn't the end of the embarrassment. The young lady had a loud laugh somewhere between a horse's whinny and a cackle, and something about the ceremony, the way the rabbi lifted his arms, something about the Hebrew, a language she might not have heard before, something about the way that Mildred had to lean way down and crane her neck to the side to kiss her husband, struck the young woman as funny, and her laugh, not the music of the gods, floated over the room. Heads turned to see who had emitted that sound, and when the young lady saw that people were staring at her, she just laughed harder and couldn't stop. This made Max laugh. He roared with her. The rabbi went on, the bride and the groom pretended not to hear, but Isaac's face burned. His brother, his brother had a way of always being there and never being helpful. But that wasn't the worse part of the story, that was just the prelude.

There was a lot of liquor pulled from the coat closet, disguised in bottles of milk. There was dancing and eating, eating and drinking, toasting and drinking, and all of sudden Max stood up on his chair, his bad leg resting on the white tablecloth. "Ladies and gentlemen, Jews and non-Jews—and with that he nodded to the lady he had escorted to the wedding—"I want to toast my niece, who in marrying so well has done the family proud, and I want to tell her that the best way to lie with a man is with your legs spread wide open, your mouth open, and your ass up in the air . . . openness. Openness, that's the secret to it."

Isaac moved to pull his brother down from the chair, Mildred shrieked in horror. The members of the Eisen family tried to pretend they hadn't heard a thing, and they clinked their glasses and knocked their silverware together to drown him out.

"What a tragedy," they whispered, "a brother like that in the family, hope it isn't inherited."

"I hear it was an accident, the leg, I mean, the rest God knows."

The young lady wasn't used to drinking or to drinking whatever Max was pouring from his private supply, and she turned a little green before Max could finish. He had more to say, and just as Isaac was not so gently pulling on his brother's sleeve, she threw up on Max's white shoes, which were resting one on the chair, the other on the table. Trying to jump out of the way of the vomit, which did not appeal to him at all, Max lurched forward and fell with a horrible bang against the table edge. He lay on the floor, and blood appeared on his forehead.

Isaac picked up his little brother, whose body had never grown straight, who had an office with his name over the door in the business but whose main function was to exchange stories with the salesmen, who had enough of their own. What I am to do with you? thought Isaac, and he pitied him even as he caught himself hoping that the accident might be fatal and his brother taken instantly off his hands. Ashamed of his thought, Isaac cradled his brother in his arms. His sister, Ruth, was there on the floor beside him, and Isaac looked at her face, healed but not healed, and he saw in her crooked eyes a grief he recognized which shamed him further.

Ruth wiped her brother's head, but the bleeding didn't stop. Ruth put Max's head in her lap and bound one of the large hotel napkins around his forehead, but the blood seeped through. "Sorry," whispered Max, "I'm no good at formal occasions."

"Yes," said his sister.

The dancers went on to the floor, stepping over the uncle, who lay on the ground, his head resting in the aunt's lap.

"Couldn't they find a suitable woman for him?" growled one of Julie's cousins.

"They tried," said someone, who claimed intimate knowledge, "but who would have him, money and all?" Who indeed.

Some young men from the company, the chief buyer of wools and the head of the Boston district who had been invited to the wedding, carried him out the door. Max's young woman was crying and crying, and only Flora was comforting her with a handkerchief dipped in champagne. Flora brought her a piece of wedding cake, and the young lady calmed down and spent the rest of the evening sitting in a corner trying to clean the considerable stains off her dress. She stopped laughing, which everyone thought was a blessing.

Max had been taken to the hospital and the doctors put a plaster on his head. "Wonderful party, wonderful wedding," he said to Isaac when he came to visit him at home the next day. "That girl that was with Arthur . . . or was it Harry? Reminds me of Peachie, a dead ringer, in fact. I was thinking of Peachie all night, that's why I got drunk. I looked happy, but I wasn't. You're my brother, you understand," said Max.

Am I my brother's keeper? thought Isaac, who knew the answer.

Bessie asked, "Why did they invite him?"

"Family," said her father. "You never turn your back on family."

The young couple sailed for France the following day. The honeymoon was uneventful; that is to say Mildred shopped in Paris at the best stores and Julie took walks along the Seine and in the evening after dinner she put on her finest lingerie and Julie reached for his bride and she closed her eyes and allowed him—wasn't this how it was supposed to be?—to touch her breasts, to open her mouth with his tongue and place it, thick and searching, down her palate. She allowed him to spread her legs and place his plump body on top of hers. Her feet extended out beyond his. He rode her, his dolphin, his mermaid, his ship of pleasure, to the point of release. She endured it bravely. She endured it the way she allowed the hairdresser to make spit curls at the side of her head, the way she soaked her feet in Epsom salts to prevent bunions, the way she endured the corset that held her stomach in tight and pushed her thighs together. Increasingly, wishing it were not so, Mildred longed for home. She didn't like the way Julie smelled after his walk. She didn't like the way he allowed a spot of sauce béarnaise to stay on his tie. She didn't find his conversation about his ninety-two par at the last club tournament intriguing. She longed for a friend to talk to about the dresses she had seen in a boutique on rue St. Pierre. She walked in the Palais Royal beside him and worried, for the first time, that others would think it odd, that such a tall girl should be with a short round man. She looked into his eyes, dark and round with black lashes that she had once found so appealing, and saw that he looked sad and would always look sad.

"Cheer up," she said to him, "be gay."

And he tried, but something held him back. The truth was, the truth that neither of them could admit was, that two weeks in Paris was too long and they were bored. They purchased presents for everyone in the family. Flora would receive a French doll with her blond hair piled up on top of her head and secured with a veil of sequins. Julie looked at his new wife and wondered if he would find something to say to her at dinner.

"Keep your eyes open," he begged her while opening the window to the Parisian air.

"All right," she said, and staring straight ahead, she made out the guest list for their first dinner party in their new home that she had furnished with beaded sofas and Tiffany lamps and rugs from Persia with her mother's help.

"Are you happy?" said Julie.

"Of course I'm happy," said Mildred. "I'm going to be happy for the rest of my life." And she believed it.

Julie grew morose. He expected less of women by the time the boat finally docked in the New York harbor. Mildred looked splendid and waved to her mother. Julie had developed a walk that included a shuffle, a sort of scraping along of the legs, that did not look so well on the future president of the New World Bank. They took up residence in the Apthorp, a large new building made to look like a Victorian castle, a fortress and a mansion combined. Their windows looked out over the Hudson River, and Mildred, when the maid drew her red velvet living room curtains, could see the very same waters that two hundred years before bore the *Half Moon* up to Albany at a time when all was wilderness and savages were adequately protected by the gods that resided in the wind and the trees.

Hedy Understands That All Dreams Do Not Come True: 1945

Hedy was sitting on the carpet beside her mother's bed. Both her knees were covered with scabs from her last fall on roller skates. She had gone down the hill leaning her body forward into the wind and had not quite made the turn at Lexington Avenue because a lamppost had appeared unexpectedly. Her mother's bed jacket, a pale blue silk with lace flowers that draped over her breasts, was speckled with silver in the morning light. The breakfast tray sat at the end of the bed, and Flora had taken the first of her morning Camels and was blowing smoke rings over the head of her daughter. It was June and the tulips were standing erect in the little islands at the center of Park Avenue. A warm breeze blew the white curtains up over the sill.

Hedy said, "I wish I could field like Pee Wee Reese."

Flora said, "I wish I could sing like Sharie Lee."

Hedy Learns How Her Mother's Cousin Sharon Herzberg Joined the Blue Onion Jazz Babies—A Great Secret: 1922

Sharon Herzberg had black hair and clear white skin and deep eyes that surrounded her slightly odd nose, a nose with a bump in the middle and a turn-up at the end that gave her a quaint look, not like something from the pages of *Vogue* magazine. She had a broad smile that seemed to quiver in her face, floating free for a second and settling back into her features in a most amazing way. Everything she felt crossed her face, so sometimes she looked like a woman waving good-bye at a railroad station or like a child who has noticed the first snowflakes of winter and stuck out a tongue so that the miracle can be confirmed. When sad, Sharon looked like one who had just seen a dead body in a coffin waiting for events to proceed.

Sharon had every moment she had ever experienced trapped in her larynx, just waiting for her to call it up, open her mouth, and release it, buried in the notes of music. Joseph still did not like to hear his daughter sing. When she was in her room practicing for the Thursday lesson, if he were home, he would put his hands over his ears. When she sang along with the radio, the songs of the day, he would walk out on the front steps or retreat into the tiny room that served as his study. What will become of Sharon? he asked his Lord, who did not answer, perhaps because he did not know.

When Ruth took Sharon to the Palladium for the talent show, she didn't tell her husband. She wrote a letter to Isaac, who said, Yes, do it, and mailed her the entrance fee. Isaac thought it was nice that his niece had a lovely voice. She will get married, he thought, probably one of those weak-eyed ones with the books and the prayers, and she will sing to her babies. However, Ruth kept on stalling when Joseph suggested a match. "She's not old enough. She has time. She can choose herself. In America women choose for themselves. I chose you," said Ruth, and kissed her husband on the lips, which made him forget the subject at hand.

Sharon was seventeen years old and she attended shul only on the High Holidays, and then her voice could be heard from the balcony through the whole congregation. Joseph would shudder and say to God, "Do something, change her voice, give it to one of my sons. How can our voice"—he never thought of it as Sharon's—"serve you in the body of a girl?" But God had no opinion on the matter.

She won the Palladium competition and was written up in the *Baltimore Times,* and there was a picture of her a quarter of a page in size. "Look at that, Mama," Sharon said, and Ruth looked and looked and clipped it out of the paper.

"No," said Joseph, "she may not go to New York to become a singer. What kind of thing is that for a good girl to do? No," said Joseph, "never. She must be married. She cannot go off alone."

"You," said Ruth, "you came to America, all alone, and found me, so it wasn't so bad, and she is only going to New York and will stay with Isaac and nothing will happen to her."

"She won't eat kosher there," said Joseph. "No," he said. "In that house, she will learn to be a whore."

Ruth got angry, and Joseph went into his study and wept. The rabbi he consulted, the wise rabbi who was said to get his rulings right from the angels' mouths, said, "No, no, she must not go to her uncle's. If she goes, she will never return."

"Just for a year," said Ruth.

"No," said Joseph, "if she goes, she will never return."

"Papa," said Sharon, "let me sing in the synagogue, from the *bimah*, like you. Let me sing with you. I know all the music." And she opened her mouth, and the sound that came out was that of Sarah, Rebecca, and Rachel and Deborah and Naomi in the desert, these were not sounds that decent Jewish men should hear, they carried with them the rolling of the body in birth and the rocking of the hips in conception and the waiting and the searching and the weariness of travel and the longing for Elijah who was coming and the promise of Elijah that had been given to men and women alike. Joseph's heart was pulled into a thousand pieces. "I cannot," he said. "You cannot," he said.

"I'm going to New York," said Sharon, and Joseph went into his study and didn't come out for three days. When he emerged, pale and his legs trembling and his eyes red, his daughter had taken the train to New York and that was that.

She was given a bed in Flora's room. Though she was older than Flora, she told the younger girl secrets, about the man she had met on the el down to music school who had promised to take her to a nightclub to hear real music, the way it was in New York. "Don't tell," she said to Flora, who didn't tell, not even when Sharon told her about her new friend, the man who played the sax in a band, a traveling band, a Negro.

"A Negro, like Willow in the laundry?" said Hedy.

"Yes," said Flora, "a Negro."

"Then he wasn't Jewish?" asked Hedy.

"Not Jewish," said her mother. "But don't tell anyone I told you. This is a secret." This is what Flora told Hedy when she asked about Sharon and how it had happened, and what happened, while they were having black-and-white sodas at Longchamps before they went to the movies to see Ingrid Bergman in *Spellbound* at the Translux 85th Street.

Reader: Have you noticed that the best stories are secret, and the best secrets are stories?

• • •

It wasn't that Sharon was able to forget her parents just like that. It wasn't that she took one breath of New York air and became intoxicated. It wasn't even that the best jobs for singers were in the nightclubs, places her father couldn't even imagine, so far were they from the opening and the closing of the ark that held the Torah. It wasn't that she didn't know how Jewish girls behaved in Baltimore, but she wasn't in Baltimore anymore and the entire world was hers to win and woo. She saw no lines that shouldn't be crossed, having crossed the threshold of her father's house, and in the wondrous openness of the world she wandered down to 42nd Street and bought a hot dog from a vendor. Her hot dog was filled with pork. She chewed it carefully and considered the likelihood that God was watching, was weeping. The street noise was horrible, especially horrible for a person who heard each note with perfect clarity, but it was also clear to Sharon, standing there in the gray dress that buttoned up to her throat that her mother had bought her to wear on the train, that God did not have time for her or her hot dog. So she wiped the mustard off her lips and said to herself over and over, I am a singer and a singer must find a place to sing.

She had gone for an audition to the Paramount Theater, where they had a chorus entertaining in the lobby. She waited a long time in line, and when it was her turn she stood up by the piano that was sitting in the lobby, underneath the golden chandeliers, to the side of the red velvet carpet that wound up the staircase and reached into the upper balcony. She sang "Who Ate Napoleons with Josephine When Bonaparte Was Away." Her pitch was perfect. She was pretty, too, and perhaps that, even more than the voice, convinced the manager.

"Yes," he said.

"Yes," she answered, hardly surprised. The voice that had begun at the Baal Shem's side was surely good enough for the Paramount. It was there she met the other girls, Meg and Constanza and Kelly, and they told her that the big stars got their starts at the jazz clubs, uptown, downtown.

She went one night when Annie and Isaac were already in bed and Flora was long asleep. She let herself out of the house and walked along Riverside Drive in the dark, afraid but not afraid enough, and she walked uptown until she found a street with a bar and some music, some real musicians playing, and she stayed outside and listened. She tapped her feet. She liked what she heard. She went in and asked for a job, a white kid with a trembling smile and black hair that looked like it had just come out of braids, a kid who wanted to sing.

In the club the smoke was thick. The second set began at midnight.

She wasn't tired. She thought of her mother and father under their quilt and her brothers, Meyer and Eli, limbs out of their beds, Hebrew books on the floor, yarmulkes on the dresser, the streetlight shining on the bare floor. Good-bye, she said to herself.

A man noticed her, a tall Negro man who played the drums. "Hey, look what came our way." He gestured and offered to buy her a drink. It was her first drink, not so long after her first hot dog. It made her feel like there was nothing, but nothing, she couldn't do. He offered her a cigarette. "A Camel. I'd walk a mile," he said, and she smiled. She took it and drew in a deep breath and began to cough. "Your first?" said the man.

She looked in the mirror and then glared at him. "Everyone has to have a first," she said.

"Okay with me," he said.

Inside the bar the people moved and talked and touched each other, men and women with low-cut blouses, and there was a smell in the air, one Sharon liked, liked a lot. It meant that there was no upstairs for women and no downstairs for men and the odors of both mingled with smoke and alcohol and food that was also not separated into milk and meat. Everything together, it excited Sharon. The light in the bar was violet, and pink and yellow globes hung above the stage where the musicians had been earlier. The smoke curled through the colored lights.

"I'm Sharon from Baltimore," she said.

"Me," said the man, "I'm Louie Alabama. Alabama's my home."

"Holy cow," said Sharon, who knew nothing about Alabama. "I don't think they like Jews down there," she said. "I'm Jewish." This much she owed her father and her mother, and this much she never forgot.

"I'm raised Baptist," he said, "but I bet we got the same stories, you and me."

She smiled. "Tell me about Baptists," she said, and he did.

After she had stood on the stage with the other musicians and sung, the way she did for her music teacher, the way she did at home in the bathtub, the way that made her father put his hands over his ears, she was on, a member, regular, a funny thing, a white girl who had a voice that knew about not getting what you want, that knew about waiting and how it was for the mamas when their children were gone and how it was for the boys when the girls betrayed them and how it was for a girl to be beaten before she had begun, and how she knew all this and how this voice came to be, they couldn't imagine.

"Hey," said the drummer, "you real good," and she was.

A few nights after her first visit to the club, it was clear that she would sing with them on their tour. After she showed that she could learn anything in a moment, one hearing and she had it, that she could improvise up and down her larynx as well as Larry on the sax, Louie took her to his room in a walk-up hotel after the last set and the bar had emptied. She was worried because she had to get back to the house before her aunt and uncle woke up. She was worried because she wasn't sure what was supposed to happen next and she knew that somewhere in Baltimore, her mother was awake, staring out the window, thinking her thoughts.

Up the stairs, with their peeling walls and the smell of urine and insect repellent, into the room with a sink and a bed and a Bible in a drawer and a bare light bulb swinging above, Louie thumped with his hands on his dresser and the rhythm was a call. Sharon sat on the bed and he offered her a drink from a bottle that appeared in a paper bag from under his bed, and he said, "Where I come from a guy can't touch a girl like you. White, like you."

"I believe," said Sharon, sitting up very straight, "that all people should love each other and that there are no rules, of who can touch who and when. . . . I think," said Sharon, who did not know that other people had thought this, too, "that there should be no rules."

"My kind of girl," said Louie Alabama.

"What happens next?" said Sharon. He asked her to take off her blouse. She was shocked.

"No rules," he said. "Why not? What are you afraid of? I won't touch unless you tell me it's all right."

And so she took off her blouse and under the bare bulb she turned toward him, and he looked and he looked and he didn't move from his place on the bed and she felt strange things in her nipples as if they were leaning out toward him, as if her genitals were pulling her apart, burning her suddenly and throbbing urgently. His hands drummed on the bed. She stood still and straightened her spine so her breasts would rise higher, and finally he said, "Let me touch with my lips," and she shuddered because here she was as the dawn was rising over the East River, in the heart of Harlem where she did not belong and there were no Jews around at all, and her mother was looking out the window at the backyard and wondering about her, and here she was in this room, about to let this man do the things that were not permitted. But there were no rules and she knew there were no rules, no rules if you had to sing, no rules if you weren't at home in your house, and she slipped off her skirt without being asked and Louie put his fingers on the tops of her thighs and beat his message straight to her heart, and she lay down with him and he hurt her and she cried, but she had no intention of going home.

Sharon had told Flora and only Flora that she was joining the Blue

Onion Jazz Babies on their tour. Flora helped her pack a few things, some underwear, a photograph of her brothers taken on Purim while they were wearing masks, a blouse she had bought in a store on Fifth Avenue, some perfume that had been Mildred's and was given to Flora, who gave it to her cousin. The gray dress she gave to Flora, who never grew tall enough to wear it and wouldn't have wanted to anyway. It hung in her closet, reminding her of Sharon, who drew air deep into her lungs and sang out the window so that people on the other side of Riverside Drive, people walking under the trees, pushing baby carriages, would stop and listen.

When Joseph found out—and it took Ruth many weeks before she could bring herself to tell him that Sharon had run off, was probably in a place called Cleveland with a band named the Blue Onion Jazz Babies and was fine and would be in touch with them all soon—he went into the bathroom and threw up in the toilet, over and over again. "No," he said, "she can't do that." But she had. It wasn't right for a girl to travel without her mother. It would make her unmarriageable. What respectable boy would want her? He knew, it had happened back in Russia, the wild ones went to Moscow, one joined a circus and was found murdered in a ditch several towns away. The girls who fooled with peasants and got bellies big and terrible, they drowned in the stream, they ran off to the whorehouses of Petrov and Vilna and were never heard from again. His beautiful Sharon, his baby who had smiled at him above all others, who had sat in his lap or played quietly at his feet as he stood before the ark and led the congregation, she was gone. It was Ruth's fault for taking her for singing lessons. Ruth's fault, he cried out, but he knew it was the fault of the voice in the body of the wrong child. It was a cruel trick, and despite himself, despite years of discipline, despite all that he had done to comfort other mourners, he found himself loving his God with less than a full heart. He also noticed for the first time that his wife's face had not become better with age but increased in its original disfigurement. . . .

The Blue Onion Jazz Babies and Their White Vocalist: 1922 and After

At first it was enough that the room quieted down when the music started, with the first drumbeat and the beginning throb of the sax, at first it was perfect. She didn't mind the hotel beds that had roaches on the sheets and the smell of urine in the hall. At first she didn't mind the bus stations at dawn with the men snoring in the seats, their flies open and their bags at their feet. Sharon had wanted to get out of Baltimore and see the world, and she was, wasn't she?

In the clubs she stood in a red velvet dress that Louie had picked out for her up at 138th Street, one that showed the things her father believed should be covered, and though the spot was up on the band, she kept her head down until four bars before she started. Then Sharon, who had changed her name to Sharie Lee, felt a tightening in the chest, a searing, burning sensation behind her eyes and a desire to open her throat and let the sound out, up and down, round and round. The audiences, in the little bars in the dark streets in the backside of towns with the bartenders serving all through the set and the smoke in the spot whirling and whirling like so many ghosts of childhoods lost, the audiences gasped. It was a real sound, a white girl with the real sound, and it cracked inside their heads and rose to the ceiling and circled the mirror behind the bar, and it made the women squeeze their thighs together and the men lean back in their chairs trying to pretend it hadn't got to them, made them make promises they could never keep. Something she did with her voice as it slid up and down the scale made the audience remember that they were in it, all of them, over their heads and would never get out till they died. And when she was finished they demanded more and more, until Alabama would signal her to leave the stage and she would, but reluctantly. She never understood why she couldn't go on and on.

They went to bigger clubs, where the women wore silk dresses and the spots were pink and blue, where the lounge seats against the wall were maroon velvet and the tables shiny ebony with chrome ashtrays as big as plates and drinks were served with maraschino cherries and the bathrooms smelled of the toilet water sprayed by an old woman who had a dish for tips and offered towels and lipstick, and sanitary pads for a fee. She got used to mirrors over her head, behind her back, and on all sides, so that if she caught the right angle, she could see herself multiplied into infinity.

They ate in diners where the waitresses looked at the white girl and sometimes spilled Coca-Cola on her dress. They rode in the back of buses so that her color wouldn't start anyone off, and still it did sometimes—a remark was made by a white guy and the bus driver would ask the whole band to get off. Once in a while this happened in between towns, and they slept folded on top of the instruments on the grass between the shoulder and the gravel, waiting for dawn and the opportunity to hitch with a Negro who had a truck going their way. Sometimes that took a long time, and they missed the date in the town ahead. It was all right with Sharie Lee. She knew she was going places. "Experience, baby, that's what it is," said Alabama, and she knew she was getting experience.

She smoked all the time now. Anything they gave her. She also took a drink, a drink from the customers who asked her to their table after the set. Bourbon, Scotch, she didn't care. Her father had made wine in the cellar for Passover. Each fall he bought the grapes at a market downtown, and then as the weather turned colder he would go down to the cellar and pound them with a board and then put the mixture in two bottles for Passover. Even the children would have a cup, and a cup of the dark red liquid was left on the table for Elijah, who might come, who did come, who should have something for his trouble. But this was different, this made a trail down the larynx, this was the elixir of the real world, of America. This was the stuff of her new life, and now she was Elijah going from table to table, throwing back her head and pouring down the liquid that was brought for her and sometimes it made her head turn and sometimes it made her stomach clutch and heave, and yet it also made her sleep anywhere as sound as if she were home in her bed in Baltimore. Louie said, "The night needs drink," and he was right.

"New York," said Sharie. "I want to go to New York."

"Soon, baby, soon we going back to New York," said Alabama.

"I want to sing in New York," said Sharie.

"You will," said Alabama, "you will."

They got to St. Louis and he looked up an old friend, and it turned out it was a she and she was a singer, too, and she didn't think so much of Sharie Lee. One night after the last set, while the boys were packing up and Sharie was sitting at a table to the side, she looked up on the stage and there was Alabama dancing and his hips were rocking back and forth attached to his old friend's hips as if the socket joints were one. Sharie Lee stood up and threw a glass at them. The lady came down from the stage and pushed Sharie Lee, not a nice playground push, not a pinch or a hair pull, like Sharie knew from when she was Sharon, but a shove and kick with a spike heel, and she went over on her face right on the pieces of glass that were lying there on the red carpet all jagged. One of them cut right into her check and blood poured out and Sharie Lee cried and Alabama walked off with his old friend and the saxophone player had to go to the hospital with Sharie. They made her wait and wait, a white girl with a nigger guy and a cut on her face, and when they asked her to give an address and she wouldn't, the nurse in attendance made a face. So Sharon Herzberg had a scar that took its own sweet time healing, and when she got up to sing, she always put some extra makeup on. Alabama bought it for her and showed her how to use it so that it was rubbed in right and didn't run under the hot lights.

After that Sharie noticed that in the mornings she had a headache and in the night when she was done singing there was a thirst in her that took a long time quenching, and that her voice had a new vibration, a high, barely audible tremor that sounded like a hand splashing in the water far off from shore, reaching for a piece of wood as the current carried her on, reaching and reaching. The audience loved the new sound. They clapped so hard that they made her do it again and again. It would come at the end of the notes, when the sax was supposed to go on without her, and somehow she didn't stop and she went with the sax as if they were twinned, as if the sax itself were her piece of wood; but it wasn't, and when she was finished she was tired.

That was when she first called Ruth to tell her she was married. It was a lie. She thought her mother would prefer it to the truth.

"Come home," said Ruth. "Leave him."

"Who are you to judge a person by appearances?" said Sharon.

Ruth was ashamed. "But he's not Jewish. He's a Negro," she said. "Something will happen to you."

"I hope so," said Sharon, and hung up the phone.

Sharon sent postcards to her cousin Flora, postcards from Detroit and Cleveland, notes on matchbooks from places called the Palms, the Coconut, the Magnolia, Dixie's, and Mama's. Flora kept the matchbooks in the box that held her hair ribbons, her extra pair of glasses, and the gold ring she had been given for her twelfth birthday. Each shiny book, red, maroon, and silver, brought a new tender tickle to her rising nipples. At night when she was asleep, her cousin Sharon was spinning out across America. It made Flora dizzy. It made Flora scared. It made Flora call her sister, Mildred, who told her that Sharon was a black sheep and never to mention her name again, not in this family. Flora took out the matchbooks that had come with a message inscribed on the white insides: "Hi, good girl, I love you." Flora opened her window that looked over the drive and saw the moon on the Hudson River, full like a belly, a shape inside it, a shadow of a mountain seen from five hundred thousand miles away. "I love you, too," said Flora out into the air.

They were on their way back to New York. Alabama and Sharon still shared a room, but sometimes he would leave the bar early and she would get back to the hotel, walk up the steps, past the sleeping night watchman, brush against the peeling wallpaper, prints of George Washington crossing the Delaware or faded roses climbing blue vines, hallways where the single light bulb hung useless on a wire and sometimes a wino set fire to his bed and they all had to climb down the stairs in the early dawn and stand drinking coffee from paper cups till it was all right to go back to bed, and she'd find Alabama had locked the door and the sounds within were unmistakable.

"All right," said Sharon, who had not loved Alabama so much as the opportunity he was giving her. "All right," said Sharon, "it's time I moved on and got back to New York." And she told Alabama she was leaving, wanted her pay, wanted out. She'd had enough.

He cried real tears dripping down into his coffee cup and promised to be faithful and, more important, promised he'd bring her to the Apollo, a star by April.

Sharon thought of her father, who never lied to her. She thought of her father whose voice she carried, and she missed the sound of his voice, practicing from his study, practicing what it had no further need to practice. She missed the sound of Hebrew, whose meanings she didn't really know, the language in which her people spoke to their God, who answered in wind bursts or burning bushes or had nothing to say for centuries. She thought about going home to her parents in Baltimore, but what waited for her there? Besides, she was someone else, not Sharon Herzberg anymore, but Sharie Lee, and Sharie Lee had other places to go.

Then she missed her period and because she was traveling, eating on the run, sleeping in different places every few days, she lost track and missed another, and then it was clear that biology follows like a shadow, biology like the mark of Cain on the human brow is everywhere, and even if you change your address frequently, it finds you and brings you low. Sharie thought, just for a moment she thought, that she had gotten pregnant because God was angry with her for using her voice, not to praise him, but to astonish the audience, to make the owner of the club give her an extra tip, to make herself into the thing that was worshiped. Because that happened, she knew it; when the applause came it was as if the people had gathered to lay goats at her feet, to burn lambs in her honor, as if she were an idol with ruby eyes who could change the weather or the chemistry of the soil. God had cause to be angry with her, she knew. But she didn't believe he had followed her out of Baltimore, here to Cincinnati. She was disguised as Sharie Lee. She decided God did not know or care that she was singing with the Blue Onion Jazz Babies. She was a free woman, and she had not been punished: she had been caught, a whole other matter.

So Sharie went with Alabama to a woman he knew in Cincinnati, where they happened to be, and she gave Sharie a big drink right out of a bottle and laid her down on a table and pulled off her skirt and her undies, and though Sharie tried to hold her legs closed to protect the thing she did not want, the woman pulled her legs apart while Alabama waited in the room outside and played gin rummy with the woman's man. Sharie screamed, and the sound set the glass beads on the lamp on the table tinkling, and the hurt was followed by the warm feeling of blood over her white thighs.

"White girl, stop being such a baby," said the woman as Sharie's cries went on and on. The woman slapped Sharie in the face. "What you think," she said, "you my first customer, this hasn't happened to anybody else in the world but you?"

Later back in the hotel room, Sharie began to get hot and dry and called out for water. Maxie, the guy on the piano, who was staying down the hall, came in and looked at her and at the blood that was seeping through the blankets, and an ambulance was called. It took its own time, the way it always did in those back streets of Cincinnati, where the porters and the bellhops and the conductors and the janitors lived, and the grandsons and the granddaughters of slaves made all their own choices as free men and free women. Finally Sharie was brought down the narrow stairs on a stretcher, her fever raging; singing, she was, in a foreign language the ambulance attendants didn't know.

The medical bill was high, and Alabama claimed he couldn't pay it, which was why Sharie called her mother and told her about the accident. When the doctor told her that she wouldn't be getting pregnant anymore, Sharie shrugged. She was a singer anyway, not a mother. If she'd wanted to be a mother, she'd have stayed in Baltimore. She didn't worry about the disciple of the Baal Shem, who would get his voice next. She had it. That was enough.

Reader: You think Sharon Herzberg should go home. A white girl, a Jewish girl, traveling with a band in a country that doesn't like the colors mixing, doesn't like niggers getting uppity and isn't so fond of Jews, not in their hotels, not in their country clubs, not in their businesses, not in their universities. Reader, I agree. Sharon Herzberg would have been much better off if she had married the son of the rabbi in Alexandria, Virginia, and moved with him to his new congregation in Duluth or Topeka, or if she had to rebel, she could have stayed in New York, married one of the young men that her aunt Annie could introduce her to, a man in investments or undergarments or vacuum cleaners. She could even have found a young lawyer in the crowd or the owner of a few houses in Brooklyn or someone with property on Fifth Avenue. Flora said so. Flora told Hedy it was her own doing, the whole thing. "She was too brave," said Flora, "that was her problem."

Max Brings Rifka Tumarkin Flowers: 1921

The secretary of the company, Rifka Tumarkin, had a blind sister whom she supported. Rifka lived in an apartment on Jerome Avenue that faced a brick wall. The fire escape was planted with geraniums that always died from lack of sun. Rifka was hardworking and never missed a day and she was cheerful and she always had a tip on the day's races, which she got from the old gentleman who lived on the floor above who had been a stable boy before his retirement and still had contacts. She had light brown hair that she wore in braids around her head. She had a space between her front teeth that brought thoughts to Max's mind about kissing and tongues and things not about business.

He offered to take Rifka to the races. She accepted. Max couldn't see above the rail line, but Rifka described it all to him. She urged her horse on with the sweetest of oohs and ahs, and when she lost she smiled and said, "Well, all right, there's always tomorrow, you know."

For the second time in his life, Max fell in love, this time with a good girl, an orphan who was supporting her sister. Max had thoughts about the three of them that made him jump up and down in his bed. He was one of the bosses. He could marry Rifka and give her a life of permanent ease, a life like his brother's wife. He had fooled around long enough. He had said he didn't want to be bored by the same face every night, but now he was worried, maybe no one would care for him if he got sick, no one would worry if he fell down a hole, was killed in the subway by a train running amok. He saw in the mirror a man with a limp, a good suit, a fine hat, a look in the eye of someone passed over. He had mourned Peachie long enough, taken trips out to Brighton Beach and watched her hang up her laundry and followed her when she went to the boardwalk and put in a penny and looked at the sea through the machines that stood every five hundred feet, tempting children and women with idle minds. He had sent her daughter presents of dresses and bracelets. He had sent Peachie a fur coat, a coat made of seals from Alaska. She had never thanked him. She never returned anything. Peachie preferred her independence to staying with Max. Someone must have knocked the sense out of that woman. Now Max was ready for love. He brought Rifka flowers each morning. He took her to the nightclubs in the evening. She wore her best dress. She allowed him to walk her up the stairs to her apartment and put his hands on her breast and squeeze just a little. She allowed him to put his tongue in the space between her teeth. She giggled.

Max asked her to marry him one lunchtime when the office was quiet and she was sitting on a chair by her typewriter redoing a long letter from Isaac to a store in Detroit explaining the change in the shipment. She looked at him, startled, and said, "Oh, no, sweetie. I can't marry someone so old."

"I'm not old," said Max.

Rifka laughed and patted him on the arm. "Old enough," she said, which was true.

Which is why Max, who never gave up entirely, over his brother's objections bought a horse and a place in New Jersey. He hired a groom from a country club to play polo with him, a game that he began to love more than business itself. Isaac sighed. Horses, he figured, were better than women; at least they were less likely to break his brother's heart.

Sharon Herzberg's Father Loses His Temper and Regains It: 1922

In the Herzberg house in Baltimore, the name *Sharon* was rarely spoken. The mother did not wish to provoke the father. The mother kept her grief to herself, and she kept the news to herself. When Sharon had called and told her that she was going to marry the drummer, Ruth had bitten her lip and kept her secret. What was the point? Joseph had been right all along. The voice lessons were a mistake. The world was going to take her child, and it would have been better, she thought to herself, if Joseph had not heard her playing the piano, the notes going down the alley to his room below, had taken another wife, one with a normal face, who might have had normal children, whose boys might have taken the voice of the disciple of the Baal Shem, and she might have spent her whole life in Isaac's house playing the piano and regretting nothing. But when Sharon called from a hospital in Detroit and said she had been in an accident and needed her mother to send her some money to pay a hospital bill, she could not keep her secret from Joseph any longer. The secret was too much of a burden for her to carry alone. She told Joseph about the marriage and the accident and the hospital.

Joseph went to shul and opened the ark as he did each Shabbos morning, and he turned to the congregation and said, "This morning I cannot proceed with the service until I tell God what is in my heart." And in his own extraordinary voice, in a combination of Yiddish and Hebrew and English, he threw up his arms and began.

"O Lord of the Universe, who is as incompetent as You, who has betrayed His people as basely as You, who has accepted my prayers all these years only to throw them back in my face like the rainwater falling from the roof? O Lord of the Universe, why didn't You protect my daughter from harm, how could You have let her marry a man who was not of us, and how could You have allowed her to suffer as she has suffered, and why did You give her the voice of the disciple of the Baal Shem, my voice, if only to mock me and my efforts to serve You? O Lord, who is rumored to be compassionate and merciful, why have You shown us Your dreadful face? Why have You allowed so many in my congregation to be without jobs or food for their young ones? Why have You brought the sickness unto death down on Mr. Israel Gershewitz, and why did You allow the baby Leibman to die before his first birthday, and what right did You have to visit blindness on the newborn of the Shapiros and the paralysis of the brothers Cohen? Why did You allow the Cossacks to enter the town of my parents, and where have You been when the Jews have been murdered in the streets of Kiev and Vilna, and why have You, if You are so almighty, permitted the car to run down the wife of the president of our shul, and if You are so powerful that we must obey Your commandment, why don't You strike down our enemies? Maybe, O Lord, You are not deserving of our praise at all. My daughter, Sharon, is in pain, in a far-off city, and it is not my fault. It is Yours."

The congregation was silent, stunned, perhaps. There was the cry of nursing baby from the women's section. There was a sound of weeping from a man in the first row, and there was a silence in the shul that mingled with the smell of damp wool and rubber boots.

Joseph bent his head. He raised it again. "That said, nevertheless, despite everything, today as we have since Sinai, we praise You, O Lord, and thank You for all that You have given us." And he went on with the prayer service, the thanking of the Lord for the gift of the Sabbath and for the creation of every living thing, the hound in the forest, the rabbit in the glade, the leaf and the flower and the cloud and the dirt and the seeds that grow and the life that is man's, and he went on to pray to God to bring all the mourners of Zion comfort just as he had every other Shabbos, and afterward, the old men, the men from the old country, shook his hand.

"Good Shabbos," they said, and to Mrs. Herzberg, too. "You told Him off," they said.

"I did," said Joseph.

The president of the shul, who had put his hands over his face throughout Joseph's unusual prayer, patted him on the back. "Well done," he said.

Joseph felt better; the pressure in his stomach had eased, and he gave Ruth the money to send to his daughter, who had married a stranger and was now in a hospital far away.

Hedy in the Corridor of the Hadassah Hospital: 1990

Hedy closed her eyes. She didn't want to see the clock with its second hand in constant motion. A reporter wanted to talk to her. There was a television camera in the downstairs lobby. They wanted to interview the family. She turned her back. Her husband sent them away. The reporter said he would wait. They were all waiting.

Mickey Makes It to Manhattan: 1921

The sea air is good for the complexion, and Mickey hung her face out the window toward the ocean breeze and let the salt and the fog from Brighton Beach wash over her. She put her elbows on her windowsill and pulled at her eyebrows, which had unruly intentions and wouldn't stay smooth the way they ought to. She slapped her back with powder that she had stolen from her mother's drawer. She stood up and stretched. She had grown so tall that her head almost hit the bedroom ceiling that sloped down over the sink. She raised her legs up in the air, running her hands up and down her calves just to make sure they were still ready for anything. They were.

Her mother, Peachie, was always telling her, "Don't let anyone touch, save it, it's your fortune. Don't make the mistake I did, don't let them near. . . . Dumpling," she said, "use it carefully."

It made Mickey angry the way her mother thought she was some kind of fool. She tilted her head and smiled into the mirror. She had no intention of giving away her ticket, the way her mother was always doing. On the other hand, who wanted to stay home and wash the floor when out there a party was waiting, a party where a girl could test her equipment, show off her ankles, and maybe sneak a cigarette or a drink, why not? A good time was not just for society girls who went around with their noses in the air, but for her, her, too; a good time was there just for the asking. If a fellow wanted to give her something pretty in return for a small favor, a little kiss or a rub in the right place, why not?

Mickey stood up as straight as she could and watched her breasts tilt upward. She felt a spike of pleasure run along her spine and then a tingle of joy in her nipples. What was wrong with joy? Nothing, she thought, and she bounced down the stairs and out of the house.

She was finished with the neighborhood boys who hung out at the corner by the candy store asking for a feel. If they offered her a cigarette, a stick of gum, all right, she'd stop and pass the time with them a while, but she wouldn't stay. Izzie and Larry and the others, what was the point, where were they going? Fifty years from now they would still be on the corner drooling into their pants. She wasn't a fool.

She was going into Manhattan to a party given by the Gruenbaum brothers in their swell house on Riverside Drive. The no-goodnik who lived with her mother these days had taken her along to the main office when he was selling to Arthur, said she was his stepdaughter, which wasn't exactly true because her mother didn't believe in marriage, which is why they were always late on the rent, and that's how she got invited to Mildred's wedding and now to this party, where opportunity beckoned. Why should a girl be buried in the back streets of Brighton Beach, a girl with a sparkling eye and legs as high as her mother's shoulders?

Arthur was a sweetie who kissed all the girls, but the one she chose was Harry. He was the one who would need her, and besides, he was the one who would be president one day. Mickey had no intention of choosing the second banana. There was something else about Harry. He understood things about Mickey that didn't show up on the surface, that other men missed. He wasn't a good-time Charlie, just wanting to take his turn and run off. He understood that she needed him to put an umbrella up over her head if it were raining and that sometimes she would need him to be quiet and hold her hand and sometimes she would need him to dance with her. She knew that Harry would answer the question, the question she'd always had but had never dared say out loud, not even to herself: Who will take care of me, who will protect me when the rocks start flying, who will pick me up if I fall down, who will stay by my bed if I am sick, who will fill the need that runs through me like the ocean at high tide in a September storm? Harry would do it, she knew. So it was Harry she chose to save her from the uncertainties of Brighton Beach, from the loneliness that even a pretty girl feels when she gets into bed and doesn't know who will remember her name tomorrow.

Harry wanted to own a sailboat. He wanted a yacht to sail across the Long Island Sound. "When you're the president of the Gruenbaum Company," said his father, "then you can spend your money any way you like."

"Jews," said Isaac, "go on ships to escape from one place to another, not to get their feet wet going back and forth, round in circles like fish."

The secretaries were very respectful of Harry and called him "Mr. Gruenbaum" and brought him apples for lunch and flowers for his windowsill. He developed a double chin and had to have his shirts specially made. They had his monogram on the pocket, and his mother made sure they were ironed perfectly and hung straight in his closet.

Arthur went to Columbia and attended classes, or some of them, some of the time, and he joined the ZBT fraternity and drank beer on warm nights with his legs hanging out the window and he dated pretty girls who allowed him certain liberties but not others, and he always had a smile for everyone and he pulled pennies out of friends' ears and he juggled three oranges at a time, a trick he would do that would set everyone at ease, especially because he would always be the first to laugh at himself when one came crashing down on his head.

Arthur looked on the bright side of things, and why shouldn't he? He knew his lot in life included good food, good clothes, pretty women, good golf greens, a little billiards, good cigars. He had a sensitive side, too. He wrote poetry in a notebook. Everything rhymed, true and blue, rain and pain. He had no interest in poetry about souls in turmoil. His literary attention turned to sunshine on the ninth hole, the way his mother ate cake, a little sliver at a time, a second and a third, till the plate was empty. He didn't show his poems to anyone, anyone except Flora, who thought they were great. He wrote poems for birthdays and poems for anniversaries. He sang to himself while he wrote. His best ideas came to him while shaving or soaking in the bath.

He dropped out of school before his third year to follow his brother into the business. He would be vice president one day and play golf. He loved golf. He bought himself suits wholesale from someone he knew in the business, and his suits were a better quality than the Gruenbaum suit, more high class, with finer fabrics. Isaac didn't like to see his youngest son walking around in competitors' clothing, but the boy just patted his father on the back. "It's all right, Dad, this is America, and I can wear a good suit if I want one."

It was spring, and Harry had his own Stanley Steamer. He drove out to Brighton Beach and picked Mickey up. Izzie and Larry and the boys at the corner touched the fender of the car, leaned against it, kicked the tires, said it wasn't as good as a Pierce Arrow, but Mickey just waved at them as she jumped in the front seat and tossed her fox wrap, the one Harry had bought her for her birthday, into the backseat. As the car pulled away from the block she rolled down the window and, turning her head toward the boys, stuck out her tongue as far as it would go.

"Have you met the uncle with the limp?" asked her mother.

"Yeah," said Mickey. "Something special about him?"

"A john," said Peachie, "just a funny-looking john. I married him once. Could've lived in the lap of luxury if I'd stayed, but you know me, I'm not the sticking type. Don't get married," said Peachie. "Then they think they own you. Then you're trapped, done for, had it."

"Yeah," said Mickey, "I could be lucky like you."

"You're my daughter," said Peachie. "You should do what I tell you. Get a profession, learn to type."

"Don't worry," said Mickey, "I can take care of myself."

Arthur carried a half-pint grudge that Harry had taken Mickey from him. He had seen her first. But he wasn't the sort to carry on about water under the bridge, milk that had spilt. Women were like summer flies, all around. Arthur whistled in his office. He was a first-rate whistler. He loved show tunes and tap dancing. He liked vaudeville and striptease. Who cares about Mickey? Not him. She was just what his brother, who let the sweat sit on his upper lip and who had taken to staring out the window and sighing as if he were eighty instead of twenty-two, needed. Besides, Harry wouldn't marry Mickey, he wouldn't. This romance between Mickey and Harry was only a good-time thing. She wasn't the right sort of girl at all. She was taller than Harry by about five inches. She was a Jewish girl, yes, but there was some question about her father. Her mother had been a whore. Isaac had said so. Something about Max. Isaac didn't want Mickey in the house. He'd slammed his fist on the table. These were not the people that Arthur and Harry were expected to mix with. Mickey had legs that seemed to come up to her earlobes. She had red nails as long as her hair, which was short, shockingly short. She chewed with her mouth open. She smoked cigarettes. She sat with her legs slightly apart. She said, "Oh, yeah," every other word.

Harry's mother, Annie, came to her son with tears in her eyes. "I came here with nothing, but never would I do what Mickey's mother did. Poor is no excuse. I will never let that woman or her daughter in my house. Don't hurt me like that." She leaned toward her son, her fingers just lightly brushing his lips.

Isaac arranged for Harry to meet a nice girl who was the younger sister of a friend of Mildred's. He took her to the Dance for the Jewish Blind, but he was bored, and he didn't know what to say. He always knew what to say to Mickey because Mickey always knew what to say to him.

Uncle Max thought Mickey was terrific and told Harry about a certain store on Delancey where a man could buy lace undies with silver zippers. "Her mother was great, too," he said. "Not faithful, that's all, otherwise perfect." He sighed. "I even married her," said Max, "but she had no respect for vows."

"Her daughter's different," said Harry, a wish as well as a statement.

Naomi said to her grandson, "What are you doing? Those girls, back in Sulvalki we knew what to call those girls."

But Harry for the first time had met a girl who liked the folds around his middle, who told him that it was all right with her if he waddled a bit when he walked. "What the hell," she said. "Meow . . ." She wiggled her shoulders. She was not the sort of girl to mind a penis on a slant or an eye that went in its own direction. What did Mickey like? Mickey liked fur coats and she liked chauffeur-driven cars and she liked gold earrings and necklaces. She liked chocolates and the movies and she loved gin with a parasol in her drink. She liked staying up till three in the morning and she liked walking in the park with her shoes off. She liked falling asleep leaning against Harry, he was all soft like a pillow. She loved Harry all over because he loved her, and he offered her everything a girl could want, to be respected above all. When she was out with Harry Gruenbaum people treated her right, waiters bowed, shopkeepers smiled. In America anybody could be a swell, even Mickey, who had dreamed of having a father like Isaac Gruenbaum, instead of the unknown who lived in St. Louis and whose name her mother never spoke. In America no one was beached forever in the backwaters, certainly not a good-looker like Mickey.

For the first time since he was born, Harry felt appreciated, just for himself, just because he was there.

Isaac ordered his older son to stop seeing the tramp from Brighton Beach. Harry slouched on his chair. He ate sugar doughnuts by the dozen. He told Mickey he couldn't see her anymore.

"So, I don't care," she said.

"I told you," said her mother. "They think their little wee-wees give them the right to everything."

Mickey got a job in a nightclub in Brighton Beach. It wasn't much of a place. She was the hatcheck girl. The tips were all right. It was kind of fun in its way, but no future at all. She was asked by the boss to be the girl in the cake at a bachelor party. She wore lace stockings and black underpants with sequins. She sat inside the box around which the cake had been made and she sweated so badly that her makeup ran. She sat with her legs pressed up against her nose and heard the men laughing and banging glasses and making rude noises while they ate. At last she was wheeled from the side of the room to its center. The maître d' banged on the backside of the box, getting white icing on his hand, and she opened the lid and jumped out.

"Hurray," she said, "for Tony, who is getting wed tomorrow."

She blew kisses to the left and kisses to the right. There was music in the background, and the men clapped and clapped and leapt to their feet and whistled and cupped their hands and made noises through their fingers. No one was allowed to touch her, the boss had insisted on that, his kind of place and all. Mickey herself thought it would be fun to just let a few of them come a little close. She had a few glasses of champagne, and when the boss wasn't looking she sat on the groom-to-be's lap. He was embarrassed and kept staring at the ceiling, which made everyone laugh, including Mickey.

"It was great, really great," Mickey explained to her mom. "Everyone was happy. They gave me some cake and the boss told me I was on for the next party. Oh, boy." And she took out a ten-dollar bill that he had stuffed in the top of her bra.

"That," said Peachie, "is the high life. Learn from my example, learn to type."

Harry couldn't stay away from Mickey. "I can't marry you," he said, "but we can be friends."

"Sure," said Mickey, who didn't believe people always meant what they said.

Isaac was furious. He hired a detective to get the full story. "She jumps out of cakes at bachelor parties, that's the kind of girl you've been seeing," said Isaac.

"I know," said Harry. "She likes her work."

Isaac said, "She's like her mother, only interested in your money, a gold digger who'll go on to the next man, that's what."

"Would you love me," asked Harry, "if I were the son of a grocer?"

"How would I know?" said Mickey. "You're not."

"But if," said Harry.

"Then you'd be somebody else," said Mickey, "and I love you, not somebody else."

Reader: What is respectability? How is it possible that Isaac and Annie Gruenbaum already felt superior to those on the ladder who were lower down than they? They must have remembered when they first arrived, *mama loshen,* knishes, the heat in summer, and the worry about the money for the rent. They must have known back in Sulvalki there were families that wouldn't speak to them, much less allow a marriage between their offspring. They had no treasure either of scholarship or coin. They were down at the bottom, where others peered at them, pointing and saying, Not like us, those poor tailors, not like us at all. They hadn't forgotten, that's just the point. Rushing away from their memories, proud of all they had accomplished, dimly perceiving that the Rockefellers themselves would have them to dine in a few generations, they had opinions about others. They had climbed out of the bottom and in climbing had developed an image of themselves that did not include a girl named Mickey whose father was a zero and whose mother was worse. You want to believe in the milk of human kindness, oozing out from the rich to the poor, go ahead. But don't forget, looking down is alarming. You could also fall.

Harry stopped sleeping. At all hours of the night he walked about in the kitchen, banging doors and opening cupboards. "I am going to join the navy," he said. "I don't want to live here anymore. I quit the business, as of now."

"You won't have a dime," said Isaac, whose hands were shaking, whose legs felt weak, who knew even as he said the words he didn't mean them.

"I'm going," said Harry, who was very frightened at the idea of not having a dime and was already worrying whether Mickey would like him in uniform.

"All right," said Isaac, "marry her." The father hugged his son, and the son had tears in his eyes.

He bought her an emerald ring, and they were married. The wedding was a small family affair at which Max was found in the coatroom banging his head against the wall because the bride was not his child and the mother no longer belonged to him.

Peachie had chucked him under the chin at the reception, but she wouldn't go home with him. When she was finished with someone she was finished. Arthur thought it was hilarious. Harry with the hatcheck girl, he roared to his sister Mildred, who was not as amused.

"So, yeah," said Mickey, "we're sisters now." And she teetered on her heels and gave Mildred a wet kiss that smelled of brandy.

"Isn't she a looker?" said Harry. Mildred nodded but made a sour face.

Flora, who was only twelve years old, thought Mickey was wonderful. "Show me," said Flora, "show me how to make my rear wiggle like yours."

But Mickey just laughed. "It ain't a thing that can be taught. The bump just follows after the twat."

Flora didn't understand but admired Mickey even though Mildred wouldn't invite her to lunch, claiming she'd bring germs into the house.

"What kind of germs?" asked Flora.

"Male germs," said Mildred, and wouldn't answer any more questions.

Hedy in the Beauty Parlor: 1945

When Flora told this to Hedy, while Hedy was sitting on a chair next to her mother's at the beauty parlor, Hedy asked, "What kind of germs did she mean, polio?"

Flora looked around and then leaned over and whispered to Hedy, "VD. Your vagina gets boils and your brain rots like an old radish and girls who give away too much, they die from it."

"How do you get it, exactly?" said Hedy.

"From men," said Flora. "Also from toilet seats in public places. Never sit down on a public toilet seat."

Hedy and her mother had been in the beauty parlor up at 125th Street for hours. Hedy was having her hair straightened. Everyone else in the beauty parlor was a Negro. Flora had explained: "You can't get your hair flattened at beauty parlors on Madison Avenue. They only do the conk in Harlem."

Hedy felt strange. She was embarrassed. "Why?" she asked.

Flora didn't have an answer. Now an oil was seeping, black and thick, into her scalp. It was going to take away the curls. Her head smelled of rotten eggs.

Hedy was tired of waiting for the brew to work. She wanted to sit on the floor with her jacks, but her mother wouldn't let her. She was the best jacks player in her class. Her hands were quick. Her eye was good. Spill them out, scoop them up, fingers picking between the spokes, grouping them in numbers, take three, leave four, everything came out even, twos, nines, backses, if you made a mistake, you started again. She beat everyone. She didn't want her hair straightened. But her mother said, "You have bad hair, it's too thick and it kinks in the rain."

"So what?" said Hedy.

"So, everything," sighed her mother.

The oil was washed off. Hedy swiveled on her chair and looked at herself in the mirror. Her black hair hung straight to her shoulders.

"That's pretty," said Flora.

"My head stings," said Hedy.

"So what?" said Flora.

Hedy didn't like her new hair. Nevertheless, she was frightened when it first began to fall out, large handfuls of hair on the pillow, in the tub, in her brush. She could see bald patches on her head in the mirror. The chemical is strong, said her mother; they used too much. Hedy wore a baseball cap till her old hair grew back, kinking its way out from under. Hedy knew it was there, prickly on her scalp, thick and black and wrong.

"I like it," she said to Ursula. "I like my old hair."

Flora Tells Hedy About the Worst Day of Her Life: 1944
The Day Itself Was November 14, 1922

Flora was in the bathtub soaping herself again and again with the dirty gray suds that rose with the scented bath oil out of the tub and spilled on the floor. She held a cigarette in one hand and on the toilet seat behind her she had placed her evening Scotch. Sitting on the bathtub rim, Hedy let her hands drip in the water, paddling back and forth as if they were duck's feet that might take her out to far-off islands. Flora told Hedy the plot of a movie she had seen the night before. Hedy told her mother the plot of the Nancy Drew mystery she had just finished reading. Flora told Hedy about the day when she was twelve years old when the police had come to the door of the house on Riverside Drive and her mother had come down the circular stairway and the police were still there when she had come home from school, with her books in a bag, and her maid told her what happened.

"What happened?" asked Hedy.

Isaac Gruenbaum had gone to his office that morning to find that his new secretary had lost the letter he had just written to the manufacturer of zippers who was late in his delivery to the factory they had just opened in Pansville. His son Arthur had been sent to Pansville to make sure that all was going on schedule. The fall suits needed to hit the streets in just a few weeks. It was a small factory, capacity for two thousand suits a week. It employed five hundred tailors, forty cutters, and thirty-five maintenance and supervisory help. It was in the old shoe factory that had been up on the hill back in the days when the Gruenbaums had stayed in Pansville. Now there were fifteen Jewish families, a drugstore as well as a general store, and a movie house had opened and two new Methodist churches and a garage and a gas station. The trains still went through, right by the house the Gruenbaums had lived in, still shaking the window frames and rattling the doors. Now those trains carried the Gruenbaum suits with the Gruenbaum label into Pittsburgh and New York.

Isaac went into his brother Max's office. Max was not there. It was too early in the week for Max, who put in his appearance around Thursday noon. Isaac saw that his brother's desk was covered with pictures of naked women in various disgusting poses. He leaned over the desk. He wanted to pick them up and throw them out before any of the secretaries came in, but one caught his eye, a young girl, maybe fourteen or fifteen, a little older than Flora, hair in blond ringlets, with deep black circles under her eyes and breasts that seemed to go in opposite directions. She was sitting on a man's knee. He was smiling above the head of the naked girl, whose legs were spread apart above his knees, and he had his finger inside her, and she was smiling out at the camera and with her own left hand she held her right breast and squeezed her nipple. Isaac felt a wave of tension, a rising up and a filling in his organ, and he was disgusted. He had never been unfaithful to his wife. He had never allowed Max to supply him with floozies, although Max offered each birthday, each anniversary of the opening of the factory, each time they made a larger sale than expected. Isaac thought of his father, wrapped in tefillin, he thought of his mother, who had bent her head over her sewing till her neck had developed a lump at the top of her spine. He tore up the pictures on Max's desk. He ripped them to shreds and went back into his office. There he got a phone call that the zipper manufacturer had run short of zippers, a miscalculation the man said, "a simple miscalculation; that happens, you know, you know how it is," said the voice.

Isaac felt a flutter in his heart, and then a roaring sound as if a waterfall had appeared in his chest, and the rocks and the water together, with the wind in the trees and the tumbling of an occasional branch, echoed in his ears. He sat down on his chair.

"We need zippers," he yelled. "When can I have them?" The voice on the phone named a date. "Too late," said Isaac. "I have to have them now."

"So what can I do?" said the voice, and hung up.

Isaac thought of his older daughter, Mildred, now married to a banker. He felt for her a tenderness so great that his head began to ache. If only he could watch over her forever, as she dressed in the evening for a party. He thought of his little daughter, Flora, just starting to thin down, just starting to get that look in her eye that promised so much. He thought of how she of all of his children made him tremble when she put her arms around him.

"Take care of her, take care of her," he prayed to an invisible presence whose power he had ignored for most of his life. He thought of his sons, two capable boys, educated, who knew so many things he did not, balancing books and managing labor, who knew about business expansion and contraction and cycles and things he had never heard of till they explained them at dinner, two boys, who could carry on. All right, they would find zippers elsewhere, it wasn't the end of the world. He had had crises before and they always found a way out. Maybe they would make their own zippers.

The roar in his chest grew louder. He thought of his wife, Annie, who lay in his bed, uncomplaining, fluffing his pillows, each night writing in a notebook the next day's shopping list, her thick legs wrapping them-selves around his night after night. He put his heavy head down on his desk. A pain, sharp as a knife, long as an eel's tail flicked down his left arm. Another pain, a squeeze of a hand, a pinch of a nerve, gentle at first and then suddenly fierce, took over his heart and he began to sweat. He tried to mop his head with his hand, but the pain was too great. He thought of Ruth before the pox, and he saw her face as clearly as if he were dreaming. She turned to him and behind her he saw Sister Abigail bending her head toward him. A great love surged through him. He thought of his death and denied that it was there. He thought of his death and felt loss so wide, so deep, that it was worse than the pain in his chest. Not now, he thought. He tried to call out for help, but his voice had disappeared into his rib cage.

When his secretary came into the office some ten minutes later with a copy of the lost letter she had found, he was lying like a scarecrow blown from its pole on his desk: he was dead.

When the funeral was over, and the rabbi had said, "May ye be comforted among the mourners of Zion and Jerusalem," and the family had gone back to the house on Riverside Drive, Harry had said to Flora, "Don't worry, I'll take care of you."

She had buried her face in his chest because she didn't want him to see in her eyes what she knew. She knew that Harry could not take care of her. She would grow up without her father: unfair. He was there at Mildred's wedding. He would miss hers. Unfair. She felt newly damaged, as if she had crushed a limb or had lost an eye in an accident. Something was wrong with her now that had been right before. She thought of her father without flesh, a skull in the ground. She would die, too. She saw across the river from life to death, the passage swift and terrible. The fear she felt that moment never left, came back in the night and was with her in the morning, followed her to school and waited for her in the park. It made her afraid of elevators, of tunnels, of bridges, of burglars and animals, of airplanes and traffic accidents. After her father died she was always expecting bad news. She was not like everyone else anymore. She was Flora, who had no father. She was not comforted among the mour-ners of Zion and Jerusalem.

Arthur Finds Happiness: 1923

The spring after his father died, Arthur met Louisa at a company picnic. She was the younger sister of a friend of Mildred's. She was blond and her eyes were green and protected by long black lashes that made Arthur's heart leap in unexpected directions. She was small, as small as his sister Flora. He thought he could lift her up with one hand and carry her easily for the rest of his life. Her father was in the shirt business, and the family lived on Jerome Avenue in a large house with thick red carpets.

At the picnic Arthur did magic tricks for the children of the salesmen. He whistled through his fingers and juggled three oranges in the air. He walked with Louisa down to the brook and told her something that he had told no one else, that he loved to watch the squirrels running up the trunks of the trees. This was true. Arthur was fond of things with fur and feathers. Each morning on his way to work, he brought a breakfast roll over to the park and crumbled it up for the birds.

Louisa had wanted to be a nurse, but her father would not allow it. She wanted to take care of those who needed her. She stared up at Arthur, searching his face for some sign of ridicule.

Arthur was hoping he would be the one deserving of her care. Arthur imagined that one day he would break par and win the club's silver trophy, and when that happened he wanted to give it to Louisa to put roses in, fresh roses every day. He told her that he wrote poetry. He had a notebook full of his poems. He recited one for her. It began with the couplet: "My heart is round, my feet are outward bound." She loved it.

This was what Louisa had been waiting for. She had no experience with boys. Her father and mother had kept her home and carefully watched her friendships. She had a soft heart that went out to all who needed. She was not vain or proud of her looks the way other young women were. She didn't know that she was uncommonly beautiful. She thought of herself as owing, owing something to the world, something of herself she should give, but what and to whom she could not imagine, and this caused her to cry unexpectedly, to wake in the night and feel lonely or restless. She had ideals, ideals of good and bad, and she thought all the time about what was good and what was bad. Good, she knew, was paying attention to others; bad, she knew, was selfishness. She had not read a good deal. She had abandoned the dance lessons that had once brought her pleasure. She was waiting, hanging in the air, shapeless as a cloud, meaning well but not knowing what action to take to translate her feelings that rolled through her soul like the fog off the sea, into deeds, deeds that would anchor her firmly to the ground. Arthur was it, the action, the deed, the purpose of her life. When this came clear she sighed with relief. She was joyous and sweet, and her arms brushed against his with tenderness. Now her life could begin.

The young couple were fortunate in their choice of each other, in the contentment that it brought their families, in the harmony of knowing that they were taking their rightful place in the human progression of birth to death, not that they thought about death. Unlike the animals entering the ark two by two, who understood that a storm was coming, Louisa and Arthur gave no thought to the weather ahead.

Hedy in the Hallway Outside Her Mother's Room: 1946

When Hedy opened the china closet in the hallway outside her mother's bedroom she could see the Worcester and Spode, the coffee cups with blue dragons circling their handles, the piles of delft and the red and blue and green of the dragon tails edged in gold scallops. The fish plates, the dessert plates, the salad plates, the settings for twenty-four, the wineglasses with gold leaf on the rim and gold tangled vines that rose all over the cups and went down the thin stems: the finger bowls with golden grapes etched on the side. Some of these Hedy knew had belonged to her grandmother in the house on Riverside Drive. When Hedy would sit in the hall and wait for her mother to wake up, she would open the closet door and, standing on her toes, reaching her arms above her head, count the dishes of one kind and another. She picked one up and looked at it closely, removing it from the closet, cradling it on her lap, turning it over and over in her hands.

The bomb had fallen on Hiroshima, and Hedy knew that in Hiroshima the dishes were all smashed to pieces. Hedy knew what had happened to the Jews in Europe. At night in her bed Hedy would think about it and marvel at the narrowness of her escape. Hedy prayed for the success of the Dodgers. She crossed her fingers. She stood on her head and leaned her feet on the wallpaper, even though she'd been told not to do that. She believed that the Dodgers would win the pennant this year, now that Cookie Lavagetto was out of the army, maybe even the World Series, if she turned the world upside down, had good thoughts. Each night she went to sleep certain that if the Dodgers could take sixty percent of the games at Ebbets Field, then Jews would never again die by the millions. Hedy worried about the bomb. She was also worried about the fact that no girl had ever made a major-league baseball team.

There was talk that Jackie Robinson, a Negro, might make it one day. So who knew what the future could bring.

Hedy thought she better put back the plate she was holding. She stood on tiptoe and carefully lined it up with the others that matched, all with gold rims and blue flowers in the center. Hedy tripped on her shoelace or Hedy tripped on an edge in the carpet, or she slipped because she had reached too high. Her arms went crashing into the shelf and the dishes fell down and the shelf fell with them on top of the crystal glasses below. Hedy lay on the floor with the pieces of china all around, and some broken glass bounced on the carpet. Flora woke up and, clutching her nightgown to her chest, opened the door.

"My God!" she screamed. "My china, the china that was given to me at my wedding!"

Hedy was crying. Her elbow was cut and bleeding. Flora sat down on the floor, weeping.

"My china, my china," she said, picking up little pieces and pressing them to her chest. "How could you?" she shouted at Hedy, who tried to explain about her foot slipping and not meaning to at all, but Flora was deaf to all but the sound of her china breaking again and again as she pictured it tumbling down. "There'll be nothing left for you," said Flora.

"I don't care," said Hedy. "I didn't want it anyway."

"You did," said Flora. "You're just saying that now because you can't have it."

"I don't care," said Hedy. "I hate china."

In Which Flora Meets Frank—Was It in the Stars?: 1928

In the ZBT house on 114th Street, the only fraternity at Columbia that was Jewish, all Jewish, the only one that would take a Jew, the one that Frank had joined in hopes of meeting the right people, the word was out that Flora Gruenbaum, eighteen years old, youngest child of the Gruenbaum family, was a real heiress and not bad-looking, either. A few of the brothers had dated her. Doesn't pet, came the word; a tease, it was said. Too small, bites her nails, twirls her hair, drops things, can't hold her liquor, talks too much, keeps her legs closed. The boys rated her "okay" and put her on the list for the spring party, the postmidterm bash, at which they would have a band, a barrel of beer, and some hard stuff gotten through the connections of brother Nate Swirling, whose father was in a business that required a lot of nighttime activity on the wharves.

Frank slicked his hair down with Vaseline till it lay like a shell on his head, black and shining. He was in his senior year and had been in fifteen fights on campus. This brought him a certain kind of acclaim among the brothers, but it also marked him as a guy with a chip, and everyone knew he had nothing, nothing but good looks and one suit and a secondhand blazer. Everyone knew he worked as a waiter over at the cafeteria and that his grades were not good enough to get him into law school. Everyone knew he was a man who might when high on too many beers put his hand through a window or throw a chair or bang his head against the bathroom stall till he bled. When the brothers put their arms around each other and told dirty jokes or shared adventures of the night before, or slipped each other papers for courses or old exams, Frank was not there. He just wasn't that sort of guy. His admission to ZBT had been based on his tall, lean body, his good-looking face, smooth like a movie star's, sure to attract girls. It happened before the brothers knew that he wasn't the sort of person to squirt in the eye with shaving cream because he might knock your teeth out. It happened because the administration had insisted that a certain number of commuters, scholarship students, be taken into the fraternities. Wasn't this a democracy, and shouldn't all that element be grouped together, where they belonged?

The night of the spring dance Flora wore her green beaded dress and she had her bobbed hair done by Mildred's hairdresser and she packed her silver purse with cigarettes, hidden from her mother, who didn't know she smoked, and she arrived at the ZBT house on the arm of Aaron Haft, whose father owned Sleep Well Pajamas, which came in all sizes for both sexes and had recently expanded into women's lingerie, the kind that was made of silk and lace and clung tight to the body whose sleep it was guarding.

Aaron had met Flora through his sister, who was a friend of Flora's from high school. Aaron was a gentle boy who collected frogs and butterflies and who hoped to go into law. His mother wanted him to go into the business, and a good business it was. His father, who knew about seasonal fluctuations, wasn't sorry his son had other ambitions. Aaron had a vision of himself. He explained it to his grandfather, who spoke only Yiddish. "I will be a kind of zaddik," he said, "a zaddik of American law."

"I will be proud of you," said his grandfather, who understood that the world of real zaddiks no longer existed and if a Jewish boy could go to law school and become a pretend zaddik, then he should.

Aaron was a quiet boy. He studied all the time. He had to take a girl from the accepted list to the party, because he also wanted to belong, to be a regular fellow. He brought Flora, who smiled at him nervously when he rang her doorbell.

When they arrived at ZBT he got her a drink and introduced her to all the guys over by the bar. The band was playing loudly. The boys were making small talk; that is to say they were arm wrestling, boasting about their tennis games, golf scores, and talking about the cars they owned or would own on graduation. They were dancing in the living room, with the huge ZBT banner hung over the mantelpiece. Frank saw Flora.

"God, what a shrimp," he said to the boy next to him.

"Some shrimp," came back the answer. "That's Gruenbaum Suits. That little shrimp is loaded right up to her antennas."

Aaron and Flora were dancing; she was smiling up at him, hoping he liked her. Somehow she was never sure. Did they like her for herself, really, or was it just obligation? She tried to be fun to be with, she laughed at all their jokes, she gulped down the Scotch that had been offered, and she lit up her cigarette, throwing her long Gruenbaum neck back and inhaling as if she were the devil's advertisement for the pleasures of sin. She pushed her glasses up on her head. She hated the way she looked in her glasses, but without them everything blurred, the colors swirled around and she groped for the wall to keep her steady. She put her glasses back down. She worried if her slip was showing. She worried if her lipstick was smeared. She worried if she had drunk too much and was getting wobbly. She worried that Aaron would not find her interesting because sometimes she couldn't think of anything to say.

Frank cut in. He introduced himself. He was dark and tall. His eyes were hooded, mysterious, as if some marauding Tatar had crossed the Ukraine and left his Mongolian seed behind. Flora looked in his eyes for a clue to his soul and saw nothing but dark pupils, cautiously looking to the left and the right. They danced. He held Flora tightly around the waist.

"You're a great dancer," he said, and smiled. It wasn't a full, open, easy smile; it had in it a pull in the opposite direction, and his eyes didn't smile with his mouth. They stayed steady, almost sad, thought Flora, and with that thought she lurched toward him. He was handsome, like Valentino. His nose was not long or irregular. His body was perfect, and he was marked, marked by some tragedy, thought Flora, and she wanted to take care of him, to make the pain better, to hold his hand.

Frank steered Flora out to the front steps and offered her another drink. The music blared over their heads. Other couples were in the street and leaning against the side of the stoops.

"I think," said Frank, whose jacket was immaculate and hung on his shoulders without a crease or a wrinkle, "you are the most beautiful girl at this party." He smiled again at her, and this time Flora thought she saw his eyes soften. Maybe she didn't, maybe it was only an illusion, but what did it matter? Flora felt excitement in every nerve of her body. He told her he was on scholarship, not one of the regular ZBT types, that he worked for what he got and that his family had come from a little town outside of Budapest twelve years before.

"You speak Hungarian?" Flora asked.

"No," said Frank, "I'm an American." He scowled and made a fist with his hands.

"You know Yiddish?" she asked timidly.

"No," said Frank, "I speak English, only English. This is my country," he said with a grimness that made Flora hold her breath.

He was dark and tall and different, and something he had seen, something he knew, made him different from her brothers, from the boys she had dated, from Aaron Haft. He was hard where they were soft. He had made his way when the others had been given everything. Her mother wouldn't like it. Her sister, Mildred, wouldn't like it and would laugh at her, but she didn't care. There comes a time when a girl jumps off a cliff and rides the currents in the river below. Aztec virgins were sacrificed this way. American girls took leaps of their own free will. This was Flora's time, and she leaned over to Frank and said, "Let's dance some more," meaning, I have fallen in love with you, do with me whatever you wish.

Reader: I should warn Flora and Frank. I could arrange a revelation, a premarriage revelation, so that Flora and Frank can go their separate ways and spare each other. I would like to put a hand on Flora's shoulder and explain to her that her father would not want her to do what she is about to do, that her mother, though busy with the others, has never forgotten her, at least not completely. It's cruel not to save Flora, not give her, there in the pinkness and roundness of her youth, to another man, one of gentle intentions, a man like Aaron Haft, perhaps, who would spend his nights admiring the roundness of her knees and the curl of her hair, a man who believed with the fervor of a Hasid dancing in his shul that women with short legs and full hips were like roses and butterflies and sea mist. Stories, because they approximate life, if not imitate it, cannot be entirely kind. If it is true that the writer is an imitator of God, then stories, like life, must have their human pain, contain no more than a thimbleful of mercy or the merest suggestion of justice. But perhaps Frank may yet surprise us, the passage of time reveal the kindness within or the love repressed. Perhaps Flora will find the way to awaken the man that is Frank, in his best moments, the man he would wish to be.

Flora Brings Frank Home: 1928

Naomi was a grandmother and a great-grandmother. Mildred had two daughters, Jill and Lydia, and Harry's wife had just given birth to a son, named Moses. Naomi lived in Isaac's house in rooms that were painted pink and had tapestry curtains that hung from the windows, and the sun set over the river, reflecting the red sky in the mirror of her dresser. She had pearls and a pair of ruby earrings and she had silk dresses and underwear in beige and white and black and negligees that folded round her small thin form. On her dresser she had five perfume bottles from Paris, one shaped like a dove and one black as onyx. She had bottles of creams for wrinkles and paste for her hair, which was silver and held in a bun at the back of her neck with a barrette made of emerald chips.

Some days when the maid brought her breakfast in bed and the satin covers were pulled up and she sat there with her head back against the pillows, tired but not too tired to appreciate the warm coffee, the fresh eggs, and the strawberry jam that her daughter-in-law had bought especially for her, she was stunned. How was it possible that what had been only an orphan's dream had actually come true? In the mirror she could see that she had lived a long time, and yet it seemed to her only a moment ago she was still there in Sulvalki at the kitchen table, opening the locket and letting the diamonds tumble into the palm of her hand. One she still had. She still carried it about her waist in a pouch attached by a velvet string that she had the dressmaker make up for her. Night and day, she kept the diamond close. It seemed to her that if she parted with it, something terrible would happen, something worse than Moses dying at the Bernstein Hotel in Greysville, New York, something worse even than Isaac dying so young at his office, something would happen to Max, to Ruth, or to the children, whose names she was beginning to have trouble keeping straight. It seemed to her that she must keep the diamond as she always had, even though it could no longer change her life, buy passage to a new place, challenge destiny. She admitted, but did not let go of it, the diamond was just a diamond, a jewel like the many her daughter-in-law kept in a box in her closet and wore to the tea parties she went to with other young widows who also had time on their hands.

When Flora brought Frank home there was disappointment in the family. Arthur was particularly concerned. "I don't think," said Arthur, "this man has a good family. He has nothing but looks, and Flora has fallen for him because he's handsome."

"No capital, no business, nothing to recommend him," said Harry.

"Don't let Flora marry him," said Mildred. "A nothing, a nobody, just got off the boat, who needs him in the family?" she added.

"It doesn't do us any good," said Annie, "to have her marry a man like Frank."

Mildred said to Flora, "Are you sure? He has no money."

Flora looked her sister in the eyes and said to her, "What do I care? I love him."

"Why do you love him?" said Mildred, who was not quite clear what love was and was not.

"Something hurts inside of him, something that he can't say. He is brave, but he needs me. I'm sure he needs me," said Flora.

"And that's what you love?" asked Mildred. "You shouldn't marry him. His family is awful. That sister of his is beyond words." Mildred rolled her eyes.

Flora said, "You should talk. Anyway, I'm not marrying his sister."

Fat Estelle Gets in Trouble: 1928

Frank's sister, Estelle, finished high school.

"Miracle," said Frank, who didn't believe in miracles at all.

She had taken a secretarial course and claimed she knew bookkeeping, bookkeeping like the back of my hand, she said, and turned her deeply creased palm up toward the sky. She wore more makeup than any other girl who still thought of herself as respectable, partially because her features were big and partially because she felt the need for disguise. She wore bracelets that jangled and earrings that caught the sun. She wore a hat that took up an entire seat on the trolley just by itself. She had big arms and wide hips, and when she came out of the bathroom she had to turn sideways to make it out the door. She had a Victrola that sat on the windowsill of the room she shared with her brother, Frank, and she danced by herself, waving her scarf around her head as if she were a fairy queen two-stepping on the forest floor under the midnight moon. She was surprisingly light on her toes, and her rhythm was perfect. She could Charleston or waltz, moving her big body between the commode and the bathroom door without missing a beat.

She got a job in a small jewelry store on Astoria Boulevard. There was a young man working there, a sales clerk whose name was Manny. He was nearsighted and shy. He dreamed about Estelle, and his dreams were steamy and involved large breasts that rose out of the tapioca pudding his mother served him. He knew that it was Estelle's breasts he was dreaming of.

He took her to the movies. They went to see Al Jolson in *The Jazz Singer*. He bought her cotton candy, and as he watched her lick it all on her lips, lipstick and spun sugar, pink tongue, all together, he felt faint. He kissed her on the platform of the elevated. He put his hand on her bottom in the hallway of her house. It was summer. Her father was traveling. Her mother slept soundly. Her brother was in the Catskills working as a lifeguard at a hotel pool. She invited Manny in and offered him a glass of milk. He took her to bed, and while she was asking him if he thought she had lips like Greta Garbo, he managed to touch her belly button and that made her giggle and then he lay down next to her and she stopped giggling.

"I want to marry him," said Estelle to her mother, who sighed.

"Marry him," said her father, who thought that he owned the jewelry store. "Don't marry him," said her father when he found out Manny was only a sales clerk.

"I love him," said Estelle, "and he loves me."

Manny wanted his bride to have all the finer things in life. He took a gold watch from the window and slipped it into his pocket. Who would ever know besides Estelle?

Estelle said, "Put it back. I don't want it."

"You want it," said Manny. "It's yours. I took it for you."

She put it on her arm. It wasn't big enough, and it wouldn't close.

"Don't worry," said Manny. "I'll get you another." This one had emeralds in the clasp.

"Oh," said Estelle. "It's beautiful." She kissed him on the forehead. He put his lips on her chin, which was soft and pink and smelled of rose water.

Lots of other things he took, too. He sold them over in Brooklyn and with the money he made a down payment on a bedroom set and he took an apartment and bought a life insurance policy in Estelle's name just in case anything should happen to him. Everything might have been all right except that old man Shapiro, who went over his inventory every Friday afternoon, found certain items missing. He wasn't so old or so blind that he didn't know that his sales clerk and his bookkeeper were exchanging looks all through the day and that when they passed each other they bumped too often for it to be merely accidental. He wasn't so stupid that he didn't call the police.

They arrested Manny, who said he was innocent, and Estelle said so, too, but she broke down and said she would give back the watch. Manny cried so hard that his glasses fogged over and the sergeant down at the station had to give him a handkerchief to wipe them dry.

"He's going to jail," said Estelle. "Help me," she said to her brother, Frank. "Your Flora has money. Get me some to give to old man Shapiro and he'll forget about pressing charges, I'm sure."

Frank looked at his sister, who was sweating, and the perspiration marks showed in a circle under her big arms. "I won't," he said. "They look down on me already. I wouldn't ask them. Never."

"All right," said Estelle, "then I'll go ask, I'll ask that snooty brother-in-law-to-be of yours. I'll walk right into the Gruenbaum Company and ask for the president and tell him I'm your sister and I need five thousand dollars or my sweetie will be put away." She shrieked, "You don't care about your own family! They'll see what kind of man you are." She could tell she was having an effect. "If they don't give me the money, I'll sit in the Gruenbaum offices until they do. I'll sit there till they call the police to carry me out and I'll tell everyone that I'm the crazy sister of Frank Sheinfold, who is about to marry Flora Gruenbaum. What do ya think of that?" she added. Her voice was flat and nasal.

"Help her," said Frank's mother.

"I'll think about it," he said.

"You'd better think fast," said Estelle. "Manny can't eat the food in jail. He has a delicate stomach. Those Gruenbaums," she added. "They won't like it that you have a crazy sister."

"You pig," said Frank, hardly raising his voice above a whisper.

"So's your anchovy," said Estelle.

Frank lay in his childhood bed, his feet now almost over the end. He listened to the trains go by one after another, the lights flickering through the window, the glass shaking in the frame. I don't deserve this. I don't deserve this at all. His head pounded. He was frightened. It wasn't just that Arthur or Harry might forbid Flora to marry him because of his fat sister whose boyfriend was going to jail. It was an old and familiar fear that came up from under the bed and wrapped itself around him, pressing tight against his chest.

When he was a boy he had accepted a dare. Jump off the pier in the East River and swim to the island that squatted out there in the dark waters. He had been scared. He had taught himself to swim imitating the other boys, but he wasn't sure he could make it, wasn't sure he was a good enough swimmer. But he couldn't turn away, go home to his mother, the way they were taunting him. He had to go. He took off his shoes and his shirt, and wearing his knickers, he jumped. He kept his eye on the island and kicked his feet and moved his arms even when they were tired, even when his eyes hurt from something in the water that stung, and even when he realized that it was far, farther than he had thought, farther than it appeared to be standing on the pier. A barge came by and the waves pushed him back and he was frightened that it would run him over, the propeller of the tug cutting his legs in two. But the barge glided past and he kept going. The current pulled him downward toward the harbor, where the ocean he had crossed only a few years before rolled, ready to swallow him up, and he pushed against it with his legs and he pulled against it with all his strength. He moved forward slowly, and each stroke took him sideward as well as ahead. Water splashed down into his throat and he knew it would be easy to drown—easier, perhaps, than churning with his arms and his legs and gasping for breath whenever he could. But he kept going. He made it. When he got close and he put his legs down and he knew was safe, he felt a joy surge through him. He had showed them, the bastards on the other shore who were watching him, even when he had become small, even when he looked like a turtle or a bobbing ball in the river, they were watching and he knew it. That afternoon, after the tugboat captain saw him waving on the island and picked him up and took him back to the pier, he felt like a hero. It didn't matter that the boys had gone home. It didn't matter that his sister didn't believe that he had done it and called him a liar. He felt celebrated. A hero. Most of the time it wasn't like that. Most of the time he felt small. Afraid of the trolley that clanged past under the el. Afraid that he would be beaten by the other boys, though he acted tough, tough enough so they left him alone. Afraid that when he woke in the morning something would be wrong with him, everyone would laugh at him, point and laugh. Shame, he often felt shame waiting for him, around the corner, in the eyes of the other boys, in the looks of the other passengers on his bus, in the way people moved away from him at parties. He pretended he didn't see it. He pretended it wasn't out there waiting for him to make a false move, but he knew it. He would be shamed someday, shamed beyond repair, a shame so deep it would break him in pieces. The hint of it, the whisper in the wind, *You're no good, not as good as the others,* would start him moving, arguing with someone, pushing against someone, just to prove it hadn't happened yet. Shame was still at bay. He kept it there by the force of his will. Whatever events filled his days, that was the plot of his life. And now if his sister had her way, he would be shamed in front of the Gruenbaums, in front of Flora, who thought she was so fine. His hands were fists.

His head pounded harder. His first migraine had come in his second year at college. Something was happening around him, something beyond grades and exams, that excluded him. He was a swimmer, a track runner. He knew the fellows at ZBT and they knew him, but when he walked into the dining room he didn't feel comfortable joining any particular group. He usually ate alone, quickly. He wished he could be easy, friendly, full of jokes, but he was always rushing, the extra job, the commute to home, the work, and then he had to be careful, careful of what he didn't know. He wished the pressure would stop, for the rushing wherever he was rushing to end, for sleep in someone's arms, for an end to the grinding of his teeth, for a way to stop worrying if his pants were spotted or his shirt wrinkled. He wished he had a friend with whom he could do twenty laps and then go to a coffee shop, nodding his head and bending his body as if unafraid, as if someone were not waiting to cut your skin, to drown you in the pool, to make a fool of you.

One evening he had been working late at his job at the cafeteria and he was clearing away the stale cigarette butts and the plates with the crumbs of chocolate cake, and he wanted to go to sleep. The exhaustion grew and with it a small sharp pain over his right eye and a weariness in his limbs, as if the adrenaline in his system had disappeared, as if he were in mourning for something or someone. By the time he had taken the two buses uptown and crosstown and had climbed the four flights of stairs and had closed himself in the room he shared with Estelle in the apartment whose front windows rattled each time the Third Avenue el came along, the pain had spread deep into his head, and in front of his eyes lights were flashing. Now it was happening again. He closed his eyes and waited for the pain to pass.

The next morning he went to Astoria and walked into the jewelry store where his sister had worked and her husband-to-be had helped himself to the merchandise. "Mr. Shapiro," he said, "I want you to drop the charges against my sister's boyfriend. I'll make it up to you, I promise. It will be a debt of mine. I'll sign a note for you."

"Nothing doing," said Mr. Shapiro. "Crooks deserve to be punished. What you think, in America there's no law?"

Frank leaned over the counter and grabbed the old man by the throat. He shook him up and down. He felt as if he had a broom in his hand, one that whimpered, "Leave me alone, leave me alone!" He picked up a paperweight from the old man's desk. It was a rock, a souvenir from a trip to Niagara Falls he had taken with his wife for their thirtieth anniversary. Frank thought quickly. He had no intention of going to jail.

"I'll kill you," he said to Shapiro. "If you press charges, I'll kill you. If you go to the police and complain about me, I'll come in the middle of the night and I'll kill you. Your arms are like sticks, I can break all your bones. Don't press charges against Manny or go to the police, or I'll kill you."

As he said the words Frank was startled. He heard them echo about the jewelry store. He heard how they sounded, not hot, not in temper, but icy, like knives just sitting in drawers waiting to be used. He was amazed at himself. If the man called the police, he would kill him. He would do it. Just then he had learned that about himself. He felt hungry and tired and, as always, afraid. Had he crossed a line? Had he always been across the line? In the museum he had seen a mummy, shrouded for thousands of years. Suddenly he felt as if he too were dead, behind glass.

Frank wasn't the only one who knew that his threats were not empty, his bluff not a bluff. Old man Shapiro dropped his charges, and Manny and Estelle were married. Old man Shapiro, at Frank's suggestion, gave Estelle the gold watch as a wedding gift.

Flora Till Death Do Them Part: 1929

Naomi called Flora to her bedside the month before the wedding. Increasingly Naomi had trouble getting up, pulling her legs over the edge of the bed, and finding her way along the thick Oriental carpet to the bathroom. Sometimes her daughter-in-law would forget to send the maid to help her get dressed, and this embarrassed Naomi, but how could she protest? Her son was no longer in the house. She was only a relic, a thing kept out of sentiment or duty. Who cared whether she came downstairs or not? It was a fact, one that Naomi acknowledged—she was going to end her life just as she began it, dependent on the mercy of strangers. It was possible that her daughter-in-law, a woman of good intentions but narrow heart, might send her, one day, to the Daughters of Jacob, the old age home founded largely by funds that Isaac and Max had contributed.

Naomi had seen the place when they had a dinner honoring her sons. There were bars on the windows so the old folks wouldn't fall out. There were bars on the beds and a smell of chlorine and witch hazel in the halls. The walls were painted a bright yellow and the nurses wore yellow caps on their heads; it was the yellow of decay, and they didn't fool Naomi, who knew that the beds were wet and fouled and that the nurses who smiled at the visitors had other thoughts when they were alone with their charges in the dimly lit halls at night. Naomi was convinced she would be murdered in the old age home, and she had good reason to fear the place, who better should know. Naomi hoped to die in her bed in the house on Riverside Drive. She considered it carefully. If she died and the maid found her, the maid could take her diamond, and who would know? If she were sent to the old age home, she would be stripped right away and the diamond would disappear.

Naomi wasn't the sort of woman to dwell on unpleasant things. She read the paper each day. She tried to get a little sunshine on Riverside Drive whenever possible. She walked carefully so she wouldn't fall and break a bone. She enjoyed her scrambled eggs cooked to order at any time of the day she wished by someone in the kitchen, someone whose name was Rosie or Mary or Meg, she couldn't remember which.

"So," said Naomi, "your young man, he's handsome?"

"Yes, Grandma," said Flora. "You met him, for dinner last week, didn't you think he was handsome?"

"No money," said Naomi to her granddaughter, who looked to her like an orphan herself, small, pale, her brown eyes blinking behind her glasses.

"No," said Flora, "but he'll work for Harry. Frank's smart. He's very smart. He won a scholarship to Columbia. Papa would have liked him, I'm sure he would."

"All right," said Naomi, "I have something for your wedding. Something for you." She pulled up her dress. Flora was embarrassed by the trembling thin legs whose skin hung wrinkled around the bone, by the petticoat that was stained with an accident the old lady had not noticed.

"Here," said Naomi, and from around her waist she took the pouch with the velvet string and she gave it to Flora. It had a strong smell, of body sweat and urine and powder. Flora held the pouch in her hand as if it were a dead mouse or one of the caterpillars that Arthur and Harry had once put on her pillow. "Open it," said Naomi. "Nobody but me has ever opened it." Flora untied the pouch. "Look, look inside," said Naomi, and Flora saw the diamond. It wasn't the biggest diamond Flora had ever seen. Mildred had one with emeralds all around it for her engagement ring. Her mother had one with rubies surrounding it like a baby's bonnet, and Flora had worried because she knew that Frank could not afford to give her a ring like that.

"Give this to your young man and have him make it into a ring for you," said Naomi, whose waist felt light, who thought her body was suddenly off center, as if the diamond carried there for so long had been the gravity that kept her anchored to the planet, upright and forward moving. Naomi said that the diamond had been given to her by a dying woman in the old age home in Sulvalki and that she had kept it all these years for an emergency, for a time when the family would need it, when it would change their lives, the way the other diamond, the one that had bought them passage to America, had changed their lives; but now she could see it would not be needed, and it had gotten smaller over the years as the business grew and she had no intention of taking it to the grave with her. Of course she was lying to her granddaughter. She would have been perfectly happy to have been buried in the plot next to Moses with the diamond still tied to her waist, but who could guarantee her possession once the angel of death had stuffed his fist down her throat? No one, no one at all.

"Flora, my love," said her grandmother, "this is my treasure, and it's for you."

Flora did not tell her mother or her sister, and she knew that her grandmother wouldn't, either.

Frank took the ring to a jeweler and he agreed to pay on time for the setting from his job as a waiter at a faculty club that overlooked Morningside Park. He was pleased he didn't have to buy a ring altogether and that the old lady had come to his rescue with her gift. When Flora put the ring on her finger and showed it to her sisters and her brothers, they admitted it wasn't a bad ring, better than they thought Frank would deliver. It caught the sunlight. In the evening it looked like a star had settled on her finger. Arthur wanted to have the ring appraised. He thought Frank might have bought an imitation, but Flora wouldn't take it off her finger. I love him, she said to herself, no matter what happens to us, I'll always love him.

The wedding was fine enough. It wasn't as big as her sister's, but then her husband did not have so many relatives, so many business acquaintances, and her father, Isaac, had died and in dying had taken some of the certainty away from the family. Still, it was a big wedding at the Plaza Hotel, and she had a dress long and white and covered with tiny pearls. There had been flowers on each table and a band and her brother Harry had given her away. Her mother wore beige silk and a lavender hat, and when Flora had walked down the aisle and seen Frank in his morning coat with its long tails and his starched white shirt, she had felt faint with anticipation. His strength would carry her. His dark eyes that did not melt or flinch or look down with pity or grief, those eyes that looked straight ahead, would admire her for the rest of her days. She saw the straightness of his back and the way his hands, waiting there at the altar, had curled into fists, as if anticipating trouble. She felt, as she stood beside him and the rabbi began in the Hebrew she could not understand

and that she knew Frank hated because it was of the old world that no longer mattered (a daring thought that made Flora shudder and yet look at him with awe), that her body was being lifted out of itself, that she was floating above the guests, above Mildred, Harry, and Arthur. Her mother was only a lavender spot on the hotel rug and she was being rocked gently into her life, her life as a woman.

At Flora's wedding the band played "The Black Bottom Stomp" as well as the hora, and the trombonist kept staring down Mildred's neckline from his perch on the stand, and the rabbi who pronounced them man and wife talked on and on about the good deeds of the family, the prosperity of the business, that Arthur and Harry, though still in their twenties, had kept steady, even increased since their father's death.

Naomi sat at a table with her daughter-in-law, whose name she now occasionally forgot. She spooned all the fruit in her compote carefully into her mouth, her hands clutching the crystal cup so that it would not move away from her, the way the family circled near her and swept away as if the currents were carrying them off, quite beyond their intentions. She watched Flora's hand, which she saw fluttering on her husband's shoulder as they danced the first dance together, tiny Flora, tall Frank, his eyes straight ahead, hers looking up trying to catch his. She watched Flora's hand and saw the ring as it turned around, whirled to the left and the right, as it moved up and down. Naomi sat at the table with her son Max, and people who passed patted her on the shoulder but avoided her face. She sat unsmiling, her eyes wet with tears as if she were at a funeral for a ring, as if her ring were her mother and father, dying once again before they could take care of her, abandoning her to a destiny that was bound to be difficult.

Spoon, June, Honeymoon—Arthur Writes a Poem for Flora: 1929

They spent the first night in the Plaza Hotel. Flora lay down on the bed expecting the things that young girls always expect, ecstasy and bliss, joy and knowledge, and fearing the things that young girls always fear, pain and rupture, tearing and ripping, blood that does not stop. Frank—who had whores in the neighborhood, who had a girl who was an orphan from Romania and lived up the stairs from them—looked at his bride in her lace panties and thought to himself, Her hips are wide, her legs are short, but when she takes her glasses off I see her brown eyes, hoping. She tilts her head up at me and smiles and she looks lost. I am responsible for her and I will take care of her. There was a lump in his chest. What if he failed her? What if she began to laugh at him? He felt the beginnings of the familiar darkness, the dark hole of an emptiness inside of him, and he leapt into action.

He knew enough to touch her nipples, but she was frightened of the way his cold hands moved across her body, as if she were a car whose hood he was inspecting, as if his mind were elsewhere. He had drunk the champagne that her brother Arthur had hidden in the men's room, many visits he made to the cubicle with the bottles placed on the seat. He had broken the glass with his foot, and he had spoken at the wedding with Harry, who, when Frank returned, would give him the corner office on 36th Street and Seventh Avenue complete with a secretary who sat at a table with a typewriter outside his door. The salary, which came with more stock in his own name each year, was enough to rent the apartment on Park Avenue and pay for the chauffeur who would take him to work. Sweet it was, sweet it tasted; America, land of the brave, had been good to him.

He entered his bride suddenly, and she cried out. Her lips were full and waited to be kissed. Frank kissed her. She tasted of strawberries. He wanted to please her. If she were pleased, then he could rest. Afterward Flora lay on the sheets that were rumpled and stained, and when she tilted her head she could see Frank over by the window, where the curtains were blowing from the late August breeze and she saw him sitting there tearing up the napkins that had been part of the wedding. A box of them had waited for them in their suite: Frank and Flora, they said in pink letters, and Frank was sitting there shredding them, one by one, in neat piles while drinking Scotch from crystal glass, as Flora, exhausted, fell asleep.

Then they boarded the *Queen Anne,* the newest ship to Europe, for a five-week trip, time to get to know each other, time to buy some essentials for their new apartment, time to begin a baby or end a childhood. There were rumors that things had gone badly in New York, the market was in flux, the papers carried stories of leapings and weepings, but Flora was not worrying about the market. She held Frank's arm tightly, as if he were a cane or a crutch, as if she has lost strength in the few weeks since they had docked at Le Havre and then arrived in Montreux for a stay at the great lake where the swans dotted the blue waters and the snow-covered mountains beckoned them from their terrace. In their hotel room there was a bathroom the size of a cathedral's nave and a tub with room for two, but Frank took showers and would not join Flora floating in the suds.

After a week of walking around the lake and taking tea in the lobby and dining in the Emerald Room with its green glass windows, they took the slow train ride down the coast of Italy, past the acres of olive groves and the houses with red tiles nestled against the hills and the donkeys pulling threshing wagons round in circles and the women all in black walking with bundles of sticks on their heads. All this time, Flora told Frank stories about her childhood. What groom would not want to hear the family jokes, the family secrets?

Frank's mind wandered when she spoke. He couldn't remember what she said. His eyes looked in her face. His thin lips were clenched. His hands were kept in fists in his lap.

"Are you listening?" she would ask.

"Yes, yes," he would say, "go on."

"Tell me something, tell me about your mother," she would say.

He would look out the window, check his watch, tell her how long it was until they arrived at the next town. He would take out his Baedeker and tell her what it was they should look at when they arrived. He would tell her about the political situation, the historical vignettes that he learned from the backs of postcards. He said his mother was fine, why did she ask?

She told him about her friends, her best friend from high school, who had gotten pregnant and had an early wedding two weeks before graduation.

"Stupid broad," said Frank. "Probably trying to trap the guy." Flora smiled at him. Frank looked at her closely. When she opened her mouth he could see that her front teeth were too large for her face and her lipstick kept smearing on them because of the way she curled her lip up when she spoke.

Before dinner he would go for a long walk by himself, a walk along the major boulevard of whatever town they were in. He needed the exercise. He moved his legs fast, like the athlete he was, swinging his arms by his side. He breathed in and out. He thought of nothing, making his mind like the slabs of the Ten Commandments before a word was carved, listening only to rhythms of his body smashing through the air. A panic rose in him. His heart beat fast. His temples throbbed. Sadness was rolling over his brain, sadness like a fog that would erase everything else, sadness that would turn his world dark.

He found a woman leaning against a doorway, half-dressed, swinging her purse at him. She made a gesture. He followed her up the stairs, and in a small room with a cot, with a bowl and pitcher of water, he threw the woman on the bed and bit her neck and, turning her over, opened her up, and screaming at her, "Whore, whore!" he rose and fell with the not precisely impassioned movements of her obedient but garlic-flavored body. She charged him more because of his choice of openings. He wouldn't pay her. When he got back to the hotel he took a long shower. "Whore," he whispered to himself. Bitch, he thought, she trapped me. But he felt better. The sadness had been beaten back down to its place in the soul, where it crouched ever ready to make an appearance, ever ready to tear him apart.

Once he found a small cemetery. Here the Jews of Padua were buried. He could tell from the names on the stones. He stood there a while in the evening chill, rubbing his hands together. A grave keeper, a little old man with a stoop and a limp, came forward.

"Are you looking for someone?" he asked in Italian, in Ladino, in Yiddish, in English. "Perhaps I can help." And he held out his hand for a tip.

"No," said Frank, backing off. "I don't know anyone here."

"Then why have you come?" said the man.

Frank wasn't sure. "All right," he said, and spent an hour walking around the cemetery with the old man pointing out the predominant families, the rabbi and his son and the children who died in the last influenza epidemic. "You want to say kaddish for someone?" asked the old man.

"No," said Frank.

She was so small, his new wife, that when he stopped in a crowded train station to buy the *Paris Herald Tribune,* when he turned around for her, he couldn't see her. She had disappeared in the crowd. He found her waiting for him at the train gate, her eyes all red from crying.

"I thought I had lost you," she said, clutching his arm.

"For God's sake," he said, "I was at the kiosk over there."

"I was worried," she said.

"Don't worry," he said, "I'll never leave you." She smiled up at him, but his face, the fine chiseled nose, the thin lips, each feature perfectly distanced from the other, remained still, creased in certain ways but un-changing.

They had a photograph taken in the Piazza San Marco, the time was fall and she wore a fox fur draped over her shoulders, her hat was black and came down across her nose, sending a shadow over her face. Her dress was tight and just right for the year. In the Piazzo San Marco, Frank stood staring into the camera with his large-brimmed fedora held in one hand, with his hair flattened down with Vaseline and his part straight, with his eyes squinting slightly from the light and the suit he was wearing newly pressed, not like a traveler at all, like a man who had been born and bred to stand in the center of the Piazzo San Marco with the pigeons all around him, hundreds on the statue behind, fluttering their wings, cooing to one another, pecking at necks and wings and hinting of copulations past and present; thousands of pigeons are in the photograph. In the picture Flora had put one foot in front of the other, knowing that the line would make her appear thinner in the picture. She had stuffed her glasses into her muff. She worried that her body was heavy. She feared that the fat child she had been was still there. She worried that Frank had not found her interesting enough. She read the guidebooks and pointed out to him details that he might have missed. They stood in the Sistine Chapel and she showed him the hand that Michelangelo painted first before he began on the faces, the hand of God reaching out to Adam. Flora looked at the hand and thought of Frank's hand pushing apart her legs, shoving up her breasts.

"See how God is reaching toward man," she said to Frank.

"Superstition," said Frank. "A cesspool of superstition, all of Italy," he said, "religious rot. They were on the side of the kaiser, these Italians, you know that, don't you?"

Flora didn't exactly. She looked at her husband in a new way. He would teach her about the world. He knew so much.

"Huns," he said. "Scum," he muttered.

"The war is over now," said Flora, "a long time."

"Still," said Frank, "don't trust them."

"It's supposed to be fun in Berlin," said Flora.

"Nothing but whores in Berlin," said Frank.

"Would you like to go home earlier?" said Flora, who thought that perhaps her sister and her mother were missing her. "Would you like to stop traveling? Perhaps we are moving too much."

"No," said Frank. "It's paid for, this honeymoon."

It worried him that he was overtipping. It worried him that his clothes might be wrong. He looked at the other men; how did they speak to the bellhops? How did they enter lobbies and cars? He made all the arrangements with the concierges. He spoke to the travel agent in the hotel. He stood as straight as he could and he smoothed down his hair and he brushed off the shoulders of his jacket and he straightened his tie, but he was uncertain. Sometimes he thought he saw people staring at him, laughing behind his back. Sometimes he thought he hadn't measured up, some custom he ignored, some way of being proper that he hadn't known. More than anything else, he feared the sting of shame. But he believed that a man should fear nothing, not a real man. Sitting on a bench on the Via Veneto, waiting for Flora to buy a set of coffee cups, he thought of Houdini. A man who was more than a man, a kind of miracle of escape, who couldn't be buried or chained or locked in a box. He was just a magician, a charlatan, it was all fake, Frank knew. There were gimmicks and gismos and ways that he did it, anybody could do it if they knew the trick.

When Frank and Flora were in Venice they received a telegram. Naomi had died. Flora cried in the café where they had gone for lunch. When she cried her nose turned red and her eye makeup ran down her cheeks. Frank gave her his handkerchief, but she got it stained and wet. He watched the waitress with the wide bottom and the tight black skirt make her way through the tight aisles between the tables. He thought of how her body would smell and hair would grow from under her arms. He was repulsed. He was aroused. He kept his eyes off his wife's face, now beginning to be swollen around the eyelids and the flesh above her cheekbones puffed out with her tears. "What did you expect?" he said. "She would live forever?"

Flora fondled her ring. "She gave it to me," said Flora. "Not to Mildred, but to me."

What diseases could you get from Italian whores? thought Frank, who wanted to go back to the hotel and take another shower.

"I've missed the funeral," said Flora.

He felt she was blaming him, as if it were his fault: the distance, the ocean, the death of the old lady. In Europe he showered four or five times a day, as if the germs of ancient civilizations could be washed down the drain, as if he could protect himself from the death that had carried off Flora's grandmother by preventing odors and stains, stains from cooking, from chimneys, from flaking buildings, from pigeons that spilled their waters wherever they felt like it, from resting on the crevices of his skin.

Her luggage included candlesticks from Paris and a set of Wedgwood dishes from a store in an alley in Venice and dresses from little shops all over and shoes and a tapestry from a store in Turin and maps and guidebooks and tablecloths and napkins with her monogram embroidered on them. At each purchase she had wondered, Is this the right thing to buy? Would Mildred like it? At each purchase she had shivered; what if she were poor and could not buy anything anymore?

Frank bought suits and ties and shoes and sent them on ahead to the boat. He bought himself ascots and hats, and when he bought something he chiseled down the price and threatened to walk out of the store, and the salespeople bowed and agreed. Frank said to Flora that the entire Roman Empire was for sale, but you had to be careful because these people were trying to cheat you, every last one of them were out to get another sucker. Frank dreamed of warriors, emperors with chariots, Caesar with his minions and Napoleon with his army, the kings and queens of Brussels and Belgium, the kaiser and the archdukes and the grafs of Poland and the ministers of the Austro-Hungarian empire; he saw them all laughing at him, a nobody Jew, a man with no army, who would never have a statue, who would die without immortality, no odes, no eulogies, except by the local rabbi who would get his name wrong. Frank woke from his dream in a sweat. Who was he, a man buried under the rubble of history, a man without a name? In Europe there were too many great men, too many gargoyles ready to fall off their columns, for his taste.

They stopped going to museums. It bored Frank. It bored Flora, who liked zoos and parks and cafes. In Paris they had watched a Punch and Judy show in the Parc Vendôme. Punch hit Judy with a bat, and Flora put her hands up to her eyes.

"It's supposed to be funny," said Frank.

"I don't think it is," said Flora. "Look how they hit each other."

"So what?" said Frank. "It's a joke."

Flora wanted to leave, but Frank made her stay till the end. He didn't laugh, but he smiled when Punch fell flat on his face over the proscenium and Judy hit her head on the arch.

Under the Arc de Triomphe, with a vendor of balloons behind her, Flora pursed her lips for the camera, her cheekbones showed better that way. She looked at the crowd, children and old men, American tourists, English schoolboys, many with bags of crumbs for the birds, and the old ladies selling pretzels from wagons. "Centuries and centuries, this place has been here," she said to Frank. "I feel as if we are intruders."

Frank sat at a cafe and ordered a Pernod. Its sweet licorice taste alarmed him. Who knew what was in it? He pushed it aside. He was waiting for Flora. He saw the man and the woman at the next table talking in Russian; intensely they stared at each other, gesturing, leaning in across the table, through the swirls of cigarette smoke, and he wished he could join them. What were they saying? Did he have an opinion, too? Were they talking about Bolsheviks? Were they White Russians? What had history done to them, how had they arrived at the cafe in Paris together?

Frank stared at them like a store mannequin looking out the window at the rush of traffic, the window shoppers, the people with destinations speeding past. The woman laughed at her companion and touched his arm, a sudden intimacy. The man sighed and leaned back in his chair. He smiled under his mustache and said something that made the lady turn pink with pleasure. Frank wanted to speak to them, to be asked to join their table, but he sat still, a handsome young American whose perfectly polished shoes were shining in the pale light of the cafe's dim bulbs. He waited. He looked in the plate-glass window and caught his own reflection. It brought him no comfort.

There were Cupids of stone and Greek goddesses holding up the corners of buildings, there were stone shields on houses whose owners had long gone to dust and flags waving and everywhere shadows, dust in the crevices, pigeon waste on the ground, white with a black curl in the center, pigeon waste on the lions and the warriors, stray feathers caught in the sweeper's broom.

During a ride on the Seine, Flora put her arm around Frank and he sat there listening to the sounds of the water lapping against the boat as it slipped under the bridges. "Darling," he said to his wife, and the sound floated to the surface of the river like a discarded piece of paper; it filled with water, dipped down, and sank. "The stock market has crashed," he said.

"People will still need suits," said Flora. She lost her passport in a hotel room, and they had to go to the embassy and wait three days and deal with functionaries who didn't believe she had just discarded it in the wastebasket with the papers from a new blouse she had bought. But in the end they gave her a new passport, and Frank and Flora sailed as scheduled from Cherbourg.

Hedy Hears the Story of the Honeymoon and Decides That When She Grows Up She Will Become a Gym Teacher— A Spinster for Life: 1944

Hedy was sitting beside her mother's bed on the soft armchair that was covered in yellow velvet. She swung her feet against the legs of the chair.

"Stop that," said her mother.

Hedy wanted to sit on the bed with her mother, to hold her hand, the one with the chipped nail, but her mother said no, stay in the chair and be quiet. So Hedy sat watching her mother breathe up and down through the negligee, watching her mother do the *Saturday Review* crossword puzzle.

Flora finished it quickly, then decided to tell Hedy the plot of the play she had seen on Broadway the night before. Hedy told Flora how she had been elected captain of the softball team by three votes. Hedy explained the game to her mother. She drew her a picture of the baseball diamond. Flora invited Hedy to sit on the bed and she took her head into her hands and pressed her nose against Hedy's nose. "An Eskimo kiss," she said. Then she told Hedy about the honeymoon—not everything, of course, but enough or too much. Hedy got the drift. She imagined her father by the window in the Plaza Hotel with the piles of paper napkins, his married life ahead, his daughter not yet born, his arms moving up and down in his dressing gown with the black velvet lapels as he picked up the napkins, folded them carefully, and tore them to bits. Hedy knew that sitting there as the pale white sky drifted over the hotel and the stars blinked and faded away, her father was feeling alone, alone in his body, the way he always did, and his bride sleeping now on the sheets, her soft thighs showing under her silk gown, had left him alone.

Hedy, at the Orthodontist, Learns of Crime and Punishment: 1948

Hedy is in the waiting room of the orthodontist. Her buckteeth with the large space between them are being fixed, buckteeth caused by excessive thumb sucking. Hedy curls up her tongue and fits it in the space. Soon she won't be able to do that anymore. Flora sits beside her, reading *Life* magazine. She has already called her broker and found out that the stock she bought in the morning has gone up three points.

Sitting across the room with her mother is a child with a cleft palate. Hedy doesn't want to stare. She doesn't want to appear not to be looking, either. She wants to be natural, but her heart is pounding. The child's face blurs the distinction between inside and outside, closed and open. The nose and the mouth are pulled together. When at last the nurse calls the child into the office and Hedy and Flora are alone in the waiting room, Hedy asks, "How did that happen?"

Flora says, "Her mother is being punished."

Hedy says, "Why?"

Flora says, "That woman did things with men she shouldn't."

"But that's not fair," says Hedy. "It's the child that's being punished," she adds.

Flora says, "My cousin Sharon told me that her father said those children are the cupbearers of the Lord in the world to come. They are his favorite angels."

"Do you believe that?" asks Hedy.

"No," says Flora.

"Why are they being punished?" asks Hedy.

Flora sucks on the earpiece of her glasses. She looks at her child. "Who knows," says Flora.

Hedy in the Corridor of the Hadassah Hospital: 1990

Time was moving, but Hedy couldn't feel it. It didn't flow through her or lift her up or lap against the edges of her body. Time was moving. She could see on the hands of the clock, the doctor had been operating over three hours; at least it was that long since they had wheeled Namah past the closed green doors. The group in the hall was silent, as if they had talked themselves out on a train trip or had been on the beach too long and were lying each on his own towel staring at the birds pecking in the sand at the edge of the sea.

If Hedy believed in God, she would feel she was being punished. Of course it was Namah who was in danger, but when the child is punished, the mother is punished, too. If Hedy believed in God, a God who judged, God who watched what she ate and knew if she had murderous thoughts about her colleagues, a God who knew just how petty and irritable, how low, her spirits could be, how unholy her appetites were, if she believed in that God, she could hate him for bringing Namah to the operating table, for bringing her to the hall to wait word from inside the operating room. If she believed, then she could hate, but since she did not believe, whom could she hate? If she believed she could call on God to rescue her child, to bring her back from oblivion, she could atone for whatever sins she may have committed, but the oblivious God she was inclined to imagine would not have noticed Namah in the vast galaxies of his creation, in the myriad moving gases and merging chemicals, molecular explosions and retractions, the light that ran through the gravitational pulls, the billion wishes of the human animals, the trillion desires of the living creatures from mollusk to elephant. God, God of the Universe, Creator of the bang or the whimper, of the first gas or the last, would not appear in Dr. Steiger's operating room, of that Hedy was certain. So there was no appeal. No ruse, no temporary illusion, no last minute papers submitted to a Supreme Being who might reconsider. There had been no consideration in the first place. Hedy stood pat. She hated without anyone to hate, and she appealed to no one, did not beg for mercy, she flattered no one. She did not offer the first fruits of her harvest, she did not expect a ram to appear on the operating table. She clenched her fist by her side. She took off her shoe and rubbed her toes, which had fallen asleep as she had pressed her foot too tightly against the leg of the chair.

Hedy, who spent her days interpreting the data gathered from the heavens, teaching others to adjust the telescopes, to chart the motions of the light and the mass, expected that her work would reveal some minute particle of truth from the entire mystery. One day, she thought, she might find a new light at the corner of her eye. Something appearing in the lens, something that no one else had ever seen, a star, or a comet, a force of some sort, a ray. It was not too late for that to happen. The universe was predictable, ordered and, at the same time, unstable. Hedy counted on that instability, but to understand punishment, who was punished and why, that she would never be able to do.

Howard Katz and the American Dream: 1922 and After

Howard Katz went with his new father-in-law to the clubhouse in the Bronx on Van Cortlandt Street. He smiled at all the fellows. He took a cigar from Finney, the largest man in the room, who leaned up against the cedar walls under the moosehead that hung on a plaque and near the framed photograph of last year's club picnic at the Bronx Zoo, where some of the members were wearing zebra ears while others sported a lion mask or a pig nose, and said to him, "So, son, you a good Democrat?"

Howard Katz looked him in the eye and said, "You bet I am. The future of this country depends on our party."

There was something in the way Howard spoke, a certain shine in his eye, that made the older man, who happened to be the treasurer of the club, uncomfortable. "Wait a minute, sonny," he said. "Not so serious. You got the rest of your life to be serious. The Irish and the Jews, up here on Spuyten Duyvil, we know how to get by. Get it? Democrats, we got Liberty's tits right here, right in this clubhouse." He held out his large hands with their perfectly manicured nails.

"Right here in our hands. Democrats, Howie, they have a good time."

Howard Katz looked at the treasurer. "Sure," he said. "Say, you got a great place here."

Ben Eisen put his arm around Howie and led him around the room. "This one," said Ben over and over, "he has a great brain. He was at the top of his class at City, he can do good for us. Tell you the truth, he's smarter than my own son," Ben confided to one man, and to another he said, "Look at him, good-looking enough to run for office, if necessary."

"Yeah," said his companion, "not bad, but a little small. Better if he had bigger shoulders."

"His shoulders are big enough," said Ben.

And Bessie got pregnant. It took time. It took time because Howard was tired in the evening and spent long hours in his office, a law practice that grew by leaps and bounds as members of the club referred relatives and friends and some of the larger clients of the bank, surprisingly, came to the young lawyer's office and had him rewrite their wills and he was always setting up contracts for business deals, for sales of buildings, and even defending criminals. He defended Finney's nephew, who was arrested for assaulting an officer in a brawl in the park, and he got him off by accusing the officer of attempting to destroy the Bill of Rights and in his final summation he threatened to take the case all the way to the Supreme Court. He was so passionate in his defense of the young man, whom he genuinely considered wronged of his basic rights as a citizen, that Judge O'Keife, who was known around the courthouse as Snoozy O'Sleep, sat up straight and kept his eyes open throughout the trial. In addition to the excellent rhetoric, Howie won that case because Snoozy was also a member of the club whose brother-in-law was the man who was in charge of bringing out the vote on election days as well as planning the annual retreat to the Catskills.

Howard's income from his law practice could not support the apartment and the servants and the clothes that Bessie needed, so Ben had placed a large amount of money in Bessie's bank account. Just as before she was married, if she wanted anything special, she asked her father, who could never say no to his only daughter. This made Howard Katz feel awkward. He couldn't explain to his poor mother and father, whom he hardly saw anymore, just how it was the young married couple had so many luxuries. The luxuries were unimportant to him. He wore better suits because Bessie insisted. He learned to let the maid pour the water and take away the dishes. He dried his body after his shower in thick towels with his initials on them, but he hardly noticed. His head was full of the glory of law, and he practiced smoking the pipe Bessie bought him because she thought it made him look more important, smoke burning his tongue hour after hour. Whatever she wanted he would do.

Mostly Howard Katz was happy. One night his happiness spilled over onto Bessie, who allowed him to pull her nightgown over her head and to pin her down against the silk sheets that had her monogram embossed on the corners and to open her legs, small as they were—almost, he thought, like a child's—and spread them apart with his fingers and, bending his mouth down, he did a thing that shocked him, a thing he hadn't thought of since a boy in junior high had told him that it was done by all the prostitutes in Odessa and he had doubted it, made a retching nose, and shoved the boy in the shoulder. He waited till she was wet and his lips felt swollen and then he entered her, and as his sperm,

propelled by the laws of biology and swathed in the chemistry of reproduction, swam the foreshortened distance to her womb, he thought about
names for his son, George for George Washington, James, for James
Madison, Oliver, for Oliver Wendell Holmes.

Bessie put her arms around her husband as he drifted off to sleep.
She too considered a child, a beautiful girl, she thought, tall and blond,
one who would make men faint and would ignore them unless they gave
her emeralds and diamonds, a girl, she thought, who would make men
love her and then discard them, one after another, like day-old bread, fit
only for pigeons or the poor. With her head back on her pillow and her
husband asleep on her breast, Bessie smiled.

The child was born, but not easily. The labor was twenty-two hours
long. Bessie was furious and frightened, and she screamed at the nurses
and spit at the doctors who approached her. She called for medication,
she threatened them all with lawsuits, she wept and clenched her teeth.
It was unfair that women bore children. She changed her mind. Not a
girl, she thought, not a child to suffer this, she thought, please God, let
the baby be a boy. And it was. Not only was the baby a boy, but his face
was not her face.

Mildred and Flora came to the hospital, and in the hall they giggled.
"He doesn't look like her."

"Swell," they said. "What luck."

The infant had wide blue eyes that stared upward as if only total
concentration could keep the ceiling from falling down onto his bassinet.
He had a ridge on his nose as if he'd already been in a fight and his skin
was olive like hers, but his features were placed in the usual way.

"All right," said Bessie, "anyone can have a son. But I have an
exceptional son. Can't you see by the way he turns his head, the way he
reaches up his hand?" Bessie didn't want him named after a president or
even a Supreme Court justice. "He needs his own name," she insisted.

"An American name," said Howard, "the kind of name a boy can
carry anywhere in this country."

They called him Will. It sounded right. Will. They could hear in it
the waters of the Mississippi turning the wheels of the great paddleboats.
They could hear the wagons moving and the axes falling on the fir trees
of Minnesota. They could hear the harvesters threshing the wheat on the
plains of Kansas. They could see the victorious men in blue walking
through the abandoned plantations of South Carolina. Will was another
name for wanting, and what was America, said Howie, but a country
wanting something for everyone? The Katz they couldn't do anything
about.

As a mother, Bessie was the equal of any woman. As a mother of a remarkable child, Bessie could only be an object of envy. The tables had been turned. Before Will entered the first grade, Howie had his judgeship. The appeals court, a fine position for a young man of talent and dedication; Howie was overwhelmed with gratitude to his father-in-law and to his wife, who threw a party in his honor the day the judgeship was announced. He put on the robes in his chambers. He met his assistants and his clerk, and he walked out into the courtroom and took his seat under the American flag and there were tears in his eyes. He would serve with honor and give back to this great country what had been given to him. He was a Democrat who believed in justice for the deprived and equality for the people and the pursuit of happiness because that's what it said in the Constitution, the most perfect document ever made by man.

That night when Ben Eisen toasted him and he lifted his glass in response, Howie told the assembled guests in the Franklin Room of the Concord Hotel that fairness was the essence of America, and he would make sure that his corner of the Bronx never violated those founding principles.

The men from the clubhouse who attended the party slapped him on the back and smiled at Ben Eisen. "Great guy, your Howie," they said. "Makes the heart sing," they said, "the way he has with words." "Let him speak at our picnic this year," said another. "He really is a Yankee doodle dandy." And they slugged down their apple juice, because this was a public party and members of the press had been invited by Bessie, who wanted to be sure that the Bronx *Eagle* and the *Herald Tribune* were aware that a new judge, amazingly young, was on the bench, a rising star was on the American scene.

Will attended the party in a velvet sailor suit, and his grandfather Eisen gave him a silver dollar to put in his piggy bank. Will kept the dollar in his pocket and kept his fingers tightly curled over it as his mother took him around the room and introduced him to everyone there. "Remember their names," she told her son. "It comes in handy to remember names."

They moved to a bigger apartment house on a steep hill where the houses had names like Trianon, Windham, and Versailles carved in stone above the front portals. There were hundreds of stairs up to the apartment front door as the buildings on the block rested against the rising earth behind them. Will would stand on the top step, and holding his mother's hand, he would wave his arm over the street below. "Guilty," he would say. "I judge you guilty." And his mother would laugh. He would climb up the steps slowly and cautiously, holding on to the guard rail and considering carefully each placement of his foot.

Will was not allowed out to play on the street because Bessie could not bear the thought of his falling on the cement and cutting his knee or scraping his hands. She did not like to think of him running with the pack, like a common wolf cub. She worried when he was out of sight that a brick might fall from a building, a kidnapper who knew that he was the child of an important judge might snatch him, a child with a running nose might put his dirty hand on a sleeve and Will might take the polio germ right into his lungs and die. Therefore Will stayed in the apartment after school and Bessie amused him by playing bridge with him at their Chippendale table. Will remembered every card that had been played. He knew the sequences of yesterday's game. He defeated his mother at cribbage and chess and checkers. He learned to read before he entered first grade. His mother had taught him.

One October just as the steam heat began to rise in the courtroom, Howie had stood in his chambers and considered removing his robes permanently. A case came before him, not a landmark case, not the kind that causes a judge to spend long hours with his law books thumbing the pages, looking up the precedents. It was a kind of open-and-shut matter. The defendant, Herschel, who had a cement factory in some old buildings at the end of Tremont Avenue, had decided to buy up the buildings next to him so that he could expand his factory and had agreed on a substantial price with the landlord, a certain Georgie Goodman. The contract had been signed. The lawyers had shaken hands. The payments were to come over two years. The first payment was made, and the buildings burned down in the middle of the night. The tenants who were still there fled down the fire escapes and some jumped and four little babies were thrown to the fire fighters, who arrived not quite in time because two old ladies who had lived together in the same apartment since coming to this country fifteen years before suffocated in the smoke and a young man who was sleeping on the roof was burned to death when a tank used to store fuel exploded near him. So Herschel was not going pay Goodman for buildings that were no longer there. Goodman said the contract was signed and a deal was a deal. Howie thought Goodman was right. There was nothing in the contract about fires that came unexpectedly in the night.

But in the middle of trial, a visitor came to Howie's chambers, just before he was leaving for the night. The courthouse was mostly empty. The janitors had started to move down the halls with their slop pails and their Medusa-haired mops that pushed the dirty water from one wall to another. The visitor was a member of the club, this year's president, in fact, who served on a special mayor's commission to combat crime in the streets and corruption in the police department. It seems it was important to the fellows that this Herschel not have to make those payments. Herschel was a good Democrat, a fine supporter of the causes that were important to Howie, the election of more Democratic officials. He was a contributor to a baseball team for the kids whose fathers worked the docks. He supplied the uniforms. He was a good citizen, said the visitor.

"Yes," said Howie, "but in this case he is wrong. He should pay Goodman."

"Young man," said the visitor, "this is not a discussion. Herschel wins."

Howie sat down, astonished. The visitor, unasked, sat down, too. "Listen here," he said, "you want to move up on the bench, don't you? You want to be a bigger judge and make your wife and son proud, don't you?"

"It won't make them proud if I don't do what I think is right," said Howie, quietly because he already knew what was going to happen.

"How," said the visitor, "do you think you got this appointment? It was us, and you owe us. I don't expect we could be disappointed in Ben Eisen's son-in-law, could we?" The visitor left and smiled at Howie from the threshold of the door. "The check, as they say, will be in the mail, and give my best to your dear wife and that fine boy of yours."

Howie took off the robe and, rolling it up into a little ball, considered resignation. But how would he explain this to Bessie, to Ben? How could he give up the thing he loved most, the courtroom as his realm? How could it be that this had happened? Had he known this was coming all along? Of course he had, he admitted to himself. He had understood, without quite understanding. He had made a deal, without quite knowing that he had.

His face by the window in the dusk grew grayer and paler, and his eyes sank deeper into his head. He was a young man who suddenly looked old, as old as the deal he had made. It won't be often, he said to himself. They can't have a side in every case that appears before my bench. The rest of the time justice will be served, he vowed, but the shadows under his eyes, the crevices along his cheeks, deepened in the evening darkness. He was a mild man, not given to anger, convinced that civilization depended on order and restraint, so he was shocked that night when he returned to his home that as the maid was bringing in the soup and Bessie was complaining to him about his lateness and Will was reciting the names of the presidents backward, Howie took the napkin off his lap and put it into his water glass, stuffed it in until water flowed over the edges and then took it out and shook it until drops of water fell on the red tulips on the velvet-flocked wallpaper and drops of water fell on the astounded face of his child. Then he let the maid take away the wet cloth and he wiped his hands on the dry napkin she brought.

That was his only outburst. Herschel won the case. Goodman and his lawyers looked up in astonishment. No judge is without stain, he thought to himself, but he had constipation for a week, and as he sat over the toilet he clasped his stomach, which was giving him great pain, and hoped that his son would never find out what kind of judge his father really was.

Two months later on a Saturday morning the doorbell rang. A boy with knickers, his cap in hand, was standing there. He had an envelope for Judge Howard Katz and he handed it to the maid, who brought it to the judge, who was playing chess with his son. The judge, after casually examining the plain unmarked envelope, opened the seal and quickly stuffed the envelope into his jacket pocket. A quick glance had shown him hundred-dollar bills. A tip, as if he were a waiter at a hotel in Monticello who had brought the coffee hot each morning: a tip, as if he were a bellhop who carried up the luggage. His face was red and his ears were shining. He should return the money, he said to Bessie, who looked at her husband as if he were a five-year-old who had spilled his milk.

"You're so rich that money doesn't mean anything to you, I suppose. You, such a big shot, you can put it in the toilet when unasked it arrives at the door." She turned her back on him and, keeping the money in her hand, slammed the door. She kept the household accounts. She knew what a dollar was worth. She knew that the diamond bracelet she saw on her sister-in-law, Mildred, cost someone a good deal. Mildred, married to her brother, Julie, had too many good things, Bessie thought. She bought herself a similar bracelet and allowed Howie to wrap it and give it to her for her birthday at the family Sunday dinner. Howie was silent when his brother-in-law hugged him and said, "Great gift you got there," and punched him in the slight protrusion beneath his belt that he had developed since the new maid insisted on making a different pastry for each night of the week.

Reader: You think Howie Katz made a bad bargain. You think he should never have agreed to marry Bessie Eisen in the first place because he knew, knew perfectly well, somewhere down the line the debt would be called. He was naive but not innocent: a Prince Mishna with a character flaw. You think that it would have been better for Howie Katz to have opened his own firm, with a few pieces of secondhand furniture. You think that Howie Katz might have become a judge, an honorable judge, by building up a law practice of indigent immigrants who were trying to get relatives into this country or of shopkeepers who were cheated by manufacturers or of friends of his father on the milk route who wanted to sue the butcher for the meat that went bad on the fire escape in two hours and made everyone in the family retch through the night. Howie Katz, who loved the Constitution and the Bill of Rights, would never have had a chance to do more than live under its umbrella, to know that it was out there, beyond his touch, out of his sight, but over him nevertheless. You say that should have been enough, you believe that Howie Katz made a tragic error by shaking Ben Eisen's hand and pledging to honor and obey his daughter and becoming a candidate for a seat on the appeals court. Who are you to make a judgment like that? Are you so perfect, so incorruptible, so without a blemish, that you can point your finger at Howie Katz? Sure, cherry trees and log cabins, what are Americans made of? Reader, do you think that anything would happen in this country, hospitals built, roads tarred and train tracks laid, oil wells drilled, factories pounding out their cars and airplanes and refrigerators, do you think anything at all would happen if everyone kept their hands in their own pockets? The economy would soon strangle, and we would all be Okies riding around in dust-stained trucks looking for a handout, for a job. Remember about Howie Katz that he was a good man, an idealist, a dreamer, a man who never pledged allegiance without hearing all the words and savoring each one, a man who thought of himself as part of a process toward a better world, where the rapacity and the indifference of some to others would finally end. Don't be too pleased at what happens to him. It might yet happen to you.

At his grandfather Eisen's funeral, Will Katz made a speech, although he was only a child. He told the guests, standing up on a stool so he could reach the lectern the funeral parlor had provided, that his grandfather had understood banking and explained it to him, and he would take that knowledge and use it well for the good of mankind.

The mourners smiled at the child. Bessie wiped away the tears that had been running down her cheeks. He should have stood up a little straighter, and perhaps spoken a little slower; otherwise, she thought, he had done well.

Bessie did not want another child. One experience with labor was enough. Most women forget, remember only the reward at the end, but Bessie did not. She had everything she needed from biology. She intended her death to be her next confrontation with the ridiculous plumbing that animated the body. Will was the only life she wished to create.

Howie was rarely allowed near her. He was permitted only those actions that would not lead to conception. He was patient and tried to convince her that normal people risked pregnancy. He promised to be careful, but she said that careful was not good enough. He finally accepted her good-night kiss on the forehead as reward enough. He went into the bathroom and sometimes with the streetlight in his eyes he would fantasize other things, his hand on his member the way one would caress an orphan found in the rubble of a bombed-out building. He was not a difficult or demanding man, but he was aware that if Bessie were not pleased with him, he could be released on the street, no severance pay, no warning. He lived with his compromise.

It pained him, though, the way his son was beginning to tell him what to do. "Sit down, Judge," he would say when his father was going on about some new case. But Bessie allowed no public disrespect for Howie. Bessie called her husband "Judge."

"The Judge wants more cream for his coffee," she said to the maid. "The Judge would like to play bridge on Thursday night," she said to the wife of the lawyer who called her expecting that a social evening might lead to some estate work falling the way of her husband. When Mildred and Julie sent invitations to dinner, she turned them down, even though Julie was her brother. "The Judge has to see the senator this week." "The Judge has to have dinner with the mayor's special prosecutor on bootlegging activities this week." "The Judge has an appointment in his chambers with someone whose name I can't reveal."

Mildred told Flora that the Judge was taking a vacation in Florida with the president-elect of the Manhattan Democratic Club, and he might even be promoted to a more important post. Bessie said the Judge was tired from so much work, so they were going to spend a month in the summer at Atlantic Beach in a house with a screened porch and it just so happened that a certain judge of the Federal District had suggested they become members of the Inwood Club and share their cabana at the pool.

"Think of Bessie in a bathing suit," said Flora to her sister. "Think of Bessie with a sunburn, she'll look like a crab."

"The Judge," said Bessie, "is too busy to see his brother-in-law until the fall."

Will went with the fifth-grade class of his private school on a field trip to the Museum of Natural History. It was a progressive school, testing the ideas of John Dewey, concerned about the growth and identity and developmental stage of each individual student. The teacher was a young man who believed that if children were not tyrannized, they would grow into flowers of civilization, artists and innovators, leaders who ruled through reason and compassion.

In the museum each member of the class was given a yellow pad and a charcoal pencil, and each was asked to draw his or her favorite animal, the one they would like to be if they were turned into an animal. The boys drew the saber-toothed tiger. The girls favored the baby bears, stuffed and standing at their mother's side, frozen behind the windows of glass in eternal childhood. One very tall girl choose the turtle, and a boy who had polio and dragged his foot permanently encased in a steel brace selected the jaguar.

Will was bored with the assignment. He wandered to the museum shop, where he found a basket of buttons, each with a picture of tyrannosaurus raised up for battle, its teeth bared at an invisible enemy. The basket was filled with hundreds of buttons. The woman behind the counter turned to take care of a customer, and in a brave moment Will scooped up all the buttons and filled his jacket pockets and dropped some in the school bag he had slung over his shoulder.

He went back to his class in the Great Room, where it was dark and hushed as if the animals caught in their boxes with fake palms and jungle flowers and rivers painted on canvas screens needed quiet in order to concentrate on their eternal pose. Inside the tomb of the great dark hall, the children were whispering to each other, showing drawings; two little girls were busy making a third feel miserable because her hair ribbons did not match. The boys were throwing baseball statistics back and forth. Will did not have a best friend. He did not belong to any of the small packs that swelled and shrank within the larger pack of the class. He was not the butt of jokes, no one would try. He was not affected by the others, as if he walked among them with an invisible glass window keeping him in a landscape of his own, permitting the others to look at him while his head never turned toward the faces that stared at him from outside. Now he took a button from his pocket and offered it to a classmate.

"Two cents," he said, "and it's yours." And she reached into her bag and paid him and put the button on her blouse. He had chosen for his first customer the girl who led the others, who had been the first to wear barrettes in her hair, the one who decided who was allowed to play in the jump rope games that were held at recess. He knew if she wore a button, the others would follow.

Within minutes, as the young teacher sat in the rotunda under the great legs of the elephants who raised their hooves and lifted their trunks in mockery of the life they lost, the buttons were sold to every member of the class, the boys, too, first the best runner in the class, and then the best hitter then Albert, the math whiz who told jokes in the bathroom that had the others falling on the floor in helpless gasps. The money rattled in Will's pocket. He made change from a dime for those who had given up their milk money. He had extra buttons for himself, which he would stick into his book at home, a scrapbook he made with his mother of all the things that interested him.

The young teacher noticed the buttons on his students as he gathered the class together for a march out the door and down the front steps. "Where did you get the button?" he asked one student. Soon it was clear that Will was the source.

"I bought them," said Will. He looked at his teacher, who, his mother had told him, did not make as much money as a doorman in the Park Avenue apartment where his uncle Julie and aunt Mildred lived.

The museum shop was there, right on the left of the entrance. The teacher walked over to the counter. He whispered to the woman behind the counter. The buttons had been taken, no doubt about it. The teacher felt the blood pound through his head. This is what a teacher did, deal with the morality of children who did not understand.

"Will," he said, "you stole the buttons, and I have to report you to the principal. I want you to return the money, and class, you must give back the buttons."

The students had already begun to take them off when Will began to shout. "My father is an appeals court judge, and he will put you in jail for lying about me. I did not steal those buttons. The sales clerk who says so will go to jail. Police, police!" he began to scream. "Arrest that woman! My father will put her in jail."

The young teacher knew that Will's father was a judge. "But, Will," he said quietly, "you took the buttons. That was wrong."

Will stood there. "My father will have you fired for falsely accusing me. My father will see to it that you never work again in New York City."

The class stood around watching, quiet. One little girl began to sob; she loved her teacher. The woman behind the counter was upset.

"He did take them. I know he did. I didn't sell them, there is no receipt. I would remember!" she was shrieking.

"All right," said the teacher, whose ears had turned red, "we'll settle this back at the school." He paid the museum shop clerk for all the buttons that his students were wearing. Will smiled. A month's salary, he thought.

The teacher talked to the principal. The principal called Will's mother, who said, "If my son said he didn't take them, he didn't take them."

Howie was never told about the episode. "Why disturb your father?" said Bessie.

Joseph Herzberg Misses His Daughter: 1930

Joseph sat in his study and considered. When is a child of yours not a child of yours anymore? What is the thing that a child does to break the link, to be as one who is dead, now to be numbered among the strangers of the world? When is it right for a parent to sever his own heart in two? What did the tradition say?

Joseph considered. Across the ocean there were families who sat in mourning when a son or daughter betrayed the people by marrying out of the faith. It happened in Baltimore, too. Just a few years ago the Olevsky family covered their mirrors, sat on wooden boxes for seven days, and walked around the block three times for a daughter who had joined the printers' union and married the Irish shop leader. Joseph had comforted the father and embraced the mother just as if a real death had occurred, but he'd had his reservations. The girl, after all, would have children, and the children would spit up orange juice and fall out of beds and run through the halls leaving fingerprints on the banister. Would God not know those children? Joseph considered but had no answer. What if my child were a murderer? thought Joseph. What if one of his sons had taken a knife and killed a rival in school, or a business partner for greed, or had robbed a man in the street and taken his life? Then would he turn his back on his son? he wondered. He would have to ask himself, Why had the boy become a murderer? Had the father not taught him right from wrong? Had the father been too busy to bring up his son in the path of righteousness? Was his son sick beyond knowing right from wrong? Would he turn his back on a child who was born missing a limb or a child who was sick? Of course not. Would he turn his back on a child whom he himself had not taught well? Would it not be better to share in the blame rather than sit in mourning? God forgave David. Was Joseph Herzberg a more righteous man than God? What if he had a daughter who committed adultery? Perhaps he should shun her. But what if she committed adultery because her husband was brutal to her? What if his daughter's husband was like the Simon boy, who pushed his bride down the stairs when she was five months pregnant? But what if he had a child who told the Cossacks where the Jews were hiding out in the fields?

Joseph took off his thick glasses and wiped his eyes. His beard was moist. His cheeks burned. This was the worse sin, to betray the people. Such a child should be shut out of the house of Israel. But then he thought, Suppose she did this because she was simple? Would he forgive his daughter then? Joseph considered all the possibilities, all the many sins of children that could provoke the death sentence from the father, and for each of them he imagined a circumstance, a possibility, that would demand forgiveness from a just man. Always there was room for forgiveness.

He left his study, and coming into the bedroom where Ruth was already asleep, he called her name. When she woke and, with dream still in her eyes and alarm at his urgency, pulled the bedclothes around her shaking shoulders, he spoke.

"Tell Sharon I want her to come home. Whatever she has done, it doesn't matter. I want to see her, and have her eat at our table."

Meyer Herzberg Rides the Ferris Wheel in Coney Island: 1930 and After

His sister, Sharon, had gone to New York. She had disappeared or, if not disappeared, been vanquished. Her name was never spoken in the family. Meyer won a fellowship to Johns Hopkins. He won the only fellowship given to Jews. It had been endowed by a smuggler, a Jewish merchant who had figured the way to get blankets and pillows, cushions and handmade sweaters, across the enemy lines during the Civil War. He died rich and childless and wanted a place for Jews in the university. After his death he smuggled Jewish boys into the citadel of learning, and Meyer was selected on the basis of his essay and his grades.

His field was the Romantics, Shelley and Keats and Wordsworth. His first biography was of Lord Byron, published before he received his B.A. After his thesis was published by an academic press and his doctorate was secured, he was invited to teach at City College. Once in New York his interest turned to the work of Alexander Pope, and from there he became one of the foremost experts on Samuel Johnson and Boswell. His colleagues were mostly Anglicans. They were gentlemen who had gone to schools in New England and learned Latin and Greek in classrooms that overlooked fields on which boys played games while overhead the geese flew north or south depending on the season. Meyer was the only member of the English Department who also knew Hebrew and whose first language had been English liberally sprinkled with a Yiddish that was used for the significant moments, the emotionally charged sentences. Meyer had learned his Latin and Greek in college, and perhaps it was because he came to these languages relatively late that he devoted himself to them with such a fierce passion and won all the prizes in translation and even composed an original elegy in Latin for a professor who died in a terrible influenza epidemic his senior year.

Meyer Herzberg was unquestionably an odd professor of English.

He wrote articles on iambic pentameter and analyzed the symbolism of daffodils and clouds, and he told jokes. He told jokes to his students and jokes to his colleagues and jokes to the Negro porter who cleaned the hallways, who also added to his stock a few of his own. Meyer was heavy and his jaws were large and always moving. He smoked cigars and pipes, and ashes were always dripping over his shirts, which weren't as clean as they should be because he also spilled soup and sauce and wine down the front of his chest while he talked and he gestured and he told his jokes, laughing himself at the punch line, sometimes laughing before the punch line, so good were his jokes that he collected, not consciously the way a man makes a library of Shakespearean folios, marking and cataloging one's property, but jokes that tumbled one after another, that were attached by association of word or item or trick of humor, thrown all tumbled and wrinkled, sometimes with pieces forgotten, into a corner of his brain, where they were always recalled and with added details told, roaringly told, again and again. "Have you heard the one . . ." and he would stick his neck forward and turn his palms outward, translating out of the Yiddish or into the Yiddish or back into German or up into Cockney and down into the dialects of Virginia, New Orleans, or the snap of Vermont or the snip of Paris. His tongue could go anywhere, and his jokes followed like obedient dogs doing tricks on a stage as soon as an audience, any audience at all, was spotted.

By the time he was an assistant professor he was perfectly capable of taking the subway on the Sabbath, and he did. He went to Flatbush, to the house of a student of his, Shelley Fine, a young man whose interests were in Marx and Lenin and the revolution, but who had a gift for the lyric line, the literary insight. He went to Coney Island with this student of his and his sister, Rose Fine. Rose had long hair tied up in a bun. She was as small as a sparrow. Her fingers were narrow as pencils. She had a small mouth that puckered and pouted and opened just a little, making Meyer think of tongues and tonsils and private parts. Rose had pale skin and green eyes that were soft and looked at Meyer eagerly. She laughed at his jokes. She couldn't remember them, but she loved them just the same. Rose was studying to be a teacher. She believed there could be equality and justice if people just worked hard enough to make it happen.

"Aha," said Meyer to Rose, "you believe in the Messiah."

Rose looked at him with horror. What kind of a man after all had she chosen to ride with on the Ferris wheel? "You're joking," she said. "I'm a socialist," she said. "I don't believe we're going to be saved by the hand of God."

The Ferris wheel stopped and Meyer and Rose were swinging at the top, looking out over the bay and over the houses of Brooklyn. "So why are we here?" said Meyer, who knew the answer but couldn't hear it enough, who heard his father's whisper and shook his head back and forth as if a mosquito were sitting on his eardrum.

Rose said, "Accident, it's all an accident."

"The butterflies, the snowflakes, the Jews, the crossing of the Red Sea, bushes that burned, the womb of women, all accident?" Meyer looked at Rose.

"An accident," she said firmly.

Meyer took her hand and put his big arm around her slight shoulders to protect against the wind that was blowing off the sea and rocking the small cart they were strapped into back and forth, like a cradle. "I believe that," he said. "An accident."

Meyer began to visit Rose every weekend. Sometimes they went to meetings with other young people who discussed Trotsky and Lenin and the events in Russia. Rose arrived with her suitcase at Meyer's apartment. Meyer heard his father's voice, and his promises broken gave him gas and headaches. They didn't believe in marriage, these young people.

"What for?" said Rose. "It's just a custom of the oppressing classes."

Meyer told his mother that he had a girlfriend. He didn't tell her where she was sleeping.

"So marry her," said Ruth, who wanted her son to be happy.

Rose got a job teaching kindergarten at a new progressive school in the village. Rose joined a group that was raising money for migrant workers.

Meyer gave a speech in a house on Fifth Avenue, where the group had been invited to tell some rich Jews about the disastrous conditions among the fruit-pickers in Florida. When Rose got pregnant he was jubilant. He laughed in her ear. He pulled at her hair. He pushed her down on their Castro convertible and tickled her under her arms till she begged for mercy.

"You have to marry me now," he said.

"Why?" she protested. But she got married after all, in City Hall.

Meyer invited his sister, Sharie Lee, to come to the wedding reception. He had found her in a cabaret in the Village. He had sat there with Rose, amazed. "That's my sister," he said to Rose, poking her in the ribs again and again.

Sharie Lee hugged her brother and introduced him to the band. She came to the celebration and brought a bottle of Scotch, which she drank herself. Meyer wanted her to sing, but she passed out in the bathtub, which was in the kitchen, which would have embarrassed another brother, but Meyer understood.

Joseph wanted to go to New York to visit his son, but Meyer always put him off. "I'm writing an article, I'm teaching four classes." Once a year for the High Holidays Meyer went home to Baltimore and he brought Rose with him and he coached her in what to wear and what to say and he made her promise not to protest sitting in the balcony or working in the kitchen while he and his father and his younger brother ate at the table.

Meyer fasted. Meyer, sleeping with his wife in his childhood room, thought about his offenses before God. He felt guilt, but he couldn't name his offense. Joseph knew. He knew without being told.

"He is not a Jew anymore," said Joseph to Ruth.

"How can a Jew not be a Jew?" said Ruth, and kissed her husband on his neck.

Meyer sent his father his articles, published in this journal and that. His father never read them, but he kept them in a pile under his desk. Sometimes his leg would press against the pile of journals, the work of his son, and it would lean there.

Meyer, having shut his ears to his father's whispers, thought of himself as a man without a childhood, and that was the same as being a man without a shadow, an unnatural thing, perhaps a ghost. But if that were so, he knew many ghosts. New York was a city of men without shadows. There was comfort in company. Good comfort. He read Freud: obsessive rituals to placate inner drives, God was a figure of the imagination, an attempt at reunion with the lost breast. Freud was a man who made his own shadow. That comforted Meyer, who worried about the news from Europe. Was this a time that a man could reasonably turn his attention to metaphor and simile?

Rose believed that the revolution would succeed. "The czar is dead. Long live the socialist republic," said Rose.

Meyer wasn't so sure. There were reports, what was happening to the Jews. A Jewish doctor has been blamed, the Politburo has lost its Jews. Meyer was worried. Rose cried in her pillow. It must be all right. Something in this world must be good. Meyer wrapped his arms around his wife.

"It's not fair," she said, "the way some people suffer."

"It's not fair," said Meyer. He told Rose what he heard from his colleague in the Political Science Department.

"It's not true," said Rose. "They can't be doing that. I don't believe it."

Meyer said, "Stalin is another false Messiah."

"Rumors," said Rose, and bit her lip and said nothing more. Who knew for sure?

Rose and Meyer had a son, whom they named Abraham after Lincoln. Abe would have the childhood that Meyer had never had, where choice and freedom from superstition and empathy with all the peoples of the world would create a new and better soul.

"Maybe an artist," said Rose.

"Maybe a doctor," said Meyer, who as he carried the infant on his shoulder, rubbing his back with his own wide palm, worried about drafts and germs and looked up bumps and lumps and coughs and aches in medical manuals he stole from the library.

Abe was two years old and still didn't talk. He made strange sounds, not like the sounds of other babies. The pediatrician said some children were slow. Ruth wouldn't let Meyer take him to a specialist. Abe did puzzles. He climbed the jungle gym. He was fine, she told herself. But then they were going to Washington Square Park, and he was walking by her side. He started ahead of her and she shouted to him to stop. He went on just as if he didn't hear her, and she knew.

They went to the specialist. Abe was deaf, totally deaf, an accident in the womb, a virus in the mother's bloodstream that passed the placenta; who knew exactly? It was too late to undo. Abe Herzberg was stone deaf.

Rose changed from a girl to a woman. She believed it now about Stalin. She believed worse would happen.

Meyer ached for his son. He told jokes about deaf people to Rose, who refused to laugh.

The Younger Brother Takes the Presidency as the Country Comes on Hard Times: 1929–30

One fall day when Flora was still on her honeymoon, a day that had started out quite like any other, the stock market crashed, and in the months that followed, it became clear why the winter orders had been going slowly.

Harry was the president of the company. He had the big office up front that had been his father's. He was particularly kind to the secretaries and knew their birthdays by heart, and he always brought them a bouquet, a box of chocolates, or a bottle of cologne. He still looked up in the air or off to the side when talking to strangers. He made decisions cautiously. He believed that disaster could come, that they could overstock on fabric bolts, extend themselves too far with promises. He was afraid that his employees would demand too much. There was always complaint in the lofts. He understood the business, the need for shaking hands and going out to stores and being seen at his club with other businessmen, but he liked best of all to stay home with his wife and watch her try on clothes. Mickey would give him a fashion show, slipping in and out of gowns, asking his opinion, sucking on his earlobe, a thing he found particularly arousing.

His uncle Max was no help. Max spent all his time with his horses, and sometimes he came in the office and complained because everyone was too busy to talk to him. Harry never wanted to talk to Max. His uncle was an obligation, not a pleasure, of that he was sure.

Harry worried about the price of buttons and the quality of zippers. He sent Arthur memos that predicted disaster. He went into Arthur's office, and making steam from his breath form on the window glass, he told his brother that business could get worse, things could fall apart. Arthur just smiled at him, patted him on the back, and offered to pay for dancing lessons. Dancing was Arthur's hobby. Harry always felt clumsy when he tried. Arthur always comforted Harry, giving him the cheerful side of all figures and possibilities. Arthur believed that his office was a part of the natural environment, like the Hudson River running down the side of Manhattan out to the sea, and would forever weather the storms.

Harry missed his father and was reminded of him every day: of course the loss was sudden, and it had happened before Harry had been able to make his father proud of him, to let him know that he was leaving the business, the family, in good hands. He thought of his father building up the Gruenbaum Company from a cart piled high with suits on Orchard Street. Harry suspected that he himself couldn't have done it. It wasn't in him, or maybe it was but he didn't know it. He doubted his own courage. He would sometimes lie down on the blue-carpeted floor of his office, a heavy man with a solemn look on his face, red pinch marks about the nose from his glasses, and fall asleep. He always fell asleep when important decisions had to be made, when he was unsure of himself, when Arthur wasn't around, when mistakes could be made. He was a man who needed more sleep than most.

Harry and Mickey gave great parties. Everyone in their crowd said so. It wasn't Harry, who never quite knew what to say and who refused to dance with anyone but his wife and got sick to his stomach from alcohol. It was Mickey, who kept the bathtubs full of gin and who grinned at everyone and allowed the fellows to watch her as she swung her hips and bounced her breasts. When she got pregnant she wore bangles, sequined maternity gowns that glittered and made metallic noises when she bent down or stood up. The pregnancy, the birth of their son, Moses, proved to Harry that his penis, although slanted, was good enough, and Mickey told him that every girl knew that the slanted kind were tops, the cat's meow, and she scratched him in just the right places. That kept Harry awake.

In the family, only Flora accepted her. Her mother-in-law wouldn't have her in the house except for holidays, when it couldn't be helped. Her sister-in-law Mildred wouldn't introduce her to any of her friends, so Mickey and Harry gave parties and all sorts of people came, and everyone agreed Mickey had the greatest, longest legs in town. Arthur and Louisa always went. Louisa disapproved of Mickey's loud laugh and the way she chewed gum if she was blowing smoke rings straight up in the air. Arthur saw these defects, but he liked the way Mickey smelled, the way she offered him straight Scotch without a blink, the way she showed off the ruby earrings Harry gave her for their first anniversary and told everybody the price.

The business continued to do well; each quarter brought more profit than the last. By the time Moses was two, Harry was beginning to suspect that he knew more about business, was more of a natural, than he had thought. He still required many naps throughout the day.

Mickey teased him, he was too fat. He did have a bulge, the bulge that he had carried with him since childhood. He tried to cut down on rich food, but each night he found himself in the kitchen after the cook had gone to sleep, having carefully placed the remains of the dinner in little bowls. Each night he emptied those bowls and left them in the sink for the maid to wash. He couldn't help it. Smoking cigars helped. Smoking cigarettes helped, but still in his mouth between puffs he placed cookies or leftover boiled potatoes. He even ate little Moses's applesauce and mashed bananas.

Arthur had a friend from school who knew a diet doctor who gave out these special pills, which would like magic take the pounds away. Arthur gave his older brother Dr. Feigen's name. He slapped him on the back.

"Go," he said. "Get rid of that bulge." And it wasn't just a bulge, it was also weights under the arms and a thickness in the neck and even the toes were broad and special shoes had to be made.

"Your golf game is terrible," said Arthur, "because of all the weight. You'd be a champion if you'd lose fifty pounds. You'd be a good dancer, a really good dancer, if you'd just lose weight." Harry imagined himself slim like his brother. He imagined dancing with Mickey and everyone watching and clapping.

So Harry went to the diet doctor, who listened to his story and gave him the pills. Mickey kissed him on his navel and rubbed his almost completely bald head and promised him she would give him a blast at the club after he lost the weight. "Such a party we'll have," she screamed. "We'll bring the police down on the place and you can eat all you want that night." She promised him that.

This was how it happened that in July, shortly before Moses's third birthday, Harry was on the golf course at the Old Oaks Club in Larchmont. He was determined to improve his game. It wasn't that he had to be better than Arthur. Arthur had always beaten him at that sort of thing, and Harry didn't mind, but it was good for him to get out on the course and walk all eighteen holes, Dr. Feigen had told him that. It was good to swing your arms and let the warm sun soak into your back. There were things that worried him that summer, and when he was worried he wanted a club sandwich, with bacon and lettuce, mayonnaise and thick slabs of turkey. The inventory of unsold suits was growing, and there was hardly room for them in the storage and shipping building in Brooklyn Heights, and the salesmen seemed to be moping in the unseasonably warm weather and the price of fabric would not go down, and there was talk in the shops among the cutters that they needed more money and he had fired the troublemakers, the outspoken ones, but always another came in their place. Business had been fair, but something about the winter orders bothered him. They were coming in slowly, too slowly. He swung his club over his head, and out of the corner of his eye he saw his caddie, a boy with a wart on the end of his nose, watching a dog that had wandered onto the green at the eighth hole, and suddenly his heart skipped a beat, then two, a pain ran down his arm, and he began to sweat. He completed the arc of his arms but then fell forward on the tee, and the ball rolled a few feet across an anthill, and Harry died at the age of thirty on the fifth hole of the golf course at the Old Oaks Country Club.

No one could believe it had happened—not Mickey, who blamed the diet doctor whose pills might have made the muscle of Harry's heart waver and pause. When Annie heard that her son was dead, her blue eyes turned gray. Her skin was the color of ash. She pulled the curtains in her room and allowed no one to enter. How could Harry have died so young? she shouted to those who paid their condolence calls, standing on the far side of her closed bedroom door. Some people have no luck, and that included Mickey. That's what Flora thought.

Isaac had left all the stock of the Gruenbaum Pants Company to Flora and her mother because the business belonged to the boys and

Mildred had married well. Flora, who had just returned some months before from her honeymoon with Frank, understood that she had all the right certificates and Mickey had nothing at all because Harry hadn't even thought of taking out a life insurance policy or purchasing a burial plot. Arthur paid for the funeral.

"Mickey will be out in the street and Moses will have nothing," Flora said.

"So," said Mildred, "that's what she gets. Don't think," she added, "anyone can count on having what they have forever. Things can change unexpectedly."

But Flora said, "Harry would want us to do something." Flora gave Mickey enough stock, and the stock was worth very little, so she had to give her a lot so she could continue living as she always had.

Frank said, "You don't owe that woman anything."

Flora said, "She was my brother's wife."

Frank said, "That stock was money." Frank got a migraine and wouldn't let anyone near him.

Flora pleaded with him: "She has no one to take care of her but me."

"You're breaking my heart," said Frank, who was frightened. What if everything went? What if the company failed? He could imagine the abyss beneath them. He could feel the hard floor of the bottom rising to meet him.

Now Flora and Moses had something in common: neither of them had a father. Flora had looked at her nephew, who had played with a blue ball on the grass-covered knoll just behind the open grave as the rabbi said the kaddish. His hair, a little long, hung almost to his shoulders in brown curls. Would he go bald? Was there a way to give him a new heart uncontaminated by the genes of his ancestors?

Arthur, who never expected to be a patriarch, was now the president of the company, and he knew that his sister and his mother and his wife expected him to do well. It made it harder for him to whistle through his fingers as he walked along the Drive in the morning. It made his shoulders bend with apprehension, and it ruined his golf game because his concentration was off. He lost his knack for rhyme. Was he going to measure up? He would try.

Reader: I know you're not surprised. The second son is the true heir, it happens all the time. Ishmael and Isaac, Esau and Jacob, Cain and Abel, the adopted son, David. We can safely conclude that God Himself must have been a second son. Why else the sympathy, the tilting of the stories to reverse the natural order of primogeniture? What happened to the firstborn God? Is our God the second-born God?

When Men Lose Their Jobs They Don't Buy New Suits: 1930

At first it seemed that, like a diver touching the ocean floor, the market would inexorably rise. But there was worry. Who knew if there was an ocean floor? Flora, who had taken to keeping records, to calling up her broker in the midafternoon, even if it meant holding up a card game, leaving the mah-jongg table, running to a phone booth in a hotel downtown, or calling for the check before dessert arrived, took the bad news with a clear head.

"Don't worry," she said to Arthur, who had taken to visiting her in the late afternoons. "Don't worry, business will get better. Think," she said, "of all the people out there." And she gestured west of the Hudson, her red nails pointing across an imaginary map that included Omaha and Santa Fe and Honolulu. "They all need suits, and not only suits, they need iceboxes and fountain pens and cars and food. They need to blow their noses and do their nails and change their shoes and get new curtains and clean the spill on the carpet and feed the cat. Don't worry," she said, "everybody needs to buy, so everybody needs to have something to sell."

Arthur admired his little sister, whose head was often clear and who said what she thought and who could be counted on to tell him the truth, like the time she told him that the green corduroy he had bought in thousands of yards was better for a couch than a suit, and she was right. But he didn't feel comforted by the wave of her hand across the Great Plains. "It doesn't look good," he said. "The fellows are saying the crash took the money out and we're in for it."

"Fire people," said Flora. "Fire everyone you can."

Arthur had already started. The cutters were cut. The pattern makers were eliminated and the loft on 14th Street was closed and the factory in Pansville, the one that employed the miners who had gotten too old to go down in the mines, and their wives and their maiden aunts, this too was cut down to half force.

"God," said Arthur. "We don't have the money to pay the suppliers for the winter wools. We don't have the money, I don't see how I can get it, I've already borrowed on the spring line to pay the mechanics to fix the machines that broke in the Borough Park loft. We might go bankrupt."

"Frank," asked Flora, "is it really that bad?"

"Worse," said Frank, and thought to himself how if it all evaporated, he would become a tennis pro at a club in Miami. He flexed his muscles and looked in the mirror. The face could get him by, he knew it. Of course he was scared, too. He wouldn't show it, not to Flora or to another living soul, but he felt like a man falling down a black hole, falling and falling. What was at the bottom? It was Arthur's fault. He also knew that. If he had been president of the company, certain decisions would have been made, the reserves would have been greater. There would be no bankruptcy. Arthur never took his advice. Arthur had moved his office to the opposite end of the building, far away from Frank. Frank fired his secretary. He had nothing for her to do.

Frank at His Club: 1932

Frank was lying in the steam room in the City Athletic Club letting the sweat out of his body. He exercised every day, squash, racquetball, tennis in the summer, he swam fifteen laps in the pool, and he did sit-ups in his gym shorts in the area outside the shower. His stomach was flat. His heart rate was steady as a fifteen-year-old boy's. He never went directly home when the day at the office was over. He had a drink in the bar of the club after he had knocked his quota of balls into the walls, over opponents' heads.

"How's it going?" the men would say to each other. "They say the market's going to rise, they say the president's going to put a lid on imports." "The unions are acting up over at my place." "The Yankees are going to make it this year." "Says who?" No women allowed except Thursday night for dinner, maid's night out.

Lying in the steam room looking through the haze at the older men, their bellies sagging, their shoulders drooping, their mustaches wet and pressed flat against their upper lips, their glasses fogged over, their penises purple-hued, mottled like mushrooms bought at yesterday's market, soft like the noses of small dogs, swinging gently as they hoisted themselves on or off the wooden benches, Frank thought of his father coming home to their apartment on Third Avenue. His salesman bag, flat and empty, every last piece of equipment sold, all the samples, he would grin, sold, orders for needles and iodine, gentian violet and gauze. He was a supplier for doctors and drugstores. His black book bulged and he held it above his head and his children begged him for the candy he should have brought home in his pocket. Frank thought of his father sitting at the kitchen table, talking to his wife in a language he could hardly remember but whose meaning was clear. The money had not come home with his father.

It had been spent. The horses had gone round and round the track and the one with the green bridle and the jockey wearing the gold colors had been first, way in front, just the way he had been told, and then, the bastard, the whore, he must have pulled back on the reins, the horse slowed in the stretch, and another one, a filly with a name like Two Lips Susan, pounded to victory.

"It won't happen again, I won't do it again," said Frank's father to his wife, who sat at the kitchen table, silent and stony-faced. She wouldn't learn English. She wouldn't leave the house except in the company of one of her children, who would speak to the shopkeepers for her and lead her across the street as if not speaking English made you blind to the horses pulling ice blocks on wagons, to the beer wagons rolling over the cobblestones, to the trolley that clanged as the bells rang and the sparks on the cables flew.

His mother sat by the window of their railroad flat and fanned herself with the newspaper. She hardly ever put on street clothes. She slept in the afternoons and stared at the walls, and she mumbled to herself when she cut the vegetables, and her hair, which once had been shining and tied in a bun at the back of her neck, hung dirty and long about her shoulders.

She waited for her husband to come home, and when he came she went to sleep. The man, with a smile on his lips, his suits amazingly pressed and his suspenders red and blue, would promise his children presents and picnics in the Bronx, but then he forgot, or he couldn't, or he disappeared for a month or so. He always came back smelling of tobacco and beer and sometimes a cheap after-shave that on hot nights filled the kitchen with bright expectations.

Frank thought of his mother in the July heat, her breasts hanging down beneath her housecoat and her legs spread apart on the kitchen chair and her slippers, now faded and the pom-poms shredded, the slippers he had bought her from his earnings at his job as a lifeguard at the pool in the Catskills, the summer he learned that in America good looks got you hired.

As a boy in the Hungarian countryside, Frank had been called Fritz; the family was trying to be German, although they were Jews. German was good, Jewish was bad. The Hapsburgs were quality folk, not like the Hungarian peasants all around. Frank's father had figured it out. Frank remembered his mother by the window of the house they had rented by the mill, where her husband was secretary to the count, her head resting against the pane. Frank pulls at her skirt. She doesn't look down. He cries out to her, "Come and see me jump in the puddles in the yard."

She smacks at his hand. He waits for her to turn around. She stays at the window. He is hungry. His baby sister is crying. Perhaps his mother is asleep, but her eyes are open. There are tears in her eyes. She does not move. What is wrong? Frank thinks he has done something. Perhaps the Gypsies had stolen her real son away, leaving him, an imposter, behind. Perhaps the Gypsies had stolen his mother away and left an imposter in her place. He goes outside in the yard and alone jumps in the puddles.

Frank looked at the men in the steam room. They would die, they would decay and die, while he, still only twenty-six, would go on, his arms flexing at his desk to keep up the muscle tone, avoiding greasy food, like the kind that came from Chinese restaurants, the sort Flora liked; no pastrami or beef with gravy. He believed a man should be trim, nothing should enter his mouth but the purest of foods. A boiled egg, a bowl of prunes, a fish with a bit of lemon. He had no fondness for the smells or tastes of foreign countries. He was an American, and Americans liked things simple.

He had hoped it would change in America, but when he came home from school he would find his mother at the kitchen table, her head in her arms, tears flowing down. He stayed in the streets as long as possible. He walked about the neighborhood chinning himself on the bars of the Third Avenue el, kicking at bottles that had fallen off the back of trucks and throwing rocks into the East River and watching them sink into the black muck of the barely moving water that was half sewage, half ocean and even when the sun was out would never look as blue as the sky. His mother said nothing to him when he came home from school with his clothes ripped and his face covered with bloody scratches. So many times he had been pushed on the stairs or attacked in the schoolyard. In 1918 it wasn't such a good thing to be a boy named Fritz, but even after he changed his name to Frank they had called him a kraut. The enemy were the Germans, and he wasn't a kraut, he was an American, two years he had been here. He turned on the attackers, and one fell down the iron steps. A boy could not run away, not if he wanted to go back to school the next day. He wiped his own blood and spilled witch hazel over his open cuts. But he was afraid, not so much afraid of the boys on the stairs as of the silence in the house when his mother was sleeping, of the walls of the house that seemed to murmur things against him, as if they didn't want him there, sheltered from the rain and the wind. His mother sat still for hours on end. His baby sister, Estelle, hung the laundry out the window and sang a song as she pulled on the rope.

His maiden aunt, Lori, moved in with them after her arrival. She took over the household and cleaned the floor and scrubbed the shelves. She made latkes and knishes and goulashes that boiled for hours on the stove, and the smell of garlic and paprika hung over his sheets as a permanent reminder of her dinners. The two sisters would whisper late into the night. Frank's mother still did not get dressed or go outside unaccompanied. She had a bad back and lay in bed day after day. Frank spoke to his mother briefly, when necessary, in English, and she looked at him, surprised. She spoke to him hardly at all. Lori made him lunch to take to school. Lori laid out his clean shirts. She ran her hands over his books and held them to the light as if the words would mean something to her. She dusted them each morning before he had breakfast. Frank didn't tell his mother when he was accepted at Townsend Harris, a public school for boys who were expected to succeed. What did she matter in this new country? She, like the faded postcard of the town they had left behind, with its church tower and its flower lady selling bunches of roses, was only a reminder of things to be forgotten; like his fat sister, whose body he could smell in the small room they had shared, everything she ate passing through, stinking up the air.

His father had admired fine suits and good cigars, and even when the rent money was in question he always dressed as if were expected at the castle for dinner. He believed that an error had been made in his case. He had been born a Jew, without a future, in a town where the railroad passed through and never stopped. He knew he was better than that, better than a secretary to a mill owner, smarter than the others, capable of great things had opportunity and luck only cooperated. If justice were done, he would be a person of stature, of rank. Each time the horses ran, each time the cards were dealt, he gave the Almighty another chance to rectify his error. Frank learned from his father that he must dress well, mark himself as one on the top of the ladder, and accept no insults from those who would drag you down to join them at the bottom.

Reader: Remember how hard it is on men, men by nature always measuring themselves by others, that someone is more powerful, has more money, counts more in the affairs of the world than you. Consider how it pressed down on them, some of them, the ones who wanted to climb but had no feet, the ones who saw the advantages at the top but had no hands to reach the rungs. Pity the humiliation of those who are climbing the ladder and look up and up at the others far ahead. The freedom of America increased the possible and so increased the illusions and disillusions of those whose only hope of rising lay in their sons.

• • •

Frank wiped his back with a towel, a soft white towel with the club monogram embedded in blue. Once, his mother had looked at him. "Handsome," she had said. He remembered everything about that moment, the color of the walls in the kitchen, the yellow flowers that were on the plates at breakfast, the curtains blowing in the wind as the train passed by.

He raced down the stairs in the morning, away from fat Estelle and away from her. It smelled in the house, a smell he loathed, like cooking grease and laundry soap and the odor of bodies that clung to the curtains even in winter when everyone was cold and his mother lay in bed under the quilt she had brought from the other side whose feathers would stick to her hair and she would forget to comb them out.

In the steam room, Frank drew deep breaths, letting the warm air into his lungs. The other men were now shadows, their whispering like the sound of wind brushing against leaves. He stretched his legs, pushing them down against the hard bench. His mother was now in Miami, in a small house with her sister that had been bought and fully paid for by Flora, who had complained because the business was not doing well and this extra expense had to be borrowed, and borrowing made her frantic.

Flora didn't like his mother. His mother didn't like Flora. She had looked at Flora and said she was almost a dwarf, fit for a circus, not a wife. She said it in Hungarian. She said it in Yiddish. She said it in German. Her sister had unfortunately translated the words for Flora. Alone, he visited his mother in Miami at least once a year. She sat on her porch and fanned herself with a paper. She blinked her eyes in the sun. She had nothing to say in any language. She waited.

His father was at the track, the dogs were running. The old man had a heart that skipped beats, that stalled and ended him up in the hospital with tubes going down his nose, and still he went out to watch the dogs go, gray streaks of ghostly promises, past him, money on their paws, money on the pencil cut of their noses, money that his father still believed would come to him, all at once, a fortune, an American fortune earned by a thirty-to-one shot in an afternoon in Florida when the pineapples were sweating on their branches and the flamingos were hiding in the shade of the hibiscus. His father told stories about farmers' wives and chickens and traveling salesmen. His father was always a man with a joke and a plan. Frank had plans, but no jokes.

In Miami his father had found a crap game. A nice, steady crap game that gave the old gentleman something to do once or twice a week. It met in the back of Louis Spitzer's garage, and Frank's dad had a debt at present of two thousand dollars and Frank wasn't sure how he was going to cover it. Flora would come through, she'd find it somewhere.

Why was it always his job to pull his father out of debt, to get his aunt to a doctor who would take care of her swollen legs? And Estelle said her husband, Manny, needed new suits and he needed them whole-sale. Why did they call him all the time? He felt it weighing on him, the burden he carried because he had married Flora, because he was an ex-ecutive in the Gruenbaum Company, because he lived in an apartment on Park Avenue. Some days he wished there was another America, one he could sail to, a stowaway, and start again.

Frank turned over on the bench and let the heat soak up through the wood into his chest. Sleep began in his outer limbs, climbed up to his brain, and he felt the warm sweat on his forehead and closed his eyes. In the moment before consciousness faded he saw himself, naked on a wooden bench. Bones and bare flesh, temporary, intended for death. Who would take care of him now? Who had ever wanted him, Frank, alias Fritz, alias the child from the town in the Hungarian mountains where a Jew deserved whatever was coming and come it would. Frank curled his fingers into his familiar fist. What if the business failed? What if he had wasted his youth and would end up with nothing, nothing but his good looks out on the road like his father trying to sell something? Frank pulled himself up and went to the showers. Nothing like a steam room to remind a man that without his clothes he had no protective shell.

Fortunes Reversed: 1932

Mildred was not given to worry. Worry made lines in the face. Worry was for those who believed they were going to live forever. Mildred took her mortality seriously and was determined to enjoy the lot that was hers. She looked in the mirror each morning at her sloping blue eyes. She curled a lock of her hair with a bobby pin above her right eye. She admired her reflection. She admired the sun outside the window on Park Avenue. She admired her young girls, who were brought in to see her before they were taken off to the park by the nanny, who had scrubbed them clean, taught them to say *"Auf Wiedersehen"* when they left her. She kissed them on the ears and the neck, and she left trails of her perfume on their clean collars. She told Jill about the rabbits she had seen in the woods near the golf course the week before, and she told Lydia about the giraffes who lived in Africa and ate the leaves off of trees and grew tall and suggested that she should eat her vegetables for a similar result.

She hugged her girls. She left lipstick stains on their cheeks that the nanny wiped off with a wet cloth before leaving the apartment.

Mildred loved dancing, and her shoes were worn out from the long nights of tapping across a wooden floor under the hot pink lights. Whenever they went to a party, and that was two or three times a week, Mildred would spot a good dancer in the crowd and bounce off with him as the music of the band played or sometimes, if they were at dinner in someone's house, as the needle of the record player scratched on. She didn't smoke because it made her cough. She didn't drink because she didn't like to feel dizzy when she swirled around in someone's arms. "A woman needs to see clearly all night long," she told Flora.

Mildred understood about the market and she understood that Julie was worried. Each night he came home and, before they went out for the evening, would take off his jacket and his shoes and lie down on the bed with his eyes closed and his hands folded across his chest but the fingers trembling slightly across his suspenders. He had stopped playing with the girls in the evening. He didn't have the energy to squeeze his wife when they were in the elevator. His skin had turned olive as if he had spent too many hours under a yellow light. He told her that banks were not like wells sunk into the countryside. The supply of money could dry up.

"Don't worry," said Mildred, stroking his forehead. "Don't be a prune," she said to him. "What can happen to a bank?" She laughed. "There's always next year," she said. "You can make more money next year, Julie," she said, "please smile." She tossed him his dinner jacket.

They were going to the opera. Mildred loved the opera. The music flowed through her. The sad parts made her cry. The costumes and the scenery amazed her. The opera, she said, was the way the world ought to be all the time. She wore her finest dress of pink silk and pearl beads to the opera. What was everyone else wearing? She craned her head back and forth during intermission. "Darling," she said to Julie, "you must stop looking so dim. No one has died."

Reader: Do not feel superior. You know now what was happening, but if you were there, what would you have known? How would you have behaved? Gone dancing, I'm sure. Made up your face; curled your hair, stuck a clean handkerchief with your monogram on it in your breast pocket and gone off to work in the car, just as always. When history is about to run you over, do you in, catch you up in its maw and mangle your bones, it doesn't announce all that with bells ringing from the churches and sirens roaring down the avenue. It doesn't alert you with an angel making a pronouncement on parchment that unfolds through the funneled end of a golden trumpet so you can read your destiny in the sky. Don't be smug because you can interpret the handwriting on the wall. That particular wall would have fallen on you, too, had you been there.

Arthur had to declare bankruptcy. He appeared in court, very thin, his shoulders hunched over. He was a young man, still under thirty, but he looked as if he were a veteran of the war and someone had blown gas down his lungs. He was already balding and his forehead shone in the courtroom lights.

He explained to the judge that he couldn't pay his creditors. He couldn't pay his employees. He had counted the assets. The stock that had been given Flora was worthless. The stock that Flora had given Mickey was worthless. The stock that was there to support his mother was worthless, and he, himself, could not support his wife or his child except by writing bad checks, which he couldn't bring himself to do. He had asked Max to sell his horses, but Max had said never.

Arthur said it was over. He talked to his father in his sleep. He begged his pardon. He grieved for the company the way one might for a wife or a mother, worse. So much work, so much time, so much thought, had gone into the company, so many people had lived off the wages and profits it brought. He was as defeated as any prince who lost his lands in battle and was about to see the treasures of his kingdom carried away by marauding strangers.

Louisa stroked his shoulders. She patted him on the arm. She lifted up her eyes and they were filled with tears, not for herself, she needed nothing, but for his anguish, for the way he banged his head against the wall, the way he seemed stooped and uncertain in his steps. "It's all right," she said. "I don't need money."

Arthur knew he was a lucky man. But he didn't feel lucky. "You do need money," he said. "Besides, the business is everything." She shook her head. "It's everything to me," he said. "It's got to be there for our son," he said. The boy, named Teddy, was only two.

Louisa said, "He doesn't need the business." Arthur was right: Louisa didn't understand. "We could go somewhere and start again," said Louisa. "I could help you. We could open a store."

The tender-hearted Louisa ached for her husband. He misunderstood. He thought she doubted him. He was insulted. Stiffly he said, "I'll take care of you somehow. I will."

"That's good," said Louisa, but she took her hand off his lap. "I'm sure you will," she said, but something stirred in her, a wish to travel, perhaps, a thought that the world was larger than she had known. A kind of boredom came over her that caused her to go to bed early and chastise herself for being less than a perfect wife and mother.

But the judge, putting the company into a temporary receivership, allowed Arthur to continue as president, allowed him to borrow the money to meet his immediate obligations. And because there was something not yet defeated in Arthur's eyes, something stubborn in the way he explained to the judge that the company had been started by his father and he would not let it go, not yet, the judge allowed him time, as much time as he needed. There were assets, the name was known, the factory in Pansville was there, and the small one in Borough Park, although now it belonged more to the bank than to the company, and the house on Riverside Drive could be mortgaged and the workers took less, those that were left, and the secretaries were down to one, who was so busy she forgot to water the plants, which withered on the office sill.

But Arthur and Frank still had a company and a fighting chance to hold on, to bring it back. Frank stretched his arms in his silk smoking jacket and smoked a cigar. Arthur wouldn't let him make any of the decisions. Arthur sent him out on the road, hand-shaking the store owners, those that were still in business. Arthur talked to Flora. Each afternoon he sat on the chair by her bedside and showed her the figures, discussed the options with her. It wasn't over yet, even though common sense, a look out the window, would tell anyone that no one was buying suits these days.

When the bankruptcy hearing was over and the small, remaining, still functioning pieces of the business were put together and Arthur and Frank sat in the office, half of which they had now rented out to Bell Lampshades with an agreement to share the salary of the switchboard operator. Arthur said to Frank, "We'll build again, we'll make it go."

Frank said, "I don't see it." He took to leaving the office for the club at about three o'clock in the afternoon.

Arthur worked until nine at night. He called every store. He visited every buyer he had ever known. He invited presidents and vice presidents to lunch. He hired a designer to make a suit for the end of the thirties, a suit that would promise a man dignity with a small dash of danger: was a gun hanging somewhere under his armpit, or was that just the hang of the suit?

Arthur took another risk—it could have bankrupted them—work pants with suspenders for the farmers and the construction workers, most of whom were laid off, but who still had to get up in the morning and cover their private parts. He made them cheap. He sold them cheap. He made money. Frank took orders over the phone. He went to the loft and watched the men working, and if he saw anyone resting at his machine, he demanded he be fired. He took out his pocket watch and timed the process of fixing one leg to the other and he insisted that with concentration everything could be speeded up. He would not sit down in the loft. There was dust everywhere. He could not go into the supervisor's office. There were beer cans and open sandwiches on his desk. When the windows were open he smelled grease from the Chinese restaurant downstairs and almost gagged. He called himself vice president in charge of efficiency.

"What kind of Jew is that?" said one of the tailors to his work partner.

"Must be a German Jew," whispered the second.

"Even German Jews are Jews," said the first. "Maybe a Romanian count who got into trouble in the old country and is here avoiding the Romanian secret police disguised as a Jew."

Arthur longed for Harry. Harry he could talk to, Harry he could complain to, Harry needed him to cheer him up. Harry would do the worrying. Harry, who was dead, would have been a far better companion in business than Frank, who didn't know how to take his jacket off and put his feet up on his desk and toss cards one by one into a hat placed in the middle of the floor. Arthur knew that if Harry were alive, he would be president and Arthur would be vice president and the decisions would be finally Harry's and he would be spending his life as second in command and that would have been all right with him, too.

Tossing cards was Arthur's favorite diversion, and whenever there was a lull, a moment between appointments, even during phone calls, he would take his hat and put it in the middle of the floor and toss. His secretary picked up the spill, the queens and jacks and deuces that slid off the fedora brim and came to rest ignominiously on the carpet.

Frank wouldn't join him in the game. "For God's sake, Arthur," he said.

Frank didn't smoke the stogies that Arthur bought in Chinatown and were top quality, ten to a box. He didn't like the musicals they went to, Arthur and Frank, Flora and Louisa, all dolled up. He only liked tennis, and that he played as if Haman were on the other side of the net. They talked about him in the clubhouse, how he smashed his racket into the ground the time Hy Brown beat him and how he yelled at Anthony Fried's wife because she giggled as he was about to serve and called her a dumb broad in front of everyone and how he practiced by the hour, smashing his serve over the net, never smiling, never easing up, just as if he were a machine, throwing the ball in the air and coming down on it as if it were an alligator trying to catch him in his jaws. Arthur had certain feelings about his business partner and his brother-in-law.

One day he stopped in to see his sister on his way home, knowing that Frank would be at the club. He sat down on the chair next to Flora's bed. It was only four o'clock, but she already had her Scotch and soda and was lying under the covers resting.

"Are you happy?" said Arthur. Flora's eyes filled with tears. "I mean," said Arthur, "Frank is not everyone's cup of tea. If he weren't your husband, I might not want to work with him."

Flora looked at her older brother. "But he is," she said, "and you have to."

"I know," said Arthur. "Are you all right? I mean, I don't want you to be unhappy."

"I'm not unhappy," said Flora, who sniffled the tears that flooded her sinuses back into the recesses inside her forehead. "I can't imagine not being married to Frank," said Flora, and she couldn't.

Arthur sighed. "I'll work with him," he said. That was the end of the conversation for a year or so.

Even in the worst year, the year of the bankruptcy hearing, two years before the charts started to show their slow swing toward the sun, Arthur never forgot the hospital or the Home for the Elderly Sons and Daughters of Jacob. He wrote out checks, not as generous as in good times, but he was determined; his father had done it and he would do it too. He wasn't going to be the sort of man who acts like a tortoise in time of trouble. He kept his neck out, he gave whatever he could, and he went to the annual hospital dinner and shook the hands of the doctors, and even though he himself ate lobster at the club whenever it was on the menu, he told them how grand it was that they gave kosher food to patients whose suffering was enough without adding to the sum total of their human guilt.

Arthur's great pleasure was his son, Teddy, who was his link into the future, his hope that the business would last forever. Arthur knew that forever was too long, that empires fall, that nations crumble, and that surely businesses must in the end do the same, but still he thought of the Gruenbaum name, printed in delicate white letters on the green label, as one that might last and last, defying the history of the Jews and defying the proclivity of matter to decay. He thought of the business living on in glory, in copious orders, in new factories, in acquisitions that he could hardly imagine and becoming increasingly weighty. Perhaps the Gentile competitors, the ones who would not allow Jewish salesmen on their staff, who sold only to the Gentile stores, perhaps one day they would all sell out to Teddy, who right now was at the boat lake at 72nd Street with his nanny, sailing the toy yacht that had been given to him for his birthday but would one day be floating life-size in Long Island Sound, with his son as captain, because of the business that had surpassed his grandmother's wildest dreams—and she, he understood, was a dreamer—and because of the business that his father had made by working day after day, long hours, with his mind and his hands and his back. Arthur came home late at night after Teddy had been bathed and put in his pajamas that had pictures of cowboys printed down the front. Smelling the sweet odor of sleeping child, he had stood by his son's bed and promised him a business that he would be proud of, one that was re- spectable, growing, vigorous in capital, and weighty in reserves. He prom- ised his son everything, even though the business was still under the shadow of bankruptcy. Aside from his sister Flora, there was no one in the world whose life he needed more than that of his son, Teddy.

Julie sat one night and looked at his annual report. He read the figures over and over. They were not good. Other bankers would see how low the reserves were, what was happening to the deposits, how little new business had come in, and they would see too that certain major loans had been issued to companies already wiped out, debtors who had no hope of ever paying the debt. When everyone saw, when it was public, things would get worse, if not fatally worse. So Julie, who missed his father so badly that he could not admit to himself that he needed advice, that he might ask his brother-in-law, Howie, for legal advice or his wife's brother Arthur, or even the staff of lawyers that his father had consulted time and again, or his old friend Ira, who was an accountant dealing with taxes and new lines of credit and new forms of finance, so Julie in the office, in the night when everyone was gone and his chauffeur was waiting outside for him in a light drizzle, altered the figures on the annual report for the better. There, he said to himself. There is the way it should be. There, he said as he changed the report and dropped it on his secretary's desk so that she could type it and bring it to the printer in the morning. There is how it should look. It did look better, much better, and the investors were reassured, and Julie was reassured. It was as if he had walked across a plank out into the sea with a pirate's sword digging into the soft muscle of his back, and he jumped into the raging waters and found himself in a bathtub after all. There, he said to himself, that was a simple matter. What is the American dream after all but wish fulfillment of the waking hours?

Later, when his sister, Bessie, called him a fool and there were tears in her eyes, something he had never seen before, he understood that perhaps he had made a mistake.

The daily reports were brought to him at his desk at four o'clock promptly each afternoon. He took off his jacket even though it was winter and he had ordered the heat kept at a minimum. He sweated through his shirt, and even his suspenders turned damp. His hair was matted on his head, thinning at the top and already far back on his forehead, the skin glistened. Drops of sweat gathered under his double chin, in the very place where Mildred had just that morning run her forefinger and called him a love apple. What to do now? If he had believed in God, he would have prayed. Not believing in God, he prayed anyway. He prayed not to the Holy of Holies, the Lord of mercy and compassion, but to his messenger, Elijah.

"Appear, appear, help," he said. "A sum of ten and a half million is needed this afternoon, or all goes under."

Elijah, who visits each home when the door is opened at the seder, Elijah, who has miraculous powers of travel and vision and who will herald the Messiah when the hour is right, Elijah, he thought, now or never. But he did not believe in his own prayer, and prayer will never levitate if the supplicant is also berating himself for the words that are in his heart. Also, prayer has seldom been helpful in achieving positive financial results.

Three o'clock at closing time, four cars pulled up in front of the bank and United States marshals in uniform with guns at their side raced up the front steps of the bank. Two stood at the front door, hurrying people out, smiling at no one, while the others bumped and pushed against each other to get into the president's office and inform him of the way things stood.

And so, Miss Blaustein, Julie's secretary, told him that the tellers were leaving, had taken their coats and were leaving. No paychecks this week. Miss Blaustein, who had an old mother to support and who had been cheated by life in matters of female entitlement, brought her boss a cup of tea and promised to stay till the doors were permanently closed, which she did.

She rinsed the tea cup in the sink for the last time. She turned out the lights in the president's office and she gave the chair a last wipe with her fingers, the chair that Ben Eisen had bought himself when the bank had opened its uptown branch. Julie sat on his brown leather couch and tried to take deep breaths, calm and easy, so as to steady his hand as he wrote the sign that he then gave to his chauffeur to post on the huge wooden doors of the bank: CLOSED BY ORDER OF THE UNITED STATES MARSHALS. He stared out into the dark street and watched the last of the women hurrying home. Everything looked normal, everything looked right. From the house on the corner came the sound of a radio playing the newest Sharie Lee song, and he could see in the apartment building across the street two girls, a little older than his girls, bouncing on their beds. The lamps were lit and they cast the usual shadows across the street, and he could see the patch of clover that had been there, by the curb on the corner, ever since he was a child and had come to visit his father at the bank. Not his bank anymore.

The chauffeur drove him home and he went right to bed, pulling the soft quilt over his head and turning his back to his wife, who put his favorite Brahms record on the Victrola in hopes of soothing them both. Silently he lay in bed and refused his dinner, or at least refused it when the maid brought it in. Hours later, his stomach curling and growling, he got up and took the tray to the table by the window and with his fingers picked at the pork chops that had turned rock cold and dry. He looked down on Park Avenue at the calm buildings, steady, wide, sure of themselves, inviting no one in, but being, just being.

At seven-thirty in the morning at the top of the front steps of the bank, in front of the large door, two marshals stood with their guns in their holsters and their hats pulled down over their eyes. At eight o'clock the ones in a rush arrived, the ones who needed to make withdrawals before getting on the trains and going downtown to work, and they saw the sign. They didn't shrug and go on their way. They stood in groups gesturing, talking. "Not this bank . . ." "I never thought . . ." "It's not possible, there's been a mistake. . . ."

The crowd got larger as the hour came near when on every other working day the doors would swing open, the tellers would be in place behind their wire cages. At the desks in the front, men wearing fresh white carnations would be ready to help borrowers borrow and purchasers purchase, and papers, papers to be completed and filed, would have rested on each desk. Now the people on the front steps looked in the windows and saw the empty bank; yesterday's flowers still sat in a vase on a desk and some teller had left a sweater on the back of her chair, but the bank was quiet. The crowd grew and the word spread through the neighborhood, and children on their way to school ran home to tell their mothers, and soon the street was filled. Everyone had money in the bank, for some a life savings, for others just a small account skimmed from every day's groceries, set aside to buy a couch, a new bed, a trip to the mountains in the summer. The mood on the street was not friendly. Julie had known it would not be. He stayed home in bed. He played the radio and listened to a Bach chorale. His head was pounding. He went to the bathroom and discovered that he had a rash on his stomach. I am really ill, he thought. This is making me ill. Tears came to his eyes.

In the Bronx, the crowd shouted at the marshals. One man tried to throw a rock, but he was quickly wrestled to the ground by the police who had come to the scene. "Never put my money in a bank," said one. "Only fools trust banks," he said.

"Lots of fools," said the other, whose savings account had been washed away when the bank on Vanderbuilt Avenue had closed some weeks before.

A woman cried out, "It's not fair!" and the others joined her, and the crowd pressed forward as if they wanted to take the bank over by storm, open its safe deposits, and claim the contents; but the marshals shot their guns in the air, the police joined arms and pressed back against the crowd.

Then everyone stood silently, as if in mourning, as if everyone there had just heard that their mother or father or spouse or child had fallen in front of a trolley and been crushed by the wheels. At noon it began to snow and the flakes came down and the children began to play at the edges of the street and it was cold and so everyone went home, except the marshals, who stood guard over the corpse of the financial empire that had been built by Ben Eisen and lost by Julie Eisen in only forty-five years, more than the time it takes to travel from Cairo to Jerusalem with the pharaoh's chariots at your back.

Mildred lay in her bath thinking. It was bad. She read the papers. She spoke to her brother-in-law Howie, who thought it would come to trial. The district attorney's office had been sent a copy of the annual report, the one that was not as accurate as such documents are supposed to be. Someone, probably an anti-Semite, in the district attorney's office had given the report as well as an interoffice memo to a reporter, and it was there, right on the front page: NEW WORLD BANK PRESIDENT CAUGHT IN FRAUD. Helen Mazur had called to tell Mildred that her dinner party was canceled because she had the flu. Did she have the flu? Or had she only canceled the Eisens for obvious reasons? Mildred considered.

"It wasn't a fraud. It was an attempt to put a good face on things," Mildred said to Flora.

"But," said Flora, "they are saying it's a crime." Flora sat next to her sister on the couch covered in tapestry fabric. She put her arm around her sister. Flora's glasses were misted because there were tears in her eyes.

The maid came in with the tea tray, and the women stopped talking.

"Are you going to keep her?" asked Flora as the maid's back in its black uniform disappeared down the hall.

"I don't know," said Mildred. "I'll sell my emeralds before I'll give up Nanny," she said.

"You can have my diamond ring," said Flora, who loved her sister at that moment more than any living creature.

"Oh, God," said Mildred. "I got a letter from the Old Oaks Club that our membership has been temporarily revoked pending an investigation."

"Who cares?" said Flora.

"I care," said Mildred.

Flora's eyes filled again with tears. She crushed her tea biscuit in her hand and spilled crumbs onto her skirt and brushed them onto the floor.

"Stop that," said Mildred. "Can't you eat a biscuit neatly?" Flora tried to put her feet over the crumbs that had now gotten onto the carpet. "You know," said Mildred, "he won't be able to survive jail. He'll get a cold and that cold will become pneumonia and he'll die."

"He won't go to jail," said Flora.

"Whatever happens," said Mildred, "we will keep our heads up, and you," she said to her sister, "will stop crying, right now. We are going to manage this. He's a stupid man, Julie," said Mildred. "I didn't know it when we got married, but I know it now. I'll despise him for the rest of his life," she said, "but he'll never know it, no one will ever know it. And you"—she pinched her sister's arm the way she had when Flora was a little girl and she on the edge of womanhood—"you forget what I said to you."

Flora hugged her sister. Her mind was filled with thoughts of revenge, of taking the district attorney and tarring and feathering him on Fifth Avenue in front of everyone who was having tea at the Plaza. She thought of the bank and its strong white pillars and its big front window and the smell of leather and cigarette smoke and golden light that came from under the green shades on the tellers' lamps, and she felt dizzy. How was it possible that the doors of a bank could shut?

Mildred shook her sister, who was staring absently at the gold swirls in the Oriental rug. "We're going to lunch," she said. "I want everyone to see us having a good time. We are going to lunch and we are going to laugh loudly."

Flora got up and followed her sister out the door. The two women were wrapped in their furs and there were sequins on the veil that Mildred wore over her face. Flora's hat was always falling off and getting tangled in her glasses.

"He won't go to jail," Flora said, "I'm sure," as they waited for the elevator to rise to their floor.

Arthur arranged for the business—the business officially in bankruptcy but already regaining some ground—to pay the household expenses for his sister Mildred. The Gruenbaum Company had increased its overalls and work jackets inventory and cut back on good suits for good times. It had opened a store of its own in Philadelphia, and because it sold cheap, honest clothes, which after all were needed, people were buying, on time, slowly, but buying.

"It's going to be all right," said Arthur to Flora.

"Of course," said Flora, "but be careful. Just work clothes, uniforms, police uniforms. Can you get a police uniform account? There will always be police."

Flora was right. Arthur got the police uniforms orders, because his were cheap, the scams were only done once, but they held, at least for the first inspection; after that the men in blue were on their own with needles and threads to keep up appearances. They got the police account in Hartford, Connecticut, and Salem, Massachusetts. The profit margin was minimal, but it was there, and in hard times a penny earned was a half a penny for your sister, and that was the way Arthur saw it. His long oval face looked haggard. He had trouble sleeping at night. What if he failed everyone? What if he couldn't pull it off? He went dancing at the Rainbow Room, and when they were on the conga line with his hands on the curve of Louisa's hips, he felt sure he could do it; somewhere out there where the lights of the city were shining and the parapets of the high buildings floated through the clouds, his father was watching out for him, would help him somehow, and all would be well. Later he danced to "Flat Foot Floogie with a Floy Floy" until he was out of breath.

Nothing much changed in the Eisen house. The children went to school. The nanny took Jill for her violin lesson each week. The food was on the table. The fur coat went to storage for the summer. The family went to Deal, New Jersey, and stayed in a rented house. But Julie came with them. There was no chauffeur waiting downstairs to take him to the bank. There was no bank. Instead there were court appearances. There were meetings with lawyers.

"Don't worry," said Howie. "After all those years that your father was in the club, the trial will be all right." And that he believed, though it hurt to believe it.

"The fix is in?" Julie asked his brother-in-law.

"I spoke to the fellows at the club," said Howie. "They said it would be hard, because of the publicity. They said of course for Ben Eisen's son, they would try everything."

This was not enough to stop Julie from waking at night with a sweat on his body and the sound of doors slamming in his ears. And a new fear had come on him that made it hard to take his wife in his arms. What if, he said to himself, I can never take care of her again? And his organ responded to the thought by trying to hide in the folds of flesh of his thigh.

Mildred lay next to him in bed, not worrying about his inactivity. She had enough to think about. "I know," she said to him, "that you meant well, and I will always respect you." She kissed him good night and turned over and turned out the light.

At least, he said to himself, my wife is on my side.

"It's all right to lie to a man," Mildred said. "They always lie to us." That's what she told Flora, who was always wanting to be honest in hopes that honesty would make her happy, clear the path, open the way. Flora believed in truth, which is why she irritated Frank by always trying to get him to tell her how he felt, if he liked her new hat, her freckles that slid down her back and over the bridge of her nose, the porcelain lamps she had bought for the night tables, the way her flesh got goose bumps when he touched her, so she would know, know absolutely, where she stood in the world.

The *New York Times,* the *Los Angeles Times,* the papers in Detroit and Cincinnati, they all carried the story. The radio in St. Paul, in Jackson, Mississippi, they all reported the trial. Front page center, there was a photo of Julie, looking sad, with bags under his eyes. A man in his mid-thirties with a double chin, a bare forehead with wisps of hair over the top that seemed to have caught in a breeze on the steps of the courthouse and stood straight up. His glasses had slipped down his nose, a nose that was exaggerated in the cartoons that filled the editorial pages. Pictures of a Jew with money bags and his hands around the throat of the small depositor. Certain priests and ministers were using Julie as an example of the Jewish vice that was breeding in the countryside, and the head of the Ku Klux Klan personally made a speech on the front steps of the Reform Temple in Atlanta, condemning Julie Eisen and all the other Jewish bankers who were raping the people. A cross was burned. The Jews said nothing. The police in Atlanta were wearing uniforms made by the Gruenbaum Company, but they said nothing.

The maid quit. She said the other maids were making remarks about her. The nanny said the other nannies wouldn't let their children play with her charges. They wouldn't sit near her on the bench in the park. Mildred said, "Don't be silly," and she invited them all to a party for Lydia's fifth birthday and she hired a clown and a magician and she planned to give each child a puppet as a party favor. But all the invitations were refused. The party was held anyway. Will Katz, who was too old for magicians, and Arthur's boy, Teddy, who was too young and ran around mashing candy into the Oriental rug, turned out to be the only child guests.

The elevator man answered the calls to their floor with increasing slowness. The doorman refused to open the door for them. Mildred ignored all this. She continued to smile at the doorman and to greet the elevator man with a cheerful wave.

It wasn't that they didn't try to bail out Ben Eisen's son. It was discussed in the clubhouse in the Bronx where Ben Eisen had introduced Howie Katz and paved the way for his selection to the bench, and it was decided that it was too risky, there was too much public attention. The bank had closed and people, registered Democrats, were too angry, their people in the Bronx had lost so much that it wouldn't be right. If it were discovered and some pup of a reporter made a stink—whose side were they on, anyway? It just couldn't be done and it wasn't and so Julie was convicted and when the judge sentenced him and the bailiffs came and put the cuffs on his wrists and his eyes watered and he looked out into the courtroom, he saw his wife, Mildred, and her sister, Flora, by her side, and Mildred was smiling at him. Be brave, said her smile, but Flora was weeping.

Hedy's Great-Uncle Max: Summer 1932

He had learned how to ride only ten years ago, but he was a spirited, determined rider, one who whipped the side of a horse with all his strength and kicked and leaned forward into the mane, yelling and patting the horse and bouncing backward and forward, in a style not quite that of the better clubs, where polo was played, but it didn't matter because they wouldn't let Max in their back door anyway, they wouldn't let his horse play on any team, they wouldn't let him in the locker room. His membership application had been turned down at every club that had a stable within one hundred miles of New York City. His name was Gruenbaum, he was clearly one of them. One look at him told the whole story. He was a self-taught polo player. He was not a graduate of Andover, Exeter, or Groton. He had never gone to college. He had retired from the suit business. He was the only man to play polo who was in the suit business. This was no comfort to the membership board, who believed that if one were admitted, thousands would demand entrance. If one thought he could wear the colors of the team, who knew what would follow? There were limits, after all, in a gentleman's sport.

Max understood all this. He wasted no time in disappointment. He bought a farm in New Jersey from a man who had gone to Argentina, and he bought a number of horses and hired a trainer, and each weekend he would pay the stable boys from the clubs with names like Homer's Acres and Nicholson Bend to play with him. Off season he would get the old jockeys from the tracks to come and play on his team. Sometimes members of the clubs would come over to Max's field. Tall and blond, younger sons of the men who sat on the admissions committees, they enjoyed the extra game, the chance to practice. They sometimes let Max make a goal and laughed as he cheered for himself. This was or should have been a humiliating arrangement. But Max enjoyed his afternoons in the sun, on the green, mallet swinging above his head. He paid for the white lines to be redrawn each week. He paid for the lemonade and the bourbon. He paid for the vans that brought the horses to him when he could not come to the horses. He would let out a huge "Oy, veh!" when he missed and a "Mazel tov!" to the man who made the shot. He got perspired and red in the face, and his clothes were always too large because he could never admit to the salesman the size he really wore, which actually existed only in the boy's department; but out on the field, hips pressed flat against the flank of the horse, his horse's name was Patrick Henry, he felt like a million dollars, a real American.

"One life for my country!" he would shout as he charged across the field. A joke that never grew tired as he repeated it week after week. He felt large and strong, towering over the blades of grass, the insects, the dogs, and the little round rolling ball, a ball that he would hit and it would go where he wanted, sort of, most of the time.

Reader: You think that at his age Max shouldn't be racing around on a horse knocking a little ball about. But he was in very good condition for a man in his fifties, who had a shortened leg from a childhood accident, who had been nourished in his early years in a town in the east of Poland known for its inability to coax fresh vegetables from its rocky soil, and whose small stature reflected the long hours his father had spent bent over his sewing machine and the thinness of his mother's milk. Max was in remarkable shape for a man who had nearly been turned back at Ellis Island when his parents presented him to the customs officer. He had coughed and sneezed and his nose had leaked and leaked and he'd kept his head down, away from the customs officer's eyes. The customs officer had thought he was retarded or dwarfed or perhaps blind, but he was only small. The whole family might have been sent into quarantine, returned on the next sailing, but his older brother, Isaac, had smiled at the officer and pointed to the pocket watch that swung from his waist and told the man the correct time in Polish, Yiddish, and English. This he had learned from a lady on the boat who was practicing from a grammar book and shared her new wisdom with the child who appeared by her elbow whenever she tried to find a quiet place to study. The customs officer had looked into the eyes of the boy Isaac, and though he agreed that the Jewish element was of inferior stock, a wave of them coming to drown the good brains of the Scotch and Irish like himself, he couldn't help but smile at this child, whose eagerness shone from every dirty cranny of his wiry frame. Another rich American, said the customs officer, and stamped the papers. Max never did grow beyond five feet and one inch. His back had something crooked, not a hunch, not a hump, but a curving bend that went both sideways and outward. For a man with those particular problems, who nevertheless went bald before he was thirty like all the other male Gruenbaums, he was in fine shape: physically, if not financially.

The business had gone bad and the money wasn't there and when Max complained to Arthur, Arthur shrugged his shoulders and told Max to sell. "Sell your horses," he said. "We need cash in the business."

Max had been furious, red in the face; his heart was racing. Never, never would he sell his horses. He'd rather sell his children, although he didn't have any, if you didn't count the one in Pansville. He borrowed money from a loan shark he knew. The hay was expensive, the grooms were costly, the bills were tucked into drawers and kept out of sight. There were certain terrible warnings. A man appeared at the door and set fire to Max's hat, and Max was worried, but not worried enough to stop playing polo on Saturdays and riding his horse in the woods.

He had dinner with Flora, the youngest of his brother Isaac's four children. Flora had come out to his place, and while she wouldn't ride with him, which disappointed him a little, and she wouldn't even give Pat an apple from her own hand, she had said to him, "I'm happy for you that you have your horse."

He said to her, "Get Arthur to give me some money, for your father's sake. I might lose my horse."

Flora lent him some money. But she couldn't convince Arthur to do the same. "Are you crazy?" he said. "That man hasn't worked a day in his life. I don't have to support horses, for God's sake."

Arthur was right, Flora knew, but she also knew that her father would have found the money to help him. Flora signed a note for him from the loan shark, who was pleased to do business on Park Avenue and tipped his hat to the doorman and tried to kiss Flora's hand, which she pulled away just in the nick of time. Flora met her payments. But a little while later, Max was back. He needed more money, that was it, he just needed more money. Flora sighed.

While she was thinking about what to do, the problem was solved. Max was riding his horse and chasing the ball and wiping the perspiration off his chin with one hand and worrying about money and thinking about the way the loan shark had set his hat on fire, when Patrick Henry reared up and Max fell backward and hit his head on a rock and never recovered consciousness. I'm going to die in the saddle, he thought as he went flying through the air.

Flora had been kind, and that was why when Max died that summer, Flora inherited all of Uncle Max's stock, though it wasn't worth much more than the paper it was written on. She also inherited his horse, Patrick Henry, who was immediately sold along with the entire New Jersey property at auction.

"Glue factory, horse meat," said Flora with a certain satisfaction, but she kept a photograph of Max with his helmet falling low over his eyebrows and his mallet swinging in the air and the horse rearing up as if to throw the rider and Max smiling into the camera as if there were nothing to fear. Flora bought a silver frame for the photograph and placed it on her dressing table, and she touched it, just at the top so as not to leave fingerprints, at least once a day. A certain Mr. Fred Wentsworth II bought the place and changed the name over the white picket gate from Green Tree Acres to High Winds Farm, and that was the last time in the twentieth century that a Gruenbaum owned a horse.

Hedy in the Corridor of the Hadassah Hospital: 1990

Hedy thought about her mother, although it was her daughter who was in danger. Hedy wanted to show her mother the picture of Namah when she was three on the swing in the Haifa park overlooking the harbor. Her brown hair was curled in a bush about her head, her brown eyes were staring at the camera with a frankness, a confidence, and an expression of surprise shaped her lips. One hand held on to the chain and the other hand waved at the person taking the picture. Hedy wanted to tell her mother about Namah, how she was taking psychology courses so she could work with troubled children, how last summer she had volunteered at the school in the Galilee for boys who had broken the law. Namah believed that everything could be fixed, that attention would help, the touch of her arms would heal, the smile and the nod of the head would heal. Namah had a shine to her face, a glow of someone ready for bliss. Hedy wanted her mother to see Namah now at the end of her childhood, a young woman not interested in abstractions, ideas, mathematical formulas, but immersed in the smallest of human vibrations, how to make a child unafraid of the dark, how to make friendship last. Namah loved dogs and gerbils and birds, babies and plants and old Beatles songs, and she believed that Arabs and Jews could live together in peace. She believed that swords could be beaten into plowshares. In the morning of her life Namah believed that she counted, what she did, what she felt, how she behaved toward others, mattered. Everything mattered. Hedy grieved that her mother couldn't see Namah, sleep in her eyes early in the morning, drinking coffee by the window, her hand on the dog's head, her sneakers crusted with dirt, her school books across the table, her curly hair falling unruly around her shoulders, and her wide mouth with the small space between the two front teeth, still surprised by everything; Namah, who was now lying on the operating table not thinking at all, not dreaming. . . . Do people dream during operations?

Hedy tried to remember her mother's face. It was hard to get it exactly right. In her head she kept seeing it only in parts, the mouth, the nose, the eyes and the glasses, the hair, but she couldn't get the parts together. There was a clock on the wall. The hands seemed not to move. There was another woman who was speaking in German, an older woman whose blue flowered dress hung on a spindle of a body. She was awaiting word about her husband, who was having an exploratory operation in his stomach. She too was attached by an invisible string to events behind the green metal doors at the end of the corridor. She was sitting with her sister and they were holding hands, the two women, bending their heads together, close like little girls.

Disgrace: 1933

Bessie did not attend her brother's Julie's trial. She kept up her appointments as if nothing extraordinary were happening at all. At the hairdresser on Convent Avenue she fancied she heard the other women whispering about her. So what? she thought. What were their husbands but cogs in the machinery? She was married to a judge, after all. So what if the family fortune were diminished one hundred percent and the maid and the cook and the fine apartment which could no longer be paid for by her share in the bank's fortunes was now being paid for by certain earnings of her husband, whose decisions on the bench—not often, just now and then, just in important matters to people of means—were swayed by large envelopes that arrived at the house, not so often, maybe only once or twice a year, delivered by hand, unmarked. She took the envelopes and took care of practical matters. Howie had a way of turning green when they arrived and pretending his back hurt and he had to lie down. Bessie had a gown made for New Year's Eve. It was draped over the hump that had gotten more conspicuous with the years, and the gown fell in a flattering way over her small hips and it was cut low, very low. She wore it to the lawyers' cotillion and carried with it a feather fan that sparkled as her hand moved it over her face. So no one wanted to be at their table. So people were embarrassed and didn't know what was the right thing to say. Bessie wasn't going to care. She knew how it would all come out in the end. Will wanted to go to court to see his uncle in the dock, but Bessie wouldn't allow it.

"He's an innocent victim," said Will.

"They hate us, for being so rich," said Bessie.

"No," said Howie, "people are angry because they lost so much money, they think it was Julie's fault."

"It was their own fault," said Bessie. "Who asked them to put money in our bank?"

Howie, who never raised his voice to his wife, who contradicted her only with the softest words, kept his head cocked to one side, like a wolf who has been bested in battle.

Bessie's face turned dark, and the violet circles under her eyes deepened. "I don't want to hear any more about it," she said.

It wasn't so bad, in prison. Not as bad as he had thought. He was in Danbury, in Connecticut, far away from his golf club and his apartment on Park Avenue and his home in the Bronx and his father's grave, which rested in a mausoleum on a grassy hill in northern Westchester. It had happened. The worst had happened, and after that he felt a kind of peace. He slept at night on the cot with the thin mattress and the bars in front and above. He ate at the mess, whatever it was, spooned out in metal trays. At first the guards had watched him carefully. They removed his belt and shoelaces. They had other types from Park Avenue who had swallowed their buttons, stuffed pillowcases down their throats, eaten chicken bones, and stabbed themselves with toothpicks. But Julie surprised them. He was cheerful and friendly and he asked only for his violin, and when that was provided him he practiced for hours by the window of his cell. Mozart and Haydn. He squeaked. He ran the notes together, his fingers plucked at two strings at a time and sometimes more. He sweated over the neck of the violin and the wood grew stained. The other men, confidence men, gamblers who lost big, a man who took widows to dinner and picked their pockets, a guy who sold insurance for a company that didn't exist, a small-time safecracker, a man whose wife claimed he had tried to murder her, although he claimed he was trying to save her from choking on a piece of steak, they made remarks about Julie. Jew, yid, kike, they called him, but they allowed him to play poker with them in the exercise yard. They laughed at him in the shower. Cut off, huh, they said, but they left him undisturbed. They banged on their cell doors sometimes when he was fiddling late into the night. He thought of it as applause. He would stop when the night guard said, "Shut it off or I'll shove it down your throat."

The hard part, the hardest part of being in prison, was visiting day. He wasn't the only prisoner who thought so. Mildred did not miss a Sunday. She got up early and dressed for the day in the best clothes she had. She wore her pearl earrings and her pearl necklace and she had the maid pack a suitcase full of sweet things for her husband, soap that was soft and smelled of roses, a new hairbrush that might if used judiciously help preserve the few hairs on his head a little longer. Vitamins so that he should not get undernourished in prison and a box of chocolates.

"What is it like?" asked Flora.

"You get used to it," said Mildred.

"Used to what?" said Flora, who was not unkind, just curious.

Mildred would sit on the green bench and wait for Julie to be brought in. He would catch sight of her as he was coming down the hall. She was taller than the other women. She was wearing her hair in perfect curls. Her earrings were real pearls. She smelled of perfume, and her white gloves were sitting, one on top of the other, on her lap. "Are you all right?" she would say.

"Fine, just fine," he would answer.

"You are pale," she would say.

"Why not," he said. "This isn't Boca Raton."

"Of course not, darling," said Mildred, "how stupid of me." And then there was silence.

Julie said, "I worked this week in the laundry. It's hot and the steam makes you think you're breathing wool, but I got the hang of it all right. I was the one who stirred up the vats when they were boiling. After a while it was easy."

"I'm glad," said Mildred. She thought of him, his round backside used to his silk pajamas, standing in a rough prison uniform over the steaming water and stirring it. She was silent. Did she pity him? Did she love him? What was it that made her hands flutter again and again to her hair as if the windowless visitors room were the backseat of a convertible driving her to an unknown destination?

She was the only visitor with a driver who waited in the parking lot. She would stop at a toy store in the Bronx. She wanted to bring the children back presents, which she told Jill and Lydia came from their father, who would see them as soon as he could. In the backseat of the car Mildred took out her gold compact with the ruby bouquet at its center and powdered her nose and colored her lips; looking in the small mirror in her hand, she would smooth the line of her hair and adjust the colors over her eyes. When the car pulled up in front of the Park Avenue building, she alighted with a jump.

"Thank you, my darling," she said to the chauffeur, who adored her for her smile, for her sweet way of nodding to him, as if he were a real person in her life, not just a chauffeur, for remembering him every Christmas and asking about his girlfriends and his beloved mongrel dog.

Mildred would greet the doorman with a cheerful wave, and only when she was alone in her bath, with soap bubbles over her knees, would she allow herself a moment of incredulity. I have just visited my husband in prison, she said to herself. A popular girl, envied and attended to by other girls, a girl loved by her father and mother and her younger sister, at least, and her brothers, she wasn't used to adversity, to people she knew having parties and not inviting her; but she'd be damned if they'd get her down. She'd remember their names, every one of them, and when the time was right, when Julie was out of prison, she'd have a huge party and invite them all, and they'd come. Mildred knew they would. She'd bounce out of the tub and spend the evening making her nails perfect, listening to records on the big Victrola in her living room and dancing with herself.

Flora said to Hedy, "You didn't know your aunt then, it was before you were born, but she was brave."

Reader: I hear you scoff. Brave, you say, in her apartment on Park Avenue with the maid in the kitchen and the cook and the nanny and the doorman and the car and chauffeur, lent by Arthur, the company's car, really, at a time when all over this country people were standing in the streets with their worldly goods packed in paper bags, not knowing where to go or how to get a job or a meal and living eight in a room, with relatives who could no longer stand them or camping in tents under bridges and by railroad tracks, homes of tar-paper roofs or ramshackle boards and mud floors, people were selling their wedding presents, their furniture, their bodies. A meal was a big thing, a hot meal an even bigger thing, and people went in trucks and old cars that broke down to cities where they knew no one, in hopes that someone was hiring, and women who had never swept their own floors were now taking in laundry and men who had sung in the church choir were now in the back alleys holding out tin cans and lying on their backs in the doorways of dark streets and the bankers came and took the farms and the dust storms came and burned the crops and the farmers went to the cities or worked the harvest up and down the coasts, alongside their wives and children, who stooped and crawled through the acres of planted land that belonged to someone else, and their girls took men into the backs of trucks and earned money to eat, and the hardware store owner and the candy manufacturer closed their doors and ate stew made from daffodils and cans of watered evaporated milk. Young men who might have gone to college were planting trees in the high dark hills of distant forests and only the poets remained as rich as always; that is to say, their prospects had not improved. So why feel sorry for Mildred, who had only to worry about Julie, who was managing in prison very well for a person who might have died of shock, developed ulcers that bled, or let the clang of the doors stop his heart from feeling altogether? Well, Mildred was brave, and Flora was right. Bravery is relative to your circumstance, and Mildred was strong and valiant, and while she never wanted in the usual sense, she wanted just the same for the respectability, even the position that had been hers when she wed, that had been hers before she wed because she was her father's daughter, a member of the Gruenbaum family. She crossed no oceans like her grandmother, Naomi, but still she was brave, she stood still and smiled at her former clubmates if she met them on Madison Avenue and she was gracious to their old parents if she met them as she sometimes did at the Thursday-afternoon Philharmonic performances. She kept her subscription seat and she walked down the aisle as if people's heads were not turning, and she sat perfectly still, talking excitedly to her guest, who was always Flora, even when she knew that others were pointing her out, whispering about her up in the first and second tier. Flora did not especially like the long afternoon of music, Flora preferred a good game of mah-jongg to the best of Bach, but she sat in the seat next to her sister and admired her. "Mildred was brave," said Flora, and she was right, dear Reader, bravery is a very individual matter.

The Younger Herzberg Follows in His Father's Path: 1908–1935

Eli Herzberg was very different from his brother, Meyer. He was an allergic baby who vomited up all but mother's milk, whose eyes puffed and closed with his first mashed carrots, who wheezed and sneezed when the windows were open and the pollen count was high. He caught cold easily and each cold settled in his chest and his mother sat by his bedside with steam kettles bubbling through the night and she fixed him special food, careful always to check his skin and keep his neck covered with a wool scarf. He was not as fast as Meyer. He learned, but in his own way and in his own time. He did not ask questions. He stared at his teachers and remembered or tried to remember what they had said.

"God has saved you for some purpose," said his father, rocking his frail son on his lap one evening.

He did not have the voice of the Baal Shem's disciple. That was clear. He did not have the capacity for extraordinary intellectual feats, that also was clear.

"Perhaps a head for business, like my brother," suggested Ruth.

"No," said Joseph, "this one has a gift for trust. That is a gift, too."

When Meyer left home to go to Johns Hopkins and it was clear to Joseph that Meyer would never return, he turned his attention to his second son. He walked with him, his arm draped over his shoulder, leaning on him, whispering into his ear, the tales of the zaddiks of Europe, the scenes of the courts of the rabbis who sang songs to the glory of God into the early hours of the morning. Eli was the chosen son. Wasn't it so in the Torah that the second son was the important one? It was true that Eli, who was not as quick as Meyer, would in the end win the blessing of the father.

Ruth sometimes worried that her second child smiled so little, ran stiffly only if asked, and prayed in his room with such intensity that his forehead was often red from the place where he had banged it against the wall as he atoned for impure thoughts or wickedness that might come to be. But when she expressed her concern to Joseph, he patted her gently and smiled. "He is a good boy. You want trouble, go worry about Meyer, go worry about the neighbor boys who have already been arrested, thrown in prison. Take pleasure in our good fortune."

So Eli went to the yeshiva in Brooklyn when he was old enough to be sent away. He studied hard, and though he showed no signs of brilliance, he was pious and decent and earnest.

In New York he visited his uncle Isaac's widow. He brought her a yellow flower and Sabbath candles that had been made in Brooklyn by a widow who dipped the wax in barrels on the porch of her house. Annie gave him money for the candles, and while he refused to drink so much as a glass of water in her house, she offered him money for his school. That is what her husband would have wanted. She wrote Ruth a letter after the visit telling her what a fine son she had and how proud she must be of him. To Flora she imitated the shrug of his shoulders, the Yiddish accent he had not lost despite being a native citizen of Baltimore in the United States of America. "I hope that's the last we see of him," she said.

Eli did well at the yeshiva. A descendant of the disciple of the Baal Shem, even a descendant without the voice, was welcomed. He was a boy who believed that if he closed his eyes and lifted his heart, he could hear the pulse of the creation, and he smiled at all his teachers and his fellow students with the innocence of one who believes himself blessed and fears only for his friends, never for himself. He had the high Gruen-baum forehead and hair that promised to recede across his scalp in time. He had long arms and thin wrists, and his feet in their hard black shoes were always stumbling, getting caught on stair steps and wrapped around the legs of chairs. He had a space between his two front teeth that was wide enough for him to curl his tongue between while he studied.

When he graduated he married a girl, named Hinda, selected by his rabbi and he joined the community of Jews in Borough Park in Brooklyn, a growing community of Jews who kept the ways of their fathers, who followed their own vision of America, one in which English was the last language after Yiddish, and Hebrew, Polish, Russian, and German. Once he went to visit his cousin Harry at his office. He took two subways and walked through the streets where the carts of dresses and coats were being pulled back and forth. His cousin Harry's office with its silver-framed photograph of his son in a sailor suit and his wife holding the baby seemed like a refuge, an oasis in the desert. Eli looked so strange to Harry that he couldn't bring himself to sit down and paced back and forth before his window while his cousin, his father's sister's child, talked to him in an accent that spoke of Poland and Yiddish and Brooklyn and seemed to Harry hardly to be speech at all. Eli wanted Harry to give money to the school he was attending.

"What are you studying?" asked Harry.

"The word of God," said Eli. "I'm studying for you."

"Don't bother," said Harry, who felt irritation turning to sweat on his forehead. "You want a suit, wholesale?" Eli shook his head. Harry sighed. Eli was his cousin, after all.

He bought a building in Borough Park for the yeshiva that Eli attended and he paid for the desks and the salaries of the teachers for two years, and in return, in return, he was invited to the dedication of the new addition, but he didn't go because he was on a business trip to Chicago that week, or so he had his secretary call to say.

"I don't understand," he said to Flora. "Why are there still Jews like that? You'd think in this country they'd go get a shave, dress right, and stop embarrassing people."

Flora said, "Are you sure that he really is our cousin?"

"Yes," sighed Harry. "He's our cousin."

A few years later Eli appeared in Arthur's office. "Do a mitzvah," said Eli, "and God will remember you."

"What is a mitzvah?" said Arthur, feeling lost in the conversation, lost in the shine of his cousin's eyes.

"How about making some suits in Borough Park?" he said. His rabbi had asked him to ask his cousin.

Arthur agreed, for his father's sake, for the sake of his aunt Ruth, whom he hardly knew, because family is family. This was how it happened that in Borough Park, in an old warehouse on Elm Street, the Gruenbaum Company set up a factory and employed 250 men, all of whom took off for the full seventeen Jewish holidays a year but were willing to work on Sundays and Christmas.

"In the summertime, they sometimes faint," Arthur told Flora, "wearing those heavy clothes, jackets and hats and scarves underneath their shirts."

Eli Herzberg had five sons and three daughters. He had listened to each of his children as they began to speak and he had taught each of them a simple song and with each he had hoped to hear the sound of the disciple of the Baal Shem, but it had not happened. His wife, Hinda, who was herself the daughter of a scholar, one of those who was himself close to the rebbe of the community whose court was at the heart of Borough Park, played the piano, like Eli's mother, but not quite, but none of her children were gifted in music. Dutiful, yes, but gifted, no.

When their first son, baby Mendel, ran a high fever and lay crying in his crib, Hinda asked Eli to take the child to a hospital in Manhattan, because the doctor in Borough Park had a worried look on his face and suggested that she ask her father to ask the rebbe for special prayers. She and Eli had taken the child into the hospital and they had stayed by his crib while the doctors, men without yarmulkes, Jewish men who couldn't complete a sentence in Yiddish without making a mistake, wrote things down on charts. Then they were told that their baby would die. They had no treatment that might divert the angel of death.

Mendel's cries grew weaker. Hinda, who slept on a chair by his crib, her wig slipping off in the night onto the linoleum floor, ate only bites of the food Eli brought her from home. She begged God for forgiveness, but none came. She searched her mind for wicked thoughts, for times she might have hurried through prayer or washed a dish with the wrong sponge. She searched for ways to take back her error, to undo what had been decreed.

Eli and Hinda took the baby home, and he died within a fortnight, his small heart stopping as she washed his diapers in the tin tub in her kitchen. Eli Herzberg's wife never trusted him again, not the way she had before. She didn't trust her father, either, who had elicited a special prayer from the rebbe. They covered the mirrors, they sat together for a week, and the men prayed in the evening and the early morning, and Hinda fixed pots of coffee and tea for her visitors and her mother helped her make cakes and breads in her oven.

At the end of the week they walked around the block, and they put away the baby Mendel's baby clothes. Hinda moved through the rooms of her apartment with her head erect, but her eyes, her eyes had changed. Before, they had been sharp like a cat on the hunt in the alley. Now they were dull. She had the eyes of a woman betrayed. But she was soon with child again, and this one they named Caleb because Caleb was the man who was sent by Moses into the Promised Land and who said that though the enemy was strong, the Israelites would triumph and the land belong to the children of God, and the name "Caleb" had a strong sound, a sound of conquering and confidence. A child with that name would not get sick, or so Eli reassured his wife and so she reassured him.

Caleb did not have an unusual voice like grandfather. He was not orderly and neat and attentive like his younger brothers. He was not a boy given to books. He learned what he had to learn, but he liked to climb the rocks in Prospect Park and jump from one to another so that his mother, who was watching below, would scream in horror.

"Don't fall!" she would yell. "Come down right now!" And the other mothers would glance up at Caleb and be thankful that their sons were sitting on the bench with their heads bent down over their books.

Caleb could throw a ball and hit it with a bat. Caleb was the fastest runner in his cheder and the other boys were afraid of him for reasons unknown to the adults. Eli looked at his son, who grew taller than the other boys—his arms were strong and he never kept his feet still but always moved them about as if ready to jump up on command—and said to himself, The people of Israel need Caleb, and he was pleased. Caleb wondered, Would his mother have preferred it if the baby Mendel had lived? Was his life the result of the other child's death? What could it mean not to have been born? Was Mendel the child with the voice? Eli too had considered and rejected that thought. "God is not a prankster," he said. "God would not be so cruel."

"You know that for a fact?" said Hinda, but she said nothing more.

Mickey Doesn't Sit Around Mourning: 1930 and After

After Harry died, Mickey moved out of town. Exactly what happened is this. The young widow with her child were well enough provided for. Flora had seen to that. Mildred and Arthur contributed. Max insisted on making a small contribution. But Mickey was not the sort just to sit around and wait and see what fortune would bring her next. She was in shock for a month or two, and then it was cold and the wind came off the river and blew up her skirts and she thought of the South and the palm leaves and the coconuts dropping from the trees and the men who wore knickers on the golf course and whose necks were red from the beating sun, and she rented a suite with room for the nanny at the Miami Beach Excelsior, a brand-new establishment with pink fla-mingos painted across the turquoise lobby and an exclusively Jewish clientele. Not the German Jews, who had their own vacation spots. This was a different crowd. The men yelled at each other in Yiddish as the money was pushed back and forth across the card tables. No one on the golf course or the tennis courts had played the game as a boy, and no one had gone to a school that taught you to congratulate the winner; no coaches who also taught French and geometry had told them it wasn't all right to throw your clubs if you missed a shot. Down in the sun for their few weeks' vacation, they threw back their heads and laughed out loud, letting everyone see the food they hadn't fully chewed and the gold teeth they could easily afford. They showed pictures of their children and grandchildren, and the ladies sitting by the pool, sipping drinks with parasols stuck on the end of straws, wiggled their red painted toes and rested their bodies in the sun. They didn't mind that their bodies were not as perfect as they had once been. Whose is? Breasts no longer pointed up and hips spread underneath wraparound skirts, why not? They ate from the breakfast table, rolls and marmalade and fruits that were orange and green and pink, and why not? When abundance cannot be taken for granted, each pat of butter and each little silver bowl of jelly is a wonder.

The mood at the Miami Beach Excelsior was very good, just what a new widow, especially one with long legs and a perfect figure, needed to get her back on her feet again. The lounge, which couldn't serve liquor but offered a punch with a cherry floating in it, had become a meeting ground for the younger crowd, daughters, sons, vacationers with a little money in their pockets. There was music, live, three Negroes in tuxedos playing until the early hours of the morning and a dance floor surrounded by potted palms and statues of the shy flamingo made of pink sponge. It was here that Mickey began to live again.

Jacob Brest had left Sulvalki shortly after the fire in the shul and some months before Naomi and Moses. In America he had found that a market in young women, kept in proper houses, fed as long as they could work, was just the sort of thing for a handsome man such as himself. He married one of his madames and moved to Brooklyn. The now apparently respectable couple had a son named Ira, who, besides having a successful businessman for a father, was also the grandson of the mitnagged rabbi of Brest. Ira, however, was in his father's business. He fell in love with a visiting nurse who took care of the health needs of the girls. She died in childbirth, leaving him with an illegitimate son named Ezra, who never finished school.

Ira saw the business opportunities of the future and he took his son with him on forays into the night, where they met with the others in the same professional line and they drank in alleys and said things that are not said in front of ladies and they exchanged large bundles of cash carried around in suitcases.

Ezra's father died in his bed—a spasm of the brain, they said—and Ezra took the stake his father had left him and bought himself a boat and a place in the Miami sun, where the liquor could be landed safely and transported north, sweet bottles of Scotch and bourbon, in unmarked trucks that looked as if they were hearses bringing the dead home from Florida. A lot of people died on vacation in Florida. Ezra was thirty-five and a big man in Miami and connected by arrangements with certain other big men in Detroit and Buffalo and New York and Chicago when Mickey was introduced to him at the Flamingo Bar and Grill by a man who thought she was going to be his for the evening but was mistaken.

Mickey liked the way Ezra's shoulders looked under his white jacket and she liked the bulge at his side of the big gun he always carried. In turn, he liked the way she walked, as if she were inviting him to touch, but she was a widow, a woman with independent funds, a respectability that he rarely came across. She had a broad mouth that was painted violet, and her suntan showed white streaks across her bare shoulders where her bathing suit straps had left their mark. After drinks, he whistled for her to follow him out onto the patio where the lights were pink and blue in paper Chinese lanterns, and they walked down to the beach, Mickey's Cuban heels catching in the grass between the patio stones, down to where fluorescent insects jumped among the grains of sand and the stars hung above the ocean, promising that death was only temporary and water was the first condition of life, wetness like the kind that Mickey began to feel between her legs when Ezra put his hand on her back and asked her to sit down with him in the dark gazebo at the end of the path.

From his jacket pocket, Ezra brought out a silver flask with his initials on it and offered it to Mickey. She brought it to her lips and threw back her head, and the muscles of her neck were taut like the lines of a ship set for sail. Ezra did not remind Mickey of Harry at all, and that was to his advantage. He came to her that night in the gazebo like deliverance; deliverance from exactly what, she couldn't have told. She said she wasn't easy and that he couldn't just have her after an hour, but she laughed and it didn't escape him that the white blouse she was wearing was heaving up and down, as if, unnoticed by its owner, certain tides were rising.

"So, what do ya really do for a living?" said Mickey, pushing Ezra's hands off her thigh.

"I take care of myself," said Ezra, "and anyone who's with me."

Mickey knew, she wasn't born yesterday. She giggled.

Ezra liked the way her hair came falling around her face when he pulled the pins out and she attempted to push his hand away but missed. It wasn't too long before her skirt was in the red hibiscus bush and her satin shoes had separated across the floor and she put her hand on Ezra's zipper and pulled it down.

"Oh, my God!" she screamed, so loudly that the people in the lounge looked up.

"That girl can take care of herself," one said.

Harry always had to be coaxed, he had to be wooed, he had to feel in the mood, and his thighs were heavy and they often covered it so that she didn't know if he wanted her or not and his belly rolled out over her hands. Also, he was slanted. Ezra was not. Ezra instead was hard and hairy and he spread her legs and he waited standing above her.

"Do what I say," he said. "Do exactly what I say."

And she did, not because he didn't remove his shirt or his holster and later she felt the steel press against her abdomen and for a moment was frightened, but then remembered where his fingers were and felt safe, guns don't go off unless they are triggered, even a girl knows that. He put his hand on her throat just over the pearls she was wearing and he put his mouth on hers and he sucked and he pulled as if her soul were the marrow of some bone that had been placed on his plate for dinner and she had trouble breathing and she gasped and thrashed her arms and he stared into her eyes and she lay still and he returned to her mouth and she arched her back and she lifted her head to his and she was grateful that death had taken Harry and left her the rest of her life—oh, glorious life!—that was beginning in the gazebo at the Miami Excelsior. Ezra got his hands tangled in her pearls and as he pulled free the string broke and the pearls, real pearls, a twenty-eighth birthday present to Mickey from Harry, scattered, rolled, and skidded in all directions. Mickey tried to get to her feet, to catch the rolling pearls as they spilled across the gazebo and out into the pink azaleas below; fun was fun, but the pearls had value.

"Let 'em go," said Ezra. "I'll get you better."

"I bet you will," said Mickey, and let her long legs spread open across the floorboards. She wasn't the sort of girl to be afraid of splinters.

Reader: So what is class in America? Our dirty little secret, that's what—the thing that was left out of the Bill of Rights. Notice that nowhere does it say that everyone has to be upper class. The guarantee of equality and opportunity and the pursuit of happiness does not include the right to belong to the country club of your choice, it doesn't promise that you'll have the same accent, way of wearing your jacket, sipping your tea, or shuffling your shoes as a person whose ancestors danced around the maypole in Concord or kissed Pocahontas on hot Virginia nights. You couldn't tell from reading the magazines and you hardly ever hear it in the newspapers of record, but how much money you have is only part of the story, who your folks were is the other part, and together they form a self-portrait, one that enables us to put you in your place, wherever that place might be. Of course we are a land of great impostors; Max and his polo field was right in that tradition, the upstarts and the newly arrived, they strut and preen, looking at the photographs in popular magazines, learning wine lists by heart, and dressing on the advice of their tailors, but everyone knows the impostor from the real thing. We admire impostors, we let them spread themselves across our society pages. We are always climbing up and down our little ladders, watching who's ahead and who's behind and who might overtake us. It's not part of the official American dream, not part of Paul Revere and his midnight ride or Abraham Lincoln's "four score and seven years ago" or Thomas Jefferson's hand on a quill or Benjamin Franklin flying his kite in the sparkling colonial skies, but it remains true that each social ladder has little ladders within it like a cabalistic diagram that if you unravel its secret will spell the name of God and bring about His presence on this disrupted earth.

Sharie Lee Sings the Blues: 1935

Sharie Lee had gotten very thin. Her dark eyes had sunk even further into her head. The fine bones on the base of her neck stood out sharp above her breasts, and when she took the air deep into her lungs, reaching for the high notes, the bones seemed to be straining to escape her body. She had conked her hair in a shop up on 125th Street and it hung, for the first time in her life, straight to her ears. Her long nose seemed to have flattened back against her face and her lips, always painted violet, rose, magenta, seemed swollen. When she held the microphone in her hands and walked in her own unsteady way across the stage, she seemed to be hanging on, the way a rider on the bus grasps the strap as the doors close and the bus lurches forward. But she had a reputation, not the million-dollar kind, not the gold record kind, but she sang in the right clubs and in New York, on 52nd Street, on Jane Street, on Greenwich Avenue, in places where the people who knew, who followed the sound, who kept the first record Louis Armstrong ever made and showed it to prospective lovers, clients, came again and again and sent her notes backstage and flowers and there were notes about her in the columns, and she had a press agent and a record company who promised but never quite delivered. She was invited to sing at benefits for the brothers in Spain, for the steel workers in Ohio, for the victims of the Schoharie flood, and wherever she was asked, she went, at least most of the time. Sharie Lee had a voice with a howl, one everyone recognized as their own but nobody else could imitate. Sharie Lee had a way in the middle of a song of abandoning the lyrics, the cry for a lost love, smarting or seeking, regretting or expecting, and letting someone come out of her throat that stunned the musicians into silence, a sound that was guttural, ancient, bloody, ferocious, and mad. When the audience heard that sound they stopped breathing, stopped drinking, stopped talking, and stared straight into the blue-and-pink spotlights, looking at the source. Holy was what it was, but of course no one could quite say that.

Sharie Lee would have been more famous if she'd managed to finish an engagement or even a full set. Sometimes she didn't make it to the club. Sometimes in the middle of the performance she would look out at the audience and yell at them, "Go home, get outa here!" and stalk off the stage. She had a manager. He tore his hair out. He begged her to be on time, to stay sober for the week, but he only had influence over her if he promised her what she needed, and what she needed was less and less money and more and more of what came in the form of powders and liquid, amber liquid.

Who loved Sharie Lee? Well, a few trombonists, a jazz pianist, some white, some Negro, some cracker from Louisiana who played the drums, one Jew, a Jew from Buffalo who owned a hot spot in downtown Brooklyn Heights who would do anything, anything at all, for Sharie Lee, who herself didn't seem to love anyone except her mother, whom she called at least twice a week and never told her anything except that she was doing well, singing here and there, wearing silk and satin, and feeling fine.

"Tell her," said Joseph, "I want her to come home and visit me."

"I'm coming soon," said Sharie Lee. "Tell Papa I'm coming soon as I can." But she couldn't.

In the early hours of the morning when the clubs had closed, she had gone with the musicians to breakfast at the diner on Twelfth Avenue, and her manager had begged her to eat the eggs and bacon he had ordered and she had pretended for his sake to swallow some but had then spit the food into her napkin and gone to the bathroom and put her head against the toilet seat and let the night flow through her, resting there till the manager had come and banged on the ladies' room door. Then he had dragged her back to her place, helped her up the stairs, and laid her out on her bed. She would lie awake listening to the occasional car, the steps of the landlord's son who worked the six A.M. shift at a pretzel factory in the Bronx, and she would smoke her last cigarette and put it out in the empty glass with the melting ice cubes that sat on the floor within hand's reach. She would put on records, those she needed each dawn, Fats Waller, Billie, Mabel, Ella. The music had to be played softly. The neighbors banged on the walls, threatened to evict her if she played it loud. She would put her head over the edge of the bed and her ear to the speaker and listen, and in listening her body would uncoil itself till she was stretched out across the whole bed. She would think about playing on the hardwood floor of the *bimah,* quietly, while her father sang to the congregation. She would remember the ark opening and closing and the silver Torah handles catching the light, the eternal light that seemed forever to glow inside the ark, above the ark, above the brass trellis in which the lion of Judah was embedded, his head back and his tail forever curved like the letter S. She wanted something, Sharie Lee, lying there on Morton Street waiting for the light of day, but what was it she wanted? She tried to find the words for the thing she wanted. She tried to remember if it was a man who had it, who had not given it to her, but if it was a man, she couldn't think who, she couldn't bring his shape into the room. Maybe it wasn't a man, this thing she wanted. "Forgive me," she would say to the beaded fringe of her lampshade. "Forgive me," she would say to her red satin shoes with the rhinestone clips, which she had flung across her floor. Outside on the street, the lamplights would turn off as if God's heart had skipped a beat, and the gray, pink dawn would be filled with the sound of the milkman's bottles rattling in their wire cages. Sharie would fall asleep, still in her dress, her lipstick thick on her lips, smearing on her pillow, so far into sleep in a place so soundless, so without form, without end, without light, that even dreams couldn't reach her.

Flora brought Frank and Arthur to hear Sharie sing. "My cousin," she said, and was proud and her eyes shone when Sharie appeared in her sequined gown on the stage and the audience clapped and clapped.

"Would you like to be Sharie Lee?" asked Arthur.

Flora nodded and her eyes filled with tears. After the performance Flora went backstage and gave Sharie roses that she had brought all the way from uptown. She kissed her.

Sharie hugged her cousin. "Thank you, thank you," she said, and offered Flora and Frank a drink.

"She was stewed," said Frank in the cab on the way home. "She's a drunk. I hate broads who drink. Who the hell does she think she is?"

"But," said Flora, "she's swell, she's a swell singer."

"She's a drunk," said Frank.

"You spoil everything," said Flora.

"You, you want to think everyone related to you is some kind of genius," said Frank.

Frank and Flora stopped talking. Sharie Lee was swell, just swell, Flora thought.

Mildred refused to go. It wasn't just that she didn't approve of Sharie Lee and her well-known association with peoples of color, communists, and anarchists; it was, she explained to Flora, that she was just too busy. She went to the opera every week and that was enough.

Flora told all her friends that Sharie Lee was her cousin. She told the doctor who was attempting to diagnose her stomach pains. She told the seamstress who came to alter her new dress. She told Frank's secretary and the dentist who wanted to give her a gold crown.

Quebec Bob was the first Negro singer to go to the Soviet Union, and he was the first Negro to have a part in a Hollywood movie that wasn't the porter or the janitor or a sharecropper with a donkey stalled in the middle of the road. He played a nightclub singer, a part patterned on his own life, and he was a huge hit. When he first heard Sharie Lee, he put back his big head and banged his arms down on the table. He knew that sound, he knew that sound too well. He took Sharie home to his apartment in the village and he gave her all she wanted to drink and he held her in his arms when she got started on a crying jag that she couldn't stop. He waited till she woke the next morning before telling her that he expected her to travel with him to France, where he was doing a film. He waited till they were in France to tell her that he was married and had three children. It didn't matter to Sharie Lee, who had never been to Paris, and she loved it almost as much as she loved the wide back of the man who rolled over her again and again and said, Sing to me or I won't touch you till tomorrow or the day after, and she sang to him, whatever he wanted, whenever he wanted, just to keep him touching.

In Paris when she woke she felt bliss, not the kind of bliss that comes from revelation, the kind that comes from a body next to yours, one that is going to be there at least for a week. "I'm thirsty," she said, and Quebec Bob answered her thirst. They made a record together in Paris and they had trouble getting it played in the United States of America. As if the voices of a man and a woman shouldn't miscegenate on jukeboxes and radios. As if it mattered that they stood on the stage of the sound studio, microphones dangling like jungle vines, one Negro and one Jewish woman, not so young as all that, but looking at each other all the time.

Louella Parsons carried the tidbit: Sharie Lee and Quebec Bob an item. "For Christ's sake, now see how your wonderful cousin is behaving," said Frank. "Stop telling people she's in the family."

"My God," said Mildred. "It's embarrassing."

Flora wrote Sharie a letter. "Let me know when you are back in New York. I want to take you to lunch. Tell me all about Paris!"

Ruth didn't read the New York papers. She received a long-distance call from Paris. She could hardly hear her daughter.

"Everything is wonderful. I'm better than ever," she said. "I'm in love. I'll tell you more when I come home."

"She's in love," said Ruth to Joseph.

He sighed. "Not a Jewish man, I suppose?" he asked.

"She didn't say," said Ruth. "Maybe."

Sharie Lee came back from Paris, and Quebec Bob rented an apartment for her on Christopher Street in a little white house with sloping green roofs and an old chimney that puffed black smoke out into the city street. Sharie told Flora that she had been to a Gypsy in Montmartre who had told her the secret of great orgasms.

"Tell me," said Flora.

"It's so simple," said Sharie. "It's all about exercise. You pull your muscles like you were trying to drink through a straw down there and you do that five hundred times a day and you get so sensitive that you can have orgasms just by thinking of chocolate sodas."

"You're joking," said Flora."

"No, said Sharie. "Try it."

Flora tried, but it didn't work. Maybe she didn't believe in it, like Dorothy and her red slippers that needed only to be knocked together to provide transportation home.

Hedy in the Corridor of the Hadassah Hospital: 1990

The dinner trays are moving out of the kitchen and up the elevators to the patients' floors. Arab men with white aprons tied over their trousers are pushing wagons through the corridors. The nurses are talking quietly at their stations, getting ready for the next shift, filling out the last of the charts. The patients are thinking about the trays that are moving toward them, clanking sounds alert them. But in the operating area no one is thinking about dinner. In the hall Hedy's husband, Elan, puts his head between his hands. His older daughter pats his shoulder, clumsily, like a teammate after a loss on the soccer field. Elan sees his wife leaning against the wall. She is standing. Her white hair tied back in a ribbon has begun to come loose around her face. His wife's cousin has gone to get coffee. He cannot sit still. All afternoon he has gone back and forth to the cafeteria as if anyone wanted the black dishwater he brings. Elan sighs. It has been too long. Something unexpected has happened. They must have failed. Why don't they just come and say so? What kindness is it to stall, to hide behind the thick doors of the operating room? Elan wants to comfort his wife, but that would mean he would have to cross the room, to unbend his legs, to reach out his arms. He can't. He is stiff. He is frozen in place. If he moves, he might break.

Hedy Going to the Park with Ursula One Saturday Morning: 1942

Hedy was afraid of nuns. This was because her mother told her to spit if she saw one.

"Nuns," said Flora, "are disappointed women."

Hedy saw the nuns walking two by two along Fifth Avenue. They lived in a convent on 96th Street. They had white hoods and long blue dresses. Hedy searched their faces, holding on to her bike handles tightly so no one could rip her off and carry her screaming into the convent. "Gypsies aren't the only ones who kidnap children," her mother had said.

Hedy was looking for disappointment. She saw that the nuns did not wear lipstick. Ursula did not wear lipstick. The cook did not wear lipstick. Were lipstick and nail polish Jewish? What was the connection between lipstick and disappointment?

How Harry's Son, Moses, Got Lost: 1932

December arrived. Back north the whole city would be decorated with pine and lights and store windows speckled with reindeer and silver ribbons on frosted panes. Mildred would be buying Christmas presents for the cook and the maid and stuffing envelopes decorated with wreaths and bells for the elevator men.

In Baltimore Joseph said to Ruth, "Wassailing, wise men, stars on treetops, were the innocent pleasures of Cossacks and czars, crusaders and royal ministers."

"The sweetness is an illusion," Frank said to Flora, who in spite of herself still believed in sweetness.

Mickey did not return to her Park Avenue apartment in March as she had planned. She moved into a house in Miami Beach that had a motorboat in the front yard, a dock that extended way out into the canal, and a view of downtown Miami to blast your eyes out. Mickey designed her days so she would have a perpetual tan. She lay on the chaise longue and covered her long limbs with coconut oil and she put bandannas printed with orange flowers in her hair and she wore a gold ankle bracelet that had Ezra's name on it in small diamonds. She wore an emerald ring the size of an ovary, and the only thing that weighted her down was her mascara, which she applied each morning with a waterproof brush.

Widowhood had its opportunities. There were guys around the house, always lots of guys, with black suits and hats and shirts, and ties. They looked odd in the sun, despite the dark glasses many of them wore, they looked uncomfortable in their black shoes and socks.

"Send 'em back to Chicago, honey," said Mickey, who didn't like the way they watched her when she spread herself out on the patio, with the latest *Silver Screen,* the newest report on Joan Crawford and her secret lover.

Ezra laughed. "We need protection," he said.

"From who?" said Mickey, kissing him and leaving a large print of her red lips across his.

He wiped himself with a handkerchief. "From the other guys," he said. "Don't worry about it," he added. "You got nothing to do but look great for me." And he took her in, the long look of the whole body, and he stretched his arms out, exposing his holster for the birds to see. He pointed at the heron that stood on one leg in the reeds by the shore. "I could shoot that bird right through the eyes," he said. "You want me to do it?"

Mickey made a face. "Naah," she said, and turned her back on him, letting her bottom swing from side to side as she retreated.

He felt that if his number was up, if worse came to worst, he would have lived, it would have been worth it. He even felt awed sometimes at his good luck, and he was a man who didn't believe in luck. He only wished he could have introduced Mickey to his father; the old man would have licked his chops, wouldn't he. He also loved her because of the way her tongue felt in his crevices of his body and the way she let her long red nails run down his vertebrae and the way she plucked at the hair around his nipples, as if she were preparing to eat him.

People in the North moved south and people in the South moved west, but Ezra and Mickey stayed put right on the canal on the Atlantic Ocean, whose waters led down the coast of Florida, through the bay of Boca Raton, filled with the sandpiper and pelican and red snapper and largemouth bass that had been there before Ponce de León had imagined the fountain of youth and bootlegging had been a business as golden as the sun that streamed through the palms and bounced off the coconuts onto the white-and-pink beaches.

There was a problem. A grain of sand in the oyster, so to speak, and that was Moses, a pale child who ran away from his nurse whenever the opportunity came and pulled on his mother's skirts and begged to be taken along when the large white car pulled up to the front of the house. His white sailor suit hung on his frail body and he kept his shoulders hunched up as if expecting a blow, though no one, certainly not Ezra, had ever hit him. He had freckles on his face and the sun burned his skin, so the nanny kept a straw hat on his head and it was tied under his chin with a ribbon.

"You sure that kid's a boy?" said Ezra to Mickey one day. Mickey kicked him in the shins and opened her mouth wide in protest.

Moses cried if he fell down and he cried when his mother went out in the evening no matter how many times she planted a kiss on his forehead, and sometimes in the middle of the night he woke screaming and had wet his bed.

"Christ," said Ezra, "this kid is going to get eaten by the sharks out there."

Mickey pouted. She thought Moses was fine. His green eyes fringed with long lashes seemed to her better than any eyes she had ever seen, including Ezra's, though she kept that thought to herself.

One afternoon that December there was talk of repeal, and the talk made Ezra nervous and he ate pistachio nuts by the handful. As Mickey and Ezra were sipping cocktails on the lawn and the guys were lounging in the boat that was tethered to their dock and cigarettes and beer bottles were floating in the reeds and Mickey was deciding what to wear out to dinner, her red silk or her green with the demure jacket, two of Ezra's men, big guys with white panama hats and identical ties with greyhounds printed up and down, dashed into the house and across the grass, past the plastic spotted fawn, and mumbled something in Ezra's ear, and he jumped up and turned pale as a ghost. The Detroit gang was here, here in Miami, and Ezra's accountant, a little fellow who walked around carrying heavy black books and who always looked as if he had water in his ears because he kept shaking his head and occasionally banging himself on the temple with the palm of his hand, was shot in his Chrysler and his brains were splattered all over the steering wheel. Dinner was canceled, and the nanny and Moses and Mickey went down to the Halcyon Hotel and had a soda in the lobby and saw Santa Claus on a bicycle wearing a red-and-white-striped bathing suit giving out balloons. Moses wanted a balloon but was too shy to join the children who pressed up close.

There was the greyhound, Ezra's own dog, who raced at the track wearing his colors, found in his kennel with his throat cut and his tongue torn out and hung from the wire post at the kennel's entrance. Ezra walked around surrounded by three men. He kept his hand in his jacket, fondling his protection. He didn't want to talk to Mickey. She thought about going back north. She called Arthur long distance and asked if he'd help her get started again in New York. He promised he would. He asked to speak to Moses. He said he would always be there if she needed him. She felt so much better that she decided to stay awhile.

"Things may get rough," said Ezra to Mickey. "We better get the kid someplace safe."

"I could send him to his father's family in New York," said Mickey.

Ezra thought of his house without the child and the nanny, and he smiled for the first time in weeks. But it turned out that Louisa's father had just died and the nanny was going on vacation.

Mildred offered to take Moses, even though this was a hard time for her. "Does he still have Harry's round thighs?" she asked Mickey.

"Naah," said Mickey. "He's thin like me, but he got Harry's eyes and that widened forehead, you know he's a Gruenbaum."

"All right," said Mildred, "the nanny won't mind one more."

But Mickey was worried that Mildred's girls, Jill and Lydia, would tease Moses, who was not used to other children. Flora, while she offered to take Moses for a visit, explained that she was trying to get pregnant herself and this wasn't the absolutely best time, would it be possible in the spring?

So it was that Mickey, who didn't want to explain the nature of the emergency to her fancy ex-sisters-in-law, couldn't think who might take Moses to keep him safe.

Ezra suggested the monks of Our Lady of the Sea. "No women around," said Ezra. "It'll make a man out of him."

"A monastery?" said Mickey. "For God's sake, this kid is a Jew."

"So what better hiding place for Jewish kid?" said Ezra, and there was a line of sweat over his upper lip and the small beads seemed pasted in the crevice under his nose.

That was the first time Mickey understood that maybe the danger was real. Her flesh prickled. She thought of the greyhound whom she had watched so many afternoons racing, usually about fourth place, streaking along on his thin gray legs, his ears plastered back with the wind, and she wept, which made Ezra mad, and he slapped her, which she didn't mind as much as one might think.

So Moses was taken early one January morning up to the monks of Our Lady of the Sea, who helped the child out of the backseat of the car and down the path lined with hibiscus and hydrangea. Moses was pale as a ghost and absolutely silent, so silent that the abbot, who saw him at lunch, reassured him that this was not a monastery in which anyone had taken a vow of silence. The abbot had gladly accepted the generous gift that Ezra offered all in cash and promised to tell no one that the child was staying just for a short while with the orphans and abandoned children who had become the merciful charges of the brothers on the hill overlooking the green sea just beyond the promenade that held the lighthouse that signaled the passing ships to steer clear of the rocky shoals below.

Moses was put in a small bare room with only a cot and told to make up his bed. He didn't know how. He sat on the floor and drew invisible circles on the floor with his finger. On the bare wall was a crucifix, and in honor of the season a branch of a fir tree had been tied to the bottom of the bleeding feet. Moses knew there was no point in calling out for his mother. She had promised him she would take him home in a few weeks. She had promised to buy him a radio of his own that he could turn on whenever he wanted, if he were brave. Moses tried to be brave, but bravery wasn't his strong suit, and the boys who soon enough found him sitting on the floor tied him up naked in his bed sheets and were shocked at his penis when it appeared bare and transparent pink before their eyes: Jew kid, for most of them their first. They left him tied up through dinner, and it wasn't until Brother Ignatius was checking the rooms at the beginning of his watch that he found Moses lying in his own urine with his eyes as blank as a child's eyes can be, still trying to be brave.

If repeal came through, then what? Unemployment lines, that's what. Gambling and whores, that's what. Penny ante stuff, that's what. The thing about the Detroit gang was that Detroit was only the point of origin, not the total description at all. The thing about the Detroit gang was that they knew what Ezra knew, that the source of the booze was out of Cuba, in the little boats that ran along the gulf, up through the inlets, and finally onto trucks that spread across America. They knew that in order to get the biggest take—and what else was worth getting up in the morning for?—they would have to control the point of entry, the source, and in order to do that they had to get one guy, one hard-to-deal-with, not properly subservient guy, out of the way. It was only what Macy's would do to Gimbel's if Gimbel's were a person and Macy's instead of having floorwalkers and salesgirls and packers in the warehouse had a band of fellows with Smith and Wessons, fast cars, and reasons for loyalty beyond the Christmas bonus and the retirement watch.

So it was after the nanny had packed and gone to visit her sister in New Jersey for what was to be a short vacation and after Ezra, who jumped each time a gull called out to his mate or a car screeched past on the road, had gone to bed with a bottle of his best bourbon in hand and after Mickey, who had applied her night cream and rubbed it in completely so that Ezra would smell it but not see it, had fallen asleep, that the guys who were playing poker in the living room with their holsters on, just in case, heard a sound outside the window. It was a crunching sound, like someone walking on glass. They jumped up and ran to the window, ready to shoot, ready to do battle, their hearts beating, their lips clenched tight over their teeth, and fear causing them to reach with their free hand for a sudden itch or a pull at their organs, when behind them the door burst open and the Siegel gang was there, not one or two or three, but many, so many that it took just a second or two and men lay on the floor, collapsing one into the other.

Even though it was three in the morning and Ezra should have been asleep, he wasn't. There was a crescent moon hanging over the canal and his boat was dipping up and down, gently pulling at its line, and there were stars in the sky. His grandfather Jacob had told him about the stars that sat over the town of Brest, "more than in America, bigger than in America," he'd added. "In America there are only imitation stars."

Ezra heard the shooting downstairs and he grabbed his gun. He climbed out the window, and from the ledge he was prepared to jump into the rose bed below, but the night was lit with stars and two of the Detroit men saw him. They fired and missed.

Ezra pulled himself up onto the roof and with his eyes cold and clear he could see the stars, too far to touch. It was the last thing he saw before falling into the flower bed.

Mickey woke up. She called for Ezra; were the shots in her dream? She rubbed her eyes and mascara came off on her hand. She rolled over and felt the empty space in the bed next to her. She got up, all naked, her fine body stretched out against the window with her breasts still firm and pointing up. She heard the steps on the stairs. Was it the boys? She grabbed for her nightie, black silk with a dragon whose tail followed the curve of her own bottom, a gift from Ezra.

They bound her hands and tied her to the bed. They'd had a tense night. They too had itches in their crotch and surges in their groin. Even tied up, even frightened, Mickey tried to respond, to make nice noises the men would like, to be soft and open for them. Why would they kill her, if they enjoyed her? They relieved themselves and then emptied their guns into the bed and the sheets turned crimson.

It was all over the papers in the week between Christmas and New Year's. Some smart reporter had posed as the coroner's assistant and taken a picture of the bed, with Mickey's cigarettes by the night table, Ezra's bottle of bourbon, and the nightgown now in shreds over what was left of the body. Fortunately the picture was grainy and the light was bad and the details were blurred.

Nevertheless, Arthur was on the phone with Mildred and Flora every day. "We have to find Moses," he said. "She must have sent him somewhere in Miami for safekeeping." Arthur went to Miami.

"Be careful, for God's sake, be careful," said Flora.

But he wasn't very careful. He asked everyone. The gardener and the nanny, who had returned from New Jersey to find that her job was over and her charge was among the missing, the headwaiters at restaurants where they were known, the pediatrician, who was also the Fontainebleau Hotel doctor, who knew Moses but hadn't seen him since he had an earache in September. GANGSTERS KIDNAP CHILD, said the headlines. But the Detroit gang, who now had houses all around Miami beach, just looked at each other. You see any kid? they asked each other.

The monks considered. They didn't read the papers every day, but the radio told them the story. Moses, who once had a mother who had a companion who was certainly not an angel, was now a child without parents, without legal guardians. He was a Jewish child who might burn in hell forever because he had the misfortune to be born into a non-Christian family. Perhaps his arrival at the monastery was part of God's plan. Certainly it took only a few moments for them to convince themselves that the child who had washed up on their beach was theirs for salvation, theirs for Christmas, a miracle child, born to be reborn in Christ. So they didn't say anything to anyone, and no one, not even Arthur, imagined that the monastery on the hill, with its small band of boy orphans, had become the permanent home of Moses Gruenbaum.

Mildred had stomach pains and headaches and lay in bed for a few days after Arthur came back empty-handed from Miami. Flora was tearful and said over and over, "Don't give up, don't give up." Flora was ashamed of herself. She should have insisted on taking the child when Mickey called. She should have known something was the matter. How could she forgive herself for letting her brother's child drop right off the face of the earth? Mildred told her to stop carrying on. What was the use of blaming yourself? Flora had nightmares about Moses. At least she thought they were about Moses; in them a little boy called out, "Aunt Flora, Aunt Flora, bring me an ice cream."

After a while everyone forgot about Moses, except Arthur, who kept apologizing for not having taken Moses, even though Louisa was not home. Eventually Arthur stopped the monthly payments to the detective firm in Miami that he had hired to trace the child. He too forgot. Jews understand that you can lose a whole tribe and the rest goes on. You can lose whole pieces of yourself and continue. It is the continuing that matters.

The Prodigal Returns: 1936

When Julie came out of prison the car was waiting, and in it was his wife, carrying a new silk tie she had bought him for the occasion. Two and a half years had passed and Julie had lost the rest of his hair and his bald head shone in the sunlight as he took his first tentative steps toward freedom. The chauffeur opened the car door for him just as he had in better days. The suit he was wearing was prison issue, and Mildred touched his collar and withdrew her hand. "You can change when we get home," she whispered in his ear. His blue eyes blinked and blinked, his pale hands clasped and unclasped.

"Aren't you happy to be going home?" said Mildred, who had prepared a celebration dinner with Flora and Frank, Arthur and Louisa, Bessie and Howard, and Will was coming, too. Even though he was still in junior high school, Bessie and Howard did not go anywhere without

Will. They took him to their Thursday bridge games and insisted he play with the adults. They took him to Democratic party dinners in the grand hotels of the Bronx and Brooklyn. He didn't fall asleep. He didn't ask for dessert the way another child might. He watched the grown-ups and listened to the speeches. He had opinions about the candidates for office, and he advised his father to speak with the cardinals and the bishops who attended these events.

"You can tell," said Will, "they count."

Mildred had spent the morning picking out her best dishes, usually saved for Passover, for the occasion. She had spent hours dressing, powdering, and perfuming every crevice of her body. Over, over and forgotten, is what she said to herself. We've had the worst, she smiled at herself in the mirror, now comes the better. In the time that her husband was doing time, she had added not a wrinkle or a line to her face. Her throat that she creamed each morning and night was as white and firm as ever.

Julie sat in the car and his shoulders slumped down. "I'll tell you," he said, and he turned to his wife.

"Don't tell me, now," she said. "Now it's over."

He sat silently as the car crossed back over the bridge into Manhattan. He sat silently through dinner, though Arthur toasted his health, told him how brave he had been, gave him the news of the business, which was hanging on, decreasing debt, looking good, not out of the woods, but in the part of the woods where the sun shines through on large patches of growing ferns and small fields of wild flowers.

"Join the business," said Arthur. "Come work with us. We could use a good mind like yours."

Julie didn't smile. He didn't agree. He didn't thank Arthur for the offer.

"Thank him," Mildred said firmly to her husband.

"Thank you," said Julie, and bent his head toward his soup. "I'm tired," he said. "Usually I go to bed before eight. I'm used to going to bed early," he said, and left the table.

"It'll take a while," said Flora, reaching for her sister's hand.

"Nonsense," said Mildred, "he'll be fine in the morning, and at work next week." And so he was.

Arthur gave Julie an office of his own and a secretary who typed his letters and brought him coffee. He was to be in charge of expansion, perhaps into long johns and socks. It was Arthur's theory that if you didn't keep growing, you shrank, and this he had learned from his father, who had told him, Don't stand still, keep building, keep building, but don't build too fast.

Julie stared out the window at the racks of clothes crossing the street, the dresses packed tight one against another and the coats covered with paper sheets that blew up in the wind, showing the red and blue and beige wools like flares in the sky on July Fourth. Julie had headaches and he took aspirin and held wet compresses to his forehead. He felt confused by the noise that roared down the avenue if he kept his window open. But he felt hot, suffocated, trapped, if he closed his window, so much of the day he went back and forth to the window, alternately raising and lowering the glass.

"All right," said Arthur to Frank, "he costs us money. We're still in trouble, but as long as I can I'm going to take care of my sister. In time, Julie will pull his weight. He's my sister's husband after all."

Julie had other plans and was biding his time.

The Clouds of War Have a Silver Lining: 1939

Something about Roosevelt made people want to buy suits, and things began to look up, but not enough to make anyone sleep easy.

"Military uniforms," said Arthur. "That's it, uniforms."

He tried to get through to the procurement officer at army head-quarters, the one in charge of garments. The name Gruenbaum did not open doors. He couldn't even get an appointment with an under-undersecretary. He wrote his congressman. He called on the phone. He sent a sample uniform, a piece of quality work that he had custom made, to his senator. There were other companies that had the same idea, and the offices of senators and congressmen were filled with uniforms, glistening buttons, shining braid, all accompanied by offers of lunch, cases of Scotch, and reminders of old school friends they had in common.

It looked as if the gates to Washington were closed, marked off limits, unscalable, unstormable, locked tight. But Arthur went to Washington and took a room in the Hay Adams Hotel opposite the White House, and he sat in the lobby and had a drink in the evening and spoke to whatever guests sat down on the big velvet chairs near him. Arthur Gruenbaum, Gruenbaum Suit Company, he introduced himself. Most often people backed away, changed their seats, put their newspapers up over their face. Arthur smiled and waited. A general came in and sat down.

"Can I buy you a drink?" said Arthur. "Arthur Gruenbaum of the Gruenbaum Suit Company," he added.

The general accepted; what the hell, this was America, wasn't it? This wasn't Germany, where the Nazis were breaking glass and burning books. It turned out the general liked golf, and even more important, the general was a card tosser, too. "Good for the mind, clears it out," he said, and the two men, in the lobby of the Hay Adams Hotel, put out the general's hat, with the braid around the rim, and with a deck of cards bought from the hatcheck girl, they tossed until the general's aide arrived for dinner and found that they were going to be three.

This was how the Gruenbaum Suit Company infiltrated the Pentagon and became a supplier of khaki for the South and heavier khaki for the North and jackets for summer and jackets for snow. It was how Arthur removed the last constraints on his business and the case was dismissed from bankruptcy court and by the time that the Japs laid down their wrath on Pearl Harbor the lawyers were already advising Arthur to take tax shelters.

Flora jumped out of bed and left a perfect red lipstick mark on her brother's high forehead when Arthur brought her the figures.

"It's for Teddy," said Arthur. "I wish Dad were here. I wish Harry were here," he added.

"They are here," said Flora. "In the business, sort of, you know what I mean."

"Maybe," said Arthur, who wasn't given to tarot cards like his sister. But of course that explained why he ached with fullness, a fullness that might break a heart, when he touched the sample suits in the storeroom at the back of the offices, why he was filled with a desire to thank someone, a desire so powerful that he sat down and wrote a check immediately to the hospital so that they could buy a new X-ray machine, a desire to sink to his knees and sing the praises of whatever power had made his business, the one he almost lost in bankruptcy court, come back to life, flex its muscles, and he noticed again the Gruenbaum suits being pushed along the avenue, loaded into trains, still swinging on their hangers, headed out across the country to Indiana and Kentucky and Oklahoma, where they sat in the best store on Main Street and said, Gruenbaum in New York knows how to make a suit. It was a thing of pride, a sanctuary this business, loved the way another man might love a woman, with devotion, attention, sensitivity to the slightest alterations in condition, a passion that could not be counted on to protect the beloved and was all the more poignant therefore.

In Which Sharie Lee Loves a Married Man: 1938

Quebec Bob and Sharie Lee had come to an understanding. He saw his wife three nights a week. He stayed at Sharie's place for two nights, and two nights were his own and neither woman knew just where he was. His wife was a Jamaican lady who had come to New York to dance, and now that Quebec Bob had made it, and money was no object, she lived in a penthouse apartment on 12th Street and danced in her living room in the dark, with one light focused on a spot on the rug in which she moved like a bird whose wings had snapped until, exhausted, she would fall asleep.

Quebec Bob wouldn't leave his wife. He wouldn't leave a girl who had trusted him with her future, who had given him three children who ran about the apartment in an endless game of cops and robbers, and when they were quiet he rocked them on his knees, held them with his hands, and ran his fingers over their eyes and mouths.

Quebec Bob thought Sharie Lee was a present that God had given him, a reward for being a dutiful husband and father, and that was that.

Sharie Lee learned to wait, to wait for Quebec Bob to call. She learned to stare back at the tourists in the village restaurants who stared at the couple and drew sharp breaths of shock. She learned not to get out of the car with Quebec Bob in midtown Manhattan because someone was sure to call her a whore. Was she a whore? Sharie Lee discussed it with her cousin Flora.

"He loves you, though," said Flora.

"I don't know," said Sharie Lee. "Who knows if a man loves you or just pretends because he wants to shut you up."

"I think," said Flora, "love isn't love at all, it's just a way of keeping yourself from falling apart.

"You should have an affair," said Sharie Lee.

"God," said Flora, "what a thing to say."

The two women were sitting on the floor of Sharie Lee's apartment, decorated with posters of Paris, patchwork quilts from Martha's Vineyard, where she had visited Max Eastman with Quebec Bob last summer. They were drinking Scotch and water, and the smoke from their cigarettes had enveloped them in a cloud.

"Do you want me to make love to you?" said Sharie Lee, putting her hand between Flora's legs, depressing the red wool skirt she was wearing till it became a valley of possibility. "In Paris, I learned the best tricks."

"I have to go home," said Flora.

Sharie Lee leaned back on the floor and asked Flora to fix her a rye and ginger ale, her afternoon drink.

Flora made two of them, and the cousins sat together listening to the sound of Sharie Lee's cat, Engels, crying in the closet where she had been locked because Flora was afraid of cats. Later, when Flora left because the company car was waiting for her on the corner of Greenwich and 10th Street, she had to steady herself on the banister of the three flights of stairs and she was red of nose and dripping for reasons she did not understand.

Quebec Bob arrived at the apartment at midnight. He had been to a party in Harlem and taken his wife. It was a big gathering after a show at the Apollo. "I'm a man of color," he said to Sharie Lee, "and that means that you think you're better than I am."

"I don't," said Sharie, "I don't."

"Prove it," said Quebec Bob, and Sharie took off all her clothes and stood before him with her pale pigment and dark eyes and sang for him a song of her father's, one he would sing to himself when he was locked away in his study, one she would hear in the kitchen and hold her hands over her stomach and rock on her heels just the way the men did, just the way her father was doing in another room. The song was the kaddish ϳf Rabbi Levi Yitzhak:

Gut morg'n dir ribbono shel olom
Ich Levi Yitzhok ben Soroh mi Berditchev

What do you want of your people, Israel
What have you demanded of your people, Israel
And I, Levi Yitzhak, son of Sarah of Berditchev
Say from my stand I will not waver
And from my place I shall not move
Until there be an end to all this

Yisgadal v'yiskadash shmei raboh

The notes rose and fell with ancient griefs, not one grief, all injustices, including the unfairness of nature that made some tall and some small, some prone to pneumonia and others to hunches of the back and squints of the eye and plagues from the distant continents and things that hid in mosquito blood and things that choked and stunted and bent the lungs into useless twigs. The sound that came from her ribs said that all was known, all was understood, all was in the hands of a force beyond understanding, beyond questioning, that grief was without end but as normal as the shoots of green grass in April and the dropping of the dried leaves in October. It was both a prayer and a protest, a call for relief and an acknowledgment that there was no relief.

Quebec Bob listened quietly and then folded Sharie Lee in his large arms. "I'm sorry," he said, "I don't know what got into me." Later he said, "Teach me that song."

Hedy and Flora at Home on Park Avenue: Fall 1941

Hedy stayed in her room, a large room that looked down Park Avenue high above the rows of uniformed doormen that stood guard over the nights and days of the street, while Ursula had a cup of coffee in the kitchen. Hedy sat on her floor on the rug the decorator had picked out for her room, a rug that prickled and left a rash if one sat too long, and waited for the maid to bring supper. If Ursula was through with her conversations in the kitchen, she would join her; if not, Hedy would eat alone at her small desk. She had a bell to ring when she was finished so that the maid would know to come back and pick up the tray.

And Flora, Flora was waiting for her handsome husband to come home from his office. He left the house each morning with his attaché case packed with orders for suits in his monogrammed shirt with his handkerchief folded in his top breast pocket.

Flora found him as handsome as a movie star. His hair was black and smooth and silky, and he was tall and athletic, and he swung his arms over his head, practicing his tennis swing. Even after twelve years of marriage, Flora knew that he was a prize, at least to look at. His nose was small, his eyes were dark and hooded, his chest was broad, his toes were perfectly groomed, and he had a massage at his club every day, so he smelled of oils and cremes. Flora was waiting for him to come home and talk to her. Meanwhile she played a game of solitaire, spreading the cards across the pink monogrammed bedspread, listening for the key in the lock, listening for the maid to come and take his hat and coat, waiting for the darkness to seal the strip of sky over Park Avenue and for her husband to come home.

Her husband, Frank, was at that very moment in the Biltmore Hotel having cocktails with a young woman who was wearing a hat with a veil, which gave her a very mysterious appearance and partially hid her round lips that were saying certain naughty things. Everyone has a story, and she would have told hers to Frank, but instead he was impressing her with his predictions of Allied victories on distant shores. She tried to pay attention. She knew she ought to take more interest in the fortunes of the army. Frank knew all the facts. She found that attractive. Her husband was away in Washington, serving the country, leaving her with the burdens of the home and the nanny and the cook and a sense that there would never be enough time for all the things she wished to do. Now everything was oiled and purring, wet where it should be wet and dry where it should be dry, shining where it should shine.

The clock at the Biltmore read seven when the two of them stepped up to the hotel registrar and signed in as "Mr. and Mrs. Frank Sheinfold." Flora had received a phone call about late work at the office and, after calling her sister, who as usual was out to dinner, had her own supper in the dining room. The maid, bringing her seconds and thirds of the delicious dessert, told her how pleased Cook would be that she had enjoyed it.

Later that night Frank came home. His wife was waiting up for him. She was wearing a pink silk nightgown decorated with lace swans that curled their long beaks delicately around her breasts. Frank was tired. He'd had enough of everything for one day: enough of keeping his eyes open, enough of watching how he was doing, enough of impressing and figuring. He had taken a shower in the hotel. There was no smell on him, no reminder of the woman, whom he'd already decided not to call again.

Flora sat up in bed and turned on her light. Her hair was messy. She smoothed it down. Her eyes blinked. She reached for her glasses. She lit up a Camel.

"Watch your ashes," said Frank. "You get them all over the sheets."

"I don't," said Flora.

"Go back to sleep," said Frank.

"Don't you want to talk?" said Flora.

Frank was silent. He was laying out his clothes for the morning.

"You must have something to tell me," Flora said, a whine rising in her throat. Don't whine, she reminded herself, and repeated the statement in a lower tone.

"No," said Frank.

"What if I have something to tell you?" said Flora.

"Oh, for Christ's sake," said Frank. "What is it?"

"Nothing in particular," said Flora, whose mind was suddenly blank.

"So shut up," said Frank.

"You can't talk to me like that," said Flora as if she were talking to a deaf man.

Two rooms away in her bed Hedy heard her mother. She sat up. Ursula was sleeping. The streetlights made patches on her floor. Hedy jumped from one to the other until she got to the door.

"Goddamn it," she heard. "You always start it!"

Hedy placed her head against the door. She wanted to go back to bed. She wanted to cover her ears, but she stayed, floating as if someone had turned the gravity off.

"Where were you?" she heard.

"Why are you asking me? she heard.

"Goddamn!" she heard, and then she heard a door slam and her mother said, "One day I'll just fly out the window and take my money with me."

Hedy's heart pounded. No, she thought, don't let her, stop her. Hedy had heard this before. She didn't believe anything would happen. Don't worry, she told herself. Nevertheless, something rose in her throat and came out her mouth and spilled down the front of her pajamas. She had stained herself. She smelled bad. She was ashamed. A big girl. Ursula would be angry. Hedy took off her pajamas. She had to go into the closet to get a clean pair. She was afraid of the closet in the dark. What was there back in the shadows? Quickly she reached into the drawer and, running out of the closet, she climbed back into bed, still listening to the sounds from down the hall.

"What do you know, what do you know about anything?" she heard. She lay in bed with the covers pulled up, her soiled pajamas thrown on the closet floor. Was there something she should do?

"Jesus," she said, "help my mother." She didn't believe in Jesus. She knew that Jesus was Ursula's God, not her own, but you never knew, you might as well try everything. Hedy had figured that out.

Estelle Loses Manny: 1941

Manny was one of those men for whom the nine-to-five job was always a sometime thing. He wasn't good at office politics. He was always passed over for a promotion. He sold watches at Macy's until they cut back. He had a job as a salesman for the Gruenbaum Company, but he never sold anything. He was shy and slight, and there was something in the quiver of his lip that made customers turn away. He worked for a while as a short-order cook, but he kept burning himself with grease.

Estelle paid the bills as best she could. She worked in an insurance firm as a bookkeeper, but then she got so heavy that she couldn't fit behind the desk anymore. She sold cosmetics door to door. She worked as a hairstylist in a store in Queens. She learned how to borrow from her brother and his wife. She got by, but always by the skin of her teeth. She had to admit she had chosen badly. Manny was a liability, not an asset. But he could dance. The two of them were a great combo on the floor. He was thin. She was large. People stared and tended to laugh at first, but when they got started how they could dance, sweat and beat, rhythm and bump. They were great.

When Manny died suddenly in a subway crash, Estelle was grief-stricken. Frank didn't come to the funeral, but Flora did. Estelle was family after all.

Reader: There are those who say that men like Manny are given the goods in the world to come, that God loves them most because they are bumblers, dreamers, and dopes, schmucks, *shlimazls,* and schlemiels all. Frank would call them jerks, and if God loves them best, perhaps He's a jerk, too.

Arthur Loses His Magic: 1941

Arthur was too old to be drafted. He had a wife and a young son. He had a business. He had moved into his brother's office years before, the office that had been his father's. He kept his golf clubs in the closet, and when he needed to think, when he needed to rest, when he needed to stretch, he would take them out and practice his swing. His secretary had removed plants, magazines, and pictures from one side of the room, and there he was able to create an imaginary fairway, one in which he always made the green, sometimes a birdie, sometimes a hole in one. He kept his old brown fedora in the closet, and when he was worried, when he was sad—sometimes he got sad for no reason at all—he would take his cards out of his desk and toss them one by one into his hat. He had a secretary who had a husband who was killed in boot camp by a mine that had been activated accidentally. Arthur wrote a poem for the memorial service. The last couplet read: "As we eat our daily bread, we will miss the men who are dead." At the company Christmas parties he would pull pennies from the ears of children, and he did a trick with yards of scarves that appeared out of a hat. Arthur made a list, and he gave every soldier's child a birthday present and set up a special fund for his workers who had served in the army. It would enable survivors to pay for memorial services, for orthodontists and dancing lessons, and for vacations for widows or a new living room rug. If a secretary was getting married to a soldier, Arthur provided the wedding cake and a handsome present for the young couple. If a salesman enlisted, Arthur gave his wife an insurance policy.

Frank thought he was a soft touch, probably a kind of secret commie, but in the office Arthur was admired, even loved. At home, however, he was less of a hero. Louisa had taken to daydreaming. She spent hours looking at the traffic below, counting the seconds between the green and red lights. She went to the beauty parlor and had her blond hair curled each week in a different style. Louisa bought dresses in three colors. She spent long hours in front of the mirror trying on her purchases. She woke in the night thinking that she had made a mistake and returned a dress and bought another. She rarely laughed at Arthur's tricks. He bought her presents. He got tickets to the best plays. He took her dancing. She was agreeable to anything he wanted. She moved slowly. She lifted her arms limply. She said very little. She bought a kitten and played with it for hours. It turned out her son was allergic to cats, and they had to give the animal away.

As the business pulled out of bankruptcy, Arthur gave his wife encouraging reports, but she just shrugged. The nanny took care of her child. The cook did the cooking. Louisa woke later and later in the morning. She had never been asked to wash her own clothes or prepare her own meals. She wasn't sure she could take care of herself.

Louisa saw the people in the street. She read the newspapers. She saw that some had no country and some had no beds to sleep in, and she was frightened. With one hand she was always placing back a lock of her hair that kept falling over her cheek. With the other hand she was brushing away wrinkles that she saw on her skirt or her blouse. Once she took her son, Teddy, to the Metropolitan Museum to see the knights in armor. He dashed from figure to figure, waving an imaginary sword about. She put out her carefully manicured hand and felt the steel breastplate. She envied the knights their impenetrable clothes. Were they safe in there? Really safe?

Her beautiful son, with his wide forehead like his father, with his feet always moving and his hands always ready to pull something down or push something away, puzzled her. When he was a baby she was afraid when the nanny put him in her arms, afraid that she might hurt him, and now that he had begun to grow she was worried that he would bump into her, crash something down on her. She wanted to read him a story, but he didn't like to sit still. She wanted to teach him the names of the animals, but Nanny had already done that. She wasn't sure what it was she was supposed to do with him. He kissed her dutifully, but he hurried off, occupied with his own business, building things in his room with the nanny, who was very patient. On the nanny's day off Louisa would let him stay in the kitchen with the cook, where he liked to be. Now that he was older he went with a boys club after school and played ball in the park. The club took him to the circus and to Ebbets Field. When he came home he went into his room and listened to the radio.

Louisa went to lunch with the wives of Arthur's friends. She played cards, but she was shy with the other women. They laughed loudly. They told stories that scared her of women who fell in love with delivery boys and women who went to hotels with other people's husbands.

Arthur and Louisa went to the club dance on Memorial Day. The chauffeur was driving them back to the city just after midnight when a raccoon appeared on the road and turned its masked face just in time to see the approaching car. The headlights caught its dark eyes in their last startle. Louisa had cried and cried. Arthur pulled a paper rose out of her ear, his favorite trick. Louisa kept on crying.

"What can I do to make you happy?" said Arthur. But Louisa didn't know.

Louisa ordered groceries from her bedside. She instructed the cook and she admonished the maid and she looked in on her son in the morning before school, but she walked through her house as if it were a mausoleum. She whispered to herself. She dusted, even though the maid had already dusted. She listened to records, Beethoven and Mozart, sounds that Arthur couldn't hear. He liked the samba and the rumba, and he liked it when she joined him in the kangaroo hop. He loved Bing Crosby, and when he shaved in the morning he would hold his brush and croon to it. Louisa sat on a chair listlessly, and when she went to the doctor to find out why she was so tired, he tested her for anemia, but her red cells and white cells were fine.

Louisa found a solution. She became a candy striper in a hospital. She pushed a tray of magazines and thumbed-through paper books through the halls. She brought to the patients' bedsides cards and pictures of movie stars that had been donated. She wore her red-and-white pinafore with a white carnation pinned to her blouse each Tuesday and Thursday afternoon, and she seemed much more cheerful.

But it wasn't the uniform and it wasn't the pushing of the cart to the patients' bedsides that strengthened the beat of Louisa's heart. It was the infectious diseases fellow on the ninth floor. He made his rounds just as Louisa was bringing her cart through. He had completed his residency and was taking an extra year to study under a doctor who was an expert in parasitic diseases of the tropics. He had a black unruly beard. He believed in socialized medicine, or so he told Louisa over coffee in the cafeteria. He believed that everyone in America had an equal right to good medical care. Louisa had never heard that before. He believed that Louisa had the saddest eyes he had ever seen and that it was his role in life to operate on those eyes and change their expression. Louisa had laughed at that. Louisa had agreed to meet him in the cafeteria. Louisa had blushed when he whispered to her in the hall that she was the best medicine his patients could have. Louisa told him the thing she had almost forgotten. She wanted to be a nurse. He said, "Why not? Go to nursing school." Louisa gasped.

His name was Rolland, and he wasn't Jewish. But what did that matter? She was married to a Jewish man already. Rolland came from West Virginia, from a small town, he said. His father had died in the mines and his mother had died of TB shortly after. His grandparents raised him and he had never wanted anything at all, except to be a doctor, to save someone. He was interested in worms, worms that entered through the bare feet of the poor, who walked to their latrines out behind rickety houses. He was interested in bowels and intestines that bloated and shrank, that ulcerated and bled. He told her amazing things about the body. It was a holy work, he said, filled with gas and decay, bile and mucus.

Louisa was fascinated. She took his hand after he told her about the colon and its malfunctions. She looked into his eyes, which were in fact too close together and had crust in the lashes from lack of sleep, and said she wished she knew how to comfort him. She wanted to comfort him as she had never wanted anything before.

Not long after that, she followed him into the supply closet on the fourth floor, the one that could be locked from the inside. He took off her candy-striped pinafore and unbuttoned the white blouse that lay underneath it and he unhooked the hooks of the brassiere and he pulled down her skirt and unhooked the garters that held her stockings up and he rolled down the girdle that kept her stomach pressed flat against her spine and he looked at her standing under the bare light bulb of the closet and he sighed. It was the sigh of a man who knew that flesh ages and that disease creeps in between the folds and that what was now pink would one day be gray and what he saw as firm would one day bulge and flop about and then stop moving altogether. He sighed because there was no way to keep Louisa in the closet forever. His sigh, he understood, was love.

Louisa, for her part, was terror stricken. What was she doing? What was she? What would her mother think of her naked in the closet with her candy-striped pinafore crumpled on the shelf next to the gauze bandages.

"Let's play doctor," said Rolland.

Louisa began to whimper. "I'm a married woman," she said. "I took a vow. I can't do this," she nearly screamed. "You're not Jewish," she added.

But Rolland, who was a real doctor and knew very well where to begin, touched each of her thighs with his lips and then took his tongue and placed it right in the center of her belly and he turned his tongue around and around and Louisa swung with him and stopped talking about being married and having a child and began to appreciate the beauty of the closet and the amazing possibilities it held. When he stood before her naked, she picked up the lid that covered his male organ.

"How peculiar," she said. "Like a hat that keeps the sun off the head. . . . My father was in shirts," she said. Rolland wasn't interested, which quite astonished Louisa.

The second time they went into the closet, he taught her how to play at being doctor. He put his stethoscope over her heart and he listened. He liked what he heard. He showed her where the fingers go and how the lips are opened, just so far, and where they move and how to keep them still, even if you want to move.

The third time she wore no panties under her uniform so that less time would be wasted. Every time she thought about Arthur, she decided to jump from her bedroom on the tenth floor and land, a heap of broken bones, on the street below. She would consider walking in front of a truck rushing down the avenue or sitting on the tracks of the Third Avenue el till the train came by and punished her for all the pleasure she was having in the closet on the fourth floor.

But after a while she stopped thinking about Arthur. She started to think about her hands. What could a woman do with her own hands? She could make a bed. She could boil water. She could change a bandage. She could plant things in a garden. Hands, Louisa realized, were more than appendages on which to hang rings or paint nails; they were tools, tools for many purposes. What, thought Louisa, should she be doing with her hands? She watched the nurses at work. She talked to the patients. She smiled at them. They smiled back at her. It wasn't just Arthur who could make people smile.

Rolland needed her. He said so. He was there on Tuesday and Thursday afternoon waiting for her to push her cart down the hall. He had only to look at her and she felt a beating, throbbing, almost pain in her place that Rolland said was beautiful, even beautiful if she were bleeding, even beautiful directly under the bare bulb, the place where Rolland had taken a mirror and made her look and she was ashamed till he said that she was beautiful and he kissed the mirror until she begged him to put down the mirror and kiss her instead. She was not a bad girl. She was not a whore, though she called herself names in the night. She was not a girl who planned the unexpected; in fact, she had always dreaded the unexpected, but it had happened and she knew that Arthur would take care of his son, and that her son would one day understand that his mother had no choice, because a real doctor had asked her to run away with him, to go off to his little town in the South where he was going to open an office and she could be his nurse. What else could she do—she who was attached to him by flushings and blushings and fillings and emptyings? Besides, it was time for her to learn how to cook. Cooking was one of the things you could do with your hands.

At the end of June, before she was supposed to move to the house they had rented for the summer at Atlantic Beach on Avenue Q near her sisters-in-law, near the Inwood Club with its cabanas around the pool and the lifeguard who would watch the nannies watching the children build sand castles by the sea, she packed her summer clothes, she left her mink in the closet, she was going south after all, to a life where no one wore mink. She left her pearls and her diamond clip that her mother had given her when she was engaged. She was going to a place where no one had diamonds. She left a note for Arthur on the dining room table. It was a short note. What was there to say? The facts, the empty closet, would speak for themselves. For Teddy she left a large stuffed bear. "Be good," she wrote on the card around its neck. "Don't give Nanny any trouble. Make lots of money," she added. "Think of me in West Virginia. Don't forget me. I had no choice."

She cried. "He's a part of me," she said to Rolland. "I am leaving a part of myself behind. I am a bad mother," she said. "What kind of a mother leaves her child behind?"

"Were you his mother," said Rolland, "or was the nanny? Mothers where I come from bathe their children, feed their children, clean their vomit, and wash their waste away. If you didn't do that, you weren't his mother. If you do that for the children we will have, you will be their mother."

Louisa felt better. Teddy was not hers. She would have others. Rolland told her that it was true that Jewish women were moister and sweeter than Christians.

"Why is that?" asked Louisa.

"I don't know," said Rolland.

Moister and sweeter; the words made Louisa happy, though she could never repeat them to another living creature.

Flora Goes to a Party: Fall 1942

"Rum and Coca-Cola," "Rum and Coca-Cola," that had been the song that had played on the rented jukebox at the Rothmans' party over and over. Flora had danced with Simon and Jerry and had laughed at their jokes. They both told her the same joke, something about Little Black Sambo and a lion. She could never remember jokes. At dinner she talked about the pinkos who were trying to get into the City Athletic Club with Michael, who was an art dealer and so the most sensitive man in the room.

Flora worried about her bra strap; was it showing, an ugly black line that everyone would know was a bra strap? She wanted to go to a bathroom to check, to see if she had lipstick on her teeth—sometimes when she talked she smudged her teeth with lipstick, Frank had told her that, she ran her tongue over her teeth as a habit now, Frank told her she looked like a chipmunk when she did that. But she had to wait to go to the bathroom because Helen's husband, Harold, was not finished talking. He had been explaining to her the new method for producing synthetic fabrics out of chemicals. He was making parachutes and windbreakers and something else top secret. It had to do with camouflage. He was proud of the new process, which was going to bring his business onto the Big Board, no kidding, going public. A government contract, the war effort, his factory helping to bring the boys home. She had told him it was wonderful, just wonderful what they could do with science. She asked him about last quarter's earnings. He told her. She sat beside him on the divan and blew smoke up at the ceiling and kicked off her high-heeled shoes and watched as the light caught in her stockings as, pulled by her garter belt, attached to her girdle that took two pounds off of her middle, they pressed tight against her rounded calf.

As Harold, encouraged, talked on about linings for raincoats and fireproof curtains for movie theaters, Flora considered her hostess's new dining table, and the red-and-white-striped silk covering the foyer chairs. Everything looked right. Flora puffed smoke in rings at Harold as he talked. She left deep red lipstick stains on the end of each Camel cigarette as she stamped it out in the ashtray. She looked at Harold, sweat on his upper lip. She leaned over and kissed him on the forehead.

"Be careful," she said, "don't expand too fast. It could be dangerous. Take care of yourself." She wanted to hold him in her arms, protect him from some invisible danger that she saw right behind him, some harm that could come. She wanted to make him smile, so she kissed him again on the tip of his nose.

"God, Flora," said Harold, "you're a great girl. Does that husband of yours appreciate what a jewel he's got?"

Flora took off her eyeglasses and wiped them with the hem of her black silk dress. She had to wear the glasses. This pair had black rims with rhinestones at the tips for parties. Without the glasses she could hardly see a foot in front of her. She held them on her lap, hoping that Harold would see her face as it was meant to be, as everyone would see it if she wasn't nearly blind. Harold's face became a blur. She reached for her Scotch and soda and her hand misjudged it and she knocked it over onto the obviously new, perfectly clean royal blue carpet. Some of it splashed onto Harold's pants and he rushed off to take out the stain. Flora replaced her glasses as the maid came with a wet cloth to clean the carpet, and Helen, black cigarette holder clenched between her teeth, glided over to assure her that no harm was done.

Frank was over in the corner talking to Elise, who had come with that bachelor from Cleveland whom all the girls were talking about. Elise was blond and had a southern accent. Frank had not left her side all evening. Out of the corner of his eye he had seen Flora spill the drink. "Oh, Christ," he said to Elise. "She should wear her damned glasses."

Flora had another drink and ate some of the shrimp and tomato aspic that sat out on the buffet. "My mother would die if she saw me eating shrimp," she whispered to Helen.

"Your mother died three years ago," Helen answered, filling her own plate high with the forbidden food.

Flora's head suddenly ached. She put down the shrimp. She thought of Hedy; if she were to die, what would become of Hedy? She felt unsteady and leaned against the wall.

In the hall the Victrola sat, like a Buddha's navel, the center of it all, on top of a Danish modern table. A maid in a starched uniform, her blue eyes blinking with responsibility, changed the record. Glenn Miller's "Chattanooga Choo-Choo" gave Flora the urge to wiggle and bump. She looked for someone else to dance with. Over in the corner a group had formed. Frank was holding on to Elise's elbow. "They're killing the Jews, all of them. There won't be one left when the war ends."

"Come on, Frank, that's only a rumor. Things are bad, but you can't kill that many people. It just isn't possible."

Frank pulled his lips together in a tight line and narrowed his eyes. "What the hell do you know?" he said. "You sit there in your office selling insurance and you think you know how many people the krauts can kill? I'm telling you I know it's true. They have killed all the Jews."

Flora stood at the edge of the group. She wished Frank could say what he wanted to say more diplomatically. What kind of a businessman insulted people all the time? She wished he would turn around and catch her eye. She would smile at him, showing she believed he was right. She heard his words. Dead, all the Jews of Europe. Children are not allowed to be killed. It couldn't be. Frank must be wrong. She thought of Hedy shot in the street, her new blue tweed coat with the velvet collar stained with mud and her mittens that Ursula had knitted for her soaked in blood. Flora's legs felt weak and she held so tight to the couch in front of her that her hands turned white. If the war were not won, if the Nazis came to Park Avenue, they would kill them all.

"Frank," said Flora, "let's dance."

"Not now, toots," said Frank.

Flora floated off and found Martin, her brother's insurance agent, sitting in a corner nursing his drink. His eyes were down on the floor and his hands were tapping the rhythm of the music against his glass. "Come on, Martin," she said. "I bet you haven't danced all night."

He blushed. He rose to his feet. It turned out that shy Martin was the best dancer of all. He and Flora began a conga line that snaked through the apartment till the dancers collapsed with beating hearts.

By the time they were in the taxi on the way home, Frank had managed to get Elise into the coat closet, where he was able to explain to her just how much he thought of her perfume. Flora had sat on Martin's lap and discussed the stock market; bull, it was just then, and Flora knew why. For some reason—luck, dumb luck, Frank called it—Flora could pick them. She read the business section, she considered the odds. She called her broker once or twice a day for news, she had a mind for it, even in the Depression, when she was a new bride and her family business rocked and sank and rose again on the waves of bankruptcy papers, even when everyone was wiped out, Flora had a way of buying when she should and selling just in time. She laughed at herself; lucky at cards, unlucky in love. Frank said she probably got her tips from her astrologer. He got his tips from the fellows at the club, at the squash court, playing tennis, relaxing on the massage table after a good sweat. His tips were always wrong, rumors, wishes, illusions. When Frank got the paper in the morning and turned to the stock market page, his head got tight, he would put down the paper, stare at his daily breakfast of prunes and toast, and curse his luck.

In the taxi Flora leaned against his shoulder. She felt dizzy. The booze had gone down to her toes, which felt numb, probably from the ordeal of squeezing together in her pointed shoes. The taxi pulled up in front of their building. It looked like a castle, an old gray Gothic castle with stone gargoyles and pointed arches like the cathedrals of France. It was one of the few buildings on Park Avenue that Jews were allowed to rent in, and therefore all the residents were Jewish. The lights out front blinked, the doorman stood at attention till it was time for him to open the taxi door.

Flora smiled. She wobbled in her high heels, and Frank squeezed her arm. "For God's sake, Flora, you can walk straight."

The doorman opened the iron gates with his key. At night the gates were kept closed, although in the day they were pushed back and cables kept them from swinging. The children would climb on the iron lattice-work while they waited for the school bus in the morning. In the circular courtyard, where the kitchen windows faced, a stone fountain bubbled and spilled and the sound echoed off the stone walls just as in the monasteries of France. The elevator men for each section stood behind their own iron gates, breathing mist against the glass panes.

Niel, the midnight-to-six A.M. man for the CD line of apartments, opened the door to the section of the building where the Sheinfolds lived. They stepped inside the mirrored lobby, its large commode with lion's heads for handles topped by a nymph holding a lily under a Tiffany lamp and a long dark green carpet letting all who entered know that this building was the home of nobility.

"Good night, sir," he said, and tipped his hat. Frank reached into his pocket and pulled out a quarter. He handed it to him, a bribe not to look at his wife, who was leaning against the commode as if she might throw up into the base of the lamp.

Once in the bedroom Frank hung his clothes carefully on the wooden valet. He took out his suit for the morning and laid out in straight lines his suspenders, his underwear, and his socks on its lower level. Flora lay on the bed, hardly having the energy to undress. God, he was handsome. His back was straight. His black hair slicked back with Vaseline shone in the light. His legs were strong from tennis, swimming, and walking. Every day he walked at least three miles. His underwear was so white, it gleamed. He turned around and looked at his wife. "Get undressed," he said.

She was short. She was somehow crumpled, and what he most admired in a woman—briskness, clean lines, long limbs, blond hair—these she did not have. She had curves everywhere and she drank chocolate milk shakes and she was soft to touch and there were powder stains on her nightgown, and she had a strange smell, a mixture of beauty products and body odor that made him faintly ill. She was his wife for better or worse, and he got into bed and reached for her.

She had managed to change into her pink silk nightgown. She had forgotten to brush her teeth or take her makeup off. His hands went right for her legs, which he spread apart. She said, "Do you think I looked pretty in the black dress I wore, or do you think I should have worn the green linen that I wore last week to the Mazurs?" As he opened her legs and lifted himself on top of her, she said, "My mother liked yellow roses. On the piano there was always a vase with yellow roses."

Frank didn't say anything. She looked into his eyes. They were not looking at her. They were following another image. She ran her hands over his back and called him "sweetheart." He said nothing. She waited till he was through, till he rolled into his own bed. They had pushed two single beds together to give the illusion of a marital bed and yet preserve the capacity to sleep alone that he had wanted, insisted on even from the beginning.

She got up and washed herself. No more babies. She was now wide awake and worrying if her sisters and brother were all right, if her child were not at this very moment developing a fever that would turn out to be typhus, or if something were happening on the war front and the Germans had crashed through Allied lines and were coming for her and hers. In the dark she smoked cigarette after cigarette, finding the ashtray on her bed table by the ember's light. She broke a carefully polished long red nail. She wanted to read the detective story by her bed, one with an ax murderer who stalked women who worked in airplane factories whose husbands were away at war, but she was afraid to put on the light and disturb Frank; he would wake with a roar and blame her for ruining his day.

She didn't fall asleep until the sky drained white behind Park Avenue and the windows turned a pinkish gold, washing them with the tenderness of a new beginning. It was then that she allowed herself to drift into sleep, and as usual she didn't hear the alarm or the careful closing of the door as Frank left in the morning. It was late, almost eleven, when with swollen eyes she woke and rang for Mary to bring her breakfast and the paper.

Hedy came in with the breakfast tray, rushing behind Mary before the maid could chase her out. "Don't bother your mother," said Mary, but Flora held up her arms and pulled her daughter onto the bed.

"Darling," she said, "you're so beautiful today. You look like an angel in that sweet pinafore. No fever, you're well, of course you're well, why should you be sick? I love your hands," she said, kissing them both. "You have hands like my mother. Let me read your palm. You have a long life line. It goes on forever. What have you done all morning? Tell me about it. I've been sleeping so long."

Reader: Frank and Flora are not the ideal couple, but after all happiness is elusive, marriage is compromise, youth is fleeting, and Park Avenue is no place for romantics. If Frank can learn to be more attentive to Flora's need to be admired, if Flora can see how frightened Frank feels, how much reassurance he needs, then perhaps everything will work out eventually. Marriage needs patience. Patience can be learned. Flora reads an article in the *Reader's Digest* on keeping your husband happy. Perhaps it will help.

Arthur Becomes Both Father and Mother to His Abandoned Child: 1941

When Louisa left him he tried to cover the scandal. The family helped. Mildred told everyone she knew that Louisa had back trouble and had gone to a sanitarium in Virginia for a cure. Flora got on the phone and said to her friends that the back trouble was serious. It might even be fatal, she whispered. The women clucked and muttered sympathetic things. They repeated stories of other early deaths. The cousin who got polio and died when the power failed on the iron lung, the sister-in-law who was operated on for appendicitis and never came out of the anesthesia. The telephone wires up and down Park Avenue carried news of legs that were amputated and breasts that had lesions, and doctors' names were given, experts in matters of back problems, a consultation was offered by the head of Mt. Sinai's orthopedic department. What is the name of the sanitarium? some friend asked. White Mountain, said Flora. Lilac Valley, said Mildred. But then the nanny told her friends, who told their mistresses, and one day Arthur was having a drink by himself at the club when a man whose business was nightgowns came over and said, "Broads, never trust em," and patted Arthur on the back.

Arthur had dark circles under his eyes. He hardly changed his clothes. It wasn't that he missed Louisa. In fact, there was something uplifting about coming home, playing a game of slapjack with his son, and having his dinner served to him without Louisa, sitting there like a toad on a rock, no longer distinguishable from her chair, waiting, making him uneasy, as if he should do something, but what? It was the humiliation, he explained to Flora. It was everyone knowing, as soon enough they knew, because a doctor at Mt. Sinai who was a member of the club knew exactly with whom and where Arthur Gruenbaum's wife had disappeared.

Hedy wished upon a star that her uncle Arthur would find a wife. Hedy wished on the same star that her aunt Louisa would catch a chill and die of pneumonia. Then Flora introduced him to the divorcée she had met at the astrologist's, and to a single woman who was heir to a lace handkerchief fortune, and he took them dancing at the Waldorf and put his hands on their backs and he bought them dinner, but he performed no magic tricks at all. Mildred invited him to parties at which lovely women with low-cut gowns were seated near him, but he hardly lifted his eyes from his plate. Flora introduced him to the young widow of an old and very wealthy banker. The young woman blinked her eyes and offered to go to art galleries with Arthur the following day, but he turned her down; he didn't like modern art.

"Is it enough to live with Teddy?" said Flora.

"You have to get married again," said Mildred. "Otherwise people will talk."

Arthur agreed. He looked more actively for a wife. But he told Flora, "I don't need love."

Teddy said he didn't miss his mother, but he did begin kicking his nanny at unexpected moments. He fought with other children at school and he hid food under his pillow, food he had slipped into a napkin at dinner. Even a child whose mother is only a shadow knows that something is wrong, badly wrong, when the shadow disappears. A boy without a shadow might be invisible in the sunlight.

Don't You Know There's a War On: Christmas Eve 1942

"Merry Christmas," Frank said to the doorman at his club. His lips made a smile. He had a few hours before dinner. He wanted some peace. He had bought Flora a present, or rather he had had his secretary buy her a gold watch at Saks Fifth Avenue. She would like it, he supposed. His secretary had said it was a good gift.

He felt in his pocket for the thin package wrapped in silver paper. She would give him something, too, something he didn't want, something he would have to return the next week. He sighed. He was in a hurry for the steam room, for the pleasure of lying naked on the table and letting his mind float and his limbs relax. His body was always coiled up, ready to strike, ready to run, ready for any emergency. He rubbed the muscles in his legs, already tensed for the game of squash he had arranged earlier.

His blue coat was taken by an attendant and he stood in the wood-paneled lobby warming his hands by a great fire. Over the fireplace was a Christmas wreath. Why not? the board of directors had said. This is a club in America, not in the Ukraine. The members were all Jewish. Twenty blocks away on the park, the large building with the blue-and-white flag that marked the New York Athletic Club sat, but that club would not have Jews through the doors, not Jews who owned Wall

Street firms, not Jews with businesses on the Big Board, not Jews who had graduated cum laude from Harvard; that club had a membership which, like cemeteries all over America, was particular. The City Athletic Club was the Jewish shadow of the New York Athletic Club, so it seemed reasonable to all its members that it have its shadow Christmas wreath.

Frank waited impatiently for the elevator that would take him up to the steam room, to the pool, to the masseur, to the paddle courts, to the locker rooms. It was a relief to be there. He was tired, bone tired, cooped up in his office, answering the phone, placating, promising, following instructions, never stretching his mind, showing what he could do if the final decisions were his. He was tired and sad, a sadness that seemed like a burn in his chest, an ache across his shoulder blades, a pull in the groin. When had he been without this exhaustion? He couldn't remember. Frank couldn't give a name to the fatigue that caught his joints. He couldn't find a cause or a culprit. He stood waiting for the elevator as if he were the last man on earth; as if only his own arms would wrap around his body and whoever he was looking for (was he looking for someone?) was in hiding far away.

"Merry Christmas," he said to the elevator man as he took an envelope marked "City Athletic Club elevator Man" and pressed it into the open palm.

Flora had a Scotch while she dressed for dinner. She and Frank were having dinner Christmas Eve with Mildred and her husband. Her brother Arthur was going to be there, too.

Flora tried on three dresses. One, a blue silk, showed the pounds she had gained around her waist and made her look as if she were wearing a rubber tire around her middle. The next was a yellow with beads around the neck. The color made her skin look like a lizard sunning on a rock. She stuck a tongue out at herself. The third was orange, and Mildred had been with her when she bought it. Flora thought it would do, but she noticed that her upper arms looked heavy. She wished Mildred were there and could tell her which dress to wear. She sat on the chair in her bedroom, dressed in her earrings and her necklace that her mother had left her, diamonds and emeralds in an Aztec design, old-fashioned now, but the best that she had. She waited for Frank. He was late. It was Christmas Eve. It was hard to get a taxi, and there was a war on. Flora sat on her chair knocking the ice cubes in her glass one against the other.

She had been to see the tarot card reader in the afternoon. The tarot cards had promised all sorts of good things for the new year. The woman had been recommended by Celia, who, after having her cards read, had converted to Christian Science, a thing that Flora would never do, believing as she did that medicine was a holy art. The tarot card reader lived in an apartment on the fourth floor of a brownstone house in the East Nineties. Flora had expected fringed lampshades and tables covered in flowered cloths and a fat old woman with a wig and Gypsy jewelry on her bodice. But instead the room had been almost bare. The tarot card reader was wearing slacks and she was young, younger than Flora, and her eyes were blue and she spoke with an accent. "In Czechoslovakia," she told her, "I was a teacher of Latin and Greek in a girls' gymnasium, but the Nazis did not want me in the gymnasium so I had to leave. Lucky that my summers had been spent in the countryside, and there I learned from the Gypsies that passed in their caravans the reading of the cards."

The tarot card reader, who said that the stars were the cards of the sky, had told Celia that her business worries would come to an end, and they had. Flora wanted good news, too, but not about business. In the war, her family business was doing just fine. She wanted good news of the heart. "Does he love me? Will he always love me?"

"I see," said the tarot card reader, "a great passion in your future. The cards tell me that you will be cherished and favored and adored."

"By my husband?" Flora had asked, afraid to say his name aloud.

The tarot reader had gathered up her cards. "The cards," she said, "don't tell you everything, but come back next week, after New Year's. Perhaps they will be clearer then, the excitement of the holiday, you know, makes the hands of the reader flutter, and things can be muddled that later will be clear. Your horoscope says, Be careful, avoid major decisions, expect surprises."

Flora looked into the woman's eyes, clear and blue. "Did you really teach Latin and Greek?" she asked.

"Why?" said the woman. "You think a reader of stars must always have been a reader of stars? You Americans," she said, "think that life is forever and forever the same. History has spoiled you so far, but who knows what lies in store."

"Are the Nazis going to win the war?" asked Flora, alarmed.

"Who knows," said the tarot card reader. "If they do, I will go read cards in China. I have my passport ready, do you?"

"Yes," said Flora. She stood up and took out her money and placed it on the bare tabletop. "I will come again after the new year. Will you remember me, Flora Gruenbaum Sheinfold?" she said.

"I will remember you," said the tarot reader. "You are the one who wants her husband to fall in love with her."

This remark brought an unexpected pain to Flora, a pain in the stomach that twitched and went into spasm and released itself all in a second's time. Flora walked down the stairs slowly, holding on to the banister with her left hand, her high-heeled shoes making the journey downward perilous.

Cherished and adored, she repeated to herself as she waited for Frank to come home from the club on Christmas Eve 1942.

Hedy and Flora Take a Trip to Grossinger's: 1942

Young men were moving, leaving home, leaving wives and mothers and jobs and schools, and they were gathering at camp bases across the forty-eight states. Frank had wanted to join. He was a fighting man. He wanted to kill the Germans with his bare hands. He wanted to protect democracy and save the Jews. He didn't want to sit out the war with a desk job, but that is what happened, because he was not such a young man as all that, one of the few who might consider themselves lucky, too young for the First World War and over the limit for the Second.

As Frank waited for the light to change on 38th and Broadway, his pigskin attaché case leaning against his blue vicuña coat, he thought about shooting, about lifting a gun to his shoulders and sighting the enemy over the hill, behind a shrub and up there on the rooftop of a barn, and he thought about blasting his target into fragments, of spilling out blood while severed limbs, bone splinters, floated over the countryside. His head was pounding, a familiar pain, the start of one of his migraines that within hours would bring a pain that would not stop, as if his head had been filled with maggots, crawling, consuming maggots, and each eating away at a vital synapse, a crucial neuron, as if he were a watermelon swollen almost to the breaking point by the rot within.

Frank wanted to be somewhere else. Over there, where the action was. Frank wanted to be on a boat in the middle of the Atlantic watching for submarines through binoculars, covering the gray, unchanging horizon with his careful eye, sleeping in his clothes in case of a night alert, commanding men, "Steady fire," and he wanted to look out at the night sea and know that the enemy was underneath waiting for the ship to come closer and that the torpedoes were out there swimming like the sharks after the object of their lust and he wanted to train the guns on the planes that would come over, hunting for the ships that were themselves hunting for the subs and the entire universe out there on the ocean would be engaged in a hunt, including the seagulls who swooped for the silver fish. The clanging of the buoys and the banging of the iron anchor would be like the bells that announce the deaths that have come; that's what Frank wanted instead of going to his desk and shuffling his papers and counting the number of sailor suits that could be packed in a carton and shipped to England in the next week. The Gruenbaum Company had won a contract to supply the army with uniforms, right off the assembly line, made in the factories that only a year before had made pants for young men to play tennis, to drive to the country club for dinner, suits to go to the office, corduroys for walks in the woods, suits for the occasions of peacetime, and now each crease, each buttonhole, each sleeve with its proper braid, these were helping win the war, part of the war effort.

It made Frank feel old to be behind his desk. His head pounded and increased its pounding as he knew it would, and before lunch he went home to his bedroom and pulled down the shades and lay in the dark.

When Flora came home and saw Frank, lying on his bed in his purple silk robe with the black lapels, she knew he had another migraine. "Can I do anything for you, darling?" she said. He didn't answer. He closed his eyes. "Well," she said, "I won forty dollars at backgammon this afternoon. Esther kept doubling when she thought she had me and I pulled her in because I knew I could get her in the last three rolls and she never thinks ahead, she's always surprised when I win. We had lunch at the Stork Club, and the martinis made her play worse than usual. It—"

Frank let out a howl, a sound not quite human. "Be quiet!" he screamed.

"I'm only trying to distract you," she said.

"Leave me alone," Frank said.

Tears came to Flora's eyes. The mascara began to run. She took off her glasses and wiped the rims that were now mascara-stained with her fingers. The freckles on her face darkened. She sat at the edge of the bed and cocked her head to one side. Her brown eyes deepened with concern. Her round face was soft, and if she had looked in the mirror, she would have seen a woman whose beauty was still shining, calling out for attention; like a small flower in a forgotten field, she bloomed without knowing she bloomed. She took off her gold earrings and put them in her jewelry box. Suddenly they had pinched, leaving red marks on her earlobes. She rubbed her lobes with her fingers, careful not to insert one of her long red nails into her ear. She took off her shoes with the straps over the ankle, the heels adding another three inches to her height.

Frank opened his eyes. "God, you are short," he said.

"You married me short," whispered Flora. "I was just as short then as I am now. You said it didn't matter to you. You said it was all right."

"I know," Frank said. The pain was now riding down his cheek and causing him to clench his mouth shut and to grind his molars. The pain settled in his jaw and burned as if his bones had turned to embers.

Flora lit up a Camel. The last of the tears were slipping into the corners of her mouth. "Should I call up the Tumarkins and tell them we can't come to dinner tonight?" she asked softly. Frank didn't answer. "For God's sake, Frank, he's working with the Supply Corps. You need his goodwill for the contract. You want to lose the contract?"

Flora took off her girdle and put her stockings on the back of the chair. Her body breathed in relief and her stomach extended out, and when Frank looked at her he felt a sorrow for himself that made the pain reach up from his jaw and move into a space behind his eyes. There it banged against his forehead, pulsed against his pupils. He reached over to the marbled-topped end table on which the Chinese lamp rested with its green-fringed shade and the cigar box that Flora had given him for his birthday and a china shepherdess with a porcelain bouquet of flowers stood, a figurine promising pastoral pleasures and suggesting the indulgences of the French court. He picked up the shepherdess and threw it, not at his wife, but at the mirror behind her above the dresser with its gold-leaf vines that circled the gold handles. In the mirror he could see the back of her head, the place where her hairdresser had pulled to make a part, the back of her neck, thicker than it was when he married her, draped in the pearls her brother had given her for her last birthday. He threw the shepherdess as hard as he could, as if it were a bomb left at his bedside by a Nazi infiltrator. The mirror shattered.

Flora let the tears flow over her face and her lipstick smeared as she attempted to wipe them off. Pieces of the shattered mirror fell over the dresser, onto the pink rug. Her lipstick, dark red, moved down her chin. "Oh, God," she cried. She was afraid to move because her bare feet could be cut by the slivers of glass that had become embedded in the tufts of the rug. Her slippers with the silk pom-poms were in the closet where the maid had put them in the morning.

Frank got out of bed. He put on his own slippers and he walked over to his wife. He picked her up under her arms and carried her to the doorsill. He threw her into the hall, and her head banged against the wall. She was crying. She was pale and her hands were shaking. In his head he could feel the squeezing of the veins and the thumping of the blood. He could have a stroke. One day he might have a stroke.

He slammed the door and returned to his bed. He closed his eyes.

What was it she wanted? Why was he always wrong? What did she expect from him? Where was it a man could do what he wanted, what he should do, without always being wrong, doing something wrong?

Flora called her sister. She told Mildred everything, and Mildred sighed. At least in the opera, Mildred thought—*Carmen,* for example— things were tragic but beautiful.

Later Frank came out into the living room. Flora was sitting with her Scotch and soda in one hand and with the other she was smoking, and her bare feet with their painted toes were wiggling in time to the Dixieland that was coming over the radio. She sat carefully on the corner of the couch. The velvet stripes on the fabric could not take rubbing or bruising or soiling. The decorator had told her to sit on the chair, not on the couch, but on the chair she felt small; its high back, the best of French provincial, seemed to mock her, as if it were a throne and she were a chambermaid pretending to be queen. She sat on the couch, but carefully.

Frank sat next to her. His migraine had not abated, that she could tell by the squint in his eyes, by the way his hands were clenched into fists and the stiff way he moved his body. "I'm sorry," he said, "I didn't mean to throw the thing. I lost my temper."

Flora turned her head away. He always said he was sorry. "I'm sorry, too," said Flora, and she touched his hand gently. He pulled his hand away and put it in the pocket of his robe. "I wish I could help when you have a headache," said Flora.

"It's all right," said Frank. "Nothing helps. I didn't mean to make you cry."

"I know," said Flora. "Maybe I will go away for a few days somewhere for fun."

"Alone," said Frank, "without me?"

"Yes," said Flora. "I could do it. I could go by myself for a few days."

Frank stretched out his legs in front of him. "Not a bad idea," he said, hoping his headache would be over before she left. "Wait a day or two," he added, "in case I need you, and then go."

"All right," said Flora. If he needed her, really needed her, she would do anything for him, anything at all, go to the North Pole and dig for herbs that grew under the ice, go to Nazi headquarters and demand their latest medicine to cure migranes. Sometimes, lying in the tub, soaping over her breasts that sometimes he touched and sometimes he didn't, she thought of things that would make him grateful to her, something that would make him look at her as if she were the heroine of his life story. She didn't mean to make him angry. It was a smallness, a meanness, a thing in her she must stop. Sitting there next to him, she felt as if she had already gone away and was sitting in a strange living room belonging to another woman, in a country where no one knew who she was and no one asked what it was she wanted or why she was there.

She shook her head. She was in her own living room. She stood up and refilled her glass. She gulped the amber liquid and carefully placed the glass on a coaster so the finish of the table would not be stained. "I'll take Hedy," she said. "I don't want to be all alone, after all."

"Good," said Frank, whose migraine was passing into his stomach and sending waves of nausea up into his throat. "Stay here," he said. "I'm going to bed."

"Shouldn't I go with you?" she asked.

"No," he said, "please, darling, don't." And he hurried out of the room.

Three days later in the early morning a long limousine pulled up into the courtyard of the building on Park Avenue and the iron gates were opened by the doorman and Flora and Hedy were helped by a driver with a blue uniform and a coat with a fur collar into the black car with its silver running board and its glass partition and wood-paneled bar that separated passenger from driver.

The driver covered their laps with a fur rug and loaded the bags in the distant trunk. They were going to the mountains for a vacation, to Grossinger's in the Catskills. Hedy was going away with her mother for the first time, alone with her mother for one of the few times in her life.

The drive was long. The winter cold frosted the windows. Flora smoked cigarette after cigarette and the ashtray overflowed and the smell of stale tobacco clung to their clothes. Hedy rubbed a spot in the window through which she could see farms and horses and black-and-white cows standing on fields of brown stubble and white patches of old snow. The car drove carefully, responsibly, up the country roads, taking the turns slowly and holding its heavy wheels steady beside the gutters that were filled with stones and branches and the still crumbling leaves of a long-gone fall.

After a while they came to the pine trees, tall firs that reached up from the road bed to the sky. Hedy leaned against her mother in the car. Flora took a piece of paper out of her purse and a pencil. "Here," she said, "let's play dots." And she built a rectangle of tiny dots, and each took a turn drawing a line. Each was trying to complete a box, and when the box was closed it would be filled with an initial, H for Hedy, F for Flora. Hedy played the game as well as she could, but Flora, Flora always had a way of tricking Hedy, of giving her a box and then taking four.

"Again," said Hedy. "Let's play again."

Flora played Hangman with Hedy. A noose was drawn, a word was invented but not shared, and Hedy had to guess the letters. With each wrong guess Flora drew another body part under the noose until Hedy guessed the word or she hung from the imaginary gallows.

"Again," said Hedy. "Let's play again."

Flora took a pack of cards out of her purse. She pulled the rug tight across their laps and dealt the cards. She taught Hedy how to play blackjack. She played gin rummy with her. At last Hedy put her head down in her mother's lap and while ashes fell in her hair and the smell of Chanel No. 5 and bath oil floated over her, she fell asleep. Flora touched her daughter's hair, now messy and tangled in her lap.

As the car pulled itself up the mountain Flora played a game with herself. How many little words could you make out of the word *Grossinger*? She got groin and ginger and ring and nose and rinse and singer. She looked out the window. Why was she going to Grossinger's?

The huge hotel with its Victorian gingerbread porches, with its green roof and its long halls with oak and maple tables and lamps with green shades and its window seats and its fringed curtains, was full to capacity and then some. The halls were thronging with servicemen on leave. They had two days between, before being shipped off, London, and then the invasion? Well, who knew when the invasion would be, but these were the boys who were going. They had on soldiers' uniforms and sailors' uniforms and some were sergeants and some were captains and some were far from home, and some had never seen a Jew before but were given a free room by the USO, who wanted them to have a good time and get out of the city into the fresh air, and some just stayed in the bar, which was full at all hours with soldiers just staring into their drinks, missing someone, dreading something, thinking or not thinking, and turning up the music from the jukebox, louder and louder.

Hedy held her mother's hand at the check-in desk. The clerk looked up the name. "Mrs. Gruenbaum," he said, "I'm sorry, we seem to have lost your reservation. We have so many soldiers, you see, wartime." He shrugged and nodded and begged her forgiveness.

Hedy and her mother were placed in a cottage just a little way off from the main house. Hedy sat on the twin bed and asked her mother, "Now can we go ice skating?"

"Later," said her mother, who was tired. Flora lay down on her bed and wondered if Frank was missing her. It was late afternoon, dinner would be soon. Flora reached into her suitcase for her silver flask and, taking a glass from the bathroom, fixed herself a Scotch.

In the dining room they were seated by the great stone fireplace above which hung a moosehead whose eyes promised Hedy it would tell her what it was like to be dead, mounted on a plaque and without the rest of your body. In the hearth logs were burning, embers crackling, and the smell of hickory and pine rose out across the room. Waiters carrying loaded silver trays dashed about, and from one end of the hall three violinists played. Hedy wore her black velvet dress with the lace collar, and her mother wore purple silk that was cut low above the curve of her breasts. Flora wore a small hat with a veil. Mother and daughter were watched by the soldiers and sailors at the nearby tables.

"They are looking at you, Mother," said Hedy.

"No," said Flora, "they are just looking around."

"There," said Hedy, and she pointed to a soldier with a crew cut that made his head look bald who was picking his teeth with a silver fork. "There," she said, "he's looking at you."

And he was. So was his friend, and so was the third man at the table. They were going off to war. This was a breather, a moment to pretend that they would go to country hotels and lean against bars while listening to dance music from the jukebox for the rest of their lives. This was time out, or time to pretend, or time that belonged to the men who were defending democracy, who were making it possible for that little girl in the velvet dress to grow up without the Nazis pasting a yellow star on her sleeve.

After dinner the men followed Flora and Hedy out into the main hall. "A drink?" said one.

"How about a dance?" said another.

Hedy held her mother's hand tightly. "She's married," said Hedy.

"I'm married," said Flora.

"It's wartime, lady," said one, and pulled a chair up. "Sit down," he said. "Join us for a drink."

"No," said Flora, and she led Hedy away, back to the cottage across from the main house. She could feel the men, the big one, the young boy, maybe one or two others, follow her with their eyes at the window.

"They are watching us," said Hedy.

"No," said Flora. "They have other things to do."

In the room, Flora locked the door and pulled the chain into its loop. She pulled the curtains even though Hedy wanted to watch the moon on the frozen lake and the few nighttime ice skaters who were circling the pond to the music that blared from a gramophone while hot chocolate was stirred in a pot at the edge of the dock.

"Let's go ice skating," said Hedy, but her mother said no. She pushed the armchair that had been by the side of the bed against the door. "Why?" said Hedy.

"For privacy," said her mother.

Reader: I can hear your thoughts. Why doesn't Flora enjoy herself? Why doesn't she pick a young man out of the dozens who are staying the week at Grossinger's? Why can't she relax and let a soldier find the curve of her body that Frank seems to have ignored? What harm would it really do? She could leave Hedy in the room for an hour or so. She could go to the bar and dance, leaning her body against the new one that pulled her close. She could have pushed her hips against the soldier's and moved from side to side with the shift of his weight. It would have been easy to steal a few hours, time out, time that doesn't count, time that rewards only for itself and makes no promises or claims on tomorrow. All over America women were taking advantage of the fact that the man you spoke to on Wednesday would likely be shipped out on Friday, and danger, death, gave an urgency to the moment, to the time, that called off the other bets, that made good girls into party girls. But it wasn't so easy for Flora. She was afraid of thunder and lightning. She believed that if you did something wrong, you were punished, and anyway she was not so hungry for the soldiers as one might think. What she was wanting they were not offering. What she was wanting you couldn't get in between ships sailing and trains leaving. Flora was afraid that if she settled for the in-between, for the glance and the tug and a little sweat on her pillow, she might never find the thing that mattered. What was that? She didn't know where it was or how to look for it. She only knew that its absence filled her day and night. Flora believed in the rules. Who would Flora Gruenbaum be in a world without rules? Reader, be patient. It is not time yet for women to go running around scoring in nightclubs and acting in the living room like pirates on the high seas. For Flora, hope lay in doing what you should. Flora hugged the shoreline of should and should not. If she let go, she feared she would drown.

Later that night, after Flora had changed into her pink nightgown with the hem of lace and after Hedy had fallen asleep counting the freckles she could see on her mother's arms, there was a banging at the door.

"Let us in, it's Bart, from the dining room," said a blurry voice. A shoulder was thrown against the door.

Flora pulled the covers up and shouted, "Go away, go away! I'll call the police." But there was no phone in the room, and the Grossinger's guards were asleep on their chairs a building away.

"C'mon, pretty lady," yelled one. "We're going to die."

"Die," screamed Flora, "and leave me alone!"

"Kike," called out a voice, but it might have been a Jewish soldier. "Let us in!"

They pounded on the door, and Hedy woke up and saw her mother white as a sheet. She had a lamp in her hand as if she might smash the first head that came through the door. "Go away," she sobbed. "My daughter is here."

There was a pushing at the door, and the latch broke. The chain fell to the floor. The wooden door, a thin latch on the wooden door, gave way. One of the men put his hand around the door and Flora threw her body with all its weight against the frame and the door shut on the soldier's hand and he screamed in pain. There were drops of blood on the floor. Flora opened the door and the men tumbled into the room. Hedy's legs were shaking under the cover.

"Help!" screamed Flora.

"Help!" screamed Hedy.

There was a moment's silence. It wasn't fun anymore, and the soldiers backed off. One was holding his hand against his chest and moaning. They cursed as they left. They banged their fists on the table and the wall. They didn't want the lady and her daughter. They wanted a good time, freely given. What the hell was wrong with that woman, and who cared? They staggered off into the night.

Flora dressed Hedy and herself. They went into the main house and spent the night on the chairs in the lobby. In the morning dark circles hung under Flora's eyes. They got into the limousine. There was a light snow falling on the road, and the driver moved slowly. A deer appeared at the roadside and, leaping in the air, crossed to the other side. But by the time the driver called out to Hedy, the deer had disappeared into the bank of high trees, stones, and twigs on the other side.

Hedy took Flora's hand and patted it again and again. Flora wrapped her arms around her daughter and rocked her back and forth. "Don't be sad," said Hedy. "I'm here."

Flora said, "Maybe I should leave your father, maybe I should get divorced?"

Hedy looked out the window. She wanted to see a rabbit running across the snow. Hedy didn't know what to say, she didn't know anyone who was divorced. Neither did Flora. Hedy said, "Do you want to play gin rummy?"

Flora took the cards out of her pocketbook and dusted off the face powder that had spilled over them, and smoothing the bear rug over their laps, they played cards all the way back to New York.

• • •

Reader: So the wife of the ex-king of England had been divorced, but who else? Artie Shaw, more than once, but he had a big band. Movie stars and directors, food for gossip columnists, but who that Flora actually knew in person? There was Louisa, who had left Arthur, a crazy woman, a disturbed person, not a woman at all. Louisa was an enemy of society, a repulsive creature. There was that woman who had run off with her dentist, a friend of Mildred's, at least before she ran away she was a friend of Mildred's. There was a member of the Sunningdale Golf Club who was seen on the train to Washington by Flora's brother Arthur with a Chinese woman who was definitely not his wife. There were women waiting all over America for men who were occupying themselves elsewhere, and there were men who longed for women who couldn't or wouldn't; but divorce itself was like pregnancy without a husband. What would everyone think? What Flora thought, as she dealt the cards in the backseat of the limousine, was that divorce was for fallen women, that divorce would leave her all alone, that everyone would talk about her and no one would invite her anywhere. What Flora thought about divorce was that it was shame, so great a shame that it was not to be considered, though she considered it all the time. Flora thought that alone she would be invisible; even her sister, Mildred, would forget her. She tucked the rug tighter around Hedy's legs. It was cold in the backseat, and Flora could see the frost on the edges of the car windows.

Although She Doesn't Know It, the Moment Hedy Became a Zionist: 1944

Flora is riding on the double-decker Fifth Avenue bus with Hedy on a Saturday morning in September. They are on their way, mother and daughter, to Saks Fifth Avenue to buy new clothes for the approaching school term.

A woman sits on the bus in front of them. She is wearing a blue silk dress that has seen better days; in fact, it looks as if it came out of a suitcase. She is heavily rouged, and her lipstick is so thick that it appears smeared and the shape of her lips has disappeared or run into the slightly hairy area beneath her nose. She has a handkerchief in her hand that she crumples again and again. Her stocking has a run in it and her pocketbook is scuffed. Flora is watching from behind her dark glasses. Hedy is watching directly. The women begins to sing to herself in German, and the man sitting next to her gets up and moves to the back of the bus. The woman is now making little gestures with her hands, which are covered with white gloves or gloves that had been white some time ago.

"What is she singing?" asks Hedy.

"Sh!" says Flora.

The bus ambles slowly along past the great white steps of the Metropolitan Museum, past the quiet, contained front of the Frick Museum, past the buildings with doormen with silver braid on their shoulders and nannies wheeling carriages in and out. The woman begins to speak loudly. "All gone," she says in heavily accented English, although no one is listening. "All gone," she shouts, and all the other bus passengers begin to shift uncomfortably on their seats.

"Who's gone?" says Hedy to her mother.

"Sh!" says Flora.

The woman catches Hedy's eye. "I had a little girl," she says. "I had a little girl, too." She looks at Hedy and says something soft in German or Polish or Yugoslavian.

"What did you say?" asks Hedy, who doesn't understand German, except for the few words Ursula has taught her. The bus pulls up to a stop directly in front of the Central Park Zoo.

"Are you a Jew?" the woman asks Hedy loudly. All the heads on the bus turn.

"Yes," says Hedy. Flora grabs Hedy's hand and pulls her off the bus. "But we're not there yet," says Hedy. "I don't want to walk."

Standing on the cobblestones on Fifth Avenue, beneath the maple trees whose leaves have not yet started to change but seem to have lost their shine, Flora says to Hedy, "Be quiet. For God's sake, just be quiet for a change."

Hedy Gets a Mysterious Rash and Flora Goes to Lunch at the Plaza: December 1944

Hedy had a fever and a rash on her chest. The steam kettle sitting on the stool beside her bed whistled hour after hour. Sheets had been placed over the headboard to make a tent so that each time she breathed the hot steam would be forced down into her lungs. She had two pillows behind her back, and her thin arms kept rising and falling with each gasp for air. Ursula sat by the bedside knitting. She was knitting Hedy a sweater, a red sweater with a pattern of tiny bears that would when the work was done march in a parade with balloons and cymbals up and down the cable stitch. Hedy had her temperature taken every few hours. It stayed the same.

Flora opened the bedroom door and got a glimpse of her daughter, pale and sweating, her mouth open like a fish, pulling air into her lungs, her small chest heaving up and down. Flora closed the door. She was frightened when Hedy was sick. She didn't like it when Hedy's brown eyes were glazed and distant, the black pupils large and blazing.

Flora was afraid that she might do something wrong. She might give the wrong medicine, she might scald Hedy with the steam kettle, she might open a window instead of closing it. She left the care of the sick to Ursula, who knew how to do things, whose hands could knit and make a bed and take a temperature.

The pediatrician came to the house. Ursula gave him a clean towel to wash his hands. He opened Hedy's pajama top and looked at her rash. "Odd," he said. "Not anything I've seen before. It will go away, when the fever goes, I'm sure." He was a tall thin man with a white mustache, the only Jewish doctor at New York Hospital. Flora was flattered that he had accepted Hedy Sheinfold as his patient.

Ursula was upset by the rash. "I've kept everything clean," she said. "The child couldn't have the rash from dirt."

"Of course not," said the doctor.

In a few days the fever went down. The rash spread from Hedy's chest to the top of her thighs and across her bottom and over to her forehead. The doctor came back. "Keep her in bed a few more days," he said.

"What is it?" asked Ursula.

"An allergic reaction to the fever," said the doctor. "It will go away in a few days."

It didn't. Hedy read books. She listened to the radio. She listened to the afternoon games of the Dodgers broadcast from Ebbets Field. She shouted when Pee Wee Reese hit a homer.

"Quiet," said Ursula. "Don't get excited or I'll turn it off."

The shades were pulled in her room. She was supposed to nap two hours each day. She was restless and bounced up and down on the bed. Slide, slide, she whispered to herself as Roy Campanella, whose knees she worried about, stole second.

The doctor came back. The rash had spread to her cheeks. The fever was long gone. She was well, well enough, except for the rash, which had turned raw and erupted in spots in pus. "Not impetigo," said the doctor. "Feed her only Jell-O and soup. Maybe it's a food allergy."

Ursula covered her body in gentian violet. She was purple all over. It didn't help. Ursula covered her with calamine lotion. She was pink all over. Ursula scrubbed at the sores with soap and water. That didn't help, either. Hedy went back to school, but the other children wouldn't sit near her or talk to her. She wanted to stay home in her room. Ursula agreed. A child with a rash like that should not go to school.

Weeks went by. The rash would fade on one arm, only to appear more fiercely on another. A specialist was called. Two dermatologists and two allergists saw her. They had no name for her rash. No one had ever seen anything like it. They took samples of blood with long needles. They attached wires to her body and had her breathe into a cup. They told her to walk on a chalk line. They pounded on her chest. Hedy didn't cry. It was important to be brave. She was silent. They examined her head and her ears and her belly. They found nothing out of place. One of the dermatologists asked permission to present her at grand rounds. Ursula went with her. In the center of an auditorium she sat on a big chair, and the dermatologist talked to the doctors who gathered around her.

"So you're the little girl with the mystery rash," said one of the doctors, patting her on the shoulder. Hedy wanted to throw herself into his arms. She sat still. Ursula took off her blouse, and the doctors looked at her under a big white light. Hedy was afraid they were going to scrape her skin or give her a shot, but they just looked. She had been very good and done everything they asked. Hedy asked, "What will happen if the rash never goes away?"

"What kind of a question is that?" said Ursula.

Flora went out for the afternoon, to lunch at the Plaza with her sister, Mildred, and then to her card game. She was worried about Hedy. She was so worried that she couldn't stay in the house, especially when there was nothing she could do to help. No one knew what had caused the rash. Flora sat on the pink upholstered circular couch, the one with the Christmas wreath strung around its back, waiting for her sister, who was as usual late. She put her mink coat by her side. The fur was long and heavy, and each time she took it off she sighed with relief. When she wore her fur she had to be careful not to bump into things, it was so wide and full. Once she had caught sight of herself in a store window. She looked like a bear, a small bear, round and fuzzy. She opened her purse and took out her gold compact with the ruby poodle in the center. She opened it and powdered her nose. Excitement, pleasure, worry, cold, heat, pride, shame, they all made her nose glisten. She covered the freckles on her face with powder, but she could see them anyway. They were hidden behind her glasses, but if you looked carefully, you could see her eyes were soft brown, like Hedy's but even gentler, like a rabbit surprised in the field. She had a long neck, and her lips, which she often ran her tongue across in a nervous gesture, were full and wide and promising.

Her hair was cut close to her head with curls coming forward above the ears. Some might say she was a dish. She was not so sure. She worried that her stockings had a run, that her slip was showing, that her jacket was wrinkled. She put dark red lipstick on her lips. Why, she wondered, did all other women have lipstick that stayed even, full-colored, in place, whereas hers, like her mascara had a way of wandering? She wore a Lily Daché hat with a lace veil that had sequins in it. The sequins caught in her glasses. She took out a cigarette, placed it in her long black holder, and lit it.

An army captain walked past, and a few ensigns went together into the Oak Room. One of the ensigns looked at her bosom swelling above the neckline of her gray linen jacket, a neckline that dipped in a heart-shaped point, just above which her pearls, her double strand, hung discreetly. Flora felt a shiver; was it pleasure or fear? She crossed her legs the other way and looked at the wallpaper, all red-and-white velvet and mirrors with gold frames everywhere.

At last Mildred appeared. Ten years older than Flora, Mildred wore her mink as if it had grown on her shoulders. She looked like the spirit of Christmas in a red suit with a green blouse. On the lapel she had pinned a sprig of holly just above the brooch made of pearls and diamonds, one that had once belonged to their mother. Her blond hair was waved just right, her nails were not broken like Flora's left pinky, which she tried to keep hidden under her purse out of sight of her sister's careful eye. Mildred was taller than Flora, thinner, too, and her voice was booming, unselfconsciously booming, her laugh and her hug for her sister was open and full, and anyone who was watching would know this was a woman who was not attracted to suffering, played a good game of golf, was eager to please and easy to please.

Mildred commanded her usual table, and the headwaiter bowed as he always did. Mildred's table was under the palm, decorated for the season with gold balls and red ribbons, just the right distance away from the violinist, who insisted on coming over to serenade them as he always did when they lunched at the Plaza. Mildred ordered their whiskey sours, their cucumber sandwiches, their tea, and directed Flora to pick out the pastry that she would have for dessert from the passing cart. There in the Plaza with Mildred, Flora felt safe, safe from what? People looking and not thinking she was pretty, ceilings falling down suddenly, electricity sparking out of irons and stoves, beams falling from construction sites, elevators tumbling to the ground floor or shooting up to the sky, germs that waited till you forgot about them and then carried you off in twenty-four hours before your children could say good-bye and kiss you for a final time. Flora believed that cars could suddenly leave the street for the sidewalk and smash you against the windowpane. She believed that the Jews were being killed in Europe. She believed that Hedy could die from the rash that no one had recognized. She was not at all certain that the war would have a happy ending.

Mildred thought none of those things and laughed at Flora when she confided her expectations. "Don't worry about things you can't change, don't listen to news you don't want to hear," Mildred would instruct her younger sister. "Don't worry about Hedy," she said. "The rash will go away. Who ever heard of a girl getting married covered with red spots?" Mildred would take care of Flora always because that's how it is between sisters.

Flora ordered the hot chocolate with whipped cream that appeared on the table in a silver bowl, and then she felt guilty. It was fattening, she should have ordered tea like Mildred. She drank it so quickly that she burned the roof of her mouth, and Mildred laughed at her and said that as soon as Hedy's rash was gone they would take her to the Plaza for tea and cake.

"Children die," said Flora.

"At least it's not polio," said Mildred, and Flora was so grateful to her sister that tears came to her eyes and her nose shone through the powder.

"Maybe I should have an affair," Flora said, to see how her sister would respond. Mildred wrinkled up her nose.

"I love Frank," said Flora.

"God knows why," said Mildred.

"Maybe I should get divorced," said Flora.

"Stop fussing," said Mildred.

Julie Eisen Recoups Some of His Fortune: 1944

The Gruenbaum offices had carpeting and soft lighting from white cans that ran across the ceiling. Potted palms, ficus, and geraniums lined the windowsills, and secretaries in spiked heels, wafting perfume down the halls, ran back and forth with pitchers of water for all the thirsty leaves. The switchboard had grown from mirror size to the length of a wall, and the operator was sometimes so frantic that her hands trembled under the pressure of incoming and outgoing calls.

Julie sat in a large, sunny office with a print of a Chagall painting over his desk. A cow was playing a fiddle in circles of orange and red above the chimney tops. His shiny head glowed in the light that beamed down from the ceiling. He had an important role in the company. He was in charge of summer suits, silk and cotton, summer seersucker and white linen and undershirts. He had a factory just for his products in Elmtown, New Jersey, and the company car would take him there to inspect the assembly line at least once a week. He had become a member of the Beach Bay Club in Mamaroneck, New York. There had been some objections when his membership was proposed, but then the civil libertarians on the board, the decent, fair-minded members of the community, argued that he had paid his debt to society, that it was all a bit of anti-Semitic Depression hysteria anyway, and that time had passed, a war had intervened. The Gruenbaum Company was a solid proposition, one that many of their members had business with in one form or another.

"What, after all, was the scandal about?" said one.

"I've forgotten," said another, and there he was out on the fifth hole with his checked pants and his yellow suspenders and his bald head hidden from the bright sun by a porkpie hat of pink-and-blue plaid.

Julie Eisen also did the books for the summer suit division of the Gruenbaum Company, and the ledger, which he kept in his neat hand, just the way his father had taught him, allowed certain discrepancies between intake and outflow, allowed certain deposits to his personal bank account that would enable him to live just a little bit better than his salary as executive vice president might have permitted and would one day buttress his old age, protect his wife, and give her what she had been guaranteed the day they married. If you had asked Julie if he had thought this wrong, he would have hugged his chest and looked at you through his wide, soft blue eyes and asked you: "What is wrong with a little justice in the world? I am only giving myself my due, my worth, my wife's worth, and her proper share, and besides," he would add, "everyone else is at it, too, a little shearing, a little back pay, a little tip for the tipster, and one for the friend who told you so. And why not? That's the way business is. Nothing in this world is flat, everything is a little shady."

Frank was on very good terms with Julie's secretary. Her husband liked the armed forces so much that he had enlisted for another term in the Philippines when the war was over. She lived with her girlfriend in Greenwich Village and thought she might try acting. She was pretty enough, after all. From Julie's secretary Frank learned about the cooked books and the special accounts.

Hedy was thinking about Phoebe Walzer, who was or was not her best friend. She was waiting for the maid to serve the potatoes when Frank began.

"Julie has done it. I'm telling you, right out from under us. He's taken enough to buy Hyde Park."

"How do you know?" asked Flora, her face pale and her eyes blinking nervously behind her glasses.

"I know," said Frank. "I've seen the books."

"We'll call the police," said Hedy.

Her father turned to her. "At least somebody has a sense of justice around here." Hedy felt warm and happy.

Flora knocked her fork against her plate in a steady rhythm. "You can't," she said.

"Why not?" said Frank.

"Because of Mildred," said Flora. "It would shame us all."

Hedy kept her eyes down on her lap. She could feel the steam rising from her father. She could feel the tears coming from her mother. She felt sick to her stomach.

Later in the living room Hedy heard them talking with Arthur. Arthur said, "We'll ignore it. It doesn't matter. Some things you don't have to know. She's my sister."

"He's taking from us," said Frank, "and it's a public company." Frank was shouting. Hedy wanted to hear what her uncle Arthur would say, but she also didn't. She covered her ears with her hands and began to sing a song.

Flora went to bed early and Frank went out for a walk and Hedy called her friend Phoebe Walzer on the phone and told her the entire plot of *20,000 Leagues Under the Sea*. She tried not to scratch at the familiar rash that appeared on the tops of her thighs.

For Mildred's forty-fifth birthday she received a pearl necklace with a ruby clip from her husband. She looked at herself in the mirror. Her long neck, her large eyes, the curls around her forehead, made her look like a woman on a Roman coin—a woman who must have a seat for the opening night of the opera. She smiled. It was hard to get older, but there was always some good mixed with the bad.

Julie practiced his violin at nights when everyone else in his apartment was asleep. Once his daughter Lydia woke and found her father in his pajamas with the violin under his chin right at the window in the kitchen. Julie had started as if he had been doing something wrong. That's because of what he was thinking, planning, had been planning for a number of years.

In January he told Mildred he had to go off on business for a few weeks. He put his bank cards, his tax information, his driver's license, in his sock drawer. He took cash out of their bank account in large bills. Holding a small suitcase and his violin, he rode the train down to Florida. In Miami he boarded a boat for South America. The country in which he found himself was filled with Jews in hats, with little luggage. They spoke German and Polish and Yiddish and Czech. They all looked stunned by the heat, by the thumping music that came from the doors of the cabarets, by the insects that swarmed large over their heads, by the lizards that crawled between the legs of the tables. They all looked as if they had lost a part of themselves, an arm or a leg or a memory. One more, one who spoke English, was no bother at all.

Julie found a small room in a hotel and, unpacking his bags, smiled, a real smile for the first time in years. Mildred would miss him. The children hardly noticed his comings and goings. He had been gone and seemed to have stayed gone, something he didn't know how to change, though clumsily he'd tried a few times. But Mildred would be all right. She could manage anything. He had to take care of himself.

He went to the Casa del Sol on the Grand Plaza and, sitting under the fronds of a palm tree, sipped coffee with cream. He asked the manager for a job. He suggested music to amuse the men at their business dinners, the drinkers, the señoras who came for lunch. The manager was a Jew from Vitebsk who had heard enough stories already and thought he knew Julie's.

Julie was hired. He wasn't the best violinist, the manager agreed with the headwaiter, but despite his awkwardness, he had charm, an earnestness that made him sweat when he worked, a pleasure in the music that was contagious even if the notes were not right and some imperfections of tone were there. Julie developed a routine. He worked late hours. He had breakfast at the same cafe each morning. He walked on the boardwalk in the afternoon. He read the papers in the evening before going out to work. His father, he thought, would be pleased. He lost weight. He was happy at last. Who would begrudge him that?

He wrote to Mildred: "Come join me. I am a violin player at the Casa del Sol. I miss you and the girls."

Mildred stared at the letter. Arthur said, "Shall I go and fetch him?" Flora held her sister's hand.

Mildred shook her head. "Let him go," she said.

Julie waited for the mail at the post office each morning. At last he gave up and invited the reservations clerk to dinner, and though she was overage and they shared no common language, they managed to comfort one another for losses that remained unnamed.

Flora and Hedy Listen to the Radio: May 1945

Flora was listening to the radio with Hedy. "Do you think God planned everything?" said Flora.

"Maybe," said Hedy. The *Inner Sanctum* door squeaked on its encrusted hinges, and the mystery began. "How," said Hedy, "does the radio work?"

"The sound comes over the air and into the radio," said Flora.

"How?" said Hedy.

Flora thought. "Somehow," she said. Flora imagined the air she was breathing full of sound broadcast from miles away. Could you swallow it? she wondered. She looked at the telephone. Was the voice she heard condensed in some way and sent through the wire? Was it sent through the air, like the radio? She thought of the bulb in the lamp by her bed. Where was the electricity—in the wall, in the air, in wires in the building? How did it get there, how exactly did it get there, how did it come when called? Why did it stay in the wires and not wander about? She thought of the stove. Where was the gas piped from? Along under the city streets, voices were moving, electricity was passing, gas was flowing. Who made gas, what was gas, anyhow? Air that was hot. How did it get hot? God, how was it done, day after day? All those currents under foot, around the ears, so many signals, crossing.

Flora felt sad and lay down on the bed. Her nylons had a rip running right up her calf. How do they make nylons? What is nylon? she thought. "Sometimes," she said to Hedy, "I feel like a savage sleeping on the floor of a cave. The sun comes up, I sleep, I age, I die, but what do I know about how it happens or why it happens? Nothing, nothing at all. I want you to understand everything. I want you to know something. Think about it, steam and electricity and airplanes, what makes them work? Don't be an idiot like me."

"Sh!" said Hedy, who had her ear pressed to the radio, waiting to hear the victim's screams. The program was interrupted. The war in Europe was over. Hitler was dead.

Hedy's rash came and went and came again. She had lotions and powders and anti-itching medicine. She scratched herself in the night. Flora consulted the tarot dealer, who suggested the curative powers of the baths in Baden-Baden.

In Which Flora Disappoints Hedy by Biting Off More Than She Can Chew: 1946

The war was over. The soldiers and sailors had kissed the girls and poured beer on their heads and jumped up and down beneath the Camel sign on 42nd Street. In front of Lindy's Flora had pressed her body against a glass window and smiled and waved as the crowd, relieved of death and destruction, whirled about like so many leaves on a bright day in September.

Ursula went home for a visit to Germany, taking with her American chocolates, nylons, and yarn. Something about a war left a country without yarn. Her temporary replacement, a Mrs. Hartung, believed that it was not enough to wash your hands once after using the toilet, but every finger needed to be scrubbed separately and inspected. Hedy thought she was old enough to be without a nanny. She was embarrassed in front of her school friends. She pretended that Mrs. Hartung was a member of the family, an old aunt of her mother's.

Flora should have been happy. The war had ended, leaving the Gruenbaum Company on the Big Board, alive and well, very well. Her husband slicked down his hair each morning and went to the office, his briefcase filled with memos about the expansions they were planning. Arthur wrote poetry to Louisa, but he didn't know where to send it. He was used to eating dinner alone. Mildred was redoing her living room in Danish modern. She had told everyone that Julie had been killed in a car crash in California, where he had gone on business. Even her children believed the story. She was an attractive widow who danced with the available men at the club but always sent them home disappointed. She had had enough of men and their odd fancies. What she liked was parties, the Philharmonic, the opera, lunch at Schrafft's with her sister, dinner after the theater with friends. She thought about Julie with a twinge of regret, the way a child might feel on seeing an old pair of ice skates in the closet that no longer fit.

Hedy's rash was on the wane, and she not been run over by a car or incarcerated in a hospital respirator, struck down with polio. But Flora woke each morning later and later, with a heavy dread sitting on her chest, as if the day were certain to bring news of fatality, of calamity so enormous that she couldn't shape its particulars but felt its weight approaching her, its shadow over her in the closet, in the bathroom, in Bonwit Teller's, at the card table. When she drove through the tunnel to her summer place in Deal, New Jersey, she watched the sides out of the corners of her eye. Water was sure to leak, the tunnel walls would crumble, and she would drown in her car, a small woman propped up on two cushions behind the wheel so that she could see the road, her dark glasses that she wore most days making her progress through the tunnel like Eurydice climbing back to a life she would never reach. Flora was suddenly incapable of taking elevators if they were automatic, and now the newer buildings, the ones with dentists' offices, brokers' offices, downtown, had installed these push-button paneled wonders. Once inside, Flora became convinced that the elevator would shoot through the roof and she would be crushed in the splintering mirrors and pressed like a cartoon cat against the sky. She took to walking up and down the fire stairs in buildings without elevator men who would say "Good morning," "Good evening," "Good weather we're having." Flora took to her bed with stomach pains that proved, after all kinds of X-rays, enemas, doctors' prodding, inside and out, not to be tumors again and again. Altogether the ending of the war, the founding of the United Nations with its promise of lions and lambs and plowshares, even the promise of a Jewish Palestine, did not ease her feeling that her child was going to fall out a window or her heart stop beating from causes unknown. Flora read in the *Reader's Digest*, in *Life* magazine, about a cure, a cure for problems just like hers.

"Maybe I should see a psychiatrist," she said to Mildred.

"Nonsense," said Mildred. "It costs too much money. Stop worrying."

Flora tried, but she failed. She continued to worry. She became the first member of the family, at the outrageous sum of $25 an hour, to visit a psychoanalyst, a refugee from Vienna who had studied with the great man himself and who understood that when she thought about leaks in cement structures it was not because she couldn't master the engineering concepts of modern society, but because she quite reasonably feared the weight of the water was too much for the tunnel walls. Dr. Saul Bergman was willing to listen to anything, no matter how preposterous it might seem. This gave Flora hope. It also gave her love. She was now hopelessly in love, unrequitedly in love, not only with Frank, but also with Dr. Saul Bergman.

So when Dr. Bergman wondered if perhaps the content of some dream she had brought him didn't mean that she had a strong desire to do something for others, she set right out to find something to do. She joined the Jewish Board of Guardians big sister program. They did not require a college degree. They did not ask her if she had any work experience. They asked her for a donation to Federation, and she increased her annual pledge. They assigned her a little girl, named Marilyn Sonnenschein, who needed to be brought from the upper Bronx, once a week, to a counseling session in midtown Manhattan. Her mother was ill, diabetic, in bed and unable to bring her child, and it was crucial because the little girl was strange, was hearing voices, and had acted peculiarly even since her father had died the year before.

Her job, Flora explained to Hedy, was to go to the Bronx once a week and accompany Marilyn on the subway to 57th Street, where the Jewish Board of Guardians had their offices, and wait while Marilyn had her appointment with a social worker and then bring her back to her home. It took up an afternoon. It meant that Flora was now busy. Once a month she was to call the social worker and talk with her about Marilyn, telling her anything she had observed in the home or any changes she had noticed in her behavior. She was a part of the team, the therapeutic team, and Dr. Bergman seemed pleased with her. She told him that she felt as if the venetian blinds in her room had been pulled up and a new light, a morning sun, still soft and mixed with mist, was falling over her.

Marilyn Sonnenschein slept on a couch in the living room of the apartment on the sixth floor. The halls were dark, and a smell of garbage hung in the air. The first time she made the trip, Flora clutched her purse and regretted wearing her pearls. The apartment walls were painted green, and the paint was chipped here and there. On the wall was a framed oil painting of a group of four old men with beards praying with their taleysim wrapped around their heads. Marilyn Sonnenschein's mother always greeted Flora in her nightgown, which smelled of medicines, and all across the floor the daily newspapers lay because it seemed Mrs. Sonnenschein did not feel up to cleaning. Marilyn was a tall girl with freckles across her face, and she wore thick glasses whose plastic earpieces were held to the frame by tape. She had a vague look in her eyes that made it hard to tell if she were really seeing the person in front of her or was gazing absently at something just beyond or on the other side. She had large teeth that needed the attention of the orthodontist, and her socks were always falling, one or another, down about her saddle shoes. She was clean and she was polite. Her hair was perfectly brushed, but she moved in her body as if she were inside a sack. She lurched forward. Her legs seemed to hang from her hips as if they had been attached by paper clips. She was failing school, and the public school wanted her to repeat the sixth grade again. She reminded Flora of rice pudding, something shapeless and pale, something bland and gluey, something unspectacular.

Sometime during the first month of their trips downtown, Marilyn Sonnenschein leaned over to Flora and, stroking the fox pelt that Flora had slung over her blue suit and kicking her shoes against the floor of the subway, ignoring the woman with shopping bags sitting on her other side, she shouted over the rumble of the wheels on the track and the shaking of the train through the darkness:

"Last night, I saw my father's shoes, under my bed. First they were under the bed and then they came up and rested on my blanket."

"Really?" said Flora, who thought for a moment that Mrs. Sonnenschein might have left her dead husband's shoes around under a pile of newspapers.

"The shoes," said Marilyn. "They spoke to me. But don't tell anyone I said that. That's my secret with you." She smiled at Flora.

She likes me, thought Flora. The next week Flora asked, "The shoes, Marilyn. Are they still there?"

"Yes," said Marilyn. "My father's black shoes, the ones he wore to synagogue on Shabbos. They are there, under my bed."

"Are they talking to you?" said Flora.

"Yes," said Marilyn. "They are sad. If they had eyes, they would cry."

"Are they sad," said Flora, "because your father died?"

"No," said Marilyn, "they are sad because I am not a good girl."

"But," said Flora, "you are, you are a good girl." The train screeched and slowed, and they pulled into the Columbus Circle station.

Flora bought Marilyn a new dress. She bought her a fuzzy bear and a pair of shining black shoes of her own. Mrs. Sonnenschein said, "No, no we don't take charity," and she made Marilyn give Flora back the package.

Flora invited Marilyn to see a Broadway play. She picked her up on a Wednesday afternoon and took her to *Oklahoma*. Marilyn sat forward on her seat and rocked back and forth with the music. She had never been to the theater before. She clutched her program to her chest and sang the songs to herself softly all the way back to the Bronx. Flora took Marilyn to Rockefeller Center to see the Christmas tree.

"Look," said Flora, "at the reindeer that line the path." Marilyn said her father did not like Christmas because it made people hate the Jews. "Well," said Flora, "you can still admire the reindeer."

When Flora took Marilyn home that afternoon Marilyn said, "You are my best friend."

Flora had kept every appointment for four months. Sometimes she would arrive in the Bronx and Mrs. Sonnenschein would tell her that Marilyn was not going today. Marilyn had a cold. Marilyn wanted to stay home. Flora would try to convince Marilyn that her appointments with Mrs. Leibowitz were important. Sometimes Marilyn would grumble and put on her coat, and sometimes she would lock herself in the bathroom and refuse to come out until Flora left.

"Helping someone else is not as easy as all that," she told Dr. Saul Bergman, who nodded sympathetically.

Besides, it frightened Flora, this look over the edge of reason, into the demon self that was Marilyn talking to her father's shoes. The subway frightened Flora with its reminder that all directions were not up. Some things just went along sideways, underground, back and forth. Flora asked Mrs. Leibowitz, "What can I do to help her?"

Mrs. Leibowitz said, "Everything can't be fixed."

Flora told Hedy, "Everything can't be fixed." Hedy patted her mother's hand.

Then Mildred was having a party, a birthday party, and it was important that Flora get her hair done in the afternoon so that it would look just right for the party and it was raining as well, so she called Mrs. Sonnenschein and told her that she couldn't come that week, and Mrs. Sonnenschein said, All right.

After that Flora decided to go to Miami for two weeks with her friend Reba, and she canceled again. When she came back she called Mrs. Sonnenschein and was told that Marilyn had been sent to the Hawthorne School for troubled youngsters because she had been talking about her father's shoes to everyone. Mrs. Sonnenschein was too tired to cry anymore, she told Flora. "Marilyn said you could come see her at her new school if you want."

Flora thought about it. The Hawthorne School was in Westchester. One thing and another came up, and her appointments with Dr. Bergman were every day now, and after a while she thought, Marilyn won't even know who I am if I visit.

"Will she be all right?" asked Hedy.

"I don't know," said Flora. "It's not a good sign to hear shoes talking."

Reader: Don't be too quick to criticize Flora. Don't jump to the conclusion that Marilyn would have been saved if Flora had continued her once weekly trips to the Bronx. The talking shoes are a serious matter. They tell us that no dear friend, no aunt, no social worker, was apt to prevent Marilyn from hearing the unsaid and proceeding to her destiny as a patient. Marilyn heard the shoes talking because her father had died before his child was ready to let him go. Marilyn heard the shoes talking because she was born without the whip that most of us have, for keeping the lions of the soul in their proper cages. Poor Marilyn, she had no whip and her lions ran free. At night at the Hawthorne School Marilyn hung her head over the edge of her cot and stared at her father's shoes, which had followed her there. "My name is Marilyn," she said, and the shoes agreed.

Flora, on the other hand, cannot be blamed for not exhibiting discipline in her voluntary job. What experience did she have? Whoever had told her that discomfort, bad smells, long subway rides, difficult children who spoke to their father's shoes, were a part of the way things were supposed to be? Don't blame Dr. Saul Bergman. He wasn't a rabbi or a teacher or a representative on this earth of Calvin's work ethic. He was a doctor, and his job was to make Flora feel whole, and that he could not do, or believed he could not do, by giving her instructions on how to behave. Understand that Flora was frightened, she was afraid she might start to talk to her own shoes. Reader, don't believe that Flora was without heart. She cared for Marilyn. It was just that she too needed care. Bear with Flora, she meant well. She did the best she could at the time.

In Miami, Flora lay on a chaise longue out in the moonlight and lifted her small but still good legs one by one up to the sky, as the exercise teacher had shown her in the morning class by the pool. Flora's brown eyes looked around with eagerness and curiosity. She admired the pelicans as they swooped down off shore and opened and closed their bucket beaks and water spilled from the sides. Flora lay back in her strapless top and longed to be touched by a man who would hold her in his arms and bend his head down to her face and take her for a walk on the moonlit beach. Lying on the chaise longue in the night, Flora had urges and hopes that made her eyes fill with water, and she began to worry about tidal waves and sharks in the water, about electric storms and tarantula bites. Dr. Bergman did not fully appreciate the dangers of the world; perhaps his escape from Europe had led him to feel safer in America than was prudent. Perhaps, she even dared to think, he lacked imagination.

Flora put in a call for Frank and, reaching him at his office just minutes before a sales meeting, asked him to come to Florida, to take a week in the sunshine with her. How wonderful he would look in his white suit and his blue shirt and his panama hat, she thought. "You could play tennis here," she said. "They have a championship golf course."

"For God's sake, Flora, I can't take a vacation now," he said before he wished her well, told her to be careful of sunburn, and promised to call in a day or two. He had to fire his secretary because there had been too much talk in the office and Arthur had said to him, "Get rid of her, now." He had found her a job in the building with an underwear company only two floors away. If he wanted her, he had only to send a message with the coffee wagon. He was having a vacation, a fine vacation, right in New York.

The Judge's Son Grows Up: 1934–1948

When Will Katz was ten years old he woke up one morning hardly able to open his mouth. His jaws seemed locked with all the treasure inside. His head pounded and his legs ached. Bessie called the doctor, who arrived within an hour. During that hour, Bessie sat by Will's bed and, taking his warm hand in hers, crooned to him, "Don't worry, don't worry, you're all I have in the world, nothing will happen to you."

And almost nothing happened. Will had mumps, and by the end of the day his face had turned into a moon and Bessie, who tried to get him to slip a spoon between his clenched teeth, was relieved. "Only mumps," she said. "You'll be all right."

The doctor told her the bad news while he waited for the elevator, his eyes on the metal hands on the half circle above the door showing its slow ascendancy. "He might not be able to have children. It could happen," said the doctor.

"Then there's no point in his marrying," said Bessie. The doctor laughed and Bessie smiled and they shook hands as the elevator doors slowly opened.

The Katzes moved to Park Avenue, to a classic seven-room apartment with two maid's rooms off the kitchen. The Judge had received a federal appointment. He was held in high esteem not only by his former colleagues at the Bronx Democratic Club, but by his new friends in Manhattan who wanted to take him out to dinner at the best restaurants and who always were calling with hard-to-get theater tickets and tickets to football or baseball games.

Howie Katz was a gentle man who rarely contradicted anyone. He had grown bald and stoop-shouldered over the years. Other lawyers admired his decisions, his obvious passion for the law, and his conviction that this country, his adopted country, was the first step in disarming the angels who stood at the gates of Eden. His blue eyes were sharp and eager, but sometimes they seemed to glaze over behind his thick glasses and his hands would nervously strum the table or the chair on which he was sitting.

"Stop that," Bessie would call out to him. "Stop making little bird noises," she would demand, and he would obediently put his hands in his lap and clasp them together as if without concentration they might again escape.

Bessie and Mildred shared a dressmaker, so Mildred knew and told Flora that Bessie had pads built right into her dresses so that her breasts, which had dropped over the years and flattened against her frame, seemed larger, more promising, than they otherwise might. She wore the emerald necklace that had been her mother's but had it reset with little diamond chips arranged in interlocking squares in a stylish way. Her living room furniture was all new, and there were large pieces of blond wood and mirrors and carved chairs that looked uncomfortable to sit on but had designer names that she was apt to tell you if you complained about the shortage of space for the human bottom or the awkwardness of rising from one of her chairs. The thing about the furniture was that it was all heavy. It made clear to all who came to the apartment that the Katzes were not going to run off in the night, that they were there, weighted by their furniture for a long time to come. All the walls had mirrors, and throughout the apartment Howie or Will or Bessie were reflected in smoky blue glass that was quilted with hexagonal little knobs of crystal.

Bessie entertained. She entertained people who she considered counted; that meant other judges of the same or higher rank. It meant members of the mayor's inner circle. The mayor himself was said to have eaten Bessie's borscht, the one the cook spent hours making the day before. She entertained certain people she felt would appreciate the important role her remarkable son was destined to have in the public affairs of his country and speed him on his way. These included the dean of the Columbia Law School and the head of the city council and the governor's right-hand man in housing.

How did Bessie know all these people, and how did she know who was worth feeding and who was not? Mildred asked Flora, and Flora said, "Everyone, absolutely everyone who Bessie met, was invited to dinner on the boat that Bessie had bought for her son's weekend amusement and was docked at a marina in City Island. Once out on the boat the guests were made to present their connections, their net worth, and their possible service to the Katz family, and the ones not worthy of a second invitation were dropped overboard and forced to swim ashore." Mildred laughed.

Bessie had a small screechy voice with the tones of the Bronx accenting her *d*'s and *t*'s. She read the columns in the tabloids and knew what was going on, but she also knew that the stream of visitors to the house, the invitations to fine restaurants and country clubs, depended on the Judge's judgeship. So she warned him each night before she turned out her light, "Don't get carried away, you're a man with family responsibilities." He knew what she meant. He knew it all too well.

With his long, slightly crooked nose and his full, sensual lips and olive skin, Will was an almost handsome boy. His mother thought he was more than that. He would perhaps have been except for a certain expression in his eyes that shone with a strange light, pale blue they were, perhaps a little uncentered, moved just a fraction of an inch out of joint with one another and seeming simultaneously fierce and frozen. He had the eyes of a boy who was listening to voices from Mars telling him to violate little girls on the back stairway. But at the same time his eyes were extremely intelligent; like a perfect radar beam, they swept around a room and detected all that needed to be detected.

He was respected by his classmates, not because he was such a remarkable student, because he often refused or ignored requests by teachers, whom he referred to as clerks or jerks. He wasn't a member of the debate club, which he considered a sandbox endeavor. He didn't date the beautiful girls or run the newspaper. He just had a way of moving through the halls, of calling for his chauffeur, who waited for him in the parking lot so he wouldn't have to worry about buses and trains, that impressed his classmates. He didn't care what they thought of him. That impressed them, too.

He didn't bother to graduate from high school. He was accepted into Columbia University after his junior year. He had no intention of wasting his time being a child. Howie thought he ought to travel around the country for a while. That was something he had wanted, but that had been beyond his reach as a young man.

"See the Grand Canyon, see the Rocky Mountains, see the plantations of the South, learn what it is that America means. He should go with some friends. A boy his age can go with some friends." Howie was flushed talking about it.

Will had no friends. He didn't want to go with friends. "All right," said Bessie, who hated sleeping in public beds and using public bathrooms. "We'll have to take him."

So it was that Howie and Bessie and Will traveled west in a first-class compartment on a train headed for California. Will stared out the window at the Great Plains, the farms of Kansas, the skyline of Chicago. Howie watched his son carefully.

In Las Vegas they stayed in a hotel with a fountain that was large enough to have trained channel swimmers. Howie took his son to a slot machine. "This," he said, "is how the little man gets cheated," he explained. "Illusion, hope, need, prompt him to throw away his hard earnings in the maw of this thing." Howie tapped the multicolored one-armed bandit on the head. "This is about greed," he said to his son.

Will took a quarter out of his pocket and put it in the slot. The wheels spun, one cherry, two cherries, and with loud ringing of bells and a clashing of metal and a grinding of gears the third cherry swung into the opening, bounced unsteadily for a moment, until the spilling quarters fell over Will's hands and onto the floor. As Howie bent to help his son gather his winnings, he caught a look of pleasure in the boy's face that made his fingers tremble as he tried to scoop up the quarters that had rolled about the red carpet.

Later, at the floor show, Will watched the girls in half-bare costumes kicking their legs into the air and wiggling up and down the runways, throwing feather boas, streamers, balloons, and bras into the audience. His face was shiny and he had pimples along the side of his nose.

Bessie said to her son, "This is not nice. This is not a nice show."

Howie said to Bessie, "Let's go. America is not Las Vegas."

"I'll go when I'm ready," said Will, and they stayed till the end.

Despite the loud music, Bessie fell asleep on her chair. Howie was worried because his son had lost interest in the girls on the stage and had not laughed at a single one of the comedian's jokes but asked about everybody in the room—what was their business, where did their money come from, how much did their pinky rings cost? This was not the America that Howie had wanted his son to explore.

Will went through college and law school in record time. He did not so much distinguish himself academically as he made connections. He let everyone know that he was the Judge's son, and he had big parties in his apartment on Park Avenue for the future lawyers of New York, for the future commissioners and congressmen and district attorneys. At these parties he would have a few of his father's acquaintances, bridge partners, a judge of the state supreme court, a Wall Street investor, a real estate tycoon.

After law school he clerked for a judge on the state appellate level, and after that he was appointed through the Democratic machinery, which by now his father knew how to use and reuse and had used and reused him, to be an assistant district attorney in the Southern District of New York State. At the age of twenty-four he was the youngest assistant DA ever. Bessie had a dinner party for him, and the entire crowd toasted him with champagne. This was the beginning.

That night as Bessie hung up her lace dress, she stood for a moment in her closet, a habit she had developed. It was quiet and dark in there and a perfect place for private thoughts, thoughts that someone might call prayer, someone else special pleading. She first looked over her shoes and then the racks of dresses, considering what more she needed for the season to come, and then she put her hands on the velvet brim of her new hat and straightened out the gloves that were piled in the corner. First he should be mayor. Mayor before he's thirty. Then governor; we've had a Jewish governor and he'll be the second.

She thought for a moment of Albany.She had been there with Howie for the inauguration of Herbert Lehman. She would be the hostess this time, she'd decide who could be invited to the dinner the night before. Mildred and Flora would be invited. Let them see who was the mother of the governor and who was not.

Then, after about ten years, maybe when he was forty, he could make a first run for the presidency. Sometime in this country there had to be a Jewish president. Things were changing. It wouldn't be impossible. Queen Victoria had a Jewish prime minister and Ahasuerus had Mordecai. America would catch up. It was time to have a Jewish president.

She ran her fingers along her best satin dress, yellow with a small rose printed in the fabric. She would move into the White House; he would need her, a hostess, to run the staff, to provide an image of family life. What closets they must have in the White House.

It wasn't just Bessie who thought that Will might be the first Jewish president. The Tammany Hall people down on 14th Street talked about it, too. Watch that kid, they said, he has a way with him. It was his eyes, the way they stared at you but seemed to go through you, the way he always seemed to have somebody more important to talk to. Why shouldn't there be a Jewish president one day? Bessie was getting better looking, Mildred said, though Flora disagreed. "Her face is less lumpy," Mildred insisted. It was primarily Bessie who believed that Will was going to make history.

Reader: Don't feel superior to Bessie. Don't for a moment think that Bessie is simply the prototype of the Jewish mother who sends her ambition out into the world wrapped in the mortified flesh of her children. Search your heart, male or female, Jew or Gentile. Haven't you expected your children, one of your children, to be exceptional? One night when you were looking into a small crib, didn't you think this child, this miracle, would do something, be a second baseman for the Baltimore Orioles, be a microsurgeon and sew severed fingers onto mangled hands, be a pianist or a composer or sail a canoe across the Indian Sea—something that would extend your own life into realms impossible for you, blocked to you, but still open, open to the small creature, flesh of your flesh, who might win the praise, the prize, the glory, the fame, that you in your sensible adulthood, your realistic adulthood, have put aside, reconciling yourself to being one mortal among many, one citizen among the voters, one body that will fall into history unnoticed, except for the final hope, the last grasp for the ring of fame, that child who sleeps before you, pacifier in mouth, lying on a sheet decorated with pink hippos, blue puppies, and yellow birds? It's not Jewish, this thing of sending little packets of one's pride, raw and vulnerable, out into the world, buried in the bloodstream of the child; it's a simple strategy to defy death. How slow and painful it is to learn that one's own dear child, miracle of protein and plasma, gene and helix, is only a mortal, if unique, combination of vice and virtue and then even more loved for that by you, who one day recognize your own ordinariness in your child.

Hedy in the Corridor of the Hadassah Hospital: 1990

Hedy felt the heat in the corridor. She had sweated through her blouse, and she could feel the damp circles under her arms. She could feel a coat of grime on her face, mostly come from her hands, from wiping her hands over her eyes, from letting her hands rest on the windowsill and then wiping them on her forehead. Hedy felt the heat of the evening falling across her neck. What did it matter to the universe if one girl lived or died, if her brain survived the operation, if her mind returned or wandered away lost forever? What did it matter? The sun would burn out one day, the galaxy would spin cold and dead, on and on, and what would Namah, her brief, flickering life, matter then? The thought did not comfort. The thought did not silence the scream that she did not scream, because professors at the Technion did not scream, women who understood that a combination of history and biology made everyone a candidate for premature extinction did not scream. Perhaps it would be all right after all. She went to the ladies' room down the corridor, the one for visitors. She splashed water on her face. She looked in the mirror above the sink but did not see her face. She returned to the corridor. She waited.

Frank Finds a Cause: 1946

Ah, the war was over. It made Frank feel better to go downtown without stumbling over soldiers and sailors and WACs and WAVEs, each a reminder that he was not over there but was here instead. It made him feel better to go to his club and find no young men stretched out in the massage room with their uniforms folded neatly on the locker benches. He slicked back his hair, he exercised his muscles by taking long walks along Park Avenue. He felt a quickening in his step. For so long, it seemed, he had been feeling under par, like a man sinking in slow motion. The thing that started his blood racing again, that began his life again, came in a double set of pictures. The first appeared in *Life* magazine, a shot of the camps, the pale faces, the barbed wire, the unbelievable that he had always believed could be. "The bastards," he said to himself. "The bastards," he said to Flora, who was white-faced and threw up in the ladies' room of a Chinese restaurant.

But then just when the facts were beginning to make him feel small, a new battle came. There was the picture of the British, guns at their side, herding a group of refugees off to the camps at Cyprus. The Arabs and the Jews and the British were coming to blows, and this time, this time, there would be no silent acceptance, this time the guns would be turned on the enemy, this time the Jews would be soldiers and, Frank thought, not in terms of trees to be planted in the desert, not in terms of tomatoes plump and red sending roots down into the sand while drops of water fell through pipes threaded under tents of plastic, but of explosives and machine guns, of British soldiers pinned against their tanks and Arabs swinging swords struck down halfway across the road, camels screaming as they rolled in the dust.

At the bar of the club he drank seltzer after seltzer, talking in long monologues about the British brutes and the Jewish homeland and the glorious fight that was to come. He also hated the commies, the pinkos, the reds that were everywhere. "This is a great country," he said, "and the whoremongers want to take it apart and we have to clean them out, out of here.

"Commies," he said to Hedy at the dinner table, "are the termites of the world."

Hedy stared at her father. She saw his eyes narrow and the tight set of his lips. She saw him throw back his shoulders, and she thought him brave. She wanted him to lead her across the sea to Jerusalem, where they could all have a new start, and he would take her hand and teach her how to shoot a gun so she could fight for Palestine by his side.

As the dessert was being served, Frank said, "Your goddamn cousin is a commie, running around with a Negro. You watch that whore of a cousin of yours, a commie."

"Sharie Lee," said Flora, "is a singer, that's all. Dr. Bergman says that singing is no crime."

"So now he's a political scientist, Dr. Know-It-All, Dr. Pay-Me-More-and-More who has made you so happy?" said Frank. Flora blew her nose in her napkin.

"What is it you admire about Sharie Lee?" asked Dr. Bergman.

"She's free," said Flora.

"So," said Dr. Bergman. "You could be free, too."

"I don't sing," said Flora.

"Is it written somewhere that only singers are free?" said Dr. Bergman.

"What is freedom?" asked Flora, and some months passed without Dr. Bergman answering the question. After a while Flora forgot that she had asked it.

The Days of Awe: 1946

The shofar had sounded, and there was a rush out the synagogue door. Flora held Hedy's hand and pulled her down the steps. They were breaking the fast at Mildred's house a few blocks down on Park Avenue. It was blowing on the street, and Flora wrapped her fox fur tightly around her neck. The small paws dangled down over her blue suit, and the small black nose bobbled around on her shoulder.

The street was filled with others rushing to dinner. Everyone was dressed up, befitting people who assumed that their names were in the book of life at least for another year. Frank had spent the afternoon at the club in the steam room. He'd eaten a sandwich in the nearly empty bar and then taken a nap on the massage table while his ribs were being coaxed up and down his trunk.

At Mildred's the lights had been turned on and the green carpet glowed and the golden threads of the lampshades shook with the steps of the people who, throwing their coats in the arms of the maid, rushed to the bar, which was near the hors d'oeuvres table where little pieces of perfectly cut smoked salmon rested on rounds of pumpernickel and small hills of chopped chicken liver rose from shining silver platters. The adults kissed and hugged, and the women went into the bedroom to reapply lipstick, to powder noses that might have turned red on the walk. The table was set with goblets of inlaid gold and dishes of greens and purples, swirls of yellow in the shape of lions and apples and geometric forms. Pearl-handled knives sat in the fruit bowl, and napkins of silk damask were folded at each place.

Will Katz stood in front of the table with the hors d'oeuvres. He blocked the others from approaching. He quickly scooped the chicken liver onto the bread, he swept up the salmon rounds, and, dropping pieces of lemon on the carpet, he ate and he ate. Bessie in the corner, smiled.

"He's such a good eater," she said.

Hedy was hungry. This was the first Yom Kippur that she had fasted. She felt dizzy. She walked up behind Will Katz. He moved his body in front of hers. She reached a hand around his side. He slapped it away.

"Wait your turn," he said.

Hedy approached from another angle. Will Katz had his mouth full of chicken liver and olives. He blocked Hedy's approach.

Teddy, her uncle Arthur's son, home from boarding school for the holiday, came up to Hedy. "I'll get you something," he said.

He walked up to the table just as Will turned around. The platter of salmon was empty. The bowls of chicken liver were scraped clean. There was nothing left. Will Katz got his coat from the maid and left. He had a meeting, an important meeting.

Hedy thanked Teddy for trying. Teddy was always there at Christmastime when the family had taken to gathering at Mildred's house and the Czech maid served them roast turkey, corn pudding, and mince pie. She sat next to him each Passover when the Czech maid would serve brisket and her father would tilt back on his chair, causing Flora to glare at him. The chairs were Louis Seize and had thin gold legs that threatened to buckle when men grew restless on their yellow tufted cushions.

Teddy asked her about her friends. He told her about cheek-to-cheek dancing, and once he had promised her she would be the best-looking Gruenbaum, the pick of the lot, when she grew up. Once, home from boarding school on some sort of temporary suspension, he waited for her in the center island of Park Avenue, which was enclosed by an iron fence and grass grew around a rusted grate through which you could see way down to the Grand Central trains heading uptown through Harlem and out to Scarsdale, Ardsley and White Plains. He had waited until she was delivered to the door by the school bus. He had helped her over the fence and thrown a football with her. Whenever she'd miss her catch and the ball bounced into the street, he would jump the fence and dash between the oncoming cars and bring it back to her so she wouldn't lose her turn to throw it. At Mildred's birthday party Teddy danced with Hedy, and there was a photograph of the two of them. Teddy, tall and straight, wearing a dark blue suit and a striped tie, holding his younger cousin in his arms, she with a yellow satin dress with puffed sleeves; she smiles into the camera, and he manages to hold her around her waist without actually bending down. Hedy would stare at Teddy's face when he wasn't looking. It seemed to Hedy that Teddy, too, was waiting. What were they waiting for?

Frank was not at Mildred's for the breaking of the fast because he was involved in secret business that required the cloak of darkness. At the bar of his club he had been introduced by a man whose company made ladies' lingerie to the fellow who had served with the British in Tripoli and had an artificial leg on which he limped or lurched. The stranger had a mustache and creases in his face as if the desert winds had rippled his skin. He stood straight, like an army man, but his dark eyes searched all the corners of the room, and when he leaned back against the bar rail, the tilt of his head, the beret that he wore, spoke of dangers unspeakable in past and future. He immediately asked Frank for a sizable contribution so that the Jews of Palestine could fly their own flag, a normal nation among the nations. Frank wrote out a small check. He didn't believe in giving money away. Flora always gave to any appeal that came in the mail. She sent checks to the March of Dimes, the Sister Kenny Foundation. She was a soft touch for any picture of an orphan child with crutches. Flora believed without question, without a shiver of irony or a tremor of doubt, that woe was not a necessary or permanent human condition. Frank did not share her convictions, her broodings over misfits, cripples, those without means or opportunity. But the man at the bar with the piercing eyes that had seen men die, he caught Frank's attention.

Wes, he said his name was, and he wouldn't give a last name. He said he needed a safe place, a hiding place, for a shipment that was coming, an urgently needed shipment. He didn't say the word *gun*, he simply lifted his arms and pantomimed aiming at the clock above the door.

Frank caught sight of himself in the mirror behind the bar. His hair was slicked down with the usual Vaseline. It shone black and flat against his head. He was wearing his blue suit with a red silk tie with a gold monogram clip and a white shirt. He felt ashamed. He wanted to look like Wes, whose fingernails were dark and whose eyes snapped and whose accent, British with a certain thickness in the throat, spoke of other places where men took what they wanted. But a man couldn't do just anything he pleased, not a man who had a wife whose family had a business in which he had a part.

The closets of the offices of the Gruenbaum Company were vacated of old files and outmoded typewriters, and new locks were purchased for the doors. The inventory books, which held records back to the early days of the thirties, were carted away and the storeroom in which they had been gathering dust was swept clean by the janitor. Arthur was unhappy. For a long time he had thought only fanatics were Zionists, but now he had changed his mind. But he wanted to leave it to diplomats, for negotiations, not guns; guns, he thought, would never accomplish anything. He said to Flora, "Your husband won't listen to me, but this is serious, this is a criminal matter. We could get arrested. It could create a scandal." Arthur believed that his responsibility was to his company, his family, and he had no intention of shooting anyone. His crazy brother-in-law, he thought, guns in the closet, it made him sick; but it also made him proud.

Flora said to Frank, "Be careful. You mustn't involve the business in this. Bring the guns to the apartment, then no matter what happens the business won't be involved."

"No," said Frank, "you can't bring guns home like a bottle of Scotch in a brown paper bag. The shipment is leaving next week. It's all arranged, don't worry."

The delivery came during the day, the week before Yom Kippur, just as if it were an ordinary shipment of sample suits, only it was marked for Frank. He put it in his own closets, the ones he had especially vacated for the purpose. The long boxes were unmarked, no postage, and the delivery men, with accents, two with numbers tattooed on their arms, heaved and pushed till three hundred M-1's rested in the office of the Gruenbaum Company awaiting transportation to the Holy Land, to be delivered to the Irgun, the ones who would take the British and whittle their empire down to size.

The delivery men said nothing to him, neither winked nor nodded. Frank signed for the packages. His secretary asked him about the cartons, and he told her he was investigating new fabrics from the Middle East. He locked his closet and kept the key on his own ring. The boxes hidden in the closet distracted him, and he lost a squash game at the club.

The night of Yom Kippur Wes came to the office and Frank met him there by the side entrance. The janitor waited to take them up the freight elevator. Wes brought three men with him. They had a rented truck. Frank leaned against the truck. "These M-1's," he said, "they're beauties, I hear."

Wes only said, "Eh," a sound from the back of his throat. They went up the elevator. Frank used his office key and let them in. He didn't turn on the lights but led them past the office cubicles where during the day secretaries sat and talked on the telephone to their mothers, past the larger offices where the designs were drawn and the books were kept, to the closets where the packages waited. In the closet Frank turned on the overhead light. The packages lined the walls. The men grabbed them and, hoisting them on their shoulders, started back toward the elevators, which were the old kind, wire cages, heavy pulleys. Soon Frank heard the familiar sound of levers and chains. He felt a strange peace, a stillness at the center of the storm. "How long till they get there?" he asked.

"A month, maybe," said Wes.

"How they getting in?" asked Frank.

"We get a boat, Libyan flag, we stop outside the three-mile limit and we swim them in, underneath the searchlights from the Brit boats, put 'em on a raft and kick."

"You swim the three miles?" asked Frank.

"Eh," said Wes, and that was all.

As they were riding down the elevator, Wes said, "Increase your check, write another larger one and I can bring in another load next month."

Frank looked at his feet. "Maybe," he said. He felt outside then, like some kind of goddamned fool, as though he'd been used.

"Thanks," said Wes, and he clapped Frank on the shoulder. This made it better.

As the men were loading the boxes into the truck, quickly so that no one would see them, one box fell, clattering to the ground, and the cardboard end tore open. Wes went over and opened the box. "Might as well look," he said.

He ripped the rest of the carton off and pulled out the pieces of the M-1. He assembled it. He ran his hands over the neck, the barrel, the trigger. "Good," he said.

Frank reached out and took the gun. He held it in his arms the way he'd seen it done in the movies. It was shiny and black, smelling of polish and unused metal, a clean barrel, innocent as the sperm before it meets the egg. "How's it fire?" he asked.

"Well enough," said Wes, who took the gun and placed it in the open cardboard box.

"Listen," said Frank, "I'll write you that check tomorrow, just let me have the gun now, that one."

Wes looked at him. Americans, he thought, should be encouraged to hold guns in their arms, with their soft bellies and their silk ties; they were the kind of Jews who were marched off, sheep Jews, not real Jews, not like the new Jews, the Jews who would take these guns that were being loaded into the back of the truck, Jews who could respect themselves.

He tossed Frank the gun. He hopped into the back of the truck and pulled from a box that had been picked up at the previous stop, a woman's Fifth Avenue apartment, where it had been stored among her furs for several weeks, a clip of cartridges. "Here," he said to Frank, "now you have the whole thing. Bring it with you if you come. Can you swim?"

Frank nodded as the truck pulled away, and he was left on Seventh Avenue and 31st Street holding an M-1 in his arms. He threw his camel-hair coat over the gun and walked to his apartment. In the bathroom he loaded the gun. He lifted it to his shoulder, knocking over Flora's night cream, shampoo, and leg wax. He aimed it out the window. "Goddamned Arab, Brit, Nazi," he said.

As he was putting the gun in the back of the hall closet, stuffing it into an old golf bag he no longer used, covering it with an old winter coat, he felt someone behind him. He turned around to see Hedy watching him. She had woken and heard him in the hall. "This is a secret," he said, "a secret between you and me." She nodded her head.

As he brushed his teeth, laid out his keys and wallet on the valet stand that stood inside his closet under his tie rack, he thought to himself, This has been the best night of my life. He put on his blue silk pajamas with his monogram on the pocket and he clipped his toenails and he picked out the white shirt and blue agate cuff links he would wear the next day and he put his head on his pillow and fell directly asleep.

Frank Incurs a Debt: 1946

When the guns were gone Arthur felt better. It had weighed on him, knowing that they were there, but even with that worry at least temporarily off his hands, he found that he was having trouble concentrating. The newspaper would blur before his eyes. He looked each morning first thing for the price of the Gruenbaum stock, but now it would take him a while to locate it among all the other G's and Gr's in the fine print. It wasn't his eyes. He had just had new glasses, tortoiseshell, that slid to just the right point on his nose. He had developed this blink that wouldn't go away: a kind of twitch that ran across his eyelids in a small but consistent spasm.

Teddy wasn't paying attention in school. He was failing again, and this despite the fact that Arthur had followed the advice of the school psychologist, who had suggested that the boy be sent to boarding school. Teddy, he had said, was the kind of young man who might do better with a little more discipline than a single father could provide.

Teddy was at Choate, and at first it had seemed to go well, but then he was caught smoking in the shower by the pool and then he was caught along with two others riding around Hartford in a stolen car, and that was serious, and the boys had beer in the backseat and the convertible top was ripped and it cost a lot of money to explain that boys will be boys to the local police and Arthur had to buy a Mr. and Mrs. James Petty a brand-new Nash before it was all over. Teddy didn't even know how to drive, and he was at the wheel. It turned Arthur's stomach when he thought about it. Images of his son smashed against concrete dividers, wrapped around traffic lights, rode through his sleep and may have partially explained his constant fatigue, his boredom with his usual bridge game, and his golf score gone all to pot so that his handicap had become embarrassing. It may also have explained why he forgot his top salesman's name just as he was awarding him the Gruenbaum bonus prize at the stockholders meeting, a name he knew perfectly well and had known for years.

Frank sent out more shipments with Wes. He also made some investments of his own. He was tired of being the second man, the brother-in-law. Something about the M-1 in the hall closet, leaning against the wall behind his old camel-hair coat and stuffed inside his plaid golf bag, gave him a sense that things could change. He had his own not yet appreciated capacities. Someone at the club had tipped him that there was oil in the bayous of Louisiana. Someone had introduced him to a man who was starting a company. Frank wrote out a check.

"Cut me in," he said. "Cut me in as a major partner."

If there was oil in the bayous of Louisiana, it was not in the bayou owned by the Hibiscus Company. By the time that became clear, Frank had written several checks. There was nothing to do but explain it to Flora. When Flora heard the amount that had disappeared in the swamp, she turned pale.

"How could you?" she said. She sold some stock. She told Arthur, who sighed.

Was Frank pleased with Flora because she had bailed him out? Only in the world to come. Maybe money is the worm in the apple, or maybe the bite Eve took of the apple was just too small. She should have opened her mouth wider and sunk her teeth in deeper. "It isn't good for women to have money. That's what's wrong with the dame, why she needs to go to a doctor three times a week," Frank said to himself, and felt trapped. He wasn't the sort to nibble on his own leg to free himself from the steel bands. He waited.

The Gruenbaum Company had a postwar growth spurt. There were two new factories in Mississippi and one in South Carolina. There was talk of starting one in Ceylon.

"Ceylon?" said Flora. "How cheap is the labor?"

Arthur worked until late at night. He was on the road visiting all the factories, all the stores that bought their label, and he talked with salesmen in little towns in Nebraska and California. He was home as little as possible. The cook and the maid had their meals in the dining room, sitting in the gilt-edged chairs that Louisa had abandoned.

Arthur dealt with the unions. Frank had no patience with unions. He didn't shake the leaders' hands and he didn't ask after their children the way Arthur did. He invested in a shoe company that was said to have the patent on a soft last that would revolutionize the business by making shoes so comfortable that you could sleep in them. He sold a lot of his Gruenbaum stock to become an officer of that corporation. He would be damned if he'd spend the rest of his life in an office with Arthur.

The shoe business turned out to have flat feet; the soft-last patent created a flexible shoe that disintegrated on the third or fourth wearing. The sole fell off of Frank's own pair of brown leather bucks while he was crossing the street midtown, and he had to flap on one foot through the traffic. Flora lay in bed the night he asked her to pay the debts that were his share of this venture and stared at the ceiling. What if one day he lost everything?

At the Atlantic Beach Inwood Country Club around the pool, Flora had played backgammon with Shelley Lipper, who had made a fortune in Manhattan real estate. Last summer she had beaten him five times and won two thousand dollars. She knew how to play the dice, unfold her cards, but she also knew that sometimes luck turned and there was nothing to be done, no way to recoup the loss. Luck was like God; no amount of prayer satisfied it.

Hedy came home from school one afternoon to find a large woman in the living room. Frank's sister, her aunt Estelle, was paying Flora a visit. It wasn't the first time the two women had met in the afternoon. Estelle was a widow, and she had a job at a hotel in Florida. She was the Sunplaza's social director, but still it was hard to make ends meet. The job was seasonal. Estelle needed to have her teeth fixed, she needed crowns, gold crowns. She needed money. If she asked Frank, she got nothing or almost nothing. If she asked Flora, she got what she needed. Estelle wasn't a moocher, but family was family, she was explaining to Flora when Hedy walked in.

Estelle's upper arms were enormous, her bottom so wide it squeezed out the side of the chair, but her smile, crooked teeth and all, was big and took you in, holding you right next to the moon face above. Her eyes beneath the dark green eye shadow flashed and jumped and were kind. Hedy liked her immediately.

Estelle put her arms around Hedy and squeezed her tight. "What a beauty," she said to Flora. "What a doll." Flora smiled.

Estelle spoke with a nasal accent, and her *d*'s and her *t*'s were hard. "How come you don't speak like my father?" said Hedy.

Estelle shrugged. "He's royalty," she said. "Me, I'm just a girl making a living. Do you know how to rumba?" she asked Hedy, who didn't exactly.

Estelle put on a record in the living room. She grabbed Flora by the waist, and the two women gave Hedy a demonstration of the rumba. Then Estelle took Hedy and, leading her firmly across the carpet, showed her how to rumba. "I win every contest I enter," said Estelle.

"Good for you," said Flora.

"Why don't we see Estelle more often?" Hedy asked after she left.

Next Year in Jerusalem: 1946

The apartment was full of people. Hedy wore her Mary Janes and a yellow velvet dress with a lace collar that her mother had bought her just that day from a store on Madison Avenue. She watched her mother's friends drinking and talking, the women in bright blue silks and little black dresses with pearls and the men, lighting cigars, dropping ashes over the turquoise rug.

Frank quieted the room. Wes stood up and spoke. "It's up to you to help us," he said. "The British will stop us as long as they can. The Arabs will attack in the night. We must be prepared. Remember," he said, "if they throw you out of this country, you have no place to go."

Hedy walked over to each of the guests. She took the checks they offered and put them in her mother's silver candy dish that she carried around with her. If someone didn't have a check, she offered a pledge card. She only went to the men. The women were in the bedroom reapplying makeup, talking, refilling drinks.

"I hope this is the right thing to do," said Arthur as he wrote out the largest check of the evening. "I hope no one is going to die because I paid for it."

In the bedroom Hedy lay down on the coats. She fell asleep. She woke as a woman in a red silk dress rustled past the bed. The woman had not seen Hedy. She was going through pocketbooks, taking money and slipping it quickly into the top of her stockings. Hedy sat up and saw her with her skirt raised over her hips and a wad of money near the garter clip. The woman came over to the bed.

"I can't help it," she said. "It's an illness. My doctor says it's not my fault." Hedy nodded. "Don't tell," said the women. "I'm counting on you."

"You can count on me," said Hedy. "Why are you doing it?"

"Because I don't feel sad when I steal," the woman replied, planting a lipstick kiss on Hedy's cheek.

Hedy took her mother's diamond pin, the one in the shape of an arrow pointing in two directions, from her jewelry box. She put it under her own pillow. She had bad dreams. She took the pin to school. She gave it to her friend Sally. "It came from a Cracker Jack box," she told her.

Flora missed the pin. "My mother's pin," she told Hedy. "It would have been yours one day." She fired the new maid and collected insurance. She talked about it with Dr. Bergman.

"Sometimes," he said, "we lose things that are valuable to us because we remember other older losses."

"Yes," said Flora, who thought he must be talking about body parts again. "But," she said, "a lot of my guests have called to say they were missing money from their purses. Do you think they were all remembering old losses?"

Dr. Bergman said, "It was wise to fire the maid."

How the Acorn Fell Far from the Tree: 1947

Teddy left Choate before the Christmas vacation. It wasn't just the American history midterm. It was the ceramic vase he tossed at the house mother who wanted to inspect his jacket pockets for hidden cigarettes. Teddy had grown tall and broad, and the muscles in his arms flexed naturally. He was first baseman on the school team when he remembered to show up for practice. He had his father's high forehead and wide smile and teeth that overlapped endearingly above his bottom lip. He was eager, eager for his life to begin, and he didn't give a damn about the Choate school and their chapel and Harold Forsythe, who had called him "Jew boy" to his face once and had ended up with a broken nose in the infirmary, another reason why the headmaster didn't think Teddy was the sort to carry the Choate name out into the world.

"He's a good enough lad," said the headmaster to Arthur, who was sitting, his shoulders hunched, his palms sweating, on a big leather chair in the head's office, with its rows of Latin books, its Oriental rug, its pipe stand on the old scuffed desk, and the huge black-and-white lithograph of some saint bent over in pain as arrows pierced all parts of his naked body. "He's just a boy who hasn't found himself yet."

"What do you mean, 'found himself'?" said Arthur. "He coming into the business with me."

"Well, yes," said the headmaster, "but perhaps he needs a little time. I've found time very helpful with this kind of young man . . . time to catch his own identity," he added. "Have you read Erich Fromm?"

"No," said Arthur.

"You should, you really should," said the headmaster.

Arthur didn't say it, but he thought the head was a touch senile. What was this business about catching identity, as if it were a germ that you breathed in while on a public bus? "How can he go to college if you don't give him a diploma?" asked Arthur. Everyone's son was getting a college degree these days. It wasn't the same as when he and Harry joined the business.

"Hard for a boy not to have a mother," the headmaster said as he stood up to show Arthur out the door, in which had been carved low reliefs of St. Paul teaching the disciples. "Perhaps the army might be just the thing for him," he called out to Arthur before he closed his study door.

How could a man like that be running a school? Arthur wondered.

Teddy came home to Park Avenue. The cook baked him his favorite chocolate swirl cake. The maid picked up his underwear off the bathroom floor and remarked to Jesus that this one was no good. He stayed in his room reading magazines with pinups of Rita Hayworth and Betty Grable. He bounced a basketball against the wallpaper, leaving dirt stains and causing the doorman to ring the bell with complaints from downstairs. The maid reported the complaints to Arthur.

"Teddy could go see Dr. Bergman," said Flora.

Arthur loved his sister beyond anyone else in the world, but he didn't believe in this talking about yourself nonsense, and to pay for it besides. What kind of man would do that? he wondered. "He'll be all right," said Arthur. "He just needs to grow up."

The third week of his return, Teddy went into the kitchen and took a can of Campbell's tomato soup from the cabinet. He walked to the window and opened it. He aimed for a spot one hundred feet from the doorman, who was helping a lady with packages from Saks and Bonwit's out of a cab. The can sailed through the air and landed on the hood of a Buick parked on the street. The doorman fainted away as he thought he saw blood everywhere. He lay on the ground, his whistle lying limply by his side. The lady screamed and clutched her packages. The cabdriver jumped out of the cab and searched the windows.

"There," he yelled. "You son of a bitch!" And he pointed his finger at Teddy.

A nanny with a baby carriage had just emerged from the archway of the building, and her white skirt was covered with splashed tomato and the cover of the carriage was stained red and she howled into the sky in terror. Teddy stood at the open window and watched. It was funny. Not the kind of funny that makes you laugh, but the kind that twists your mouth in a thing that must be a smile. Teddy enjoyed the scene.

"You could take an accounting course," said Arthur, "and then in the fall come in the business. I need you. You can be in charge of the younger salesmen. You can help your uncle Frank."

Teddy took the accounting course. He had no gift for numbers that belonged between little lines. He found a young kitchen maid just over from Poland on the floor below and began kissing her in the stairwell.

In the fall Teddy started out in the business with a small office of his own. He could see his father's office down the hall with its ficus tree and its windows overlooking Seventh Avenue. He brought his uncle Frank coffee and followed him around as he went to the factory in Borough Park and the stores in the new mall in Scarsdale. Sitting in the company car, while the chauffeur drove up the Hutchinson Parkway, Frank told his nephew about the storeroom with the M-1's hidden there and he asked him to meet Wes that night. Frank had an appointment with a former army nurse who had promised to play with him till dawn, which he explained to Teddy as dental work that would lay him low and he explained to Flora was business out of town. The original thrill had gone from the encounter with Wes. Frank didn't like the way Wes used the occasion of their midnight meetings to ask for more and more money.

Frank was still interested in his own M-1, which he would take out of the hall closet and caress from time to time when everyone else in the apartment was deep in sleep. Several times Hedy uncovered the gun in the back of the closet in the golf bag. She didn't touch it. A secret, she thought, one that she shared with her father.

Teddy didn't stand in the street watching while Wes's men loaded the guns into the truck. He picked up boxes himself and jumped in and out of the truck. When everything was loaded, he looked at Wes and asked him if he could come along to their next stop. He was strong. He could help. At Choate they hadn't told him much about the struggle for a homeland for the Jewish people. He listened to Wes, who spoke of the promise that God had made in the Bible to Moses and of the destruction of the temple, the first and the second. He spoke of the ghosts of Europe who needed the land of refuge and he spoke of the justice that was wanting, that there would come a time when the Jewish people had a state of their own and would no longer be blown about the globe like the dust of the dead.

Teddy listened and he told Wes that he was a good swimmer. He didn't know how to shoot, but he had taken archery up at Choate and he was sure he could learn.

Three weeks later he left a letter on his father's desk. He was going to Palestine. He was going to fight the British and the Arabs, and he was doing this because he was needed, because it was right. "Shalom," he signed his letter.

"Shalom," said Arthur. For God's sake, his son was supposed to take his place in the business. "What is everything for?" he asked Flora. "What is the point if Teddy isn't here? What am I working for?"

Flora sat on her bed with her solitaire game spread out on the covers. She looked at her brother's twisted face, his eyes blinking at her over and over. "He'll come back," she said. "I'm sure he'll get tired of it over there. It's supposed to be full of mosquitoes. He hates bugs." That was true. Arthur felt better. "I give him three months," said Flora. "He's a playboy, not a soldier," she added.

"Please God," said Arthur, "don't let my boy die in the sand."

"He won't," said Flora. "I'm sure he won't."

It was shortly after midnight when the rafts were lowered into the water just outside the three-mile limit. The British boats were patrolling the shores and their lights swung back and forth over the darkened ocean, picking up the occasional whitecap, the high swells of the waves, and sometimes in their glare a seagull, dipping its wings, opening its beak to the stars. The moon made its own path on the water.

The boat was silent. The motor was cut. The men stripped to their shorts and waited in the cool air. Then one by one they plunged, splashed as silently as possible, and hung on to the rafts loaded with boxes and began to swim for the shore that they couldn't see, with the tide helping them with a gentle shove but the darkness hiding their faces one from the other.

The British boat came back and the lights covered the water, the men ducked under, and the raft itself, dark and small, looked only like a piece of floating wood, something dropped off a passing boat, nothing for concern. The British sailors were joking to each other, their voices carried long distances over the water, and one was talking about a woman, his voice whining as he complained into the night.

Teddy pushed and kicked and took deep breaths. If they were caught, they would be imprisoned. If they were caught, the guns would not arrive. If they were caught, the members of the Irgun, waiting hidden in the brush by the sand just above the cove, would not be able to protect, to achieve, to take what was theirs. It made Teddy's mouth dry to think of it. It made the muscles in his legs tense to think of it. He had a cramp. The raft stopped its forward glide as he went under the water and massaged his calf. He swallowed some ocean water, salt on his lips and tongue. Quietly the men pushed the rafts through the warm waters. Teddy brushed a clump of red algae out of his way and stared at the black humping shoreline that now pushed up against the dark blue of the sky. Moving forward under the moon and riding over the crest of the sloping waves by the time the British boat had made its last pass, the rafts landed with small scraping sounds on the pebbles of the beach. Lying breathless in the dark, shivering now from the wind that was blowing down from the hills of the Galilee, watching the shadows of men move back and forth across the beach, Teddy felt the joy of knowing exactly what he was doing.

He sent Hedy a postcard. On the front of the postcard was a photograph of a camel and a bedouin, his face hidden behind his headdress and his long robes blowing in the desert wind. "This is the Negev," said the postcard. "I am here with my friends. Shalom, Teddy," and under the signature it said, "Ari," and then in parentheses in a big scrawl, a schoolboy who had never learned to get his letters all the same size, it said, "In Hebrew I am called Ari. It is the Hebrew word for lion. From now on call me Ari Gruenbaum." Teddy was catching identity.

Hedy put the postcard in a box with her charm bracelet and her locket and the letter her bunk counselor had written her after camp was over.

Hedy Gets a Present from Bessie: 1947

Flora and Mildred had lunch with Bessie. Flora didn't like the way Bessie hoarded things. She didn't like the way Bessie added up the check twice if they had lunch in a restaurant, figuring out exactly how much everyone owed and it always turned out she owed a little less.

Bessie had a new passion, collecting weather vanes. Flora had not known that the iron roosters, the horses' heads, the ducks with arrows issuing from their beaks that sat on top of old barns had a name and a value and were in fact collector's items, antiques that people admired, treasured, and even went to museums to see. "Oh," said Flora when Bessie explained to her that her newest acquisition was a priceless treasure from a barn in Utah put up by one of the first Mormon families to settle in Salt Lake. "What do you do with them?" she asked.

"Keep them," said Bessie. "Like gold in the bank, like rare stamps."

The busboy poured water for the women, and Bessie complained about the service at the restaurant. Flora turned her attention to her Caesar salad.

"Don't you see," said Bessie, "it's folk art, valuable folk art." She had learned about this from an antique dealer outside the town in Vermont that she visited for a week or so each spring. Now weather vanes were sitting on her coffee tables, resting on bookcases, two on the dining table and three in each of the bathrooms.

After lunch Flora and Mildred walked up Madison Avenue, stopping every now and then to price a lamp or a dress that had enticed them from the window. "Dr. Bergman thinks this weather vane thing is a problem she has with sexual identity," said Flora.

Mildred said to Flora, "When are you going to finish with Dr. Bergman?"

"When I'm happy," said Flora.

The next day a box arrived, delivered by Bessie's chauffeur for Hedy. In it were two Chanel suits that Bessie no longer wore, and under the Chanel suits were layers of sanitary napkins. A note was included. "I bought these napkins at Klein's and no longer need them, thought you could use them." Hedy couldn't, not yet; she was only ten years old, but it was thoughtful. Hedy wrote Bessie a thank-you note on stationery with a picture of a purple puppy chewing a rag doll.

Sharie Lee Goes Traveling: 1947

Quebec Bob went to Moscow to give a concert and he took Sharie Lee with him. The trip had been arranged by friends of friends who had connections in the Party. Quebec Bob was well known in the Soviet Union. His song "Bodies Swinging in the Night Wind" was playing over and over on the radio, not in the South, of course. The white woman who accompanied him everywhere was photographed by the *Paris Herald Tribune* when they stayed at the Plaza Athénée en route. The photograph was reprinted in the *Daily News*, a titillation, a proof that commies miscegenated and that Sharie Lee, whose own reputation had faded, who knew who she was, had crossed all boundaries.

"In public," said Mildred to Arthur. "I don't believe it."

Arthur sighed. Flora cut out the clipping and pasted it in the album with pictures of Hedy's kindergarten class and Hedy at camp.

In the hotel room, whose window looked out on chimneys and rooftops and arched windows and in the distance the bells from the tower on the Île de la Cité rang out over the heads of the American students who flocked like pigeons in their heavy sweaters, in their new berets, to the cafes on the edge of the Seine, Sharie Lee lay on the huge soft quilt and invited Quebec Bob to join her. She wanted to take off his suit, his red silk tie, and his white shirt. Quebec Bob was too excited.

"The goddamned Soviet Union," he said. "We're going to see it, day after tomorrow, the revolution at work, the dream. Justice, equality, a place where it doesn't matter if a man's grandfather was a slave or a serf." His eyes shone.

Sharie Lee wasn't so sure. "My brother Meyer says that the Hitler-Stalin pact was a devil's contract. Meyer says that Hitler and Stalin are the same person," she said.

"Don't listen to Meyer," he said.

"But maybe it's true," she said.

"Someone is always trying to tell you it won't work, it can't get better, Cain and Abel ever after. Someone is whispering bad things so they won't have to look at themselves in the mirror. Don't listen to Meyer, listen to me."

Quebec Bob sat on the edge of the bed and he sang the "International" and his deep voice rose and fell and Sharie thought, Maybe, maybe, and she was tired and fell asleep, aided by two Scotches and a couple of Seconals.

In Russia, bundled in her new fur coat that Quebec Bob had bought her for the trip, she asked the tour guide to take them to Grodno, where her father had come from once upon a time, to the village where his father had prayed each morning with the prayer shawl over his shoulder and each evening as dusk settled over the one main street and the peasants were bringing their cows in from the fields.

"No such place," said the Intourist guide.

"Yes," said Sharie, "my father told me, a big Jewish community there."

"No Jews there," said the tour guide, "no Jews in Grodno."

Sharie had Quebec Bob ask his connection in the Kremlin, who took them to dinner at a hotel and served them champagne and caviar. "There were very few Jews in the countryside of Russia," said the man in perfect English, accented like an Oxford don. "The Jews all left for America before the turn of the century."

"Are you sure?" said Sharie.

Quebec Bob cast her a look. "There are more important things to talk about here," he said. "What about hydraulic dams?" The man from the Kremlin was an expert on hydraulic dams.

Sharie Lee wanted to see where the Nazis had killed the Jews in trenches, she heard, in forests. "The Nazis murdered many Soviet citizens," said the guide. "Maybe some Jews were among them. In Russia we don't separate our people."

"Of course not," said Sharie Lee, who didn't want anyone to think she was the sort who would, who could think that of her; after all, she was traveling with a Negro. "Please," she said to Quebec Bob, who arranged it three days before the concert.

They went by train, in a first-class compartment, through the rows of cypress, the snow-covered hills, the stretches of empty Russia with high firs climbing up from the railroad bed as far as the eye could see. Then a black limousine, a government car, drove them out into the country to the town that her father had come from.

When they got there and the car stopped in the middle of the plaza, all the children came running. The car, of course, was an event, but the large Negro man was an even bigger one. He was led by the guide into the church, which had been stripped of its crucifix and had a portrait of Stalin above the baptismal font and was obviously used now for town meetings. A few old men stopped playing cards on tables set up in the former nave and stared at their visitor.

The guide asked Quebec Bob to sing to the people, who quickly gathered there, and he did, he sang "Bodies Swinging" and for the children he sang "The Hokey Pokey" and "Pickin' up Paw Paws in the Paw Paw Patch." Finally he sang "The Internationale," and meanwhile Sharie walked around. Where is the synagogue, where is the shul, where did the Jews live? she had the guide ask everyone. They shook their heads; no Jews, no Jews, never any Jews.

Before the concert Quebec Bob was asked to give the authorities a list of the songs he was going to sing. They wished to be familiar with them. He told them "Swing Low, Sweet Chariot," two African freedom songs in Swahili, the song of the French Resistance, and a Jewish song. A man in a gray suit came to the hotel room in late afternoon before the concert.

"No need," he said, "to sing a Jewish song; there will be no one in the audience who understands Yiddish. We do not consider Yiddish a language here."

It was cold in the concert hall, and the audience kept their coats over their shoulders and their gloves on. The piano was out of tune and Quebec Bob insisted on making everyone wait until the tuner had been called and fixed it as best as he could. Sharie Lee sat in a box on the side of the auditorium. There were sounds in her throat, too, but she held them back. He sang his songs from the Congo and a few from Ghana and he sang his spirituals and he sang, to a standing ovation, "Bodies Swinging," and then he announced that he was going to sing an old antiimperialist song and he began, "*Gut morg'n dir ribbono shel olom, Ich Levi Yitzhok ben Soroh mi Berdichev bin tzu dir gekoomen mit a din Torah far dein folk Yisroel.* And I, Levi Yitzhak, son of Sarah of Berditchev, say, From my stand I will not waver and from my place I shall not move until there be an end to all this." And from her seat in the side of the auditorium, Sharie Lee rose and opened her mouth and sang as if this were the last song she were ever going to sing, and here and there in the large hall others joined in and soon many joined and it seemed as if at least half the audience had known the words, had always known the words, and the crystal chandeliers swung on their gold chains and the Negro in black tie and tails raised his arms to the heavens, "*Far dein folk Yisroel . . .*" and a woman began to weep and even the man from the Kremlin had to blow his nose as he and several others rushed onstage to announce to the audience that the concert was now over.

After returning to the United States, Quebec Bob found his popularity in sharp decline. Sharie Lee too was not called for club dates. Record companies weren't interested. Flora sent Sharie a check to meet the rent. Quebec Bob took his children on a trip out west. He sent Sharie a postcard of the Grand Canyon.

How Hedy Learned to Eat Quickly: 1947

Flora was having dinner with Frank and Hedy. She looked tired and was wearing her blue robe, which meant she was going to bed right after the meal. She said to Frank, "Let's go away together, just you and me. Maybe we could go to Venice, like on our honeymoon."

Frank blinked. "What is it you want now?" he asked.

Flora flushed red. "I just thought we ought to try to be kinder with each other," she said.

"I am kind," said Frank. "If you would stop nagging me all the time, everything would be all right."

"But you're not satisfied," said Flora.

"Yes, I am," said Frank. "I am completely satisfied. . . . Your mother," he said to Hedy, "can't leave a man alone."

"That's not true," said Flora. "You have no capacity for normal conversation."

"Oh, God," said Frank, who felt a familiar lump in his chest, blocking his airways. "I'm talking to you now, I am talking to you, what more do you want?"

"Stop shouting," said Flora. "Why can't you ever talk to me without shouting?" She had tears in her eyes. Her mascara began to run down her checks. "Your sister called again. She wants us to pay for her cruise to Haiti," she said in a voice that seemed perfectly controlled.

"You're bringing my sister up, to use her against me," said Frank.

"You never want to see her. You avoid her," Flora shouted.

"You and your fancy family. You want to see her, I suppose."

"She's your sister," said Flora, lifting up her glasses and wiping her eyes with her napkin.

"Stop that goddamned crying," said Frank.

"If you could talk to me like a real man would, a real man, then I wouldn't cry," said Flora.

Frank looked at the bowl of tomato soup that the maid had set before him. He stared at the pieces of tomato and toasted crouton. He went to the window and opened it. "Hot in here," he said.

"No, it's not," said Flora. "I'm fine. Aren't you fine?" she said to Hedy.

Hedy was sitting at the table, steadily stirring her soup. She'd heard all this before. It was just noise, she told herself. Keep your head down, she told herself. But her father turned to her.

"Your mother started it, didn't she? Your mother started the fight. I want an answer." He put his hand under Hedy's chin and pulled her face around to look directly at him. "Answer me," he said, his voice cold and empty.

Hedy said, "I don't know who started it, I wasn't listening."

"Don't bring in Hedy, she knows that you started it, ruining a good dinner the way you do all the time," said Flora, almost whispering. She added, "You were the one who yelled. I never yell. I just asked if you wanted to go to Venice."

Frank curled his hands into fists and banged them on the table. The water shook in the glass and the vase of flowers rocked on its base. "You know that's a rotten question. I can't just leave your stinking business whenever I feel like it." He turned to Hedy. "Your mother started this fight."

Hedy said nothing. Flora got up from the table, just as the maid asked if she should bring in the rest of dinner.

"Yes," said Frank. "I'm not going to starve because this broad can't be civil."

Flora wept, great sobs coming from her small chest. "I'm going to bed," she said, and she went, closing the bedroom door.

"I'm going for a walk," said Frank. "I'll get supper at the club." He got up from the table.

Hedy didn't feel like eating, either, but the cook had worked all afternoon on a stuffed veal roast and the maid was bringing in the platter. Hedy sat at the table, a long blond art deco table with a bowl of red flowers in the middle, and ate her dinner as quickly as she could.

Hedy Does the Mexican Hat Dance: 1948

When Hedy was twelve years old her mother sent her to Viola Wolf's dancing class. There the boys wore white gloves and the girls wore dresses with velvet ribbons that clutched their waists and hung down their backs. Hedy's aunt Estelle was a rumba queen. She won prizes at dance contests in the Catskills. She won a trophy at a hotel in Miami Beach. She had not learned to rumba at Viola Wolf's. She was self-taught. Hedy wanted to teach herself how to dance, too, but her mother had insisted that Viola Wolf was as important as the orthodontist, as important as school.

Viola Wolf was a tall lady with lavender-blue hair, and she always wore a ball gown and three strands of pearls. She had silver slippers with sequins on them, and the room in which she taught the children had mirrors on all four walls and rows of gilt chairs with velvet cushions.

In this room, said Viola Wolf to her charges, are the finest children in New York. Your parents have sent you here to learn how to dance and how to be gracious to each other, and some of you, the lucky ones, will find as we change partners that one of the nice persons of the opposite sex in this very class will be your husband or wife.

With that she signaled the pianist, and he, dreaming perhaps of a solo debut on Carnegie's stage, a repertoire of Mahler and Stravinsky, leaned his pale hands over the keys and began the Mexican hat dance.

"Take your partners," Viola Wolf commanded, and her voice was deep as a cavern, windy as the nights in the Sinai, and clouded with whiskey and tobacco, and no one, not the most rebellious of little boys, the ones who smoked in the cloakroom, not the ones who placed sticks of firecrackers on the steps as the girls arrived with their nannies or maids, dared to disobey.

Some of these children came from families who had been in America not one generation, not two generations, but the best of them, the ones whose descendants had been German, came from five generations of American citizens, and they had amazing names, names that ricocheted down on Wall Street, names that caused bankers to blink and nod, names that were chiseled in hospital lobbies and engraved on seat backs in synagogues along Park Avenue and Fifth Avenue and inscribed on golden trophies that proclaimed the winners of tennis tournaments and golf tournaments representing the founding members of the fine Jewish clubs in the city, on Weaver Street in Scarsdale, in Bedford and Greenwich, Connecticut.

When Viola Wolf lifted from her neck a long gold chain from which a whistle hung and, puffing her cheeks, which were painted pink up over the earlobes, blew that whistle with the same energy as an army trumpeter calls his men to charge, the little boys, who dropped their partners like they were hand grenades with the pins pulled and rushed to the side of the wall to await her next command, were named Lehman and Loeb and Warburg and Schiff or they were the newest buds on the branches of the women who had once carried these illustrious names. Then there were others, ordinary names, like Schwartz and Levy and Roth and Blotstein and Wineburg. These were the names of the newly arrived, mostly Russian or Polish, mostly garment business, or jewelry business or perhaps real estate. These were the aspirants, the social climbers, the almost there, the if-they-marry-right theres. Not that the children thought about this: the concerns of the young people who were learning how to do the box step, how to lead and how to follow and how to speak to the opposite sex, what is your name, what school do you go to, what is your favorite sport, what camp do you go to, what baseball team do you like, the gathering of the statistics, the girls doing the talking as they looked down for the most part on the heads of the boys shining with Vaseline, parts neatly in place and palms with sweat beneath the white gloves, were all about being liked. Sometimes there were more girls than boys, and then when the boys made their choices the leftover girls stood on the side, not wanting to sit on the chairs and crush their dresses, not wanting to be noticed but watching their reflection in the mirror four times over as they stood with frozen smiles. Caryatids supporting the temple of maidenhood, fearful that this moment was an omen, a prelude to a comedy of rejection, of failure in the only marketplace that counted. Sometimes a boy would ask a girl to dance, and she, her eye on someone else, someone a few inches taller, the captain of the Horace Mann sixth-grade soccer team, the one who had offered her a cigarette when his chauffeur left him off in front of Viola Wolf's that afternoon, would say no and turn away. The boy, his hand extended, ready to begin to form with his uncertain feet the exact box in which he was to move from one end of the floor to the other, returned to the sidelines to look over the crowd. Who was left? Who would have him? Could he go to the bathroom and wait out this dance?

Viola Wolf knew all about bathrooms, and she had an assistant, a pale thin lady who always wore the same pink dress and dyed her hair pink to match, who would go through the bathrooms, rounding up the boys and girls, one flush and you were chased out. She would open the door to the boys' bathroom and call in, "I'm giving you thirty seconds and then I'm coming in. Out on the floor; everyone out on the floor." All the boys and girls at the six o'clock Thursday class at Viola Wolf's knew there was no escape.

At Christmastime there was a big dance. There were Christmas decorations on the mirrors, and the girls were expected to wear particularly fine dresses. Hedy and her mother had picked out a yellow strapless dress that came down to the floor, and Hedy wore her hair up in a barrette that had pearls across the top. Hedy wore heels that made her wobble and she worried how she could ever do the Mexican hat dance, how she could conga without slipping. Hedy worried that the lipstick she wore would smudge on her teeth the way it did on her mother's. She worried that she might be one of the leftover girls.

She had an escort for the evening. A boy whose name had been given to her mother by the secretary at Viola Wolf's arrived at her door at five-thirty to take her to the dance. His nanny came, too. He brought Hedy a flower with a pin and she was supposed to put the flower on her dress. It was a perfect orchid, yellow and white. His mother had called the day before to find out what she was wearing. In the ladies' room at Viola Wolf's, Hedy put the flower on her waist, and it was hard through the folds of the dress to get the pin to stick. Under her dress she was wearing a corset that held her stomach in tight, and her stockings, shiny and irritating, were attached by garters to the corset. There was silence in the ladies' room, as if the girls were preparing for war, not a dance, as if something terrible had happened already.

Hedy went out onto the floor, and her escort asked her for the first dance, as he was obligated to do, and as she started to move, to fox-trot across the floor, one-two-three-four, one-two-three-four, her heels shaking and her ankles turning inward with each step, she felt the pin from her flower pierce her skin sharply. She had put it too far in, through the corset, through the dress, and when she moved forward and backward, it wounded her. When the boy let her go at the sound of the whistle and the pianist was playing "O Little Town of Bethlehem" while the boys and girls caught their breath each on their own side of the room, Hedy caught sight of herself in the mirror and there she saw a splotch of blood at her waist, staining her yellow satin dress, forming a kind of red flower of its own, underneath her crushed corsage, a spot that was growing as she watched.

Hedy ran to the ladies' room and pulled out the pin, but the stain was still there. She tried to wipe it out with water, but it wouldn't fade. There was blood on her dress and Hedy began to weep. She wept not from shame or sorrow. She wept in anger. It wasn't fair that she should be pinned to herself, wavering on her new shoes, trying to allure, to bring about the exact thing she did not want. What she wanted was to run across the basketball court and dunk the ball through the hoop. What she wanted was to take the barrette out of her hair and let her black curls rise upward and outward like a shield to protect her brain, to disguise its thoughts. What she thought of in the ladies' room was the gun her father had hidden in the back of the closet. A secret between them. It was their secret from her mother and the rest of the world. When she was frightened she thought of the gun and felt reassured. Her father had a gun after all. The stab of the corsage, the sight of the blood on her dress, had made her tremble, so she ran to the coatroom and grabbed her coat, wrapped it tightly around her, and was waiting just like that on the front steps in the December cold when the boy's nanny showed up several hours later with a waiting taxi. Hedy's hands were locked one into the other, her velvet coat was pulled up over her neck and mouth, and she said nothing all the way home, not even a polite "Good night" and "Thank you."

Caleb Herzberg Returns Home: 1948 and On

When the state of Israel was founded, Caleb was in the yeshiva studying the Book of Kings. Caleb felt as if a hand had picked him up and thrown him in the air. Triumph and glory, he felt. When in the following weeks the Arabs attacked and the small band of Jews fought back, he held his breath as he leaned toward his radio.

"I must go," he said to his father, and Eli nodded. His son Caleb had a mission of his own, and Eli knew it. It was just the way it should be; the son would do things the father could not, and in that way, slowly but surely, the world would move forward toward the time when the shekinah would no longer lie in splinters across the globe and God would be whole and the vessels of the earth would be whole and the purpose would be revealed. Some of the rabbis said to wait for the Messiah, that the state was an unholy imitation, a false Messiah that would break the heart of the Jewish people. But Eli didn't believe that. He told his children that if their hearts were to be broken, why not in the Promised Land?

So Caleb and some friends went on a boat along with a shipment of arms, and in Italy they loaded some refugees who had been living in tents along the beach, and when they landed in Haifa, Caleb used his strong arms to help the dockworkers unload the guns and he took one of the guns for himself as he made his way up the road to Jerusalem where the fighting was taking place. He kept his yarmulke on his head. He kept his young beard curled and growing. He kept his black jacket on even when he crawled behind the tanks and shot at the enemy across the hill. He kept his black shoes polished as best he could. He wore his white shirt that his mother had washed for him daily when he was in Brooklyn, a Brooklyn that soon seemed a dream, an imaginary land in which Jews had pretended to exist while waiting for the return, a Brooklyn that seemed like an appendix, unnecessary and capable of causing infection.

Caleb, lying in the field along the road to Jerusalem with the other soldiers, saw his mother's face in the shape of the clouds overhead, but after a while the clouds became just clouds and he was slapped on the back and congratulated for the mortar attack on an Arab position by a boy from Krakow who had spent the last years of the Third Reich hiding in a pig trough in the farm of a local peasant. Caleb was not seduced by all the talk of the boys around him of justice in a new society and a government of equals. Equality for women was an idea that made him spit in the dust. Democracy cut no ice with Caleb, who believed that someone needed the authority to punish the wicked. He was not fighting for the communists and the socialists who shared their rations with him. He was fighting to restore the days of the temple when the holiest of holies waited for the annual sacrifices of the priest. He was always fighting for God, not against him.

When the green line was drawn and the fighting was over, he did as he had promised his father he would do. He went to a yeshiva in Safed and continued his studies, but he was still an indifferent student whose mind wandered to the streets outside and whose hands tapped the desk top and who opened and closed books with undue haste. He wanted to live in Judea and claim the land for his people, but the government did not encourage him. Partition was a fact. Compromisers and cowards, these too were Jews, or so he wrote his father.

He married and he had children of his own and he worked as a stonemason, like his father-in-law, repairing and restoring the buildings of the city. He would rub his hands over the bullet holes in the stone walls, bullets from the British and the Arabs. In the morning when he woke as his young wife was preparing coffee and the baby was mewing in his crib, he would go to the window and look out over the hills and watch the cypress trees take shape out of the mist and clouds. He would run his hands across the sill and, smelling the lemon tree in the courtyard and the winds that blew off the distant lake carrying the smell of pine and cedar, watching the rocks turn pink with the rising sun, he would hit his head against the wall, its loveliness so overcame him. In the evenings he would smell the cooking oils and the leavings of the goats that were kept in a pen down the street. In the night he would watch the stars come up in the sky and the moon hang over the old synagogue where the mosaics showed Romans marching under an arch, and his heart would beat with a joy that he had come to this place where everything began, and he knew he would serve it with his entire soul.

Caleb's eyes were clear as the pools of rainwater that gathered in the rocks about the Red Sea, and other young men believed him. "It was not a portion of the land of Israel that had been promised, but all of the land of Israel. Just as in the time of Moses, the land was occupied by the enemy and the soldiers of Israel stormed down from the hills and seized what belonged to them, took the enemy captive, and appropriated their wells and orchards, so," said Caleb, "the time will come again when the Jews will have a kingdom worthy of the Messiah."

Caleb wrote to his father in Brooklyn: "Here G-d is in every stone. Here we are close to Sinai, where the tablets were given to us. My children will eat the fruits of the land of Israel, no longer 'Next year,' no longer will they kill us like chickens in the barnyard. Now if we die, they die, if one of us is killed, we will kill ten of them. Our time is now."

Eli read his son's letter and he walked along Avenue P toward his shul with his face shining. It is true that the Lord is with us every day, he said to himself. Nevertheless some days are better than others.

When Caleb had his second son, Eli and his wife flew to Israel, and they brought with them a toaster oven and a hair dryer and a television set because appliances were cheaper and better in the diaspora. When the plane landed and Eli felt the hot wind of the desert as it blew through the palm trees that lined the airport exit, he grasped his wife by the shoulder until his knuckles were white and she pulled his fingers off. "I wasn't sure," he said, "it was real. Maybe only words in a book, I thought. Forgive me for doubting," he mumbled as the taxi headed through the crowds. "Holy one, blessed be He."

Hedy Learns That Golf Is Not a Jewish Game: 1949

Hedy's old friends abandoned her. They joined a group of girls who all wore cashmere sweaters and giggled when the boys snapped the bra straps that were clearly visible in the back. Hedy played basketball as if winning would bring the Messiah. Hedy tried to comb her hair like the other girls, but it kept rushing unruly, curly, and thick out of all containers. Hedy was not ready for the boys who wanted to play post office in the back of the school bus. She wanted to discuss the baseball scores. She daydreamed in class. She stopped doing work. She seemed frozen in some iceberg of her own making. She had no partner for lunch. She forgot to tie her shoelaces. Her breasts grew. Her hips came and she refused to look in the mirror. At night she had trouble sleeping and she would sit by the window and look at the slice of sky that hung above Park Avenue. She wanted to see a falling star. But she never did. In the morning her rash was worse. It would cover her chin, and now she was ashamed and kept her head down.

Flora was worried about her. Dr. Bergman suggested a change of schools. This new school was only for girls and it had few Jewish children in it and most of those had names of mansions or Wall Street firms attached to them, but nevertheless Hedy was accepted. Flora told Arthur that this was a step up, a new beginning for the Gruenbaum family. Frank didn't care. He was not interested in conversations about education.

In this new school Hedy learned that her mother looked peculiar, peculiar in her fur coat and her big gold earrings and her bracelets that jangled when she walked, peculiar in her high Cuban heels with the thin straps over the ankle, and peculiar in her mascara and red nails and red mouth and hair now dyed a ripe strawberry blond and combed and sprayed to look like a bonnet. The other mothers wore sensible shoes and suits in tweeds and dark plaids. The other mothers all had volunteer jobs with Planned Parenthood or the Thanksgiving Day dinners of the Trinity Church or the Playschool program of New York, which brought toys to poor children on Christmas. They worked for the Fresh Air Fund and they held dinners to support the ballet and the opera. They had all gone to Bryn Mawr or Vassar or Smith, and they liked to bicycle and garden and they played tennis. Some of them rode horses. Hedy loved horses, but her mother had forbidden her to ride at camp.

"Beasts," said her mother, "with terrible teeth and huge hooves that trample: riding is for people who don't mind jouncing their brains around, or people like my uncle Max," she said with a grin, "who had no brains at all. Riding is for people who want to trample others."

These mothers at her new school had riding outfits with jodhpurs and black boots, and her new best friend, Bonnie, showed Hedy her mother's box with red and blue ribbons won at horse shows. Hedy knew that these were mothers who had very good values. They were on committees for dances with names like the Golden Ball and the Junior Galaxies, and they held dinners before the dances for the girls and their dates. Hedy was not invited to those events, but she didn't mind. She had no date to take her there, anyway.

Hedy soon realized that all her new friends' mothers had read Toynbee and Darwin and they had old leather-bound copies of Tolstoy in the library. Flora read all the time. She read mysteries and best-sellers and *The New Yorker* and she told Hedy the stories of everything she read, but it wasn't the same as the leather books in her new friends' houses. It wasn't the same at all. Flora did the crossword puzzles or played cards— the other mothers didn't, not canasta, anyway, not for money, not two or three times a week. In her new friends' apartments there were drawings of eighteenth-century women and paintings of Revolutionary War figures, and one friend had a Henry Moore statue in the hall just in front of the elevator. On the Gruenbaum walls there were silk screens from China that the decorator had purchased. Everything in the Gruenbaum living room matched the turquoise and gold of the Chinese screens. In her new friends' home everything was faded brown or yellow and the chairs were comfortable and the rugs had bald spots. If you knew how to ride, Hedy realized, you decorated your house so that a horse would feel comfortable in it. Hedy understood that you needed to have a lot of money, you needed to have a lot of money for a very long time, to have good values. Hedy would have preferred her mother to pick her up a few blocks away from the school building on those occasions when she came to school.

Once, when Hedy sprained her wrist playing touch football in the park, she didn't go to the school nurse. She didn't want them to call her mother. Hedy was the team quarterback. She had an arm that could cover the entire field. She ran as though her life depended on it, and she dodged the oncoming team as if she were carrying the Holy Ark through the lines of the Russian army. She ran until she felt the cold October air pulling at her lungs as they squeezed together and a sharp pain cut across her chest. The pain felt good, a sign of effort, of vitality, proof she hadn't collapsed yet. Her school uniform was grass-stained and dirt-smeared and her socks hung loose at her ankles and she smelled of sweat. She was happy.

At the school assembly each morning, the headmistress, a Scottish lady with a fine-boned face clear of makeup, clear of pretension, interested only in the moral character of her charges, would lead the Lord's Prayer, Hedy said the words, but she didn't believe them. At Christmastime she kept her mouth closed when they sang carols. She didn't believe them, either. Were the good values of the women who were the mothers of her new friends connected with the words of the Lord's Prayer and the words of the Christmas carols? This was a question Hedy was not prepared to answer, so in the meantime, before she was clear on the matter, she decided to close her mouth but keep her eyes open. She had acne: ordinary acne. Her peculiar rash subsided.

Frank Meets Englewood's Beauty Queen: 1950

Frank met Maria at a wedding. Maria Weil and her husband, Hugo, were seated at the same table because Hugo and his wife were the next-door neighbors of the groom's parents and Flora and the bride's mother's were in the same Thursday-afternoon canasta game. Maria wore a single rose attached to her blond ringlets by a bow of diamond chips. She was wearing a white dress that hissed and rustled with each turn of her body. She smelled of bath oil and talcum powder. She spoke with a flat heartland twang. Also she lisped her *s*'s and slurred her *t*'s. Sometimes she searched for the right word and she would look helplessly around the table till someone supplied it for her. She admired everything, the flower arrangement in the middle of the table, the lace tablecloth, the fruit cocktail, the saxophone player in the band, and Frank's jacket, not Gruenbaum at all, but Brooks. She was from Missouri, she told everyone. The woods outside Columbia where she had spent her childhood summers, fishing in the inlets of the river with her four brothers, were full of wildflowers, but none as beautiful as those in the table centerpiece. She leaned forward to talk to the men, but her voice was shy and she kept her eyes slightly averted. Her round breasts, just lightly tanned and accented with a gold chain that slid down the center just out of sight, moved forward, letting off a warmth, a shine, a prediction of nipples that rose on speckled pads and followed a man's hand like a dog watching a biscuit held between the thumb and the forefinger. "Whore," said a woman in the ladies' room to Flora, who nodded agreement and held on to the edge of the porcelain sink as if it were trying to escape her grasp.

Maria had grown up in a small town where her father had owned a used-car lot. The lot was their backyard. In it old Fords, trucks and sedans, rusted in the rains that came in the fall and sank in the snows of winter. Occasionally customers would come and poke at the wheels or pinch the worn upholstery. Sometimes a car would leave, only to be brought back some days later. Her father sat on the couch collecting beer bottles under his feet while Maria's mother rushed off to work at the pocketbook factory down the highway. She came back wiping the matted strands of hair off her face and with her eyes glazed and unfocused. The boys drove the cars back and forth in the dirt road behind the house. Once in a while they hit a tree.

Maria slept on a cot in the kitchen. She wouldn't share a room with the boys. When she wanted something she let them take a look. If she wanted something badly she let them touch. There was a calendar over the stove that had a picture of Christ raising Lazurus. Maria was not interested in Christ. She wanted to be a cheerleader in high school with red pom-poms on her shoes. She was. Her blond curls bounced up and down as she shouted into the sky, "Rah, rah, rah." She grew tall and large-boned and her eyes were deep blue. In her junior year of high school she was chosen homecoming queen. She wanted to be a model. She was too big-boned, too heavy, too broad in the hips. She got a job in the bosses's lunchroom at her mother's pocketbook factory. She was the salad girl. She sat on a high stool and smiled and smiled.

Hugo was learning the family business. He was visiting the Columbia plant. He looked into her eyes and saw himself, no longer a skinny shy boy with a slight astigma and the remains of acne but a real American with big muscles cooking hamburgers on a barbecue and whistling through his teeth. He saw himself, the only son of immigrants from Alsace, throwing a baseball across home plate, hitting it out of sight, like Hank Greenberg. From Maria's body came the faint odor of perfume and sweat, of corn and milk and rice pudding. As he held his tray up to her and she scooped out the greens with little bits of carrot shreds onto his plate he lost his heart.

His parents were desperate. They wanted him back in New York. He wouldn't come without her. In the end they gave in. He was their only son. They begged her to convert. She converted. She told the rabbi with tears in her eyes that she was happy that God had selected her to join the chosen people. She had a gold bracelet with a heart on it that said, "From Hugo, your darling." He was a darling. One brother became the foreman of the factory. Two others went out on the road as salesmen, and the third, who had no gift for anything but gambling, received a check from Maria whenever the spot he was in got tight. Her parents received as a present, perhaps for not going to the wedding, enough money to go down to Florida and buy a trailor in which they hung up pictures of the grandchildren who never did get down to visit.

Maria admitted to Frank that the Weil son was not perhaps as handsome as she might have hoped. He was very tall, with an adam's apple of considerable dimensions and a chin that seemed to be trying to tuck itself back out of sight. He had lost most of his hair, and he combed the remains over the top and it lay there like wisps of wheat that had blown out of the stack. He had thin arms and spindly legs. His eyes were always watery from an allergy to trees, plants, dust, and chocolate, and hairs grew from nostrils like reeds along the riverbanks. She shuddered when she told Frank about the hairs and he felt his own face, smooth from a careful shave, his clipped firm features and his slicked-down hair all in place. In the evening she would sit naked at the dressing table and cream her neck and throat and Hugo would lie in bed watching the curve of her back and the arch of her neck as she tossed her blond curls forward over her face. She would feel his eyes on her and she would shift on the small pink-tufted seat so that he would see the line between her buttocks move in the moonlight that filtered through the maple outside their bedroom window, but her flesh had bumps, her teeth were clenched tight, and a taste of the evening's dinner would rise in her throat. She imagined herself chained to her dressing table. Hugo adored Maria. Maria had two children and with each child her husband grew more satisfied, as if he were the luckiest of men in the best of all possible worlds. He bought a house on a lake in the Poconos. He bought a motorboat and had the salesman show him how to water-ski. From early spring into late fall, when the family arrived for the weekend in the chauffeur-driven car he would immediately run down to his dock and jump in his boat and with one of the neighbors' boys running the motor he would put on his skis and glide across the lake, bending his knees, lurching over the wake, rushing by the maples and the oaks whose green leaves trembled in the boat's vibrations. "Yeah," he would scream like an American cowboy. "Like Christ across the water," he said to his wife, who smiled at him. He wanted Maria to learn to water-ski, but she wouldn't. In the winter-time he played with the toy train set he had built in the library. He made it go through tunnels and up hills. At dinner he quoted baseball statistics and sometimes he tested Maria's memory. She often failed. "He thinks I love him," said Maria. "Do you?" said Frank. "I did," said Maria. "I never expected to meet someone like him," said Maria. "I'll bet you didn't," said Frank, whose skepticism about Greek gods included Cupid. "He has been good to me," Maria sighed. "Are you happy being Jewish?" asked Frank as he led her upstairs to her bedroom. "Jewish?" She shrugged. "I don't mind." "Do you believe?" said Frank. "I mean the Ten Command-ments and all?" "No," she said. "Is that all right with you?" she added. It was all right with him. It was also all right with the next-door neighbor, whose wife suffered from headaches, and the golf pro at the club, and it was just fine with the dentist, who scheduled a series of two-hour ap-pointments that lasted through the spring. At the sales convention in

Bangor, Maine, Maria disappeared for a few hours; perhaps it was with the salesman for the northern district of the United States or perhaps it was simply the desk clerk. Maria knew how to please and thought it her necessity.

Her flesh was pinker and rounder than in her youth. She saw a wrinkle or two around the eyes and grew frightened. She read in a beauty magazine that sleep would stave off the signs of age. She slept till noon, never opening her eyes till the sun was past its midpoint. She had a massage twice a week to smooth out the imperfections that appeared in the joints of her knees, in the grainy places on her elbows, in the crook of her neck, where she feared a bump might be rising. Her weekend house overlooked the lake and she saw the birds flying out seeking candy and pieces of hot-dog buns from the concessionaire down on the public beach. She watched the fog come in over the distant rocks and listened to the sound of tennis balls knocking against the practice wall beside her court. Hugo almost always had a Saturday-morning doubles game. By dinnertime she was always dressed and her hair was done and her nails were shining in hues of violet and peach.

In Englewood, where the Weils lived in a Tudor house with a gardener and a cook and a nanny for the children, Maria went shopping and frequently she went to the beautician, who fluffed her blond curls up and back, around and to the side. She went to the chiropodist, who held her feet in his hands and told her she was a remarkable woman. She went to the doctor, who found she was anemic from too many carrot sticks and too few proteins. He insisted on seeing her every other week for a year to make sure her nutrition was adequate.

At first the affair was no different from any of the others Frank had enjoyed over the years, and the fact that Maria was tall, fifteen years younger than his wife, and thought that everything he said was clever touched him hardly at all. Maria smelled of perfume and bath oil and body lotions made from coconuts and mangoes. Flora ate without discretion, pastrami and onions and Chinese eggrolls, and sometimes in between her teeth little bits of garlic-flavored shredded pork were embedded. Flora's hair was going gray at the roots and she changed the color of her dye each week. When Frank saw Flora in Maria's shadow he saw what he had sacrificed as a young man, and it made him angry. The unfairness of it made him angry. The fact that a woman, a perfect woman, like Maria existed, but not for him, made him furious. Was he not entitled to the best? Divorce—he thought of divorce, but then he would be removed from the Gruenbaum Suit Company. He would be taken off the payroll as soon as the word "divorce" was out of his mouth. The stock he had, the bonuses each year, the stock that Flora gave him when their daughter was born, had been sold to pay for his less successful ventures. The apartment lease was in Flora's name. The club membership would be lost, in both the city and the country. And what could he offer Maria without his salary, his position in the Gruenbaum Company? He too was chained to a dressing table, to Flora's dressing table.

One late June weekend he went to Maria's house in Pennsylvania to play tennis. He had joined a regular foursome, including Hugo, who was the weakest partner. At noon Maria stretched out in a bathing suit on a chair; she wore a gold chain on her ankle that flashed in the sun. She offered the men, when they were done with their tennis, drinks from a bar that the butler wheeled to the side of the court. "Do you water-ski, Frank?" asked Hugo. Frank shook his head. "Easy," said Hugo. "I'll show you how. Come out in my boat." Maria smiled at Frank. In Hugo's bathing suit, which pinched around the waist and hung at the knees, Frank climbed into the boat. He wasn't used to boats. He looked around calmly and noticed that the gray water was choppy and the sun had disappeared behind some clouds. "Maybe another time," he suggested. But Hugo just started up the boat. Maria was coming along for the ride. Hugo took the first turn while one of the tennis partners held the wheel steady and drove the boat in wide circles halfway across the lake, so far that Frank had to strain to see the house or the cove in which it rested. It was his turn, way out in the water. He jumped off the boat. Hugo had crossed in and out of the water's wake. He had ridden on one ski. He had taken one hand off the bar that attached him to the boat and waved his arm in circles. Showoff, thought Frank. Frank wasn't worried. He was a good swimmer, after all. His back muscles were strong and he could do it. He held the rope. He put his skis up the way they told him, but then just as the motor started he tilted forward and the points of his skis went down toward the bottom. The force of the motor pulled him rapidly down under the water instead of up over the surface. He should have let go. In the boat they were yelling at him to let go, but he wouldn't. If Hugo could do it he would do it too. He held on as the boat lurched forward and the man driving the boat assumed he was up behind him and Maria and Hugo were screaming into the air. In only a few seconds' time, Frank rode to the bottom and his skis stuck in the mud and his feet were locked in the rubber slippers that were attached to the skis. He held fast to the rope and waited for them to pull him to the surface. The water at the bottom of the lake was ice cold. They cut the motor. They circled back. Frank felt a crashing pain in his chest and finally he let go of the rope and pulled his feet away from the skis and floated to the surface gasping for breath, vomiting small amounts of bile into the dark lake water. He said, "You should have kept going. I would have gotten up." Shame was on him as he dried with the towel. Shame was in him as he sat in the boat and with shame came its familiar escort: a storm of rage blowing in every part of his body, stomach knotted in pain, arms locked in one against another lest they should fly out and attack.

Reader: Frank is a hard man to understand. He looks strong and clean and sure of himself, but pity him his fragility, his skin as thin as the first petal of spring. Look how easily he feels himself unmoored, ridiculed, unmanly. Think how he would like to rest his body against a true love and know that he was safe, protected from the winds within and the winds without. Flora would cherish him through all eternity, yes, but Flora, every time she breathes, reminds him that the money is not his, and every time she moves across the floor, he sees his humiliation coming and going. Besides, he needs a woman with a body that will assure him of immortality, youth and vitality. The unraveling of age is more than he can bear. Frank is a man who bites the hand that feeds him, but pity him nevertheless because he too cannot help himself.

Hedy Falls into the Pit of Desire: 1950

Hedy writes to Teddy, who is now named Ari, and he answers her. "Here," he says, "is a different world. Someday you will come and visit me and see for yourself how Jews are meant to be."

Hedy was going to a New Year's Eve party at the Lehmann town house. Every New Year's Eve the Lehmann family had a party for all the generations. This was the first year that a Gruenbaum would be there.

"It's very important," said Flora to Hedy, "important for all of us." Flora bought her a red dress and shoes with a small heel to match. Flora explained to Hedy that the Lehmanns were very important people, a very important family, someone in the family had been governor of the state of New York, but the family, everyone in the family, including the third cousin who had invited Hedy, were very special people. Flora explained to Hedy that the world was changing. The war had made it different, someone like Hedy could actually go to the Lehmanns' New Year's Eve party. "Maybe," said Flora, "you'll marry a Lehmann. It could happen. If they invite you to a party, it could happen. It would be very nice," she added, "if you could be friendly with those people."

The grandmother sat on a blue velvet chair, and all the children and their dates were introduced. Hedy blushed when the grandmother nodded to her. "What was your name again, dear?" she asked.

Hedy repeated her name and then moved with the other young people up to the top floor, where they played spin the bottle and another Lehmann cousin kissed her and pushed his tongue in her mouth. Hedy felt faint. She must not anger him, but she must not let him do that. If she did, he wouldn't respect her, he would tell the others that she was easy. If she were rude and shoved him away, he would not like her. Hedy did nothing. While he had his tongue in her mouth, Hedy wondered if there was intelligent life on another planet, if falling stars were flying coffins for alien beings.

At midnight they went downstairs and everyone had champagne. The adults were dancing and clinging to the staircase, and some woman in a green dress was kissing all the young people. She kissed Hedy, too. There was a long table with golden plates and pink salmon and strawberries and cream puffs, and the knives and forks were gold and the sconces on the wall flickered on the embroidered chairs and the maids carried trays back and forth and Hedy's date played cards with his cousins while Hedy and some other girls danced with each other while "Smoke Gets in Your Eyes" played on the Victrola. At one-thirty in the morning on New Year's Day, Hedy and her date got in the back of the chauffeur-driven car that was waiting downstairs and the date brought her up the elevator to her door.

"Happy New Year," said Hedy.

"See you around," said her date after putting his lips to hers and pressing them together so long that Hedy gasped for air. When the elevator came back for her date, his mouth and nose were covered with lipstick, which got all over the handkerchief he used to wipe himself.

"Did you have a good time?" asked Flora the next morning.

"It wasn't heaven," said Hedy.

Will Katz Defends America: 1950 On

Will Katz was doing brilliantly. That is to say, he was shining in the district attorney's office. He was shining because he managed to get appointed to the best cases, the ones that would get the attention of the press, and he knew how to talk to the press, get them excited, drop a hint of a big fish being brought in, letting them in on a secret or two, and announcing that he had everything under control, would take them on tours, leak them the facts, and take them to dinner at Toots Shor's. The DA might have resented his very young associate who had a way with headlines, whose picture began to appear in the tabloids almost as regularly as his own, but he was a man who served his party and he knew that the young Will Katz was going places. Although he acted like a man twice his age and offered certain rewards to people who pleased him that perhaps weren't entirely his to offer, he was the Charles Lindbergh of the Tammany future: sure to set new records. The DA wanted a judgeship for his crown and he wanted it badly enough to select Will Katz for his team to prosecute a pair of notorious spies. The item appeared in Earl Wilson: BRILLIANT YOUNG LAWYER TO FIGHT FOR AMERICA AGAINST THE LEFTIES WHO WOULD STAB US IN THE BACK. Will Katz had given the columnist the inside tip himself as he prowled the nightclubs, always drinking club soda, staying clear-headed, checking out the crowd and moving from table to table. MOST ELIGIBLE BACHELOR IN TOWN, said Leonard Lyons, SEEN WITH MODEL JILL MOYERS LAST NIGHT AT THE RED SLIPPER. Always a different model, always there until the bartender began to wipe off the bar and turn up the lights, always at work early in the morning, he was a man to watch.

Bessie sat with him at the breakfast table while the maid brought him his juice and eggs. There were those who said he should move out, have his own apartment. Howie was among them.

"He's a grown man," he said.

Bessie said that an apartment for Will would be a waste of money. "Another apartment, what for? He has plenty of room here, and the same maid can do his laundry and change his sheets here, and what for? If he wants privacy, I'll give him privacy. I don't listen to his phone calls. He can breakfast alone if he wants."

Will didn't mind having breakfast with Bessie. He didn't move out even though it was not quite true that she didn't listen to his phone calls.

The night the traitors were convicted, Will Katz had a celebration dinner party, black tie, at the 21 Club. There was champagne for all the guests. The aspiring actress who came with Will was wearing a red, white, and blue dress with pearls roped through her hair. Howie and Bessie came to the party, and everyone congratulated them on the triumph of their extraordinary son.

Bessie accepted the compliments graciously, bowing her head slightly to the commissioner of housing, the city councilman, and the managing editor of the *Daily News*.

Howie sat at a back table stirring his whiskey sour. The radio behind the bar played dance music and a few couples swayed back and forth between the tables. Howie held his head. He was losing his hearing and the sounds blurred and he couldn't tell what anyone was saying. It was too dark to read lips. He somehow didn't think it was a good thing for a judge to be in the 21 Club, but Bessie refused to go home till Howie fell asleep with his head down on the table and Will thought people would think his father was drunk and so bundled his parents off into the night.

Security men in plain clothes circulated through the party. A bomb threat had been received. Security men, extra police, had followed Will Katz throughout the trial, and their presence, explicit at the doorways or hidden behind the potted palms, posted in the men's room endlessly washing their hands, added to the excitement. America had been placed in danger, and danger is the greatest aphrodisiac of them all. It added to the glamour, to the shine of the briefcase, the perfectly creased line in the trouser. It made the crowd on 14th Street that had gathered to watch the clock on the night of the execution clasp hands, rock back and forth on their heels, and look over their shoulders. Who in the crowd was foe and who was friend? That night someone was orphaned. That night someone threw a rock at the statue of Justice over the courthouse on Chambers Street and chipped the right-hand scale. There was weeping on certain corners and speech makers clenched their fists and promised an international investigation and the ultimate victory of the oppressed, but most Americans—"Good night, Mr. and Mrs. North America"—felt safer from sabotage and subversion. That night Will Katz made a reputation; a slayer of dragons had made his first kill.

It was three-thirty in the morning when Will Katz emerged into the dawn with the actress on his arm. He put her in the car and told the waiting chauffeur to take her home. He would walk. She took off her pearls and put them around his neck in a gesture of invitation, or was it a thank-you for introducing her to the producer of last year's hit musical? As the car pulled away from the curb and the actress collapsed on the backseat, Will took the pearls from around his neck, looked at them carefully, and slipped them over the head of the first little black-faced, pink-lipped jockey who stood in a row with all the others in front of the 21 Club, shining in the lamplight, his colors blazoned on his shirt and his arm outstretched to receive the reins of a horse. The pearls were obviously costume jewels.

There was an aching inside Will, up beyond the place where the testicle the doctor had said would never descend lay tucked up against the top of his groin. There was a longing for a way to end the night, arms, flesh, a flash of sensation, a need that made no promises for tomorrow, not roses or diamonds, or anything more than itself. He didn't care if he had to pay for it or if it were given freely. He didn't care if it spoke Haitian or cockney or Fiji. He just wanted.

He heard the newspaper trucks moving out of 43rd Street up and down to the newsstands by the subway stops. He knew what they'd say. Christ, he had told them what to say. He walked quickly because now he could see his shadow on the pavement. A man can't take his own shadow in his arms. He walked uptown with the lamplight glowing on his face as the night turned to history and it was afternoon in Berlin. Will Katz was a name, a name that was being mentioned around, the first Jewish president. He looked in all the darkened doorways; something somewhere for me?

Will Katz had been rewarded, recognized, and suggested for the job of counsel to the chairman of the committee. It was a plum assignment. Such a young man might not have been considered under ordinary conditions, but it suited the chairman to have a Jew on his team. It suited the chairman that the young man had friends in high places, particularly friends among the press.

Will Katz took a suite at the Hay Adams Hotel, and weekends he went home to his Park Avenue apartment, where his mother made sure that he was eating balanced meals and getting enough sleep. He walked along Pennsylvania Avenue, down Massachusetts Avenue past the stately mansions that housed the diplomatic staffs, the long limousines, the butlers and the cooks and the secret agents and the cultural attachés of half the world, and he tossed his cigarettes into the bushes and took out his note pad and made notes to himself on whom to call and whom to have lunch with and who might be significant in the matter at hand. He called the head of the FBI and invited him to dinner in his suite. He came, and what's more, he had a good time. Patriots know how to give each other pleasure. He was seen in the best restaurants with one or another tall woman on his arm. Sometimes they were wives of out-of-town senators, but more often they were secretaries to newspapermen or sometimes hatcheck girls at other restaurants. One remarkable redhead gave lectures to schoolchildren at the Washington Monument. They all had long legs and wore high heels with straps over the ankle.

Bessie read about them in Walter Winchell. Bessie read about the movie directors, the actors, the writers who appeared before the committee. She read how most of them named only their lawyer's name and recited the Fifth over and over. "Why don't they put them in jail?" she asked her husband.

Howie shook his head. "They have a right," he said, "not to incriminate themselves."

"Some right," said Bessie. "Puts us all in danger."

Howie put his hand on his wife's arm. "They have a right," he said.

She stared at him. He was pale and there were beads of sweat on his upper lip. "All right," she said, "calm down."

"I'm fine, dear," he said.

Frank said, "We'll get the commie bastards and drive them out of the country."

Flora wasn't happy. "Maybe they didn't do anything," she said. "Maybe they have the wrong names." She told Dr. Bergman, "I feel sad for the people on lists who can't work anymore."

Dr. Bergman said, "Are you thinking about getting a job?"

"What could I do?" asked Flora.

Casualties of the Cold War: 1951

Rose Herzberg had become head of the lower school, and she interviewed parents and their children in an office covered with drippings of paint, dabs of clay, and books on child development that lay scattered among the folders of applications, test results, conference announcements, and sales pitches of textbook publishers. Abe had graduated from a school for the deaf and was in art school. He drew cartoons. Meyer had three of them framed in his office. Meyer was in line to be chairman of the English Department at City College. Everyone knew his work on Boswell. Everyone knew he was an essayist whose articles ranged from the obscure line in Keats to the not-so-obscure questions of democracy and its implications for the literary mind.

Meyer had grown larger with the passing years, and his heavy hands waved about as he told his jokes to his students, to his colleagues in the cafeteria, and home in bed to his wife. In the morning he told the jokes to his son in sign language, although most of the time they were not funny in signs and further explanations had to be given. Then Meyer was summoned to a committee hearing in Washington. His name appeared on a list that Will Katz was holding up in front of the television cameras on the evening news.

"This man," said Will, "this name I have here, is the brother of a notorious singer who has traveled, not simply fellow-traveled"—and the reporters laughed— "behind the lines of those who would take us over, destroy our way of life, and turn us into slaves for the socialist machine. This man"—he waved his list again—"is teaching our children, teaching in a major college, in New York, untouched by criticism, he is free to turn each of his students into soldiers in the army of the subverters, the traitors who are linked together in common evil purpose across this great nation of ours. This man claims to be a professor of English, but what is he, really?"

In a nightclub in downtown Santa Fe, Quebec Bob met a young singer, half Indian, half Mexican, who accompanied her songs on the drum. Under the stars on the Great Plains, women may once have danced the way she danced, made sounds, wails, thumps, and the calls of birds the way she did. She was young and her black eyes had no wrinkles around them. She had no stains on her hands, and her fullness and ripeness made Quebec Bob feel that he could leap mountains, swim the Grand Canyon down to the sea. He tried to explain to Sharie Lee that he was a man who needed renewing like the moon. He told her that artists were not meant for bonds and chains and routines that bury the senses under mounds of ordinariness.

"I am not," he said to her, "an ordinary man." She had not thought so. "It would be better for me," he said, "to go to Mexico for a while."

She wasn't surprised. She didn't cling or write pleading letters. She packed up Quebec Bob's things. She dusted the spaces they exposed. She found it hard being alone when the streetlights went out and each new day abruptly began. She called her manager. She called her mother. She called Meyer. She called Flora. She went on a bender that lasted a month, and no one could find her anywhere.

Meyer had dinner with his sister in an Italian restaurant on Bleecker Street. "I'm not a party member," he said. "I never have been. I'm not a dyed-in-the-wool capitalist, either."

"What are you?" asked Sharie Lee, who had never had a head for politics.

"I believe that God, or what is left of God, is in the stories men write. That's why I read so carefully."

Sharie wasn't sure if her brother was joking or not. She smiled at him with a smile that both recognized the possibility of irony and yet carefully considered his words.

"So, how to fight back?" said Meyer. Sharie shrugged. "Ask your cousin Flora," Meyer said, trying to keep his voice steady, "to get Will Katz to release me from his hook."

As the cannoli were served, Meyer cheered up. "So what's with you?" he asked.

"I'm not drinking," said Sharie, which was only partly true. "I'm absolutely reliable, but no one believes me. I could do three sets a night, but no one trusts me." Her fingers were stained with nicotine. Her lipstick was bright and rouge was slashed across her cheekbones, but the makeup seemed to rest uneasily on her pale skin. She looked worn. "Is it my fault," she asked Meyer, "if I'm not a young bird anymore?" Meyer reached out and touched her hand.

Mildred called her nephew Will in his office on Capitol Hill. "Meyer Herzberg is a cousin of mine. He's only a professor. He can't harm the country. Clear his name so he doesn't lose his job."

"He's on a list," said Will. "His sister went to Russia with a Negro. His wife teaches at a progressive school that teaches union songs instead of long division. His wife has signed too many petitions. We have their names on petitions going back fifteen years. I didn't know your family was involved with people like this. I'll have to follow up this lead," he added before hanging up.

Mildred sent Will a note on her purple stationery, apologizing for bothering him. She sent him a cashmere cardigan sweater for his birthday. This was no time to be associating with known traitors, participants in the conspiracy to overturn the elected democratic free government of the United States. Infiltrators, spies, those who met in little cells to debate the fall of Congress and the collapse of Wall Street. They were not welcome, especially by those who had insomnia when it came to the American dream.

Meyer testified, but he didn't give any names of members of the English Department whose politics were also dubious. There had been a moment when he had nearly joined the Party. He and Rose had gone to some meetings. Then the Stalin-Hitler pact was announced and he felt he needed more time to work on his article on the Romantic poets.

"The Romantic poets?" a friend had asked. "The world is falling apart and you want to work on the Romantic poets?"

"Yes," said Meyer.

But that changed nothing in the eyes of Will Katz and his committee. Meyer admitted he had signed all the petitions for the Abraham Lincoln Brigade and he had made contributions. He said he believed in democracy, but Will had asked him if that meant that he believed in our economic system, and Meyer was silent.

"What are you?" he yelled at Meyer.

Meyer felt the heat of the camera lights on his face. There was sweat on his upper lip. He was a man who had broken a promise made long ago to his father. He didn't answer. There was turmoil in the department. There was financial cutbacks. There were pressures to appear patriotic.

Meyer, who had tenure, was asked to leave. The provost claimed that he was entitled to fire him on grounds of gross criminal behavior.

Rose cried. Meyer said, "Please God, Rose, don't cry." It hurt him to see her eyes averted, her hands twisting a strand of matted hair again and again. He sat on the worn armchair in their apartment on Morton Street and tried to read. He had planned to teach Coleridge the following fall. His notes were ready. "In Xanadu did Kubla Khan a stately pleasure-dome decree. . . ." He had thoughts about where this pleasure-dome really existed; was it the mind, the paradise of Christian promise, or the moment of sexual pleasure, as Freud might have it? Was it possible that Coleridge was writing about death? Meyer couldn't concentrate. He would have no students in the fall. He would have no income in the fall. He thought of his father. What was the punishment for a broken promise? He was tired. He ate too much. He forgot the punch lines to jokes. He paced back and forth in the apartment.

He went for a walk in Washington Square Park, but a former colleague looked away when he saw him coming. After that he kept his eyes down on the ground as he moved along, watching the candy wrappers blow under the benches. He played chess at the table under the maple on the west side of the park. He lost frequently. He mumbled apologies. He explained to the men at the chess board that he was a professor, a professor of English.

"Oh, yeah," said one of them. "I used to be a chicken farmer."

Meyer got a job teaching English as a second language in a school on 14th Street. His class was at night. He heard stories from refugees that made him ashamed to have pitied himself. He got a second job as a waiter in a luncheonette on Christopher Street. What did he care if his former students saw him wiping counters? He signed to his son, A man is what is in his soul, not his occupation. As he was making the hand gestures, his child had looked away. Meyer knew he was embarrassing. He embarrassed himself.

Meyer called his mother and tried to explain it all. She didn't understand. "If you didn't do it, why are they blaming you?" She was an old lady, what did he expect? Then the board of trustees of Rose's school asked her to resign. "We know you didn't do anything," they said, "but in these times, it would be better for the school." They were sure she would understand.

Rose used her maiden name and got a job teaching first grade in a school in a Westchester for the deaf. The head of that school had no ear for politics and had trouble getting decent teachers. It was a long commute. Rose was exhausted when she came home in the evening.

Meyer lay in bed with Rose. They were holding each other tightly. Rose's small form was almost lost in Meyer's hulk. His glasses were on the night table, and his eyes were not clearly focused. She was touching his bare back, feeling for the mole on the left shoulder, the way a sailor looks for the buoy at the harbor's entrance. Meyer's large body was trembling. Rose held him till he quieted down.

"We are lucky," she said, "to have each other."

Meyer opened his mouth and gulped down drafts of air. He put his heavy hands on her small breasts, and rubbing his fingers over her nipples, he sighed, "Our bed is our raft," he said.

"Watch out for sharks," said Rose, rocking him gently.

Sharie Lee Makes a Sensible Choice At Last: 1951

Flora invited her cousin to dinner. Frank objected. "I don't want that commie broad with the commie brother in this house," he had yelled. He had banged his fist on the door.

Flora told him he had no right to tell her who she could have to dinner. She reminded him that she had just paid his back taxes and she told him that Dr. Bergman didn't think that married people had to have the same friends. Frank said he wouldn't come home the night of the dinner party, and Flora said that was all right with her. Flora was experimenting with expressing her opinion. It made her giddy. It made her joyous.

Flora told Hedy she could have her father's place at the dinner table, but he arrived and even told Sharie Lee that she was looking well. Flora had invited Lenny Fisher to dinner. Lenny was a bachelor, and Frank thought he was probably a faggot because he also liked the theater and ballet and had kept his mother's box seat at the opera and went at least twice a year. Lenny was the extra man always invited to dinner by their crowd, a member of the club, a good golfer, and everyone admitted he had brought his appliance business along very well for a man who seemed to be in something of a daze most of the time. He had big eyes behind thick glasses and perfect thin lips set in a round face that was settling graciously into its middle years. He was built low to the ground but solid. He had recently developed a slight bulge over his belt, and his left knee was stiff from an old football injury. Above his socks varicose veins had begun to climb, but his smile was promising and there was still a sweetness in his face that made everyone want to sit next to him. He was easy to talk to, and he made each of his women partners feel that somewhere out there was a man who could be a friend. Lenny had told Flora that he had been in psychoanalysis for a number of years because of women problems. He was ready now, he told her, ready for anything. Not cured, of course, psychoanalysis is not about curing, but improving. Flora knew. She was improved, too.

Sharie Lee came that night wearing her best low-cut black silk dress. She had braided her hair around her head and hardly sipped her Scotch. Lenny Fisher found her exotic, her past, as Flora whispered it to him as he took off his coat, excited him, and he looked at her white throat and was stirred in a way he had never been before. He took her home to Jane Street, although it was out of his way and he had an early meeting with a toaster manufacturer from Pittsburgh. He took her to the opera and to the new Rodgers and Hammerstein musical and he took her to bed with him in his apartment overlooking the Central Park reservoir and he was with her when the streetlights went out and the sun came up over the East River. He begged Sharie Lee to marry him and live forever after in his apartment, his house in Westport that had a greenhouse and a swimming pool.

While she didn't immediately say yes, she didn't say no. She was tired, after all, and when Lenny put his arms around her, she felt the opposite of the earth moving, and that was just what she wanted, the earth to stay still for a while. Sharie introduced Lenny to Meyer and Rose, and at dinner at Lenny's apartment in which a Negro maid in uniform served them perfectly done roast beef from a silver platter, Meyer said he was happy for his sister and lifted his glass in honor of her new relationship. Rose told stories about the children she was teaching that interested Lenny, who offered to make a contribution to the school.

On the subway back to Greenwich Village, Meyer put his arm around his wife and he put his large head on her shoulder. "Is that what Sharie wants?" he asked.

"Yes," said Rose.

"Ah," said Meyer, who thought he felt ill from the roast beef jouncing along in his intestines.

Reader: Amazing how fast time runs in this century. The miscegenation of Sharie Lee and Quebec Bob, which was scandalous at the time, which caused Mildred to shut her eyes in shock, which once seemed to offer the promise of brotherly love, a world of light brown, half Christian, half Jewish, melted children, the vision of the Left as they groped for a way toward equal opportunity and the pursuit of universal happiness, has been rejected and the goal of color-blind America has been replaced by the fierce loyalty of tribe to tribe, stripe to stripe, and humanitarians these days believe in social fission, not fusion, as the source of energy, the electricity of the future.

Amazing how out of date Flora seems all dressed up with her corset holding in her stomach muscles, the seams of her stockings always wavering up her legs, her hairdresser appointments that provided respite and renewal and endless anxiety as her reflection was multiplied in the rows of mirrors in front and in back of her chair. Imagine how Flora's closet hung with dresses that she no longer wore because she had lost at cards the day she wore the blue one or had a fight with Frank while wearing the gray suit. Imagine Flora's closet floor, where the maid came each morning and picked up the items she had thrown down in disgust, in a haste, in uncertainty. Imagine the hats with veils, the satins and the silks and the embroidered gowns, and think of Flora sitting on her pink monogrammed bed cover spreading out the solitaire cards, playing them out over and over, until she won, never cheating, believing that the fall of queens and jacks and tens were predicting something, appeasing something, sending her word of her status in the world to come, the days to come. Think of Flora, whose ashtray overflowed and whose sheets had bed crumbs from her midnight snacks of pickle and corned beef, think of what she had to tell Dr. Bergman. Would she be amazed at how times have changed? Her tarot cards spread across her bed sheets in the early hours of the morning never told her that she could toss out her troubles in an old black bag, that she didn't need white gloves every time she went out, that her grief would have an end, if she would only end it. The astrologer who read Flora's horoscope never told her that seeing double when it comes to standards was going out of style.

Sharie Lee was planning to get married, and Flora was happy for her. "There is such a thing," she told Dr. Bergman, "as a happy ending."

There was a problem. Sharie Lee was unable to sing. It wasn't that she didn't remember the notes or the words or the way you contracted your muscles in the diaphragm or in the neck, the way you blew through your nose and let the sound rise from the top of your head. It was that the sounds that she made were now unlike any she had made before, the voice of the disciple of the Baal Shem had left her—disgusted, perhaps, by her worldly ways; eroded, perhaps, by cigarettes or Scotch, or disinterested in her now that she was about to be happy, to be married to Lenny Fisher and have a home of her own with five bedrooms and a Negro maid to serve tea in the afternoon and a laundress to wash out her undies.

"Your voice will come back," said Lenny, "After we're married. I didn't fall in love with you because of your voice."

His kindness embarrassed her. Why was she worrying about her voice now, now that she would no longer need it, now that she could live for herself and not for the voice that had been her albatross, her hunchback, her joy for so long? A Jewish wedding, she told her mother, and her mother wept because Sharie's father, Joseph, had died before the miracle and had died of something that made his hands shake and his feet tremble and finally had made his lungs grow stiff.

Sharie grew very thin. "Are you eating enough?" Flora asked.

"I eat all the time," said Sharie, "but I keep losing weight. There seems to be a lump in my throat where my voice gets knotted up."

It was true that Sharie Lee now sounded hoarse, and suddenly Flora began to worry. They were at Lindy's with Hedy, sharing one large piece of strawberry cheesecake. They had just bought Sharie's wedding dress in Bergdorf Goodman's. Hedy was complaining. She didn't want to wear a pink bridesmaid's dress. "Pink," said Hedy, "is a disgusting color."

Flora, who visited a doctor at least once a month to put her mind at ease about a cough, a bump, a stomach pain, a backache, a slight yellowing of the eyeballs, fatigue—she was always fatigued—ignored Hedy's objections. She turned to Sharie Lee. "See a doctor, see my doctor," she added, convinced that only the fleet of mind, the adequately suspicious, would survive into old age.

Flora Takes to Ice Skating Sunday Mornings at Rockefeller Center: 1952

Flora had another peculiar pain in her head. She thought about mortality. It was time to make out her will.

She went to Arthur's lawyer, Aaron Haft. He was a full partner in the firm of Haft, Herz, and Wilentz. In his office were pictures of his wife and children at the beach, on a camping trip in Maine. He had rounded shoulders that sloped under his jacket. He had a long face and his hair was turning gray. He wore thick glasses and kept his head tilted to one side when he listened. He spoke softly. He looked intently at his clients. He thought about them after they left the office. His clients had trouble with their mates, they had trouble with their taxes, they had trouble with their business partners. They sighed. They were wronged. They didn't have control over things they believed they should. They needed him to calm them down, to assure them that justice would be done and justice was on their side. He believed that if he practiced law, advised his clients of the options, lent the system the muscle of his mind, all would be well. It was fortunate that he loved law the way he did because his wife had died two years before Flora entered his office, and he mourned her still, circling around her dressing table, never opening her closet door, talking about her all the time to his children, saying, If only your mother could see or hear you now. He came home to be with his children for dinner but often went directly back to the office to read papers, to browse through his law library, to sit on his leather chair and watch the lights of the city blinking across the rooftops. In his office he would make late night phone calls, read *The New Yorker* stories, watch the cleaning women work, avoiding the solitude of his bed.

His wife had died of multiple sclerosis. It had taken years. He had watched her change from a tennis player, a girl who ran across the sand at the beach and danced with him in their bedroom with the radio playing loud, to a bent and twisted figure that he hauled out of her chair into bed, whose mouth was frozen in a grimace, and whose hands couldn't hold a pencil or a cup. It had made him quiet. Inside his head he kept revolving images of his wife before the illness came, and he talked to her often now that she was dead. He felt cheated, but he knew that others were cheated, too. He tried to be brave, to take what had happened in stride, to be there for his children, who needed him. His children, a boy and a girl, were too quiet, as if they could stave off further disaster by barely moving, as if thunderbolts could not find you hiding close to the ground.

Flora Sheinfold, his secretary had announced. But when she entered his office and sat on the leather chair opposite him, he recognized her immediately.

"Flora Gruenbaum . . ." He smiled, and when he smiled a tenderness came over his face and a whisper of joy eased from the corners of his mouth. "I took you to a dance at the ZBT house, remember me?"

Flora blushed. She had remembered but assumed he would forget. He got up from behind his desk and pulled up a chair next to her.

"Tell me," he said, "what brings you to me?" She told him. While he was taking notes, he said, "You were so sweet the night of the dance. You were beautiful that night, did you know it?"

Flora didn't know it, and his words seemed to mock her. "I'm not beautiful now," she said.

Aaron Haft thought Flora was still beautiful, but he thought it unprofessional to say so. She was married, of course, but she touched him, moved him somehow, perhaps only because she reminded him of the time before he was a lawyer, before he had a wife and children, and his wife was still alive although he hadn't met her yet.

He invited Flora to lunch. Sitting at a corner table, he told her about his wife, Reba. It was hard to speak of her to another woman, but something about Flora, the way she waited for him to finish his sentences and paused before speaking herself, the way her eyes filled with tears when he told her about Reba, how she looked at his pictures of his children and touched the photographs carefully, as if she understood how much they meant to him, something about Flora made him quiver inside in a way he had forgotten. She told him stories about her sister, Mildred, whose husband, Julie, had run off to South America, about Arthur, about her nephew Teddy, who had gone to Israel. She made him laugh. She told him she could do the *NYT* crossword puzzle in fifteen minutes. He was awed.

Flora told Dr. Bergman about the lunch. Dr. Bergman smiled. "You feel guilty, I suppose?" he said.

Flora shook her head. "Not very," she said.

"Good," said Dr. Bergman, who believed that progress was slow, the art of healing at his disposal flawed, and the years passing by like constant reproaches.

Aaron Haft told Flora that he wanted to take her to the theater.

"You can't," she said. "I'm a married woman."

"Please," he said. "Let me take you ice skating with my children one Sunday morning."

Flora considered. She went bundled up in scarves and dark glasses so no one would recognize her. She did not skate well, she hardly remembered how. Aaron Haft held her up by the elbow. The music in Rockefeller Center made her wish she could twirl and float like the others in tights and short skirts doing flips and tangos in the center of the ice.

"I'll take lessons," she said to Aaron.

"Not necessary," he said. "I'll teach you."

His children circled around, watching their father with wide eyes. They all had hot chocolate together. Flora told the children about Hedy. "Next time I'll bring my daughter, Hedy," she said.

Dr. Bergman said, "Ice skating is a fine kind of foreplay, makes you long for a cup of hot chocolate." So it happened one weekend when Aaron's children were at their grandparents' house that Flora appeared for dinner at Aaron's apartment wearing her newest silk dress and her heart beating so loud that she thought she might die before the elevator reached his floor.

He couldn't bring her into his bedroom, the one he had shared with Reba, but in the living room on the floor, beside the fireplace, he brought her a brandy and sat down on the rug beside her. He was shy and fumbling. His hormones were welcoming him back by jumping and leaping through his body and he had a mighty need to make her happy, to heal everything, to make up to her for the time that had passed since he took her to the ZBT dance and never called again.

She kicked off her heels and stood before him at full stature. "I'm short," she said.

"You're just right," he said. "Here, I can put my arms around you and pull you against my chest and we fit. Don't we fit, just right?" he asked.

Flora took his face in her hands and stared at his eyes. "Why are you so good to me?" she asked. "Do you pity me?"

He wondered at her question. "Why would I pity you?" he asked. "I want you. I need you. I want to be with you."

Flora decided to believe him. This was the most important decision of her life. She made it in an instant, although it was years in coming. She let Aaron Haft undo the buttons of her new dress and she slipped it off her head and he undressed her slowly until she was naked before him and he was naked and the two of them touched and rocked and allowed the moment to grow between them until it erupted and her mouth was on his and his hands were on her hips and although they were not young and although they both knew enough to expect disappointment after pleasure, they let themselves go. Reba was abandoned to her grave, Frank was dismissed as a mistake, and the only thing that mattered was the movement between them, the rushing force of nature, the added poignancy of finding after waiting, and the miracle that was the two of them on the carpet.

Dr. Bergman was not the sort of man to thank God. He wasn't the sort to take too much credit, either. It might have happened without him, but nevertheless he stretched out his legs and massaged his lower back, which sometimes stiffened up from so much sitting in one place, and felt grateful.

Escape: 1952

It was Hedy's spring vacation. Hedy and her mother went to Nassau for a vacation. Flora wore a flowered dress with white sandals when they went to dinner the first night. Hedy had gotten sunburned, and she shivered in the cool patio air. They sat at a small table covered with a white cloth, and the stars seemed so low that Hedy wondered if the sky was coming down on them like the bed in the story by Edgar Allan Poe in which a visitor to an inn is crushed by the canopy of the bed. A white egret sat on the sand just beyond the hotel path that was lined with red and white hibiscus. At other tables couples were toasting each other with glasses of wine, and a family with three small girls all dressed in yellow pinafores with blue ribbons in their hair were laughing together at something the father had said. Flora sipped at her tequila sunrise. "You had a cousin named Moses. We lost him."

"How?" said Hedy.

Flora told her. "Maybe someday you'll find him," said Flora.

"I think he's dead," said Hedy, who didn't care much one way or the other.

The waiter came with their food, and Flora thanked him for taking such good care of them. She looked at the waiter, whose light brown skin matched his brown jacket, and she smiled at him. "Doesn't he have a sweet face," she said.

Three musicians came to the bandstand, and after setting up their equipment, they began "Yellow Bird in Banana Tree." They sang loud and plucked on their instruments with more energy than accuracy. Flora sang along in a soft voice. Hedy looked at her mother, whose lipstick was mostly on the wineglass in front of her but whose eyes, behind her red plastic glasses, were shining. Hedy was taller than her mother. She was thin and long like her father. Her mother looked up at her when they walked side by side.

"I'm glad you're tall," said Flora.

"It's better for basketball," said Hedy.

"Men like long legs," said Flora.

"Why?" asked Hedy.

The musicians began the limbo music. Two of the waiters stood holding a pole and the diners marched around, bending backward going under the pole. The music got louder. Hedy joined in the limbo and she bent down and bent her knees forward and staggered under the pole. She could see her mother laughing and clapping each time she made it through. A young woman fell and knocked the pole out of the waiters' hands and the guests applauded her as she limped off the dance floor. The musicians made the music increase in speed, and it seemed as if the music too were lowering closer to the ground. Hedy was still in the game along with a loose-limbed boy whose arms dangled out of his sleeves but whose head rolled back, missing the pole again and again. Only, two people had not been eliminated—Hedy, who could bend her back down to the floor, and this strange boy, who was shorter than Hedy by several inches.

Flora puffed on a cigarette. She waved encouragingly to her daughter. The waiters were now on their knees, holding the pole only a foot above the floor. A lizard scampered by, and the little girls at the next table screamed with excitement. Hedy laid her spine backward, put her hands behind her head like an inside-out frog, and crawled under the pole. The musicians banged out their amazement. The boy put his body in the same position, but his knees moved upward and he hit the pole and the winner of the game was Hedy and Flora's eyes filled with sudden tears. Hedy was standing with the musicians, and they gave her a basket of fruit for a prize and she brought it back to the table as the musicians began yet another round of "Yellow Bird in Banana Tree."

Flora looked at her daughter, flushed with triumph. Leaning across the table, she said, "Let's stay another week, what do you say?"

Hedy nodded, and they did, swimming out in the blue water, at dusk watching the fishermen at the pier. One morning they paid for a ride on a glass-bottomed boat. The boat had a tent roof to protect the passengers from the full heat of the day and along the sides were wooden benches and you could sit and stare at the glass panel in the center through which they saw at the bottom of the sea red and yellow and blue fish, striped and spotted and rippled with white and gray and strange things with small arms waving in the current growing on the coral. The boat owner sold them Coca-Cola and orangeade as well as fresh pineapple slices that came each with its own little spear. Juice spilled on Hedy's shirt and she reached into the warm water and splashed it away. Flora cupped her hands and scooped up some water and cooled off her face. The drops stuck to the rims of her glasses.

Through the glass bottom they saw gliding along above the pink coral a creature that looked like a gray platter with a long tail. A stingray, said the man who was sitting beside Flora and kept mopping his brow with the bandanna he had tied around his neck. The fish moved through the water without a sound, hunting, searching for something to kill. Hedy stared at it and followed it to the end of the boat when it disappeared beyond the view of the glass bottom.

Flora sat on the small wooden bench as the boat rocked on the gentle sea, turned, and headed for shore. She put her arm around her daughter, covering her shoulders from the sun. "I wish I could sing like Sharie Lee," said Flora.

"You do sing," said Hedy. "It's just that I'm the only one who hears you."

"I might leave your father," said Flora.

Hedy stared at the blue-spotted silver fish that had swum into view. She had heard this before. She paid no attention.

Then Flora said, "I might have found someone else." Hedy felt a sinking in her stomach.

• • •

Reader: Hedy should have been pleased, but what child is pleased at the news that the whole of the home is going to be a half? Remember that scandal and shame were a part of the deal, and Hedy didn't want everyone to know the secret of her house. Hedy was old enough, you say, to understand. She should have said to her mother, Go ahead, hurry up, it's about time. But Hedy said nothing because her thoughts weren't clear. What she wanted was not to talk about it. Amazing, the colors of the fish that swam beneath their glass-bottomed boat, eating and being eaten in the shifting currents.

Maria and Frank: New Attachments: 1952

Maria and Frank began to see each other every Wednesday afternoon. Maria saw no one in the mornings because she was sleeping, or at least lying in bed with pads over her eyes so that the light would not reach her skin. She touched Frank's arm gently. She told him how she loved the muscles that she felt moving under the skin. She told him that when she was a child in the center of America, she had imagined that one day a man with dark hair, a tall handsome man, would come to her and take her away, and here he was, he had come at last, and she would lie back on the bed and her soft breasts would fall out of her blue slip and her eyes that seemed clear in the afternoon grew wet with tears. "I am so glad you came," she would say, and Frank would feel that he had at last understood what he wanted.

One Wednesday she held on to his hands and searched in his eyes. Hugo had been told something. Hugo had more than suspicions. Hugo's mother was asking for a return of certain family necklaces. It was necessary, absolutely necessary that she find someone to provide, in case of a storm, in case she should be abandoned. She lifted her eyes to the sky. "Who will take care of me?" she asked in a small-girl voice, her lisp blending the words backwards into childhood. "Perhaps," she added, "I will accept the invitation of the president of Seidman Cushions to travel with him on his yacht in April. "You can't," said Frank, who felt violated. "I can," said Maria. "You have no claim on me."

Frank told Arthur he needed a larger salary. Arthur agreed. Frank was his sister's husband. After Frank left his office, Arthur paced up and down. He practiced pulling an egg out of his ear. When Teddy was a boy he loved that trick. He would shout out loud and tip himself backward on the bed. Arthur's tricks were rusty, and he had promised to perform on the children's ward at Beth Israel.

If only his son would return, would get tired of his army life. But the boy kept getting promoted. He seemed to be good at whatever it was he was doing out there in the new towns at the edge of the sand. At the club everyone slapped Arthur on the back, as if having a corporal in the Israeli army was some kind of wonderful thing. His son's place was by his side, not five thousand miles away.

A Jewish homeland was important, sure. Arthur was as excited as anyone else when the United Nations vote came over the radio. When there was fighting and the Arabs were on the road to Jerusalem, he had stayed home and sat by the radio all day. He hadn't slept at all, and every time the phone rang his heart sank with fear, but it had been all right and they had won after all and his son had apparently been braver than necessary and done things that his father would never have expected, not of such a boy who had never done anything particularly remarkable in his whole life, except perhaps drop a can of tomatoes at the doorman's feet.

A photograph arrived in the mail, a picture of Teddy, who was now named Ari, with four other boys standing on top of a captured British tank that had been used by the Arabs as they pushed up the road from Tel Aviv. Teddy was smiling into the camera, his face was sunburned and his cap was pushed back on his head, but his smile was so open, so wide, so full of the joy of triumph, that his father almost wished he were the boy, not the father. The eyes in the picture—Arthur kept it in a silver frame on his desk—were the eyes of an old man older even than his father. They had seen something, something that was not so simple, something that altered the nature of the triumph. Leaning on his friend, waving with his free hand, Teddy looked like a man who had grasped that breathing was a temporary matter and survival a question of luck, not virtue. "Come home," Arthur said to the photograph at least once a day. "Come home and I'll make you vice president of the company," he repeated, once in the morning and once at the end of the day as his secretary was putting on her coat in the outer office.

But Arthur knew Corporal Ari Gruenbaum wasn't coming home, not soon. "Yeah," he said to his golf partner, the one he won the club championship with the year before, "I'm proud of him, what father wouldn't be."

Arthur thought of his nephew Moses. He was the one who should one day take over the company. Where was he? Dead!

Hedy in the Corridor of the Hadassah Hospital: 1990

"It's been too long," said Hedy to no one in particular. "Something has gone wrong. They can't get it. They can't take it out," Hedy was whispering.

"No," said Hedy's cousin Ari, who had arrived back in the corridor holding a paper cup of coffee, his army uniform soaked with perspiration, "you told me the surgeon said he would be four hours at least. He said he had to work slowly. If anything was wrong, they would have told us. Everything is going fine."

Hedy looked up. "What does the government say?"

"Nothing yet," said Ari. "There will be an investigation. It has started already."

Ari had to push his way into the hospital past the TV reporters. "No comment, no comment," he had shouted as the mike was placed in front of him. They had called him back from Hebron, where he was trying to keep some streets open for the army vehicles coming in that evening. "My cousin's daughter," he had said to his lieutenant. "Just out of the army, at the university, good girl," he said, "in the wrong place at the wrong time."

"Eh," said the lieutenant, "aren't we all."

What a Mother Shouldn't Have to Hear: 1952

Sharie Lee called her mother. "It's bad news," she said.

"You're not getting married," said Ruth, who was suffering from angina herself and was thinking that she had lived longer than was right, longer than either her mother or father, longer than a person who was nearly lost before her tenth birthday ought to live.

"No," said Sharie Lee, "it's not about Lenny."

"Thank God," said Ruth.

Sharie Lee had something growing in her larynx. Something the doctors had to remove. Something that could kill.

"In your throat?" said Ruth, who never quite believed bad news even when it was certainly true. "That can't be," she said. "I never heard of that."

Neither had Sharie Lee, but the doctor had said smoking and drinking and genetics had done it. The bad gene had not come from the disciple of the Baal Shem, Ruth knew that as clearly as she knew her name.

"I'm in the hospital. Everyone is especially nice, since Uncle Isaac's portrait is hanging in the lobby."

"Is it, really," said Ruth. "I'd forgotten that."

"I won't be able to speak afterward," said Sharie Lee, "or sing." The phone was quiet on both sides.

Sharie Lee called her brother Meyer. He was eating his fourth sugar doughnut of the morning and considering writing a letter to *The New York Times* about the irony of Jews being crucified as communists at the same time that communists were crucifying Jews. Where was the ram in the thicket now that he was the one being sacrificed? Meyer tried to think of a joke about the binding of Isaac on Mt. Moriah, but he couldn't. A joke would be the perfect way to begin the letter. Sharie called Meyer from the hospital and he sat down in his chair and plucked at the tufts of stuffing that were emerging from a rip in the seat.

"You are not being punished," said Meyer, "not for anything you have done." After he hung up the phone he sat still like a rabbit frozen in the headlights' glare. An unnamed, unmanageable, unspecific weight pressed against his chest. He knew what it was. His house was not kosher. Even on the holiest day he stayed out of synagogue. No man breaks a promise without paying for it. Did he believe that? Was that a rational thought? How long could a man stay rational?

Reader: Listen to what Meyer told Sharie Lee. Ignore the fears that overcame him later. Don't believe that God is punishing Sharie Lee for having abandoned the path of her fathers. If that were true, there are other people we all could name who ought to be languishing in hospitals, waiting in doctors' offices for reports of X-rays, calling their lawyers, and saying their final good-byes. Most of them are dining on lobster and shrimp marinara in the best restaurants on both coasts and may well outlive you and me. Most likely, as Rabbi Levi of Berdichev said, sometimes God is in error and it's reasonable, even justified, to call Him to account, for all the good that it does.

Reader, don't think that God punished Sharie Lee because she was about to be happy. Unhappy people get cancer of the lip and the lung, the marrow and the blood, all the time. Don't think that he punished Sharie Lee because she had used her gift for the profane, for the drinkers and whoremongers, the drifters and the con men, for the denizens of the night, instead of the holy spirit. The Baal Shem taught that the Holy Spirit was everywhere, not just in the synagogue where the men expected it to be, not just sitting in the ark or resting on the Torah cover or sliding on the Torah pointer, or flickering with the eternal light that never goes out. Many people abandon the gift that God gave them, misuse it, turn it into a weapon to harm themselves or others, and some of them get cirrhosis of the liver and some of them get nosebleeds and agoraphobia and kleptomania and fear of flying, but very few of them get cancer of the writing hand or cancers of the calf muscle or tumors of the brain, and those who do are no more gifted than the population in general. All this is to say that God was not punishing Sharie Lee for her life. Meyer was right. Rationally speaking, nothing that happened was Sharie Lee's responsibility.

Sharie Lee lay in her bed in the hospital and she listened to the radio. If she wanted something, she wrote it down on a pad she kept on the night table by her bedside. Lenny Fisher sat up straight on the chair that was pushed in close so that the curtain that separated Sharie from the woman in the next bed could be pulled around. Sharie was pale—not pale, exactly, but without the colors that shape the face, that mottle the skin, that give signs of blood and membrane just beneath the surface. She looked drained, puffy, empty. Lenny considered that perhaps she had become hollow, like the chocolate bunny he had once smashed on the floor and discovered that what he had thought was solid was only a shell. Sharie's eyes were different. They stared at the ceiling, they seem to have dropped back into their sockets. They would not look at him, but they were not empty, they were full, so full he couldn't bear to look at them. She reached over for her pad. He could see the effort it took for her to raise her arms. "Too late," she wrote.

It was too late. He knew it, but he came every day, and when she went back to the apartment on Jane Street, he paid for a nurse to stay with her and he arrived after dinner, bringing flowers and magazines, finally only staying for five minutes until she closed her eyes and drifted into sleep. It had spread from the throat. She was coughing, and no matter how carefully the nurse boiled the egg or spread marmalade on a piece of toast, she vomited it all into the pan on the floor and the doctor came and gave her injections for pain and Flora came and held her hand. Flora bought chocolate ice cream and a new nightgown with pink lace at the collar.

Sharie wrote a note to her cousin. "Go away," she said.

"You don't mean that," said Flora.

"Stay," wrote Sharie Lee, and fell asleep.

Sharie wanted to see her brother Eli, who lived in Borough Park. He came and stared at his sister. There were tears in his eyes. He said Hebrew prayers by her bedside until she told him to stop. The sound of the Hebrew grated against her ears. It filled her with impossible wishes and memories that stung. He showed her pictures of his children, boys with payess and girls with long-sleeved dresses and bows in their hair. He showed her a picture of Caleb in Israel. "Can you imagine, in the Holy Land?" he asked her. Sharie nodded.

"We are different," said Eli, "but you are my sister and I will ask God for a miracle." None came.

Meyer came in the mornings to spell the nurse while she went to have coffee in the local delicatessen. He sat by his sister's bedside. He held her small hand in his large one. He quoted Shelley and he read her drafts of the article he was writing on due process and the literary mind. She closed her eyes and fell asleep. Rose came after school and brought flowers she put in vases by the bed. Meyer stroked his sister's bed cover.

"It's an accident," said Rose.

"Yes," agreed Meyer, who rehearsed the rusty words to the kaddish for when they would be needed.

Ruth prayed as her husband would have done. She cursed as her brother would have done. She was an old lady who had not walked up the stairs to the second floor of her house for over two years. One son was kosher, and that was more than many of the women in the neighborhood could say. Ruth felt as if she were not quite there, as if she were only a memory her children had: one she did not share. The amazement she had felt when they were young, that the children ran and cried and spoke, the pleasure they had given Joseph when they said the Hebrew phrase, when they stood beside him on the *bimah,* when the white satin tallis was placed on their shoulders, all this she remembered. But now, now that the scars on her face had somehow sunk into the lines of age and she looked almost like other women, now she had lost everything— the sheen of her black hair, the bend of the knee, the music that once she heard so keenly came to her as if muffled, as if God were hiding his face. And wasn't he? She wanted to go to her daughter. She thought about her every waking moment. She imagined her face and her body and her bed covers and her thoughts; the last was the most difficult of all. Please God, at least be merciful enough to let me stop thinking her thoughts.

There were reprieves, of course. Hadn't she recovered from the pox and returned from the hospital that no one returned from? But this time her brother Isaac wasn't there to fight off the angel of death. She told herself that she was not the first woman to outlive her child, that people die in their prime before they had done the thing they wanted to do, regularly, of typhus and diphtheria, of flu and train accidents and lightning bolts and mysterious illnesses that bring fever and choke the breath away, of appendixes bursting and tumors growing, that the common condition of people is to lose someone they love or to lose themselves.

This view of mass death, of the mourners of Zion going back to the exodus of Egypt, was comforting. She added to it the camps and the ovens and the cruelty of man and the babies who died in transportation trains and her own loss, her Sharon, lying in a bed in Greenwich Village without a voice and with her hands weakly pushing away the cup of broth that her brother's wife tried to give her, her Sharon became just like one raindrop among the billions that fall from the sky and disappear into the ground.

The comfort she gave herself with this thought did not last long, and soon she was back at the memory of the little girl who would sing in the kitchen as she helped set the table: the little girl whose hand she held in the bus trip across Baltimore to the music teacher. Was it her fault, this life that had happened to her daughter? Yes, it was her fault, she said to herself as she folded herself into a small ball and tried each night to find sleep in the bed she had shared for so many years and which now seemed in each corner, in each dip of the mattress, to accuse her of failure. And the tenderness that she felt for her child swelled within her and covered her entirely like the blisters of the pox puffed and ready to burst.

Fame: 1952

Will Katz went on a trip with his friend Johnny Pommer. They went as part of the commission to investigate Communist party infiltration in the army posts in Paris and Hamburg and Athens. Everywhere they went, the two men under thirty were greeted by cameras, reporters, and dignitaries of the local government and generals and colonels and lieutenants who drove them to the best hotels and invited them to the best night spots for evenings with long-legged, big-breasted, good-smelling women who knew why they had been asked along.

Johnny Pommer had been introduced to Will Katz at a party in New York given by the real estate developer Irwin Pommer. Irwin owned the great buildings with gargoyles on the green-and-white roofs that marched along upper Broadway. He owned four blocks of midtown Manhattan and he was building along Third Avenue, adventuring into a no-man's-land of tenements and hardware stores that would either make his fortune or send him tumbling to his knees. Johnny was his son and destined to go into the business as soon as he had a little experience in the world of finance and politics, both of which were required in equal proportions for the trade. Johnny was short but muscular, and his square jaw and gray eyes, which sat under a shag of curly blond hair, made him look just a little like Michelangelo's *David,* a statue Will Katz had admired so much that he kept a small reproduction of it in his office on his shelf along with the law books from his last year of school.

Johnny Pommer admired Will Katz, who seemed always to attract newspapermen, who knew everyone and who could fix anything from a parking ticket to a restaurant violation, and who would one day, his father had said it, be governor of New York and maybe the first Jewish president. Johnny Pommer knew that one day, as sure as the five fingers on his hand, he himself would surely be chairman of Pommer Enterprises, and he sincerely hoped that by then he would understand what was expected of him. He had problems with left and right, and he had trouble on the football field remembering which way he was supposed to run and who it was he was supposed to block. He smiled at everyone eagerly and he always paid for drinks and he ordered limousines to take his friends to the theater. If someone at his table looked sad, he would get up from his seat and give them a hug. He wanted to make things right for everyone.

When Johnny Pommer and Will Katz got to Paris, he bought a Marie Antoinette doll for his favorite sister and he had the army fly it back in the diplomatic pouch so that she could have it before the week was out.

Will Katz had asked Johnny to be his assistant on the committee for reasons that even Will Katz, who was never at a loss for explanations, did not clearly understand. Johnny played with his collection of baseball cards, which he carried in a leather wallet in his jacket pocket. He shook his curly head from side to side and always agreed with everything Will said. He had given the senator a bottle of Dom Pérignon and talked about his father's office building in Puerto Rico, which had been built to withstand typhoons and hurricanes up to 600 MPH. The senator, who liked a man who promised to take him deep-sea fishing on his father's yacht, which wintered in the turquoise sea off of Key West, had warmed to him immediately. He was a good-looking addition to the staff.

In Paris the two young men had eaten at the Tour D'Argent and gone dancing in a dark club at the top of Montmartre, where they had stood above the city and stared down at the lights and sung with the general and his aide, who had accompanied them, the Army football song. They had announced to the papers, or rather Will had announced, that they had names, actual names of men on the NATO staff who had fornicated with East German women and had handed over to the enemy documents of grave importance to the security of the United States. They had names of Party members who were employed at army headquarters and had infiltrated into the highest level on the chain of command. The Paris offices of the Stars and Stripes were a hotbed, Will's term, a hotbed of fellow travelers with access to secret information. Will's words made headlines in newspapers from Bonn to Boise. The generals were afraid of losing their jobs. Wasn't it their fault that commies had risen through the ranks on their watch? The generals were afraid of being named by Will Katz. Men who had landed at Normandy, men who had led battalions through the Dordogne, up through the hill towns outside of Milan, men who saluted God in their sleep and who knew what it was like to sit in the trenches in the rain and pick bugs from the eyes of men who had bled out their lives in the night, these men showed Will Katz pictures of their wives and their children, of their mothers and fathers, in hopes that he would remember them kindly and not mention their names.

Bessie hired a secretary just to cut things about Will out of the papers. She pressed all the photographs of Will between the pages of a leather album. The album sat on the bookshelf next to the complete works of Shakespeare Howie had used in his sophomore year at City. It leaned against the Bible that her mother had given her as a wedding present.

Howie said to Bessie, "He's chasing some communists that aren't there. He's ruining reputations that may not deserve to be ruined."

"Sometimes," said Bessie, "I wonder what kind of an American you are."

Howie wiped the steam on his glasses and turned back to his newspaper. Only the slight trembling of his hands as he held the pages between his fingers might have revealed that he wished his son would visit more cathedrals and art galleries and fewer army bases on the remainder of his trip.

At four in the morning in Hamburg on their way to Rome, the two men staggered into their adjoining bedrooms in the hotel that had been rebuilt, just a few years before, the one that had housed Hitler's headquarters on the lobby floor when he came to Hamburg. Where Hitler's receptionist once sat painting seams up her stockingless legs, now the maître d' of the restaurant stood at a podium and directed diners to the tables that filled the room where once Hitler's desk had rested. Near the desk Goering and Goebbels and Himmler had sat on leather chairs and pored over maps, offering strategies that were ultimately less successful than the new chef's sauce béarnaise and his Wiener schnitzel international, which was served on a yellow china plate garnished with gherkin and radish.

After a long night of Scotch and sodas, hardly ever with ice—ice being, after all, an American luxury—after Johnny had danced with a girl in a bar who licked her tongue in his ear and said things to him that he didn't understand in German or English, after Will had put his arm around a little fräulein just up from the Bavarian countryside whose father was killed on the Russian front—all the dead soldiers had been killed by the Russians—and later pushed her away on the street when she attempted to get into the car with him, after a long day of press conferences and promising names that were being wired to him the next morning from the senator's office, after telling the local press that the communist conspiracy to overthrow the government of the United States was a threat to every man, woman, and child on this globe who valued the freedom to think and write and worship as they wanted, Will Katz led a young soldier who was his liaison with his office in Washington, relaying messages back and forth, into his bedroom. Will Katz's new friend stood by the window with the curtains blowing above his shoulder and his naked body bent over as he had promised. Will Katz felt an urge that was beyond repressing, that shook him to the core, that was for the first time since his early childhood a thought without thought, a feeling without calculation, that rose from the groin and flowed through the whole of his body. It was almost happiness; so urgent was the moment, so thoroughly was he living in that moment, so needful he was, that he cried out to the soldier, "Help me." So four stories above Hitler's former office, above the Restaurant FierYahrZeiten, Will Katz finally understood why everyone said travel was broadening.

It wasn't that everyone approved, just that everyone was alarmed and eager not to be named themselves. There were some cartoons that showed the two young men like bad kids putting gum on the teacher's seat. There was some talk of the true Constitution and the rights of citizens to due process and some questioning about the communists under the bed that like so many cooties kept getting trapped in the hairs of the broom just in time for the evening news. Certain Jews, lay officers of the major Jewish organizations, were biting their fingernails. "If Will Katz becomes the first Jewish president, we'd better pack our bags." Jews, of course, always have their bags packed, so that was just a manner of speaking.

His eyes with their slight cross, the whites gleaming as if they were part of a fried egg, Will Katz appeared night after night on the evening news. He called his new enemies "commie symps," "pinko wimps," and he went to dinner at the White House and he had lunch at least once a week with the head of the FBI, who was a man who trusted very few people, and young Will Katz was one of them. They shared certain tastes. The young soldier became an aide de camp, a general factotum, a secretary to Will Katz. He was delivered by chauffeur one night to the house in Alexandria where the head of the FBI lived, and although it was wintertime he was wearing only his GI overcoat and his galoshes, inside of which his bare toes had turned blue with cold.

There were rumors. Mildred heard them. "It couldn't be true," she said to Flora.

Flora said, "Dr. Bergman said that sons who were attached to their mothers might have difficulty making the transition to women."

"So why should they make the transition to men?" said Mildred.

When Flora repeated the question to Dr. Bergman, he asked her, "What are you avoiding talking about?"

Arthur said he didn't like Will. "Not because of the fag thing," said Arthur, who had grown more tolerant since Louisa had left him, "but because," he said to Flora, sitting at her bedside one dusk, "because he makes everyone feel guilty. I never signed anything, and I feel guilty."

"I know what you mean," said Flora, who was about to lose the solitaire game spread out before her. "I feel guilty, too. Everyone feels as if they'd betrayed someone, their country or something."

"I don't know," said Arthur. "I don't understand Picasso and I don't understand politics. That shouldn't make me a traitor to my country. When I see him on television, whispering into the senator's ear, I keep thinking he's going to name me."

Flora laughed, but Arthur looked worried. "Do you suppose Will could use his contacts with the FBI to find Moses?" Arthur asked, not seriously, but not joking, either. His eyes blinked.

Hedy came home from school, her uniform stained with ink. "I hope she turns into a girl one of these days," said Arthur. It was Flora's turn to look worried.

Jerusalem: 1952

It was hard for Teddy, now Ari, to remember the face of his nanny, who had read him a book in German about a little boy whose fingers were chopped off because he had stolen a cookie. It was hard for him to remember the face of the doorman, who had pulled him off of his friend Alan when they were both waiting for the school bus on Park Avenue and Alan had said that Teddy's front teeth looked like elephant tusks and Teddy had pushed him down and was ready to pound his skull into the pavement when the doorman in his blue uniform and gold braid had picked him up under his arms and held him kicking and screaming up in the air. It was just possible for Teddy to remember the apartment with its long yellow walls, the velvet chairs, and the rose-colored couch in the living room where his mother sat leaning against the embroidered cushions, with yellow flowers and blueberries climbing up their sides. It was easy to remember the dining room with its long mahogany table and the crystal chandelier that came from France, his mother had said, but it was impossible to picture the kitchen. He had hardly ever been to the kitchen, but he could remember the dining room door swinging open and the maid with the silver tray stopping at his place. "Here, master Teddy, some lamb chops," she had said, and he remembered the smell of baking soda and ammonia that lay on her hands and spoiled his appetite.

"Come back," his father wrote him, "the business needs you. Frank is a hothead and he will lose all we have built if anything should happen to me. The business is for you. Your grandfather began it. You would be the fourth generation of Gruenbaums in the business. Doesn't that mean something to you? This is our family. We have accomplished this. Don't throw it away. The War of Independence is over, you did what you wanted, now come back and lead a real life, in the real world. Think about it," said Arthur in his letter. "Write me if there is any chance you would return, even for a visit. You are, after all, my son."

Ari walked to the army headquarters on Rehoboth Street, past an Arab pulling a goat with a rope along the narrow sidewalk. His khaki pants, his white shirt, his sandals, were drenched with sweat. The dust in the street rose and fell as if someone were shaking a blanket over all Jerusalem. He breathed deeply, pulling hot air into his lungs. The cypress trees on the hills seemed to float in the heat, and the white houses and the pink stones seemed to flow one into another. He passed a woman talking in German to her male companion. She spoke to Ari in accented Hebrew. She wanted to find the orphans' building, the one where new refugees were arriving that morning.

"Who knows who is coming?" she said to him with a small light in her eye.

As he walked past the market where the Arabs were selling oranges and dates that they pulled from huge baskets and wrapped in brown paper, Teddy thought of his father, "Come here," he would write. "Here is the real world. Here is my home." He would tell his father about Shulamit, whose arms and neck were dark brown from the sun and who could drive a tractor and crawl for hours in the rows of tomatoes and who had told him stories he had never heard before. Here, he wanted to tell his father, the rocks were white and the goats that climbed them had horns that curled in circles, and these horns were speckled the color of rocks, golden and gray, and the streets were white and the new buildings in Tel Aviv were white and the waves in the harbor of Haifa were white and in the ruins of Caesarea, where his army unit had camped for a week, the stones were surrounded by white sand, by columns and pillars and steps that had once held Roman soldiers who sacked Jewish cities but could not destroy the people.

Ari wished his father would understand. He didn't want the business. He didn't want a Cadillac car with fins. He didn't want an apartment like his father's with two maid's rooms behind the kitchen. He didn't want to marry a woman who knew how much to tip the doorman at Christmastime. He didn't want a maid to bring him lamb chops. He wanted a woman who could use her own hands and children who wore sandals and whose arms were brown and who were safe in the land that was theirs.

By the time Ari reached headquarters and received his orders and had taken the jeep and the driver that was his past the walls of the old city, out on to the road to Elath, into the desert where the mounds of sand dipped and flowed and an occasional hermit cried out to his God from the protection of a hidden cave above the long wadis, he had forgotten his father.

Maria and Frank—At the Edge of a Precipice: 1952

Maria combed her hair in front of her dressing table. Frank watched her. She was naked. He was full of desire. Her limbs smelled of coconut oil and her pubic hair curled in even rows and her white arms rose and fell with each stroke of the brush.

"Hugo has spoken to a lawyer," she said.

Maria rose from the table and lay down beside him. She put her hands on his stomach and stroked him carefully. "We may not be together forever," she whispered as she pulled up his shirt and traced with her fingers, nails perfectly shaped and painted rose, little circles around his nipples. He moaned in anticipation of her next gesture.

The Conversion of Moses Gruenbaum: 1932 and After

Moses Gruenbaum had waited in the monastery for the return of his mother with infinite patience, and when the other boys would tease him, "She's not coming for you, she forgot about you," he would close his eyes and put his hands over his ears. He learned to look his tormentors in the eye and not move a muscle. In his mind he held a picture of his mother, her red shoes with the silver buckles coming up the long path to the monastery, her hair blowing behind her, tied in a red-and-white scarf, and her skirt hiked up past her knees as she climbed the road. He always imagined her without Ezra, but with her white car waiting at the base of the cliff, and in the car, his nanny, with her blouse buttoned up to her neck, would be twisting a handkerchief in her hand, waiting for him.

The monks were patient with the child. They decided not to tell him exactly what they had learned from the *Miami Herald* and the *Miami World* centerfold. They decided not to announce to anyone that the child was among them. In the interest of the child's immortal soul, they kept his presence there a matter of conscience between them and their confessors. It was morally complicated, but then what is not? Besides, the child had appeared at Christmastime, a sure sign of God's intention.

The abbot sat in his study and talked to the little boy. The abbot had large eyes that seemed to sink back into his large head, which bobbed up and down on a small and frail body. "We think you will be staying with us a while. Would you like that? he said.

Moses said, "Yes, I would like that."

The abbot's eyes were kind. He put his arm around the child and drew him close. He brought him to the crucifix that hung behind his desk and he said to the child, "Jesus Christ takes care of children who need him. He will protect you and guide you, and He loves you."

Moses said to the abbot, "I am Jewish and I don't think Jews are allowed to believe in Jesus."

The abbot offered the boy some lemonade that he poured from a silver pitcher. It tasted cool and sweet. Moses wanted some more but wasn't sure it was all right to ask. The abbot took his glass and poured more just as if he could read the child's mind. "Here in the Monastery by the Mouth of the Bay, the mother of Jesus will also watch over you. Your mother cannot come back to take you, so you will be one of us and you will not be Jewish anymore because here we are not Jewish and we will arrange it so that you will be one of us. Would you like that?" he asked the child.

"Yes," said Moses.

"Do you have any questions?" asked the abbot.

"Yes," said Moses. "Will Jesus make the other boys like me?"

The abbot smiled. "Jesus will help you make the other boys like you. When you have accepted our Lord, you will be liked by them. It's important to have friends," said the abbot. "Jesus understands that, and so do I."

Moses replaced his lemonade glass on the desk and said, "When will I see my mother again?" The abbot took the child out on the terrace that looked down the cliff into the sea that whirled and banged on the rocks below. "See the sky," he said to the child. "See the clouds and the whole edge of the world that curves out there over the horizon." Moses saw. There was a small fishing boat just at the edge where the sea curved out of sight, blue of the water lifting into the paleness of air. "It is all God's creation, God's power that has made this." A seagull flew past, cawing out his hunger and snapping at the breeze. "Jesus Christ is God's son, and right now, as we are speaking, he is holding out his arms to you."

The abbot stared out over the horizon. He was a small man whose capacity for stillness, for concentration, for holding his spirit aloft and waiting, had become over the years as certain as the ocean itself. The boy, whose mother had not returned for him as she had promised, looked into the sky and saw the arms of Jesus. Perhaps it was only the clouds and the sun, perhaps it was the abbot's arms he saw raised up toward him, but he rushed into the abbot's cloak and hid his head in its dark folds, lifting it up only to whisper into the crash of the waves, "I believe that Jesus died for me."

The abbot stroked the boy's head. The child, he realized, needed a haircut.

It happened shortly after the baptism and after he had learned the catechism from Brother Mark. It happened in the dining hall after prayers. One of the boys, an older boy who was beginning to need to shave, called out to Moses to come and tie his shoelace, which had come undone. Moses got up from his seat and, kneeling before the older boy, began to make his knot when the boy leaned back in his chair, kicking his foot up and knocking Moses onto his back. Lying on the floor, Moses saw the stained-glass window with the dove holding the olive branch shining in the noon sun and he felt the trickle of blood on his neck from the spot where his head had hit the wooden boards. He rose to his feet and began punching and biting and kicking and screaming, "Jesus hates you," he said again and again as he raised his fists in a fury.

The older boy blocked his blows, but the smile was gone from his face. The other boys watched as Moses ran in circles, punching the air, yelling for Jesus, and bleeding down the back of his shirt.

Brother Mark intercepted him and led him off to the infirmary, where Brother Luke, who had dropped out of medical school after a few months, bandaged his head.

After that, the boys called him Mose, and they let him play baseball in the field with them, although he was small and it took him a while to learn how to catch and throw. He made a new friend whose name was Algernon, whose mother had died and whose father had disappeared. Moses gained weight. He grew. He lost the hunch to his shoulders and the pallor in his face. He was the best student of them all when it came to Latin and Greek.

He told Brother Mark that he missed his mother, who said, Don't we all, and Isn't that the way it is for man, to be always wanting a mother and never having one, and he felt better that Brother Mark too was without a mother and that missing your mother did not make you a bad Catholic. "Mary is our mother now," said Brother Mark, and Moses stayed longer in the chapel, telling Mary the things that concerned him, like the men who were following Ezra. Did anything happen? he asked her again and again, until he forgot the question and spoke to her about improving his ability at second base and asked her to help him learn to swim. Brother Paul helped him, and he was soon swimming in the surf with the other boys and he would swim out farther than the others and dive under the biggest waves and Brother Paul would be standing on the shore in his hassock, screaming out into the ocean, "Moses, that's far enough, enough," until the boy caught the next wave in and was washed up, sandy and sturdy, on the beach.

The second Christmas he spent at the monastery, he was one of the three wise men who came to visit baby Jesus in his stable, at the pageant that was given for the Catholics of Miami and used as a fund-raising event for the orphanage, since tickets were ten dollars or more. This was an honor given as a reward only to boys who deserved special recognition here on earth as well as in heaven.

"Christ was a Jew, too," said the abbot at dinner to his assistant.

"He'll always be circumcised," said the assistant making a face like a man discovering a bug in his sandwich.

"So was Christ," said the abbot, who thought too much could be made about a small flap of skin.

In Which Frank Finds His Way Out of a Tight Spot: 1952

Flora felt guilty meeting Aaron Haft in the stolen time between lunch and dinner, in the evenings when Frank had told her he was working, but was he? Flora felt that the sweetness that was hers was tainted by its secretness. She didn't like dishonesty. She didn't like lying to Frank.

She met Frank at the club on a Thursday night when women were allowed in the dining room. She ordered a Scotch and drank it fast. She was frightened. Her glasses kept fogging over with moisture that seemed to pour out of her body, a mixture of tears and sweat. But she was sure. She had discussed it carefully with Dr. Bergman. He had not encouraged her, but he hadn't discouraged her, either. "It's your choice," he had said.

She made it. She was going to tell Frank. She had someone else, someone she might marry. She felt sorry for him sitting there opposite her at the table, his hooded eyes hardly moving, like a snake sensing danger. She thought how her words would sound to him. It hurt her to think of the shame that would sweep over him. He tapped on his spoon. She knew that once she had left Frank, Arthur would fire him. He had no stock, no resources, no means to keep living. She would change her will. She was going to tell him. She had every right. She loved Aaron Haft. But the words didn't come out of her lips. It was hard. Frank was her husband after all. She was used to him, used to the life they had together. Every-thing else, even the joy that beckoned her, was uncertain. She wasn't quite ready, not yet, to tell him. Soon, she would. Next week, she would. She promised herself. Dr. Bergman understood how hard it was for her to let go of the way things were. Besides, she felt sorry for Frank. She saw that he was handsome still, but now she knew, hard-earned knowl-edge, that you shouldn't judge a book by its cover. She looked across the table and saw Frank alone, far away, sealed off in a glass tomb. He was sad, she thought, really sad, and next week, next week, she would tell him. Next week, she thought. I will tell him and he will leave and I will marry Aaron Haft. Happiness, happiness is coming to me, she thought as she silently ate her dinner.

The next morning Maria called Frank at the office. "You have to meet me," she whispered into the phone.

It wasn't the first such call Frank had received. He clenched his teeth. He hoped she wasn't pregnant. He didn't need any more trouble. He arranged to have lunch with Maria at the Oyster Bar at the Plaza. If they met anyone they knew, he would say were discussing the potential em-ployment of an uncle of hers who had survived the war in Buenos Aires and now wanted to come to the States. They were in fact discussing that uncle, but he doubted if that was the reason she had called him.

He arrived at the Plaza and went immediately into the men's room, where he smoothed his hair and straightened his already straight tie. He pushed his shoulders back and pulled in the muscles of his abdomen. He was flat, absolutely flat, but nevertheless he checked several times a day. Before a man knows what's happening, deterioration can set in, muscle tone can go. The skin at the base of the throat can sag. The upper arms can grow fleshy and limp. Frank wanted to be hard, hard as the oak floor on which he was walking with his perfectly polished black shoes and his handkerchief appearing above his pocket, just exactly one and one-quarter of an inch so that the monogram, the blue interlocking letters, would show. He saw her sitting at a table by the window, a bowl of iris and tiger lilies on the shelf behind her head. The sun splashed down on the crystal water glass, reflecting fragments of light as if diamonds had spilled across the white cloth.

"Darling," she said to him, her voice hushed and deep in her throat, the soft slur of her voice adding mystery to the word. "The lawyer will get me nothing. I am poor." She sighed. The word floated out between them.

Frank thought about being poor, poor like his father and mother in the rented rooms by the elevated, poor when you considered each purchase of shoes as if it weighed against dinner. That kind of poor he had forgotten, but not quite. Poor, his beautiful Maria poor, himself, too, poor, and the thought made him ill. Why do all the wrong women have money? he thought. Short women with baggy circles under their eyes, those are the kind that have money.

Maria looked at him with her hands fluttering nervously over her plate. "I'll have to find someone else," she said, looking down at her lap.

"Ria," he said, using the name he called her at their most intimate moments, "give me time."

Reader: You wonder was it love or simple sexual attraction that made him promise at the Oyster Bar at the Plaza Hotel to save Maria. Frank was not a man to make promises rashly. Sexual attraction was not novel enough for him to have gulped his lunch and rushed off to his office to think through his options, to make up his mind. Love, on the other hand, was not one of his illusions. Women were more or less appealing, grating, ingratiating, pleasurable, necessary, decorative, soothing, or abrasive, but he had never burned in the kind of religious flames that might require the word *love*. He had used the word, of course, whenever convenient, and Flora herself had extracted it from him on anniversaries and birthdays, but it no more directed his actions than pulling an earlobe set the feet running, or pressing the belly button caused an erection. He had easily avoided love, or perhaps it had avoided him, so he had been spared the concomitant mess that such entanglements suggested. It was rather that Maria, whose skin was pale and perfect, whose long legs quivered under her skirt, made him bitter about his bondage to Flora, made him see that he was pushed and belittled and demeaned. Sitting next to Maria and smelling her perfume, he thought himself entitled, justified. He saw himself in the mirror behind their table, a man whose elegance was unquestioned, whose taste was fine, who deserved the best. Which is when he remembered his M-1 in the closet of the Park Avenue apartment and he remembered Wes standing in the bar telling him, one foot up on the rail, his sunburned arms in a short-sleeved khaki shirt, that it was time to take action, time to bring things to an end, time not to wait for the favors of others, but to insist on one's rights. Of course he was talking politics, but the words Frank remembered so clearly took flight from the Zionism of their intentions and gathered other resonances. Freedom, after all, is not an abstraction, a noun for the rhetoric of office holders and would-be office holders, for army manuals and enlistment advertisements, for Will Katz to protect against the weasels of the Fifth Amendment, and antitrust lawyers and union leaders to evoke when their back is pushed to the wall. Freedom is the stuff of manhood, the essence of breathing; to grow old, to grow flabby, without knowing freedom, that would be a tragedy. This is the realization that made Frank clench his teeth and grind his back molars.

Emma, the cook, had swollen knees. She was hauling herself around from the kitchen table to the stove with perspiration dripping down her face and her hands reaching for the backs of chairs to guide her along the way. She wanted to go home to her sister, who worked in the five-and-ten in Harrisburg, Pennsylvania, and whose six children, her nieces and nephews, were the only family she had. "A vacation," she said to Flora. "Two weeks is all I want."

Flora sighed. Emma had just taken a vacation a few months ago. She wasn't going to be able to stay with them much longer. Emma made biscuits in the morning and they were still warm when they arrived on Flora's breakfast tray. She made a good roast beef, although she didn't understand the concept of rare. Whatever she cooked was always too well done, which was all right with Frank, who hardly ate meat anyway. He preferred grains and fish, no gravy, no sauce. "Do you think you should go to the doctor about your knees?" said Flora.

"I will," said Emma. "When I go home, I'll go to my sister's doctor."

So Emma left for a vacation. Bridget was in charge of fixing breakfast. Bridget not only couldn't make biscuits, she couldn't even make coffee. Flora was irritated with her. Thursday was her day off.

"Go Wednesday night," she said to her. "Never mind about breakfast, I'll skip it this Thursday, it will be good for me."

Bridget had a boyfriend who worked on the docks in Brooklyn, and while Flora wasn't sure, she suspected the two were planning on a wedding in the spring. She envied Bridget the blush on her face when she spoke of Ed. She worried for Bridget, what lay ahead, she pitied Bridget's husband-to-be: he would never have a decent cup of coffee. She told Frank that he would have to have breakfast at his office on Thursday. She gave Hedy a dollar to buy a doughnut on her way to school.

Frank woke at seven-thirty as usual. He showered and dressed and as usual slipped out of the room, leaving his wife asleep in her bed, her sheets and blankets snarled about her ankles, her silk nightgown pulled up over her hips, and her lipstick-smeared pillow lying on the floor. The ashtray was full as usual with Camels smoked down to their ends, and her copy of John Hersey's best-seller, half-finished, which she had marked with a pencil, lay on the edge of the bed. Hedy said good-bye to her father and rushed out the door, hoping to meet her friend Sally at the bus stop. They were both going early to school to practice shooting baskets in the gym before their first class.

Carrying an attaché case that held the orders for spring suits from the Midwest that had come into the office the day before, a clean hand-kerchief, a change of shirt, and his Parker fountain pen, Frank wished the doorman a good day and walked around the corner, pacing up and down, his vicuña coat collar pulled close to his neck over his Brooks Brothers silk scarf, keeping the wind that ripped up over the hill on Park Avenue away from his ears. His gray fedora with its broad brim tilted over his forehead threatened to blow off. He kept it on his head by holding it down with one hand.

He waited till he saw his daughter disappear down the block, then walked to Third Avenue and back to the building to give himself some time. He waited in the alley in front of the delivery entrance, which led to the basement corridors, past the laundry rooms and the storage rooms, and opened onto the gray cement fire stairs that provided passage up to the apartments and down to the street in case of emergency. He waited till he saw the back doorman, who was wearing work clothes, turn away and head down the corridor that led, Frank knew, to the underground locker rooms, where the superintendent had meetings with his staff, where a pot of coffee sat on a burner. It was only eight-fifteen in the morning, but the fellow had been on duty since six. In the moment he turned his back, Frank slipped in the door and followed the corridors to the stairway, walking casually along. It wasn't unusual for tenants to use the basement access to their sections of the building, especially in the wintertime when the hot air from the furnace was welcome on cold hands and reddened ears.

On the third-floor landing he heard the service door to the D apart-ments open. He quickly backed down the stairs, and when a maid carrying a large carton and a paper bag with coffee grounds opened her garbage can and dropped her load, she did not know he was close. Two floors up he heard the back elevator creak to a standstill on the landing above. He waited till the elevator man had rung the doorbell and spoken to the cook at great length, something about a friend of his who had a complaint about her behavior the night before. The elevator bell rang and the elevator doors creaked closed, and Frank could hear the chains and gears grinding downward. After hearing the apartment door slam, Frank let himself into his own apartment. He put down his attaché case but kept his gray suede gloves on. He walked to the hall closet, and from behind Flora's mink and his own old camel-hair coat, stuffed into the extra bag of golf clubs behind four umbrellas and Flora's blue velvet coat that she wore to the opera and the theater, he pulled out his M-1. He had loaded it the night before while Flora had sat on her bed reading her mystery story.

Frank walked down the hall to his bedroom. He opened the door carefully, lightly, as if his wrist were not really turning the knob, as if his feet were not really settling down on the heavy rose carpet in the hallway, as if he were not carrying the M-1 cradled against his chest. The caution he exercised was not because it mattered if she woke. The apartment walls were thick. He moved like his own shadow because he felt numb, like a body emptied of mind, as if he were moving on automatic pilot, as if radar were guiding him, as if he were not a flesh-and-blood man on a mission not so uncommon as all that.

He stood in the doorway, picked up the gun, and, holding it with his gloved hand, aimed at Flora, who tossed in her bed, neither more nor less than usual, the sunlight hitting her face through the slit at the corner of the linen shade and showing Frank a deep crease where she had been sleeping against the folded lace of her gown.

There was a terrible sound. He had missed and shattered the Chinese lamp on the bed table. Flora awoke and sat straight up, confusion on her face. Frank took three steps into the room. He aimed again. This time his hand was steady and blood and membrane and shattered bone flew over the pillows. Frank was a free man.

He knocked over the night table, emptied all the drawers, took Flora's jewelry box, and grabbed her diamond necklace, the diamond engagement ring that had been given her by her grandmother, her gold charm bracelet, her pearls, and emptied the costume rings and earrings, loops and loops of fake gold on the floor. He opened all the drawers of her desk and spilled the contents, and he threw the two lamps made of porcelain in the bathtub. He pulled one of the lace curtains down. Then he carefully closed the bedroom door. He put the gun back in the closet. He put the valuable jewelry in his attaché case. He went down the fire stairs and, waiting until the back doorman was busy signing for a package, he slipped out into the street.

Hailing a cab, he arrived at his office, said good morning to his secretary, and, in the privacy of a men's room stall, threw the diamonds and the pearls into the toilet and flushed them away. As the water rushed from the rim of the bowl, he had a second's regret and considered thrusting his hand down after the jewels. He decided to let them go. Naomi's diamond joined the rest of the sewage under the city's streets, moving sluggishly through ancient pipes toward the river and the tides that would carry it out to sea.

Back at his desk, he began to open his mail, most of which was complaints about damaged or incomplete orders. At noontime he called Maria. She was still asleep. The maid took the message.

Later that afternoon Hedy, who had a test the next day on the War of 1812, rang the bell of her apartment. She had forgotten that Emma was on vacation and Bridget had her day off. When no one answered she put down her school bags and searched among the books for her keys. She let herself in.

The apartment was quiet. She went into the kitchen and made herself a ham, cheese, pickle, and leftover tuna-fish sandwich, eating as she walked down the darkened hallway to her mother's room, dropping pieces of tuna fish on the carpet. Sometimes her mother was home in the early afternoon, already napping, or playing solitaire on her bed. The quiet of the house made Hedy think her mother was still out.

The door was open, but the room was not light. The shades must still be pulled down. Hedy walked across the threshold and saw first the empty drawers and the jewelry box, green leather with gold engraving and her mother's initials on the lid, lying on the floor. Then she saw the bed with Flora's limbs stiffening and the blood drying and the bones of her skull showing and her face gone, and Hedy didn't scream, she didn't run, she walked slowly down the hall. She opened the door and rang the elevator bell, and only when she saw Patrick, who gave her his usual smile and said, "Going out without your coat, young lady?" did she find her voice. Sitting, on the little bench in the elevator to prevent the dizziness from causing her to fall, she told Patrick what she had seen in her apartment. The superintendent had to open the door with his master key because she had closed it behind her. The police came. They called Frank at his office and he came home immediately. He put his arm around his daughter in a gesture so unusually intimate, she stiffened.

Mildred held Hedy tight and kept saying again and again, "I don't believe it." Arthur felt his heart missing beats, going loud and then soft in his chest. He lay down on the Victorian chaise in Flora's living room, trying to get his pulse steady.

Hedy couldn't think clearly. She couldn't eat. Her old rash appeared on her breasts and broke out across her belly. She scratched all through the night. She couldn't stop seeing the bed and her mother lying on the bed and her broken glasses on the floor and she couldn't sit and she couldn't lie down and she couldn't stand. She roamed about. She wasn't crying, but she wasn't all right. She was not all right at all.

The following day Detectives Ross and Barney were all over the building questioning everyone. They sat in the kitchen and drank cup after cup of Bridget's awful coffee, asking questions. They talked to Arthur and his cook, too. Detective Barney showed up at the club and, flashing a badge, appeared in the locker room, asking questions. Detective Ross took the receptionist at the Gruenbaum Company to the Automat for a private conversation. Over a cheese sandwich he heard about Frank and the secretaries that had come and gone over the years. Detective Ross asked Hedy if her parents got along. Hedy shrugged. She stared at Detective Ross. She had nothing to say. Hedy thought that the FBI and New York's finest always got its man. Hedy thought that no one got away with murder. She expected the police to catch the intruder. She knew that none of the elevator men or doormen or janitors had seen any unknown person enter the building. But she figured that fingerprints would do it. Hedy asked Detective Ross if he had a wife. He did. She asked Detective Ross if he had children. He did. Hedy thought he would be a good father. Everyone remarked on how brave Hedy was, considering that she was the one who found the body.

Will Katz and Bessie and Howie came to the funeral. Hedy shook Will's hand. Bessie kissed her on the cheek. Flora's astrologist came and offered to read Hedy's stars for free, anytime. Mildred and Arthur sat on either side of Hedy during the service and kept turning their heads to stare at her with caution in their eyes as if they expected her to behave badly, to fidget or make a scene in public. The rabbi leaned forward to speak directly to Hedy, telling her that her mother would live on in her thoughts, that she was to be comforted among the mourners of Zion. Dr. Bergman came and sat in the back row. Afterward, standing on the street waiting for the long black limousines to fill up, he introduced himself to Hedy, who was surprised. He looked like an ordinary man, not the way she had pictured him at all.

On the way to the cemetery, in the black car, the rabbi told Hedy that she must not lose her faith in God, who would watch over her now as a mother would, near her in all her times of trouble. Hedy thought that God should reveal the name of her mother's murderer. Hedy thought that God should have led the murderer to the apartment next door where an old lady who had no children lived. Or He should have tripped him on the stair so that he shot himself in the head. Hedy was unimpressed by God or his emissaries, but she was polite to the rabbi and stood by his side at the grave, standing very straight, almost as tall as her father, in her camel-hair coat and her white-and-black saddle shoes. She threw the shovel of dirt on the disappearing coffin when the rabbi instructed her. She looked up at the blue, cloudless sky. How long until the sun burned out? How far away was the nearest star? She smelled her aunt Mildred's perfume and put her hand in the pocket of Mildred's fur coat, but that was the only sign she gave that she was herself actually present at the funeral. In fact, Hedy was embarrassed that everyone was looking at her. She wished her uncle Arthur would stop blinking and blinking.

In the days that followed the funeral, she returned to school and took a makeup test on the War of 1812 and with a cold look and a shrug of her shoulders brushed aside her friends' attempts to console her. Detective Ross hinted to Hedy that the police thought it might have been Bridget or Bridget's boyfriend from the docks in Brooklyn since there didn't seem to be a break-in. But of course some of these guys could jimmy locks so that they were hardly damaged. Bridget sometimes left the door open when she went to put the garbage out and talk with the back elevator man. Maybe, Bridget had admitted, she had forgotten to lock the door. She cried and her ears got all red and her skin was blotchy and her Irish accent got so thick they had to get a cop from the old country to translate what she was saying. Emma, whose knees were so swollen that she decided not to return to her job, was interviewed by Detective Barney, who made a special trip to see her and cleared her of any complicity. They interviewed her nephews and nieces, too, just in case, but found no suspects. The tabloids called it the "Park Avenue Blast," and there was some talk that the family might have been involved with gangsters. It was remembered by one clever reporter that Arthur Gruenbaum's brother Harry's widow had been connected with the Miami gangster Ezra Brest, but that was ancient history and no one could tell anyone why the gangs would go after Flora Gruenbaum in her bed on Park Avenue. There was some talk again about the bank closing and that perhaps some investor who had lost everything was taking it out on Flora, mistaking her for Mildred. But that was improbable. They considered that it might have been the union, the one that was pressing the Gruenbaum factories in Pennsylvania and North Carolina. But what help would it have been to the union to have killed Flora? Robbery was the likely motive; $20,000 worth of diamonds and pearls were missing. Hedy was told by the chief of detectives, who made a personal appearance at the scene of the crime, that when the murderer went to sell the jewels, someone would tip them off.

But there was another possibility. Detective Ross had made himself at home in Arthur's office. Arthur had told him that his sister's husband had some dealings with gunrunners some years back, before the founding of the state of Israel. Arthur had also let it slip that Frank was not the best of husbands. The receptionist had told Ross about Frank's extramarital interests. It turned out that the bullet that had killed Flora came from an army-issue gun, just like the ones that passed through the Gruenbaum office some years before. Detective Barney was cheerful. Detective Ross figured it was always this way. "The husband did it," he said to his wife.

"How do you know?" she said.

"I can smell it," he answered.

But smelling and proving are two different things. Detective Ross found out by following the phone bills that Frank had a relationship with a Maria Weiss. Of course, lots of guys cheat on their wives, and that doesn't make them murderers. Maria Weiss welcomed the detectives into her home. Yes, she admitted, she had a special relationship with Frank Sheinfold. But what did that prove? Detective Ross found her very attractive himself.

The Saturday after the funeral, Frank carried his old clubs down to his car, which had been brought round from the garage, and drove up to Westchester for his first outing since his wife's death. Some of the members questioned whether it was all right for him to be out on the course just one week later. They didn't know that he had stopped the car on the Hutchinson Parkway, over on the shoulder of the road, where the river runs under a bridge. There he spotted a drainpipe, broken and abandoned under a pile of old fall leaves, rocks, and broken branches. He had taken his bag of clubs out of the trunk and removed his M-1 from the bag, carrying it down into the ravine and stuffing it into the pipe that was gradually sinking into the sludge at the bottom of the muddy water.

Arthur thought about Detective Ross's questions. He shivered. He called Mildred. What did she think? Mildred thought it was too awful and didn't want to hear any more about it. No one in the building had seen anyone come in or out the morning of the murder. Frank had been on his way to his office when it happened. He couldn't prove that he wasn't at home, but on the other hand no one could prove that he was.

Detective Barney was waiting for Hedy by the front door two weeks after the funeral. Hedy sat down with him in the turquoise living room. His large frame seemed uncomfortable on the gilt chairs. His face reflected in the mirror. He mopped his forehead with a handkerchief. He asked Hedy about the guns that went to Israel. Hedy knew it wasn't legal. She didn't want to say anything. She shook her head. "I don't know," she answered to everything.

Detective Ross thought she knew something. "Your father have a gun?" he asked. "A gun of his own?"

Hedy understood what the detective was saying. It wasn't possible. She wouldn't believe it. He did have a gun. She didn't say anything. She didn't want to get her father in trouble for sending guns for the liberation of Palestine. After Detective Ross left, she opened the closet door and, pushing through the old coats, found the golf bag where her father had put the gun, their secret. The bag was there, but it was empty. There was no gun inside.

Hedy waited for the New York City detectives to get the murderer. She considered whether or not she believed in capital punishment for him when he was caught. She began to play solitaire as soon as her homework was finished. She spread the cards out on her own bed and played till she won, night after night.

Detectives Ross and Barney came back. "Was your mother happy with your father? Was your mother planning to go on a trip, or change her life in any way? Did your mother have a special man friend?"

"Yes," said Hedy, but she didn't know his name. Hedy told the detectives that her mother and father had fights.

"He ever hit her?" asked Detective Ross.

"No," said Hedy.

"You're sure he didn't have a gun?"

"He had a gun," said Hedy, "but it's gone."

Hedy was afraid of her own words. She was afraid of her own thoughts. She stopped thinking. She was only able to do her math home-work. Everything else was too difficult. Her notebooks remained blank. When Frank came home from the office after stopping at his club for a game of squash, he found Detectives Ross and Barney in the living room with his daughter.

"No," Frank answered Detective Ross, "I never had a gun. Hedy"— he turned to his daugher—"what made you say that?" Hedy was silent.

"Did you make that up, about the gun?" asked Detective Ross.

Hedy was silent. "Maybe," she said.

Her father smiled at her. "Good girl," he said. "It takes a mature person to admit to a mistake." Later Frank said to Hedy, "I threw that gun out a long time ago."

But Hedy knew he hadn't because every now and then she rummaged in the closet to feel it there, the long barrel cold on her hand.

Detective Ross believed Hedy had seen a gun, but how could he prove it? He got Frank's permission to search the house, and his men turned everything upside down. They emptied all the closets, finding Flora's unlucky dresses wrinkled on the floor, finding Hedy's old ice skates and her baseball glove that she no longer used, finding a note from Maria Wald tucked into the pocket on one of Frank's suits, finding Bridget's letters from her mother under her black stockings. They did not find a weapon that could blast the face off a woman before breakfast. Detective Ross believed he knew who had killed Flora, but all he had was motive and not a very compelling one at that; half the world cheated on their wives, half the world fought with their spouse, half the world had access to a gun at one time or another, but to put it together into an indictment, to bring it to the DA, to get the grand jury excited, that he couldn't do.

The detectives tried to pursue the robbery line. The jewels had disappeared. The murder weapon had not surfaced in a sewer or a garbage truck or a pawn shop. The newspapers stopped speculating. Justice was blind, thought Hedy. He had a gun, thought Hedy, and when she heard him come in at night she jumped out of her bed and stood for a while in the dark corner of her room behind the curtains. But he never opened her door.

She slept at her friend Sally's. She slept in Teddy's old bedroom in Arthur's apartment. Even there the sound of a car backfiring in the street, a siren calling down the avenue, woke her and she sat holding her knees to her chest, trying to calm herself. Sometimes she took her blanket and pillow and, locking the bathroom door, curled up in the tub. There she was able to sleep.

Arthur came home late one evening to find Hedy with her books spread out around her on his living room couch. He fixed himself a Scotch and soda. "What is there to say?" said Arthur, whose eyes kept twitching and whose hands trembled.

"You were a good brother," said Hedy.

"I was," said Arthur.

Frank spent his evenings with Maria. Her rent was paid by Frank. Detectives Barney and Ross knew this. They dropped in on Maria from time to time. She was always glad to see them. She offered them brandy and chocolate cake. They admired her ankles, and Detective Ross asked her the name of her perfume. It didn't change anything, that Frank wanted that woman; every man on a jury would understand that. They needed a weapon. They needed a witness. They had neither.

The Limits of Psychoanalysis: 1952

Dr. Bergman sat in his office and twirled his envelope knife. It was Flora Sheinfold's hour, and he had not yet filled it with another patient. It sat in the middle of his day, confronting him again and again with the fact that his work had its limits, that the body had its end. Discouraged, he noticed the ivy plant on his windowsill was turning brown. He hadn't thought he could stop death or change history or alter the equinox or make the rain come. But a little change, a little freedom, a deep breath that opened the lungs, that he had hoped for. He was tired of worrying the edges of dreams, the slips and the contradictions of love, and the irregularities of childhood memory. Perhaps he had not provided enough trust. He wanted her to spring from him the way a squirrel uses one branch of a tree to reach another. Maybe if he had ten more years? He sat in his office thinking about death and how would he feel when his turn came and how hard it must be to let go into nothingness. He thought of how frightened Flora must have been when she saw the intruder at her door and his head pounded and he twirled the envelope knife. He missed Flora Sheinfold, who amused him always in the ways she tried and the ways she failed and her habit of chewing on the stem of her glasses and the way her makeup would never stay in place. He felt somehow that the movement of her lipstick onto her teeth was a statement of hope, she had not, after all, assumed her final shape. Now it was too late, and Dr. Bergman, sitting at his desk, remembered Flora and sighed. Against intruders, insight and interpretation, his only weapons, didn't have a chance.

Rockefeller Center: 1952

Aaron Haft puts on his skates and moves slowly out onto the ice. He is alone. It is nighttime and the lights of the office buildings bounce off the square of sky above. People are standing at the rail above watching the skaters in their costumes go round and round the rink, and the center the dancers bend and twirl, cutting the ice with the sharp blades of their skates. The music plays. Aaron glides forward and, bending his knee, turns around and around. He wears his blue topcoat and a red scarf against the cold. He wears a wool cap his children had given him for his birthday. Solitary, he moves among the skaters. He is mourning Flora.

Mildred at Bonwit Teller's: 1952

Mildred is at the pocketbook counter buying a black alligator purse. She sees the pocketbooks hanging on their racks, the more expensive ones displayed in their glass cases. She is suddenly dizzy. She holds onto the countertop and steadies herself.

Without Julie she has managed very well. She has many friends who call each morning and constant luncheon and dinner engagements. She has her daughters, who are good as gold. She has, thanks to her brother, if not as much money as she once had, enough for an alligator purse, enough to go to Florida each winter and Deal in the summer. She is no longer a beauty but still desired, a good dancer, party girl. She has season tickets to the opera and the Philharmonic. She stands at the counter grieving for Flora, wondering for the first time, Why am I here, what is the point?

Reader: Consider the gallantry of women who live without husbands, who are not coupled or bonded like pigeons and deer or most of the human species, women who are single figures, responsible for their own pleasures and pains, and bank accounts. These days it is fashionable to envy them their singleness, their freedom from conventional intimacies and boring repetitions, but even today they are living on nerve and driven by harsh winds that don't touch the coupled, the merged, the ones with life insurance and matching pajamas. Consider how they arrive at parties and speak gaily and laugh in the face of the loneliness that must welcome them home each evening. They are the heroines of our domestic scene.

Hedy Finds Her Aunt Estelle: 1952

Hedy was not sleeping. Hedy was not doing her schoolwork. The school understood, but they thought she should leave for a while, repeat the year. Hedy didn't care. She packed up her books and cleaned out her desk. She sat in Arthur's living room watching the cars move up and down Park Avenue. Her rash came back.

Detective Ross stopped by. He asked Hedy where her father's sister, Estelle, might be. He wanted to talk to Estelle. He was grasping at straws. He had discovered that Estelle's husband, Manny, had once been in trouble with the law. Perhaps there was a connection with Flora's death.

Hedy told him, "My father doesn't like Estelle. He never says her name." Detective Ross said, "She's still your aunt. Nothing changes that."

One morning Hedy was gone. She had packed her clothes in a bag and left. She left a note for Arthur. "I am going south for a while. I'll call you. Don't worry." Arthur worried. Hedy was only sixteen years old. She was a girl, and girls shouldn't. He couldn't stand any more women running away. He blinked.

Frank shrugged. "She'll show up," he said.

Flora's mink coat, which had been hanging in the closet, was gone. Hedy had sold it in a pawnshop on 45th Street and Eighth Avenue. She bought a train ticket for Miami. The train took two days, and Hedy curled up on her seat watching the rivers and the trees, the small towns and the telephone poles, swim past. She slept. She felt safe on the train.

In Miami she took a taxi to the Sunplaza Hotel. She was wearing a sweater and her camel-hair coat. She was hot in the warm Florida sun. In the hotel lobby she asked the concierge, "Estelle Kravitz, is she here?"

Estelle was out by the pool. Her huge body was covered with oil, and with her bathing suit she wore gold earrings, a gold necklace, and her diamond watch. She wore high heels and her toes were painted red.

Estelle had read about Flora's death. She had called her brother to offer her condolences, but he had cut her off abruptly. So she wasn't a Park Avenue swell, she was the only sister he had, but if that's how he felt, what could she do? Now here was Hedy all red with the heat and some rash on her face, tall like her brother, thin, too thin, and looking like something the cat wouldn't even drag in.

Estelle took Hedy to her room and told her she could stay as long as she liked and she bought a tanning cream that would keep her from burning and she bought her a bathing suit because the child had forgotten hers and she introduced Hedy to everyone in the hotel lobby, My niece from New York, Hedy, meet Dr. Hans Snabel, meet Gloria Howrwich, and so on. It seemed the social director of the hotel knew every one of the regulars, the ones there for two weeks or two months.

"Use my makeup," urged Estelle. "You could use a little brightening up."

Estelle told everyone Hedy had come home and seen her mother on the bed. Poor child, they said. What a shock, they said. Of course some of the women had seen worse, the ones with the accents and the numbers on their arms. Even they said, "Poor child. Oh, no. Have they a suspect?" It didn't surprise them, of course, that even in America a Jewish woman could come to a bad end.

Estelle had no children. She was delighted to take the plucked chicken that was named Hedy and feed it and fuss over it and bring her chewing gum, movie magazines and romance comics, and cigarettes, and yellow barrettes for her hair. She bought Hedy a big box of saltwater taffy. Each candy was wrapped in a pink pastel paper. Hedy wasn't hungry, not even for saltwater taffy.

Hedy was grateful that her aunt Estelle had let her stay. What she was staying for and what she wanted she did not know. The sun wasn't good for her skin because her rash was worse. She called Arthur and Mildred. "Tell Daddy I'm going to stay a while with his sister."

Mildred said, "Estelle must weigh two hundred pounds and she still gets up on a dance floor and wiggles like she was Ginger Rogers. It's disgusting, that's what."

Arthur said, "I wonder if Moses is still in Miami?"

Hedy sent Arthur a box of oranges, which arrived in a package with a pink flamingo painted on the cover.

There were shuffleboard games and Ping-Pong and in the evening there was bingo and canasta and bridge. There was a dance and a barbecue on Tuesdays, and Thursdays was ladies' choice on the dance floor. There were clowns to amuse the grandchildren who came during school vacations and magicians all through the season for the adults. Estelle went through the crowd smiling at everyone. Everyone smiled at her. "Have a good time," she said. "You only live once." Hedy considered once could be too much.

She was lying on a chaise by the pool watching the senior ladies water ballet class that met twice a week. The women had learned how to make stars with their arms and legs spread out as they floated in a circle. They had learned how to somersault backward and come out in the center, all of their raised arms looking like petals of a rose, or so said the instructor, who was a young woman with a perfect body who was a lifeguard as well as a water ballet instructor. From a loudspeaker at the side of the pool came the sound of the Boston Pops providing music for the ballet. The women had passed the age of glamour, but they did exercises in the pool, waving arms and legs to the music, images of Esther Williams in their heads. Widows or soon-to-be widows, mothers, and grandmothers, these old ladies doing the sidestroke in formation were enjoying the winter in Florida, why not? Hedy stared at the ocean just beyond the path. It was calm and turquoise blue like the walls and the rug of the Sheinfold living room on Park Avenue. She was wearing red lipstick. Estelle had insisted. Her toes were painted, too.

A weight was on her too great for her frame. She felt as if she were sinking. She felt as if she wanted to sink. She got up and walked to the beach and past Mrs. Fine, who had had one of her nosebleeds that morning and so was not in the water ballet class. She walked into the ocean, which lapped at her feet, little waves that welcomed her, warmed in the sun, white froth about her ankles. She walked out in the water, feeling the clams and the pebbles underneath, feeling a sweep of seaweed brush by her thigh. She lifted her legs and let herself float. She was not frightened. She would just drift out until she reached the horizon's edge and then she would sink, holding her breath, and she would be gone, gone wherever her mother was gone, gone where the picture in her head couldn't follow, gone where she wouldn't keep thinking about the gun in the closet and what had happened to it, gone where it was quiet, better than here. That's what she wanted. Hedy was drifting out. Every once in a while she used her arms to paddle herself a bit farther, but mostly she waited for the gently ebbing tide to take her.

Mrs. Fine got up from her chair under the palm tree and rushed to the pool. The water ballet class was over. The women were wrapped in towels, their terrycloth slippers stuck under their chairs. Mrs. Goodman and Mrs. Kramer, Mrs. Levine and Mrs. Miller as well as Miss Ornstein, who had never married beause of madness in the family, moved together toward the ocean. They went right in the waves, not splashing themselves with water on the wrists or the chest the way they usually did. They pulled their bathing caps over their hair; their caps all had rubber flowers in pink, blue, and yellow on the top. Hedy, looking back at the shore, saw a line of flowers bobbing in the water as the women dunked their heads into the gently rippling waves. Mrs. Fine was wearing her tiger-print suit with the long skirt that kept getting caught in her legs. She did the breaststroke, nice and smooth; steadily she moved away from the shore. Mrs. Goodman's legs were not so good because of veins that showed blue on her calves and she moved slowly in the shallow water, but then she flopped her body straight down and did the dead man's float until the water was deeper. Mrs. Levine was last. Her stroke was the elementary back. Mrs. Kramer had been recently widowed and her eyes often filled with tears, but now she was clear-eyed and determinedly paddling out to the place where Hedy was drifting, quite far now from the shore. Miss Ornstein, who had retired after forty years as a secretary at the insurance company owned by her brother-in-law, was the star of the water ballet troop because she could stay underwater for the longest time and when she found her place in the formation she never lost it like some of the others who giggled or confused the beat and couldn't tell if they should turn left or right. Miss Ornstein now did a determined crawl, humming to herself as she swam. She was the first to reach Hedy.

Hedy was surprised to see the women, all of them older much older than her mother. Mrs. Fine said, "You been to Paris?" Hedy realized she was talking to her. She shook her head while treading water. "Neither have I," said Mrs. Fine, "but next year, God willing, Mo and I are going."

Mrs. Levine said, "I hear Paris is beautiful. Not as beautiful as Tel Aviv, but beautiful."

Mrs. Kramer rolled over on her back and, pulling up the straps of her bathing suit, which kept slipping down over her shoulders, said, "Once I got for my birthday a red sequined dress. It had little lines on the bosom that wiggled. What a dress, what a gorgeous dress. I looked like a tramp, my sister said, she was jealous. What a dress. I'll remember it till the day I die. You got a dress like that?" Hedy shook her head. Mrs. Kramer swam right up against Hedy. Her breasts were large and on land they hung down stretched and deflated, but in the water they floated up on top of the waves. "When I walked on the boardwalk at night, all the men turned around, and my Willie, he said, Don't wear that dress anymore. But I did."

Miss Ornstein said, "You seen the mountains in a storm? I saw last year in the Catskills."

"Not as good," said Mrs. Miller, "as the fog on the lake in Maine where my son-in-law built a cabin." Mrs. Miller kicked her leg and her gold ankle bracelet caught a flash of sunlight above the water. She said, "You know what's the best feeling in the world, sweetheart? Holding a sleeping baby, that's what. Say the baby has been crying and it took you a while to get her to stop and all of sudden she puts her arms around your neck and the weight of her body is up against yours. What a feeling. Better than anything. Don't you think?"

"I don't know," said Hedy, who had never held a baby.

Mrs. Levine came swimming up on the other side. The pink flower on her bathing cap bobbed up and down. "I remember when my Hershey brought me an ashtray from first grade, a smile on his face like he brought me my first million."

Mrs. Miller said, "But, darling, a sleeping baby whose whole weight lies on you, what a thing that is, just think of it."

Mrs. Goodman said, "That's good, but not the best. The best is a man who sleeps against you in the morning and when you move to get up he follows your body to the end of the bed trying to hold on to you."

"Nice," agreed Mrs. Kramer.

Mrs. Miller, sneezing from the water that had gotten up her nose, said, "My Harry, bless his heart, would smile when I brought him an applesauce cake, that was his favorite. Taking out of the oven, putting on a plate, watching as someone smiles all the while it goes down the throat, that's something."

"You cook, *maidele*?" asked Mrs. Miller. Hedy shook her head.

"You could learn," said Mrs. Fine.

Mrs. Levine said, "You have a boyfriend?" Hedy shook her head. "You will," said Mrs. Levine.

Mrs. Goodman said, "Tell her about the garden you made in Far Rockaway with a border of pansies and black-eyed Susans."

"Yes," said Mrs. Fine, "I used to garden before my legs got stiff. You have a garden?" she asked Hedy. "You don't, you should."

Miss Ornstein was doing a steady crawl around Hedy; her arms were like sticks, but they were strong. "You type?" she asked. "I type a hundred and twenty words per minute. I was the best in the office. I supported myself for forty years. A paycheck I earned. You earn any money yet?" Hedy shook her head. The women were around her now, holding hands, kicking their feet, the rubber flowers bobbing up and down.

"So," said Mrs. Goodman, "no babies, no husband, no cooking, no planting, no typing, what have you done?"

Hedy was getting tired. "I'm only sixteen."

"Oh," said Mrs. Kramer, "then you have everything ahead."

"Yes," said Mrs. Goodman. "Women do things more these days, vote even. It's not so hard to learn to cook."

Mrs. Levine, who did the dog paddle and could do it for hours, poked Hedy in the back right between her shoulder blades. "I won once a set of dishes at the Saturday matinee. What a surprise. My number was called. The plates were for me, blue-and-white china. My momma laughed so hard when I come home carrying them. What a day that was. I won. The movie had Joan Crawford. I always liked Joan Crawford after that."

The women were nudging her with their arms and their legs, pushing her, sort of, and pulling her, kind of, and blocking her way forward and leading her back to the sand. Hedy was happy to let Mrs. Goodman put her arm around her waist when they got to the place where the water was shallow. Hedy wanted to say "Thank you," but she was so tired she lay down on her beach towel and fell right asleep. The senior water ballet class watched her, pulling up their own chairs in a circle around her.

"She'll be all right," said Mrs. Fine.

Hedy Doesn't Get to Dance at Her Father's Wedding: 1953

A year and a half after Flora's death, Frank and Maria were married on a vacation in Palm Beach. Hedy wasn't there because she had gone off the summer before to visit her cousin Teddy in Israel. He and his wife, Shulamit, lived on a kibbutz in the north of Israel near the Golan

Heights, and when the invitation had come, Hedy said yes because she had nowhere else to go. At dinner one night Arthur told her that the people in Israel had none of the comforts of America, that toilet paper was rough, the plates on the kitbbutz were like those in Automats in the United States, the women had no silk dresses and most of the girls didn't even wear makeup. Also, the Arabs smelled peculiar and animals walked around in the streets and the sanitation was primitive and the desert was hot, Tel-Aviv was hot in the summer, so hot you couldn't breathe till nightfall, and people were always making you go look at ruins. Arthur preferred new buildings, of which there were some but not enough. There wasn't a first-class hotel, not by European standards, he reported.

Hedy decided to accept Teddy's invitation. Arthur told her to visit the trees he had planted, whole forests of trees he had paid for. He told her they were only saplings, but one day they would turn whole acres green. He told her to visit an eye clinic in Haifa. He had given the young doctor who had arrived at his office with a letter from Teddy the money to build the clinic. "It helps the Arabs, too, flies make them blind, and we can cure them. Make Teddy take you to the Home for the Young David, where I paid for the dormitory. The boys there came from camps." Arthur blinked rapidly. "Just go for a short visit, that's all."

Hedy in the Corridor of the Hadassah Hospital: 1990

In the hospital corridor Elan and Hedy, their children, Tova and Yehuda, and Hedy's cousin Ari were waiting.

Hedy on Kibbutz Hyrat: 1953

The girl from Yugoslavia, who had survived in the mountains with the partisans, hid food under her bed. During the war her nights had been spent moving back and forth above the Adriatic coast. Her older sister had brought her into the hills after a neighbor had hidden them in the cellar for two weeks, and when the girls came out into the street, their eyes blinking and squinting in the suddenness of light, their parents were gone and their house occupied by strangers who had already changed the curtains and taken down the window box their mother had planted with rosemary and thyme. Often when she woke at night, Hedy could hear the sound of crunching, chewing, crumbling. She would go outside and wait for the eating to be over. Sitting on the step of the cabin, while the girl from Yugoslavia sat up on her cot, her skin white and full and her breasts still flushed with dreams, Hedy watched the sky.

She traced the path of the morning star and the slide of the ghost moon as it faded in the silver light of the approaching sun. She stood up to watch the eastern edge of the kibbutz, out by the hut where the tractors, the sheets of dark plastic that would cover the green shoots of lettuce, the sharp shears and the lines of wire and rubber tubing, sat, next to the trucks that carried the workers out to the fields and the orchards that sometimes bore fruit and sometimes did not. Hedy watched the first red glow hit the metal roof of the quonset huts that squatted in the dry grass like ageless turtles who had lost their way to the sea.

She forgot her mother. Once, the girl from Yugoslavia had told her she could not remember her own mother's face. She could picture a blue dress with cherries on it, and she remembered her mother's handkerchief, white lace with a monogram, crumpled on the top of a bureau. Hedy had listened. In the kitchen when they washed plates together, in the children's house where they held babies over their shoulders and sang songs to four-year-olds who didn't want to lie down or eat lunch, they talked to each other in broken Hebrew, each accent different, each learning, each knowing words the other had not yet caught; but Hedy never spoke about her life in America. When the girl from Yugoslavia asked, Hedy would shrug. "I don't remember," she would say. "I don't know," she would answer. She never thought about her mother. She watched the sky and considered the distance from star to star. The question of dead stars worried her: Which were alive and which were mere illusions of life? Were light and death compatible? Could space be cold or hot? Where was the end, the very end, or was there no end?

Ari had married Shulamit. They lived together on the kibbutz, and Shulamit was pregnant. Ari went off for weeks at a time. He was a lieutenant first grade in the army. In the fields where he worked he would sing songs he had learned in the sands on the shore of the Jordan, where he and his men had been on patrol, watching in the sand for footsteps of intruders. One hot night in his cabin while they were lying naked on the bed and the smell of Shulamit's body, sweat and earth and cooking oil, rose through the room, he took his wife in his arms and, pressing her close, told her that if she left him, if she found another man more worthy, he would die. His lips trembled. He cried on his wife's shoulder. He knew he was pitiable. He lay on top of her so she could not move, push him away. He begged her to be loyal.

That was her intention. She imagined no other man, but listening to Ari, she understood that men were like children, expecting always to be left behind. She laughed at his shaking hands. "What is this, all of a sudden?" she said. "You think because we are having a baby, I will leave you?"

"History repeats itself," he said.

"Not exactly," she said. "Don't count on it."

She put his head against her full breasts, enlarged from the pregnancy. She let his hands roll down over her round abdomen. He felt their child move beneath her skin. He saw her navel suddenly push forward. He kissed her stomach. He turned his face away from her. He did not want her to see that he was clinging to her belly, a child abandoned, adrift, afraid.

They planted trees, Ari on leave from the army and Shulamit so full with child that she needed help getting up from her knees. Together they planted trees on the north side of the kibbutz, to make shade in the summer, to make a cool place for the children to play. Hedy helped, her hands in the soil, pulling out bits of rock and stone. Hedy thought about the trees, the quality of fir, the thickness of the branch of pine, she thought about soil, its mineral content, its salt density, she thought about water, everyone on the kibbutz thought about water, how to bring it, how to pipe it uphill, how to ration it, how to store it, how to spill it slowly through the hose that snaked through the plantings. Everywhere she saw guns. Ari's rested in a corner of his cabin. The men went off in the trucks carrying guns. At first Hedy couldn't look at them. But after a while she forgot what they were for and they became objects, like belts and shoes, like canteens to hold the water, like the purse her mother carried under her arm when she went downtown. She did not think about Flora. What was there to think?

Mildred wrote to Hedy. The envelope was purple and the stationery smelled of perfume. "Come home," she said, "your mother would not want you digging in the dirt like a peasant girl. You can spend the summer with me at the shore and then go to college in the fall. We will buy you a wardrobe. It will be fun." Mildred enclosed an article from a magazine with pictures of girls in Bermuda shorts and shirts with yellow circle pins, and their hair was blond and their lipstick shone. Hedy put the pictures up on the wall by her bed. She stared at them.

The girl from Yugoslavia was leaving the kibbutz. "I want to look for my aunts and uncles, maybe in Haifa," she said. "I will get a job and I will get an apartment. You want to come?" she asked Hedy.

"No," said Hedy. "I will stay."

She stayed through the winter when the sun disappeared right after supper and it was cold enough to wear her old camel-hair coat. She stayed to help plant the vegetables the following spring.

Arthur wrote her a letter. It came on business stationery. His secretary had typed it. "Come home," he said. "You belong here. I will give you a party at the Harmonie Club as soon as you return. Your mother would not want you in Israel. She would be worried about your safety. What kind of future can you have on a farm? A girl has to be married. Trust me, your uncle."

She now shared a cabin with a girl from Cleveland who had taken a year off from Wellesley College to find herself and who read long passages of Martin Buber to Hedy, who began as a result to long for a thou of her own, although the idea of a real thou made her feel quite uneasy.

The girl from Cleveland took up with a young man, named Elan, who had come to the kibbutz from the Home of the Young David in Jerusalem, where he had been placed after he arrived with a group of orphans who had been rounded up on the beaches of Trieste. Hedy saw the boy at dinner eating his food, his head bent down over the plate and his feet tapping against the floor as if they had thoughts of their own. Hedy watched the boy when he passed her on the path to the greenhouse and she hoped he would speak to her, but he didn't. Often Hedy would wake in the morning and see the sheets of the girl from Cleveland flat and white under the undisturbed blue blanket. "Aren't you worried about getting pregnant?" Hedy asked.

The girl from Cleveland laughed. "Jews need babies. I am a Zionist, so I will make babies. You should, too," she added.

Hedy wanted to move to another cabin. In the meanwhile she watched the girl from Cleveland to see if her body looked different, if her walk had changed. In the dining room a boy who came with a visiting official put his hand on Hedy's back as she walked with her tray. She turned red and everyone laughed at her.

"I am in love," said the girl from Cleveland.

"I am happy for you," said Hedy. "It is time," she told Shulamit, "that I leave the kibbutz."

Hedy's hair curled in thick black bunches. It brushed across her forehead, dry and stiff. It was not soft hair, not the kind of hair a man might want to run his fingers through. Hedy looked in the mirror in the cabin where Shulamit was lying on her bed playing with her baby before returning him to the children's house. Hedy saw that her own skin was brown and her arms strong and full, and she saw her own face, the mole above her cheekbones, not like the faces of the young women wearing Bermuda shorts and saddle shoes that her aunt had sent, a face that seemed to be like the morning moon, fading out of sight. Now she had freckles from the sun and they spotted her chin and ran across her nose and she took off her blouse and cupped her breasts in her hands, holding them high up so that she could see their reflection in the mirror. The nipples were dark, the circles were round. Nothing was wrong. She looked, she thought, like a mermaid carved of wood on the prow of a boat that had sunk to the bottom of the sea, a boat long forgotten, whose treasure had floated off in the tides. Perhaps, she thought, she was homesick. Years ago at camp in Maine, one of her bunkmates had been homesick and had cried all night and her mother came for her in a car and her cot was empty for the rest of the summer. She wrote Emma, the cook, a postcard. She said, "I am here, planting tomatoes. I hope you are well and that your knees are not bothering you." She received the announcement of Frank and Maria's wedding. She sent them a note.

"Congratulations," it said. "Please feel free to use my old room any way you like."

Shulamit went to Tel Aviv, to a conference on new words in Hebrew. She came back and said that in Israel every hour there were ten new words invented to turn the language of the Torah into speech for people who had microscopes and electromagnetic waves and toxins and antitoxins and could travel in the sky without Elijah's assistance.

Hedy wanted to learn the new words. She wrote to her father and asked him to send the money so she could go to the Technion in Haifa. He wrote back that he didn't see the reason for it. Why not get a job? he said. Soon you'll be married anyway.

Arthur sent Hedy money. He wrote to Hedy: "Don't stay in school too long. Take care of yourself, brush your hair, wear makeup. Don't end up like those girls who look like boys. Come back to America. Tell Teddy I think of him every day. Tell him to send more pictures of the baby. I need a large one for my desk."

Where Frank Was When Kennedy Was Shot: 1963

Frank was in Miami in the condominium he had bought and mortgaged heavily for a business investment that didn't work out. The terrace with its orange tree planted in a porcelain pot perched above the rocky sand and the black teeth of the jetty that stretched out into the crashing waves of the Atlantic Ocean. The pool was turquoise and the beach chairs were flamingo pink. There was a Jacuzzi on the main floor and a shower to wash off the sand from your feet, and all around the pool the owners of their apartments sat covered in zinc and PABA and hats that came down to the bridge of their noses. Maria was by far the youngest of the women there, and when in the waning hours of the afternoon she stretched out on her lounge chair and put baby oil on her legs, the men would watch, covertly, over the tops of their newspapers, putting down their spy stories, taking off their dark glasses, and rubbing their eyes. Palm trees bordered the walk to the lobby and gold fixtures hung in front of blue mirrors even in the garage where the Cadillacs and Mercedes rested from their labors while an occasional lizard darted between the parked wheels.

Frank had gone to the judge in Tampa and made his offer. It was the best offer he could make. He hoped it would be good enough. Maria's daughter had been caught with a friend in a van that was not theirs and in the van there were drugs. The girl, Daisy, had gone down south to make her fortune. She would be in jail maybe fifteen years. Maria had cried. Frank had called Will Katz. Will Katz had told him what to do. He did it. The judge accepted his phone call. He had accepted an envelope, but he wouldn't set bail, so who knew if it worked or it didn't work. Frank couldn't care less. Let the bitch rot in jail, he thought. Maria said it wasn't her fault. She had made some bad friends. She was a good girl who would work hard if she were given a second chance. She told Frank that she would do anything he wanted if he would just rescue Daisy.

Frank had found Maria a better companion than Flora. She never questioned him. She listened quietly as he explained to her the events on the nightly news. His headaches had eased. The girls had been at boarding school. She devoted herself to her clothes, her body, her sleeping. She didn't complain if he stayed long hours at the club. She didn't protest if he went off on the weekends to play golf, to have time for himself. His appetite for women had lessened, although now and then he would take a young secretary to a hotel and spend the afternoon watching her change her stockings, pulling her underwear on and off. He was still handsome. But now he liked best of all to talk with men in the bar, about the state of Israel, about the conditions in the South, about the Democratic party and its promises. He had strong opinions. When someone disagreed with him he was apt to let his voice rise and his fists clench, and once or twice he had leapt to his feet when some ignoramus had challenged him. Arthur had bought him out of the business. It had cost Arthur a lot. He'd had to borrow to do it, and that pleased Frank. He didn't work at the Gruenbaum Company anymore. He spent his time in Florida investing here and there, buying what he pleased when he pleased.

Maria, whose figure was broadening despite her constant efforts to eat only wheat germ and fresh oranges, was always there when he came home. She brought him a drink. She asked what he thought. Other men envied him. He knew it. But he felt her breath on him in the morning and jumped up out of bed. He felt her hands on him at night when he stood on the terrace and watched the moon slide across the sky. He didn't like the odor of her body that lingered in the bathroom. Once he had seen her sleeping in her bed, the heavy white flesh of her arms lying across her face and her hair, pressed tight to her scalp in the net she wore to hold her curl, and he felt alone, alone and in need. He knew that the need was beyond answer and the alone was forever. He thought that people were ignoring him. He talked louder and had more opinions. His love, like a fungus on a wall, attached itself to his own person and could neither fly nor float nor drift in the air toward another. He felt weighted down by his love but had no means to drive it away. In the meanwhile he saw that Maria was stuck to him, like a hump on the back of a hunchback. He tried to remember how he had admired her in the beginning. It was her long legs. It was perfume and silk underwear. It was her slight lisp that made her slur and mumble and wait for him to complete her sentences. It was her contrast to Flora. Now he interrupted her if she started to talk when they were with other people. Once he hit her in the face when she forgot to tell him he had received a call from a business contact. She didn't look him directly in the eye anymore. She kept her head lowered and turned slightly to one side, like a dog who had lost the taste for the fight. "He's so handsome and strong," she said to the manicurist who came to the apartment twice a week. "I'm so lucky," she said. She accepted an invitation for drinks with one of the men around the pool. Why not? Frank didn't notice.

In the meantime he had gone to Tampa and given the judge an envelope the way Will Katz had told him, and now the phone call came from Daisy. She had been set free, but her friend was sentenced to ten to fifteen years. "That's luck," said Daisy.

"Yeah, luck," said Frank.

Maria came out of her shower and kissed Frank on the mouth, letting her tongue wander over his teeth. "Dumb broad," said Frank. Maria's hands shook.

The television was on. "The president's been shot," a frantic voice was saying. There was a blurred scene of an open car, a parade, bodies falling.

Frank said, "I'm going out for a walk." He walked along the ocean's edge, a tall, handsome man despite the liver spots on his hands and arms, whose black hair was slicked down and carefully parted on the left and whose dark eyes with their heavy Tatar lids were half-closed in the bright sun. As he swung his arms and let the calves of his legs tense and relax he breathed deeply through his mouth, in and out. A man has to take care of himself, exercise, eat carefully, avoid fatty foods.

The Afterlife of an American Hero, or Fame Unquenchable: 1955 On

Will Katz was forced out of the national limelight. The jokes had gotten broader. The wave of fear had crested, and those he had named and wounded, those he had named and caused suffering, became an army of their own. The senator who began it all made statements on TV so bizarre that even his friends thought perhaps it was time for him to retire, to visit a sanitarium, to write a memoir. Will Katz, while still a hero in some circles for having hunted down the wild dogs of democracy, was considered in other circles as the master of the inquisition, a man who himself rode a broom across the night sky doing the work of the Devil while wearing the collar of the Church. At any rate, it was not very Jewish, this thing that he had done. The talk of his becoming governor stopped. The odds on his being the Democratic presidential candidate equaled Jimmy the Greek's odds on Doris Day lying down with her costar on their first date.

Will returned to New York and his old room, which Bessie had repainted for him, a lovely red like the hotel rooms in Vienna where he had enjoyed himself so thoroughly. He became a partner in a law firm, some older lawyers who often brought litigation before Judge Katz, who appreciated that Will Katz had made lots of friends in his months in the public eye, and who hoped that the young man whose energies were obviously boundless would increase their treasure; at least they figured they would have an interesting ride on his magic carpet.

They were right. Leonard Lyons, Walter Winchell, and Earl Wilson reported on all Will Katz's dinners at Toots Shor's, Lindy's, and the 21 Club. They reported when he went to court with a major divorce and they reported when he was litigating for business clients like Rocky Mountain Trains, or the Gruenbaum Company, which was having some kind of contract trouble with its overseas partners. Once again he became a lion of the night. He was a familiar figure known to the headwaiters from one side of town to another. He never looked anyone directly in the eye, partly because his left eye had slipped a millicentimeter more out of focus and partly because he wasn't interested in the nuances of faces, the way the nose wrinkled or the mouth turned up and down. He was concerned with potential worth measured in publicity or dollars, in support or its opposite. His chauffeur drove him from spot to spot, a young actress on his arm, till the lights went dim and the waiters were emptying the ashtrays for the last time. He had dark circles under his eyes, but he would get up and have breakfast with his mother each morning and head off to his office, where he would make phone calls to all the contacts, new and old, he had made the night before.

Johnny Pommer had returned from Washington and entered his father's business. He had married a young woman whose family was in banking. He didn't return Will's phone calls. His father had threatened to send him off to Thailand, where the firm was building a convention center, if he appeared in public with Will Katz.

Will found that love was not so hard to find. His chauffeur, for instance, would come upstairs with him at the end of the night and they would walk quietly to Will's bedroom and sometimes the chauffeur would have his breakfast in the kitchen with the cook while Will read the newspaper and talked with his father. Will discovered the night pleasures of Riverside Drive and the clubs on the wharves of lower Manhattan, where a man could pick and choose just what appealed and when. He discovered the bathhouses, where everyone was anonymous but willing, and the thing that ached, the thing that made him cartwheel through the night as if he were sent from the mouth of the cannon, all burning powder, would ease in the steam and the sauna and the curve of the male waist. The shift of the male shoulder blades hooked him onto a chase that never ended but provided diversion, diversion enough.

He made friends with women reporters and TV stars, and he introduced them one to another. He made friends with the younger judges and the new members of the political parties. He had no preference for Democrats over Republicans, no feeling of loyalties or boundaries. He was interested in muscle, the kind that flexed on the body and the kind that worked in the boardroom and that bought you a house in the country where you could lie beside your pool and let the butler serve canapés to your guests. He was interested in women who were divorcing giants of industry because their settlements would involve endless appearances in court and delays and arguments over the damask curtains and the Kandinsky paintings and the Porsche that had or had not been a wedding gift.

"What is marriage?" he asked his mother, who had heard some rumors, some things that Mildred had hinted, which had started her thinking perhaps he should find a wife and stay at home in the evenings because he was getting too old for all this running around. "Marriage," he said, "is the treasure hunt of the times, it's the pirate king boarding the passenger ship and throwing the jewels into a sack and the maidens into the sea. Marriage is an inferior sort of economic arrangement." He wasn't interested.

Howie Katz listened to his son and he held on to the glass of wine that he had each night before he went to bed. He held on to the stem of the glass till it snapped in his hands and the wine was spilled on the beige carpet and the maid came with seltzer and salt and rags and Bessie muttered under her breath.

There was talk of indictment, of illegalities here and there, a certain matter of forging of papers, of fudging of tax documents, of colluding with other lawyers against his own clients. There was talk of disbarment. "Just talk," Will told his mother. "Don't worry, they're jealous or else they're pink, pink to the gills, and it'll come out just how pink they are, if they try to get me."

He liked it somehow, the threat that was always there. They were after him and he led them a chase through the law courts. He would grind his teeth and write out his own defense statements. They would leak certain facts to the papers and he would counterattack. The rich ladies came to him weeping into their sleeves; they were being robbed. The rich men came to him: "You're the only one who will understand what's she's doing to me." He bought a yacht that he kept in a marina off the isle of Capri. On long vacations he would take young sailors, waiters, workers in the stone quarry at the top of the mountain, for a cruise around the high rocks and into the distant deserted coves. While the captain discreetly kept his eyes on the sea, he would take his visitors downstairs and rub their shoulders with suntan oil and offer them good wines from the vineyard of one of his clients.

Mildred went to his New Year's Eve party every year. She wandered among the actors and actresses and the producers and the movie agents, among the real estate tycoons and the journalists and the owners of casinos in Las Vegas, among the handsome young men in tuxedos who seemed French or Italian and had places in Ravenna and Martinique. She always wore her best dress, one that she selected months before, and she wore her diamonds and her hair was dyed to match the color of corn in mid-summer. She sat with Bessie in the dining room. "Would you believe that the Princess Borghese is here," said Mildred. Bessie just nodded; why not? It was only what she'd expected.

Will began to collect cats, Siamese cats with strange voices and long legs, eyes the color of the sea off St. Croix where he had gone with a client who was buying bauxite mines across the Caribbean. His first cat he called Jefferson, and his second he called Delano after the man his father had always revered. The cats rose to their feet when he came in the door and wound themselves around his legs. They slept on his bed and allowed him to run his hand down their backs as they arched and preened and used their sandpaper tongues to clean between their claws, which extended sharp and uncut onto the rugs and the upholstered chairs. Bessie complained, but Will insisted. Jefferson, Delano, and Will, between them there was some unconditional bond, some understanding, that gave him peace. More and more he needed his cats to sit on his lap, to run between his legs, to be warm under the covers when he woke. He added Lewis and Clark to the household and the anchorwoman on a major TV network gave him Tippecanoe, who was only a kitten. Will Katz would sit on his chair in his bedroom and rock the kitten in his arms, burrowing his nose in its soft fur. It would whine the high-pitched cry of its breed and stretch out its belly for his fingers to stroke.

When he went to the country he took all his cats with him. When he went to Capri to sail on his boat, the cats flew in the special box in the cargo hold. On Capri he always rented a young man, younger than fifteen, older than twelve, whose job was to sit naked on the side of the boat and dive in the water on command, arranging shells and pink coral on the wooden hull. In the evenings Will would sit at a cafe with his companions, and letting the cool evening air brush over his tanned arms, he would lift his head to the mountain ridge behind him and toss down Pernod after Pernod until his eyes closed shut and his friends had to carry him back to the hotel room. Holding him up in the elevator, which looked like a bird cage and had red velvet seats, they would bring him to his room.

Bessie had no fondness for cats but endured them for Will's sake and insisted they remain in the apartment despite the fact that Howie developed a chronic stuffed nose.

Hedy Begins Her Life as a Student at the Technion in Haifa: 1954

Hedy began to dream in Hebrew. She lived in the dorm in the Technion and each day in the cafeteria, breakfast of yogurt and cucumber, she would go over words in her dictionary that she had not understood during the previous day. She wore khaki pants and a white shirt like the other girls on the campus. She wore no makeup and she let the sun burn her nose until it blistered. She wrote to her uncle Arthur in America:

"I am studying the stars and the gases of the universe. I am also studying calculus and physics. My professors speak German or Russian or French and they try to teach in Hebrew, which sometimes works out and sometimes doesn't. Numbers at least are the same in all languages. I have a friend whose name is Yael. She is the only person I know who was born here. Her great-grandfather came here from Lvov in 1870. He had been widowed and was an old man, so he sold everything he had and came to Safed to be buried on the land. When he got here the community, seeing he had some money, immediately married him off to a seventeen-year-old girl who was orphaned and had no prospects. He didn't die and he became the father of five sons, one of which was my friend Yael's grandfather. She is teaching me how to act like a sabra. She and I talk all night until we are so tired that we fall asleep in our chairs and can hardly make class the next morning. She thinks I am not strong enough and so we do exercises each day. She is studying aerodynamics. She thinks Israel will soon design a fighter plane that is invisible to enemy radar. I hope you will come and visit this spring. I think of you and Aunt Mildred and know that you would love to see the new buildings that are rising everywhere in Haifa. It is so busy here that I walk the streets always looking up to make sure that no hammer falls on my head."

Arthur put the letter away in a box where he collected Teddy's letters. When Frank was finally gone, he had walked into Frank's old office and breathed deeply, like a man held hostage for years and just granted his freedom. He missed his sister. He missed her in the evenings when he returned from work and he entered his apartment where the maid had cleaned everything and laid out his pajamas on the bed covers and was waiting in the kitchen to serve him dinner whenever he rang. He still thought of Louisa, who had never phoned or written him, who the detective he had sent after her claimed had disappeared in the mountains of West Virginia. He imagined her now with folds of flesh under her chin, with hands rough from washing and glasses slipping down her nose. Why was he working? Why was he buying stores in the suburbs in order to have a new market for his suits? What was he working for? He thought about Moses. If the gangsters had taken him, if someone finally told him who he really was: he might appear one day at the office and ask for his share of the business. Moses might want the business. Arthur would keep it going for him. But maybe he had died. Maybe he would never find out that a suit company was his for the asking. If his own son wouldn't come home and take over the business, what was he doing?

Mildred told him to stop asking questions that had no answers. "Enjoy yourself," she said.

Arthur went to Temple Emanu-El on Fifth Avenue and up the red carpet to the rabbi's study on the third floor. He asked the rabbi, "What does God want of me?"

"You're a good man," said the rabbi in his deep voice that echoed through the corridors of time and rose from his diaphragm just as if he had been trained as a Shakespearean actor. "You have continued your father's interest in the hospital and you have contributed to all our fund-raising drives. You are good to your employees and your business has done well. You have done all that is required."

"So why, then," said Arthur, "do I feel at loose ends?"

"Loose ends?" said the rabbi. "That is not my business. I have no special authority in the area of loose ends."

In the evenings Arthur, with his eyes on *The Ed Sullivan Show* or watching Milton Berle on the new television set he had bought, would take out his old fedora and toss cards over the brim. He tried to teach the new maid how to toss the cards, but she would stand there and laugh.

"Oh, Mr. Gruenbaum," she would say, "I can't do it."

"Practice," Arthur would say. But she never did. He missed Hedy; he remembered her smile when he pulled a rose out of his sleeve and gave it to her for her twelfth birthday. He sent her a present. It was a large check.

The girl from Cleveland asked Hedy to meet her in the park near the Technion. She wore dark sunglasses and her bright red toenails showed between her sandal thongs. She was breaking up with her boyfriend, who had come to the kibbutz from the juvenile home. He never talked to her. He treated her like a tree. He said that love was imperfect and that she was going home to her mother's house and then, when the new semester began in January, she was going home to Wellesley.

"Going home to Wellesley," Hedy said, repeating her words.

The girl from Cleveland lit a cigarette. "The thing is I can't tell him I'm leaving. He might stop me. He might tell me he loves me and then I won't be able to go and I want to go." Hedy's former roommate explained and explained some more. Hedy listened, but she didn't understand.

"So I have this letter," said the girl from Cleveland. "Will you deliver it to him after I'm on the plane?"

"Put it in the mail?" said Hedy.

"No," said her friend. "That's too cruel. I can't bear to think of him finding the letter in his mailbox. It will hurt him too much. I want you to be there for him, to stay while he reads it so that he will have to be brave. If someone is there, he won't cry. Enough has happened to him already."

"What happened?" asked Hedy.

"I don't know," said her friend. "He doesn't talk about it."

"Why me?" asked Hedy.

"He knows you," said the girl, whose hand clutched her passport and whose palate was longing for a cheeseburger with a chocolate milk shake. "He remembers you from the kibbutz, and now he's in your physics class."

So Hedy and Elan Aloni sat down together at a table by the window in the cafe where the students met after, between, and during classes. "I have something for you," she said. She handed him the envelope, and, steeling herself for his tears, his cry of anger, his throwing of his books, his smashing of his fist on the table, she waited. She was curious. He spoke Hebrew heavily with the thickness of German or Polish, Hedy could not yet distinguish.

He was silent. He handed Hedy back the letter, replaced in its envelope. Hedy sipped at her coffee. She waited for Elan to speak. he was silent. He took a spoonful of sugar from the bowl and stirred his cup. He leaned back in his chair and looked around the room, examining each of the Formica tables, the orange plastic chairs.

"I'm sorry," said Hedy.

"Why?" said Elan. "It was not forever. It was for the hormones, you understand."

Hedy did not, not exactly. She wasn't sure if he had used the Hebrew word for hormones or the one for oceans. She took out her pocket dictionary to look it up. Elan waited. It was hormones.

"I didn't want to be the one to give you the letter," said Hedy.

"Why not?" said Elan. "Since the first class I have been wanting to talk to you."

"Why?" said Hedy.

"Hormones," said Elan, and smiled.

When he smiled something cracked inside of Hedy, something sprang out of the crack and raced through her body looking for its place. It settled low in an area below the stomach, above the legs, a place that Hedy wouldn't name, but when Elan smiled she had discovered that it was there, heavy, vast, almost burning, but not burning.

He had a head of dark curls, a head that seemed large for his slim body. His hands were always in motion, fingers tapping on the tabletop, flying upward or downward in gesture. His shoulders were not broad and his chest seemed to sink inward as if his ribs were on backward, but his eyes looked out with an alertness that Hedy had never seen before. They stared at her with a hunger that made the muscles in her thighs tremble. His eyes took her in and sent her sprawling down into their own darkness. In the smile, in the curve of the cheek, in the way the chin came forward and the curls on the forehead fell, Hedy saw a sweetness, a center of sweetness, like the smell of bread in the oven, like the way the babies in the children's house smelled after their bath, like the olive grove just before harvest.

"What was your name, before?" said Hedy.

"I've forgotten," said Elan.

"You haven't forgotten," said Hedy. "Nobody forgets their name."

"Where I came from," said Elan, "we did not have name tapes. It was possible to forget your name."

At the Technion Elan had a reputation. It was for numbers. It was not just that he could do anything in his head as if he were a calculator. He could do that, but he also had formulas and hypotheses and theorems solved that had not yet been presented to the others. He had ideas of his own about the places of parallel lines and the infinity in which the curves and the digits tumbled not at random, but in order, in the order of his mind. He was interested, he told Hedy, in the working of the atom, the spinning of the quark, the gyroscoping form of proton linked, he said, to the blast of neutrons rubbing. In the smallest of forms lay the greatest power, like in the smallest of nations. "And one day," said Elan to Hedy, "we in Israel must have our own power."

"No," said Hedy, who understood him perfectly. "We will be strong enough without it."

Elan smiled at her. It was the smile of a child when its mother's face appears after a nap. It was the smile of a boy who had found his way to the top of a hill and looks down on the city below. It was the smile of a man who remembered the child whose mother was there after the nap. "We will be stronger with it," he said.

Some weeks later they went out together into the hills of sand and walked up the wadi in Ein Gedi. They had packed their knapsacks with oranges and chocolate and they sat on the rocky ledges above the road, dust on their faces and in the lines of the palms of their hands, and they dripped orange over their mouths and down their chins. Hedy's hair stood thick like a nest of wire in the hot, unmoving air, and she had a stain on her shirt where the seeds of the orange had fallen and under her arms perspiration formed dark lakes. Elan ran his hands over her face and he felt each of her features with his eyes closed as if he were a blind man.

"What are you doing?" She pushed him away.

"I am memorizing you," he said. "One sense at a time is better."

She put her hands on his face and closed her eyes. She felt his nose and his brow and the sticky area below his lips where the juice had been and she felt the new stubble of his hours-old beard and she put her fingers in his mouth and ran them over his teeth and she felt the hairs of his nostrils and the ridges of his ears. She felt the drops of sweat that came from his forehead and slid down his cheek. She opened her eyes and saw him staring at her.

"This time," he said, "it's not just hormones."

"It's hormones, too," said Hedy, who believed in honesty and was afraid of illusion and distrusted words that covered instead of exposed.

What Elan saw in the sand in the shade of a rocky ledge that hung overhead and was pockmarked underneath with the dark green of desert moss was a tall girl, naked, with her breasts sinking back into her body, her thick black hair untied and filled with grains of sand. He saw the lines of her waist and the roll of the hip as she turned toward him. He saw the pink flush of her skin and the white strap marks where her shirt had protected from the sun and he saw the dark hole of her navel which folded itself inward toward the dormant womb and the curl of fallopian tube. He heard her sigh. He saw her calf muscles round and lengthen as she arched and stretched till her fingers touched his ankle and he was close enough to see the roller-skating scar on her knee. Elan saw Hedy and trusted her to do him no harm and he knelt beside her and covered her body with his own; nothing was to happen to her that would not happen to him also. He pulled himself up on her body and, carrying the density of a black hole in his heart, put his full weight on her chest, and when he was exhausted he slept.

What Hedy saw was a man near her, a man so young that he might still grow but wouldn't because in the years when he should have been eating proteins and carbohydrates, such things were not easily found, a man whose shoulders were hunched even without the pull of his knapsack and whose legs, though tan and muscular, bowed away one from the other. She saw a man whose lips were cracked from the sun. His nose was burned red and over his eyes dripped the sweat from his forehead. There were ridges under his eyes where his sunglasses had pressed into his flesh. His nakedness hurt her as if a rock might tumble and hit him, as if a thorn from a cactus might pierce him, as if he might disappear in the sand, become bone and flaking cartilage like the femur of a goat that they had seen farther down the gully. He was a man who would not hurt her. She trusted him and turned everything over, opening all that could be opened, waiting. She knew that what was happening was fatal. After a while she felt his body crushing her backbone into the ground. She felt the hard root of a bush that was bruising her shoulder. She heard his heart beat against hers. She tried to count backward from one thousand by sevens. She could no longer reason. She could no longer think. She tried to remember the word for "enough" in Hebrew, but the mingle of yearning and wonder swept her under. She rode the tide in and out. Finally she felt his body on her chest like a stone pressing the air out of her lungs. She gasped. He was asleep.

She pushed him over, and feeling the hot air against her breasts, she smiled. Cradling him in her arms, she rocked him gently back and forth. She stopped only to brush away the insects that kept crawling up her arm, smelling perhaps with their rapidly swiveling antennae the odors of human affection.

After that they went everywhere together. The American girl who was named for a movie star and the boy who had come from a place he wouldn't name, whose parents were never spoken of, who had no relatives, and who spoke only of a certain Eshol, a counselor at the Home of the Young David, who was the one who had taught him how to play soccer and kicked a ball with him in the evenings after supper until he became good enough to join the team. The home had a team of its own and it played the high school, and Elan kicked many goals. This much he told Hedy.

Moses Gruenbaum in the Holy Land: 1949 On

Moses Gruenbaum was due to graduate from the Monastery by the Mouth of the Bay, and there was no question in any of the brothers' minds what would become of him. He was to be a priest. He had expressed no interest in applying for the scholarship to Notre Dame that was awarded to an orphan at the monastery each year. He told his confessor. He told the abbot, who had walked with him along the cliff's edge and questioned him carefully, questioned him especially about the issue of celibacy. It was not a choice everyone could or should make, but Moses Gruenbaum was not deterred. His decision was final.

He was sent to the seminary in Westchester that had trained the abbot himself. There he put on for the first time the black cassock and he walked in silence about the grounds that bordered the highway on one side and the new shopping mall on the other. He disliked the cold winters of the North and missed the sound of the ocean as it beat against the rocks of the monastery. His Latin was among the best. His knowledge of church law was good, but his piety was exceptional, exceptional even among the handful of young men who were still coming for training in the priesthood, all of whom had been summoned, all of whom had passions and desires they had embedded in the body of Christ and its remarkable history. Often he went without food, often he took vows of silence that lasted days at a time, often he knelt on the hard wood and said rosary after rosary. He believed that the Virgin heard his prayers. He believed that he was not alone in the universe. He believed that he had a mission to complete on this earth, a mission for his savior. He couldn't imagine what it was.

In his final year, about to be ordained and perhaps given a parish, he won the seminary prize for writing an essay in Latin on the thirteen steps of humility, and he was granted a stipend to visit the Holy Land, to pilgrimage to the birthplace to mark the Stations of the Cross through the winding streets of Jerusalem at Eastertime. He was given lodging with the Brothers of the Crown, who had kept their order going for three centuries by tending fields filled with the plants and fruits mentioned in the Bible and sending herbs from their garden to sufferers around the world, who would receive in return for a small payment a package of dried herbs that were said to bear the breath of Jesus into a sickroom. The Brothers of the Crown lived in an abandoned fort and made weekly journeys by foot to the birthplace in Bethlehem. They also searched the stars, someone on watch every night, for signs of angels who might be sending messages of the divine will.

Just after the British soldiers had departed and the state of Israel was founded and the Arabs had taken the fort and held it for a few hours until the Israelis pushed them back, Moses Gruenbaum arrived at the monastery and saw the expanse of sky, unlike anything he had ever seen before, rose-colored, hills with cypress waving in the heat and white stones of graves tumbling in every direction. He walked around the edge of the fort, running his hand over the stones once lifted in place by the soldiers of Antioch, torn down by the Romans, built again by the Turks, who aimed cannons at the Crusaders as they climbed in bloody glory up the steep face of the small mountain, finally to send word to the Vatican that the building was theirs for any Christian purpose the pope should wish. The Brothers of the Crown had lent their building to the British, who camped their men in the long halls and dug latrines in the rocky ground by the fields that they appropriated for their wastes and in so doing made more fertile the garden of the biblical plants that the brothers returned to tending when the British moved their men on to other, higher points along the road to Sinai.

Moses Gruenbaum felt closer to Christ in the field of biblical plants than he had ever felt before. Eastertime he walked the Stations of the Cross. He visited the church in Bethlehem and saw the spot where the wise men had stood. He stood in the crypt in Jerusalem while the Armenian priests went by, swinging the silver chalices of incense, and he wept for the death of his Lord, who had been so cruelly treated by the Jews.

The streets were full of soldiers, new soldiers in the Israeli army. They were younger even than the boys in the seminary in Westchester. The girls wore their Uzis strapped over their arms and their young breasts heaved up and down beneath their open blouses. In the stream by the Brothers of the Crown, the Jewish soldiers would take off their clothes and splash in the water, and Moses Gruenbaum would cover his eyes and put his head against a tree till they had moved on.

"Make me worthy, O Christ," he prayed. "Let me not fall into temptation."

Moses had visions of hell, nightmares with his eyes open. He saw the flames that were never extinguished, he saw the ripping and the tearing of limbs, and he saw doors closing and gas rising until body after body tumbled down only to rise again and stand naked next to its neighbor until the gas again hissed from the vents on the floor. In his hell the trains with no windows were eternally traveling across a green and plowed farmland, each packed full with bodies that called out for water as the wheels turned and the sparks flew off the tracks.

"Have pity on me, O Lord," he prayed. "I am an orphan abandoned on your doorstep."

At the end of the afternoon, as the shafts of light turned white and the plum-colored rocks shone like handprints against the drifting sky, Moses was struck with dread. He shivered. He held his arms around his chest. He prayed. He counted his beads. He counted his footsteps, but he could not remove the shroud that had fallen on him from an unexpected source, a grief not like mourning, a grief like terror. He held his hand before his face and knew that he would soon disintegrate, separate cell from cell, soul into air. Only at the table of the Brothers of the Crown did he feel safe. Only at the evening prayers when out of the corners of his eyes he could see the soft motion of his neighbor's cassock as he knelt and stood, as he moved slowly toward the nave of the chapel and back toward the carved wooden pews with lions' heads on the armrests and bird claws at the base, only then did he feel that Christ was not angry with him, that he had done what was asked, that the shivers of foreboding were banished from his soul and would not return. But they did, day after day.

He extended his stay at the Brothers of the Crown and he learned how to tend the plants, even the smallest of them that grew in the desert sand and needed no water or shade but perished if the rains came down too strong or the air off the mountain blew with unexpected cold. He wrote to the seminary in Westchester. Perhaps he did not want to be a parish priest after all. Perhaps his service was in the Holy Land.

"He had heard a whisper while he was praying," he wrote Father Bernard, who was in charge of the students, "a whisper that seemed to be coming from the white stones in the chapel, telling him to stay, it was here he belonged."

Father Bernard did not want any more students who heard voices, had visions, whose palms bled and who starved themselves for the glory of Christ; that kind always ended in the hospital, and the order would end up with an increase in their insurance, or else that kind ended up in police stations and explanations had to be made. Father Bernard graciously allowed Moses Gruenbaum to stay in Jerusalem at the Brothers of the Crown.

"Let the heat fry his Jewish brains," said Father Paul, teacher of the Latin language and liturgy class, who was disappointed because Moses had been his prize student, so apparently comfortable with his calling, so steady in his work.

The years flowed from Christmas to Easter and back again, and Brother Moses led the pilgrims who came from various churches around the United States along the Stations of the Cross. He walked them through the garden of the biblical plants and showed them the box in which they could make their offerings to continue the brothers' good work. The dread that he experienced in the dusk never left him entirely, but he had grown used to it, a companion, his own cross, a way in which he could share in the pain of his Lord. He had learned to pause and look down at his feet when it came on him, and gradually the sight of his sandals, splashed with the dirt of the road and stained by the rain, would reassure him. He had grown in his place and was content. With his hands stretched out he could press his palms on either wall of his cell, like the one he had spent his childhood in, although now he had no roommates and could fall on his knees stark naked before the first rays of the morning sun and bow his head as the bells in the tower rang the matins over the field and into the sand-filled canyons below.

It was this position of his, prayer without the protection of the cassock, that brought about the trouble. Brother John, suffering from stomach problems, walked through the beaded curtain that sealed off each cell to tell Brother Moses that he would have to substitute for him in the kitchen that morning. He saw Moses standing up in front of him, his member without its foreskin, and he gasped. "That's why you are named Moses," he said. "You are a Jew."

"No," said Moses. "In America everyone is circumcised. I am a Catholic, baptized in Christ. I was born a Jew, but my mother left me with the fathers in Miami when I was just a child."

"A Jew," said Brother John, shaking his head, "is always a Jew."

"No," said Moses.

"We'll have to watch you," said Brother John, "when it comes to handling the shopping. Perhaps you are taking a little extra for yourself."

"No," said Moses.

But after that the voices started to plague him.

"Go away," said Saint Teresa, who appeared to him in a dream. "Go into the desert and atone for the sins of your people. Stay in the desert one hundred years and talk only to the insects under the rocks."

"Don't drink when you are thirsty," said Saint Francis. "Don't eat when you are hungry. Let yourself bleed into the dust from sores on your skin. That's what Christ wants."

During the evening prayers he heard Mary Magdalene call him. He turned and saw her beckoning him in the archway of the chapel. "Go away into the desert," she said, "and I will comfort you at night when it is cold. Let your skin be exposed to the moon and the stars."

The voices were not there all the time. They came and they went. He was free of them for days at a time, and just when he began to think he had been returned to himself, he would hear them again, sometimes all at once, sometimes one at a time. He would go right up to the bell tower and let the sound of the bells blast in his ears. The voices were tricky. They waited till the bells had stopped and then they began again.

Once a group of Jordanians, army men on a mission of terror, came into the monastery and ate at the table and drank water from the well. "We have a Jew here," said Brother John to the captain. "He is disguised as a brother, but he is a Jew, just lift his cassock and you will see."

"No," said Moses, "I am not a Jew. I am a Catholic."

The Jordanian captain was not interested in Jews. He was interested in the oranges that grew in the orchard and he told his men to pick them and pack them in their knapsacks, which they threw into their jeeps before disappearing in the dust of the road.

Moses packed up his Bible and his rosary. He left behind his blanket and warm shirt and he walked deep into the desert, through the wadis that the bedouins roamed with their camels while their tents rested on the sand like childhood memories in the mind. Moses walked for days in the crevices between the mounds of sand and rock, and he ate from the occasional tree, a piece of the bark and a drop of the rainwater that had gathered here and there in the wells of the rocks. Everything was white under the stars, and the voices spoke comforting words to Moses most of the time. Once in a while he would wake to hear voices, high-pitched, speaking in Latin, English, Hebrew, screaming at him. "Vile stink," they would say. "Sacrament of shit, prayer of pus, stick it in your ass."

At last somewhere deep in the Negev, beyond Ein Gedi, south of the new town of Arad, high above the Dead Sea, whose sulfurous waters rose from a crack in the earth's surface that lay between the Israeli soldiers who walked the sandy shore at dawn and dusk looking for footprints of intruders and the Jordanian women who washed their laundry on rocks and listened for the sound of their children who played in the olive groves behind, Moses found a cave large enough for a man to lie down in and stretch out his limbs, his arms touching its walls and his head protected from the sand.

How Hedy Didn't Get Married: 1955

Yael took an engineering course. "I am a builder of airplanes," she said to Hedy. "I am a flyer."

They had not let Yael fly in the army. She had served as an instructor in the assembly and cleaning of guns. She had walked in the hills and lain down in the dirt and on her back with her eyes closed put together weapons whose parts she knew the way she knew her own body. Now Yael studied wind charts and spoke of the effect of lightning on the tip of the wing, the terror of the wind shear on take off. Yael thought of the plane as the outer layer of skin, the first line of protection, the thing that held the whole nation together. Yael was amazed that Hedy was unimpressed by the differences between F-10's and DC-3's. Hedy, however, was only interested in the rotation of the universe, the theories of origin, bangs and gases, meteors falling and exploding.

"You are looking for God," said Yael.

"No," said Hedy. "I just believe the future depends on our knowing the beginning. "If the sun dies—"

"Please," said Yael, "I have enough to do worrying about the Syrian army moving over the Golan. I am not going to worry about the sun."

"I'll worry for you," said Hedy, who believed in a division of labor.

Elan was going to work for the government, in a secret place in the desert. He could not tell Hedy where. He could not tell Hedy what he was doing. He could not tell Hedy when he was coming back to Haifa. Hedy spoke of shadows on the ground, shadows that had been flesh. Hedy spoke of danger. She lay in bed with him the night before he was to leave, his bags packed, and she asked him if this was what his parents would have wanted. Is this what they had you for? Is this what you were saved to do? Hedy kissed his arm, his neck his shoulder. She rubbed his belly where the hairs curled around his upper thighs. She kissed his eyes. She combed his hair with her fingers. He lay still.

"Don't go," she said.

"What do you know?" he said to her in a voice she did not recognize. "You don't understand."

"What don't I understand?" asked Hedy.

"Them," said Elan. "You don't understand them."

"I do," said Hedy. "I do." But he didn't believe her.

Elan came back to Haifa and he said nothing about his work. Hedy had decided to teach: teach at the Technion. She would be able to work at the secret observatory several hours outside of Haifa. A rich American had given the money for a powerful instrument that would enable them to participate with others around the world in the gathering of data, the analyzing of information, astronomers around the globe sitting shiva for dead stars. Elan held her in his arms.

"What happened to you?" she said. "What happened there?"

Elan lay on the bed. He looked at Hedy, who was staring at him, pinning him down with her eyes, accusing him of evasion, of distortion, of lying. "Nothing happened," he said.

Elan came back from the desert. "It is time for us to get married," he said to Hedy. "It is time for us to have a wedding."

He brought her a ring, a silver ring he had bought from a bedouin who had sold it to him from a pack that slid off the hump of his camel. Hedy held the ring in the palm of her hand.

"Not yet," she said. "Not now. I can't get married."

"Why not?" said Elan.

"I am afraid of you," said Hedy.

Elan laughed. "Now, you are afraid of me?"

"Yes," said Hedy, who did not understand herself. She cried, and Elan held her, and they spent the night holding each other, and Elan had stomach cramps.

In the early morning when he finally fell asleep, Hedy went to the window to watch Venus sink in the sky and she saw an Arab walking in the street with a young boy running behind him. In the white light of the new day she put her hands on her stomach and hoped, but her hope met a stone wall. She could not get married. Not yet, she said to the ladies of the Sunplaza water ballet class, to whom she felt she owed an explanation.

New Year's Eve: Florida, 1965

Frank took Maria to the club for New Year's Eve. She was wearing gold lamé and gold sandals. She had a Chinese comb stuck into the top of her hair. She smiled at everyone. Her arms were dimpled and her chin line was no longer clear. Frank had caught her praying to the Virgin the night before. She had a small statue that she kept out on the terrace near the orange tree. He found her on her knees, mumbling. She smelled of coconut oil and lavender power. He hated the smell of coconut oil. "Some conversion," he said.

At the club she piled her plate high with salmon and roast chicken and potatoes au gratin served from a silver chafing dish. He looked at his watch. Maria was dancing with the retired eye doctor from Cleveland. Frank walked about the terrace underneath the swinging lights that twinkled on strings above his head. When he was a child the lights from the Third Avenue el had flashed through his bedroom along with the rattling and the roaring and the shaking of the building all through the night, and he had stopped hearing it, stopped seeing the light, learned how to sleep rolling from side to side in his bed. Now sometimes, after he'd had a drink or two, he would hear the trains coming, one after another, as if he were still a child in his bed in the apartment by the el. It seemed to be taking forever for the New Year to arrive and for the balloons that were packed in a net pulled tight across the ceiling to fall down and the waiters to come by with champagne, and the orchestra to play "Auld Lang Syne."

Someone dropped a paté cracker on his white pants and he was in the men's room wiping off the stain when the hour came. There were tears in his eyes: inexpressible grief, mourning for something he had lost and could not find as he heard the bells ring and the shouts rise from the patio.

A Second Chance: 1960

The security police were at the door of Hedy's apartment waiting for her. They pushed their way in. They asked for her papers. They were white-faced and brusque and they refused her offer of tea. She sat down on her chair by the window and they surrounded her, all five of them, in turn, overlapping, together, one in English, though she assured them she understood Hebrew. "Where is Elan Aloni? When did you last hear from him? Has he written you letters? Who are his friends? Where did he take you on vacations? You are his girlfriend? Your address, your phone, was found in his papers."

"What has happened to Elan?" she asked.

They didn't answer. "If he contacts you, tell the man by your door immediately. We will have someone near you twenty-four hours a day."

"Why?" said Hedy. "What is it?"

"Listen to the news," said one officer.

Hedy rushed to her radio. An hour later while a security officer sat on her couch flicking his cigarette ashes over her rug, the radio announced that a prominent Israeli scientist was missing from a government defense project. He was feared kidnapped. He was last seen hitching a ride on the road to Elath, wearing a white shirt open at the collar and jeans, carrying a knapsack, army issue, wearing sunglasses and canvas boots. The government suspected terrorists or hostile forces might have taken him. They did not announce his name.

She had not wanted to marry him because she had known something was going to happen to him. No, that was not it. She didn't want to marry him because he was silent so long so often that she was lonely with him. Sometimes she forgot he was there in her bed, by the table, at the window. Sometimes he stared down at the floor so long that she thought he had drowned inside himself. She didn't want to marry a man who talked to her only when he felt like it. She didn't want to marry and stay on her side of the wall. What was the point of getting married if you couldn't scale the wall? Marriage was dangerous, she knew that. Now that he was missing, she remembered everything. The taste of his mouth, the look in his eye when she had handed him back his ring, the way they lay together on the bed, the way he studied his books with his hand stroking her thigh, the way he smiled when she came out of the shower.

She remembered her mother lying on the bed with the sheets stained in blood and her head no longer her head and her face no longer her face, and Hedy grew pale and sat on the floor and held her arms around herself, trying to bring herself comfort for the things that had fallen away. She drank a beer from the refrigerator and offered one to the soldier. She tried to remember her mother, but it was hard to remember her mother's face and Elan's kept coming to her mind and she wanted him there in her apartment, to hold her and tell her that the past was done and it was time for their story to begin, not end, not end, not now. She could not comfort herself, so deep was the regret and so sharp was the terror and so swiftly was she falling, alone. From some other planet, not yet discovered, so far away that it remained for now uncharted, out across the smooth microwaves, quasars and quasars away, its properties unnamed; on that planet had she already aged and turned to dust.

She went to her classes. She went to the observatory. She called her friend Yael, and Yael told her to stay calm. "The Arabs will not kill him.

They will ransom him, a thousand terrorists for one Israeli scientist. Don't worry," said Yael, "our security people will find him."

"I told him I would not marry him," said Hedy.

"They haven't found his body." said Yael. "You can still marry him."

In the morning when Hedy went to buy her milk, an Arab with a dark beard and a caftan wrapped around his head followed her to the store and back to her apartment. She told the soldier who had walked with her. He looked back, but several Arabs, many children on their way to school, and a bus filled with American tourists with cameras raised blocked his view of the other side of the street.

She walked to the university to pick up her papers from her study there. The Arab, the same Arab, was following her. She told the soldier who had waited for her on the steps of the campus. He looked and saw no Arabs, only Israeli students, and maybe a Druze or two hurrying off and a vendor of nuts who was making change for some women who were speaking French.

At night, Hedy opened the windows, hoping for a breeze, and leaning out over her sill, she saw in the lamplight below the same Arab, staring up at her window. She woke the soldier who was sleeping on her couch and he jumped to the window, straightening his T-shirt, which had bunched up around his chest, and pulling his gun from the holster that he had draped over a chair. But when he got to the window the street was empty. The sound of a car rounding the corner ricocheted off the stone walls and up the balconies.

Hedy sat by the window and an hour later she saw the Arab again, but this time she saw him walk, she saw that under his caftan his legs were bowed. She held her breath. She watched him. He watched her. Quietly she eased her way out the apartment door. Wearing only her nightgown, her sandals, and a shawl, she walked down the stairs, not turning on the lights that would illuminate the halls, one after another for a few seconds, holding tight to the banister, she walked down the stars, hoping.

On the street she saw him, still staring up at her window, and she crossed over. He saw her coming. He did not run. She put her hand on his face just as he tried to turn away, bend his head down. "Elan," she said, "what is it?"

He looked at her and his lashes were wet and his eyes were red. "I have left the project," he said. "I didn't want to be there anymore."

"It's all right," said Hedy.

Later, after the security officers had left and Elan had promised to appear in their headquarters the next day and he had explained that he was dizzy and unwell and unable to work and had wanted to leave but hadn't known how to say it and to whom and the officers had written down what he said in a note pad and they had conferred with each other locked in the bedroom while Hedy and Elan held hands on the couch and the darkness of the night eased and the officers had grown tired and called their superiors and packed up their briefcases and gone home, Elan told Hedy everything.

He had tried to find another woman after she had said they would not be married. He had gone to a prostitute in Arad, but he had wept when she touched him and he had hit her when she bent her head forward to kiss him. He was ashamed. He had hit her and there was blood on her lip. He had gone to the Home of the Young David to find his old counselor, Eshol, and talk to him, but Eshol had left the home and was in Tiberias in charge of delinquents in a new school and Elan was not sure he would remember him. He had gone back to the project and sat in his room and he couldn't think and he couldn't sleep and he became frightened that his mind was failing and he decided he had to leave the project before all of his mind was gone. What use would he be without a mind? He wanted to say good-bye, to explain to the men he was working with that he needed to leave for a while, but he couldn't speak to them. He was afraid he would cry. He was afraid he would laugh when he shouldn't laugh. He left without telling anyone and he lived in the streets and slept on the campus under the cypress trees and disguised himself as an Arab and watched Hedy come and go and he couldn't explain what had happened or why it had happened.

Hedy rocked him in her arms and she fixed him breakfast, an American breakfast with eggs and juice, and then he told her the rest: the things that he had never said. Hedy listened. She listened to repeat the events over and over, each time adding another detail, a memory more difficult than the one that had preceded it.

Hedy heard: His name had been Aaron. He had been born in Kiev and his family had fled to the country and lived for a while in a small town far from the city with several cousins and a grandfather, and then his mother had wrapped him in his coat and told him they were going into the forest. He had walked with the others. He had held his cousin's hand. She had told him she believed in angels and he had said he did not. There was a big ditch. He heard guns. His mother undressed him. He was naked next to his cousin. He was in the ditch. He was breathing. He heard the Germans shouting to each other. Later he was walking alone in the cold naked. There was a fire. There were men. He stayed with them for years. He told Hedy about the blueberries in the summer and he told her about the bird that was strangled by the hands of the woman who cooked in the camp and saved the blood of the bird in a cup for the boy so he could grow strong. He told her about the boots that he wore that cramped his toes till his friend cut an opening in the leather with his knife. He told her about coming into the city and seeing the soldiers in the streets waving and smiling, and the trucks going by and a big wagon with the bodies of Germans piled high. He told her of following the others down to the sea and waiting there on the beach, sitting by big fires in the night and huddling one against the other in the mist while they waited for the boats to take them to Palestine.

"A big boy gave me his bread. Women came to the beach from the Jewish Agency. They gave us blankets and chocolate. Then the boats came and took us away. We could not land during the day because of the British, so we came in at night, quietly, in rowboats. The boat next to ours hit a rock and turned over and there were children in the water, but they didn't cry out because we had been told to be quiet. Some of them we saved. They clung to our oars and we pulled them into shore. As soon as we reached land we were told to run."

Hedy heard everything, and his words became part of what she knew and who she was and how she would see ever after. She canceled her class. She stayed with him until it was time for him to go to the authorities. She watched him shave. She pressed his shirt. She went with him and waited outside the door as he met with a captain and a lieutenant. Several young men carrying Uzis guarded the door behind which they were talking.

He came out of the room and said he was leaving the project. They thought he was better suited for civilian work. Hedy bought an ice and licked it carefully in its paper cup. It was sweet and tasted of raspberries. Elan bought a container of nuts, pistachio nuts with their blushing shells. They sat in the park in the sun and they leaned their legs against each other.

Reader: It is true that stories can weigh people down, right into their graves. But it is also true that two people carrying each other's stories can manage. They can manage even to jump, leap, dance, do the dishes, mop the floor, change diapers, teach little children the word for bird, ice, nuts, park bench, love.

Elan and Hedy were married, and Ari and Shulamit came to the wedding. Yael gave them a salad bowl, and Arthur sent them a big check with which they bought a small house with a garden and Elan became a teacher in a high school and he was the coach of the soccer team and each Sunday he wore his whistle and his sneakers and he went with the boys to play in the fields.

Anxiety: The 1967 War

Ursula was an old lady living in the Bronx. She went to mass every Sunday and she still sent packages home to her village. She sent sweaters that she had knit with cables going up the front to grandnieces and grandnephews who had never seen their aunt in America. She sent watches and electric coffeepots at Christmastime. The nieces and the nephews had moved, many of them to Munich, and they had their own coffeepots and television sets and they didn't wear hand-knit sweaters anymore but preferred the latest fashion from the Paris designers. Still, they wrote Ursula thank-you notes each year and asked her to come and visit. She talked about going home, but the family farm was sold. Where would she stay? She wrote to her brother, who had been paralyzed during the war and who sat in a hospital in a wheelchair and watched television night and day. He was not eager to see her. Mildred sent Ursula a Christmas check each year. Arthur paid her medical insurance. Mildred wrote Ursula that Hedy had gone to Israel to become a scientist. Ursula wondered if Hedy still had a rash.

When the war broke out in 1967 and the television news told of the Arabs marching on Israel, and the eighty million Arabs were pointing their guns at Israel, Ursula sat on her chair and wouldn't move through the night. She listened to every report. At last she heard that the Israelis had crossed the Jordan, had crossed the Golan Heights; there was talk of them going all the way to Damascus. She crossed herself. She thanked God. She had not taken care of Hedy so many years to have her killed by an Arab, a savage, in a savage land. "*Gott seit Dank*," she said to herself on the morning of the sixth day. Israel would be all right.

Arthur was in Taiwan arranging for a factory to make Gruenbaum suits when he heard the news on Radio Hong Kong while he was sitting at the bar thinking about using the card that had been given him by a taxi driver that morning that promised satisfaction the Oriental way. He put in a call to the American embassy in Tel Aviv and couldn't get through. He wanted to know if his son was all right. He was unable to sit still, unable to eat, unable to shave himself. He needed to know if his son was all right. But the long-distance operators couldn't get the phone to ring.

He called the Israeli consulate in Washington. Someone answered and promised to try to find his son but reported that the consulate was swamped with calls exactly like his. "It might be a while," the voice told him, "before we can notify you."

"I've given an operating room to the Hadassah Hospital," Arthur said as calmly as he could. "I've given money for your planes and your tanks."

"All right, sir," said the voice.

Arthur called the Israeli consul in Hong Kong. The operator there cut him off. He called his friend Fred Harmon, who had donated a wing to the Hadassah Hospital, and whose testimonial dinner he had just attended, paying three hundred dollars for a platter of cold roast beef. Fred promised to try to get information, but, shouting to Arthur across a crackling phone line, he explained that his own son had left for Israel to pick fruit. "Fruit, for God's sake!" he said.

Eli tried to reach his son Caleb by phone, but he could not get through. He rocked back and forth on his feet. He kissed his prayer book a thousand times. He told his wife it would be all right, God would protect. She kept her hands busy and her mind as empty as possible. Eli longed for his father, to hear him sing. It seemed as if his father's prayers would carry further, would mean more.

Eli called his brother, Meyer. Meyer said, "They are strong. They will win."

Eli said, "They are surrounded by enemies. They are few and the others are many. They will die."

"Have faith," said Meyer.

"Be realistic," said Eli. He went to the rabbi. There were others in the study, all with the same grief in their hearts.

"Pray," said the rabbi. They prayed.

Later Meyer said to Rose, "We won."

"So now it's we," said Rose.

"It's we," said Meyer. "It always was."

"Tell it to the marines," said Rose, who had no grand causes left in her, had used up her allotted amount.

The green line moved. Jerusalem was returned, at last a whole, to the people of Israel, a symbol of the wholeness to come. Eli called his son on the phone.

"It was God's plan," he said.

Caleb went to the government. "I want to build," he said, "a town, in Judea, near Hebron. I want to make it Jewish with my body and my hands and my family and I want to consecrate my town to the people of Israel. It is our land, not theirs," he said.

Frank stood at the window of his apartment and let the morning sun fall across his chest. He slipped off his monogrammed robe and lay back on the chaise. We did it, he said to himself. He stretched out his legs, strong from walking along the beach day after day. I should have been there. I should have gone. Then the pleasure of the swift victory came back and he lay there watching the gulls scavenge the shore. Joy was in his heart.

The Last Course—The Just Dessert: 1961–1984

After his father and mother had died, Will Katz bought a brownstone in the East Sixties and he had a prominent decorator fill it with country chintz pillows, French antiques, and solid armchairs of the sort that belonged in English manors where lords and their spotted dogs sat by blazing fires. He had a valet who in addition to tending clothes foraged in the bars of Provincetown, in the corners of Brooklyn and Staten Island, to bring young men to Will. Often they stayed on to serve as bartenders at his parties or gardeners at his country home, and if they were particularly well formed, he sometimes introduced them to owners of modeling agencies or theatrical directors and some of them relocated to Hollywood. Jefferson and Delano had grown old and deaf, and lost bladder control. They had been replaced by Willkie and Coolidge, and Tippecanoe had spawned an entire generation of Siamese, one named Studio 54 and the other Palladium after night spots of the moment.

He was accused of bringing a will to a dying man that he later changed to leave himself a consideration in excess of his fee. It was not proved, but it was hinted. The ethics committee of the bar wanted to remove him, but they didn't have the evidence, only the word of an associate in his firm who had left disgruntled when he found he wouldn't be made partner.

Will always made time to sit down with famous women and discuss the disposition of their houses in Bel Air, Santa Fe, and Monaco in the wake of divorces. He returned the phone calls of all publicists, commentators, journalists, and photographers. He invited female clients for the weekend at his country home, and sitting around the pool playing with his Caesar salad, he told them that the sons of bitches who had promised them everything would pay, pay through their noses for the treachery that was theirs, for the assumption that they would shed a bride as easily as a snake sheds its skin. The women let tears slip down their cheeks and stuck out their tongues to lick away the salt of despair while he outlined a strategy guaranteed to bring tycoons to their knees and equitable distibution to all.

He sat in his office and thumbed through papers, the ones that were being served on politicians accused of bribery, racketeering, taking a hoodlum out to lunch, going to Miami in the private jet of a corporate tycoon. The pinko bastards were after anyone who was earning a living, and Will Katz was there to fight back, to take the politician's hand in his and squeeze it hard to encourage him to revive him, to make the man stand tall and look at the jury and swear on his children's lives that the account in the Swiss bank was there only because he feared nuclear war and needed a deposit box to keep his mother's letters to him when he was in the army safe from the singe of potential radiation.

If a television star was having a party, Will appeared in black tie and a white silk scarf and he had his chauffeur wait for him downstairs, in case he was bored, in case the photographers were elsewhere that night. If a Broadway producer was opening a new musical, he was at the party at a table down front, and his presence was noted by the lady columnist, who told all to everyone who was not invited but wished they were. He fixed subpoenas and he fixed jury notices and he fixed it when a client's son wanted to get into an Ivy League college and was put on the waiting list and he fixed it when the judge wanted tickets to the Giants' game and he always had an extra ticket for a journalist pal who might go with him to the fights at Madison Square Garden. If his favorite restaurant was cited for cockroaches or liquor violations, he fixed that, too.

Then he got sick. A little boy, a busboy at Le Cirque, who had been recruited for an early-morning encounter, pointed out the bluish green spot on his ear. Affectionately, with the sweetness of youth, he tried to rub it away. Will didn't have time to go to the doctor, so it wasn't until another spot appeared on his shoulder and he saw it himself in the mirror that he grew alarmed.

The ethics committee of the bar association had a new case against him. Before he could fall asleep at night he needed a body to give him release. He needed to hold on to that body as he drifted off, otherwise no amount of alcohol, no Valium or sleeping pill, would work. His staff brought him boys, a new one every few days. He got thinner. He had pains in his chest. He was hospitalized with pneumonia and he lay there in the oxygen tent, breathing up and down, fighting for air, and when his law partner came to visit and stood by his bedside feeling awkward in his street clothes, embarrassed by the tube that entered Will's nose, and upset by the bones of his head that now protruded through the vulnerable skin, Will said to him, "Be sure that my cats have good homes, all of them. I've left you enough money to pay for their care. Don't put my cats out on the street. Don't let my enemies get my cats."

"I won't," said the law partner.

But he recovered and seemed to gain strength, and when there were rumors about his illness and what had caused it, he went on television on a prime-time talk show and he said "No, not me. What kind of malicious gossip is that? I have enemies," he said, "who'd say anything at all, libel and falsehood."

He was thin, but not too thin. His face was pasted with makeup so the spots that had spread looked only like the aging blotches of men who spend time in bars and whose blood pressure rises and falls with the passing moment. "I'm in great condition," he said. "I have a personal trainer come to my house every morning and I do exercises in the gym I have built on my fourth floor." This was true enough, but the nature of the exercises was not explained on prime-time television.

"He's got it," said Arthur, who had come through a bypass operation and was recovering in Palm Beach, sitting in a chair by the poolside next to his sister Mildred, whose flowered dress covered her wrinkled ankles. She wore a big straw hat to keep the sun off her face because she had two skin cancers already.

"No," said Mildred. "He said he had pneumonia, that's all."

Will was hospitalized and given chemotherapy in Washington, D.C. He was directed to the best doctors there by a former client, an ex–FBI man who had been accused of exceeding the Constitution in his zeal to find something on Martin Luther King. The fellow who always invited Will to lunch whenever he was in town was having an affair with someone on the White House staff, and the hospitalization was arranged quietly. He had a private room, and late at night, when the staff was down to its minimum, his valet would arrive and lie down in the hospital bed with him so that he could sleep. "The patient does not accept the necessity for safe sex," said the chart at the end of his bed.

Now more than ever he needed his friends. He made lists of his enemies and he laughed at them. "Pinko, civil liberties pansies, do-good-ers, and Boy Scouts. What could you do to me?" He conjured up their images in the early hours of the morning when he couldn't sleep and the pain in his muscles made it hard to turn over, to pull up his head. "I know all the secret passages, all the tunnels and the shortcuts. You could never catch me."

He thought about his death, and it seemed to him unfair. It seemed to him that his enemies had planned it, the liver swelling and the bluish spots on his skin opening and spreading over his shoulders. He thought about death and he stared at it straight, without illusions of a life to come or reunions with the boys he had opened and speared for so long, no illusions of his mother holding his head and promising him that he was an exception, name the rule, he was the exception. He had no need for visions of angels and clouds and judgments pronounced. He had no fear of Gehenna and no conviction that others' bones would rise, leaving his in the dust. Sometimes he faced death directly. The running—the long run, the run to get there first, with the most, with the best, with the papers always mentioning what you did and who you knew—the running was over. So what? So who cared? So what was he leaving? Although there were days even when he was so weak that the private nurse had to turn him over in bed to prevent sores, to wipe the sweat off the flesh that seemed to stick now to the bones, even then it sometimes seemed possible to him that he might fix this. He had connections everywhere. He knew all the major donors of the hospitals. He knew and was personally owed a favor by most of the members of the city council. He knew the man who had bought up all the real estate in the New York Hospital area. He had connections in the Pentagon and he had a secret Rolodex with the names of congressmen who would enjoy a good lunch, a night on the town. But when it was finally clear to him that he could not change the changes that had come to him, when he faltered getting up from a chair and slept through the afternoon that a certain senator had come to discuss a matter of defense contracts with a company he was connected with in Omaha, he went back to his house in the country and he lay in his bed with his cats all around and he said to his cook who had been the cook on a merchant ship in the China seas and had a tattoo on his arm of a lady entwined in a snake, who was bringing him a vitamin drink made in the blender in a tall glass on a silver tray, "I've had everything but a long life," and he died.

The newspapers reported his death on the front page, and Mildred went to the funeral. Flying back from Palm Beach, she sat in the temple while the rabbi spoke of the remarkable career of this most remarkable man who had become a part of the American fable as it would be told generation to generation. Mildred noted that three movie stars, two big producers, several men in dark suits and dark glasses who were clearly somebody, though she didn't know who, were there. It was the most exciting funeral Mildred had ever been to, more like the opening night of the opera than anything else, she explained to Arthur, who was sitting on the terrace of his hotel room overlooking the Atlantic Ocean, his lips set tight when his sister called to distract him with news of the funeral.

"Say what you will about him," said Mildred, "but he is the only member of this family to become famous." She had cheerfully forgotten that her husband, Julie, had also managed a brief moment in the public eye.

Tippecanoe's descendants, Siamese voices raised in protest, were carried off by his law partner's butler in cages in the back of the limousine in which they had ridden back and forth to the house in Connecticut, to the brownstone in the East Sixties, and brought to the local ASPCA, where they perished only days after their master, in circumstances less luxurious than those they had become accustomed to.

God's Real Estate: 1978

Caleb Herzberg's family and forty others packed themselves up, left their apartment in Judea just beyond the city of Hebron, near the graves of Rachel, Rebecca, and Sarah. They did this with money from the government, supplemented by money from an American religious organization located in Brooklyn dedicated to the principle that God had promised not a half a loaf, but a whole one.

Caleb and his settlers put up houses and built a school and on the edges of the land they had been granted by the Interior Ministry, they put up a barbed-wire fence that was taller than two men. They built a small synagogue in the center of the settlement with a bare wall that partitioned off the section for women, which had no window and no benches so the women would have to stand pressed one against another during the prayers. Caleb painted the synagogue building a pale blue.

Some of the settlers worked in Jerusalem and would get in their cars each morning and leave for the day and return over the winding roads as night fell. The women watched their infants play along the boardwalks that connected the houses and the school. Except for the sky, which hung low overhead, and the distant hills of rock and sand, the settlement looked familiar, a combination of army post and shtetl in Poland. The settlers were comfortable with both images.

Outside the barbed wire the Arabs would wander after goats that had grazed too far. All the settlers carried guns at their hips and the children at play would fight in dramatic hand combat an enemy always named Farouz or Kahli. When Shabbat came and the men were at home in their houses, the sound of prayer would float up over the settlement and from each small house with its latrine in the back would come the rocking melody, caressing, soft, holding and floating, rising and sinking, that was the welcome for the Sabbath queen, who arrived down the planks of wood that connected the houses and visited each just as she had on the slopes of the Dnieper and the hills of Alsace. This made the settlement not just an extension of Jewish property, not a matter of national real estate, but a tribute to the work of the Holy One, blessed be He.

Caleb's father, Eli, visited the settlement. When he saw the barbed wire he sighed. When he saw the gun on the hip of his son, he sighed. "I am too old for this cowboy and Indian," he said to his wife.

"It is good for Jews to have guns," said his wife. "When they had only prayers, look what happened."

Eli bent his head, gray hair falling over his forehead. "It does not look nice," he said, "not nice at all."

Caleb showed his father how they kept watch on the settlement with wires that if tripped would set off an alarm. Up on the far hill some Arab in Jordan had built a house with blue tiles in geometric designs across a wide turret and a design of fig trees planted in the mosaic pottery on either side of an arch.

"Look," Caleb said to his father, "some Arab who never comes here built that house just to stop us from growing, but we won't be stopped by a checkbook in Amman."

"Maybe," said Eli, "God intended the land to be shared among brothers."

Caleb said to his father, his voice like a dropping stone, "Like Esau and Jacob, like Cain and Abel, like Joseph and his brothers, everything should be equally divided? That's not," said Caleb, "what God had intended. Jordan they can have, Egypt they can have, Syria for the Syrians if it must be, but the land of Israel, the Holy Land, is ours as it was drawn in the maps of the kings and as it is drawn in my heart."

"All right," said Eli, who knew when to argue with a child and when to retreat.

An Enemy of the Jews: 1970

Moses found a green patch where berries grew. He found that he could survive on the rainwater that had gathered in the rocky pools. His beard grew wild and long. His hair was matted and he spoke to his voices as he made his way up and down the canyons of the desert, looking for a bird that had fallen, for a rabbit snared in some brush, for the fruit of some tree, for the bark of a branch that he could chew. Every now and then he would see a snake and he would bash it to pieces with his stick and eat its flesh. His teeth were blackened and his gums were red and his molars fell from his mouth. He dreamed that the Devil spoke to him and he was wearing a white suit and a broad-rimmed white hat and he had a gun in a holster he wore at his hip. He recognized the Devil's face, but he could not place it. One day he found an abandoned campsite. An army troop on a training mission had been through the cliffs and had left behind a radio that did not work, a pot, and two bent forks. He gathered those up and brought them to his cave.

He survived in the desert for many months. The voices did not ease. Sometimes he banged his head against the side of the cave in hopes that the pain would shut them out. He couldn't tell if the angels of God blamed him for a great crime or were asking him to commit a crime. "Peace," he would plead, "leave me in peace." He prayed morning, noon, and night, and when his lips were moving in prayer, the voices let him alone. I am a holy man, he said to himself, like St. Jerome.

Two bedouins roaming through the empty land found the cave. Moses was sleeping at its entrance in the early morning when the moon was pale and low and the stars had all disappeared but one hanging over the edge of the horizon. The desert air was cold and in his sleep Moses rocked back and forth. He smelled of sweat and feces and the damp of the rock. One of the bedouins noticed the pot and the radio. He picked it up as Moses woke and saw him. Moses screamed as if he had come to the end of the earth and was about to fall. This frightened the bedouins, one of whom pulled a knife from under his shirt and in a quick and practiced gesture slit Moses's throat from ear to ear. The bedouins stripped the wounded man of his cassock, because everything had value, and fled up the ravine. As the sun blundered rose-colored out of the east and the waves of heat began to dance over the mounds of sand, Moses in his cave bled out his life. "For the glory of God," he said before losing consciousness.

Ari and his sons were camping. It was something he did with the boys at least twice a year. There was something about being in the cool night and the hot sun that turned a man into his essence, that would teach a boy that he could stand up and be counted. The desert was a place to learn how small you are and how swiftly you can move. Ari wanted his boys to know that the land, the Jewish land, was for people who could make fires with nothing more than sticks, who could eat out of small tin cans and could ration their water with reason. He also liked to be with his boys, watching their limbs move, holding them close to him at night by the fire, and telling them stories they would not believe about his own childhood when he was named Teddy and lived in America and had a nurse who picked up his dirty socks and washed his underwear.

"Grandpa Arthur," asked one of the boys, "what kind of a gun did he have?"

Ari laughed. "None," he said, "none at all."

On the third day of their camping trip, when Ari's beard was shaggy and the boys were beginning to fight with each other, they found a naked man with his throat cut, stiff and smelling of death, lying in the mouth of a cave. Ari allowed the boys to look.

"Not pretty," he said. White-faced, they agreed.

"Who did it?" asked the older boy.

Looking down at the naked body, Ari answered, "An enemy of the Jews."

The army came and took away the corpse. It was never identified.

Ever After: 1960–1985

Hedy and Elan had a house in Haifa with a yard. Hedy weeded and planted and grew roses around her back fence. The children had colds, and once Tova had a sore throat that did not go away, but finally it did. Hedy made costumes for Purim. The children dressed as Greeks and Romans and one year they shared the front and back end of a horse. Once Namah was an Indian princess, and when she was nine she was a tiger whose mask had whiskers made from a broom.

Several times a month Hedy worked late at night at the observatory, and when she was gone Elan would open the door to the children's room and he would watch them sleeping. Alert, he stared into the corners and into the closet, as if he expected terrorists to jump out of dark corners.

Hedy sent pictures of the children to Arthur and Mildred. Elan taught science in the high school. He told his students that science was not good or bad, it was like a sword, you could use it on your enemies or on yourself. "Be careful with science," he said. He was known to raise grades, to give a failing student a boost, to work extra hours with a child who was lonely. He knew about children. They wanted something to trust. Every six months he put on his uniform and went off for three weeks. Hedy liked the smell of him when he came home, a mixture of dirt and smoke from a fire and sweat that had been washed not so carefully in river water and army-issue shaving cream.

Namah's best friend abandoned her for another and for weeks Namah refused to go to school. Tova and Yehuda built a rocket in the backyard that misfired and burned the neck of the dog, who then succeeded in tearing the bandage off his neck. Hedy and Elan cut orange slices for breakfast and scooped yogurt out of a container into bowls. At night they turned toward each other and Elan put his hands in familiar places and Hedy rolled over, open and full, heavy with wanting, damp with desire, again and again.

"Can this go on forever?" Hedy asked.

"Yes," said Elan. "It isn't written anywhere that only nightmares are eternal."

Yehuda completed high school and entered the army. He was chosen to work a radar machine in the Golan Heights. Their daughter Tova completed her service and entered the university. Namah was reading Jane Austen in English class. She didn't like it.

Elan was asked to run for the city council and Hedy worked on his campaign. He lost because he belonged to the party that was held responsible for inflation that year, though the financial problems of the country would not be decided in the council of Haifa. Elan wanted the army to increase radar protection on the Golan and his opponent wanted the army to use its money for additional tanks. The defense budget would also not be decided in the council of Haifa, but the two candidates had very strong and differing opinions and the electorate decided on tanks. After the election returns were in, Hedy brought Elan a cup of coffee. Sitting in their bed, naked, with her feet wound around his, she told him that he deserved to be councilman and would have been a far better councilman than the man who took the seat. Elan was disappointed.

"What will I do with myself?" he asked.

"What you have always been doing," said Hedy.

He lay next to her and saw that the skin under her chin was sagging and her hair was gray at the temples. Good, he said to himself, then she'll have to stay with me forever.

All I Want Is Out: 1972

Frank had been taking medication for two years. It had stalled the cancer, but now his stomach was bloated and the doctor wanted him to return to the hospital. It was going to be over soon. The bastards, he thought to himself, the bastards would go on drinking their coffee in the morning long after he was gone. The bastard doctors, he thought, they charge what they want and they do nothing, nothing at all.

He turned away from Maria when she came to sit by his side. He didn't want her to know what his abdomen looked like full like a woman's and pressing against his spine. He had pain. "All I want is out, just out," he said.

Maria didn't know what to do. Daisy came and brought him some drug that came from the street. It gave him a few hours of rest. He was grateful to Daisy.

Frank insisted on combing his own hair and shaving his face. Maria tried to help him, but he didn't want her in the room. "Keep the gold digger out," he shouted at the nurse, who didn't know what he wanted or whom he meant.

Maria tried to convince him to say a prayer, just once, just in case. She tried to convince him that Jesus would take him in his arms, and he looked at her. "Please," he said, "I want a light on in the room all the time. I want all the lights on."

"Are you afraid for your soul?" asked Maria.

Frank looked at his wife. She was like a child, believing in ghosts. "I'm not afraid," he said.

Maria put her hand to her mouth and was quiet. In the last hours, long after he had refused to eat any more food or drink any more liquid or allow the doctor to start an IV in his arm, his good tennis arm, he put his head in his hands and there were tears in his eyes. "Nothing has worked out right for me," he said. "Nothing has ever worked out."

"I'm here," said Maria.

"Yes," said Frank, "you are."

"Do you love me?" asked Maria expecting the answer he had always given. He surprised her.

"I can't," he said. "I don't know how." Then, as he drifted off into a morphine sleep, small puffs of wordless fury filled his mind like the smoke of a fading fire.

Hedy and Elan and their three children came to America for Frank's funeral. Hedy had called each year on her father's birthday and she called him when her children were born and he had always sounded distant, not just the miles of ocean and sky between them, but vague as to who she was and what she wanted from him. "I think he did it," Hedy had told Elan.

"Don't think about it," said Elan.

"I can't help it," said Hedy. "Sometimes when I hear you in the dark getting up in the middle of the night, I roll over in the bed ready to spring up, just in case."

"My God," said Elan, who held his wife in his arms and let her memories fold with his.

So it was that Hedy stood on a grassy hill on Long Island, some way down the highway from New York City, in a city of stones, large and small, patches of dead clumped together by name, Rosenbaum, Lifton, Berg, and Tannen.

"Why is everybody in this cemetery Jewish? If America is such a melting pot, why do the bones get separated out?" Elan asked.

The children were exhausted from the plane trip. Tova was wearing a brassiere for the first time. She thought people were staring at her.

Namah stood by her mother and held her hand. "I never knew my grandpa," she explained to anyone who would listen.

The wisteria bush at the corner of the plot was in bloom and the purple blossoms drifted over the gravesite. A set of pines at least one hundred years old were planted just up the hill. The plot had belonged to Hedy's mother. Flora had bought three graves when the synagogue offered them in a prime location. She wanted a place for her husband and child near her for all eternity. She was buried there and Hedy walked over to her gravestone and ran her hand over it. She had been to this place before, when her tears wouldn't come and she had held her uncle Arthur's hand because her father kept his hands in his pocket. At the time of the *yahrzeit*, the unveiling, she had been in Israel, in the kibbutz, and Frank had said, "Don't bother to come. We're not having a ceremony." Now she asked the rabbi if he would say a memorial prayer for her mother.

"I can't," said the rabbi. "It would not be right. Your stepmother is in mourning now."

Maria was supported between her children. She didn't look at Hedy or Elan or their children. The coffin was lowered. The cars that were parked on the side of the road pulled away. Hedy came over to Maria. "I am sorry we didn't get to know each other better," she said.

"When I die," said Maria, her face white as a new widow's should be, "your father wants me to be buried in the third grave. It's cheaper that way. He didn't want me to waste money on a grave of my own."

"In the same plot with my mother?" asked Hedy. She repeated the fact all through the night as the plane flew toward Tel Aviv.

"It doesn't matter," said Elan. "Your mother won't know."

"I think it matters," said Hedy, "but I can't prove it."

"So forget it," said Elan, who was unconcerned about life after death.

Frank had lost most of Flora's money in the years since her death. He had made curious investments in precious metals that took dives in the market, and he bought a chain of drugstores that had soda fountains and went bankrupt inside of a year. He had sold all of Flora's stock. What was left, he had willed to Maria and her children. "He must have loved her," said Hedy.

"Or hated your mother," said Elan.

A package arrived in Israel from America. It was a small china dachshund that had belonged to Hedy, a gift, in fact, from Ursula. It had sat on her dresser until she had left for Israel to visit Teddy. There was a note in the package signed by Maria: "I found this little dog in the closet. I thought you might want it." So it happened that all of the Gruenbaum fortune that would come to Hedy was a little china dachshund given her originally by her German nanny.

Hedy considered disinterring her mother's body from its grave and flying it to Israel for burial. But who spent such money on flying bodies across the sea? No sane person, surely. And what did Flora know of Israel? She would be a stranger, a dead stranger. Hedy stopped thinking about it. A body was an empty shell and the soul, Flora's soul, Hedy believed, was gone, disintegrated into waves of matter that carried no name, so what did it matter where you were buried or who was buried with you.

Romance on the Lower East Side: 1898

Ruth sat at the piano playing the same notes again and again. She had a Chopin piece to work on. It was hard. It needed the pedal and the hands to work together. Her fingers were not yet warmed up. She couldn't get it right, not the swoop of the downward scale and the sound of the warble that came between and the swaying in the notes that made you want to laugh. It was there, she just couldn't get it. She started over and over. She could feel the perspiration fall over her face and catch in the dent above her lip where her father had said the angels pressed their thumbs on the about-to-be born child so the baby would forget all it knew of Paradise. She could feel the way her thighs were sticking to the piano bench. She started again. She could do it if she kept on trying. The window above the fire escape was open. Downstairs across the courtyard in the apartment on the first floor, the young man whose voice she had heard at his morning prayers while she still lay in her bed might be listening. She tried again, and it was all right. Not perfect, not with everything, but the notes and the swoop and the warble and the laugh were there and she sighed with relief. She got up from the bench to get a glass of water. Music made her thirsty. Below, standing by his window that opened on the alley, Joseph bent his head and, rocking back and forth on his heels, felt the bite of happiness sting the back of his neck, causing a flush to spread across his chest.

A Walk on the Drive: 1919

Isaac walked along Riverside Drive. It was Saturday and his wife was visiting her sister in the Bronx and his children all had plans. He watched a young girl, just a little older than Flora, roll her hoop carefully over the cobblestones until it bumped into a shiny black baby carriage, where, shaking for a moment, it fell. He watched the girl pull up her falling stocking and run to a nearby bench, where her nanny took a cloth out of a pocketbook and wiped the child's face. He watched a skinny squirrel climb one of the huge maples that lined the Drive and leap into the next tree, its paws poised, outstretched, for a split second, like wings, its tail stiff and straight, and its nostrils quivering with the wind that blew upward.

Isaac sat down on a bench and watched the chauffeur in the nearby Packard pull a bag from his pocket and lift something to his lips. He saw the Irish maid from the building next door, the one who was always putting out the garbage in the mornings when he left for his office. She was leaning on the stone fence and looking down at the river. Her hair was tied in a black ribbon and she lifted herself up and down on her toes, tensing the muscles in her calves again and again. Isaac leaned back against the boards of his bench and tilted his face toward the sun. He took out his notebook and calculated again. The spring season would be good. It was only fall, but the orders were coming in better than expected. He felt the weight of his legs press against the bench.

Is there something I want? he wondered. Is there something I need that I don't have? The sun played across his face. His wife was always pressing him to take a vacation, to go to Venice or Paris. "We can afford it," she would say. "The Kaplans have booked themselves aboard the *Queen Mary*. We could go, too." But Isaac always said no. What for? Who wanted to ride on a boat, to eat food that slides about on a plate? He had everything he wanted right here, on Riverside Drive. Can one thank a God whose commandments one has been ignoring? Why not?

On Riverside Drive, in the sun, as the pigeons pecked each other and scratched in the grass that grew in patches on the side of the walk, as a bicycle horn blew, deep-throated, a warning to make way, Isaac, who had forgotten the Hebrew words that he had heard from his father so often he thought they were carved in his heart, but they weren't because he couldn't remember them now, said in English, "Thank you." He bowed his head and rocked it slightly up and down, and his bowler hat slipped forward over his bald forehead and he pushed up the rim with his thumb and looked at the sky. "Thank you," he said again.

Good Times: 1925

Harry leaned over in bed. His bulky chest rolled with him. "Hey, Mickey," he said, "give me a break, make me some room."

"So whaddya want, you lug?" said Mickey, who wiggled her bottom and blew air in his ear.

"I'm going to this diet doctor that Arthur recommends. Says his friend Hersh lost sixty pounds."

"Yeah," said Mickey.

"I'm going to look great," said Harry.

"You already look great to me," said Mickey. "But a girl can have too much of a good thing," she added.

Harry felt her silk nightgown brush against his belly and found with his fingers the place where it plunged in the front and the lace caught his nails as he pulled down.

"Easy," said Mickey, "that's a fifty-dollar nightgown you're tearing." She pulled it over her head and snuggled next to him, running her nipples up and down on his face while he gulped and snorted and breathed in her perfume beneath.

Romance in Greenwich Village: 1931

Sharie Lee and Quebec Bob were sitting in a bar in the West Village and the walls were brick and a large painting hung over a fireplace of a street painted in the rain as the drops fell across the grocer's window and made puddles around the cars parked at the curb. Sharie Lee looked at Quebec Bob, who was wearing a flannel shirt open at the neck and a beret made of blue felt. "God, you're fine," she said. "A fine man."

"Oh," he said, "me and who else?"

"Just you," said Sharie Lee. She took her Scotch and she poured it down her throat and waited for the warm swell feeling to rise to her brain.

Quebec Bob reached for her arm. "White girl," he said, "go slow." She looked at him. "No hurry to get where you're going. I'm going with you, you know."

"Says who?" said Sharie Lee.

The door to the bar opened and a blast of cold air blew across the table. Sharie was wearing a red silk dress with a rhinestone belt that cut tight across her waist. Quebec Bob stood up and said to the eight other people in the room, including the two who had just entered, "This here white bird goes home with me. Is that clear?"

No one paid any attention, but Sharie Lee, who felt the tickle down in her toes, spread her legs just a little, discreetly, under the table, to let the steam escape so she wouldn't explode before her time. "My daddy would have liked you, he would have liked you a lot," she said.

Meyer: 1956

Meyer had been having trouble sleeping. That is to say, he fell asleep all right, but then he would wake at two or three in the morning and stare at the ceiling for hours. He was too tired to read, too tired to do anything but wait for morning. He was without work, and that exhausted a man who had been a teacher for so long, who had once possessed an office with a file cabinet, with papers to get ready for publication and colleagues to meet at lunch and students to dress down or encourage. He had the kind of exhaustion that made it impossible to sleep.

Then one morning he woke at three when the sky was still dark and his wife was sleeping, her ponytail tied in a bandanna, by his side, and he went to the window and he looked up at the tree that had lost its leaves some months ago but still stood in its wire enclosure, surrounded by cement, bending in the wind. He could see the traffic light at the corner change. He heard nothing. He stood still, leaning his weight against the sill, his forehead pressed to the glass, while the light came up in the sky, first white, then pink, then darker rose, and finally, as his wife stirred in the bed, putting her arms out, searching for his body in her sleep, he saw the first shades of day, the pale blue of winter light seeping upward from behind the buildings. He saw the sliver of white moon fading, slipping down, until, blurred, it disappeared behind his head. He saw the star of morning. It hovered a silver blink above. It drifted off. He forgot about himself, the I that was watching. He had seen the holy at work. He had seen the sacred day begin. It had nothing to do with his father. He had no urge to say words or mumble in the air. He was content to be quiet and watch. He knew he had seen something ordinary, banal, random, causeless, unnoticing of him, something vast and impersonal, cold and indifferent, something he had seen before, and yet it was holy and he knew it was holy and he knew he would be able to sleep the next night and the night after. When a man remembers that the sacred is there, right in front of him, every day, then he can close his eyes at night and get a proper rest.

Victory in New Jersey: 1933

A fall day. Max rides his chestnut horse, the one with the white stripe down his nose, named Patrick Henry. The colors of the field are already faded green, pale rust, brown, the brown of sun-baked dirt and dung. Ribboned through the trees at the far edge, the yellows and reds fold over each other. Max wears a big sweater and his glasses are tied to his head with a string. He wears a leather cap, a jockey's cap, but it had earflaps that he had especially made for the cold weather. They are fleece-lined. Now they are flapping free against his head, with the rhythm of the horse's gallop, bang, bang, his earflaps hit the side of his head. He swings his mallet as hard as he can and he hits the little ball that had come to a stop in a mound of late blooming daisies whose yellow centers were eaten by bugs who crawled, not for exercise, but for necessity, over the petals. Max had to lean way off the saddle in order to hit the ball, but he fearlessly bent, lifted himself up and over, as if he were an acrobat in a circus performance, not a man retired from the suit business, a man with a limp, a man with a crook in his back, a man whose height was a matter of speculation among the grooms at the stable who had bets with each other that they could never confirm.

Max was red in the face. He pulled himself back to the center of the saddle and put his heels in the flanks of his horse and cantered forward across his field toward the goalposts he had told the stable boy to paint just that morning so that they would glisten in the sun, glisten just as brightly as the posts at the polo clubs that had not admitted him, just as brightly as the polo clubs that flew their colors on flagpoles and set their tables with napkins embossed with the club monogram.

He imagined the team, his own and the other. He heard the hooves of the horses gaining on him. He saw out of the corner of his eye a black horse with its teeth bared and its forelegs raised in the air. He urged Patrick Henry on. "We can do it," he yelled in the air. He swung his mallet again and for a moment he seemed to slip too far and the horse, feeling the uncertain balance of the rider, pranced and lost his step. Holding tight with one hand to the reins and grasping the saddle post with the other, Max pulled himself back to center and, leaning forward, called out to the air, "Go, go, make it, hurray for Max, hurray for Max," and he followed the ball till it rolled past the goalpost. He heard the cheering of the crowd. He saw the disappointment on the face of the captain of the opposing team.

"Well done," he said to his horse. "Well done," he said to himself, though he was breathing hard as his horse trotted back to the center of the field. He imagined the colored shirts of his team blazoning in the sun and he imagined applause that filled the field and the neighboring field, applause that reached all across New Jersey and floated over the Hudson River right into Manhattan, where his brother's children would hear it. "Hurray for Max, hurray for Max!"

He dismounted. He handed his horse over to the stable boy. He took off his hat. He held it in one hand and in the other he held his riding crop. He stood a moment in the field. What a fortunate man I am, he thought in one of those rare moments when we realize how much worse things could be, that others do not own horses. He smiled. A split in his face appeared from ear to ear. His smile was not an idiot's smile. It included the knowledge that he was humped and small and would never own a ranch in Montana. It included also his certainty that he was, whatever anyone wanted to think, a real American.

In Every Generation: 1990

Caleb went into Jerusalem to talk to the interior minister about additional funding for the twenty more families that were waiting to join them on the settlement. He had agreed to allow tour buses of visiting Americans to come to the settlement. "We will show them how Jews build the land," Caleb said. "Those whose hearts bleed for the Arabs, they will see that we need barbed wire to protect ourselves. They will see that Jews live again near the graves of the matriarchs and they will be proud." Caleb wanted money from the ministry to paint all the houses. "Americans will not like it if our settlement is shabby and worn," he argued.

Meanwhile his youngest child, Amos, and his friend Noah had been playing with a baseball and a bat that had been given to Amos by his grandfather Eli, who had been visiting just the week before. Noah hit the ball over the barbed wire and into a ravine, and the two boys saw their ball roll down the hill outside of the settlement where they were not permitted to go, not without adults, not on foot, but in cars only. But the ball was new and the game was good and the boys climbed over the fence and followed the line of the settlement around to its back where they could see their ball in the gully below. Carefully picking their legs up over the warning wire, they made their way down the hill.

A passing Arab saw the boys slipping and sliding down the ravine, trying to keep their balance by holding on to the ragged brush that grew from the dry earth. He saw their yarmulkes on their heads, Amos's had been embroidered by his grandmother with little red birds and white hearts. The Arab waited until the boys were down at the bottom of the hill, their faces red from the effort of keeping their balance on the sharp incline. Behind him his donkey put his head down and munched on the weeds that grew sparsely among the stones. He had not planned it. It came to him suddenly, a commandment, a way to please, to tame the burning in his chest. He picked up a rock and smashed first one child and then the other. Allah understood that this was for his mother, who had lost her house in Jaffa, and for his uncle, who was killed in the village. He smashed the boys the way his father had once killed a dog that had gone mad and was eating chickens in the yard. When he was done he wiped his hands on his jacket. He looked up at the sun that had slipped in the sky and he bent down on his knees and leaned back on his calves and with his head near the dirt he thanked Allah for the creation of life. The bodies were found later that night when the men in groups, their guns pulled out of their holsters, began looking outside the barbed wire.

Caleb and his wife and his three other sons and his two daughters sat at the table in their kitchen and received the hugs and the pats and the food brought by their neighbors. They tore their lapels and they cried through the night. How to explain how Caleb felt: as if his heart had been mangled by a vulture who was consuming him live on the road. Amos had been the youngest and his eyes had been bright blue and his lashes black and his father had taught him the Shema when he was three and had held him in his arms when he cried in the night with a pain in the ear. How was he to live without this son?

The men in the settlement stood by Caleb's side when the coffin was lowered into the ground, and they clenched the guns at their hips and they looked outside the wire of the settlement and they promised to avenge the child that was taken from them. They promised Caleb that.

Caleb spoke to his father, Eli, on the phone. Eli offered to come to the settlement. Eli's wife, Hinda, wept. She remembered the baby she had lost. Eli said to his son, "Be strong for the sake of the others." Caleb promised. Eli said, "Don't forget your wife; she suffers, too." Caleb promised. Caleb sobbed into the phone and his father said, "This costs too much. I will call tomorrow."

Namah Looks for Peace: 1990

Hedy and Elan were pleased when Namah, after serving her two years in the army, went to the university to major in mathematics. She had her father's mind for the way numbers made patterns and danced in the face of infinity and marched parallel to destinies that could be figured or approximated or squared or divided and theorems that showed that while the first bang might have been random, after that there was reason and form and the stars might be light-years distant, but their rotations through the heavens could be counted, measured, predicted.

"Mathematics," said Elan, "is as close to God as man is ever going to get." And his youngest child, Namah, agreed.

Namah joined with a group of students who believed it was important to make friends, to build bridges, to work together for peace with the Arabs. The group was not popular on the campus and its numbers were small, but they encouraged each other and they spoke to the Arab students and they became counselors at a camp for Arab children and Jewish children where the two groups would come together and tell each other about their traditions and their parents and what games they like to play. They learned each other's songs. Namah believed this was the road to peace.

Elan said, "Don't trust the Arabs. It is not so easy as you think. I know them better than you do. I know them longer."

Namah looked at her father and said to him, "You are being unreasonable."

"So you feel sorry for them," he said. "Who felt sorry for us? No little bands of university students played games with me by my ditch. I have no sorrow left for my enemies. I have enough to do to take care of myself."

"I don't care," said Namah, "it's different now."

"Sure," said Elan, "I believe that."

But Hedy was proud of her daughter. "This is the way," she said, and she invited a class from an Arab school to the Technion, where she lectured them on the cosmos, a place in which claims to particular olive groves and specific wells were erased out by electromagnetic waves that spread like spilled wine about the galaxies.

Namah loved the Beatles and the Stones and Sting and she owned a Walkman that had been sent her by her great-uncle Arthur, who lived in the United States. She wanted to fall in love, but so far the closest she had come was a crush on a physics teacher in high school who had left for America.

So it happened that Namah was with two friends from the university in the town of Nablus one afternoon in the early spring. She was there recruiting campers for the Arab-Jewish camp that would open, supported by some American money, in the month between school sessions. It was not so hard to find Jewish families who wanted to send their children off to learn about the Arabs. But it was hard to find Arab parents who did not think the camp was a plan to take their children away from them or a means of teaching them not to obey the rules of Allah or to weaken their bones by not giving them milk. The group had agreed it wanted to have some children from the West Bank. It was Namah's task, since her Arabic was good, to win the confidence of the mothers and hand out a brochure of the camp that was printed in both Hebrew and Arabic.

About four o'clock, just as the young people were sitting in a cafe at the corner of the village square, drinking sodas and ice coffee, Caleb, his older sons, and a group of about ten men from his settlement entered the village in a battered farm truck. The truck pulled to a stop in the square in front of the old tree that had bent in a thousand ways since its birth some centuries before. The men from the settlement wanted to find the murderer of their children, but not expecting to find the particular murderer, they wanted to make it clear that justice, an eye for an eye, would be done, and the Israeli army, which was conducting an investigation, was not to be relied on to be the avenging hand of a just God.

A small Arab boy was passing on his bicycle. He was balancing a loaf of bread on his handlebars. He brought his bike to an instant stop when he saw the settlers, their black coats, their black hats, their white shirts, their guns waving in the air. Caleb, jumping from the cab of the truck, his boots dusty and his black coat still ripped in mourning, grabbed the boy by the neck and lifted him up from his bike as the child howled in terror. The cafe owner tried to close his shutters, but one of the settlers screamed at him to stand still. An Arab man threw a grapefruit from the basket at his side at Caleb, who wheeled around to confront his attacker. Caleb's son Eliezar, not yet sixteen, raised his gun to his shoulder. He aimed his gun at the child, who, held by Caleb in a firm grip, was crying for his father and his uncles and was kicking his feet in the air.

Namah jumped out of her seat. "No," she shouted, "the child didn't do anything." She ran toward Caleb and Eliezar and the pack of Jews in black coats standing in the center of the village. At that moment either a car backfired two streets away, or a gun was triggered from an open window above the cafe, or a pot was dropped in the back patio by the frightened cook. But before the sound had a chance to form and echo, Eliezar began to shoot, and a bullet went into Namah's head and a second brushed her side and she fell in a pool of blood in the sidewalk.

There was a moment of stunned silence. The Arab boy broke free and ran down an alley. "She's Israeli!" called out her comrades.

The army was called from a pay phone in the back of the cafe and an ambulance came, and Namah, who was still breathing, was brought to the hopital and Elan and Hedy were called.

The settlers said she was shot by the Arab who had opened the window and was firing on Caleb. Eliezar claimed he never fired at all, but the villagers said there was no sniper and that Eliezar's gun had gone off and the army was investigating and the afternoon's TV newscaster reported that efforts were being made in the highest ranks of the ministry to keep the army from releasing its report. In a disciplinary action by the Israeli Defense Force, several houses, one belonging to the cook at the café, were to be blown up within hours.

Hedy in the Hadassah Hospital: 1990

In the hospital the daylight had turned to a metallic gray. The night nurses had reported for duty. The waiting room ashtrays were full. Styrofoam cups of coffee, their plastic stirrers lost under the seats, lined the windowsill.

"How much longer can this be?" said Hedy. Elan touched his wife's shoulder and felt its hardness, the bone beneath the sweater.

The lights in the waiting room flickered on. It was not yet dark. There was a reporter in the corridor. There were TV crews waiting in the lobby. What were her last words? they wanted to ask. Who do you blame? One had prepared his question and stood by the elevator door, rehearsing it. He would say it softly, sweetly, as if he were asking if the family had a preference in the national soccer playoffs that were to be held that weekend.

Ari closed his eyes. He wanted to believe it would be all right. After all, the pursuit of happiness must be more than a way to pass the time. Some bullets do not find their mark. A protective hand still stays some disasters. But not, Ari reminded himself, others.

Then there was a banging of doors, the green doors that separated the sterile area from the rest of the hospital. First two nurses hurried past, anxious to get home, pulling on their jackets as they walked. Behind them came the surgeon and his first and second assistant. Their eyes were tired. The surgeon kept rubbing his thumb against his cheek. The second assistant took off his surgical hat and crumpled it in his hands. The surgeon walked over to Hedy, who stood frozen in the spot.

"It's all right," he said. "We got everything. The bullet in the brain was not deep. She was lucky. No permanent damage. Everything's fine."

Elan felt the air rush through his lungs. Now he wanted to cry. Hedy took his hand.

"She'll be coming out soon," said the surgeon. "We'll keep her in intensive care a few days, but she should recover, be good as new. You have my word."

"Why did it take you so long?" asked Hedy

"We work carefully," said the surgeon. "Invite me to her wedding," he added as he headed down the hall.

Later that night Hedy sat by the bedside of her daughter. There were tubes everywhere. There were machines that followed the beat of the heart. There were bleats and electronic bleeps that occurred every few minutes. There was silver chrome everywhere, on the bars on Namah's bedside, on the machines, on the chair that Hedy pulled over, and there was blue, blue sheets on the bed, blue paper of the sterile shoes the nurses wore, blue papers on the pillow. There were no windows to the street or the yard below. Namah's breathing was steady. She was sleeping. "Just sleeping," said the nurse. "You should go home."

"Later," said Hedy.

Namah's dark hair had been shaved and a surgical band covered her brow, and her wrists were punctured by needles attached to tubes that dripped glucose and antibiotics in a steady stream into her veins.

Hedy sat by her daughter's side and began to tell her stories, family stories that went on and on.

In Which the Narrator Removes Her Mask and Discloses the Method in Her Madness

Yes, Reader, I am Hedy, the child in Maine whose mother was afraid of the storm. My family story unfolded through the structures of an alien culture and and alien language. After all, English was not spoken on the Temple Mount. The struggle to survive in another culture was the sublime work of my characters' lives. Forgive me my mask. So many masks were necessary.

In science, when the theories do not account for the observable facts, when the facts dangle unexplained, we go back to the beginning and examine all assumptions, do the calculations again, and weave alternate designs that might accommodate the whole more simply. So I am addressing you, Reader, laying it out before you. Perhaps you can find cause and effect, purpose and reason; maybe if you add the numbers of pages in which the word *God* appears and divide them by the numbers of pages on which the word God does not appear, a whirlwind will rush through your living room or your ficus tree will burn.

As for me, I live with the sequence of events as they fell out, memories, inventions, connections forced and natural. I still see my mother's face on the bed sheets and the gun in the closet and I see Isaac on the boat and Max in the whorehouse and Mildred at her wedding, Sharie Lee leaning against the piano, Moses in the desert listening to his voices.

This book is my mourning for my mother. How will my children mourn for me?

About the Author

Anne Roiphe is the author of *A Season for Healing, Lovingkindness*, and several other books. She is a frequent contributor to a number of national magazines. She lives in New York City.